THE BEST
SCIENCE FICTION AND
FANTASY OF THE YEAR
Volume Nine

Also Edited by Jonathan Strahan

Best Short Novels
(2004 through 2007)
Fantasy: The Very Best of 2005
Science Fiction: The Very
Best of 2005
The Best Science Fiction and
Fantasy of the Year: Volumes 1 - 9
Eclipse: New Science Fiction
and Fantasy (Vols 1-4)
The Starry Rift: Tales of New
Tomorrows
Life on Mars: Tales of New
Frontiers
Under My Hat: Tales from the
Cauldron (forthcoming)
Godlike Machines
Engineering Infinity
Edge of Infinity
Fearsome Journeys
Fearsome Magics
Reach for Infinity
Meeting Infinity (forthcoming)
Drowned Worlds, Wild Shores
(forthcoming)

With Lou Anders
Swords and Dark Magic: The New
Sword and Sorcery

With Charles N. Brown
The Locus Awards: Thirty Years
of the Best in Fantasy and Science
Fiction

With Jeremy G. Byrne
The Year's Best Australian Science
Fiction and Fantasy: Volume 1
The Year's Best Australian Science
Fiction and Fantasy: Volume 2
Eidolon 1

With Jack Dann
Legends of Australian Fantasy

With Gardner Dozois
The New Space Opera
The New Space Opera 2

With Karen Haber
Science Fiction: Best of 2003
Science Fiction: Best of 2004
Fantasy: Best of 2004

With Marianne S. Jablon
Wings of Fire

EDITED BY **JONATHAN STRAHAN**

THE BEST SCIENCE FICTION & FANTASY OF THE YEAR

VOLUME NINE

First published 2015 by Solaris
an imprint of Rebellion Publishing Ltd,
Riverside House, Osney Mead,
Oxford, OX2 0ES, UK

www.solarisbooks.com

US ISBN 978 1 78108 309 3
UK ISBN 978 1 78108 308 6

Cover by Dominic Harman

Selection and "Introduction" by Jonathan Strahan.
Copyright © 2015 by Jonathan Strahan.

Pages 611-614 represent an extension of this copyright page

10 9 8 7 6 5 4 3 2 1

A CIP catalogue record for this book is available from the
British Library.

Designed & typeset by Rebellion Publishing

Printed in the US

For Marianne, with love, as always.

ACKNOWLEDGEMENTS

MY SINCERE THANKS to the publishers and writers who have sent me their work, and to the authors who generously have allowed their stories to appear here. Special thanks to Jonathan Oliver, Ben Smith and David Moore at Solaris Books, who have given the *Best Science Fiction and Fantasy of the Year* such a great home. My thanks, too, to my agent, Howard Morhaim, who stood with me through a long and difficult year. And finally, as always, my sincere thanks to my loving wife Marianne, and daughters Jessica and Sophie. Every moment working on this book was stolen from them, and I am grateful to them for their kindness and understanding.

CONTENTS

Introduction, Jonathan Strahan — 11

Slipping, Lauren Beukes — 17

Moriabe's Children, Paolo Bacigalupi — 37

The Vaporization Enthalpy of a Peculiar Pakistani Family,
Usman T. Malik — 55

The Lady and the Fox, Kelly Link — 71

*Ten Rules for Being an Intergalactic Smuggler
(The Successful Kind)*, Holly Black — 97

THE LONG HAUL from the ANNALS OF TRANSPORTATION,
The Pacific Monthly, *May 2009*, Ken Liu — 117

Tough Times All Over, Joe Abercrombie — 137

The Insects of Love, Genevieve Valentine — 171

Cold Wind, Nicola Griffith — 195

Interstate Love Song (Murder Ballad No.8), Caitlín R. Kiernan — 205

Shadow Flock, Greg Egan — 227

I Met a Man Who Wasn't There, K. J. Parker — 255

Grand Jeté (The Great Leap), Rachel Swirsky — 275

Mothers, Lock Up Your Daughters Because They are Terrifying,
Alice Sola Kim — 329

Shay Corsham Worsted, Garth Nix — 347

Kheldyu, Karl Schroeder — 361

Caligo Lane, Ellen Klages — 393

The Devil in America, Kai Ashante Wilson — 401

Tawny Petticoats, Michael Swanwick — 439

The Fifth Dragon, Ian McDonald — 469

The Truth About Owls, Amal El-Mohtar — 489

Four Days of Christmas, Tim Maughan — 503

Covenant, Elizabeth Bear — 509

Cimmeria: From The Journal of Imaginary Anthropology,
Theodora Goss — 525

Collateral, Peter Watts — 543

The Scrivener, Eleanor Arnason — 571

Someday, James Patrick Kelly — 587

Amicae Aeternum, Ellen Klages — 601

INTRODUCTION

Jonathan Strahan

EVERY CHRISTMAS I take a short vacation with my family. It's a time of year when the city gets hot and uncomfortable, making the cooler, greener southwest a tempting holiday retreat. This year we headed to a small town about 300km south of Perth where, between long mornings at the beach and longer evenings by the pool, I worked late into the night assembling the annual recommended reading list for *Locus* magazine.

I've been part of the group that compiles the *Locus* list for nearly twenty years, starting as a book reviewer in 1997 and continuing after I became reviews editor in 2002. The nature of the job has changed over the years: what started as a few additions by a newcomer became long summer days sitting around arguing over inclusions and exclusions with publisher Charles Brown, who would fly to Australia so we could work on the list together. All these years later it's evolved into a process where I compile a list of short fiction with a panel of experts and then discuss book recommendations with current publisher Liza Trombi, after which I retreat to work on my year in review essay.

It's also a time when I work on this book, reading stories that arrive at the last minute, and making final story selections, something that used to happen much earlier in the year. I look back to compiling *Science Fiction: Best of 2003* with Karen Haber, which we submitted to our publisher in August of 2003, with some amazement. With digital publishing dominating the short fiction market, stories now appear right up to the very last minute of December, and often aren't selected or edited until moments before that. Delivery dates for volumes in this series have moved from August to October to December and into January. And so, what was once pure vacation time has now become time for a little vacation and a lot of reflection on the state of science fiction and fantasy.

To help make my vacation seem more like a vacation I usually take something with me to read that has nothing to do with the SF field. This year it was Carl Wilson's fascinating discussion of taste and the music of Celine Dion, *Let's Talk About Love: Why Other People Have Such Bad Taste*. In a fascinating book Wilson talks about how consensus views of art grow and change over time, how critics and commentators striving for standards of 'objective excellence' lead to the formation of a canon of accepted excellence, and how that canon is and needs to be broken down and reformed over time. He says at one point that though "... science fiction fans may believe strongly in their own tastes, in aggregate they are acclimatized to the notion that separate taste groups can coexist peacefully, without the need for external, official inspection and verification." That is to say, without affirmation from a cultural elite that their tastes are acceptable. However, he goes on to talk about how the interaction between taste groups, between self-appointed cultural elites and so on has the positive effect of allowing a new consensus of excellence to evolve, become widely accepted, challenged and then broken down again, regardless of whether that conversation is uniformly welcomed or not.

Wilson's book struck a chord with me, as I wrote about the state of the science fiction field. It seemed quite clear to me that the reviewers, editors and commentators I'd read in my youth – from James Blish to Terry Carr to Charles N. Brown – were the sort of cultural Brahmins who argued for and helped with the formation of a science fiction canon. Best of the Year annuals, like those edited by Donald Wolheim or Harry Harrison or Gardner Dozois, lists of award nominees and winners, and assorted end of year round-ups, are all part of the discussion that leads to a consensus view, one that needs constantly to be built up and torn down as science fiction evolves and changes.

And the SF field is changing in interesting and exciting ways. Where it once presented an almost wholly white male worldview pretty much exclusively sourced from North America and the United Kingdom, it is now increasingly diverse and varied. Fiction from China, India, Africa, and South America is slowly (too slowly!) becoming available, as is work in English translation thanks to the work of Ken Liu and others, and we are seeing fiction written by and from the viewpoint of non-white, non-male, non-cisgendered people become more widely published and more widely read than ever before. This diversity of writers and of perspectives comes at a time when SF needs a fresh influx of ideas and perspectives to rejuvenate itself.

While diversity is to be nurtured and encouraged and is enriching our field, I suspect that the conversation around it is yet to reach the stage where we see taste groups break down and new consensuses emerge about what the SF canon should and should not be for the coming years. But I can see that time coming.

When I entered SF back in the mid-1980s I heard a lot about that 'conversation', the dialogue between individual works of science fiction and fantasy and between readers and commentators on the field who were engaged in identifying the SF/F literary 'canon'. I also rather absorbed the compelling narrative that sees SF start in the 'Golden Age of SF' with Hugo Gernsback, glance off Heinlein and Campbell, and make its way to the present with a ricochet here and there off the New Wave and Cyberpunk. I certainly didn't think much about what happened outside that narrative, or how that narrative itself might change, or how it needed to be challenged from time to time. That came later.

Looking around the field now, it seems to me that we are at as stage where the evolution of that main conversation – the discussion of where SF comes from, where it is today and where it's going tomorrow – is being set to one side as discrete taste groups form, evolve and change, a process greatly assisted by changes to publishing and distribution that have empowered new voices and alternate viewpoints and reduced the influence of traditional elites. Discussions are going on within those groups about what is and is not excellent, and those discussions are perhaps not yet completely ready to move outwards to change the field at large. It certainly seems to me that at the same time the field is becoming more diverse, the barriers of cost and access to the means of publication have been removed, and as a result fiction is being published in ever increasing quantity. That means it's more and more possible to read within a taste group, and to not engage with the wider field. This atomizing of the field seems to me to be a natural part of the cycle of forming a new consensus view of SF. The SF conversation I loved when I became active in the field is only enriched when more people take part, and when it is fully open to others taking part. I'm optimistic that will happen more in coming years.

I believe that a small part of the process of moving to a broader more inclusive conversation of SF and fantasy is the regular inclusion of new voices in best-of-the-year annuals like this one. With so much work being published in some many different places and in such quantity it can be challenging for casual readers to find interesting work and to see how the consensus is evolving on what is and is not of interest. Books like this one, and the valuable ones compiled by my colleagues Ellen Datlow, Gardner Dozois, Rich Horton, Stephen Jones, Nisi Shawl and others, become important simply because they present manageable selections to be consumed, considered and both argued with and applauded.

As to the short fiction market, it was a difficult year. Unless something changes, it seems destined for a niche status. A lot of what happened was familiar, with magazines opening and closing, new editors being appointed and old editors retiring, but some markets looked better than others.

It seemed to me that anthologies were the most reliable source of good original short fiction this year, something that's not always true, with a strong diverse set of books being published. Certainly *Hieroglyph*, *Monstrous Affections*, *Rogues*, *Kaleidoscope*, *Upgrade*, *Long Hidden*, *Twelve Tomorrows*, and others stood out. Print magazines, which featured a lot of good work, were less impressive than usual. *Asimov's* was the best out there, but seemed a little weaker to me than in recent years. *Analog* continued to deliver its particular brand of hard SF to a dedicated readership, but encouragingly continued to change under the editorial direction of Trevor Quachri. *The Magazine of Fantasy & Science Fiction,* once the gold standard for SF/F short fiction but somewhat disappointing of late, had a solid but unremarkable year. Interestingly publisher Gordon Van Gelder announced the appointment of a new editor at year's end and I wish Charles Coleman Finlay great success with rejuvenating this well-loved and much-respected publication.

Tor.com published a wide variety of excellent short fiction and was the best of the online magazines this year. While it doesn't have a clear focus, and while I couldn't tell you what makes a *Tor.com* story a '*Tor.com* story', it's always worth reading. *Subterranean*, which sadly closed at the end of the year ending a seven year run, published some very fine work during 2014, including major novellas by KJ Parker, Rachel Swirsky, and others. It will be missed. Both *Clarkesworld* and *Lightspeed* also had good years, but were a little indistinguishable from one another at a story level. Newly launched *Uncanny* seems promising, but is yet to really establish a personality. Also of interest were *Terraform*, *Beneath Ceaseless Skies*, and *Apex*.

And now, it's time for me to step out of the way and let you get to the stars of this show: the stories. I hope you'll enjoy reading them as much as I have, and that at the end of it, you'll have a bit of an idea of the year that was. And, of course, I'm already reading for next year and hope you'll join me when volume ten hits the shelves. Till then, enjoy!

Jonathan Strahan
Perth, Western Australia
January 2015

SLIPPING
Lauren Beukes

Lauren Beukes (www.laurenbeukes.com) is an award-winning, best-selling novelist who also writes comics, screenplays, TV shows and, occasionally, journalism. She is the author of *Broken Monsters, The Shining Girls, Zoo City, Moxyland, Maverick: Extraordinary Women From South Africa's Past* and the graphic novel, *Fairest: The Hidden Kingdom* with Inaki Miranda. As a screenwriter, she is currently adapting *Zoo City* for South African producer Helena Spring. She's worked on the satirical political puppet show, *Z News*, and the travelogue of *Archbishop Desmond Tutu: The South African Story*, and written on kids shows for Disney, including *Mouk and Florrie's Dragons* and was the showrunner on South Africa's animated TV series, *URBO: The Adventures of Pax Afrika*, which ran for 104 episodes from 2006-2009. In 2010, she directed the documentary *Glitterboys & Ganglands*, about Cape Town's biggest female impersonation beauty pageant. The film won Best LGBT film at the San Diego Black Film Festival.

1. High life

THE HEAT PRESSES against the cab, trying to find a way in past the sealed windows and the rattling air-conditioning. Narrow apartment blocks swoop past on either side of the dual carriageway, occasionally broken up by a warehouse megastore. It could be Cape Town, Pearl thinks. It could be anywhere. Twenty-three hours' travel so far. She has never been on a plane before.

"So what's the best part about Karachi?" Tomislav says, trying to break the oppressive silence in the back – the three of them dazed by the journey, the girl, her promoter, and the surgeon, who has not looked up from his phone since they got in the car, because he is trying to get a meeting.

The driver thinks about it, tugging at the little hairs of his beard. "One thing is that this is a really good road. Sharah e Faisal. There's hardly ever a traffic jam and if it rains, the road never drowns."

"Excellent." Tomislav leans back, defeated. He gives Pearl an encouraging smile, but she is not encouraged. She watched the World Cup and the Olympics on TV; she knows how it is supposed to be. She stares out the window, refusing to blink in case the tears come.

The road narrows into the city and the traffic thickens, hooting trucks and bakkies and rickshaws covered in reflecting stickers like disco balls, twinkling in the sun. They pass through the old city, with its big crumbling buildings from long ago, and into the warren of Saddar's slums, with concrete lean-tos muscling in on each other. *Kachi abaadi,* the driver tells them, and Pearl sounds it out under her breath. At least the shacks are not tin and that's one difference.

Tomislav points out the loops of graffiti in another alphabet and taps her plastic knee. "Gang signs. Just like the Cape Flats."

"Oh, they're gangsters, all right," the driver says. "Same people run the country."

"You have gangsters in your government?" Pearl is shocked.

The cab driver clucks and meets her eyes in the rearview mirror. "You one of the racers?"

"What clued you in?" Dr. Arturo says, without looking up. It's the first thing he's said all day. His thumbs tap over the screen of his phone, blunt instruments. Pearl rubs her legs self-consciously where the tendons are visible under the joint of her knee, running into the neurocircuitry. It's a showcase, Dr. Arturo told her when she asked him why it couldn't look like skin. Some days she thinks it's beautiful. Mostly, she hates seeing the inside-out of herself.

"Why do you think you're in Pakistan?" The driver laughs. "You think anyone else would let this happen in *their* country?" He rubs his thumb and fingers together and flings it to the wind.

*   *   *

2. Packed with goodness

PRE-RACE. A huge +Games banner hangs above the entrance of the Karachi Parsi Institute, or KPI. It's a colonial building that has been extended to accommodate them, the track built over the old cricket ground and into the slums. The school has been turned into the athletes' village, classrooms converted to individual medical cells to cater to their unique needs. Pearl's, for example, has hermetic bio-units and sterile surfaces. The window has been fused shut to prevent the polluted air from leaking in.

In the room next door, they installed extra generators for Charlotte Grange after she plugged in her exo-suit and tripped the power on the whole building. Pearl can hear her grunting through the walls. She doesn't know what Siska Rachman has.

She sits on the end of her bed, paging through the official program while Tomislav paces the room end to end, hunched over his phone, his hand resting on his nose. "Ajda! Come on!" her promoter says into the phone, in that Slavic way, which makes the first part of the sentence top-heavy. Like Tomislav himself, still carrying his weight-lifter bulk all squeezed up into his chest and neck. He doesn't compete anymore, but the steroids keep him in shape. The neon lights and the white sheen off the walls makes his eyes look bluer, his skin paler. 'Peach,' she was taught in school, as if 'peach' and 'brown' were magically less divisive than 'black' and 'white' and words could fix everything. But Tomislav's skin is not the warm orange of a summer fruit – it's like the milky tea she drinks at home.

Tomislav has thick black hair up his arms. She asked him about it when they first met at the Beloved One's house on the hill. Fourteen and too young and too angry about everything that had happened to mind her elders, even though her mother gasped at her rudeness and smacked her head.

Tomislav laughed. *Testosterone, kitten.* He tapped the slight fuzz over her lip. *You've got it too – that's what makes you so strong.*

He's made her laser all her unsightly hair since. Sports is image. Even this one.

He sees her looking and speaks louder. "You want to get a meeting, Arturo, we gotta have something to show." He jabs at the phone dramatically to end the call. "That guy! What does he think I'm doing all day? You all right, kitten?" He comes over to take her by the shoulders, give them a little rub. "You feeling good?"

"Fine." More than fine, with the crowd's voices a low vibration through the concrete and the starting line tugging at her insides, just through that door, across the quad, down the ramp. She has seen people climbing up onto the roofs around the track with picnic blankets.

"That's my girl." He snatches the program out of her hands. "Why are you even looking at this? You know every move these girls have."

He means Siska Rachman. That's all anyone wants to talk about. Pearl is sick of it, all the interviews for channels she's never heard of. No one told her how much of this would be *talking* about racing.

"Ready when you are," Dr. Arturo says into her head, through the audio feed in her cochlear implant. Back online as if he's never been gone, checking the diagnostics. "Watch your adrenaline, Pearl. You need to be calm for the install." He used to narrate the chemical processes, the shifting balances of hormones, the nano-enhancing oxygen uptake, the shift of robotic joints, the dopamine blast, but it felt too much like being in school: words being crammed into her head and all worthless anyway. You don't have to name something to understand it. She knows how it feels when she hits her stride and the world opens up beneath her feet.

"He's ready," she repeats to Tomislav.

"All right, let's get this show pumping."

Pearl obediently hitches up her vest with the Russian energy drink logo – one of Tomislav's sponsors, although that's only spare change. She has met the men who have paid for her to be here, in the glass house on the hill, wearing gaudy golf shirts and shoes and shiny watches. She never saw the men swing a club and she doesn't know their names, but they all wanted to shake her hand and take a photograph with her.

She feels along the rigid seam that runs in a J-hook down the side of her stomach, parallel with her hysterectomy scar, and tears open the Velcroskin.

"Let me," Tomislav says, kneeling between her legs. She holds her flesh open while he reaches one hand up inside her abdomen. It doesn't hurt, not anymore. The Velcro releases a local anesthetic when it opens, but she can feel an uncomfortable tugging inside, like cramps.

Tomislav twists off the valves on either side and gently unplugs her stomach and eases it out of her. He sets it in a sterile biobox and connects it to a blood flow. By the time he turns back, she is already spooling up the accordion twist of artificial intestine, like a party magician pulling ribbons from her palm. It smells of the lab-mod bacteria and the faintest whiff of feces. She hands it to Tomislav and he wrinkles his nose.

"Just goes to show," he says, folding up the slosh of crinkled plastic tubing and packing it away. "You can take the meat out of the human, but they're still full of shit!"

Pearl smiles dutifully, even though he has been making the same joke for the last three weeks – ever since they installed the new system. "Nearly there." He holds up the hotbed factory and she nods and looks away, because it makes her queasy to watch. It's a sleek bioplug, slim as a communion wafer and packed with goodness, Dr. Arturo says, like fortified breakfast cereal. Hormones and nanotech instead of vitamins and iron. Tomislav pushes his hand inside her again, feeling blindly for the connector node in what's left of her real intestinal tract, an inch and a half of the body's most absorbent tissue for better chemical uptake.

"Whoops! Got your kidney! Joking. It's in."

"Good to go," Dr. Arturo confirms.

"Then let's go," Pearl says, standing up on her blades.

3. Forces greater than you

YOU WOULD HAVE to be some kind of idiot. She told her mother it was a bet among the kids, but it wasn't. It was her, only her, trying to race the train. The train won.

4. Why you have me

THE SPRINGKAAN DRONE flits in front of Pearl's face, the lens zooming in on her lips to catch the words she's saying under her breath and transmit them onto the big screen. *"Ndincede nkosi undiphe amandla."*

She bends down to grab on to the curved tips of her legs, to stretch, yes, but also to hide her mouth. It's supposed to be private, she thinks. But that's an idea that belonged to another girl before Tomislav's deals and Dr. Arturo's voice in her head running through diagnostics, before the Beloved One, before the train, before all this.

"It's because you're so taciturn, kitten," Tomislav says, trying to comfort her. "You give the people crumbs and they're hungry for more. If you just talked more." He is fidgeting with his tie while Brian Corwood, the presenter, moves down the starters' carpet with his microphone, talking to Oluchi Eze, who is showing off her tail for the cameras. She doesn't know how to talk more. She's run out of words, and the ones Dr. Arturo wants her to say are like chewing on raw potatoes. She has to sound out the syllables.

Pearl swipes her tongue over her teeth to get rid of the feeling that someone has rigged a circuit behind her incisors. It's the new drugs in the hotbed, Tomislav says. She has to get used to it, like the drones, which dart up to her unexpectedly. They're freakish – cameras hardwired into grasshoppers, with enough brain stem left to respond to commands. Insects are cheap energy.

Somewhere in a control room, Dr. Arturo notes her twitching back from the springkaan and soothes in her head. "What do you think, Pearl? More sophisticated than some athletes we know." She glances over at Charlotte Grange, who is also waiting for her interview. The big blonde quakes and jitters, clenching her jaw, her exo-suit groaning in anticipation. The neural dampeners barely hold her back.

The crowd roars its impatience, thousands of people behind a curve of reinforced safety glass in the stands, raised high above the action. The rooftops are packed, and there are children climbing the scaffolding around the old church like monkeys.

The people in suits, the ones Dr. Arturo and Tomislav want to meet, watch from air-conditioned hotel rooms five kilometers away. Medical and pharmaceutical companies looking for new innovations in a place where anything goes: any drugs, any prosthetics, robotics, nano. That's what people come for. They tune in by the millions on the proprietary channel. The drama. Like watching Formula 1 for the car crashes.

"All these people, kitten," Tomislav says. "They don't want you to win. They're just waiting for you to explode. But you know why you're here."

"To run."

"That's my girl."

"Slow breaths," Dr. Arturo says. "You're overstimulated."

The springkaan drone responds to some invisible hand in a control room and swirls around her, getting every angle. Brian Corwood makes his way over to her, microphone extended like a handshake, springkaans buzzing behind his shoulder. She holds herself very straight. She knows her mama and the Beloved One are watching back home. She wants to do Gugulethu proud.

"Ndincede nkosi." She mouths the words and sees them come up on the big screens above the track in closed captions below her face.

They'll be working to translate them already. Not so hard to figure out that she's speaking Xhosa.

"Pearl Nit-seeko," the presenter says. "Cape Town's miracle girl. Crippled when she was 14 years old and now, here she is, two years later, at the +Games. Dream come true!"

Pearl has told the story so many times that she can't remember which parts are made up and glossed over. She told a journalist once that she saw her father killed on TV during the illegal mine strikes in Polokwane, saying she covered her ears so she didn't have to hear the popcorn *pa-pa-pa-pa-pa* of the gunshots as people fell in the dust. But now she has to stick to it. Grand tragedy is a better story than the reality of a useless middle-aged drunk who lived with a shebeen owner's daughter in Nyanga so that he didn't have to pay off the bar tab. When Pearl started to get famous, her father made a stink in the local gossip rags until Tomislav paid him to go away. You can buy your own truth.

"Can you tell us about your tech, Pearl?" Brian Corwood says, as if this is a show about movie stars and glittery dresses.

She responds on autopilot. The removable organs, the bath of nano in her blood that improves oxygen uptake. Neural connectivity blows open the receptors to the hormones and drugs dispatched by the hotbed factory. Tomislav has coached her in the newsworthy technical specs, the leaks that make investors' ears prick up.

"I can't show you," she apologizes, coyly raising her vest to let the cameras zoom in on the seam of scar tissue. "It's not a sterile environment."

"So it's hollow in there?" Corwood pretends to knock on her stomach.

"Reinforced surgical-quality graphene mesh." She lightly drums her fingers over her skin, like in rehearsal. It looks spontaneous and shows off her six-pack.

She hears Arturo's voice in her head. "Put the vest down now," Arturo instructs. She covers herself up. The star doesn't want to let the viewers see too much. Like with sex. Or so she's been told. She will never have children.

"Is that your secret weapon?" Corwood says, teasing, because no one ever reveals the exact specs, not until they have a buyer.

"No," she says, "but I do have one."

"What is it, then?" Corwood says, gamely.

"God," she says, and stares defiant at the insect cameras zooming in for a close-up.

5. Things you can't hide

HER STUMPS ARE *wrapped in fresh bandages, but the wounds still smell. Like something caught in the drain. Her mother wants to douse the bandages in perfume.*

"I don't want to! Leave me alone!" Pearl swats the teardrop bottle from her mother's hands and it clatters onto the floor. Her mother tries to grab her. The girl falls off the bed with a shriek. She crawls away on her elbows, sobbing and yowling. Her Uncle Tshepelo hauls her up by her armpits, like she is a sack of sorghum flour, and sets her down at the kitchen table.

"Enough, Pearl," he says, her handsome youngest uncle. When she was a little girl she told her mother she was going to marry him.

"I hate you," she screams. She tries to kick at him with her stumps, but he ducks away and goes over to the kettle while her mother stands in the doorway and covers her face.

Pearl has not been back to school since it happened. She turns to face the wall when her friends come to visit and refuses to talk with them. During the day, she watches soap operas and infomercials and lies in her mother's bed and stares at the sky and listens to the noise of the day; the cycles of traffic and school kids and dogs barking and the call to prayer buzzing through the mosque's decrepit speakers and the traffic again and men drunk and fighting at the shebeen. Maybe one of them is her father, who has not been to see her since the accident.

Tshepelo makes sweet milky tea, for her and her mother, and sits and talks: nonsense, really, about his day in the factory, cooking up batches of paté, which is fancy flavored butter for rich people, and how she should see the stupid blue plastic cap he has to wear to cover his hair in case of contamination. He talks and talks until she calms down.

Finally, she agrees that she will go to church, a special service in Khayelitsha Site B. She puts on her woolen dress, grey as the Cape Town winter sky, and green stockings, which dangle horribly at the joint where her legs should be.

The rain polka-dots her clothes and soaks into her mother's hat, making it flop as she quick-steps after Tshepelo, carrying Pearl in his arms like an injured dog. She hates the way people avert their eyes.

The church is nothing, a tent in a parking lot, although the people sing like they are in a fancy cathedral in England like on TV. Pearl sits stiffly on the end of the pew between her uncle and her mother, glaring at the little kids who dart around to come and stare. "Vaya," she hisses at them. "What are you looking at? Go."

Halfway through the service, two of the ministers bring out the brand-new wheelchair like it is a prize on a game show, tied with a big purple ribbon. They carry it down the stairs on their shoulders and set it down in front of her. She looks down and mumbles something. Nkosi.

They tuck their fingers into her armpits, these strangers' hands on her, and lift her into it. The moment they set her down, she feels trapped. She moans and shakes her head.

"She's so grateful," her mother says, and presses her into the chair with one hand on her shoulder. Hallelujah, everyone says. Hallelujah. The choir breaks into song and Pearl wishes that God had let her die.

6. Heat

PEARL'S BRAIN IS microseconds behind her body. The bang of the starting gun registers as a sound after she is already running.

She is aware of the other runners as warm, straining shapes in the periphery. Tomislav has made her study the way they run. Charlotte Grange, grunting and loping, using the exo-suit arms to dig into the ground like an ape; Anna Murad with her robotics wet-wired into her nerves; Oluchi Eze with her sculpted tail and her delicate bones, like a dinosaur bird. And in lane five, farthest away from her, Siska Rachman with her face perfectly calm and empty and her eyes locked on the finish line, two kilometers away. A dead girl remote-controlled by a quadriplegic in a hospital bed. That is the problem with the famous Siska Rachman. She wins a lot, but there is network lag time.

You have to inhabit your body. You need to be in it. Not only because the rules say, but because otherwise you can't feel it. The strike of your foot against the ground, the rush of air on your skin, the sweat running down your sides. No amount of biofeedback will make the difference. "Pace yourself," Arturo says in her head. "I'll give you a glucose boost when you hit 800 meters."

Pearl tunes in to the rhythmic huff of her breath and she stretches out her legs longer with each stride and she is aware of everything, the texture of the track, and the expanse of the sky, and the smell of sweat and dust and oil. It blooms in her chest – a fierce warmth, a golden glow within, and she feels the rush of His love and she knows that God is with her.

She crosses third, neck and neck with Siska Rachman and milliseconds behind Charlotte Grange, who throws herself across the finish line with a wet ripping sound. The exo-suit goes down in a tumble of girl and metal, forcing Rachman to sidestep.

"A brute," Arturo whispers in her ear. "Not like you, Pearl."

7. Beloved

The car comes to fetch them, Pearl and her mother and her uncle. A shiny black BMW with hubcaps that turn the light into spears. People come out of their houses to see.

She is wearing her black lace dress, but it's 40 degrees out and the sweat runs down the back of her neck and makes her collar itch.

"Don't scratch," her mother says, holding her hands.

The car cuts through the location between the tin shacks and the government housing and all the staring eyes, out onto the highway, into the winelands and past the university and the rich people's townhouses which all look alike, past the golf course where little carts dart between the sprinklers, and the hills with vineyards and flags to draw the tourists, and down a side road and through a big black gate which swings open onto a driveway lined with spiky cycads.

They climb out, stunned by the heat and other things besides – like the size of the house, the wood and glass floating on top of the hill. Her uncle fights to open the wheelchair Khayelitsha Site B bought her, until the driver comes round and says, "Let me help you with that, sir." He shoves down hard on the seat and it clicks into place.

He brings them into a cool entrance hall with wooden floors and metal sculptures of cheetahs guarding the staircase. A woman dressed in a red-and-white dress and a wrap around her head smiles and ushers them into the lounge, where three men are waiting: a grandfather with two white men flanking him like the stone cats by the stairs. One old, one hairy.

"The Beloved One," her mother says, averting her eyes. *Her uncle bows his head and raises his hands in deference.*

Their fear makes Pearl angry.

The grandfather waves at them to come, come, impatiently. The trousers of his dark-blue suit have pleats folded as sharp as paper, and his shoes are black like coal.

"So this is Pearl Nitseko," the Beloved One says, testing the weight of her name. *"I've heard about you."*

The old white man stares at her. The lawyer, she will find out later, who makes her and her mother sign papers and more papers and papers. The one with thick shoulders fidgets with his cuffs, pulling them down over his hairy wrists, but he is watching her most intently of all.

"What?" she demands. *"What have you heard?"* Her mother gasps and smacks her head.

The Beloved One smiles, gently. "That you have fire in you."

* * *

8. Fearful tautologies

TOMISLAV HUSTLES PEARL past the Muslim protestors outside the stadium. The sects have united in moral outrage, chanting, "Un-natural! Ungodly! Unholy!" They chant the words in English rather than Urdu for the benefit of the drones.

"Come on!" Tomislav shoulders past the protestors, steering her toward a shuttle car that will take them to dinner. "Don't these cranks have bigger things to worry about? Their thug government? Their starving children?" Pearl leaps into the shuttle and he launches himself in after her. "Extremism I can handle." He slams the door. "But tautology? That's unforgivable."

Pearl zips up the hood of her tracksuit.

The Pakistani crowd surges to the shuttle, bashing its windows with the flats of their hands. "Monster!" a woman shouts in English. "God hates you."

"What's tautology?"

"Unnecessary repetition."

"Isn't that what fear always is?"

"I forget that you're fast *and* clever. Yeah. Screw them," Tomislav says. The shuttle rolls and he claps his hands together. "You did good out there."

"Did you get a meeting?"

"We got a meeting, kitten. I know you think your big competition is Siska, but it's Charlotte. She just keeps going and going."

"She hurt herself."

"Ripped a tendon, the news says, but she's still going to race tomorrow."

Dr. Arturo chimes in, always listening. "They have backup meat in the lab, they can grow a tendon. But it's not a good long-term strategy. This is a war, not a battle."

"I thought we weren't allowed to fight," Pearl says.

"You talking to the doc? Tell him to save his chatter for the investors."

"Tomislav says –" she starts.

"I heard him," Dr. Arturo says.

Pearl looks back at the protestors. One of the handwritten banners stays with her. *I am fearfully and wonderfully made*, it reads.

*   *   *

9. She is risen

PEARL WATCHES THE *buses arrive from her bed upstairs in the church. A guest room adapted for the purpose, with a nurse sitting outside and machines that hiss and bleep. The drugs make her woozy. She has impressions of things, but not memories. The whoop of the ambulance siren and the feeling of being important. Visitors. Men in golf shorts and an army man with fat cheeks. Gold watches and stars on the uniform, to match the gold star on the tower she can see from her window and the fat tapered columns like bullets at the entrance.*

"Are you ready?" Dr. Arturo says. He has come from Venezuela especially for her. He has gentle hands and kind eyes, she thinks, even though he is the one who cut everything out of her. Excess baggage, he says. It hurts where it was taken out, her female organs and her stomach and her guts.

He tells her they have been looking for someone like her for a long time, he and Tomislav. They had given up on finding her. And now! Now look where they are. She is very lucky. She knows this because everyone keeps telling her.

Dr. Arturo takes her to the elevator where Tomislav is waiting. The surgeon is very modest. He doesn't like to be seen on camera. "Don't worry, I'll be with you," he says, and taps her jaw just below her ear.

"It's all about you, kitten," Tomislav soothes, wheeling her out into a huge hallway full of echoes under a painted sky with angels and the Beloved One, in floating purple robes, smiling down on the people flowing through the doors, the women dressed in red and white and the men in blue blazers and white shirts. This time she doesn't mind them looking.

They make way for the wheelchair, through the double doors, past the ushers, into a huge room with a ceiling crinkled and glossy as a seashell and silver balconies and red carpets. She feels like a film star, and the red blanket over her knees is like her party dress.

From somewhere deep in the church, women raise their voices in ululation and all the hair on Pearl's body pricks up as if she were a cat. Tomislav turns the wheelchair around and parks it beside a huge gold throne with carved leaves and flowers and a halo of spikes around the head. He pats her shoulder and leaves her there, facing the crowd, thousands of them in the auditorium, all staring at her. "Smile, Pearl," Dr. Arturo says, his voice soft inside her head, and she tries, she really does.

A group of women walk out onto the stage, swaying with wooden bowls on their hips, their hands dipping into the bowls like swans pecking at the water and throwing rose petals before them. The crowd picks up the ululating and it reverberates through the church. Halalala.

The Beloved One steps out and onto the stage and Pearl has to cover her ears at the noise that greets him. A hail of voices. Women are weeping in the aisles. Men too, crying in happiness to see him.

The Beloved One holds out his hands to still them. "Quiet, please, brothers and sisters," he says. "Peace be with you."

"And also with you," the crowd roars back, the sound distorted, frayed. He places his hands on the back of the wheelchair.

"Today, we come together to witness a miracle. My daughter, will you stand up and walk?'

And Pearl does.

10. Call to prayer

THE RESTAURANT IS fancy with a buffet of Pakistani food, korma and tikka and kabobs and silver trays of sticky sweet pastries. The athletes have to pose for photographs and do more interviews with Brian Corwood and other people. The girl with purple streaks in her hair and the metal ring in her lip asks her, "Aren't you afraid you're gonna die out there?" before Tomislav intervenes.

"Come on! What kind of question is that?" he says. "Can't you be normal?"

But the athletes don't really eat and there is a bus that takes them home early so they can be fresh, while the promoters peel away, one by one, looking tense, in fancy black cars that take them to other parts of the city. "Don't you worry, kitten." Tomislav smiles, all teeth, and pats her hand.

Back in her room, Pearl finds a prayer mat that might be aligned toward Mecca. She phones down to reception to ask. She prostrates herself on the square of carpet, east, west, to see if it is any different, if her God will be annoyed.

She goes online to check the news and the betting pools. Her odds have improved. There is a lot of speculation about Grange's injury and whether Rachman will be disqualified. There are photographs of Oluchi Eze posing naked for a men's magazine, her tail wrapped over her parts.

Pearl clicks away and watches herself in the replay, her strikes, her posture, the joy in her face. She expects Dr. Arturo to comment, but the cochlear implant only hisses with faint static.

"Mama? Did you see the race?" she says. The video connection to Gugulethu stalls and jitters. Her mother has the camera on the phone pointed down too low, so she can only see her eyes and the top of her head.

"They screened it at the church," her mother says. "Everyone was very excited."

"You should have heard them shouting for you, Pearl," her uncle says, leaning over her mother's shoulder, tugging the camera down so they are in the frame.

Her mother frowns. "I don't know if you should wear that vest – it's not really your color."

"It's my sponsor, Mama."

"We're praying for you to do well. Everyone is praying for you."

11. Desert

SHE HAS A *dream that she and Tomislav and Jesus are standing on the balcony of the Karachi Parsi Institute looking over the slums. The fine golden sand rises up like water between the concrete shacks, pouring in the windows, swallowing up the roofs, driven by the wind.*

"Did you notice that there are only one set of footsteps, Pearl?" Jesus says. The sand rises, swallowing the houses, rushing to fill the gaps, nature taking over. "Do you know why that is?"

"Is it because you took her fucking legs, Lord?" Tomislav says. Pearl can't see any footsteps in the desert. The sand shifts too quickly.

*   *   *

12. Rare flowers

WIDE AWAKE. HALF past midnight. She lies in bed and stares at the ceiling. Arturo was supposed to boost her dopamine and melatonin, but he's busy. The meeting went well, then. The message on her phone from Tomislav confirms it. *Good news!!!! Tell you in the morning. Sleep tight, kitten, you need it.*

She turns the thought around in her head and tries to figure out how she feels. Happy. This will mean that she can buy her mother a house and pay for her cousins to go to private school and set up the Pearl Nitseko Sports Academy for Girls in Gugulethu. She won't ever have to race again. Unless she wants to.

The idea of the money sits on her chest.

She swings her stumps over the bed and straps on her blades. She needs to go out, get some air.

She clips down the corridors of the school building. There is a party on the old cricket field outside, with beer tents and the buzz of people who do not have to run tomorrow, exercising their nerves. She veers away from them, back toward the worn-out colonial building of the IPC, hoping to get onto the race track. Run it out.

The track is fenced off and locked, but the security guard is dazed by his phone, caught up in another world of sliding around colorful blocks. She clings to the shadows of the archway, right past him and deeper into the building, following wherever the doors lead her.

She comes out into a hall around a pit of sunken tiles. An old swimming pool. Siska Rachman is sitting on the edge, waving her feet in the ghost of water, her face perfectly blank with her hair a dark nest around it. Pearl lowers herself down beside her. She can't resist. She flicks Rachman's forehead. "Heita. Anyone in there?"

The body blinks, and suddenly the eyes are alive and furious. She catches Pearl's wrist. "Of course I am," she snaps.

"Sorry, I didn't think –"

Siska has already lost interest. She drops her grip and brushes her hair away from her face. "So, you can't sleep either? Wonder why."

"Too nervous," Pearl says. She tries for teasing, like Tomislav would. "I have tough competition."

"Maybe not." Siska scowls. "They're going to fucking disqualify me."

Pearl nods. She doesn't want to apologize again. She feels shy around Siska, the older girl with her bushy eyebrows and her sharp nose. The six years between them feels like an uncrossable gap.

"Do they think Charlotte is *present?*" Siska bursts out. "Charlotte is a big dumb animal. How is *she* more human than me?"

"You're two people," Pearl tries to explain.

"Before. You were half a person before. Does that count against you?"

"No."

"Do you know what this used to be?" Siska pats the blue tiles.

"A swimming pool?"

"They couldn't maintain the upkeep. These things are expensive to run." Siska glances at Pearl to make sure she understands. In the light through the glass atrium, every lash stands out in stark relief against the gleam of her eyes, like undersea creatures. "They drained all the water out, but there was this kid who was... damaged in the brain, and the only thing he could do was grow orchids, so that's what he did. He turned it into a garden and sold them out of here for years, until he got old and now it's gone."

"How do you know this?"

"The guard told me. We smoked cigarettes together. He wanted me to give him a blowjob."

"Oh." Pearl recoils.

"Hey, are you wearing lenses?"

She knows what she means. The broadcast contacts. "No. I wouldn't."

"They're going to use you and use you up, Pearl Nit-seeko. Then you'll be begging to give some lard-ass guard a blowjob for spare change."

"It's Ni-tse-koh."

"Doesn't matter. You say tomato, I say ni-tse-koh." But Siska gets it right this time. "You think it's all about you. Your second chance, and all you got to do is run your heart out. But it's a talent show, and they don't care about the running. You got a deal yet?"

"My promoter and my doctor had a meeting."

"That's something. They say who?"

"I'm not sure."

"Pharmaceutical or medical?"

"They haven't told me yet."

"Or military. Military's good. I hear the British are out this year. That's what you want. I mean, who knows what they're going to do with it, but what do you care, little guinea pig, long as you get your payout."

"Are you *drunk?*"

"My *body* is drunk. I'm just mean. What do you care? I'm out, sister. And you're in, with a chance. Wouldn't that be something if you won? Little girl from Africa."

"It's not a country."

"Boo-hoo, sorry for you."

"God brought me here."

"Oh, that guy? He's nothing but trouble. And He doesn't exist."

"You shouldn't say that."

"How do you know?"

"I can feel Him."

"Can you still feel your legs?"

"Sometimes," Pearl admits.

Siska leans forward and kisses her. "Did you feel anything?"

"No," she says, wiping her mouth. But that's not true. She felt her breath that burned with alcohol, and the softness of her lips and her flicking tongue, surprisingly warm for a dead girl.

"Yeah." Siska breathes out. "Me neither." She kisses her again. "News flash, Pearl Ni-tse-koh. There's no God. There's only us. You got a cigarette?"

13. Empty spaces

LANE FIVE IS empty and the stadium is buzzing with the news.

"Didn't think they'd actually ban her," Tomislav says. She can tell he's hung over. He stinks of sweat and alcohol and there's a crease in his forehead just above his nose that he keeps rubbing at. "Do you want to hear about the meeting? It was big. Bigger than we'd hoped for. If this comes off, kitten..."

"I want to concentrate on the race." She is close to tears but she doesn't know why.

"Okay. You should try to win. Really."

The gun goes off. They tear down the track. Every step feels harder today. She didn't get enough sleep.

She sees it happen, out of the corner of her eye. Oluchi's tail swipes Charlotte, maybe on purpose.

"Shit," Grange says and stumbles in her exo-suit. Suddenly everything comes crashing down on Pearl, hot metal and skin and a tangle of limbs and fire in her side.

"Get up," Dr. Arturo yells into her head. She's never heard him upset.

"Ow," she manages. Charlotte is already getting to her feet. There is a loose flap of muscle hanging from her leg, where they tried to attach it this morning. The blonde girl touches it and hisses in pain, but her eyes are already focused on the finish line, on Oluchi skipping ahead, her tail swinging, Anna Murad straining behind her.

"Get up," Dr. Arturo says. "You have to get up. I'm activating adrenaline. Pain blockers."

She sits up. It's hard to breathe. Her vest is wet. A grey nub of bone pokes out through her skin under her breast. Charlotte is limping away in her exo-suit, her leg dragging, gears whining.

"This is what they want to see," Arturo urges. "You *need* to prove to them that it's not hydraulics carrying you through."

"It's not," Pearl gasps. The sound is somehow wet. Breathing through a snorkel in the bath when there is water trapped in the U-bend. The drones buzz around her. She can see her face big on the screen. Her mama is watching at home, the whole of the congregation.

"Then prove it. What are you here for?"

She starts walking, then jogging, clutching her top to the bit of rib to stop its jolting. Every step rips through her. And Pearl can feel things *slipping* inside. Her structural integrity has been compromised, she thinks. The abdominal mesh has ripped, and where her stomach used to be is a black hole that is tugging everything down. Her heart is slipping.

Ndincede nkosi, she thinks. Please, Jesus, help me.

Ndincede nkosi undiphe amandla. Please, God, give me strength. *Yiba nam kolu gqatso.* Be with me in this race.

She can feel it. The golden glow that starts in her chest, or if she is truthful with herself, lower down. In the pit of her stomach.

She sucks in her abdominals and presses her hand to her sternum to stop her heart from sliding down into her guts – where her guts used to be, where the hotbed factory sits.

God is with me, she thinks. What matters is you feel it.

Pearl Nitseko runs.

MORIABE'S CHILDREN
Paolo Bacigalupi

Paolo Bacigalupi (www.windupstories.com) has been published in *Wired, High Country News, Salon.com, OnEarth Magazine, F&SF*, and *Asimov's Science Fiction*. His short fiction has been collected in Locus Award winner and PW Book of the Year *Pump Six and Other Stories* and has been nominated for three Nebula Awards, four Hugo Awards, and won the Theodore Sturgeon Memorial Award for best science fiction short story of the year. Debut novel *The Windup Girl* was named by *Time Magazine* as one of the ten best novels of 2009, and won the Hugo, Nebula, Locus, Compton Crook, and John W. Campbell Memorial Awards, among others. His debut young adult novel, *Ship Breaker*, is a Printz Award Winner, and a National Book Award Finalist, and was followed by *The Drowned Cities, Zombie Baseball Beatdown*, and *The Doubt Factory*. His new novel for adults, *The Water Knife*, will be published later this year. He currently lives in Western Colorado with his wife and son, where he is working on a new novel.

ALANIE HAD NEVER seen a kraken, but her people spoke of them often. The kraken were out beyond the breakwaters of Serenity Bay, the hungry children of Moriabe. They writhed in the depths and sometimes rose to the surface to hunt. A kraken's tentacles could encircle a sailing ship and crack its spine. Kraken snapped masts like kindling, and swallowed sailors whole. None but the most foolhardy and desperate hunted kraken. But sometimes, it was said, a captain might return from the open ocean with the prize of one of Moriabe's children, his ship wallowing low in the waters as he tied to the Prince's Pier, his fortune assured thanks to the bloody mountain of flesh piled in his hold. Alanie sold oysters in

Greyling Square, and she had seen hopeful ships set sail on hunts, but she had never seen one return with a kraken in its hold – and most ships never returned at all.

ALANIE SOLD OYSTERS and accepted whatever prices High Street cooks offered when they came down from the mansions that ringed the white cliffs of the bay. After her father died, Alanie prayed to Moriabe that she might find and sell enough oysters so that she and her mother would not be forced from their home on Middle Street, and each day she returned home with too little for her efforts.

Alanie often lingered in Greyling Square until darkness fell and then stumbled home by the light of the stars. And while she lingered, she listened to the talk of the other fishmongers as they compared their business days and their netted catch, and sometimes they would speculate on what it might be like to return to port with a hold overflowing with kraken spoils.

"I saw Greyling when he caught his prize, so long ago," old Bericha said, as she plucked out the last of her flankfish and beheaded it for Tradi Maurch's cook.

"The prince threw a fete. Maidens tossed rose petals at his feet as he went up the cliffs to the prince's manor on the point. And behind him, his sailors came, too. Urn after urn, full to the neck with reddest blood and greyest poisons and blackest inks."

The ink went to lovers' notes, a syrup-sweet filigree to the protestations of devotion that suitors spilled on vellum. The blood went to wealthy bedrooms and was mixed with wine, an aphrodisiac said to besot lovers for days. And, of course, the poison also had its place. Wrung from the kraken's tentacles, the grey viscous poison was slipped via servant entrances to the betrayed – the ones who had been foolish enough to believe the sweet calligraphy of love, and yielded to the madness of trust. Kraken poison found its way into Calagari wine and Rake Point mead and flankfish stuffing, and former lovers thrashed and collapsed, frothing blood and spittle, praying for forgiveness as they gave up their lives.

Ink and blood and poison, tender meat, powdered tentacles – all found ready markets in the High Street mansions where they ringed the bay atop white marbled cliffs and kept sharp eye over the prince's commerce.

The fishmongers gossiped and wished, and packed up their water carts and dragged them sloshing from the deepening shadows of Greyling Square, with copper bits in their pockets and visions of untold wealth in their tired dreams.

ALANIE HAD NEVER seen a kraken, but her mother spoke of them often. Sinolise spoke bitterly of the creatures that had taken the *Sparrow* and her crew. She spoke of Alanie's father, whom Alanie remembered as a giant of a man, black-bearded and laughing.

Alanie's mother said the kraken were always hungry, spawned from a cold trysting between Moriabe and Stormface, an object lesson that lovemaking in anger resulted in terrible things.

Sinolise said the kraken were always hungry, and it wasn't just a man's body they sought to consume, but his mind.

A man could lose his head hunting kraken, mad for the profit that might result. He forgot wife and child, love and life. Kraken muddled a man's thoughts until he dreamed of becoming another Orin Greyling, a legend who might be spoken of for generations. It happened all the time. A man lost his wits in pursuit of kraken, and when he did, it was his family who suffered. It was his family who were forced to flee to pastures far beyond the city. It was his wife who was forced to find a new man who would accept a pauper woman and daughter into his home.

The kraken stole not only sailors' lives, but also the lives of all those people who had been foolish enough to believe in them.

ALANIE HAD NEVER seen a kraken, but her father had spoken of them often.

"I saw them, Alanie. With my own eyes, close as touching, just beneath our *Sparrow*'s beam."

He told her how the *Sparrow* had wallowed, half drowned, leaking between her boards as Moriabe and Wanem clashed in a lovers' battle and the *Sparrow* was trapped in the heart of the tempest.

"Half of Moriabe was down in our hold. Every time a wave crested, I was sure poor *Sparrow* would founder and we'd all be dragged down.

"For two days and two nights, we fought that storm. We bailed and bailed. We lost Tomo and Relkin to Moriabe's and Wanem's fury. We fought Moriabe's waves, and we battled Wanem's torrents, and none of us believed that we could survive. Waves taller than our masts, Alanie! Winds yanking us about like a toy on a string. It was all I could do to keep the *Sparrow*'s prow to the rise of Moriabe's next embrace. Every time we climbed a wave, I was sure it would be our last. . ."

He trailed off, and then abruptly smiled.

"When dawn came, we were so exhausted and waterlogged and broken down that at first we thought we had drowned and gone to the distant shore, but instead of the warm song of the Rising Lands, it was the sun, giving us all her warmth.

"The waves steamed mist, and the sky was bluer than the shell of a bluestem clam, and Moriabe was as still and calm and loving as a cat nursing kittens, and our only company was a pair of dolphins bearing Tomo back to us. It was as if Moriabe herself had decided old Relkin was enough sacrifice, so she gave us back our skinny cabin boy.

"We thought we were blessed that day, Alanie. We bailed water from our hold, and every time we dumped a bucket into the sea, we thanked Moriabe for making peace with Stormface. She was so still and calm in that moment, just sunshine and wavelets, all the way to the horizon. Bitty little wavelets, gleaming like mirrors...

"That's when we saw them. Just below our hold. Huge, Alanie, so big... I've seen a black whale breach and knock a frigate aside like a toy, and a black is nothing to the kraken. A snack, perhaps. The kraken are so large, you can't fit them in your eye. You cannot see the whole of them, not when you're close. Nothing holds a candle to the size of them, except maybe bluebacks, and no one dares hunt them.

"We stood there, staring. Me and all the rest of the men, jam-jawed, every one of us. All of us looking down into the water, and not a one of us making a sound as they passed and passed and passed. It was something extraordinary, seeing Moriabe's children. Huge long tentacles trailing behind them, down there in the water. Dozens of them, and any one of them might have dragged our mortal *Sparrow* down without a second thought. They are greater than we, by far."

He paused. "Everyone talks of kraken, but no one knows the truth. That prize Orin Greyling brought home in his hold? The one they say was as big as his ship?" Her father shook his head. "It was but a babe, Alanie. Nothing but a tiny little babe."

Alanie's father had seen the kraken, and he never forgot its awe. And when he was near poverty, ruined by poor trade, and with hundreds upon hundreds of useless black-whale oil casks turning rancid in his warehouse, he remembered how the kraken surfaced after Wanem and Moriabe fought in a tempest and then made amends, and he would hunt.

Armored with his own desperation, armed with poisoned harpoons and the lore of Greyling's triumph, Alanie's father sailed the *Sparrow* into the teeth of a building storm, his crew a band of hopeless souls who anticipated nothing but debtors' labor in the marble quarries of the white cliffs if they failed in their mission – a ragged band of gamblers, betting on a future that was already beyond their reach.

Alanie had never seen a kraken, but they spoke to her often.

In her dreams the kraken spoke to her, and when they did, they called her by name.

Alanie. Alanie.

In the darkness of her new father's chink-stone manor, wrapped in quilts before his hearth, listening to her mother and the man she had chosen for shelter as they rustled and groaned in the man's bedroom, Alanie stared into the flickering fires as the kraken called to her.

The kraken sang of ocean currents and cities beneath the waves. They sang of shipwrecks and gold and the lost wines of ancients. They sang of urns of olives and whale oil, the marbled statuary of Melna and Calib, a carpet of treasures spread across the seafloor, woven with the bones of sailors.

The kraken called to Alanie when she was asleep and stalked her when she was awake. They sang to her as she walked the pastures learning the trade of shepherd from her stepbrother, Elbe. They whispered to her when she scrambled down the cliffs to the beach where she hid from her new family and hunted for oysters. They chuckled predatory in her mind when she straightened from scrubbing shells and caught her stepfather standing too close, his gaze lingering too long on her body.

Every night as the embers of the kitchen fire turned to ash and glow, the kraken came calling.

Alanie, Alanie.

*   *   *

ALANIE HAD NEVER seen a kraken, but she remembered the first time she heard their song.

She'd stood at the end of Prince's Pier, a tiny girl alone on the longest finger that poked into the bay, looking out across calm waters to the froth of the breaks and the channel where her father would return. Around her, sailors loaded bales of wool brought into the city from the pastureland. The great storm rains had soaked the bales, and the sailors and stevedores cursed the weight of the wool, while owners and captains argued over the merits of drying the wool or shipping it immediately.

All across the pier's oiled planks, water beaded and steamed as the sun rose and warmed the white cliffs that ringed Serenity Bay, and it was then that Alanie heard the singing. She heard the snap of timbers and felt the prick of barbed steel in her skin and tasted blood in her mouth.

Alanie stood at the tip of the pier, bathed in sunlight, trembling, listening to the delighted singing of the kraken as they fed.

That night she told her mother that Father was dead and would not be returning, and her mother beat her for the news. Her mother beat her for cursing a sailor beyond the breaks, and beat her for telling lies, and beat her for her lack of faith; and Alanie fled her home for the streets, and all the time Alanie heard the kraken singing as they ran their tentacles through the shattered *Sparrow* and ferreted out the last drowned bodies of her father's crew.

When Alanie returned home, she found Sinolise sitting in the shadows, a single candle flickering on her mother's face, turning her bones to hard, sharp angles. The woman did not look up at Alanie's return, and Alanie saw that her mother was afraid.

Her mother – who had seemed so important and authoritative as she ran her Middle Street household and its servants – was now adrift. A bit of storm wood tossed into an ocean of uncertainty.

With a surge of fear, Alanie realized that her mother was weak. Sinolise was not a woman who supported herself as the fishmongers in Greyling Square. She was a woman who wanted others to care for her. She'd chosen a man with a ship to his name on the assumption that her marriage would bring her servants and a house farther up the white cliffs, far away from the fish guts among which she'd been raised. Sinolise had chosen a man of the sea in order to abandon it, and more foolish she to have thought that way.

Alanie went to bed, knowing that she was lost in an ocean greater than any her father had ever navigated. She wondered how she was meant to sail its currents and shallows with no knowledge or skill of her own.

A week later news came of the *Sparrow* wreckage, and Alanie found her mother down on her knees in the kitchen, burning her father's clothing in the fire. Alanie saw her mother's hatred and fear – that Alanie had known of her father's death before it could be known.

A month after that, without money to pay them, their two servants were gone, and not long beyond, just before Summerturn, Alanie's mother announced that they would be living in the country.

Alanie would have a new father – a stepfather – a man who was a widower, and who had lands and sheep.

Eliam was a man who didn't mind a woman who brought with her the child of another man, and came without means to his doorstep.

ALANIE HAD NEVER seen the kraken, but she remembered the first time they spoke her name.

The man who was meant to replace her father called himself Eliam. His wealth was known, his generosity as well. He was tall and strong, his beard was brown, and he kept his hair in a long braid. He was as powerful as her father, but different in the eyes in a way Alanie couldn't name.

Eliam smiled as Alanie's mother presented her. He touched Alanie's hand and exclaimed over her and complimented her dress and tresses.

"Why, you're nearly a woman," he said.

"You look the age of my son, Elbe," he said.

"Such a lovely daughter," he said.

Sinolise took Eliam's attention as a compliment, but Alanie turned rigid with fear, for she heard the kraken whispering.

Do you know how we hunt blueback, Alanie? That whale is greatest and most powerful, but we together are stronger. We do not hunt the blueback – we hunt the blueback's young, for the blueback must forget herself, then.

We hunt and poke at the children of old blueback, and of course she must defend. Parents must save their little ones, and so the great ones forget themselves and dive deep, chasing us away, and then we seize a great mother and we hold her to us, and we twine our tentacles in seafloor corals, and we hold her fast.

All our kinfamily come, and we hold that mother to us, and we nip at her flesh, and the salt water turns misty black with the blood of her great heart, and at last she tires and sips of Moriabe, and then we have her to us.

And later, if we like, we snack on her children, too. Once we've drowned the mother, the children are no match.

That is how we hunt the blueback. We trick the mother and seize her and drag her down.

We are the children of Moriabe, and the blueback, though she swims in Moriabe's embrace, she is not one with the sea. We breathe the waters, but old blueback must needs breathe the air above, and if we hold blueback tight enough, she may thrash and twist and beg, but in time, the great one breathes of our mother, and once a creature has sipped of Moriabe, that one is ours.

See how your mother sips and drowns?

She is gone, and you are vulnerable.

Above or below the waves, it is the same.

The hunt is the same.

The kraken whispered to her, and Alanie saw it was true. Her mother fluttering to impress the man, using words to tend and flatter, while the man's eyes lingered only on Alanie. Eliam was no husband and no father, Alanie realized. He was a wolf who tended lambs.

Alanie bolted for her room and slammed her door, and plastered her body against its planks, and wished that her father was not dead in the embrace of Moriabe, and that the kraken did not speak true, and that she had not tasted her father's own blood in her own mouth as he died.

ALANIE SOBBED AND wished for impossible things while the kraken whispered that her father was no salvation. His *Sparrow* lay beneath the waves, and they themselves nested within its hold.

Alanie's mother pounded on the door and begged to be allowed in, and Alanie heard her apologizing to the man who would devour her.

"This isn't like her," Alanie's mother said, again and again. "Alanie is a good girl. She will listen to you. I will make her listen."

Terror of abandonment made her mother's voice rise and crack as she sought to assuage her future husband, and Alanie heard her mother's words and Eliam's indulgent chuckle, and knew that her mother was lost. Sinolise would sacrifice anything for this new man. Eliam was meant to preserve Sinolise from fish guts and sea, and she would do anything to serve him.

The kraken chuckled and rolled lazily in the deeps of Moriabe.

The young blueback is the sweetest to consume. No gristle at all. They drown easy once the mother's gone. We wrap our tentacles around them and drag them down, whenever we like.

ALANIE HAD NEVER seen a kraken, and yet she swam among them.

She tumbled in the fast black flows of Moriabe's currents and nested in tangled writhing piles of kin beneath the ancient shells of massacred cathedral crabs. Alanie felt the grit of sand on her skin as she buried herself up to her eyes for ambush, and she tasted blood in her mouth when the kraken fed.

Sometimes the kraken songs were so loud that they drowned Alanie's ears with their feeding joy. When Sinolise instructed Alanie as to which belongings they would take to their new home, Alanie could only stare at her mother's lips and guess at the woman's words, for kraken voices crashed and foamed inside her skull like surf off the breaks.

At other times the kraken voices were only whispers, as when they pursued narwhal pods beyond the icy northern horizons, their voices faint as fingers on Alanie's coverlet. But more and more the kraken were with her, sometimes close and sometimes far, tidal in their company, but never gone entirely.

When Alanie rode the cart to her new home, kraken rode with her, amused at the wheeled conveyance piled precarious with her and her mother's belongings, and when the kraken saw the chinkstone and thatching of Eliam's hall, with its storm-shutter windows and heavy wooden door, they murmured to themselves as to how it might be pried open for the food within.

But they were most impressed when they spied Eliam's sheep in his lush green fields – they marveled at prey that waited so contentedly to be slaughtered.

The kraken watched and listened as Alanie was taken into her new father's household, but they recoiled and flooded Alanie's sight with black-ink flight at the sight of Eliam's son.

Elbe was a boy of Alanie's age, and yet his eyes were those of a Graybane warrior's, returned from shoreline slaughter, and they seemed to laugh and mock her when he called her sister. A ghost of a boy, haunting the dark silences of his father's hall. Elbe's ancient knowing eyes clung to Alanie as he shadowed her through the echoes and stone of Eliam's manor.

Bluebacks beget bluebacks. Eels beget eels, the kraken murmured. *Beware.*

Room after room, hall after hall, Elbe stalked behind her as Alanie explored the kitchens and libraries and examined her spare clean room, where no lock barred her door. Always Elbe's knowing eyes followed her.

At last Alanie paused in Eliam's great hall and stood staring up at hunted trophies upon the walls. Byre elk with barbed ivory antlers, and snarling grey wolves, and the heads of mountain apes arranged by tribe and mounted in studied lines. Snow-lion pelts sprawled across granite flagstones, three times Alanie's length, and their white lush furs smothered her footsteps as she walked from kill to kill.

"In winter, he goes to the edge of the Scarp," Elbe murmured in Alanie's ear, standing so close that she flinched and drew away. "He hunts with bow and knife," Elbe said. "He likes the chase. The look of a heart draining in the snow. I've seen him stand and watch a stag bleed out for hours."

Alanie shrank further from the ghostly boy, but Elbe ignored her retreat and instead pointed to the dead and told their tales.

Eliam ranged forests where wind pines towered and forged through waist-deep snows where none but snow lions laired. He followed blood-spattered trails, relentless, undaunted by the worst of Wanem's ice-blind storms and careless of the Scarp's avalanches. Eliam ran his prey until at last it collapsed exhausted in the drifts, ribs heaving with its last living breaths, finally willing to give up life and flight, in favor of rest and death.

"He likes surrender in his toys," Elbe said. "He wants their welcome when his knife finally cuts them true. He likes to see them lift their throats to him.

In the end, they all lift their throats and make his cutting easy. They're like your mother that way. So very desperate to please."

Alanie blanched at his words and turned to flee, but Elbe seized her arm and yanked her close. His lips pressed to her ear. "Make no sound," he whispered. "Make not a sound. Listen to me while you still can. Listen like a rabbit, for surely you are prey. Do you not hear their trysting? Listen silent, sister, listen close. Already my father consumes your mother. If we slip to his chamber door, we'll hear her as she groans. But she is not the prey he most desires. I've seen his eyes on you, Alanie. You are the one he desires to hunt."

The boy drew away, and to Alanie's surprise, she saw pity in his eyes. Pity of what was to come. And the sight of his grieving eyes frightened Alanie more than any of his words.

"We're not so different, you and I," Elbe whispered. "We see the monsters others deny. We know what comes knocking at our chamber door. Run now, sister. Run and never look back."

"But my mother –"

"– is weak and wants to feel his teeth."

He pulled her to the manor door. "Don't make me earn a bloody back for nothing. Run, Alanie. Run for the ocean and follow the cliffs to the bay. Find a ship and sail, and remember that my father has never failed to catch his prey."

Still Alanie hesitated, but the kraken whispered in her ear.

A young blueback is easy to catch once its mother has sipped of Moriabe. So soft in our beaks. So easy to drag deep. Drown the parent first, then dine on the child. Sea or land, the hunt is the same. The hunt is always the same. First the parent, then the child.

Alanie fled.

She fled across green fields and rolling hills, sobbing with fear and running still. When she reached the sea, Alanie bore north, following the rise and fall of white marbled shores. The sun sank toward the ocean as Alanie ran. Shadows lengthened and fields reddened. Moriabe wrapped the sun in her quilt, turning day to night, and still Alanie ran. She plunged through black pine forests and scrambled up and down ragged cliffs, and still she ran, her breath burning in her lungs and her legs turning weak. Her guts knotted, and still she ran. When she broke through the last of the forest and saw the burning lanterns of Serenity Bay and the white cliffs of the town luminous under the moon, she fell to her knees with relief.

In the end, it was for naught.

Eliam caught her on the Prince's Pier begging for work or berth or pity as the morning sun broke above the white cliffs. He seized her wrists in one strong hand and dragged her away from the docks, joking with the sailors and warehouse owners that children were always headstrong. He tossed her over the back of his horse as easily as tossing a sack of oats, and when still Alanie fought, he struck her face until her lips broke and bled.

When they arrived home, Alanie's mother stood at the manor door, wringing her hands with concern. But when Alanie fled to her, Sinolise struck her for a defiant child and returned her to Eliam's waiting hand. The boy Elbe watched with his ancient warrior's eyes as Eliam led Alanie into the manor, and said nothing at all.

Later, Elbe stripped his clothes to show Alanie what his father had wrought on his skin, and she traced the wounds of his bloody battles with her fingertips. The boy's flesh hung from his ribs in tatters and the coral knots of his spine showed through the shredded meat of his back.

But by then, Alanie hardly cared, for her own back was bloody as well.

ALANIE HAD NEVER seen a kraken, but they called out to her often. When Eliam whipped her bloody, the kraken thrashed and disappeared in clouds of blackest ink, calling for her to flee as well. When Eliam pinned Alanie in the kitchens and fumbled at her skirts, they lashed out with poisonous tentacles and snapped sharp beaks and called for her to fight.

And Alanie did flee, and she did fight. She fought until she was exhausted. She fled once and once and once again, and each time Eliam dragged her back, and finally she fled no more.

Eliam hunted too well, and his belt bit too deep.

The kraken recoiled at being hunted down. They lashed out at the monster that pinned them, and each time they shrieked that they had warned her about the beast who stalked her.

We told you, they said. *We told you how the hunt was done.*

Moriabe's children were not creatures to be preyed upon. They reviled the monster who ran them down, and they were with Alanie less and less. They went distant hunting for narwhal pods or else sank deep in Moriabe's blind trenches. The kraken nested in the wreckage of the sailing ships they'd broken and slept beneath shifting seafloor sands, and when Alanie called for them, they sang, *We are of the sea, and you are of the shore. We are Moriabe's children. No one hunts our kind.*

My father hunted you, Alanie retorted, but the kraken only laughed.

It was we who hunted him, they sang, and their voices were faint and fading.

ALANIE HAD NEVER seen a kraken, and she heard their voices not at all. So silent were they that Alanie began to wonder if she had been simply mad, fooling herself into believing that Moriabe's children had spoken to her in the wake of the storm that had reshaped her life. She called to the kraken and she cursed them and she cajoled, but nothing moved them, if indeed they had ever been moved at all. Alanie was alone.

Alone she learned to bar her bedroom door with cedar chests, and alone she took the whippings for her new defiance. Alone she learned to ghost the halls, as silent and careful as a rabbit, alert for the wolf that stalked her. Alone she learned to survive as best she could. Her eyes became sunken and ancient, and she became watchful and fearful, but she survived.

And still she remembered the kraken and how they'd called to her. And no matter how much she hated herself for seeking their voices, still she tried.

Alanie, Alanie.

She remembered the first time she'd heard their song, and so she waited, implacably patient, hoping to find them once again, waiting for one of the great storms that brought the kraken to the surface. Waiting for Moriabe and Stormface to clash in a lovers' quarrel, just as they had when her father had seen the kraken in his own time.

Alanie waited and survived, and at last a night came when Wanem lashed the manor's shutters with wind and rain, and Moriabe's waves rose high. That night Alanie dreamed of kraken in the deeps, and in the morning she ran across the rain-drenched fields to the cliffs, to look out across the blue calm waters of Moriabe's quilt as it shimmered with golden sunshine.

Alanie scrambled down rocky trails to the beaches far below and picked her way across the kelp-draped stones to the water's edge. She waded out amongst crystal tide pools, stepping barefoot past anemones and bluestem clams. She hiked her skirt as Moriabe's waters rushed and foamed about her knees, and she closed her eyes and listened, straining for the taste of blood in her mouth and the rising strain of kraken song.

She listened for her name.

Alanie. Alanie.

If she listened close, she imagined she could hear them still, their voices tumbling in the surf. If she listened close, she could imagine great vast creatures swimming in the depths of Moriabe. She could imagine that Eliam did not squeeze her wrists until they bruised and pretend that Sinolise never turned away from a daughter pressed against a kitchen block. Alanie could imagine and pretend, and listen for the sound of kraken, and hours could pass. The sun could climb in the sky, and gulls could wheel and bank and hunt, and dolphins could cut the far blue waters, but if kraken called her name, their voices were drowned in foam and surf.

When Alanie at last opened her eyes, the rising tide had soaked her to the waist, and Elbe squatted on the shore, his knowing eyes upon her.

By reflex Alanie searched the cliffs, afraid he had been followed, but she spied no sign of Eliam.

"I thought you might keep walking," Elbe said.

Alanie waded back to shore and spread her skirts to dry. "I was listening to the ocean."

"My mother said the same. And then one day she walked out into the heart of Moriabe. She walked out into the waters, and when it became too deep to walk, she swam. And then she kept on swimming. Father was in a rage at that. Nothing escapes him on land, but she was in the sea. He called to her and shouted. I watched him waving his arms and raging, but he was too much the coward to swim after her into the deep ocean. He stood on the shore and screamed and screamed like Wanem, and she kept swimming. And then she stopped, and Moriabe took her. In the end, it was easy. She ducked her head and sipped of Moriabe, and it was done. And I was alone with him."

"Why didn't you tell me?"

"And tell you the one true escape?" Elbe laughed. "If you go swimming, sister, then there is only me. There aren't enough cedar chests to block a door that he wants open. What wouldn't you do to keep from hearing that man's knock? What wouldn't you do to keep his attentions focused elsewhere?"

"But you told me to run, when we first met."

"I hoped..." He shook his head. "I liked your eyes. You did not look like someone hunted, then. I knew your mother wouldn't save you, but I thought, perhaps..." He shrugged. "I was a fool. My father never fails to catch his prize."

They were quiet for a while. At last Alanie asked, "Why do you not go swimming, too?"

"I tried once. Soon after. I couldn't breathe the water the way she did. I'm a coward, I think. I swam back to shore. He whipped me for it. He was terrified that he would lose his heir. He keeps a boat close now, to row after me in case I try to follow her."

He was quiet awhile and then said, "I know that everyone says that the great storms are caused by Moriabe's and Stormface's love quarrels. But I think they're wrong."

"Oh?"

"I think Stormface is like my father."

"And what is Moriabe, then, if Wanem is such a creature?"

"Moriabe..." Elbe fell quiet for a long time. "I think that when the great storms rise, she is fighting to defend her children. Moriabe isn't like our mothers at all. She is something else. Stronger. Fearless. And when Stormface comes to her door as my father does to ours, she battles him and fights him, and she forces him to flee." He nodded out at the blue waters. "And then, when she turns calm like this, it's because her children are safe again. Moriabe defends her children – that's what I think."

Above them on the cliffs, Eliam called out, and Elbe flinched. Alanie looked up at the man who stalked her nights, and her skin crawled. She thought of Elbe's mother, swimming out in the deeps, and wondered at parents who would do anything to save a child.

Eliam called out again, and Sinolise appeared as well, demanding that they return.

Alanie reached for her brother's hand. "Come with me," she said. "We'll swim together. We don't have to be afraid." And though Elbe looked at her with terrified eyes, he followed where she led.

The waters rushed around Alanie's ankles as she strode into the ocean. It swirled about her knees and clutched at her thighs and tangled her skirts. From high on the cliffs, Eliam shouted for their return, and Alanie's mother begged for their obedience in her high frightened voice, but they were far away, and the waves were loud, drowning out demands.

A wave came crashing in, frothing up around Alanie's ribs, and she gasped at the chill of soaking clothes. She kicked free of skirts and blouse, and pulled Elbe deeper into the waters. He seemed to struggle for a moment between the pull of her hand and his father's voice, and then he, too, was tugging off his clothes, and the ocean rose to their chests, and they pressed on, and Alanie thought she heard Elbe laughing as if suddenly free.

The next wave lifted Alanie's feet from the stones, and then she was swimming, letting Elbe's hand go so she could stroke hard through the surf. She dived through an oncoming wave and surfaced on the far side, shaking her head to clear water from her eyes. Elbe surfaced beside her, swimming hard, and then they were swimming together, matching each other stroke for stroke, swimming with all their will.

Behind them, Eliam galloped down the path to the shore. His threats and demands echoed across the waters, but the ocean spread between them, blue and wide, and he stood powerless on the shore.

Alanie swam and Elbe kept pace, and then the ocean's current caught them, and they were swept away from shore. Moriabe cupped them in her currents and carried them fast away from where Eliam dragged his boat into the surf.

Alanie turned on her back, resting and treading water and staring up at blue sky as the current carried them. Beside her, Elbe was smiling. His eyes seemed almost young. The white cliffs of shore were distant now, but when Alanie checked Eliam's progress, she found to her surprise that he gained upon them.

"He's quick," Alanie said, trying not to despair.

"He was born to hunt."

Eliam used his great strength to advantage as he leaned into his oars, and his boat fairly shot across the waves.

"I don't have the will to drown myself," Elbe said quietly.

"You won't have to," Alanie said, wanting to believe it was true. "Just swim with me. All we have to do is swim."

She tugged his shoulder and kicked off again, and Elbe cursed and followed. Stroke after stroke, they swam through blue glittering waters, rising and falling on Moriabe's waves. Panting and paddling still. Kicking, always kicking deeper into the blue, until at last their strength gave out and there was nothing left to do but float.

The two of them bobbed on Moriabe's quilt, flotsam specks on the open ocean. Alanie's limbs felt loose and sinuous in the waters, limp and used. She didn't resent the exhaustion, but wished she could have swum deeper. She wondered if she had done enough. She wondered if Moriabe truly cared for anything at all. She wondered if kraken were close or far. She wondered if she had ever heard their voices.

Eliam closed the distance, straining at his oars. On the waves, he looked small. Not the monster that Alanie had known on land, but only a tiny man in a tiny little boat, far out upon a wide, deep ocean, a man who thought he was a hunter.

Alanie narrowed her eyes as she stared at him, and then she lay back and spread her arms wide to float on Moriabe's quilt, and she called to the kraken. Alanie imagined them in the deeps, lying in tangled piles of kin. She imagined them swimming sinuous through the dark shadow waters, and she called to them.

Do you know how I hunt the blueback? I seize his child, and he forgets himself. Come and see what I've baited forth. Come and see how I have learned to hunt.

Alanie could hear Eliam's cursing as he drew nearer, and Elbe had begun to sob with fear, but Alanie cared only for the deeps.

Again and again she called out to the kraken.

The hunt is the same on sea or shore. The hunt is always the same. I have listened; I have learned. Come and see what follows me.

Again and again she called, and down in the deeps great shadow creatures stirred and shifted. Alanie felt the currents change, and she redoubled her calls, and Moriabe's children slid from beneath ocean sands and eased from night-black trenches.

The hunt is the same on sea or shore, Alanie sang. *A great blueback has forgotten himself in the chase to save his child. Come and hunt; come and see.*

The ocean currents shifted and swirled. The waters around Alanie began to froth as kraken surged upward.

Come and hunt; come and see.

She could feel the kraken rising from the depths, feel the ocean rushing past her skin, faster and faster, see the sunlight streaming down through the waters, and the specks that floated far above, so small so small.

See what I have baited forth, Alanie called. *He is soft. No gristle at all. He is soft.*

Moriabe's children surged for the surface.

Eliam was still shouting and Elbe had grabbed Alanie's arm to point at the boiling waters all around, but all their words were lost. The ocean's roar drowned them out completely. The only sounds in Alanie's ears were the voices of the kraken, rising.

Sister, the kraken called. *Sister.*

Alanie spread her arms wide, welcoming her kin.

THE VAPORIZATION ENTHALPY OF A PECULIAR PAKISTANI FAMILY

Usman T. Malik

Usman T. Malik (www.usmanmalik.org) is a Pakistani writer resident in Florida. He reads Sufi poetry, likes long walks, and occasionally strums naats on the guitar. His fiction has appeared or is forthcoming in *Tor.com*, *Strange Horizons*, *Black Static*, *Daily Science Fiction*, *Exigencies*, and *Qualia Nous*, among other places. He is a graduate of Clarion West.

1

THE SOLID PHASE of Matter is a state wherein a substance is particulately bound. To transform a solid into liquid, the intermolecular forces need to be overcome, which may be achieved by adding energy. The energy necessary to break such bonds is, ironically, called the *heat of fusion*.

ON A FRIDAY after jumah prayers, under the sturdy old oak in their yard, they came together as a family for the last time. Her brother gave in and wept as Tara watched, eyes prickling with a warmth that wouldn't disperse no matter how much she knuckled them, or blinked.

"Monsters," Sohail said, his voice raspy. He wiped his mouth with the back of his hand and looked at the sky, a vast whiteness cobblestoned with heat. The plowed wheat fields beyond the steppe on which their house perched were baked and khaki and shivered a little under Tara's feet. An earthquake or a passing vehicle on the highway? Perhaps it was just foreknowledge that made her dizzy. She pulled at her lower lip and said nothing.

"Monsters," Sohail said again. "Oh God, Apee. Murderers."

She reached out and touched his shoulders. "I'm sorry." She thought he would pull back. When he didn't, she let her fingers fall and linger on the flame-shaped scar on his arm. *So it begins*, she thought. *How many times has this happened before? Pushing and prodding us repeatedly until the night swallows us whole.* She thought of that until her heart constricted with dread. "Don't do it," she said. "Don't go."

Sohail lifted his shoulders and drew his head back, watched her wonderingly as if seeing her for the first time.

"I know I ask too much," she said. "I know the customs of honor, but for the love of God let it go. One death needn't become a lodestone for others. One horror needn't –"

But he wasn't listening, she could tell. They would not hear nor see once the blood was upon them, didn't the Scriptures say so? Sohail heard, but didn't listen. His conjoined eyebrows, like dark hands held, twitched. "Her name meant a rose," he said and smiled. It was beautiful, that smile, heartbreaking, frightening. "Under the mango trees by Chacha Barkat's farm Gulminay told me that, as I kissed her hand. Whispered it in my ear, her finger circling my temple. *A rose blooming in the rain.* Did you know that?"

Tara didn't. The sorrow of his confession filled her now as did the certainty of his leaving. "Yes," she lied, looking him in the eyes. God, his eyes looked awful: webbed with red, with thin tendrils of steam rising from them. "A rose God gave us and took away because He loved her so."

"Wasn't God," Sohail said and rubbed his fingers together. The sound was insectile. "Monsters." He turned his back to her and was able to speak rapidly, "I'm leaving tomorrow morning. I'm going to the mountains. I will take some bread and dried meat. I will stay there until I'm shown a sign, and once I am," his back arched, then straightened. He had lost weight; his shoulder blades poked through the khaddar shirt like trowels, "I will arise and go to their homes. I will go to them as God's wrath. I will –"

She cut him off, her heart pumping fear through her body like poison. "What if you go to them and die? What if you go to them like a steer to the slaughter? And Ma and I – what if months later we sit here and watch a dusty vehicle climb the hill, bouncing a sack of meat in the back seat that was once you? What if..."

But she couldn't go on giving name to her terrors. Instead, she said, "If you go, know that we as we are now will be gone forever."

He shuddered. "*We* were gone when *she* was gone. We were shattered with her bones." The wind picked up, a whipping, chador-lifting sultry gust that made Tara's flesh prickle. Sohail began to walk down the steppes, each with its own crop: tobacco, corn, rice stalks wavering in knee-high water; and as she watched his lean farmer body move away, it seemed to her as if his back was not drenched in sweat, but acid. That his flesh glistened not from moisture, but blood. All at once their world was just too much, or not enough – Tara couldn't decide which – and the weight of that unseen future weighed her down until she couldn't breathe. "My brother," she said and began to cry. "You're my little brother."

Sohail continued walking his careful, dead man's walk until his head was a wobbling black pumpkin rising from the last steppe. She watched him disappear in the undulations of her motherland, helpless to stop the fatal fracturing of her world, wondering if he would stop or doubt or look back.

Sohail never looked back.

MA DIED THREE months later.

The village menfolk told her the death prayer was brief and moving. Tara couldn't attend because she was a woman.

They helped her bury Ma's sorrow-filled body, and the rotund mullah clucked and murmured over the fresh mound. The women embraced her and crooned and urged her to vent.

"Weep, our daughter," they cried, "for the childrens' tears of love are like manna for the departed."

Tara tried to weep and felt guilty when she couldn't. Ma had been sick and in pain for a long time and her hastened death was a mercy, but you couldn't say that out loud. Besides, the women had said *children*, and Sohail wasn't there. Not at the funeral, nor during the days after. Tara dared not wonder where he was, nor imagine his beautiful face gleaming in the dark atop a stony mountain, persevering in his vigil.

"What will you do now?" they asked, gathering around her with sharp, interested eyes. She knew what they really meant. A young widow with no family was a stranger amidst her clan. At best an oddity; at her worst a seductress. Tara was surprised to discover their concern didn't frighten her. The perfect loneliness of it, the inadvertent exclusion – they were just more beads in the tautening string of her life.

"I'm thinking of going to the City," she told them. "Ma has a cousin there. Perhaps he can help me with bread and board, while I look for work."

She paused, startled by a clear memory: Sohail and Gulminay by the Kunhar River, fishing for trout. Gulminay's sequined hijab dappling the stream with emerald as she reached down into the water with long, pale fingers. Sohail grinning his stupid lover's grin as his small hands encircled her waist, and Tara watched them both from the shade of the eucalyptus, fond and jealous. By then Tara's husband was long gone and she could forgive herself the occasional resentment.

She forced the memory away. "Yes, I think I might go to the city for a while." She laughed. The sound rang hollow and strange in the emptiness of her tin-and-timber house. "Who knows I might even go back to school. I used to enjoy reading once." She smiled at these women with their hateful, sympathetic eyes that watched her cautiously as they would a rabid animal. She nodded, talking mostly to herself. "Yes, that would be good. Hashim would've wanted that."

They drew back from her, from her late husband's mention. Why not? she thought. Everything she touched fell apart; everyone around her died or went missing. There was no judgment here, just dreadful awe. She could allow them that, she thought.

2

THE LIQUID PHASE of Matter is a restless volume that, by dint of the vast spaces between its molecules, fills any container it is poured in and takes its shape. Liquids tend to have higher energy than solids, and while the particles retain inter-particle forces they have enough energy to move relative to each other.

The structure therefore becomes mobile and malleable.

*   *   *

IN THE CITY, Tara turned feral in her pursuit of learning. This had been long coming and it didn't surprise her. At thirteen, she had been withdrawn from school; she needed not homework but a husband, she was told. At sixteen, she was wedded to Hashim. He was blown to smithereens on her twenty-first birthday. A suicide attack on his unit's northern check post.

"I want to go to school," she told Wasif Khan, her mother's cousin. They were sitting in his six-by-eight yard, peeling fresh oranges he had confiscated from an illegal food vendor. Wasif was a Police hawaldar, and on the rough side of sixty. He often said confiscation was his first love and contraband second. But he grinned when he said it, which made it easier for her to like him.

Now Wasif tossed a half-gnawed chicken bone to his spotted mongrel and said, "I don't know if you want to do that."

"I do."

"You need a husband, not –"

"I don't care. I need to go back to school."

"Why?" He dropped an orange rind in the basket at his feet, gestured with a large liver-spotted hand. "The City doesn't care if you can read. Besides, I need someone to help me around the house. I'm old and ugly and useless, but I have this tolerable place and no children. You're my cousin's daughter. You can stay here forever if you like."

In a different time she might have mistaken his generosity for loneliness, but now she understood it for what it was. Such was the way of age: it melted prejudice or hardened it. "I want to learn about the world," she said. "I want to see if there are others like me. If there have been others before me."

He was confused. "Like you how?"

She rubbed an orange peel between her fingers, pressing the fibrous texture of it in the creases of her flesh, considering how much to tell him. Her mother had trusted him. Yet Ma hardly had their gift and even if she did Tara doubted she would have been open about it. Ma had been wary of giving too much of herself away – a trait she passed on to both her children. Among other things.

So now Tara said, "Others who *need* to learn more about themselves. I spent my entire childhood being just a bride and look where that got me.

I am left with nothing. No children, no husband, no family." Wasif Khan looked hurt. She smiled kindly. "You know what I mean, Uncle. I love you, but I need to love me too."

Wasif Khan tilted his head back and pinched a slice of orange above his mouth. Squeezed it until his tongue and remaining teeth gleamed with the juice. He closed his eyes, sighed, and nodded. "I don't know if I approve, but I think I understand." He lifted his hand and tousled his own hair thoughtfully. "It's a different time. Others my age who don't realize it don't fare well. The traditional rules don't apply anymore, you know. Sometimes, I think that is wonderful. Other times, it feels like the whole damn world is conspiring against you."

She rose, picking up her mess and his. "Thank you for letting me stay here."

"It's either you or every hookah-sucking asshole in this neighborhood for company." He grinned and shrugged his shoulders. "My apologies. I've been living alone too long and my tongue is spoilt."

She laughed loudly; and thought of a blazing cliff somewhere from which dangled two browned, peeling, inflamed legs, swinging back and forth like pendulums.

SHE READ EVERYTHING she could get her hands on. At first, her alphabet was broken and awkward, as was her rusty brain, but she did it anyway. It took her two years, but eventually she qualified for F.A. examinations, and passed on her first try.

"I don't know how you did it," Wasif Khan said to her, his face beaming at the neighborhood children as he handed out specially prepared mithai to eager hands, "but I'm proud of you."

She wasn't, but she didn't say it. Instead, once the children left, she went to the mirror and gazed at her reflection, flexing her arm this way and that, making the flame-shaped scar bulge. *We all drink the blood of yesterday*, she thought.

The next day she enrolled at Punjab University's B.Sc program.

In Biology class, they learned about plants and animals. Flora and Fauna, they called them. Things constructed piece by piece from the basic units of life – cells. These cells in turn were made from tiny building blocks called atoms, which themselves were bonded by the very things that repelled their core: electrons.

In Physics class, she learned what electrons were. Little flickering ghosts that vanished and reappeared as they pleased. Her flesh was empty, she discovered, or most of it. So were human bones and solid buildings and the incessantly agitated world. All that immense loneliness and darkness with only a hint that we existed. The idea awed her. Did we exist only as a possibility?

In Wasif Khan's yard was a tall mulberry tree with saw-like leaves. On her way to school she touched them; they were spiny and jagged. She hadn't eaten mulberries before. She picked a basketful, nipped her wrist with her teeth, and let her blood roast a few. She watched them curl and smoke from the heat of her genes, inhaled the sweet steam of their juice as they turned into mystical symbols.

Mama would have been proud.

She ate them with salt and pepper, and was offended when Wasif Khan wouldn't touch those remaining.

He said they gave him reflux.

3

THE GASEOUS PHASE of Matter is one in which particles have enough kinetic energy to make the effect of intermolecular forces negligible. A gas, therefore, will occupy the entire container in which it is confined.

Liquid may be converted to gas by heating at constant pressure to a certain temperature.

This temperature is called the *boiling point*.

THE WORST FLOODING *the province has seen in forty years* was the one thing all radio broadcasters agreed on.

Wasif Khan hadn't confiscated a television yet, but if he had, Tara was sure, it would show the same cataclysmic damage to life and property. At one point, someone said, an area the size of England was submerged in raging floodwater.

Wasif's neighborhood in the northern, hillier part of town escaped the worst of the devastation, but Tara and Wasif witnessed it daily when they went for rescue work: upchucked power pylons and splintered oak trees smashing through the marketplace stalls; murderous tin sheets and iron rods slicing through inundated alleys; bloated dead cows and sheep eddying in shoulder-high water with terrified children clinging to them. It pawed at the towering steel-and-concrete structures, this restless liquid death that had come to the city; it ripped out their underpinnings and annihilated everything in its path.

Tara survived these days of heartbreak and horror by helping to set up a small tent city on the sports fields of her university. She volunteered to establish a nursery for displaced children and went with rescue teams to scour the ruins for usable supplies, and corpses.

As she pulled out the dead and living from beneath the wreckage, as she tossed plastic-wrapped food and dry clothing to the dull-eyed homeless, she thought of how bright and hot and dry the spines of her brother's mountains must be. It had been four years since she saw him, but her dreams were filled with his absence. Did he sit parched and caved in, like a deliberate Buddha? Or was he dead and pecked on by ravens and falcons?

She shuddered at the thought and grabbed another packet of cooked rice and dry beans for the benighted survivors.

THE FIRST WARNING came on the last night of Ramadan. *Chand raat.*

Tara was eating bread and lentils with her foundling children in the nursery when it happened. A bone-deep trembling that ran through the grass, flattening its blades, evaporating the evening dew trembling on them. Seconds later, a distant boom followed: a hollow rumbling that hurt Tara's ears and made her feel nauseated. (Later, she would learn that the blast had torn through the marble-walled shrine of Data Sahib, wrenching its iron fence from its moorings, sending jagged pieces of metal and scorched human limbs spinning across the walled part of the City.)

Her children sat up, confused and scared. She soothed them. Once a replacement was found, she went to talk to the tent city administrator.

"I've seen this before," she told him once he confirmed it was a suicide blast. "My husband and sister-in-law both died in similar situations." That wasn't entirely true for Gulminay, but close enough. "Usually one such attack is followed by another when rescue attempts are made. My husband used to call them 'double tap' attacks." She paused, thinking of his kind, dearly loved face for the first time in months. "He understood the psychology behind them well."

The administrator, a chubby short man with filthy cheeks, scratched his chin. "How come?"

"He was a Frontier Corps soldier. He tackled many such situations before he died."

"Condolences, *bibi*." The administrator's face crinkled with sympathy. "But what does that have to do with us?"

"At some point, these terrorists will use the double tap as decoy and come after civilian structures."

"Thank you for the warning. I'll send out word to form a volunteer perimeter patrol." He scrutinized her, taking in her hijab, the bruised elbows, and grimy fingernails from days of work. "God bless you for the lives you've saved already. For the labor you've done."

He handed her a packet of boiled corn and alphabet books. She nodded absently, charred bodies and boiled human blood swirling up from the shrine vivid inside her head, thanked him, and left.

The emergency broadcast thirty minutes later confirmed her fear: a second blast at Data Sahib obliterated a fire engine, killed a jeep-ful of eager policemen, and vaporized twenty-five rescuers. Five of these were female medical students. Their shattered glass bangles were melted and their headscarves burned down to unrecognizable gunk by the time the EMS came, they later said.

Tara wept when she heard. In her heart was a steaming shadow that whispered nasty things. It impaled her with its familiarity, and a dreadful suspicion grew in her that the beast was rage and wore a face she knew well.

* * *

4

WHEN MATTER IS heated to high temperatures, such as in a flame, electrons begin to leave the atoms. At very high temperatures, essentially all electrons are assumed to be dissociated, resulting in a unique state wherein positively charged nuclei swim in a raging 'sea' of free electrons.

This state is called the *Plasma Phase of Matter* and exists in lightning, electric sparks, neon lights, and the Sun.

IN A RASH of terror attacks, the City quickly fell apart: the Tower of Pakistan, Lahore Fort, Iqbal's Memorial, Shalimar Gardens, Anarkali's Tomb, and the thirteen gates of the Walled City. They exploded and fell in burning tatters, survived only by a quivering bloodhaze through which peeked the haunted eyes of their immortal ghosts.

This is death, this is love, this is the comeuppance of the two, as the world according to you will finally come to an end. So snarled the beast in Tara's head each night. The tragedy of the floodwaters was not over yet, and now this.

Tara survived this new world through her books and her children. The two seemed to have become one: pages filled with unfathomable loss. White space itching to be written, reshaped, or incinerated. Sometimes, she would bite her lips and let the trickle of blood stain her callused fingers. Would touch them to water-spoilt paper and watch it catch fire and flutter madly in the air, aflame like a phoenix. An impossible glamor created by tribulation. So when the city burned and her tears burned, Tara reminded herself of the beautiful emptiness of it all and forced herself to smile.

Until one morning she awoke and discovered that, in the cover of the night, a suicide teenager had hit her tent city's perimeter patrol.

AFTER THE OTHERS had left, she stood over her friends' graves in the twilight.

Kites and vultures unzipped the darkness above in circles, lost specks in this ghostly desolation. She remembered how cold it was when they lowered Gulminay's remains in the ground. How the drone attack had torn her limbs clean off so that, along with a head shriveled by heat, a glistening, misshapen, idiot torso remained. She remembered Ma, too, and how she was killed by her son's love. The first of many murders.

"I know you," she whispered to the Beast resident in her soul. "I know you", and all the time she scribbled on her flesh with a glass shard she found buried in a patrolman's eye. Her wrist glowed with her heat and that of her ancestors. She watched her blood bubble and surge skyward. To join the plasma of the world and drift its soft, vaporous way across the darkened City, and she wondered again if she was still capable of loving them both.

The administrator promised her he would take care of her children. He gave her food and a bundle of longshirts and shalwars. He asked her where she was going and why, and she knew he was afraid for her.

"I will be all right," she told him. "I know someone who lives up there."

"I don't understand why you must go. It's dangerous," he said, his flesh red under the hollows of his eyes. He wiped his cheeks, which were wet. "I wish you didn't have to. But I suppose you will. I see that in your face. I saw that when you first came here."

She laughed. The sound of her own laughter saddened her. "The world will change," she said. "It always does. We are all empty, but this changing is what saves us. That is why I must go."

He nodded. She smiled. They touched hands briefly; she stepped forward and hugged him, her headscarf tickling his nostrils, making him sneeze. She giggled and told him how much she loved him and the others. He looked pleased and she saw how much kindness and gentleness lived inside his skin, how his blood would never boil with undesired heat.

She lifted his finger, kissed it, wondering at how solid his vacant flesh felt against her lips.

Then she turned and left him, leaving the water and fire and the crackling, hissing earth of the City behind.

Such was how Tara Khan left for the mountains.

THE JOURNEY TOOK a week. The roads were barren, the landscape abraded by floodwater and flensed by intermittent fires. Shocked trees, stripped of fruit, stood rigid and receding as Tara's bus rolled by, their gnarled limbs pointing accusatorially at the heavens.

Wrapped in her chador, headscarf, and khaddar shalwar kameez, Tara folded into the rugged barrenness with its rugged people. They were not unkind; even in the midst of this madness, they held onto their deeply honored tradition of hospitality, allowing Tara to scout for hints of the Beast's presence. The northerners chattered constantly and were horrified by the atrocities blooming from within them, and because she too spoke Pashto they treated her like one of them.

Tara kept her ears open. Rumors, whispers, beckonings by skeletal fingers. Someone said there was a man in Abbottabad who was the puppeteer. Another shook his head and said that was a deliberate shadow show, a gaudy interplay of light and dark put up by the real perpetrators. That the Supreme Conspirator was swallowed by earth soaked with the blood of thousands and lived only as an extension of this irredeemable evil.

Tara listened and tried to read between their words. Slowly, the hints in the midnight alleys, the leprous grins, the desperate, clutching fingers, incinerated trees and smoldering human and animal skulls – they began to come together and form a map.

Tara followed it into the heart of the mountains.

5

WHEN THE ELEMENTARY particle boson is cooled to temperatures near absolute zero, a dilute 'gas' is created. Under such conditions, a large number of bosons occupy the lowest quantum state and an unusual thing happens: quantum effects become visible on a macroscopic scale. This effect is called the macroscopic quantum phenomena and the 'Bose-Einstein condensate' is inferred to be a new state of matter. The presence of one such particle, the Higgs-Boson, was tentatively confirmed on March 14th, 2013 in the most complex experimental facility built in human history.

This particle is sometimes called the *God Particle*.

* * *

WHEN SHE FOUND him, he had changed his name.

There is a story told around campfires since the beginning of time: Millennia ago a stone fell from the infinite bosom of space and plunked onto a statistically impossible planet. The stone was round, and smaller than a pebble of hard goat shit, and carried a word inscribed on it.

It has been passed down generations of Pahari clans that that word is the *Ism-e-Azam*, the Most High Name of God.

Every sect in the history of our world has written about it. Egyptians, Mayans. Jewish, Christian, and Muslim mystics. Some have described it as the primal point from which existence began, and that the Universal Essence lives in this *nuktah*.

The closest approximation to the First Word, some say, is one that originated in Mesopotamia, the land between the two rivers. The Sumerians called it *Annunaki*.

He Of Godly Blood.

Tara thought of this oral tradition and sat down at the mouth of the demolished cave. She knew he lived inside the cave, for every living and nonliving thing near it reeked of his heat. Twisted boulders stretched granite hands toward its mouth like pilgrims at the Kaaba. The heat of the stars they both carried in their genes, in the sputtering, whisking emptiness of their cells, had leeched out and warped the mountains and the path leading up to it.

Tara sat cross-legged in the lotus position her mother taught them both when they were young. She took a sharp rock and ran it across her palm. Crimson droplets appeared and evaporated, leaving a metallic tang in the air. She sat and inhaled that smell and thought of the home that once was. She thought of her mother, and her husband; of Gulminay and Sohail; of the floods (did he have something to do with that too? Did his rage liquefy snow-topped mountains and drown an entire country?); of suicide bombers, and the University patrol; and of countless human eyes that flicked each moment toward an unforgiving sky where something merciful may or may not live; and her eyes began to burn and Tara Khan began to cry.

"Come out," she said between her sobs. "Come out, Beast. Come out, Rage. Come out, Death of the Two Worlds and all that lives in between. Come out, Monster. Come out, Fear," and all the while she rubbed her eyes and let the salt of her tears crumble between her fingertips. Sadly she looked at the white crystals, flattened them, and screamed, "Come out, ANNUNAKI."

And in a belch of shrieking air and a blast of heat, her brother came to her.

THEY FACED EACH other.

His skin was gone. His eyes melted, his nose bridge collapsed; the bones underneath were simmering white seas that rolled and twinkled across the constantly melting and rearranging meat of him. His limbs were pseudopodic, his movement that of a softly turning planet drifting across the possibility that is being.

Now he floated toward her on a gliding plane of his skin. His potent heat, a shifting locus of time-space with infinite energy roiling inside it, touched her, making her recoil. When he breathed, she saw everything that once was; and knew what she knew.

"Salam," she said. "Peace be upon you, brother."

The *nuktah* that was him twitched. His fried vocal cords were not capable of producing words anymore.

"I used to think," she continued, licking her dry lips, watching the infinitesimal shifting of matter and emptiness inside him, "that love was all that mattered. That the bonds that pull us all together are of timeless love. But it is not true. It has never been true, has it?"

He shimmered, and said nothing.

"I still believe, though. In existing. In *ex nihilo nihil fit*. If nothing comes from nothing, we cannot return to it. Ergo life has a reason and needs to be." She paused, remembering a day when her brother plucked a sunflower from a lush meadow and slipped it into Gulminay's hair. "Gulminay-jaan once was and still is. Perhaps inside you and me." Tara wiped her tears and smiled. "Even if most of us is nothing."

The heat-thing her brother was slipped forward a notch. Tara rose to her feet and began walking toward it. The blood in her vasculature seethed and raged.

"Even if death breaks some bonds and forms others. Even if the world flinches, implodes, and becomes a grain of sand."

Annunaki watched her through eyes like black holes and gently swirled.

"Even if we have killed and shall kill. Even if the source is nothing if not grief. Even if sorrow is the distillate of our life."

She reached out and gripped his melting amebic limb. He shrank, but didn't let go as the maddened heat of her essence surged forth to meet his.

"Even if we never come to much. Even if the sea of our consciousness breaks against quantum impossibilities."

She pressed his now-arm, her fingers elongating, stretching, turning, fusing; her flame-scar rippling and coiling to probe for his like a proboscis.

Sohail tried to smile. In his smile were heat-deaths of countless worlds, supernova bursts, and the chrysalis sheen of a freshly hatched larva. She thought he might have whispered sorry. That in another time and universe there were not countless intemperate blood-children of his spreading across the earth's face like vitriolic tides rising to obliterate the planet. That all this wasn't really happening for one misdirected missile, for one careless press of a button somewhere by a soldier eating junk food and licking his fingers. But it was. Tara had glimpsed it in his *nuktah* when she touched him.

"Even if," she whispered as his being engulfed hers and the thermonuclear reaction of matter and antimatter fusion sparked and began to eradicate them both, "our puny existence, the conclusion of an agitated, conscious universe, is insignificant, remember . . . remember, brother, that mercy will go on. Kindness will go on."

Let there be gentleness, she thought. *Let there be equilibrium, if all we are and will be can survive in some form. Let there be grace and goodness and a hint of something to come, no matter how uncertain.*

Let there be possibility, she thought, as they flickered annihilatively and were immolated in some fool's idea of love.

For the 145 innocents of the 12/16 Peshawar terrorist attack and countless known & unknown before.

THE LADY AND THE FOX
Kelly Link

Kelly Link (www.kellylink.com) published her first story, "Water Off a Black Dog's Back", in 1995 and attended the Clarion writers workshop in the same year. A writer of subtle, challenging, sometimes whimsical fantasy, Link has published more than forty stories, some of which have won the Hugo, Nebula, World Fantasy, British SF, and Locus awards, and been collected in *4 Stories, Stranger Things Happen, Magic for Beginners*, and *Pretty Monsters*. Link is also an accomplished editor, working on acclaimed small press 'zine *Lady Churchill's Rosebud Wristlet* and publishing books as Small Beer Press with husband Gavin J. Grant. Link's latest books are anthology *Monstrous Affections: An Anthology of Beastly Tales* (co-edited with Grant), and new collection *Get in Trouble*.

SOMEONE IS IN the garden.

"Daniel," Miranda says. "It's Santa Claus. He's looking in the window."

"No, it's not," Daniel says. He doesn't look. "We've already had the presents. Besides. No such thing as Santa."

They are together under the tree, the celebrated Honeywell Christmas tree. They are both eleven years old. There's just enough space up against the trunk to sit cross-legged. Daniel is running the train set around the tree forwards, then backwards, then forwards again. Miranda is admiring her best present, a pair of gold-handled scissors shaped like a crane. The beak is the blade. *Snip, snip,* she slices brittle needles one by one off the branch above her. A smell of pine. A small green needle rain.

It must be very cold outside in the garden. The window shines with frost. It's long past bedtime. If it isn't Santa Claus, it could be a burglar come to steal someone's jewels. Or an axe murderer.

Or else, of course, it's one of Daniel's hundreds of uncles or cousins. Because there isn't a beard, and the face in the window isn't a jolly face. Even partially obscured by darkness and frost, it has that Honeywell look to it. The room is full of adult Honeywells talking about the things that Honeywells always talk about, which is to say everything, horses and houses and God and grouting, tanning salons and – of course – theater. Always theater. Honeywells like to talk. When Honeywells have no lines to speak, they improvise. All the world's a stage.

Rare to see a Honeywell in isolation. They come bunched like bananas. Not single spies, but in battalions. And as much as Miranda admires the red-gold Honeywell hair, the exaggerated, expressive Honeywell good looks, the Honeywell repertoire of jokes and confidences, poetry and nonsense, sometimes she needs an escape. Honeywells want you to talk, too. They ask questions until your mouth gets dry from answering.

Daniel is exceptionally restful for a Honeywell. He doesn't care if you are there or not.

Miranda wriggles out from under the tree, through the press of leggy Honeywells in black tie and party dresses: apocalyptically orange taffeta, slithering, clingy satins in canary and violet, foamy white silk already spotted with wine.

She is patted on the head, winked at. Someone in cloth of gold says, "Poor little lamb."

"Baaaah humbug," Miranda blurts, beats on. Her own dress is green, fine-wale corduroy. Empire waist. Pinching at the armpits. Miranda's interest in these things is half professional. Her mother, Joannie (resident the last six months in a Phuket jail, will be there for many years to come), was Elspeth Honeywell's dresser and confidante.

Daniel is Elspeth's son. Miranda is Elspeth's goddaughter.

THERE ARE TWO men languorously kissing in the kitchen. Leaning against the sink, where one of the new Honeywell kittens licks sauce out of a gravy boat. A girl – only a few years older than Miranda – lays soiled and tattered Tarot cards out on the farmhouse table. Empty wine bottles tilt like cannons; a butcher knife sheathed in a demolished Christmas cake. Warmth seeps from the stove: just inside the Aga's warming drawer, Miranda can see the other kittens, asleep in a crusted pan.

Miranda picks up a bag of party trash, lipstick-blotted napkins, throwaway champagne glasses, greasy fragments of pastry, hauls it out through the kitchen door. Mama cat slips inside as Miranda goes out.

Snow is falling. Big, sticky clumps that melt on her hair, her cheeks. Snow on Christmas. None in Phuket, of course. She wonders what they give you to eat on Christmas Day in a Thai prison. Her mother always makes the Christmas cake. Miranda helps roll out the marzipan in sheets. Her ballet flats skid on the grass.

She ties the bag, leaves it against the steps. And here is the man in the garden, still standing before the window, looking in.

He must hear Miranda. Surely he hears her. Her feet upon the frozen grass. But he doesn't turn around.

Even seen from the back, he is recognizably a Honeywell. Lanky, yellow-haired; perfectly still, he is somehow *perfectly* still, perfectly posed to catch the eye. Unnaturally natural. The snow that is making Miranda's nose run, her cheeks blotchy with cold, rests unmelted upon the bright Honeywell hair, the shoulders of the surprising coat.

Typical Honeywell behavior, Miranda thinks. A lovers' quarrel, or else he's taken offense at something someone said, and is now going to sulk himself handsomely to death in the cold. Her mother has been quite clear about how to behave when a Honeywell is being dramatic when drama isn't required. Firmness is the key.

At this last thought of her mother, Miranda has some dramatic feelings of her own. She focuses on the coat, sends the feelings away. It is *quite* a coat. A costume? Pilfered from some production. Eighteenth century. Beautifully cut. Not a frock coat. A *justacorps*. Rose damask. Embroidered all over with white silk thread, poppies and roses, and there, where it flares out over the hips, a staghorn beetle on a green leaf. She has come nearer and nearer, cannot stop herself from reaching out to touch the beetle.

She almost expects her hand to pass right through. (Surely there are ghosts at Honeywell Hall.) But it doesn't. The coat is real. Miranda pinches the damask between her fingers. Says, "Whatever it is that happened, it isn't worth freezing to death over. You shouldn't be out here. You should come inside."

The Honeywell in the *justacorps* turns around then. "I am exactly where I am supposed to be," he says. "Which is here. Doing precisely what I am supposed to be doing. Which does not include having conversations with little girls. Go away, little girl."

Little girl she may be, but Miranda is well armored already against the Honeywell arsenal of tantrums, tempests, ups, downs, charm, strange.

Above the wide right pocket of the *justacorps* is a fox stitched in red and gold, its foreleg caught in a trap.

"I'm Miranda," she says. And then, because she's picked up a Honeywell trick or two herself, she says, "My mother's in jail."

The Honeywell looks almost sympathetic for the briefest of moments, then shrugs. Theatrically, of course. Sticks his hands in his pockets. "What's that got to do with me?"

"Everyone's got problems, that's all," Miranda says. "I'm here because Elspeth feels sorry for me. I hate when people feel sorry for me. And I don't feel sorry for you. I don't know you. I just don't think it's very smart, standing out here because you're in a mood. But maybe you aren't very smart. My mother says good-looking people often don't bother. What's your name?"

"If I tell you, will you go away?" the Honeywell says.

"Yes," Miranda says. She can go in the kitchen and play with the kittens. Do the dishes and be useful. Have her fortune told. Sit under the tree again with Daniel until it's well past time to go to sleep. Tomorrow she'll be sent away home on a bus. By next year Elspeth will have most likely forgotten she has a goddaughter.

"I'm Fenny," the Honeywell says. "Now go away. I have things to not do, and not a lot of time to not do them in."

"Well," Miranda says. She pats Fenny on the broad cuff of the sleeve of his lovely coat. She wonders what the lining is. How cold he must be. How stupid he is, standing out here when he is welcome inside. "Merry Christmas. Good night."

She reaches out one last time, touches the embroidered fox, its leg caught in the trap. Stem stitch and seed stitch and herringbone. "It's very fine work, truly," she says. "But I hope he gets free."

"He was stupid to get caught," Fenny says, "you peculiar and annoying child." He is already turning back to the window. What does he see through it? When Miranda is finally back inside the drawing room where tipsy Honeywells are all roaring out inappropriate lyrics to carols, pulling Christmas crackers, putting on paper crowns, she looks through the window. The snow has stopped. No one is there.

BUT ELSPETH HONEYWELL, as it happens, remembers Miranda the next year and the year and the year after that. There are presents for Miranda under the magnificent tree. A ticket to a London musical that she never sees. A makeup kit when she is thirteen.

The year she is eleven, Daniel gives her a chess set and a box of assorted skeins of silk thread. Under her black tights, Miranda wears a red braided leather anklet that came in an envelope, no letter, from Phuket. The kittens are all grown up and pretend not to know her.

The year she is twelve, she looks for the mysterious Fenny. He isn't there. When she asks, no one knows who she means.

The year she is thirteen, she has champagne for the first time.

The Christmas she is fourteen, she feels quite grown up. The man in the *justacorps* was a dream, or some story she made up for herself in order to feel interesting. At fourteen she's outgrown fairytales, Santa Claus, ghost stories. When Daniel points out that they are standing under the mistletoe, she kisses him once on each cheek. And then sticks her tongue in his ear.

IT SNOWS AGAIN the Christmas she is fifteen. Snow is predicted, snow falls. Something about the chance of snow makes her think of him again. The man in the snowy garden. There is no man in the garden, of course; there never was. But there is Honeywell Hall, which is enough – and seemingly endless heaps of Honeywell adults behaving as if they were children again.

It's exhausting, almost Olympic, the amount of fun Honeywells seem to require. She can't decide if it's awful or if it's wonderful.

Late in the afternoon the Honeywells are playing charades. No fun, playing with people who do this professionally. Miranda stands at the window, watching the snow fall, looking for something. Birds. A fox. A man in the garden.

A Honeywell shouts, "Good god, no! Cleopatra came rolled up in a carpet, not in the Sunday supplement!"

Daniel is up in his room, talking to his father on Skype.

Miranda moves from window to window, pretending she is not looking for anything in particular. Far down the grounds, she sees something out of place. Someone. She's out the door in a flash.

"Going for a walk!" she yells while the door is swinging closed. In case anyone cares.

She finds the man navigating along the top of the old perimeter wall, stepping stone to stone. Fenny. He knocks a stick against each stone as he goes.

"You," he says. "I wondered if I'd see you again."

"Miranda," she says. "I bet you forgot."

"No," he says. "I didn't. Want to come up?"

He holds out his hand. She hesitates, and he says, "Suit yourself."

"I can get up by myself," she says, and does. She's in front of him now. Walks backwards so that she can keep an eye on him.

"You're not a Honeywell," he says.

"No," she says. "You are."

"Yes," he says. "Sort of."

She stops then, so that he has to stop, too. It isn't like they could keep on going anyway. There's a gap in the wall just behind her.

"I remember when they built this wall," he says.

She's probably misheard him. Or else he's teasing her. She says, "You must be very old."

"Older than you anyway," he says. He sits down on the wall, so she sits down, too. Honeywell Hall is in front of them. There's a copse of woods behind. Snow falls lazily, a bit of wind swirling it, tossing it up again.

"Why do you always wear that coat?" Miranda says. She fidgets a little. Her bum is getting cold. "You shouldn't sit on a dirty wall. It's too nice." She touches the embroidered beetle, the fox.

"Someone very. . . special gave it to me," he says. "I wear it always because it is her wish that I do so." The way he says it makes Miranda shiver just a little.

"Right," she says. "Like my anklet. My mother sent it to me. She's in prison. She'll never get out. She'll be there until she dies."

"Like the fox," he says.

"Like your fox," Miranda says. She's horrified to find that her eyes are watering. Is she crying? It isn't even a real fox. She doesn't want to look at the man in the coat, *Fenny,* to see if he's noticed, so she jumps down off the wall and begins to walk back toward the house.

When she's halfway to the Hall, the drifting snow stops. She looks back; no one sits on the wall.

THE SNOW STOPS and starts, on and off all day long. When dinner is finished, Honeywells groaning, clutching their bellies, Elspeth has something for Miranda.

Elspeth says, wagging the present between two fingers like it's a special treat, Miranda some stray puppy, "Someone left it on the doorstep for you, Miranda. I wonder who."

The wrapping is a sheet of plain white stationery, tied with a bit of green thread. Her name in a scratchy hand. *Miranda.* Inside is a scrap of rose damask, the embroidered fox, snarling; the mangled leg, the bloodied trap.

"Let me see, sweet," Elspeth says, and takes the rose damask from her. "What a strange present! A joke?"

"I don't know," Miranda says. "Maybe."

It's eight o'clock. Honeywell Hall, up on its hill, must shine like a torch. Miranda puts on her coat and walks around the house three times. The snow has all melted. Daniel intercepts her on the final circuit. He's pimply, knobbly at present, and his nose is too big for his face. She loves him dearly, just like she loves Elspeth. They are always kind to her. "Here," he says, handing her the bit of damask. "Secret Santa? Secret admirer? Secret code?"

"Oh, you know," Miranda says. "Long story. Saving it for my memoirs."

"Meanwhile back in there everyone's pretending it's 1970 and they're all sweet sixteen again. Playing Sardines and drinking. It'll be orgies in all the cupboards, dramatic confessions and attempted murders in the pantry, under the stairs, in the beds and under them all night long. So I took this and snuck out." Daniel shows her the bottle of Strongbow in his coat pocket. "Let's go and sit in the Tiger. You can tell me all about school and the agony aunt, I'll tell you which Tory MP Elspeth's been seeing on the sly. Then you can sell the story to *The Sun.*"

"And use the proceeds to buy us a cold-water flat in Wolverhampton. We'll live the life," Miranda says.

They drink the cider and eat a half-melted Mars bar. They talk and Miranda wonders if Daniel will try to kiss her. If she should try to kiss Daniel. But he doesn't, she doesn't – they don't – and she falls asleep on the mouse-eaten upholstery of the preposterous carcass of the Sunbeam Tiger, her head on Daniel's shoulder, the trapped fox crumpled in her fist.

CHRISTMAS AFTER, ELSPETH is in all the papers. The Tory MP's husband is divorcing her. Elspeth is a co-respondent in the divorce. Meanwhile she has a new thing with a footballer twenty years her junior. It's the best kind of Christmas story. Journalists everywhere. Elspeth, in the Sunbeam Tiger, picks up Miranda at the station in a wide-brimmed black hat, black jumpsuit, black sunglasses, triumphantly disgraced. In her element.

Miranda's aunt almost didn't let her come this year. But then, if Miranda had stayed, they would have both been miserable. Her aunt has a new boyfriend. Almost as awful as she is. Someone should tell the tabloids.

"Lovely dress," Elspeth says, kissing her on the cheek. "You make it?"

Miranda is particularly pleased with the hem. "It's all right."

"I want one just like it," Elspeth says. "In red. Lower the neckline, raise the hem a bit. You could go into business. Ever think of it?"

"I'm only sixteen," Miranda says. "There's plenty of room for improvement."

"Alexander McQueen! Left school when he was sixteen," Elspeth says. "Went off to apprentice on Savile Row. Used to sew human hair into his linings. A kind of spell, I suppose. I have one of his manta dresses somewhere in the Hall. And your mother, she was barely older than you are now. Hanging around backstage, stitching sequins and crystals on tulle."

"Where's Daniel?" Miranda says. She and her mother have been corresponding. Miranda is saving up money. She hasn't told her aunt yet, but next summer Miranda's going to Thailand.

"Back at the house. In a mood. Listening to my old records. The Smiths."

Miranda looks over, studies Elspeth's face. "That girl broke up with him, didn't she?"

"If you mean the one with the ferrets and the unfortunate ankles," Elspeth says, "yes. What's her name. It's a mystery. Not her name, the breakup. He grows three inches in two months, his skin clears up, honestly, Miranda, he's even better looking than I expected he'd turn out. Heart of gold, that boy, a good brain, too. I can't think what she was thinking."

"Preemptive strike, perhaps," Miranda says.

"I wouldn't know about the breakup except for accidentally overhearing a conversation. *Somewhat* accidentally," Elspeth says. "Well, that and the Smiths. He doesn't talk to me about his love life."

"Do you *want* him to talk to you about his love life?"

"No," Elspeth says. "Yes. Maybe? Probably not. Anyway, how about you, Miranda? Do you have one of those, yet? A love life?"

"I don't even have ferrets," Miranda says.

ON CHRISTMAS EVE, while all the visiting Honeywells and cousins and wives and boyfriends and girlfriends and their accountants are out caroling in the village, Elspeth takes Miranda and Daniel aside. She gives them each a joint.

"It's not as if I don't know you've been raiding my supply, *Daniel*," Elspeth says. "At least this way, I know what you're up to. If you're going to break the law, you might as well learn to break it responsibly. Under adult supervision."

Daniel rolls his eyes, looks at Miranda. Whatever he sees in her face makes him snort. It's annoying but true: he really has become quite spectacular looking. Well, it was inevitable. Apparently they drown all the ugly Honeywells at birth.

"It's okay, Mi*randy*," he says. "I'll have yours if you don't want it."

Miranda sticks the joint in her bra. "Thanks, but I'll hang on to it."

"Anyway I'm sure the two of you have lots of catching up to do," Elspeth says. "I'm off to the pub to kiss the barmaids and make the journos cry."

When she's out the door, Daniel says, "She's matchmaking, isn't she?"

Miranda says, "Or else it's reverse psychology?"

Their eyes meet. *Courage, Miranda.* Daniel tilts his head, looks gleeful.

"In which case, I should do this," he says. He leans forward, puts his hand on Miranda's chin, tilts it up. "We should do this."

He kisses her. His lips are soft and dry. Miranda sucks on the bottom one experimentally. She arranges her arms around his neck, and his hands go down, cup her bum. He opens his mouth and does things with his tongue until she opens her mouth, too. He seems to know how this goes; he and the girl with the ferrets probably did this a lot.

Miranda wonders if the ferrets were in the cage at the time, or out. How unsettling is it, she wonders, to fool around with ferrets watching you? Their beady button eyes.

She can feel Daniel's erection. Oh, God. How embarrassing. She pushes him away. "Sorry," she groans. "Sorry! Yeah, no, I don't think we should be doing this. Any of this!"

"Probably not," Daniel says. "Probably definitely not. It's weird, right?"

"It's weird," Miranda says.

"But perhaps it wouldn't be so weird if we smoked a joint first," Daniel says. His hair is messy. Apparently she did that.

"Or," Miranda says, "maybe we could just smoke a joint. And, you know, not complicate things."

Halfway through the joint, Daniel says, "It wouldn't have to complicate everything." His head is in her lap. She's curling pieces of his hair around her finger.

"Yes, it would," Miranda says. "It *really, really* would."

Later on she says, "I wish it would snow. That would be nice. If it snowed. I thought that's why you lot came here at Christmas. The whole white Christmas thing."

"Awful stuff," Daniel says. "Cold. Slippy. Makes you feel like you're supposed to be singing or something. In a movie. Or in a snow globe."

"Stuck," Miranda says. "Trapped."

"Stuck," Daniel says.

They're lying, tangled together, on a sofa across from the Christmas tree. Occasionally Miranda has to remove Daniel's hand from somewhere it shouldn't be. She doesn't think he's doing it intentionally. She kisses him behind the ear now and then. "That's nice," he says. Pats her bum. She wriggles out from under his hand. Kisses him again. There's a movie on television, lots of explosions. Zombies. Cameron Diaz unloading groceries in a cottage, all by herself.

No, that's another movie entirely, Miranda thinks. Apparently she's been asleep. Daniel is still sleeping. Why does he have to be so irritatingly good-looking, even in his sleep? Miranda hates to think what she looks like asleep. No wonder the ferret girl dumped him.

Elspeth must have come back from the pub, because there's a heap of blankets over the both of them.

Outside, it's snowing.

Miranda puts her hand in the pocket of her dress, feels the piece of damask she has had there all day long. It's a big pocket. Plenty of room for all kinds of things. Miranda doesn't want to be one of those designers who only makes pretty things. She wants them to be useful, too. And provoking. She takes the prettiest blanket from the sofa for herself, distributes the other blankets over Daniel so that all of him is covered.

She goes by a mirror, stops to smooth her hair down, collect it into a ponytail. Wraps the blanket around herself like a shawl, goes out into the snow.

He's there, under the hawthorn tree. She shivers, tells herself it's because of the cold. There isn't much snow on the ground yet. She tells herself she hasn't been asleep too long. He hasn't been waiting long.

He wears the same coat. His face is the same. He isn't as old as she thought he was, that first time. Only a few years older than she. Than Daniel. He hasn't aged. She has. Where is he, when he isn't here?

"Are you a ghost?" she says.

"No," he says. "I'm not a ghost."

"Then you're a real person? A Honeywell?"

"Fenwick Septimus Honeywell." He bows. It looks better than it should, probably because of the coat. People don't really do that sort of thing anymore. No one has names like that. How old is he?

"You only come when it snows," she says.

"I am only allowed to come when it's snowing," he says. "And only on Christmas Day."

"Right," she says. "Okay, no. No, I don't understand. Allowed by whom?"

He shrugs. Doesn't answer. Maybe it isn't allowed.

"You gave me something," Miranda says.

He nods again. She puts out her hand, touches the place on the *justacorps* where he tore away the fox. So he could give it to her.

"Oh," Miranda said. "The poor old thing. You didn't even use scissors, did you? Let me fix it."

She takes the piece of damask out of her pocket, along with her sewing kit, the one she always keeps with her. She's had exactly the right thread in there for over a year. Just in case.

She shows him the damask. A few months ago she unpicked all of the fox's leg, all of the trap. The drops of blood. The tail and snarling head. Then she reworked the embroidery to her own design, mimicking as closely as possible the feel of the original. Now the fox is free, tongue lolling, tail aloft, running along the pink plane of the damask. Pink cotton backing, a piece she cut from an old nightgown.

He takes it from her, turns it over in his hand. "You did this?"

"You gave me a present last year. This is my present for you," she says. "I'll sew it back in. It will be a little untidy, but at least you won't have a hole in your lovely coat."

He says, "I told her I tore it on a branch. It's fine just as it is."

"It isn't fine," she says. "Let me fix it, please."

He smiles. It's a real smile, maybe even a flirtatious smile. He and Daniel could be brothers. They're that much alike. So why did she stop Daniel from kissing her? Why does she have to bite her tongue, sometimes, when Daniel is being kind to her? At Honeywell Hall, she is only as real as Elspeth and Daniel allow her to be. This isn't her real life.

It's ridiculous, of course. Real is real. Daniel is real. Miranda is real when she isn't here. Whatever Fenwick Septimus Honeywell is, Miranda's fairly sure it's complicated.

"*Please*," she says.

"As you wish it, Miranda," Fenny says. She helps him out of the coat. Her hand touches his, and she pushes down the inexplicable desire to clutch at it. As if one of them were falling.

"Come inside the Hall," she says. "Just while I'm working on this. I should do it inside. Better light. You could meet Daniel. Or Elspeth. I could wake her up. I bet Elspeth knows how to deal with this sort of thing." Whatever this sort of thing is. "Theater people seem like they know how to deal with things like this. Come inside with me."

"I can't," he says regretfully.

Of course. It's against the rules.

"Okay," Miranda says, adjusting. "Then we'll both stay out here. I'll stay with you. You can tell me all about yourself. Unless that's against the rules too." She busies herself with pins. He lifts her hand away, holds it.

"Inside out, if you please," he says. "The fox on the inside."

He has lovely hands. No calluses on his fingertips. Manicured nails. Definitely not real. His thumb smooths over her knuckles. Miranda says, a little breathless, "Inside out. So she won't notice someone's repaired it?" Whoever *she* is.

"She'll notice," he says. "But this way she won't see that the fox is free."

"Okay. That's sensible. I guess." Miranda lets go of his hand. "Here. We can sit on this."

She spreads out the blanket. Sits down. Remembers she has a Mars bar in her pocket. She passes that to him. "Sit."

He examines the Mars bar. Unwraps it.

"Oh, no," she says. "More rules? You're not allowed to eat?"

"I don't know," he says. "I've never been given anything before. When I came. No one has ever talked to me."

"So you show up when it snows, creep around for a while, looking in at the windows. Then you go back wherever when the snow stops."

Fenny nods. He looks almost abashed.

"What fun!" Miranda says. "Wait, no, I mean how creepy!" She has the piece of embroidery how she wants it, is tacking it into place with running stitches, so the fox is hidden.

If it stops snowing, will he just disappear? Will the coat stay? Something tells her that all of this is very against the rules. Does he want to come back? And what does she mean by *back*, anyway? Back here, to Honeywell Hall? Or back to wherever it is that he is when he isn't here? Why doesn't he get older?

Elspeth says it's a laugh, getting older. But oh, Miranda knows, Elspeth doesn't mean it.

"It's good," Fenny says, sounding surprised. The Mars bar is gone. He's licking his fingers.

"I could go back in the house," Miranda says. "I could make you a cheese sandwich. There's Christmas cake for tomorrow."

"No," he says. "Stay."

"Okay," she says. "I'll stay. Here. That's the best I can do in this light. My hands are getting too cold."

He takes the coat from her. Nods. Then puts it around her shoulders. Pulls her back against his chest. All of that damask: it's heavy. There's snow inside and out.

Fenny is surprisingly solid for someone who mostly isn't here. She wonders if she is surprising to him, too.

His mouth is just above the top of her head, blowing little hot circles against her hair. She's very, very cold. Ridiculous to be out here in the snow with this ridiculous person with his list of ridiculous rules.

She'll catch her death of cold.

Cautiously, as if he's waiting for her to stop him, he puts his arms around her waist. He sighs. Warm breath in her hair. Miranda is suddenly so very afraid that it will stop snowing. They haven't talked about anything. They haven't even kissed. She knows, every part of her knows, that she wants to kiss him. That he wants to kiss her. All of her skin prickles with longing. Her insides fizz.

She puts her sewing kit back into her pocket, discovers the joint Elspeth gave her, Daniel's lighter. "I bet you haven't ever tried this, either," she says. She twists in his arms. "You smoke it. Here." She taps at the side of his face with the joint, sticks it between his lips when they part. Flicks the lighter until it catches, and then she's lunging at him, kissing him, and he's kissing her back. The second time tonight that she's kissed a boy, the first two boys she's ever kissed, and both of them Honeywells.

And oh, it was lovely kissing Daniel, but this is something better than lovely. All they do is kiss, she doesn't know how long they kiss; at first Fenny tastes of chocolate, and she doesn't know what happens to the joint. Or to the lighter. They kiss until Miranda's lips are numb-ish and the *justacorps* has come entirely off of her, and she's in Fenny's lap and she has one hand in Fenny's hair and one hand digging into Fenny's waist, and all she wants to do is keep on kissing Fenny forever and ever. Until he pulls away.

They're both breathing hard. His cheeks are red. His mouth is redder. Miranda wonders if she looks as crazed as he looks.

"You're shivering," he says.

"Of course I'm shivering! It's freezing out here! And you won't come inside. Because," Miranda says, panting, shivering, all of her vibrating with cold and with *want, want, want,* "it's against the rules!"

Fenny nods. Looks at her lips, licks his own. Jerks back, though, when Miranda tries to kiss him again. She's tempted to pick up a handful of wet snow and smush it into his Honeywell face.

"Fine, fine! You stay right here. Don't move. Not even an inch, understand? I'll get the keys to the Tiger," she says. "Unless it's against the rules to sit in old cars."

"All of this is against the rules," Fenny says. But he nods. Maybe, she thinks, she can get him in the car and just drive away with him. Maybe that would work.

"I *mean* it," Miranda says. "Don't you *dare* go anywhere."

He nods. She kisses him, punishingly, lingeringly, desperately, then takes off in a run for the kitchen. Her fingers are so cold she can't get the door open at first. She grabs her coat, the keys to the Tiger, and then, on impulse, cuts off a hunk of the inviolate Christmas cake. Well, if Elspeth says anything, she'll tell her the whole story.

Then she's out the door again. Says the worst words she knows when she sees that the snow has stopped. There is the snow-blotted blanket, the joint, and the Mars-bar wrapper.

She leaves the Christmas cake on the window ledge. Maybe the birds will eat it.

DANIEL IS STILL asleep on the couch. She wakes him up. "Merry Christmas," she says. "Good morning." She gives him his present. She's made him a shirt. Egyptian cotton, gray-blue to match his eyes. But of course it won't fit. He's already outgrown it.

DANIEL CATCHES HER under the mistletoe when it's past time for bed, Christmas night and no one wants to go to sleep yet, everyone tipsy and loose and picking fights about things they don't care about. For the sheer pleasure of picking fights. He kisses Miranda. She lets him.

It's sort of a present for Elspeth, Miranda rationalizes. It's sort of because she knows it's ridiculous, not kissing Daniel, just because she wants to be kissing someone else instead. Especially when the person she wants to be kissing isn't really a real person at all. At least not most of the time.

Besides, he's wearing the shirt Miranda made for him, even though it doesn't fit.

In the morning, Daniel is too hungover to drive her down to the village to catch the bus. Elspeth takes her instead. Elspeth is wearing a vintage suit, puce gabardine, trimmed with sable, something Miranda itches to take apart, just to see how it's made. What a tiny waist she has.

Elspeth says, "You know he's in love with you."

"He's not," Miranda says. "He loves me, but he's not in love with me. I love him, but I'm not in love with him."

"If you say so," Elspeth says. Her tone is cool. "Although I can't help being curious how you've come to know so much about love, Miranda, at your tender age."

Miranda flushes.

"You know you can talk to me," Elspeth says. "You can talk to me whenever you want to. Whenever you need to. Darling Miranda. There's a boy, isn't there? Not Daniel. Poor Daniel."

"There's nobody," Miranda says. "Really. There's nobody. It's nothing. I'm just a bit sad because I have to go home again. It was such a lovely Christmas."

"Such lovely snow!" Elspeth says. "Too bad it never lasts."

DANIEL COMES TO visit in the spring. Two months after Christmas. Miranda isn't expecting him. He shows up at the door with a bouquet of roses. Miranda's aunt's eyebrows go almost up to her hairline. "I'll make tea," she says, and scurries off. "And we'll need a vase for those."

Miranda takes the roses from Daniel. Says, "Daniel! What are you doing here?"

"You've been avoiding me," Daniel says.

"Avoiding you? We don't live in the same place," Miranda says. "I wasn't even sure you knew where I lived." She can hardly stand to have him here, standing in the spotless foyer of her aunt's semidetached bungalow.

"You know what I mean, Miranda. You're never online," he says. "And when you are, you never want to chat. You never text me back. Aren't you going to invite me in?"

"No," she says. Grabs her bag.

"Don't bother with the tea, Aunt Dora," she says loudly, "We're going out."

She yanks at Daniel's hand, extracts him violently from her life, her *real* life. If only.

She speed walks him past the tract houses with their small, white-stone frontages, all the way to the dreary, dingy, Midlands-typical High Street. Daniel trailing behind her. It's a long walk, and she has no idea what to say to him. He doesn't seem to know what to say, either.

Her dress is experimental, nothing she's ever intended to wear out. She hasn't yet brushed her hair today. It's the weekend. She was planning to stay in and study. How dare he show up.

There's a teashop where the scones and the sandwiches are particularly foul. She takes him there, and they sit down. Order.

"I should have let you know I was coming," Daniel says.

"Yes," Miranda says. "Then I could have told you not to."

He tries to take her hand. "Mirandy," he says. "I think about you all the time. About us. I think about us."

"Don't," she says. "Stop!"

"I can't," he says. "I like you. Very much. Don't you like me?"

It's a horrible conversation. Like stepping on a baby mouse. A baby mouse who happens to be your friend. It doesn't help that Miranda knows how unfair she's being. She shouldn't be angry that he's come here. He doesn't know how she feels about this place. Just a few more months and she'll be gone from here forever. It will never have existed.

They are both practically on the verge of tears by the time the scones come. Daniel takes one bite and then spits it out onto the plate.

"It's not that bad," she snaps. Dares him to complain.

"Yes it is," he says. "It really truly is that bad." He takes a sip of his tea. "And the milk has gone off, too."

He seems so astonished at this that she can't help it. She bursts out laughing. This astonishes him, too. And just like that, they aren't fighting anymore. They spend the rest of the day feeding ducks at the frozen pond, going in and out of horror movies, action movies, cartoons – all the movies except the romantic comedies, because why rub salt in the wound? – at the cinema. He doesn't try to hold her hand. She tries not to imagine that it is snowing outside, that it is Fenny sitting in the flickering darkness here beside her. Imagining this is against the rules.

MIRANDA FINISHES OUT the term. Packs up what she wants to take with her, boxes up the rest. Sells her sewing machine. Leaves a note for her aunt. Never mind what's in it.

She knows she should be more grateful. Her aunt has kept her fed, kept her clothed, given her bed and board. Never hit her. Never, really, been unkind. But Miranda is so very, very tired of being grateful to people.

She is sticky, smelly, and punch-drunk with jetlag when her flight arrives in Phuket. Stays the night in a hostel and then sets off. She's read about how this is supposed to go. What you can bring, how long you can stay, how you should behave. All the rules.

But, in the end, she doesn't see Joannie. It isn't allowed. It isn't clear why. Is her mother there? They tell her yes. Is she still alive? Yes. Can Miranda see her? No. Not possible today. Come back.

Miranda comes back three times. Each time she is sent away. The consul can't help. On her second visit, she speaks to a young woman named Dinda, who comes and spends time with the prisoners when they are in the infirmary. Dinda says that she's sat with Joannie two or three times. That Miranda's mother never says much.

It's been over six months since her mother wrote to either Elspeth or to Miranda.

The third time she is sent away, Miranda buys a plane ticket to Japan. She spends the next four months there, teaching English in Kyoto. Going to museums. Looking at kimonos at the flea markets at the temples.

She sends postcards to Elspeth, to Daniel. To her mother. She even sends one to her aunt. And two days before Christmas, Miranda flies home.

On the plane, she falls asleep and dreams that it's snowing. She's with Joannie in a cell in the prison in Phuket. Her mother tells Miranda that she loves her. She tells her that her sentence has been commuted. She tells her that if Miranda's good and follows the rules very carefully, she'll be home by Christmas.

SHE HAS A plan this year. The plan is that it will snow on Christmas. Never mind what the forecast says. It will snow. She will find Fenny. And she won't leave his side. Never mind what the rules say.

Daniel is going to St. Andrews next year. His girlfriend's name is Lillian. Elspeth is on her best behavior. Miranda is, too. She tells various Honeywells amusing stories about her students, the deer at the temples, and the girl who played the flute for them.

Elspeth is getting *old*. She's still the most beautiful woman Miranda has ever seen, but she's in her sixties now. Any day she'll be given a knighthood and never be scandalous again.

Lillian is a nice person. She tells Miranda that she likes Miranda's dress. She flirts with the most decrepit of the Honeywells, helps set the table. Daniel watches everything that she does as if all of it is brand new, as if Lillian has invented compliments, flirting, as if there were no such thing as water glasses and table linens before Lillian discovered them. Oh newfound land.

Despite all this, Miranda thinks she could be fond of Lillian. She's smart. Likes maths. Actually, truly, *really* seems to like Miranda's dress, which, let's admit it, is meant as an act of war. Miranda is not into pretty at the moment. She's into armor, weaponry, abrasiveness, discomfort – hers and other peoples'. The dress is leather, punk, studded with spikes, buckles, metal cuffs, chain looped round and around. Whenever she sits down, she has to be careful not to gash, impale, or skewer the furniture. Hugging is completely out of the question.

LILLIAN WANTS A tour, so after dinner and the first round of cocktails, Miranda and Daniel take her all through Honeywell Hall, the parts that are kept up and the parts that are falling into shadow. They end up in one of the attics, digging through Elspeth's trunks of costumes. They make Lillian try on cheesecloth dresses, hand-beaded fairy wings, ancient, cakey stage makeup.

Take selfies. Daniel reads old mail from fans, pulls out old photos of Elspeth and Joannie, backstage. Here's Joannie perched on a giant urn. Joannie, her mouth full of pins. Joannie, at a first-night party, drunk and laughing and young. It should hurt to look at these pictures. Shouldn't it?

"Do you think it will snow?" Lillian says. "I want snow for Christmas."

Daniel says, "Snowed last Christmas. Shouldn't expect that it will, this year. Too warm."

Not even trying to sound casual about it, Miranda says, "It's going to snow. It has to snow. And if it doesn't snow, then we're going to do something about it. We'll make it snow."

She feels quite gratified when Lillian looks at her as if Miranda is insane, possibly dangerous. Well, the dress should have told her that.

"My present this year," Miranda says, "is going to be snow. Call me the Snow Queen. Come and see."

Her suitcases – her special equipment – barely fit into the Tiger. Elspeth didn't say a word, just raised an eyebrow. Most of it is still in the carriage house.

Daniel is game when she explains. Lillian is either game, or pretending to be. There are long, gauzy swathes of white cloth to weave through tree branches, to tack down to the ground. There are long strings of glass and crystal and silver ornaments. Handcut lace snowflakes caught in netting. The pièce de résistance is the Snowboy Stage Whisper Fake Snow Machine with its fifty-foot extending hose reel. Miranda's got bags and bags of fake snow. Over an hour's worth of the best quality fake snow money can buy, according to the guy who rented her the Snowboy.

It's nearly midnight by the time they have everything arranged to Miranda's satisfaction. She goes inside and turns on the Hall's floodlights, then turns on the snow machine. A fine, glittering snow begins. Lillian kisses Daniel lingeringly. A fine romance.

Elspeth has been observing the whole time from the kitchen stair. She puts a hand over her cocktail. Fake snow dusts her fair hair, streaks it white.

All of the Honeywells who haven't gone to bed yet, which is most of them, *ooh* and *ah*. The youngest Honeywells, the ones who weren't even born when Miranda first came to Honeywell Hall, break into a spontaneous round of applause. Miranda feels quite powerful. Santa Claus exists after all.

*   *   *

ALL OF THE Honeywells eventually retreat back into the house to drink
and gossip and admire Miranda's special effects from within. It may not
be properly cold tonight, but it's cold enough. Time for hot chocolate, hot
toddies, hot baths, hot water bottles and bed.

She's not sure, of course, that this will work. If this is playing by the
rules. But isn't she owed something by now? A bit of luck?

And she is. At first, not daring to hope, she thinks that Daniel has come
from the Hall to fetch her in. But it isn't Daniel.

Fenny, in that old *justacorps*, Miranda's stitching around the piece above
his pocket, walks out from under the hawthorn tree.

"It worked," Miranda says. She hugs herself, which is a mistake. All
those spikes. "Ow. Oh."

"I shouldn't be here, should I?" Fenny says. "You've done something."
Miranda looks closely at his face. How young he looks. Barely older than
she. How long has he been this young?

Fake snow is falling on their heads. "We have about an hour," Miranda
says. "Not much time."

He comes to her then, takes her in his arms. "Be careful," she says. "I'm
all spikes."

"A ridiculous dress," he says into her hair. "Though comely. Is this what
people wear in this age?"

"Says the man wearing a *justacorps*," she says. They're almost the same
height this year. He's shorter than Daniel now, she realizes. Then they're
kissing, she and Fenny are kissing, and she isn't thinking about Daniel
at all.

They kiss, and Fenny presses himself against her, armored with spikes
though Miranda is. He holds her, hands just above her waist, tight enough
that she thinks she will have bruises in the shape of his fingers.

"Come in the Hall with me," Miranda says, in between kisses. "Come
with me."

Fenny bites her lower lip. Then licks it. "Can't," he says.

"Because of the rules." Now he's nibbling her ear. She whimpers. Tugs
him away by the hair. "Hateful rules."

"Could I stay with you, I vow I would. I would stay and grow old with you, Miranda. Or as long as you wanted me to stay."

"Stay with me," she says. Her dress must be goring into him. His stomach, his thighs. They'll both be black and blue tomorrow.

He doesn't say anything. Kisses her over and over. Distracting her, she knows. The front of her dress fastens with a simple clasp. Underneath she's wearing an old T-shirt. Leggings. She guides his hands.

"If you can't stay with me," she says, as Fenny opens the clasp, "then I'll stay with you."

His hands are on her rib cage as she speaks. Simple enough to draw him inside the armature of the dress, to reach behind his back, pull the belt of heavy chain around them both. Fasten it. The key is in the Hall. In the attic, where she left it.

"Miranda," Fenny says, when he realizes. "What have you done?"

"A crucial component of any relationship is the capacity to surprise the one you love. I read that somewhere. A magazine. You're going to love women's magazines. Oh, and the Internet. Well, parts of it anyway. I won't let you go," Miranda says. The dress is a snug fit for two people. She can feel every breath he takes. "If you go, then I'll go, too. Wherever it is that you go."

"It doesn't work that way," he says. "There are rules."

"There are always ways to get around the rules," Miranda says. "That was in another magazine." She knows that she's babbling. A coping mechanism. There are articles about that, too. Why can't she stop thinking about women's magazines? Some byproduct of realizing that you're in love? 'Fifteen Ways to Know He Loves You Back.' Number eight. He doesn't object when you chain yourself to him after using fake snow in a magic spell to lure him into your arms.

The fake snow is colder and wetter and heavier than she'd thought it would be. Much more like real snow. Fenny has been muttering something against her neck. Either *I love you* or else *What the hell were you thinking, Miranda?*

It's both. He's saying both. It's fake snow and *real*. Real snow mingling with the fake. Her fake magic and real magic. Coming down heavier and heavier until all the world is white. The air, colder and colder and colder still.

"Something's happening, Fenny," she says. "It's snowing. Really snowing."

It's as if he's turned to stone in her arms. She can feel him stop breathing. But his heart is racing. "Let me go," he says. "Please let me go."

"I can't," Miranda says. "I don't have the key."

"You can." A voice like a bell, clear and sweet.

And here is the one Miranda has been waiting for. Fenny's *she*. The one who catches foxes in traps. Never lets them go. The one who makes the rules.

It's silly, perhaps, to be reminded in this moment of Elspeth, but that's who Miranda thinks of when she looks up and sees the Lady who approaches, more Honeywell than any Honeywell Miranda has ever met. The presence, the *puissance* that Elspeth commands, just for a little while when Elspeth takes the stage, is a game. Elspeth plays at the thing. Here is the substance. Power is something granted willingly to Elspeth by her audience. Fenny's Lady has it always. What a burden. Never to be able to put it down.

Can the Lady see what Miranda is thinking? Her gaze takes in all. Fenny keeps his head bowed. But his hands are in Miranda's hands. He is in her keeping, and she will not let him go.

"I have no key," Miranda says. "And he does not want to go with you."

"He did once," the Lady says. She wears armor, too, all made of ice. What a thing it would be, to dress this Lady. To serve her. She could go with Fenny, if the Lady let her.

Down inside the dress where the Lady cannot see, Fenny pinches the soft web between Miranda's thumb and first finger. The pain brings her back to herself. She sees that he is watching her. He says nothing, only looks until Miranda finds herself again in his eyes.

"I went with you willingly," Fenny agrees. But he doesn't look at the Lady. He only looks at Miranda.

"But you would leave me now? Only speak it and I will let you go at once."

Fenny says nothing. A rule, Miranda thinks. There is a rule here. "He can't say it," she says. "Because you won't let him. So let me say it for him. He will stay here. Haven't you kept him from his home for long enough?"

"His home is with me. Let him go," the Lady says. "Or you will be sorry." She reaches out a long hand and touches the chain around Miranda's dress. It splinters beneath her featherlight touch. Miranda feels it give.

"Let him go and I will give you your heart's desire," the Lady says. She is so close that Miranda can feel the Lady's breath frosting her cheek. And then Miranda isn't holding Fenny. She's holding Daniel. Miranda and Daniel are married. They love each other so much. Honeywell Hall is her home. It always has been. Their children under the tree, Elspeth white-haired and lovely at the head of the table, wearing a dress from Miranda's couture label.

Only it isn't Elspeth at all, is it? It's the Lady. Miranda almost lets go of Daniel. Fenny! But he holds her hands and she wraps her hands around his waist, tighter than before.

"Be careful, girl," the Lady says. "He bites."

Miranda is holding a fox. Scrabbling, snapping, blood breath at her face. Miranda holds fast.

Then: Fenny again. Trembling against her. "It's okay," Miranda says. "I've got you."

But it isn't Fenny after all. It's her mother. They're together in a small, dirty cell. Joannie says, "It's okay, Miranda. I'm here. It's okay. You can let go. I'm here. Let go and we can go home."

"No," Miranda says, suddenly boiling with rage. "No, you're not here. And I can't do anything about that. But I can do something about this." And she holds on to her mother until her mother is Fenny again, and the Lady is looking at Miranda and Fenny as if they are a speck of filth beneath her slippered foot.

"Very well then," the Lady says. She smiles, the way you would smile at a speck of filth. "Keep him then. For a while. But know that he will never again know the joy that I taught him. With me he could not be but happy. I made him so. You will bring him grief and death. You have dragged him into a world where he knows nothing. Has nothing. He will look at you and think of what he lost."

"We all lose," says an acerbic voice. "We all love and we all lose and we go on loving just the same."

"Elspeth?" Miranda says. But she thinks, it's a trap. Just another trap. She squeezes Fenny so hard around his middle that he gasps.

Elspeth looks at Fenny. She says, "I saw you once, I think. Outside the window. I thought you were a shadow or a ghost."

Fenny says, "I remember. Though you had hardly come into your beauty then."

"Such talk! You are going to be wasted on my Miranda, I'm afraid," Elspeth says. "She's more for the doing of things than for the telling of them. As for you, my lady, I think you'll find you've been bested. Go and find another toy. We here are not your meat."

The Lady curtseys. Looks one last time at Elspeth, Miranda. Fenny. This time he looks back. What does he see? Does any part of him move to follow her? His hand finds Miranda's hand again.

Then the Lady is gone and the snow thins and blows away to nothing at all.

Elspeth blows out a breath. "Well," she says. "You're a stubborn girl, a good-hearted girl, Miranda, and brighter than your poor mother. But if I'd known what you were about, we would have had a word or two. Stage magic is well and good, but better to steer clear of the real kind."

"Better for Miranda," Fenny says. "But she has won me free with her brave trick."

"And now I suppose we'll have to figure out what to do with you," Elspeth says. "You'll be needing something more practical than that coat."

"Come on," Miranda says. She is still holding on to Fenny's hand. Perhaps she's holding on too tightly, but he doesn't seem to care. He's holding on just as tightly.

So she says, "Let's go in."

TEN RULES FOR BEING AN INTERGALACTIC SMUGGLER (THE SUCCESSFUL KIND)
Holly Black

Holly Black (blackholly.com) is the author of bestselling contemporary fantasy books for kids and teens. Some of her titles include *The Spiderwick Chronicles* (with Tony DiTerlizzi), the *Modern Faerie Tale* series, the Curse Workers series, *Doll Bones*, and *The Coldest Girl in Coldtown*. She has been a finalist for the Mythopoeic Award and for an Eisner Award, and the recipient of both an Andre Norton Award and a Newbery Honor. Her new books are *The Darkest Part of the Forest*, a return to faerie fiction, and *The Iron Trial*, the first book in a middle grade fantasy series, *Magisterium*, co-authored by Cassandra Clare. Holly currently lives in New England with her husband and son in a house with a secret door.

1. *There are no rules.*

THAT'S WHAT YOUR uncle tells you, after he finds you stowing away in his transport ship, the *Celeris,* which you used to call the *Celery* when you were growing up, back when you only dreamed of getting off the crappy planet your parents brought you to as a baby. No matter how many times you told them their dumb dream of being homesteaders and digging in the red dirt wasn't yours, no matter how many times you begged your uncle to take you with him, even though your parents swore that he was a smuggler and bad news besides, it wasn't until you climbed out of your hidey-hole with the vastness of space in the transparent alumina windows behind you that anyone really believed you'd meant any of it.

Once you're caught, he gives you a long lecture about how there are laws and there's right and wrong, but those aren't *rules*. And, he says, there are especially no rules for situations like this. Which turns out to be to your advantage, because he's pissed but not that pissed. His basic philosophy is to laugh in the face of danger and also in the face of annoyance. And since he thinks his brother is a bit of a damp rag and likes the idea of being a hero to his niece, it turns out that *no rules* means not turning around and dumping you back on Mars.

He also turns out to be a smuggler. Grudgingly, you have to admit that your parents might not be wrong about everything.

2. *Spaceports are dangerous.*

YOUR UNCLE TELLS you this several times as you dock in the Zvezda-9 Spaceport, but it's not like you don't know it already. Your parents have told you a million stories about how alien races like the spidery and psychopathic Charkazaks – fugitives after their world was destroyed by InterPlanetary forces – take girls like you hostage and force you to do things so bad, they won't even describe them. From all your parents' warnings about spaceports, when you step off of *Celeris,* you expect a dozen shady aliens to jump out of the shadows, offering you morality-disrupting powders, fear inhibitors, and *nucleus accumbens* stimulators.

Except it turns out that spaceports aren't that interesting. Zvezda-9 is a big stretch of cement tunnels, vast microgravity farms, hotel pods, and general stores with overpriced food that's either dehydrated or in a tube. There are also InterPlanetary offices, where greasy-looking people from a variety of worlds wait in long lines for licenses. They all stare at your homespun clothes. You want to grab your uncle's hand, but you already feel like enough of a backworld yokel, so you curl your fingers into a fist instead.

There are aliens – it wasn't like your parents were wrong about that. Most of them look human and simultaneously inhuman, and the juxtaposition is so odd that you can't keep from staring. You spot a woman whose whole lower face is a jagged-toothed mouth. A man with gray-skinned cheeks that grow from his face like gills or possibly just really strange ears loads up a hovercart nearby, the stripes on his body smeared so you know they are paint and not pigmentation. Someone passes you in a heavy, hairy cloak, and you get the impression of thousands of eyes inside of the hood. It's creepy as hell.

You do not, however, see a single Charkazak. No one offers you any drugs.

"Stop acting stupid," your uncle growls, and you *try* to act less stupid and keep from staring. You try to act like you stroll around spaceports all the time, like you know how to use the gun you swiped from your mother and strapped to your thigh under your skirt, like the tough expression you plaster on your face actually *makes* you tough. You try to roll your hips and swagger, like you're a grown lady, but not too much of a lady.

Your uncle laughs at you, but it's a good kind of laughter, like at least you're sort of maybe pulling it off.

Later that night, he buys you some kind of vat-meat tacos, and he and some of his human 'transporter' buddies get to drinking and telling stories. They tell you about run-ins with space pirates and times when the InterPlanetary Centurions stopped their ships, looking for illicit cargo. Your uncle has a million stories about narrow getaways and hidey-holes, in addition to a large cast of seedy accomplices able to forge passable paperwork, but who apparently excel at getting him into dangerous yet hilarious situations. You laugh your way into the night.

The next day your uncle buys you a pair of black pants and a shirt like his, made from a self-cleaning material that's both hydrophobic and insulating, plus a shiny chromium steel clip for your hair. You can't stop smiling. And although you don't say it out loud to him, in that moment you're sure that the two of you are going to be the greatest smuggling duo of all time.

3. *When someone says they'll pay double your normal rate, they're offering to pay at least half what you'd charge them if you knew the whole story.*

THE CELERIS STAYS docked in the spaceport for a couple of weeks while your uncle buys some used parts to repair the worst of wear and tear to her systems and looks for the right official job – and then an unofficial job to make the most of that InterPlanetary transport license.

You try to keep out of your uncle's way so he doesn't start thinking of you as some kid who's always underfoot. You don't want to get sent back home. Instead, you hang around the spaceport, trying to make yourself less ignorant. You go into the store that sells navigational charts and stare at the shifting patterns of stars. You go into the pawnshop and look at the fancy laser pistols and the odd alien gadgets, until the guy behind the counter gets tired of your face and orders you to buy something or get out.

After a while the spaceport seems less scary. Some of your uncle's friends pay you pocket money to run errands, money that you use to buy caff bars and extra batteries for your mother's gun and holographic hoop earrings that you think make you look like a pirate. Just when you start to feel a little bit cocky and comfortable, your uncle informs you that it's time to leave.

He's lined up the jobs. He's found a client.

A little man with a red face and red hair sits in their eating area on the ship, sipping archer ethanol, booze culled from the Sagittarius B2 cloud, out of a coffee can. The man tells your uncle that he supplies alien tissue to a scientist who has his laboratory on one of the outer worlds, where the rules about gene splicing and cloning are more lax. The little man has come across a particularly valuable shipment of frozen alien corpses and needs for it to get where it's going fast, with few questions asked.

The assignment creeps you out, but you can tell that your uncle has been distracted by the ludicrously high offer the man is waving around. It's more money than you've ever imagined being paid for anything, and even with the cost of fuel and bribing Centurions, you're pretty sure there would be enough to refit the *Celeris* in style. No more used parts, no more stopgap repairs. He could have all new everything.

"Half now," the man says. "Half when the cargo arrives *intact*. And it better get there inside a month, or I will take the extra time out of your hide. I am paying for speed – and silence."

"Oh, it'll be there," your uncle says, and pours a little archer ethanol into a plastic cup for himself. Even the smell of it singes your nose hair. "This little ship has got hidden depths – *literally*." He grins while he's speaking, like the offer of so much money has made him drunker than all the booze in the sky. "Hidden depths. Like me."

The red-haired man doesn't seem all that impressed.

You have lots of questions about where the alien bodies came from and what exactly the scientist is going to do with them, but a quick glance from your uncle confirms that you're supposed to swallow those and keep pouring drinks. You have your guesses, though – you've heard stories about space pirates with alien parts grafted on instead of their own. New ears and eyes, new second stomachs tough enough to digest acid, second livers and new teeth and organs humans don't even have – like poison glands or hidden quills. And then there were worse stories: ones about cloned hybrids, pitiless and monstrous enough to fight the surviving Charkazak and win.

But you're a stupid kid from a backworld planet and you know it, so you quash your curiosity. After the client leaves, you clean up some and fold your stuff so it tucks away in the netting over your bunk back in your room. You go down to the cargo hold and move around boxes, so the way to the secret storage compartment is clear for when the redhead comes back with his alien parts in the morning. That night you look out through the transparent alumina windows at ships docking on Zvezda-9, and you get excited about leaving for your first mission in the morning.

But in the morning, the *Celeris* doesn't depart.

It turns out that it takes time to get ready for a run like this – it takes supplies and paperwork; it takes charting a course and new fuel and lots of batteries and a ton of water. The whole while you careen between sadness over leaving Zvezda-9 now that you've become familiar with it and wishing you were in space already. You visit your favorite spots mournfully, unsure if you'll ever see them again, and you pace the halls of the *Celeris* at night until your uncle orders you to your bunk. His temper is a short-sparking fuse. He sends you to buy supplies and then complains loudly about what you get, even though you're the one who'll be doing the reheating and reconstituting.

The client arrives in the middle of the night. You sit in the shadows above the cargo bay and watch what he loads – a long cylindrical casket, big enough for several human-size bodies. Smoke curls off of it when it's jostled, as though it is very, very cold inside.

An hour later you're back among the stars. There, your uncle starts to relax, as though space is his real home and being on a planet for too long was what was making him tense. Over the next week, he teaches you a few simple repairs he has to do regularly for the *Celeris,* shows you a few of his favorite smuggling hidey-holes, teaches you a card game and then how to cheat at that card game, and even lets you fly the ship for an hour with him hanging over your shoulder, nagging you about everything you're doing wrong.

Considering that he turns on autopilot while he sleeps, letting you put your hands on the controls while he watches isn't that big of a vote of confidence, but sitting in the cockpit, gazing out at the spray of stars, makes you feel important and wholly yourself, as though all your time laboring in that red dirt was worth something, because it brought you to this.

Mostly the trip is uneventful, except for an evening when your uncle comes up from the cargo hold and won't look at you. He downs a whole bottle of archer ethanol and then gets noisily sick while you watch the computer navigate and fiddle with your earrings. He never says what set him off, but the next day he's himself again and you both try to pretend that it never happened.

Then you wake up because the whole ship is shaking. At first you think you're passing through an asteroid field, but then you realize something bad is happening. There's the faint smell of fire and the sound of the ship venting it. Then the gravity starts going crazy – lurching on and off, bouncing you against the floor and the walls.

Once it stabilizes, you manage to crawl out into the corridor. Your heart is pounding like crazy, fear making you light-headed. You clutch your mother's gun to you like it's some kind of teddy bear. There's shouting – more voices than there should be on board. You think you hear your uncle calling your name and then something else. Something loud and anguished and final.

You head automatically for the cockpit when a man runs into the corridor, skidding to a stop at the sight of you. Based on the mismatched array of weapons and armor, you figure he's got to be a pirate – if he was a Centurion, he'd be in uniform. He reaches for his weapon, like he's just shaking off the shock of seeing a kid in her nightgown aboard a smuggling ship, but you've already swung your mother's gun up. You blast him in the head before you allow yourself to consider what you're doing.

When he drops, you start trembling all over. You think you're going to throw up, but you can hear more of them coming, so you try to concentrate on moving through the ship, on remembering all the hidey-holes your uncle pointed out to you.

The lights go out all of a sudden, so you have to feel your way in the dark, but soon you've found one big enough for you to fit yourself into and you're shut up inside.

Snug as a bug in a rug, your mom would say.

You start crying, thinking about her. You know your uncle is probably dead, but you don't want to admit that to yourself yet, so you pretend you're not thinking of him when you wipe away your tears.

4. If your ship gets raided by space pirates, don't hide in the cargo hold, because everybody wants what's in the cargo hold.

THE *CELERIS* IS a small enough ship that you can hear the pirates walking through it, talking to one another. You try to count different voices, but all you can figure out is that there's more than five and probably less than ten. Which doesn't mean that much, since they boarded from another ship and there could be any number of them back there.

Did you find it? you hear them say, over and over again. *We've got to find it before it finds us.*

Which doesn't mean anything to you. You wonder if they attacked the wrong ship. You wonder if your uncle got murdered for nothing, for less than nothing, since the credits he got paid are in his bank account and not anywhere aboard the ship.

You hear the acceleration of the engines and feel the odd sensation of forward momentum. Which means they're probably taking the whole ship, not just gutting it for parts and leaving it to spin endlessly in the void – which would have meant no life support for you. Maybe you'll survive this, you think. Maybe no one even knew you were aboard, maybe they thought the guy you shot was shot by your uncle. If they docked on a planet, even a terrible planet, maybe you could sneak off the ship and hide in the station.

To do that, you need to make sure you stay hydrated. You'll need food too, but not right away. A bathroom, ideally. You and your uncle usually ate in the little kitchen area – he called it the galley – off the main cockpit, where there's a small burner, lots of packages of freeze-dried food, tubes of paste, and a jar of nutrient powder. You're sure that some of the pirates have raided it by now, drinking through your uncle's supply of archer ethanol – you've heard them, rowdy and full of good cheer, like they'd done something heroic instead of something awful.

If they catch you, they'll most likely kill you. You're using up oxygen, just breathing. But you know all the other things pirates might do instead – sell you, use you, cook you, eat you. Your parents loved to tell you how bad things could get when you talked about wanting to have adventures in space.

There's food in the cargo hold, you know – those were the supplies that went on the official roster as his official shipment. Your uncle had the papers to sell that stuff to a homesteader planet. He'd been planning on sending you down to haggle with them – and had loaded you down with plenty of pieces of dubious bargaining wisdom in preparation.

Don't be afraid of silence, he'd told you. *Silence shows your strength. Have a bottom line,* he'd told you. *Sometimes to make a deal, you've got to walk away from a deal.*

But it turned out that pirates didn't care about negotiating. Just like your uncle had told you in the beginning, there aren't any rules.

You doze impatiently waiting for your chance to slip down to the cargo hold. Your leg cramps from the position you've folded yourself into, and finally you decide that even though you can still hear voices, they're faint, and you're going to have to go for it.

You unfold yourself and step into the hallway. The floor is cold against your feet, and you feel light-headed from being in one position so long, but you begin to pad your way toward the cargo bay. There's a steel ladder to a crow's nest above the cargo bay, and as you climb down it, you know that if there's a pirate patrolling beneath you, he's going to see you before you see him, your pale nightgown fluttering around you like a white flag of surrender. There's nothing you can do about it, though, so you just try to keep on going and stay quiet.

You're in luck. There's no one there. You climb all the way down and start to open up the shipping crates. You find luxuries that settlers love – caff bars, tins of coffee, jars of spicy peppers, fermented soy, and plenty of both salt and sugar. Ripping into one of the caff bars, you realize the stuff won't keep you fed until the pirates dock, unless they dock very soon. Worse, there's nothing to drink.

Despairing, you grab another caff bar and begin to look over the few remaining crates. You find some machinery – farming stuff – and what appears to be an array of tents suitable for a desert environment.

You're freaking out, sure that you're about to be caught, when you remember the secret hold, where the alien bodies are being stored. There might not be anything particularly useful there, but it's at least a little more spacious than your last hiding place, and if you keep to the corners, you'll have a great shot at picking off any pirates who discover the compartment before they can spot you.

It takes you a few tries to get the hatch open, but you manage it and slide down into the darkness. The only lights are the dim blinking green and blue and red buttons on the side of the cylindrical casket. You crawl over to it and look at the buttons. Maybe, you think, maybe it has life support built into it. Maybe you could dump out the contents and put yourself inside if things got really bad.

You squint at the control panel. There's a large button, clearly labeled: VIEW SCREEN.

You press it.

5. *If your ship gets raided by space pirates and you wind up hiding in the cargo hold, even though you know it's a bad idea, don't go poking through the secret cargo.*

A SQUARE OF the shiny white case turns clear and the inside glows. The whole thing hums a little, as though expecting more instructions, a thin mechanical whine. You lean down, looking at what's inside, and then it's all you can do not to scream.

There's a Charkazak, its eight terrible black legs drawn up against the shiny black carapace of its chest. Its humanoid face, with black lips and red tattoos along its cheekbones. A chest that rises and falls with breath.

That thing is alive.

You stumble back, falling against the steel, more scared than you were when you faced down the pirate in the hallway, more scared than when you felt the blast hit the side of the ship and realized the *Celeris* was being raided.

You've heard horror stories about the Charkazaks all your life, on the news, whispered about at slumber parties of kids on the farm, and even on Zvezda-9. They were a race of warriors who worshipped death, becoming bodyguards for the most corrupt merchants and glorying in being soldiers on the front lines of the most awful wars just so they'd have more opportunities for bloodshed. They were so awful that they wouldn't follow InterPlanetary laws regarding who it was okay to kill and who it wasn't, nor did they believe in things like surrender or mercy. They invaded planets, brought down ships, and generally behaved like the monsters they appeared to be. When Centurions were dispatched to discipline the Charkazaks, they fought back with such viciousness that the only way to keep them from overrunning the galaxy was the obliteration of their planet and all the Charkazaks on it. Those that were off-planet when the Charkazaks' homeworld was destroyed became even more vicious than before. And as you look at the living one cocooned in metal, you feel like a child hearing those stories for the first time – more like a child than you've felt since you stowed away after that last stupid fight with your parents.

This – *this* must have been what the pirates meant when they worried about it finding them before they found it. You wonder how the redheaded dirtbag who hired your uncle acquired such a thing and where you'd really been transporting it. That Charkazak is the reason your uncle is dead.

The whine gets a little louder, and one of the red buttons on the side of the case begins to blink, like a throbbing pulse. Between that and the dim light from the screen, the secret cargo area feels too bright, but you wait and wait and finally all the lights switch themselves off.

You wouldn't think you could sleep with that thing near you, but you're so relieved to be able to stretch out your limbs that you sleep after all. You dream of someone calling your name from very far away. When you wake, your body is stiff with cold and everything is still dark. You realize that you're freezing and that if you don't get warmed up fast, you might be in serious trouble.

Tents, you remember. There are tents up in the regular cargo hold. But as you feel around in the dark, you can't quite make out how to open up the hatch. Then you remember that the casket lit up – surely that would be enough for you to find the latch by – so you go over and press the green button again.

It lights up the case and you try not to look inside. You scuttle up instead and grab a couple of tents. You're dragging them back down when you hear the tramping of heavy footfalls. They speed up, like maybe they heard the thud of the material hitting the floor, and you swear under your breath. You move as quickly and quietly as you can, back under the floor, yanking the cover of the hidden compartment into place.

The light is still shining from the casket, and you're afraid that the glow will show through the seams and reveal your hiding spot. You press the green button again, hoping that will turn off the view screen, but it doesn't. The other light – the red one – starts blinking again, and you're panicking, because it's brighter and more obvious than the glow from the casket.

Push to open, the red button says. And as the footfalls come closer, as you hear the pirate feel around for the latch, a sudden strange calm comes over you. Since you're going to die – or worse – you figure, screw everything. Screw the pirates, screw yourself, screw every goddamn thing. You owe your uncle some final revenge. You're not going out like some dumb farmer kid. You're going to give those pirates exactly what they were looking for.

So you press the button. Twice. There is a horrible loud sound, like a giant exhalation of breath. The top of the casket slides open.

6. *And if you do go ahead and poke through the secret cargo, then for the love of all that is holy, watch out which buttons you push.*

For a moment, you almost believe that you can take back the last five minutes. It seems so impossible that you could have done what you did. You were tired and freaked out, but you'd been pretty clever right up until then, clever and quiet and careful. Not crazy. No death wish. For a moment, you're just angry, so angry – at yourself, at the world. It feels so unfair that you're going to die because of one stupid decision, one bad moment.

"Hey," the pirate calls. "Kid, we know you're on board. We knew you'd show yourself eventually. Now come on out, and we'll go easy on you."

You snort, because it's a ridiculous thing to say. What does that mean – *go easy on you* – like surely he knows that implies nothing easy at all? Plus, it's too late. He's swaggering around, cocky, without realizing that you're both about to be dead. You're all about to be dead.

"Come out, come out, wherever you are," he calls, a laugh in his voice.

From the casket the Charkazak unfolds itself, bathed in the glow of the light from within. It rises, up and up and up. Eight legs, two sets of arms with six-jointed fingers on its shining onyx chest, and large luminous eyes. It might have human features, but you can't read its expression. It seems to shudder all over, then swings its head your way.

Fear makes you nearly pee your pants. You freeze so completely that you don't even draw in breath. It moves toward you – fast, its legs a blur – and leans down, all wide eyes and flaring nose slits.

Your mother's gun is lying beside you, but you don't grab for it. You released the Charkazak, after all. There's no point fighting it.

You whimper.

"Come on, girl," calls the pirate. "You think I've never been on a cheap old smuggling ship before? You think I can't find you? Come out or I'm going to make you sorry."

You close your eyes, but you can still hear the scratch of Charkazak feet against the floor, can smell the medicinal odor that clings to it from its containment, can hear its ragged breaths.

"I know you killed Richard," says the pirate, his voice falling into a false, honeyed tone. He's come closer to the grate that conceals the hidden cargo area. Maybe he knew where it was all along. Maybe you were a fool, thinking they didn't know where you were. He laughs. "You did me a favor there. I owed him money."

You hear the slide of metal on metal and open your eyes. The Charkazak is no longer in front of you. You let out your breath all at once, so fast that you feel dizzy.

"Hey, there, you –" the pirate says, then there's a gasp and a wet, liquid sound.

You sit in the cargo hold for a while – you don't know for how long – too scared to move. But then you force yourself numbly to your feet. You walk past the body of the pirate, with a massive bloody hole in his chest like that Charkazak thrust a clawed hand into his chest and pulled out his heart. The pirate's gurgling a little, but his eyes are shut, and you wouldn't know how to help him, even if you wanted to, which you don't.

You go straight to the galley, passing two more bodies. They are bent at odd angles, one missing the top of her head, her long red-blond hair in a cloud around her face. There is an odd spatter of red along one wall, and laser blasts have blackened the corridor.

In the galley, you wash your hands and then make yourself a cup of tea. You eat an entire sleeve of sugar cookies and then you heat up a freeze-dried package of salty, soy-drenched noodle soup and eat that, too. There's no point in dying on an empty stomach.

After that, you feel super sleepy, your eyes heavy, so you go back to your tiny room, climb under the covers, and close your eyes.

7. *On a spaceship, there really aren't that many places to hide.*

THE CHARKAZAK ISN'T like the pirates. It's a monster, and you can't hide from monsters. So you don't.

But it doesn't come for you.

You go into the bathroom and take a shower. You change your clothes and check your mother's gun for ammo.

Out in the hallway, the bodies are gone. You return to the galley and drink more tea, noting how the food has been picked over. You didn't count the night before, though, so you're not sure what was eaten by pirates and what was eaten by the alien.

You make some oatmeal with powdery reconstituted milk.

While you're eating, there's movement in the hallway. You duck down under the table, hoping that you're not worth the Charkazak's notice. Maybe you're like a rat to it, some kind of ship vermin. Maybe you don't matter. You wrap your arms around your legs and *hope* you don't matter.

It skitters into the room, and you can't help noticing that as large as it is, there is a certain gliding elegance to its movements.

Then the Charkazak's body crouches low, bending forward, two pairs of arms reaching to the floor to take its weight. Its head tilts under the table, looking straight at you.

It blinks. Twice.

"Um, hi," you say, because you don't know what else to do.

It keeps looking at you, tilting its head the other way this time. *Don't be afraid of silence,* your uncle told you, but you are afraid.

You don't have the upper hand in this situation. You don't have anything to bargain with in trade for your life.

8. *You'll catch more Charkazaks with salt than with sugar.*

"I COULD MAKE you something," you say, "if you don't know how to cook."

"I know how," it says after a long moment, and you're completely startled by its voice, which has a little hiss behind it and an accent you're not used to but that you understand easily enough. It's a young voice, a not-much-older-than-you voice, and you have no idea what to make of that.

Of course some part of you knew that Charkazaks could talk – or at least understand commands. They couldn't have betrayed any treaties if they didn't talk, couldn't have committed treason if they hadn't sworn fealty to the InterPlanetary government, but you're still surprised. Monsters aren't supposed to sound like everybody else.

It – *he* – leans up and begins to move things on the counter, turning on the water heater and setting out two tin cups. His many legs move, swift as a centipede's, and equally disturbing.

"I am going to make some of this red fern tea," he says, opening one of the tins of leaves. "You will drink it."

You listen to the crinkle of paper, the whine of the steam, and the sound of water splashing into the cup. Tea making is confusing, because you associate it with comfortably curling up with your holo-reader and sleeping off a minor illness. Monsters aren't supposed to be able to make tea. If monsters can make tea, then nothing's safe.

"What happened to their ship?" you ask, because he *hasn't* killed you so maybe he'll *keep on* not killing you.

You heard the metal spoon clank against the sides of the cup. "Their ship is unharmed."

Which meant that everyone who'd once been inside of it was dead.

The Charkazak leans down again and passes you a cup with his delicate, multi-jointed fingers. It's warm in your hands.

"Th-thank you," you manage, and take a sip. Then you start to cough. It's *salty*, like your mother described the seas of old earth.

"Is there something wrong with it?" the Charkazak asks, folding his limbs under him, so he can look at you.

You shake your head, terrified. You force yourself to take another swig and try not to choke. You don't think you quite pull it off, though, because he looks oddly stricken, studying you with those large, pale eyes.

"Was this your parents' ship?" he asks, taking the cup from you and drinking deeply, as though he's not afraid of tasting your spit or getting your germs. As though he really, really likes salt.

"How do you know the *Celeris* isn't mine?" you ask. Then you remember that you're trying to get him to think of you as some kind of ship vermin, entirely unimportant, and wish you could take back those words.

"*Is* it yours?" he asks, not seeming unwilling to believe it, just confused.

"No," you admit. "The ship belonged to my uncle, but I'm pretty sure he's dead."

He tilts his head and narrows his eyes, studying you. "You freed me," he accuses softly. "By accident?"

You don't want to tell him that you thought of him as a bullet to the head. Your big murder-suicide plan, now staring at you with that implacable gaze. "I –" you begin, but you can't think of a lie fast enough.

He nods and picks up something from the counter. Then he leaves, the sharpness of his many steps across the floor a reminder of just how fast and lethal the Charkazaks are.

Once he's gone, you draw up your legs, wrap your arms around them, and feel smaller and stupider than ever.

You no longer believe that he'll just kill you outright, but that makes you realize how bleak your future has become. Even if the Charkazak dumps you off at some space station, even if you drain your uncle's bank account of all his credits, the only place you have to go is home. You didn't learn enough from your uncle to fly the *Celeris* yourself. You've got no way to make any money back on Zvezda-9. You're just a farming kid with delusions of grandeur.

Of course, you're not sure that the Charkazak will let you off the ship. He's from a fugitive race, hunted by InterPlanetary Centurions – he might want to keep you around so he could shove your face in front of any call screens until he moved outside regulated space. Then you'd be in the same situation you were in with the pirates; he could sell you or eat you or... well, you've heard stories about Charkazaks ripping humans apart in a sexual frenzy, but you're trying not to think about that.

You decide you're going to make dinner for him. You break out more rehydratable noodles and start in on making a vat-meat goulash. There's a tube of apple-quince jelly and some cheese that you figure you can either make into a dessert or some kind of first course.

Halfway through, you think about cooking for your uncle, and tears come to your eyes. You have to sit down and sob for a little while, but it passes.

Once the food's done, you pad through the halls of the ship to find the Charkazak. A smear of blood still marks one of the walls, wiped by something but not wiped clean.

9. *The dead are a lot less trouble than the living.*

YOU LOOK FOR the Charkazak in the cargo area, but you find dead bodies instead. They're lined up on the floor, the cold keeping them from decaying quickly, but they're still a mess. Eleven pirates, men and women, scarred and tough-looking, and your uncle, all with their eyes open, staring at a nothing that's even bigger than space. Your uncle's shirt is blackened from blaster fire. They must have shot him soon after boarding. You lean down and take out his identification card from his pocket, running your finger over the holo-picture of him, the one where he's not horribly pale, the one where his lips aren't blue and his eyes aren't cloudy. The one where he isn't dead.

You wanted to be just like him – you wanted to have adventures and see the universe. You didn't want to believe there were rules.

See where it got him, your mother would say. *See where it got you.*

Leaning over his body, you close his eyes. "I love you," you tell him, brushing his hair back from his face. "I love you and all your hidden depths."

On your way out, you can't help but notice how nine of those eleven pirates died, though. They were sliced open or stabbed through. One was missing a limb as though it had been pulled clean off her.

You find the Charkazak in the cockpit, pressing buttons with those long, delicate fingers, his dagger-like feet balanced easily against the floor. He turns toward you swiftly, a blur of gray skin and gleaming black carapace, his body hunched, as if braced for flight.

"I made dinner," you say lamely, heart pounding.

He doesn't immediately respond. You watch as he slowly relaxes and wonder if, for a moment, he'd thought you were stupid enough to attack him.

"It's ready, b-but I could j-just bring you a plate if you're b-busy." You're stammering.

He touches the screen again, twice, quickly, then begins to unfurl toward you. "I am honored by your hospitality," he says, and each time he speaks, you are startled anew that he sounds almost human. "We will eat together."

You go together through the hall, with you walking in front. You can hear him behind you, can hear the clattering sound of his many feet, and you steel yourself not to look, because you're afraid that if you do, despite everything, you'll run. You'll scream.

10. *Good food is universal. And it's universally true that you're not going to get any good food in space.*

IN THE GALLEY, he manages to perch on the bench while you plate the goulash. He waits, watching.

Finally, he says, "I'm called Reth."

Which is odd, because of course you knew he must have a name, but you'd never have asked him for it. "I'm Tera."

"Tera," he echoes, and then begins to eat, his long fingers making him seem like a mantis.

You wait until you've pulled out the cheese and apple-quince paste to ask him the question that's been haunting you. "What are you going to do with me?"

He tilts his head, studying you. "I know you're afraid. I even know why."

You are silent, because of course you're scared. And of course he knows why.

"They caught me off the salty sea of Callisto – and I heard them talking while they processed me. I am on my way to be harvested for experiments and organs, just like the rest of my race."

You study his strange face – those luminous eyes, the grayish color of his skin, those tattooed marks that remind you of the stripes on a tiger, his high cheekbones, and the sharp elegance of his features, which make him both almost human and very alien. You hear the anger in his voice, but he's got something to be angry about.

"I know what they say about my people. I know the rumors of savagery and horror. Not all of it is untrue, but the war – the reasons you have heard it was declared, those are *lies*. The InterPlanetary government wanted us to fight their wars, wanted our own government to sacrifice its children, and when the Charkazaks would not become a slave race, they decided to destroy us and engineer the army they desired from our flesh."

He could be lying, but he doesn't sound like he's lying.

He could be mistaken, but he doesn't sound like his knowledge is secondhand.

"I'm sorry," you say, because you can't imagine being hunted across the galaxy, whatever the reason.

Reth shakes his head. "No, don't say that. Because I have become like your legends about my people. I can kill quickly and surely now – and as for where I am taking this ship, I am completing the course that your uncle had set. I am planning on docking and destroying those scientists who would have cut me open and used my body for their experiments. I am going to destroy their laboratory, and I am going to free whatever creatures are being tormented there." He slams down two of his fists on the table and then seems startled by the action. He looks over at you with haunted, hunted eyes. He was trying to stop you from being scared, and he thinks he's scared you worse.

But he hasn't really. He's just startled you. You never heard of any Charkazaks saving anyone, and the anger in his voice is righteous fury, not the desire for bloodshed. He might not sell you to anyone, you realize. Might not rip you apart or eat you. Might not even mean you any harm at all, despite being the scariest thing you've ever seen.

You force yourself to reach across the table and touch his arm. His skin feels smooth, almost like patent leather. He tenses as your fingers brush up his arm and then goes entirely still.

"This dish you made is very good," he says suddenly, and you can hear in his voice a shy nervousness that fills you with a sudden giddy power. "I told you I knew how to work the cooking things – but all the food was unfamiliar. I ate one of the green packages and found it entirely strange. I feel sure I was supposed to do something more to it, but I wasn't sure what . . . ."

You keep your hand on his arm a moment more, fingers dragging over his skin, and his words gutter out. You wonder when the last time it was that someone touched him – or touched him without anger. You wonder how lonely it's possible to become out in the void of space.

The comm crackles at that moment, a voice booming from the speakers in the wall. "Centurion ship *Orion* hailing the *Celeris*. Are you there, Captain Lloyd?"

Reth's eyes narrow and he rises, looming above you on those long black legs.

"I know what you're thinking," he says softly. It makes you try to imagine what it would be like to grow up with all the world against you. "But if they know I'm here, they will destroy your ship. They won't face me – they've heard the same stories you have. They'll kill us both to avoid facing me."

Don't be afraid of silence, your uncle told you. *Silence shows your strength.*

You know it's not the nicest thing you've ever done, especially because you're pretty sure Reth's correct about the Centurions' likelihood of blowing up the ship rather than fighting him, but you make yourself stay quiet as the seconds tick by. Reth needs you to go to that comm, but you need things from him, too. Promises.

"Please," he says again.

"If you want my help, you have to agree to my terms," you say. "Agree that you'll teach me how to fly. That we will split the salvage profits from the pirate ship fifty-fifty. And that we'll be partners."

"Partners," he echoes, as though he's trying out the word, as though he doesn't know what to do with it. As though you're giving him something, instead of asking for something from him.

Have a bottom line, your uncle told you. *Sometimes to make a deal, you've got to walk away from a deal.*

But there isn't going to be any walking away this time. There was nowhere to walk to, not for either one of you.

"Agreed," he says, and the relief in his voice is enormous. You probably could have asked him for a *lot* more, and he would have agreed. You're even worse at this bargaining thing than you thought.

"And you have to agree that once we finish attacking the planet of the mad scientists, we'll take some actually profitable jobs," you amend, trying your best to sound tough. "Since I don't think we're going to get paid for the last one."

The comm crackles again. "Captain Lloyd, are you there? Please respond."

"Agreed, Tera," Reth says softly, like a vow.

11. *One more for the road. There really are no rules. There's laws and there's right and wrong, but those aren't rules. You make it up the best you can as you go along.*

YOU GRIN AT Reth and go over to feed your uncle's ID into the comm. "This is Captain Tera Lloyd of the *Celeris*," you say, once you get the right frequency. "Captain David Lloyd – my uncle – is dead, and I have taken control of the ship. We were in distress, but you're a little late to be of much help, *Orion*."

Reth watches you speak, smiling a fierce alien smile as you tell the Centurions to buzz off, swearing up and down that they don't need to board and you don't need a tow. Finally, you agree to a small bribe, pull out your uncle's ID card, and wire the credits over.

The whole thing reminds you of one of your uncle's stories. You hope it would have made him laugh. You hope it would have made him proud.

You know you've been wrong a lot since you left home, but as you look out at the stars and the Charkazak begins to explain how the controls work, you begin to believe that you might still have a chance to become one-half of the best smuggling duo of all time.

THE LONG HAUL
From THE ANNALS OF TRANSPORTATION, *The Pacific Monthly*, May 2009

Ken Liu

Besides writing and translating speculative fiction, Ken Liu (kenliu.name) also practices law and develops software for iOS and Android devices. His fiction has appeared in *The Magazine of Fantasy & Science Fiction*, *Asimov's*, *Clarkesworld*, *Strange Horizons*, *TRSF*, and *Panverse 3*, among other places. His story "The Paper Menagerie" is the only work ever to receive the Hugo, Nebula and World Fantasy Awards. Liu has become a significant translator of Chinese science fiction in recent years, translating works like Liu Cixin's *The Three Body Problem* among others. His long-awaited debut novel *The Grace of Kings*, first in a series, will be published in 2015 along with a collection of his short fiction. Liu lives near Boston, Massachusetts, with his wife, artist Lisa Tang Liu.

Twenty-five years ago, on this day, the Hindenburg *crossed the Atlantic for the first time. Today, it will cross it for the last time. Six hundred times it has accomplished this feat, and in so doing it has covered the same distance as more than eight roundtrips to the Moon. Its perfect safety record is a testament to the ingenuity of the German people.*

There is always some sorrow in seeing a thing of beauty age, decline, and finally fade, no matter how gracefully it is done. But so long as men still sail the open skies, none shall forget the glory of the Hindenburg.

– John F. Kennedy, March 31, 1962, Berlin.

*　　*　　*

IT WAS EASY to see the zeppelins moored half a mile away from the terminal. They were a motley collection of about forty Peterbilts, Aereons, Macks, Zeppelins (both the real thing and the ones from Goodyear-Zeppelin), and Dongfengs, arranged around and with their noses tied to ten mooring masts, like crouching cats having tête-à-tête tea parties.

I went through customs at Lanzhou's Yantan Airport, and found Barry Icke's long-hauler, a gleaming silver Dongfeng Feimaotui – the model usually known in America, among the less-than-politically-correct society of zeppeliners, as the 'Flying Chinaman' – at the farthest mooring mast. As soon as I saw it, I understood why he called it the *American Dragon*.

White clouds drifted in the dark mirror of the polished solar panels covering the upper half of the zeppelin like a turtle's shell. Large, waving American flags trailing red and blue flames and white stars were airbrushed onto each side of the elongated silver teardrop hull, which gradually tapered towards the back, ending in a cruciform tail striped in red, white, and blue. A pair of predatory, reptilian eyes were painted above the nose cone and a grinning mouth full of sharp teeth under it. A petite Chinese woman was suspended by ropes below the nose cone, painting over the blood-red tongue in the mouth with a brush.

Icke stood on the tarmac near the control cab, a small, round, glass-windowed bump protruding from the belly of the giant teardrop. Tall and broad-shouldered, his square face featured a tall, Roman nose and steady, brown eyes that stared out from under the visor of a Red Sox cap. He watched me approach, flicked his cigarette away, and nodded at me.

Icke had been one of the few to respond to my Internet forum ad asking if any of the long-haulers would be willing to take a writer for the *Pacific Monthly* on a haul. "I've read some of your articles," he had said. "You didn't sound too stupid." And then he invited me to come to Lanzhou.

After we strapped ourselves in, Icke weighed off the zeppelin – pumping compressed helium into the gasbags until the zeppelin's positive lift, minus the weight of the ship, the gas, us, and the cargo, was just about equal to zero. Now essentially 'weightless,' the long-hauler and all its cargo could have been lifted off the ground by a child.

When the control tower gave the signal, Icke pulled a lever that retracted the nose cone hook from the mooring mast and flipped a toggle to drop about a thousand pounds of water ballast into the ground tank below the ship. And just like that, we began to rise, steadily and in complete silence, as though we were riding up a skyscraper in a glass-walled elevator. Icke left the engines off. Unlike an airplane that needs the engines to generate forward thrust to be converted into lift, a zeppelin literally floats up, and engines didn't need to be turned on until we reached cruising height.

"This is the *American Dragon*, heading out to Sin City. See you next time, and watch out for those bears," Icke said into the radio. A few of the other zeppelins, like giant caterpillars on the ground below us, blinked their taillights in acknowledgment.

Icke's Feimaotui is 302 feet long, with a maximum diameter of 84 feet, giving it capacity for 1.12 million cubic feet of helium and a gross lift of 36 tons, of which about 27 are available for cargo (this is comparable to the maximum usable cargo load for semis on the Interstates).

Its hull is formed from a rigid frame of rings and longitudinal girders made out of duratainium covered with composite skin. Inside, seventeen helium gasbags are secured to a central beam that runs from the nose to the tail of the ship, about a third of the way up from the bottom of the hull. At the bottom of the hull, immediately below the central beam and the gasbags, is an empty space that runs the length of the ship.

Most of this space is taken up by the cargo hold, the primary attraction of long-haulers for shippers. The immense space, many times the size of a plane's cargo bay, is perfect for irregularly shaped and bulky goods, like the wind generator turbine blades we were carrying.

Near the front of the ship, the cargo hold is partitioned from the crew quarters, which consists of a suite of apartment-like rooms opening off of a central corridor. The corridor ends by emerging from the hull into the control cab, the only place on the ship with windows to the outside. The Feimaotui is only a little bit longer and taller than a Boeing 747 (counting the tail), but far more voluminous and lighter.

The whole crew consisted of Icke and his wife, Yeling, the woman who was re-painting the grinning mouth on the zeppelin when I showed up. Husband-wife teams like theirs are popular on the transpacific long haul. Each of them would take six-hour shifts to fly the ship while the other slept. Yeling was in the back, sleeping through the takeoff. Like the ship itself, much of their marriage was made up of silence and empty space.

"Yeling and I are no more than thirty feet apart from each other just about every minute, but we only get to sleep in the same bed about once every seven days. You end up learning to have conversations in five-minute chunks separated by six-hour blocks of silence.

"Sometimes Yeling and I have an argument, and she'll have six hours to think of a come-back for something I said six hours earlier. That helps since her English isn't perfect, and she can use the time to look up words she needs. I'll wake up and she'll talk at me for five minutes and go to bed, and I'll have to spend the next six hours thinking about what she said. We've had arguments that went on for days and days this way."

Icke laughed. "In our marriage, sometimes you *have* to go to bed angry."

The control car was shaped like an airplane's cockpit, except that the windows slanted outward and down, so that you had an unobstructed view of the land and air below you.

Icke had covered his seat with a custom pattern: a topographical map of Alaska. In front of Icke's chair was a dashboard full of instruments and analog and mechanical controls. A small, gleaming gold statuette of a laughing, rotund bodhisattva was glued to the top of the dashboard. Next to it was the plush figure of Wally, the Green Monster of Fenway Park.

A plastic crate wedged into place between the two seats was filled with CDs: a mix of mandopop, country, classical, and some audio books. I flipped through them: Annie Dillard, Thoreau, Cormac McCarthy, *The Idiot's Guide to Grammar and Composition.*

Once we reached the cruising altitude of 1,000 feet – freight zeppelins generally are restricted to a zone above pleasure airships, whose passengers prefer the view lower down, and far below the cruising height of airplanes – Icke started the electrical engines. A low hum, more felt than heard, told us that the four propellers mounted in indentations near the tail of the ship had begun to turn and push the ship forward.

"It never gets much louder than this," Icke said.

We drifted over the busy streets of Lanzhou. More than a thousand miles west of Beijing, this medium-sized industrial city was once the most polluted city in all of China due to its blocked air flow and petroleum processing plants. But it is now the center of China's wind turbine boom.

The air below us was filled with small and cheap airships that hauled passengers and freight on intra-city routes. They were a colorful bunch, a ragtag mix of blimps and small zeppelins, their hulls showing signs of make-shift repairs and *shanzhai* patches. (A blimp, unlike a zeppelin, has no rigid frame. Like a birthday balloon, its shape is maintained entirely by the pressure of the gas inside.) The ships were plastered all over with lurid advertisements for goods and services that sounded, with their strange English translations, frightening and tempting in equal measure. Icke told me that some of the ships we saw had bamboo frames.

Icke had flown as a union zeppeliner crewman for ten years on domestic routes before buying his own ship. The union pay was fine, but he didn't like working for someone else. He had wanted to buy a Goodyear-Zeppelin, designed and made 100% in America. But he disliked bankers even more than Chinese airship companies, and decided that he would rather own a Dongfeng outright.

"Nothing good ever came from debt," he said. "I could have told you what was going to happen with all those mortgages last year."

After a while, he added, "My ship is mostly built in America, anyway. The Chinese can't make the duratainium for the girders and rings in the frame. They have to import it. I ship sheets of the alloy from Bethlehem, PA, to factories in China all the time."

The Feimaotui was a quirky ship, Icke explained. It was designed to be easy to maintain and repair rather than over-engineered to be durable the way American ships usually were. An American ship that malfunctioned had to be taken to the dealer for the sophisticated computers and proprietary diagnostic codes, but just about every component of the Feimaotui could be switched out and repaired in the field by a skilled mechanic. An American ship could practically fly itself most of the time, as the design philosophy was to automate as much as possible and minimize the chances of human error. The Feimaotui required a lot more out of the pilot, but it was also much more responsive and satisfying to fly.

"A man changes over time to be like his ship. I'd just fall asleep in a ship where the computer did everything." He gazed at the levers, sticks, wheels, toggles, pedals and sliders around him, reassuringly heavy, analog, and solid. "Typing on a keyboard is no way to fly a ship."

He wanted to own a fleet of these ships eventually. The goal was to graduate from owner-operator to just owner, when he and Yeling could start a family.

"Someday when we can just sit back and collect the checks, I'll get a Winnebago Aurora – the 40,000 cubic feet model – and we and our kids will drift around all summer in Alaska and all winter in Brazil, eating nothing but the food we catch with our own hands. You haven't seen Alaska until you've seen it in an RV airship. We can go to places that not even snowmachines and seaplanes can get to, and hover over a lake that has never seen a man, not a soul around us for hundreds of miles."

Within seconds we were gliding over the broad, slow expanse of the Yellow River. Filled with silt, the muddy water below us was already beginning to take on its namesake color, which would deepen and grow even muddier over the next few hundred miles as it traveled through the Loess Plateau and picked up the silt deposited over the eons by wind.

Below us, small sightseeing blimps floated lazily over the river. The passengers huddled in the gondolas to look through the transparent floor at the sheepskin rafts drifting on the river below the same way Caribbean tourists looked through glass-bottom boats at the fish in the coral reef.

Icke throttled up and we began to accelerate north and east, largely following the course of the Yellow River, towards Inner Mongolia.

THE MILLENNIUM CLEAN Energy Act is one of the few acts by the "clowns down in D.C." that Icke approved: "It gave me most of my business."

Originally designed as a way to protect domestic manufacturers against Chinese competition and to appease the environmental lobby, the law imposed a heavy tax on goods entering the United States based on the carbon footprint of the method of transportation (since the tax was not based on the goods' country-of-origin, it skirted the WTO rules against increased tariffs).

Combined with rising fuel costs, the law created a bonanza for zeppelin shippers. Within a few years, Chinese companies were churning out cheap zeppelins that sipped fuel and squeezed every last bit of advantage from solar power. Dongfengs became a common sight in American skies.

A long-haul zeppelin cannot compete with a 747 for lifting capacity or speed, but it wins hands down on fuel efficiency and carbon profile, and it's far faster than surface shipping. Going from Lanzhou to Las Vegas, like Icke and I were doing, would take about three to four weeks by surface shipping at the fastest: a couple days to go from Lanzhou to Shanghai by truck or train, about two weeks to cross the Pacific by ship, another day or so to truck from California to Las Vegas, and add in a week or so for loading, unloading, and sitting in customs. A direct airplane flight would get you there in a day, but the fuel cost and carbon tax at the border would make it uneconomical for many goods.

"Every time you have to load and unload and change the mode of transport, that's money lost to you," Icke said. "We are trucks that don't need highways, boats that don't need rivers, airplanes that don't need airports. If you can find a piece of flat land the size of a football field, that's enough for us. We can deliver door to door from a yurt in Mongolia to your apartment in New York – assuming your building has a mooring mast on top."

A typical zeppelin built in the last twenty years, cruising at 110 mph, can make the 6900-mile haul between Lanzhou and Las Vegas in about 63 hours. If it makes heavy use of solar power, as Icke's Feimaotui is designed to do, it can end up using less than a fraction of a percent of the fuel that a 747 would need to carry the same weight for the same distance. Plus, it has the advantage I'd mentioned of being more accommodating of bulky, irregularly-shaped loads.

Although we were making the transpacific long haul, most of our journey would be spent flying over land. The curvature of the Earth meant that the closest flight path between any two points on the globe followed a great circle that connected the two points and bisected the globe into two equal parts. From Lanzhou to Las Vegas, this meant that we would fly north and east over Inner Mongolia, Mongolia, Siberia, across the Bering Strait, and then fly east and south over Alaska, the Pacific Ocean off the coast of British Columbia, until we hit land again with Oregon, and finally reach the deserts of Nevada.

*　　*　　*

BELOW US, THE vast city of Ordos, in Inner Mongolia, stretched out to the horizon, a megalopolis of shining steel and smooth glass, vast blocks of western-style houses and manicured gardens. The grid of new, wide streets was as empty as those in Pyongyang, and I could count the number of pedestrians on the fingers of one hand. Our height and open view made the scene take on the look of tilt-shift photographs, as though we were standing over a tabletop scale model of the city, with a few miniature cars and playing figurines scattered about the model.

Ordos is China's Alberta. There is coal here, some of the best, cleanest coal in the world. Ordos was planned in anticipation of an energy boom, but the construction itself became the boom. The more they spent on construction, the more it looked on paper like there was need for even more construction. So now there is this Xanadu, a ghost town from birth. On paper it is the second richest place in China, per capita income just behind Shanghai.

As we flew over the center of Ordos, a panda rose up and hailed us. The panda's vehicle was a small blimp, painted olive green and carrying the English legend: 'Aerial Transport Patrol, People's Republic of China.' Icke slowed down and sent over the cargo manifests, the maintenance records, which the panda could cross-check against the international registry of cargo airships, and his journey log. After a few minutes, someone waved us on from the window in the gondola of the blimp, and a Chinese voice told us over radio that we were free to move on.

"This is such a messed up country," Icke said. "They have the money to build something like Ordos, but have you been to Guangxi? It's near Vietnam, and outside the cities the people there are among the poorest in the world. They have nothing except the mud on the floor of their huts, and beautiful scenery and beautiful women."

Icke had met Yeling there, through a mail-order bride service. It was hard to meet women when you were in the air three hundred days of the year.

On the day of Icke's appointment, he was making a run through Nanning, the provincial capital, as part of a union crew picking up a shipment of star anise. He had the next day, a Saturday, off, and he traveled down to the introduction center a hundred kilometers outside Nanning to meet the girls whose pictures he had picked out and who had been bused in from the surrounding villages.

They had fifteen girls for him. They met in a village school house. Icke sat on a small stool at the front of the classroom with his back to the blackboard, and the girls were brought in to sit at the student desks, as though he was there to teach them.

Most of them knew some English, and he could talk to them for a little bit and mark down, on a chart, the three girls that he wanted to chat with one-on-one in private. The girls he didn't pick would wait around for the next Westerner customer to come and see them in another half hour.

"They say that some services would even let you try the girls out for a bit, like allow you to take them to a hotel for a night, but I don't believe that. Anyway, mine wasn't like that. We just talked. I didn't mark down three girls. Yeling was the only one I picked.

"I liked the way she looked. Her skin was so smooth, so young-looking, and I loved her hair, straight and black with a little curl at the end. She smelled like grass and rainwater. But I liked even more the way she acted with me: shy and very eager to please, something you don't see much in the women back home." He looked over at me as I took notes, and shrugged. "If you want to put a label on me and make the people who read what you write feel good about themselves, that's your choice. It doesn't make the label true."

I asked him if something felt wrong about the process, like shopping for a thing.

"I paid the service two thousand dollars, and gave her family another five thousand before I married her. Some people will not like that. They'll think something is not altogether right about the way I married her

"But I know I'm happy when I'm with her. That's enough for me.

"By the time I met her, Yeling had already dropped out of high school. If I didn't meet her, she would not have gone on to college. She would not have become a lawyer or banker. She would not have gone to work in an office and come home to do yoga. That's the way the world is.

"Maybe she would have gone to Nanning to become a masseuse or bathhouse girl. Maybe she would have married an old peasant from the next village who she didn't even know just because he could give her family some money. Maybe she would have spent the rest of her life getting parasites from toiling in the rice paddies all day and bringing up children in a mud hut at night. And she would have looked like an old woman by thirty.

"How could that have been better?"

THE LANGUAGE OF the zeppeliners on the transpacific long haul, though officially English, is a mix of images and words from America and China. *Dao*, *knife*, *dough*, and *dollar* are used as interchangeable synonyms. Ursine imagery is applied to law enforcement agents along the route: a panda is a Chinese air patrol unit, and a polar bear Russian; in Alaska they are Kodiaks, and off the coast of BC they become whales; finally in America the ships have to deal with grizzlies. The bear's job is to make the life of the zeppeliner difficult: catching pilots who have been at the controls for more than six hours without switching off, who fly above or below regulation altitude, who mix hydrogen into the lift gas to achieve an extra edge in cargo capacity.

"Whales?" I asked Icke. How was whale a type of bear?

"Evolution," Icke said. "Darwin said that a race of bears swimming with their mouths open for water bugs may eventually evolve into whales." (I checked. This was true.)

NOTHING CHANGED AS an electronic beep from the ship's GPS informed us that we crossed the international border between China and Mongolia somewhere in the desolate, dry plains of the Gobi below, dotted with sparse clumps of short, brittle grass.

Yeling came into the control cab to take over. Icke locked the controls and got up. In the small space at the back of the control cab, they spoke to each other for a bit in lowered voices, kissed, while I stared at the instrument panels, trying hard not to eavesdrop.

Every marriage had its own engine, with its own rhythm and fuel, its own language and control scheme, a quiet hum that kept everything moving. But the hum was so quiet that sometimes it was more felt than heard, and you had to listen for it if you didn't want to miss it.

Then Icke left and Yeling came forward to take the pilot's seat.

She looked at me. "There's a second bunk in the back if you want to park yourself a bit." Her English was accented but good, and you could hear traces of Icke's broad New England A's and non-rhoticity in some of the words.

I thanked her and told her that I wasn't sleepy yet.

She nodded and concentrated on flying the ship, her hands gripping the stick for the empennage – the elevators and rudders in the cruciform tail – and the wheel for the trim far more tightly than Icke had.

I stared at the empty, cold desert passing beneath us for a while, and then I asked her what she had been doing when I first showed up at the airport.

"Fixing the eyes of the ship. Barry likes to see the mouth all red and fierce, but the eyes are more important.

"A ship is a dragon, and dragons navigate by sight. One eye for the sky, another for the sea. A ship without eyes cannot see the coming storms and ride the changing winds. It won't see the underwater rocks near the shore and know the direction of land. A blind ship will sink."

An airship, she said, needed eyes even more than a ship on water. It moved so much faster and there were so many more things that could go wrong.

"Barry thinks it's enough to have these." She gestured towards the instrument panel before her: GPS, radar, radio, altimeter, gyroscope, compass. "But these things help Barry, not the ship. The ship itself needs to *see*.

"Barry thinks this is superstition, and he doesn't want me to do it. But I tell him that the ship looks more impressive for customers if he keeps the eyes freshly painted. That he thinks make sense."

Yeling told me that she had also crawled all over the hull of ship and traced out a pattern of oval dragon scales on the surface of the hull with tung oil. "It looks like the way the ice cracks in spring on a lake with good *fengshui*. A ship with a good coat of dragon scales won't ever be claimed by water."

The sky darkened and night fell. Beneath us was complete darkness, northern Mongolia and the Russian Far East being some of the least densely inhabited regions of the globe. Above us, stars, denser than I had ever seen winked into existence. It felt as though we were drifting on the surface of a sea at night, the water around us filled with the glow of sea jellies, the way I remember when I used to swim at night in Long Island Sound off of the Connecticut coast.

"I think I'll sleep now," I said. She nodded, and then told me that I could microwave something for myself in the small galley behind the control cab, off to the side of the main corridor.

The galley was tiny, barely larger than a closet. There was a fridge, a microwave, a sink, and a small two-burner electric range. Everything was kept spotless. The pots and pans were neatly hung on the wall, and the dishes were stacked in a grid of cubbyholes and tied down with Velcro straps. I ate quickly and then followed the sound of snores aft.

Icke had left the light on for me. In the windowless bedroom, the soft, warm glow and the wood-paneled walls were pleasant and induced sleep. Two bunks, one on top of another, hung against one wall of the small bedroom. Icke was asleep in the bottom one. In one corner of the room was a small vanity with a mirror, and pictures of Yeling's family were taped around the frame of the mirror.

It struck me then that this was Icke and Yeling's *home*. Icke had told me that they owned a house in western Massachusetts, but they spent only about a month out of the year there. Most of their meals were cooked and eaten in the *American Dragon*, and most of their dreams were dreamt here in this room, each alone in a bunk.

A poster of smiling children drawn in the style of Chinese folk art was on the wall next to the vanity, and framed pictures of Yeling and Icke together, smiling, filled the rest of the wall space. I looked through them: wedding, vacation, somewhere in a Chinese city, somewhere near a lake with snowy shores, each of them holding up a big fish.

I crawled into the top bunk, and between Icke's snores, I could hear the faint hum of the ship's engines, so faint that you almost missed it if you didn't listen for it.

I WAS MORE tired than I had realized, and slept through the rest of Yeling's shift as well as Icke's next shift. By the time I woke up, it was just after sunrise, and Yeling was again at the helm. We were deep in Russia, flying over the endless coniferous Boreal forests of the heart of Siberia. Our course was now growing ever more easterly as we approached the tip of Siberia where it would meet Alaska across the Bering Sea.

She was listening to an audio book as I came into the control cab. She reached out to turn it off when she heard me, but I told her that it was all right.

It was a book about baseball, an explanation of the basic rules for non-fans. The particular section she was listening to dealt with the art of how to appreciate a stolen base.

Yeling stopped the book at the end of the chapter. I sipped a cup of coffee while we watched the sun rise higher and higher over the Siberian taiga, lighting up the lichen woodland dotted with bogs and pristine lakes still frozen over.

"I didn't understand the game when I first married Barry. We do not have baseball in China, especially not where I grew up.

"Sometimes, when Barry and I aren't working, when I stay up a bit during my shift to sit with him or on our days off, I want to talk about the games I played as a girl or a book I remember reading in school or a festival we had back home. But it's difficult.

"Even for a simple funny memory I wanted to share about the time my cousins and I made these new paper boats, I'd have to explain everything: the names of the paper boats we made, the rules for racing them, the festival that we were celebrating and what the custom for racing paper boats was about, the jobs and histories of the spirits for the festival, the names of the cousins and how we were related, and by then I'd forgotten what was the stupid little story I wanted to share.

"It was exhausting for both of us. I used to work hard to try to explain everything, but Barry would get tired, and he couldn't keep the Chinese names straight or even hear the difference between them. So I stopped.

"But I want to be able to talk to Barry. Where there is no language, people have to build language. Barry likes baseball. So I listen to this book and then we have something to talk about. He is happy when I can listen to or watch a baseball game with him and say a few words when I can follow what's happening."

*   *   *

ICKE WAS AT the helm for the northernmost leg of our journey, where we flew parallel to the Arctic Circle and just south of it. Day and night had lost their meaning as we flew into the extreme northern latitudes. I was already getting used to the six-hour-on, six-hour-off rhythm of their routine, and slowly synching my body's clock to theirs.

I asked Icke if he knew much about Yeling's family or spent much time with them.

"No. She sends some money back to them every couple of months. She's careful with the budget, and I know that anything she sends them she's worked for as hard as I did. I've had to work on her to get her to be a little more generous with herself, and to spend money on things that will make us happy right now. Every time we go to Vegas now she's willing to play some games with me and lose a little money, but she even has a budget for that.

"I don't get involved with her family. I figure that if she wanted out of her home and village so badly that she was willing to float away with a stranger in a bag of gas, then there's no need for me to become part of what she's left behind.

"I'm sure she also misses her family. How can she not? That's the way we all are, as far as I can see: we want that closeness from piling in all together and knowing everything about everyone and talking all in one breath, but we also want to run away by ourselves and be alone. Sometimes we want both at the same time. My mom wasn't much of a mom, and I haven't been home since I was sixteen. But even I can't say that I don't miss her sometimes.

"I give her space. If there's one thing the Chinese don't have, it's space. Yeling lived in a hut so full of people that she never even had her own blanket, and she couldn't remember a single hour when she was alone. Now we see each other for a few minutes every six hours, and she's learned how to fill up that space, all that free time, by herself. She's grown to like it. It's what she never had, growing up."

There is a lot of space in a zeppelin, I thought, idly. That space, filled with lighter-than-air helium, keeps the zeppelin afloat. A marriage also has a lot of space. What fills it to keep it afloat?

We watched the display of the aurora borealis outside the window in the northern skies as the ship raced towards Alaska.

*   *   *

I DON'T KNOW how much time passed before I was jolted awake by a violent jerk. Before I knew what was going on, another sudden tilt of the ship threw me out of my bunk onto the floor. I rolled over, stumbled up, and made my way forward into the control cab by holding onto the walls.

"It's common to have storms in spring over the Bering Sea," Icke, who was supposed to be off shift and sleeping, was standing and holding onto the back of the pilot's chair. Yeling didn't bother to acknowledge me. Her knuckles were white from gripping the controls.

It was daytime, but other than the fact that there was some faint and murky light coming through the windows, it might as well have been the middle of the night. The wind, slamming freezing rain into the windows, made it impossible to see even the bottom of the hull as it curved up from the control cab to the nose cone. Billowing fog and cloud roiled around the ship, whipping past us faster than cars on the autobahns.

A sudden gust slammed into the side of the ship, and I was thrown onto the floor of the cab. Icke didn't even look over as he shouted at me, "Tie yourself down or get back to the bunk."

I got up and stood in the back right corner of the control cab, and used the webbing I found there to lash myself in place and out of the way.

Smoothly, as though they had practiced it, Yeling slipped out of the pilot chair and Icke slipped in. Yeling strapped herself into the passenger stool on the right. The line on one of the electronic screens that showed the ship's course by GPS indicated that we had been zigzagging around crazily. In fact, it was clear that although the throttle was on full and we were burning fuel as fast as an airplane, the wind was pushing us backwards relative to the ground.

It was all Icke could do to keep us pointed into the wind and minimize the cross-section we presented to the front of the storm. If we were pointed slightly at an angle to the wind, the wind would have grabbed us around the ship's peripatetic pivot point and spun us like an egg on its side, yawing out of control. The pivot point, the center of momentum around which a ship would move when an external force is applied, shifts and moves about an airship depending on the ship's configuration, mass, hull shape, speed, acceleration, wind direction, and angular momentum, among other factors, and a pilot kept a zeppelin straight in a storm like this by feel and instinct more than anything else.

Lightning flashed close by, so close that I was blinded for a moment. The thunder rumbled the ship and made my teeth rattle, as though the floor of the ship was the diaphragm of a subwoofer.

"She feels heavy," Icke said. "Ice must be building up on the hull. It actually doesn't feel nearly as heavy as I would have expected. The hull ought to be covered by a solid layer of ice now if the outside thermometer reading is right. But we are still losing altitude, and we can't go any lower. The waves are going to hit the ship. We can't duck under this storm. We'll have to climb over it."

Icke dropped more water ballast to lighten the ship, and tilted the elevators up. We shot straight up like a rocket. The *American Dragon*'s elongated teardrop shape acted as a crude airfoil, and as the brutal Arctic wind rushed at us, we flew like an experimental model wing design in a wind tunnel.

Another bolt of lightning flashed, even closer and brighter than before. The rumble from the thunder hurt my ear drums, and for a while I could hear nothing.

Icke and Yeling shouted at each other, and Yeling shook her head and yelled again. Icke looked at her for a moment, nodded, and lifted his hands off the controls for a second. The ship jerked itself and twisted to the side as the wind took hold of it and began to turn it. Icke reached back to grab the controls as another bolt of lightning flashed. The interior lights went out as the lightning erased all shadows and lines and perspective, and the sound of the thunder knocked me off my feet and punched me hard in the ears. And I passed into complete darkness.

BY THE TIME I came to, I had missed the entire Alaskan leg of the journey.

Yeling, who had the helm, was playing a Chinese song through the speakers. It was dark outside, and a round, golden moon, almost full and as big as the moon I remember from my childhood, floated over the dark and invisible sea. I sat down next to Yeling and stared at it.

After the chorus, the singer, a woman with a mellow and smooth voice, began the next verse in English:

But why is the moon always fullest when we take leave of one another?
For us, there is sorrow, joy, parting, and meeting.
For the moon, there is shade, shine, waxing and waning.
It has never been possible to have it all.
All we can wish for is that we endure,
Though we are thousands of miles apart,
Yet we shall gaze upon the same moon, always lovely.

Yeling turned off the music and wiped her eyes with the back of her hand.

"She found a way out of the storm," she said. There was no need to ask who she meant. "She dodged that lightning at the last minute and found herself a hole in the storm to slip through. Sharp eyes. I knew it was a good idea to repaint the left eye, the one watching the sky, before we took off."

I watched the calm waters of the Pacific Ocean pass beneath us.

"In the storm, she shed her scales to make herself lighter."

I imagined the tung oil lines drawn on the ship's hull by Yeling, the lines etching the ice into dragon scales, which fell in large chunks into the frozen sea below.

"When I first married Barry, I did everything his way and nothing my way. When he was asleep, and I was flying the ship, I had a lot of time to think. I would think about my parents getting old and me not being there. I'd think about some recipe I wanted to ask my mother about, and she wasn't there. I asked myself all the time, *what have I done?*

"But even though I did everything his way, we used to argue all the time. Arguments that neither of us could understand and that went nowhere. And then I decided that I had to do something.

"I rearranged the way the pots were hung up in the galley and the way the dishes were stacked in the cabinets and the way the pictures were arranged in the bedroom and the way we stored life vests and shoes and blankets. I gave everything a better flow of *qi*, energy, and smoother *fengshui*. It might seem like a cramped and shabby place to some, but the ship now feels like our palace in the skies.

"Barry didn't even notice it. But, because of the *fengshui*, we didn't argue any more. Even during the storm, when things were so tense, we worked well together."

"Were you scared at all during the storm?" I asked.

Yeling bit her bottom lip, thinking about my question.

"When I first rode with Barry, when I didn't yet know him, I used to wake up and say, in Chinese, *who is this man with me in the sky?* That was the most I've ever been scared.

"But last night, when I was struggling with the ship and Barry came to help me, I wasn't scared at all. I thought, it's okay if we die now. I know this man. I know what I've done. I'm home."

"THERE WAS NEVER any real danger from lightning," Icke said. "You knew that, right? The *American Dragon* is a giant Faraday cage. Even if the lightning had struck us, the charge would have stayed on the outside of the metal frame. We were in the safest place over that whole sea in that storm."

I brought up what Yeling had said, that the ship seemed to know where to go in the storm.

Icke shrugged. "Aerodynamics is a complex thing, and the ship moved the way physics told it to."

"But when you get your Aurora, you'll let her paint eyes on it?"

Icke nodded, as though I had asked a very stupid question.

LAS VEGAS, THE diadem of the desert, spread out beneath, around, and above us.

Pleasure ships and mass-transit passenger zeppelins covered in flashing neon and gaudy giant flickering screens dotted the air over the Strip. Cargo carriers like us were constricted to a narrow lane parallel to the Strip with specific points where we were allowed to depart to land at the individual casinos.

"That's Laputa," Icke pointed above us, to a giant, puffy, baroque airship that seemed as big as the Venetian, which we were passing below and to the left. Lit from within, this newest and flashiest floating casino glowed like a giant red Chinese lantern in the sky. Air taxis rose from the Strip and floated towards it like fireflies.

We had dropped off the shipment of turbine blades with the wind farm owned by Caesars Palace outside the city, and now we were headed for Caesars itself. Comp rooms were one of the benefits of hauling cargo for a customer like that.

I saw, coming up behind the Mirage, the tall spire and blinking lights of the mooring mast in front of the Forum Shops. It was usually where the great luxury personal yachts of the high-stakes rollers moored, but tonight it was empty, and a transpacific long-haul Dongfeng Feimaotui, a Flying Chinaman named the *American Dragon*, was going to take it for its own.

"We'll play some games, and then go to our room," Icke said. He was talking to Yeling, who smiled back at him. This would be the first chance they had of sleeping on the same bed in a week. They had a full twenty-four hours, and then they'd take off for Kalispell, Montana, where they would pick up a shipment of buffalo bones for the long haul back to China.

I lay in bed in my Downtown hotel room thinking about the way the furniture in my bedroom was arranged, and imagined the flow of *qi* around the bed, the nightstands, the dresser. I missed the faint hum of the zeppelin's engines, so quiet that you had to listen hard to hear them.

I turned on the light and called my wife. "I'm not home yet. Soon."

This story was inspired in many ways by John McPhee's Uncommon Carriers. *Some liberty has been taken with the physical geography of our world: a great circle flight path from Lanzhou to Las Vegas would not actually cross the city of Ordos.*

The lyrics of the song that Yeling plays come from a poem by the Song Dynasty poet Su Shi (1037-1101 A.D). It has remained a popular poem to set to music through the centuries since its composition.

TOUGH TIMES ALL OVER

Joe Abercrombie

Joe Abercrombie (www.joeabercrombie.com) attended Lancaster Royal Grammar School and Manchester University, where he studied psychology. He moved into television production before taking up a career as a freelance film editor. His first novel, *The Blade Itself,* was published in 2004, and was followed by sequels *Before They Are Hanged, Last Argument of Kings,* and stand-alones *Best Served Cold, The Heroes, Red Country,* and YA fantasy *Half a King.* His most recent novel is sequel *Half a World.* Joe lives in Bath with his wife, Lou, and his daughters, Grace and Eve. He still occasionally edits concerts and music festivals for TV, but spends most of his time writing edgy yet humorous fantasy novels.

DAMN, BUT SHE hated Sipani.

The bloody blinding fogs and the bloody slapping water and the bloody universal sickening stink of rot. The bloody parties and masques and revels. Bloody fun, everyone having bloody fun, or at least pretending to. The bloody people were worst of all. Liars and fools, the lot of them. Rogues every man, woman and child.

Carcolf hated Sipani. And yet here she was again. Who, then, she was forced to wonder, was the fool?

Braying laughter echoed from the mist ahead and she slipped into the shadows of a doorway, one hand tickling the grip of her sword. A good courier trusts no one, of course, and Carcolf was the very best, but in Sipani she trusted... less than no one.

Another gang of pleasure-seekers blundered from the murk, a man with a mask like a moon pointing at a woman who was so drunk she kept falling over on her high shoes. All of them laughing, one of them flapping his lace cuffs as though there never was a thing so funny as drinking so much you couldn't stand up. Carcolf rolled her eyes skyward, and consoled herself with the thought that behind the masks they were hating it as much as she always did when she tried to have fun.

In the solitude of her doorway, Carcolf winced. Damn, but she needed a holiday. She was becoming a sour arse. Or, indeed, had become one, and was getting worse. One of those people who held the entire world in contempt. Was she turning into her bloody father?

"Anything but that," she muttered.

The moment the revellers tottered off into the night she ducked from her doorway and pressed on, neither too fast nor too slow, soft boot heels silent on the dewy cobbles, her unexceptional hood drawn down to an inconspicuous degree, the very image of a person with just the average amount to hide. Which in Sipani was quite a bit.

Over to the west somewhere, her armoured carriage would be speeding down the wide lanes, wheels striking sparks as they clattered over the bridges, stunned bystanders leaping aside, driver's whip lashing at the foaming flanks of the horses, the dozen hired guards thundering after, streetlamps gleaming upon their dewy armour. Unless the Quarryman's people had already made their move, of course: the flutter of arrows, the scream of beasts and men, the crash of the wagon leaving the road, the clash of steel, and finally the great padlock blown from the strongbox with blasting powder, the choking smoke wafted aside and the lid flung back to reveal... nothing.

Carcolf allowed herself the smallest smile, and patted the lump against her ribs. The item, stitched up safe in the lining of her coat.

She gathered herself, took a couple of steps and sprang from the canal-side, clearing three strides of oily water and onto the deck of a decaying barge, timbers creaking under her as she rolled and came smoothly up. To go around by the Fintine Bridge was quite the detour, not to mention a well-travelled and well-watched way, but this boat was always tied here in the shadows, offering a short cut. She had made sure of it. Carcolf left as little to chance as possible. In her experience, chance could be a real bastard.

A wizened face peered out from the gloom of the cabin, steam issuing from a battered kettle. "Who the hell are you?"

"Nobody." Carcolf gave a cheery salute. "Just passing through!" and she hopped from the rocking wood to the stones on the far side of the canal and was away into the mould-smelling mist. Just passing through. Straight to the docks to catch the tide and off on her merry way. Or her sour arsed one, at least. Wherever Carcolf went, she was nobody. Everywhere, always passing through.

Over to the east that idiot Pombrine would be riding hard in the company of four paid retainers. He hardly looked much like her, what with the moustache and all, but swaddled in that ever-so conspicuous embroidered cloak of hers he did well enough for a double. He was a penniless pimp who smugly believed himself to be impersonating her so she could visit a lover, a lady of means who did not want their tryst made public. Carcolf sighed. If only. She consoled herself with the thought of Pombrine's shock when those bastards Deep and Shallow shot him from his saddle, expressed considerable surprise at the moustache, then rooted through his clothes with increasing frustration and finally no doubt gutted his corpse only to find... nothing.

Carcolf patted that lump once again, and pressed on with a spring in her step. Here went she, straight down the middle, alone and on foot, along a carefully prepared route of back streets, of narrow ways, of unregarded shortcuts and forgotten stairs, through crumbling palaces and rotting tenements, gates left open by surreptitious arrangement and, later on, a short stretch of sewer which would bring her out right by the docks with an hour or two to spare.

After this job she really had to take a holiday. She tongued at the inside of her lip, where a small but unreasonably painful ulcer had lately developed. All she did was work. A trip to Adua, maybe? Visit her brother, see her nieces? How old would they be now? Ugh. She remembered what a judgemental bitch her sister-in-law was. One of those people who met everything with a sneer. She reminded Carcolf of her father. Probably why her brother had married the bloody woman...

Music was drifting from somewhere as she ducked beneath a flaking archway. A violinist either tuning up or of execrable quality. Papers flapped and rustled upon a wall streaked with mould, ill-printed bills exhorting the faithful citizenry to rise up against the tyranny of the Snake of Talins. Carcolf snorted. Most of Sipani's citizens were far more interested in falling over than rising up, and she had other business.

She scratched at her groin, trying to find a comfortable position, but it was hopeless. How much do you have to pay for a new suit of clothes before you avoid a chafing seam right in the worst place? She strode along a narrow way beside a stagnant section of canal, long out of use, gloopy with algae and bobbing rubbish, plucking the offending fabric this way and that to no effect. Damn this fashion for tight trousers! Perhaps it was some kind of cosmic punishment for her paying the tailor with forged coins. But then Carcolf was considerably more moved by the concept of local profit than that of cosmic punishment, and therefore strove to avoid paying for anything wherever possible. It was practically a principle with her, and her father always said that a person should stick to their principles –

Bloody hell, she really was turning into her father.

"Ha!"

A ragged figure sprang from an archway, the faintest glimmer of steel showing. With an instinctive whimper Carcolf stumbled back, fumbling her coat aside and drawing her own blade, sure that death had found her at last. The Quarryman one step ahead? Or was it Deep and Shallow, or Kurrikan's hirelings... but no one else showed themselves. Only this one man, swathed in a stained cloak, unkempt hair stuck to pale skin by the damp, a mildewed scarf masking the bottom part of his face, bloodshot eyes round and scared above.

"Stand and deliver!" he boomed, somewhat muffled by the scarf.

Carcolf raised her brows. "Who even says that?"

A slight pause, while the rotten waters slapped the stones beside them. "You're a woman?" There was an almost apologetic turn to the would-be robber's voice.

"If I am, will you not rob me?"

"Well... er..." The thief seemed to deflate somewhat, then drew himself up again. "Stand and deliver anyway!"

"Why?" asked Carcolf.

The point of the robber's sword drifted uncertainly. "Because I have a considerable debt to... that's none of your business!"

"No, I mean, why not just stab me and strip my corpse of valuables, rather than giving me the warning?"

Another pause. "I suppose... I hope to avoid violence? But I warn you I am entirely prepared for it!"

He was a bloody civilian. A mugger who had blundered upon her. A random encounter. Talk about chance being a bastard. For him, at least. "You, sir," she said, "are a shitty thief."

"I, madam, am a gentleman."

"You, sir, are a dead gentleman." Carcolf stepped forward, weighing her blade, a stride length of razor steel leant a ruthless gleam from a lamp in a window somewhere above. She could never be bothered to practice, but nonetheless she was far more than passable with a sword. It would take a great deal more than this stick of gutter trash to get the better of her. "I will carve you like –"

The man darted forward with astonishing speed, there was a scrape of steel and before Carcolf even thought of moving, the sword was twitched from her fingers and skittered across the greasy cobbles to plop into the canal.

"Ah," she said. That changed things. Rather materially. Plainly her attacker was not the bumpkin he appeared to be, at least when it came to swordplay. She should have known. Nothing in Sipani is ever quite as it appears.

"Hand over the money," said the mugger.

"Delighted." Carcolf plucked out her purse and tossed it against the wall, hoping to dart past while he was distracted. Alas, he pricked it from the air with impressive dexterity and whisked his sword-point back to prevent her escape. It tapped gently at the lump in her coat.

"What have you got... just there?"

From bad to much, much worse. "Nothing, nothing at all." Carcolf attempted to pass it off with a false chuckle but that ship had sailed and she, sadly, was not aboard, any more than she was aboard the damn ship still rocking at the wharf for the voyage to Thond. She steered the glinting point away with one finger. "Now I have an extremely pressing engagement, so if –" There was a faint hiss as the sword slit her coat open.

Carcolf blinked. "Ow." There was a burning pain down her ribs. The sword had slit her open too. "Ow!" She subsided to her knees, deeply aggrieved, blood oozing between her fingers as she clutched them to her side.

"Oh... oh no. Sorry. I really... really didn't mean to cut you. Just wanted, you know..."

"Ow." The item, now slightly smeared with Carcolf's blood, dropped from the gashed pocket and tumbled across the cobbles. A slender package perhaps a foot long, wrapped in stained leather.

"I need a surgeon," gasped Carcolf, in her best I-am-a-helpless-woman voice. The Grand Duchess had always accused her of being over-dramatic, but if you can't be dramatic at a time like that, when can you? Probably she really did need a surgeon, after all, and there was a chance the robber would lean down to help her and she could stab the bastard in the face with her knife. "Please, I beg you!"

He loitered, eyes wide, the whole thing plainly gone further than he had intended. But he edged closer only to reach for the package, the glinting point of his sword still levelled at her.

A different and even more desperate tack, then. She strove to keep the panic out of her voice. "Look, take the money, I wish you joy of it." Carcolf did not, in fact, wish him joy, she wished him rotten in his grave. "But we will both be far better off if you don't take that package!"

His hand hovered. "Why, what's in it?"

"I don't know. I'm under orders not to open it!"

"Orders from who?"

Carcolf winced. "I don't know that either, but –"

KURTIS TOOK THE packet. Of course he took the packet. He was an idiot, but not so much of an idiot as that. He snatched the packet and ran. Of course he ran. When didn't he?

He tore down the alleyway, heart in mouth, jumped a burst barrel, caught his foot and went sprawling, almost impaled himself on his own drawn sword, slithered on his face through a slick of rubbish, scooping a mouthful of something faintly sweet and staggering up, spitting and cursing, snatching a scared glance over his shoulder –

There was no sign of pursuit. Only the mist, the endless mist, whipping and curling like a thing alive.

He slipped the packet, now somewhat slimy, into his ragged coat and limped on, clutching at his bruised buttock and still struggling to spit that rotten-sweet taste from his mouth. Not that it was any worse than his breakfast had been. Better, if anything. You know a man by his breakfast, his fencing master always used to tell him.

He pulled up his damp hood with its faint smell of onions and despair, plucked the purse from his sword and slid blade back into sheath as he slipped from the alley and insinuated himself among the crowds, that faint snap of hilt meeting clasp bringing back so many memories. Of training and tournaments, of bright futures and the adulation of the crowds. *Fencing, my boy, that's the way to advance! Such knowledgeable audiences in Styria, they love their swordsmen there, you'll make a fortune!* Better times, when he had not dressed in rags, or been thankful for the butcher's leftovers, or robbed people for a living. He grimaced. Robbed *women*. If you could call it a living. He stole another furtive glance over his shoulder. Could he have killed her? His skin prickled with horror. Just a scratch. Just a scratch, surely? But he had seen blood. Please let it have been a scratch! He rubbed his face as though he could rub the memory away, but it was stuck fast. One by one, things he had never imagined, then told himself he would never do, then that he would never do again, had become his daily routine.

He checked again that he wasn't followed then slipped from the street and across the rotting courtyard, the faded faces of yesterday's heroes peering down at him from the newsbills. Up the piss-smelling stairway and around the dead plant. Out with his key and he wrestled with the sticky lock.

"Damn it, fuck it, shit it – Gah!" The door came suddenly open and he blundered into the room, nearly fell again, turned and pushed it shut, and stood in the smelly darkness, breathing.

Who would now believe he'd once fenced with the king? He'd lost. Of course he had. Lost everything, hadn't he? He'd lost two touches to nothing and been personally insulted while he lay in the dust but, still, he'd measured steels with his August Majesty. This very steel, he realised, as he set it against the wall beside the door. Notched, and tarnished, and even slightly bent towards the tip. The last twenty years had been almost as unkind to his sword as it had been to him. But perhaps today marked the turnaround in his fortunes.

He whipped his cloak off and tossed it into a corner, took out the packet to unwrap it and see what he had come by. He fumbled with the lamp in the darkness and finally produced some light, almost wincing as his miserable rooms came into view. The cracked glazing, the blistering plaster speckled with damp, the burst mattress spilling foul straw where he slept, the few sticks of warped furniture –

There was a man sitting in the only chair, at the only table. A big man in a big coat, skull shaved to greying stubble. He took a slow breath through his blunt nose, and let a pair of dice tumble from his fist and across the stained table top.

"Six and two," he said. "Eight."

"Who the hell are you?" Kurtis' voice was squeaky with shock.

"The Quarryman sent me." He let the dice roll again. "Six and five."

"Does that mean I lose?" Kurtis glanced over towards his sword, trying and failing to seem nonchalant, wondering how fast he could get to it, draw it, strike –

"You lost already," said the big man, gently collecting the dice with the side of his hand. He finally looked up. His eyes were flat as those of a dead fish. Like the fishes on the stalls at the market. Dead and dark and sadly glistening. "Do you want to know what happens if you go for that sword?"

Kurtis wasn't a brave man. He never had been. It had taken all his courage to work up to surprising someone else, being surprised himself had knocked the fight right out of him. "No," he muttered, his shoulders sagging.

"Toss me that package," said the big man, and Kurtis did so. "And the purse."

It was as if all resistance had drained away. Kurtis had not the strength to attempt a ruse. He scarcely had the strength to stand. He tossed the stolen purse onto the table, and the big man worked it open with his fingertips and peered inside.

Kurtis gave a helpless, floppy motion of his hands. "I have nothing else worth taking."

"I know," said the man, as he stood. "I have checked." He stepped around the table and Kurtis cringed away, steadying himself against his cupboard. A cupboard containing nothing but cobwebs, as it went.

"Is the debt paid?" he asked in a very small voice.

"Do you think the debt is paid?"

They stood looking at one another. Kurtis swallowed. "When will the debt be paid?"

The big man shrugged his shoulders, which were almost one with his head. "When do you think the debt will be paid?"

Kurtis swallowed again, and he found his lip was trembling. "When the Quarryman says so?"

The big man raised one heavy brow a fraction, the hairless sliver of a scar through it. "Have you any questions... to which you do not know the answers?"

Kurtis dropped to his knees, his hands clasped, the big man's face faintly swimming through the tears in his aching eyes. He did not care about the shame of it. The Quarryman had taken the last of his pride many visits before. "Just leave me something," he whispered. "Just... something."

The man stared back at him with his dead fish eyes. "Why?"

FRIENDLY TOOK THE sword too, but there was nothing else of value. "I will come back next week," he said.

It had not been meant as a threat, merely a statement of fact, and an obvious one at that, since it had always been the arrangement, but Broya's head slowly dropped, and he began to shudder with sobs.

Friendly considered whether to try and comfort him, but decided not to. He was often misinterpreted.

"You should, perhaps, not have borrowed the money." Then he left.

It always surprised him that people did not do the sums when they took a loan. Proportions, and time, and the action of interest, it was not so very difficult to fathom. But perhaps they were prone always to overestimate their income, to poison themselves by looking on the bright side. Happy chances would occur, and things would improve, and everything would turn out well, because they were special. Friendly had no illusions. He knew he was but one unexceptional cog in the elaborate workings of life. To him, facts were facts.

He walked, counting off the paces to the Quarryman's place. One hundred and five, one hundred and four, one hundred and three . . .

Strange how small the city was when you measured it out. All those people, and all their desires, and scores, and debts, packed into this narrow stretch of reclaimed swamp. By Friendly's reckoning, the swamp was well on the way to taking large sections of it back. He wondered if the world would be better when it did.

... seventy-six, seventy-five, seventy-four...

Friendly had picked up a shadow. Pickpocket, maybe. He took a careless look at a stall by the way and caught her out of the corner of his eye. A girl with dark hair gathered into a cap and a jacket too big for her. Hardly more than a child. Friendly took a few steps down a narrow snicket and turned, blocking the way, pushing back his coat to show the grips of four of his six weapons. His shadow rounded the corner, and he looked at her. Just looked. She first froze, then swallowed, then turned one way, then the other, then backed off and lost herself in the crowds. So that was the end of that episode.

... thirty-one, thirty, twenty-nine...

Sipani, and most especially its moist and fragrant Old Quarter, was full of thieves. They were a constant annoyance, like midges in summer. Also muggers, robbers, burglars, cut-purses, cut-throats, thugs, murderers, strong-arm men, spivs, swindlers, gamblers, bookies, moneylenders, rakes, beggars, tricksters, pimps, pawnshop owners, crooked merchants, not to mention accountants and lawyers. Lawyers were the worst of the crowd, as far as Friendly was concerned. Sometimes it seemed that no one in Sipani made anything, exactly. They all seemed to be working their hardest to rip it from someone else.

But then Friendly supposed he was no better.

... four, three, two, one, and down the twelve steps, past the three guards, and through the double doors into the Quarryman's place.

It was hazy with smoke inside, confusing with the light of coloured lamps, hot with breath and chafing skin, thick with the babble of hushed conversation, of secrets traded, reputations ruined, confidences betrayed. It was as all such places always are. Two Northmen were wedged behind a table in the corner. One with sharp teeth and long, lank hair had tipped his chair all the way back and was slumped in it, smoking. The other had a bottle in one hand and a tiny book in the other, staring at it with brow well-furrowed. Most of the patrons Friendly knew by sight. Regulars. Some come to drink. Some to eat. Most of them fixed on the games of chance. The clatter of dice, the twitch and flap of the playing cards, the eyes of the hopeless glittering as the lucky wheel span.

The games were not really the Quarryman's business, but the games made debts, and debts were the Quarryman's business. Up the twenty-three steps to the raised area, the guard with the tattoo on his face waving Friendly past.

Three of the other collectors were seated there, sharing a bottle. The smallest grinned at him, and nodded, perhaps trying to plant the seeds of an alliance. The biggest puffed himself up and bristled, sensing competition. Friendly ignored them equally. He had long ago given up trying even to understand the unsolvable mathematics of human relationships, let alone to participate. Should that man do more than bristle, Friendly's cleaver would speak for him. That was a voice that cut short even the most tedious of arguments.

Mistress Borfero was a fleshy woman with dark curls spilling from beneath a purple cap, small eyeglasses that made her eyes seem large, and a smell about her of lamp oil. She haunted the anteroom before the Quarryman's office at a low desk stacked with ledgers. On Friendly's first day she had gestured towards the ornate door behind her and said, "I am the Quarryman's right hand. He is never to be disturbed. *Never*. You speak to me."

Friendly, of course, knew as soon as he saw her mastery of the numbers in those books that there was no one in the office, and that Borfero was the Quarryman, but she seemed so pleased with the deception that he was happy to play along. Friendly had never liked to rock boats unnecessarily. That's how people ended up drowned. Besides, it somehow helped to imagine that the orders came from somewhere else, somewhere unknowable and irresistible. It was nice to have an attic in which to stack the blame. Friendly looked at the door of the Quarryman's office, wondering if there was an office, or if it opened on blank stones.

"What was today's take?" she asked, flipping open a ledger and dipping her pen. Straight to business without so much as a how do you do. He greatly liked and admired that about her, though he would never have said so. His compliments had a way of causing offence.

Friendly slipped the coins out in stacks, then let them drop, one by one, in rattling rows by debtor and denomination. Mostly base metals, leavened with a sprinkling of silver.

Borfero sat forward, wrinkling her nose and pushing her eyeglasses up onto her forehead, eyes seeming now extra small without them.

"A sword, as well," said Friendly, leaning it up against the side of the desk.

"A disappointing harvest," she murmured.

"The soil is stony hereabouts."

"Too true." She dropped the eyeglasses back and started to scratch orderly figures in her ledger. "Tough times all over." She often said that. As though it stood as explanation and excuse for anything and everything.

"Broya asked me when the debt would be paid."

She peered up, surprised by the question. "When the Quarryman says it's paid."

"That's what I told him."

"Good."

"You asked me to be on the lookout for... a package." Friendly placed it on the desk before her. "Broya had it."

It did not seem so very important. It was less than a foot long, wrapped in very ancient stained and balding animal skin, and with a letter, or perhaps a number, burned into it with a brand. But it was not a letter that Friendly recognised.

MISTRESS BORFERO SNATCHED up the package, then immediately cursed herself for seeming too eager. She knew no one could be trusted in this business. That brought a rush of questions to her mind. Suspicions. How could that worthless Broya possibly have come by it? Was this some ruse? Was Friendly a plant of the Gurkish? Or perhaps of Carcolf's? A double bluff? There was no end to the webs that smug bitch span. A triple bluff? But where was the angle? Where the advantage?

Friendly's face betrayed no trace of greed, no trace of ambition, no trace of anything. He was without doubt a strange fellow, but came highly recommended. He seemed all business, and she liked that in a man, though she would never have said so. A manager must maintain a certain detachment.

Sometimes things are just what they seem. Borfero had seen strange chances enough in her life.

"This could be it," she mused, though in fact she was immediately sure. She was not a woman to waste time on possibilities.

Friendly nodded.

"You have done well," she said.

He nodded again.

"The Quarryman will want you to have a bonus." Be generous with your own people, she had always said, or others will be.

But generosity brought no response from Friendly.

"A woman, perhaps?"

He looked a little pained by that suggestion. "No."

"A man?"

And that one. "No."

"Husk? A bottle of –"

"No."

"There must be something."

He shrugged.

Mistress Borfero puffed out her cheeks. Everything she had she'd made by tickling out people's desires. She was not sure what to do with a person who had none. "Well, why don't you think about it?"

Friendly slowly nodded. "I will think."

"Did you see two Northmen drinking on your way in?"

"I saw two Northmen. One was reading a book."

"Really? A book?"

Friendly shrugged. "There are readers everywhere."

Deep and Shallow were sitting near the entrance. If one had been reading, he had given up. Deep was drinking some of her best wine straight from the bottle. Three others lay scattered, empty, beneath the table. Shallow was smoking a chagga pipe, the air thick with the stink of it. Borfero did not allow it normally, but she was obliged to make an exception for these two, as she had to with so much else. Why the bank chose to employ such repugnant specimens she had not the slightest notion. But she supposed rich people need not explain themselves.

"Gentlemen," she said, insinuating herself into a chair.

"Where?" said Shallow, and gave a croaky laugh. Deep slowly tipped his bottle up and eyed his brother over the neck with sour distain.

Borfero continued in her business voice, soft and reasonable. "You said your... *employers* would be *most grateful* if I came upon... *that certain item* you mentioned."

The two Northmen perked up, both leaning forward as though drawn by the same string, Shallow catching an empty bottle with his boot and sending it rolling in an arc across the floor.

"Greatly grateful," said Deep.

"And how much of my debt would their gratitude stretch around?"

"All of it."

"The whole party," said Shallow, tapping the embers from his pipe across her polished tabletop.

Borfero felt her skin tingling. Freedom. Could it really be? In her pocket, even now? But she could not let the size of the stakes make her careless. The greater the payoff, the greater the caution. "My debt would be finished?"

Shallow leaned close, drawing the stem of his pipe across his stubbled throat. "Killed," he said.

"Murdered," growled his brother, suddenly no further off on the other side.

She in no way enjoyed having those scarred and lumpen killer's physiognomies so near. Another few moments of their breath alone might have done for her. "Excellent," she squeaked, and slipped the package onto the table. "Then I shall cancel the interest payments forthwith. Do please convey my regards to... your employers."

"Course." Shallow did not so much smile as show his sharp teeth. "Don't reckon your regards'll mean much to them, though."

"Don't take it personally, eh?" Deep did not smile. "Our employers just don't care much for regards."

Borfero took a sharp breath. "Tough times all over."

"Ain't they, though?" and Deep stood, and swept the package up in one big paw.

THE COOL AIR caught Deep like a slap as they stepped out into the evening. Sipani, none too pleasant when still, had a decided spin to it of a sudden.

"I have to confess," he said, clearing his throat and spitting, "to being somewhat on the drunk side of drunk."

"Aye," said Shallow, burping as he squinted into the mist. At least that was clearing somewhat. As clear as it got in this murky hell of a place. "Probably not the bestest notion while at work, mind you."

"You're right." Deep held the baggage up to such light as there was. "But who expected this to just drop in our laps?"

"Not I, for one." Shallow frowned. "Or for... not one?"

"It was meant to be just a tipple," said Deep.

"One tipple does have a habit of making itself into several." Shallow wedged on that stupid bloody hat. "A little stroll over to the bank, then?"

"That hat makes you look a fucking dunce."

"You, brother, are obsessed with appearances."

Deep passed that off with a long hiss.

"They really going to score out that woman's debts, d'you think?"

Deep hardly even cared enough to discuss it. "For now, maybe. But you know how they are. Once you owe, you always owe." He spat again and, now the alley was a tad steadier, started walking off with the baggage clutched tight in his hand. No chance he was putting it in a pocket where some little scab could lift it. Sipani was full of thieving bastards. He'd had his good socks stolen last time he was here, and worked up an unpleasant pair of blisters on the trip home. Who steals socks? Styrian bastards. He'd keep a good firm grip on it. Let the little fuckers try to take it *then*.

"Now who's the dunce?" Shallow called after him. "The bank's this way."

"Only we ain't going to the bank, *dunce*," snapped Deep over his shoulder. "We're to toss it down a well in an old court just about the corner here."

Shallow hurried to catch up. "We are?"

"No, I just said it for the laugh, y'idiot."

"Why down a well?"

"Because that's how he wanted it done."

"Who wanted it done?"

"The boss."

"The little boss, or the big boss?"

Even drunk as Deep was he felt the need to lower his voice. "The bald boss."

"Shit," breathed Shallow. "In person?"

"In person."

A short pause. "How was that?"

"It was even more than usually terrifying, thanks for reminding me."

A long pause, with just the sound of their boots on the wet cobbles. Then Shallow said, "We better hadn't do no fucking up of this."

"My heartfelt thanks," said Deep, "for that piercing insight. Fucking up is always to be avoided when and wherever possible, wouldn't you say?"

"Y'always aim to avoid it, of course you do, but sometimes you run into it anyway. What I'm saying here is we'd best not run into it." Shallow dropped his voice to a whisper. "You know what the bald boss said last time."

"You don't have to whisper. He ain't here, is he?"

Shallow looked wildly around. "I don't know. Is he?"

"No he ain't." Deep rubbed at his temples. One day he'd kill his brother, that was a foregone conclusion. "That's what I'm saying."

"What if he was, though? Best to always act like he might be."

"Can you shut your mouth just for a fucking *instant*?" Deep caught Shallow by the arm and stabbed the baggage in his face. "It's like talking to a bloody –" He was greatly surprised when a dark shape whisked between them and he found his hand was suddenly empty.

KIAM RAN LIKE her life depended on it. Which it did, o' course.

"Get after him, damn it!" And she heard the two Northmen flapping and crashing and blundering down the alley behind, and nowhere near far enough behind for her taste.

"It's a girl y'idiot!" Big and clumsy but fast they were coming, boots hammering and hands clutching and if they once caught a hold of her...

"Who fucking cares? Get the thing back!" And her breath hissing and her heart pounding and her muscles burning as she ran.

She skittered around a corner, rag-wrapped feet sticking to the damp cobbles, the way wider, lamps and torches making muddy smears in the mist and people busy everywhere. She ducked and wove, around them, between them, faces looming up and gone. The Blackside night-market, stalls and shoppers and the cries of the traders, full of noise and smells and tight with bustle. Kiam slithered between the wheels of a wagon limber as a ferret, plunged between buyer and seller in a shower of fruit then slithered across a stall laden with slimy fish while the trader shouted and snatched at her, caught nothing but air and she stuck one foot in a basket and was off kicking cockles across the street. Still she heard the yells and growls as the Northmen knocked folk flying in her wake, crashes as they flung the carts aside, as though a mindless storm was ripping apart the market behind her. She dived between the legs of a big man, rounded another corner and took the greasy steps two at a time, along the narrow path by the slopping water, rats squeaking in the rubbish and the sounds of the Northmen now loud, loud, cursing her and each other. Her breath whooping and cutting in her chest and running desperate, water spattering and spraying around her with every echoing footfall.

"We've got her!" the voice so close at her heels. "Come here!"

She darted through that little hole in the rusted grate, a sharp tooth of metal leaving a burning cut down her arm, and for once she was plenty glad that Old Green never gave her enough to eat. She kicked her way back into the darkness, keeping low, lay there clutching the package and struggling to get her breath. Then they were there, one of the Northmen dragging at the grating, knuckles white with force, flecks of rust showering down as it shifted, and Kiam stared and wondered what those hands would do to her if they got their dirty nails into her skin.

The other one shoved his bearded face in the gap, a wicked-looking knife in his hand, not that someone you just robbed ever has a nice-looking knife. His eyes popped out at her and his scabbed lips curled back and he snarled, "Chuck us that baggage and we'll forget all about it. Chuck us it now!"

Kiam kicked away, the grate squealing as it bent. "You're fucking dead you little piss! We'll find you, don't worry about that!" She slithered off, through the dust and rot, wriggled through a crack between crumbling walls. "We'll be coming for you!" echoed from behind her. Maybe they would as well, but a thief can't spend too much time worrying about tomorrow. Today's shitty enough. She whipped her coat off and pulled it inside out to show the faded green lining, stuffed her cap in her pocket and shook her hair out long, then out onto the walkway beside the Fifth Canal, walking fast, head down.

A pleasure boat drifted past, all chatter and laughter and clinking of glass, people moving tall and lazy on board, strange as ghosts seen through that mist and Kiam wondered what they'd done to deserve that life and what she'd done to deserve this, but there never were no easy answers to that question. As it took its pink lights away into the fog she heard the music of Hove's violin. Stood a moment in the shadows, listening, thinking how beautiful it sounded. She looked down at the package. Didn't look much for all this trouble. Didn't weigh much, even. But it weren't up to her what Old Green put a price on. She wiped her nose and walked along close to the wall, music getting louder, then she saw Hove's back and his bow moving, and she slipped behind him and let the package fall into his gaping pocket.

HOVE DIDN'T FEEL the drop, but he felt the three little taps on his back, and he felt the weight in his coat as he moved. He didn't see who made the drop and he didn't look. He just carried on fiddling, that Union march with which he'd opened every show during his time on the stage in Adua, or under the stage, at any rate, warming up the crowd for Lestek's big entrance. Before his wife died and everything went to shit. Those jaunty notes reminded him of times past, and he felt tears prickling in his sore eyes, so he switched to a melancholy minuet more suited to his mood, not that most folk around here could've told the difference. Sipani liked to present itself as a place of culture but the majority were drunks and cheats and boorish thugs, or varying combinations thereof.

How had it come to this, eh? The usual refrain. He drifted across the street like he'd nothing in mind but a coin for his music, letting the notes spill out into the murk. Across past the pie stall, the fragrance of cheap meat making his stomach grumble, and he stopped playing to offer out his cap to the queue. There were no takers, no surprise, so he headed on down the road to Verscetti's, dancing in and out of the tables on the street and sawing out an Osprian waltz, grinning at the patrons who lounged there with a pipe or a bottle, twiddling thin glass-stems between gloved fingertips, eyes leaking contempt through the slots in their mirror-crusted masks. Jervi was sat near the wall, as always, a woman in the chair opposite, hair piled high.

"A little music, darling?" Hove croaked out, leaning over her and letting his coat dangle near Jervi's lap.

JERVI SLID SOMETHING out of Hove's pocket, wrinkling his nose at the smell of the old soak, and said, "Fuck off, why don't you?" Hove moved on, and took his horrible music with him, thank the Fates.

"What's going on down there?" Riseld lifted her mask for a moment to show that soft, round face well-powdered and fashionably bored.

There did indeed appear to be some manner of commotion up the street. Crashing, banging, shouting in Northern.

"Damn Northmen," he murmured. "Always causing trouble, they really should be kept on leads like dogs." Jervi removed his hat and tossed it on the table, the usual signal, then leant back in his chair to hold the package inconspicuously low to the ground beside him. A distasteful business, but a man has to work. "Nothing you need concern yourself about, my dear."

She smiled at him in that unamused, uninterested way which for some reason he found irresistible.

"Shall we go to bed?" he asked, tossing a couple of coins down for the wine.

She sighed. "If we must."

And Jervi felt the package spirited away.

SIFKISS WRIGGLED OUT from under the tables and strutted along, letting his stick rattle against the bars of the fence beside him, package swinging loose in the other. Maybe Old Green had said stay stealthy but that weren't Sifkiss' way anymore. A man has to work out his own style of doing things and he was a full thirteen, weren't he? Soon enough now he'd be passing on to higher things. Working for Kurrikan maybe. Anyone could tell he was marked out special – he'd stole himself a tall hat that made him look quite the gent about town – and if they were dull enough to still be entertaining any doubts, which some folk sadly were, he'd perched it at quite the jaunty angle besides. Jaunty as all hell.

Yes, everyone had their eyes on Sifkiss.

He checked he weren't the slightest bit observed then slipped through the dewy bushes and the crack in the wall behind, which honestly was getting to be a bit of a squeeze, into the basement of the old temple, a little light filtering down from upstairs.

Most of the children were out working. Just a couple of the younger lads playing with dice and a girl gnawing on a bone and Pens having a smoke and not even looking over and that new one curled up in the corner and coughing. Sifkiss didn't like the sound o' those coughs. More'n likely he'd be dumping her off in the sewers a day or two hence but, hey, that meant a few more bits corpse money for him, didn't it? Most folk didn't like handling a corpse but it didn't bother Sifkiss none. It's a hard rain don't wash someone a favour, as Old Green was always saying. She was way up there at the back, hunched over her old desk with one lamp burning, her long grey hair all greasy-slicked and her tongue pressed into her empty gums as she watched Sifkiss come up. Some smart-looking fellow was with her, had a waistcoat all silver leaves stitched on fancy and Sifkiss put a jaunt on, thinking to impress.

"Get it, did yer?" asked Old Green.

"Course," said Sifkiss, with a toss of his head, caught his hat on a low beam and cursed as he had to fumble it back on. He tossed the package sourly down on the tabletop.

"GET YOU GONE, then," snapped Green.

Sifkiss looked surly, like he'd a mind to answer back. He was getting altogether too much mind, that boy, and Green had to show him the knobby-knuckled back of her hand 'fore he sloped off.

"So here you have it, as promised." She pointed to that leather bundle in the pool of lamplight on her old table, its top cracked and stained and its gilt all peeling but still a fine old piece of furniture with plenty of years left. Like to Old Green in that respect, if she did think so herself.

"Seems a little luggage for such a lot of fuss," said Fallow, wrinkling his nose, and he tossed a purse onto the table with that lovely clink of money. Old Green clawed it up and clawed it open and straight off set to counting it.

"Where's your girl Kiam?" asked Fallow. "Where's little Kiam, eh?"

Old Green's shoulders stiffened but she kept counting. She could've counted through a storm at sea. "Out working."

"When's she getting back? I like her." Fallow came a bit closer, voice going hushed. "I could get a damn fine price for her."

"But she's my best earner!" said Green. "There's others you could take off my hands. How's about that lad Sifkiss?"

"What, the sour-face brought the luggage?"

"He's a good worker. Strong lad. Lots of grit. He'd pull a good oar on a galley, I'd say. Maybe a fighter, even."

Fallow snorted. "In a pit? That little shit? I don't think so. He'd need some whipping to pull an oar, I reckon."

"Well? They got whips don't they?"

"Suppose they do. I'll take him if I must. Him and three others. I'm off to the market in Westport tomorrow week. You pick, but don't give me none o' your dross."

"I don't keep no dross," said Old Green.

"You got nothing but dross, you bloody old swindler. And what'll you tell the rest o' your brood, eh?" Fallow put on a silly la-de-da voice. "That they've gone off to be servants to gentry, or to live with the horses on a farm, or adopted by the fucking Emperor of Gurkhul or some such, eh?" Fallow chuckled, and Old Green had a sudden urge to make that knife of hers available, but she'd better sense these days, all learned the hard way.

"I tell 'em what I need to," she grunted, still working her fingers around the coins. Bloody fingers weren't half as quick as they once were.

"You do that, and I'll come back for Kiam another day, eh?" And Fallow winked at her.

"Whatever you want," said Green, "whatever you say." She was bloody well keeping Kiam, though. She couldn't save many, she wasn't fool enough to think that, but maybe she could save one, and on her dying day she could say she done that much. Probably no one would be listening, but she'd know. "It's all there. Package is yours."

FALLOW PICKED UP the luggage and was out of that stinking fucking place. Reminded him too much of prison. The smell of it. And the eyes of the children, all big and damp. He didn't mind buying and selling 'em, but he didn't want to see their eyes. Does the slaughterman want to look at the sheep's eyes? Maybe the slaughterman don't care. Maybe he gets used to it. Fallow cared too much, that's what it was. Too much heart.

His guards were lounging by the front door and he waved them over and set off, walking in the middle of the square they made.

"Successful meeting?" Grenti tossed over his shoulder.

"Not bad," grunted Fallow, in such a way as to discourage further conversation. *Do you want friends or money?* he'd once heard Kurrikan say and the phrase had stuck with him.

Sadly, Grenti was by no means discouraged. "Going straight over to Kurrikan's?"

"Yes," said Fallow, sharply as he could.

But Grenti loved to flap his mouth. Most thugs do, in the end. All that time spent doing nothing, maybe. "Lovely house, though, ain't it, Kurrikan's? What do you call those columns on the front of it?"

"Pilasters," grunted one of the other thugs.

"No, no, I know pilasters, no. I mean to say the name given to that particular style of architecture, with the vine-leaves about the head there?"

"Rusticated?"

"No, no, that's the masonry work, all dimpled with the chisel, it's the overall design I'm discussing – hold up."

For a moment Fallow was mightily relieved at the interruption. Then he was concerned. A figure was standing in the fog just ahead. The beggars and revellers and scum scattered round these parts had all slipped out of their way like soil around the plough 'til now. This one didn't move. He was a tall bastard, tall as Fallow's tallest guard, with a white coat on and the hood up. Well, it weren't white no more. Nothing stayed white long in Sipani. It was grey with damp and black-spattered about the hem.

"Get him out of the way," he snapped.

"Get out of the fucking way!" roared Grenti.

"You are Fallow?" The man pulled his hood back.

"It's a woman," said Grenti. And indeed it was, for all her neck was thickly muscled, her jaw angular and her red hair clipped close to her skull.

"I am Javre," she said, raising her chin and smiling at them. "Lioness of Hoskopp."

"Maybe she's a mental," said Grenti.

"Escaped from that madhouse up the way."

"I did once escape from a madhouse," said the woman. She had a weird accent, Fallow couldn't place it. "Well... it was a prison for wizards. But some of them had gone mad. A difficult distinction, most wizards are at least eccentric. That is beside the point, though. You have something I need."

"That so?" said Fallow, starting to grin. He was less worried now. One, she was a woman, two, she obviously was a mental.

"That is so. I know not how to convince you, for I lack the sweet words, but it would be best for us all if you gave it to me willingly."

"I'll give you something willingly," said Fallow, to sniggers from the others.

The woman didn't snigger. "It is a parcel, wrapped in leather, about..." she held up one big hand, thumb and forefinger stretched out. "Five times the length of your cock."

If she knew about the luggage, she was trouble. And Fallow had no sense of humour about his cock, to which none of the ointments had made the slightest difference. He stopped grinning. "Kill her."

She struck Grenti somewhere around the chest, or maybe she did, it was all a blur. His eyes popped wide and he made a strange whooping sound and stood there frozen, quivering on his tiptoes, sword half-way drawn.

The second guard – a Union man big as a house – swung his mace at her but it just caught her flapping coat. An instant later there was a surprised yelp and he was flying across the street upside down and crashing into the wall, tumbling down in a shower of dust, sheets of broken plaster dropping from the shattered brickwork on top of his limp body.

The third guard – a nimble fingered Osprian – whipped out a throwing knife but before he could loose it the mace twittered through the air and bounced from his head. He dropped soundlessly, arms outstretched.

"They are called Anthiric columns." The woman put her forefinger against Grenti's forehead and gently pushed him over. He toppled and lay there on his side in the muck, still stiff, still trembling, still with eyes bulgingly focused on nothing.

"That was with one hand." She held up the other big fist, and had produced from somewhere a sheathed sword, gold glittering on the hilt. "Next I draw this sword, forged in the Old Time from the metal of a fallen star. Only six living people have seen the blade. You would find it extremely beautiful. On the downside I would kill you with it."

The last of the guards exchanged a brief glance with Fallow, then tossed his axe away and sprinted off.

"Huh," said the woman, with a slight wrinkling of disappointment about her red brows. "Just so you know, if you run I will catch you in..." She narrowed her eyes and pushed out her lips, looking Fallow appraisingly up and down. The way he might have appraised the children. He found he didn't like being looked at that way. "About four strides."

He ran.

She caught him in three and he was suddenly on his face with a mouthful of dirty cobblestone and his arm twisted sharply behind his back.

"You've no idea who you're dealing with you stupid bitch!" He struggled but her grip was iron, and he squealed with pain as his arm was twisted still more sharply.

"It is true I am no high thinker." Her voice showed not the slightest strain. "I like simple things well done and have no time to philosophise. Would you like to tell me where the parcel is, or shall I beat you until it falls out?"

"I work for Kurrikan!" he gasped out.

"I'm new in town. Names work no magic on me."

"We'll find you!"

She laughed. "Of course. I am no hider. I am Javre, First of the Fifteen. Javre, Knight Templar of the Golden Order. Javre, Breaker of Chains, Breaker of Oaths, Breaker of Faces." And here she gave him a blinding punch which, he was pretty sure, broke his nose and filled the back of his mouth with the salt taste of blood. "To find me, you need only ask for Javre." She leaned over him, breath tickling at his ear. "It is once you find me that your difficulties begin. Now, where is that parcel?"

A pinching sensation began in Fallow's hand. Mildly painful to begin with, then more, and more, a white hot burning up his arm that made him whimper like a dog. "Ah, ah, ah, inside pocket, inside pocket!"

"Very good." He felt hands rifling through his clothes, but could only lie limp, moaning as the jangling of his nerves gradually subsided. He craned his neck around to look up at her and curled back his lips. "I swear on my fucking front teeth –"

"Do you?" As her fingers found the hidden pocket and slid the package free. "That's rash."

Javre pressed finger against thumb and flicked Fallow's two front teeth out. A trick she had learned from an old man in Suljuk and, as with so many things in life, all in the wrist. She left him hunched in the road struggling to cough them up.

"The next time we meet I will have to show you the sword!" she called out as she strode away, wedging the package down behind her belt. Goddess, these Sipanese were weaklings. Was there no one to test her anymore?

She shook her sore hand out. Probably her fingernail would turn black and drop off, but it would grow back. Unlike Fallow's teeth. And it was scarcely the first fingernail she had lost. Including that memorable time she had lost the lot and toenails too in the tender care of the Prophet Khalul. Now *there* had been a test. For a moment, she almost felt nostalgic for her interrogators. Certainly she felt nostalgic for the feeling of shoving their chief's face into his own brazier when she escaped. What a sizzle he had made!

But maybe whatever preening crime-lord, sinister slum master or corrupt Sipanese nobleman employed Fallow would be outraged enough to send a decent class of killer after her. Then she could go after them. Hardly the great battles of yesteryear, but something to while away the evenings.

Until then Javre walked, swift and steady with her shoulders back and the parcel dangling from her loose fingers. She loved to walk. With every stride she felt her own strength. Every muscle utterly relaxed yet ready to turn the next step in a split instant into mighty spring, sprightly roll, deadly strike. Without needing to look she felt each person about her, judged their threat, predicted their attack, imagined her response, the air around her alive with calculated possibilities, the surroundings mapped, the distances known, all things of use noted. The sternest tests are those you do not see coming, so Javre was the weapon always sharpened, the weapon never sheathed, the answer to every question.

But no blade came darting from the dark. No arrow, no flash of fire, no squirt of poison. No pack of assassins burst from the shadows.

Sadly.

Only a pair of drunk Northmen wrestling outside Pombrine's place, one of them snarling something about the bald boss. She paid them no mind as she trotted up the steps, ignoring the several frowning guards, who were of a quality inferior even to Fallow's men, down the hallway and into the central salon, complete with fake marble, cheap chandelier and profoundly unarousing mosaic of a lumpy couple fucking horse-style. Evidently the evening rush had yet to begin. Whores of both sexes and one Javre still was not entirely sure about lounged bored upon the overwrought furniture.

Pombrine was busy admonishing one of his flock for overdressing, but looked up startled when she entered. "You're back already? What went wrong?"

Javre laughed full loud. "Everything." His eyes widened, and she laughed louder yet. "For them." And she took his wrist and pressed the parcel into his hand.

POMBRINE GAZED DOWN at that unassuming lump of animal skin. "You did it?"

The woman thumped one heavy arm about his shoulders and gave them a squeeze. He gasped as his bones creaked. Without doubt she was of exceptional size, but even so the casual strength of it was hardly to be believed. "You do not know me. Yet. I am Javre, Lioness of Hoskopp." She looked down at him and he had an unpleasant and unfamiliar sensation of being a naughty child helpless in his mother's grasp. "When I agree to a challenge I do not shirk it. But you will learn."

"I keenly anticipate my education." Pombrine wriggled free of the crushing weight of her arm. "You did not... open it?"

"You told me not to."

"Good. Good." He stared down, the smile half-formed on his face, hardly able to believe it could have been this easy.

"My payment, then."

"Of course." He reached for the purse.

She held up one calloused hand. "I will take half in flesh."

"In flesh?"

"That's what you pedal here, no?"

He raised his brows. "Half would be a great quantity of flesh."

"I get through it. And I mean to stay a while."

"Lucky us," he muttered.

"I'll take him."

"An excellent choice, I –"

"And him. And him. And her." Javre rubbed her rough palms together. "She can get the lads warmed up, I am not paying to wank anyone off myself."

"Naturally not."

"I am a woman of Thond, and have grand appetites."

"So I begin to see."

"And for the sun's sake someone draw me a bath. I smell like a heated bitch already, I dread to imagine the stink afterward. I will have every tom cat in the city after me!" And she burst out laughing again.

One of the men swallowed. The other looked at Pombrine with an expression faintly desperate as Javre herded them into the nearest room.

"... you, remove your trousers. You, get the bandages off my tits. You would scarcely credit how tightly I have to strap this lot down to get anything done..."

The door snapped mercifully shut.

Pombrine seized Scalacay, his most trusted servant, by the shoulder and drew him close.

"Go to the Gurkish temple off the third canal with all haste, the one with the green marble pillars. Do you know it?"

"I do, master."

"Tell the priest that chants in the doorway that you have a message for Ishri. That Master Pombrine has the item she was asking after. For Ishri, do you understand?"

"For Ishri. Master Pombrine has the item."

"Then run to it!"

Scalacay dashed away leaving Pombrine to hurry to his office with hardly less haste, the package clutched in one sweaty hand. He fumbled shut the door and turned the key, the five locks closing with a reassuring metallic clatter.

Only then did he allow himself to breathe. He placed the package reverently upon his desk. Now he had it, he felt the need to stretch out the moment of triumph. To weigh it down with the proper gravitas. He went to his drinks cabinet and unlocked it, took his grandfather's bottle of Shiznadze from the place of honour. That man had lived his whole life waiting for a moment worthy of opening that bottle. Pombrine smiled as he reached for the corkscrew, trimming away the lead from the neck.

How long had he worked to secure that cursed package? Circulating rumours of his business failings when in fact he had never been so successful. Placing himself in Carcolf's way again and again until finally they seemed to happen upon each other by chance. Wriggling himself into a position of trust while the idiot courier thought him a brainless stooge, clambering by miniscule degrees to a perch from which he could get his eager hands around the package, and then... unhappy fate! Carcolf had slipped free, the cursed bitch, leaving Pombrine with nothing but ruined hopes. But now... happy fate! The thuggery of that loathsome woman Javre had by some fumbling miracle succeeded where his genius had been so unfairly thwarted.

What did it matter how he had come by it, though? His smile grew wider as he eased the cork free. He had the package. He turned to gaze upon his prize again.

Pop! An arc of fizzy wine missed his glass and spurted across his Kadiri carpet. He stared open mouthed. The package was hanging in the air by a hook. Attached to the hook was a gossamer thread. The thread disappeared through a hole in the glass roof high above where he now saw a black shape spread-eagled.

Pombrine made a despairing lunge, bottle and glass tumbling to the floor and spraying wine, but the package slipped through his clutching fingers and was whisked smoothly upwards out of his reach.

"Guards!" he roared, shaking his fist. "Thief!"

A moment later he realised, and his rage turned in a flash to withering horror.

Ishri would soon be on her way.

WITH A PRACTICED jerk of her wrist Shev twitched the parcel up and into her waiting glove.

"What an angler," she whispered to herself as she thrust it into her pocket and was away across the steeply-pitched roof, knee pads sticky with tar doing most of the work. Astride the ridge and she scuttled to the chimney, flicked the rope into the street below, was over the edge in a twinkling and swarming down. Don't think about the ground, never think about the ground. It's a nice place to be but you wouldn't want to get there too quickly...

"What a climber," she whispered to herself as she passed a large window, a garishly decorated and gloomily lit salon coming into view, and –

She gripped tight to the rope and stopped dead, gently swinging.

She really did have a pressing engagement with not being caught by Pombrine's guards, but within the room was one of those sights that one could not simply slide past. Four, possibly five, or even six naked bodies had formed, with most impressive athleticism, a kind of human sculpture – a grunting tangle of gently shifting limbs. While she was turning her head sideways on to make sense of it the lynch-pin of the arrangement, who Shev took at first glance for a red-haired strongman, looked straight at her.

"Shevedieh?"

Decidedly not a man, but very definitely strong. Even with hair clipped close there was no mistaking her.

"Javre? What the hell are you doing here?"

She raised a brow at the naked bodies entwined about her. "Is that not obvious?"

Shev was brought to her senses by the rattle of guards in the street below. "You never saw me!" And she slid down the rope, hemp hissing through her gloves, hit the ground hard and sprinted off just as a group of men with weapons drawn came barrelling around the corner.

"Stop thief!"

"Get him!"

And, particularly shrill, Pombrine desperately wailing, "My package!"

Shev jerked the cord in the small of her back and felt the pouch split, the caltrops scattering in her wake, heard the shrieks as a couple of the guards went tumbling. Sore feet they'd have in the morning. But there were still more following.

"Cut him off!"

"Shoot him!"

She took a sharp left, heard the flatbow string an instant later, the twitter as the bolt glanced from the wall beside her and off into the night. She peeled off her gloves as she ran, one smoking from the friction, and flung them over her shoulder. A quick right, the route well-planned in advance, of course, and she sprang up onto the tables outside Verscetti's, bounding from one to the next with great strides, sending cutlery and glassware flying, the patrons floundering up, clutching at her, at each other, tumbling over in their shock, a ragged violinist flinging himself for cover.

"What a runner," she whispered to herself, and leaped from the last table, over the clutching hands of a guard diving from her left and a reveller from her right, catching the little cord behind the sign that said *Verscetti's* as she fell and giving it a good tug.

There was a flash like lightning as she rolled, an almighty bang as she came up, the murky night at once illuminated, the frontages of the buildings ahead picked out white. There were screams and squeals and a volley of detonations. Behind her, she knew, blossoms of purple fire would be shooting across the street, showers of golden sparks, a display suitable for a baron's wedding.

"That Qohdam certainly can make fireworks," she whispered to herself, resisting the temptation to stop and watch the show and instead slipping down a shadowy snicket, shooing away a mangy cat, scurrying on low for three dozen strides and ducking into the narrow garden, struggling to keep her quick breath quiet. She ripped open the packet she had secured among the roots of the dead willow, unfurling the white robe and wriggling into it, pulling up the cowl and waiting in the shadows, the big votive candle in one hand, ears sifting at the night.

"Shit," she muttered. As the last echoes of her fiery diversion faded she could hear, faintly, but coming closer, the calls of Pombrine's searching guards, doors rattling as they tried them one by one.

"Where did he go?"

"I think this way!"

"Bloody firework burned my hand! I'm really burned, you know!"

"My package!"

"Come on, come on," she muttered. To be caught by these idiots would be among the most embarrassing moments of her career. It might even make the top five, which was saying something. That time she'd been stuck in a marriage gown half way up the side of the Mercers guildhall in Adua with flowers in her hair but no underwear and a steadily growing crowd of onlookers below would take some beating, but still. "Come on, come on, come –"

Now, from the other direction, she heard the chanting, and grinned. The Sisters were always on time. She heard their feet now, the regular tramping blotting out the shouting of Pombrine's guards and the wailing of a woman temporarily deafened by the fireworks. Louder the feet, louder the heavenly song, and the procession passed the garden, the women all in white, all hooded, lit candles held stiffly before them, ghostly in the gloom as they marched by in unison.

"What a priestess," Shev whispered to herself, and threaded from the garden, jostling her way into the midst of the procession. She tipped her candle to the left, so its wick touched that of her neighbour. The woman frowned across and Shev winked back.

"Give a girl a light, would you?"

With a fizzle it caught and she fell into step, adding her own joyous note to the chant as they processed down Caldiche Street and over the Fintine Bridge, the masked revellers parting respectfully to let them through. Pombrine's place, and the increasingly frantic searching of his guards, and the furious growling of a pair of savagely arguing Northmen dwindled sedately into the mists behind.

It was dark by the time she slipped silently through her own open window, past the stirring drapes, and crept around her comfortable chair. Carcolf was asleep in it, one strand of yellow hair fluttering around her mouth as she breathed. She looked young with eyes closed and face relaxed, shorn of that habitual sneer she had for everything. Young, and very beautiful. Bless this fashion for tight trousers! The candle cast a faint glow in the downy hairs on her cheek, and Shev felt a need to reach up and lay her palm upon that face, and stroke her lips with her thumb –

But, lover of risks though she was, that would have been too great a gamble. So instead she shouted, "Boo!"

Carcolf leaped up like a frog from boiling water, crashed into a table and nearly fell, lurched around, eyes wide. "Bloody hell," she muttered, taking a shuddering breath. "Do you have to do that?"

"Have to? No."

Carcolf pressed one hand to her chest. "I think you might have opened the stitches."

"You unbelievable baby." Shev pulled the robe over her head and tossed it away. "It barely broke the skin."

"The loss of your good opinion wounds me more deeply than any blade."

Shev unhooked the belts that held her thief's tools, unbuckled her climbing pads and started to peel off her black clothes, acting as if it was nothing to her whether Carcolf watched or not. But she noted with some satisfaction that it was not until she was slipping on a clean gown that Carcolf finally spoke, and in a voice slightly hoarse besides

"Well?"

"Well what?"

"It has always been a dream of mine to see a Sister of the White disrobe before my eyes, but I was rather wondering whether you found the –"

Shev tossed over the package and Carcolf snatched it smartly from the air.

"I KNEW I could rely on you." Carcolf felt a little dizzy with relief, not to mention more than a little tingly with desire. She had always had a weakness for dangerous women.

Bloody hell, she really was turning into her father...

"You were right," said Shev, dropping into the chair she had so recently frightened Carcolf out of. "Pombrine had it."

"I bloody knew it! That slime! So hard to find a good expendable decoy these days."

"It's as if you can't trust anyone."

"Still. No harm done, eh?" And Carcolf lifted up her shirt and ever so carefully slid the package into the uppermost of her two cash belts.

It was Shev's turn to watch, pretending not to as she poured herself a glass of wine. "What's in the parcel?" she asked.

"It's safer if I don't tell you."

"You've no idea, have you?"

"I'm under orders not to look," Carcolf was forced to admit.

"Don't you ever wonder, though? I mean, the more I'm ordered not to look, the more I want to." Shev sat forward, dark eyes glimmering in a profoundly bewitching way, and for an instant Carcolf's head was filled with an image of the pair of them rolling across the carpet together, laughing as they ripped the package apart between them.

She dismissed it with an effort. "A thief can wonder. A courier cannot."

"Could you be any more pompous?"

"It would require an effort."

Shev slurped at her wine. "Well, it's your package. I suppose."

"No it isn't. That's the whole point."

"I think I preferred you when you were a criminal."

"Lies. You relish the opportunity to corrupt me."

"True enough." Shev wriggled down the chair so her long, brown legs slid out from the hem of her gown. "Why don't you stay a while?" One searching foot found Carcolf's ankle, and slid gently up the inside of her leg, and down, and up. "And be corrupted?"

Carcolf took an almost painful breath. "Damn, but I'd love to." The strength of the feeling surprised her, and caught in her throat, and for the briefest moment she almost choked on it. Not just lust. Much more. For the briefest moment, she almost tossed the package out of the window, and sank down before the chair, and took Shev's hand and shared tales she had never told from when she was a girl. For the briefest moment. Then she was Carcolf again, and she stepped smartly away and let Shev's foot clomp down on the boards. "But you know how it is, in my business. Have to catch the tide." And she snatched up her new coat and turned as she pulled it on, giving herself time to blink back any hint of tears.

"You should take a holiday."

"With every job I say so, and when every job ends, I find I get... twitchy." Carcolf sighed as she fastened the buttons. "I'm just not made for sitting still."

"Huh."

"Let's not pretend you're any different."

"Let's not pretend. I've been considering a move myself. Adua, perhaps, or back to the South –"

"I'd much rather you stayed," Carcolf found she had said, then tried to pass it off with a carefree wave. "Who else would get me out of messes when I come here? You're the one person in this whole damn city I trust." That was a complete lie, of course, she didn't trust Shev in the least. A good courier trusts no one, and Carcolf was the very best. But she was a great deal more comfortable with lies than with truth.

She could see in Shev's smile that she understood the whole situation perfectly. "So sweet." She caught Carcolf's wrist as she turned to leave with a grip that was not to be ignored. "My money?"

"How silly of me." Carcolf handed her the purse.

Without even looking inside Shev said, "And the rest."

Carcolf sighed once more, and tossed the other purse on the bed, gold flashing in the lamplight as coins spilled across the white sheet. "You'd be upset if I didn't try."

"Your care for my delicate feelings is touching. I daresay I'll see you next time you're here?" she asked as Carcolf put her hand on the lock.

"I shall count the moments."

Just then she wanted a kiss more than anything, but she was not sure her resolve was strong enough for only one, so she blew a kiss instead, and pulled the door to behind her, and slipped swiftly across the shadowed court and out the heavy gate onto the street, hoping it was a while before Shevedieh took a closer look at the coins inside the first purse. Perhaps a cosmic punishment was thus incurred, but it was worth it just for the thought of the look on her face.

The day had been a bloody fiasco, but she supposed it could have been a great deal worse. She still had ample time to make it to the ship before they lost the tide. Carcolf pulled up her hood, wincing at the pain from that freshly stitched scratch, and from that entirely unreasonable ulcer, and from that cursed seam in her trousers, then strode off through the misty night, neither too fast nor too slow, entirely inconspicuous.

Damn, but she hated Sipani.

THE INSECTS OF LOVE
Genevieve Valentine

Genevieve Valentine's (www.genevievevalentine.com) first novel, *Mechanique: A Tale of the Circus Tresaulti,* won the 2012 Crawford Award and was nominated for the Nebula. Her second, *The Girls of the Kingfisher Club,* appeared in 2014 to acclaim. Coming up is science fiction novel, *Persona.* Valentine's short fiction has appeared in *Clarkesworld, Strange Horizons, Journal of Mythic Arts, Fantasy, Apex,* and others, and in the anthologies *Federations, The Living Dead 2, The Way of the Wizard, Teeth, After,* and more. Her story "Light on the Water" was a 2009 World Fantasy Award nominee, and "Things to Know about Being Dead" was a 2012 Shirley Jackson Award nominee; several stories have been reprinted in Best of the Year anthologies. Her nonfiction and reviews have appeared at NPR.org, *Strange Horizons, Lightspeed, Weird Tales, Tor.com,* and *Fantasy Magazine,* and she is a co-author of *Geek Wisdom* (Quirk Books). She has also been known to write *Catwoman* comics for DC! Her appetite for bad movies is insatiable.

BEFORE FAIRUZ GOT the tattoo, I'd never even heard of the beetles.

I just knew that the tattoo she wanted was enormous, and that it would take all night, and even as I agreed to come with her I said, "This is a bad idea."

"Good," she said, and hit the gas.

I expected some shithole off the main drag, the kind of place Fairuz would go to make a point. But it was clean as a dentist's office, and they gave us paper caps and told us to watch what we touched.

Inside was even cleaner, and the man waiting for us was in a work suit that zipped up to his neck.

"Lie down," he said, turning on the projector.

As Fairuz pulled off her shirt and settled onto her stomach, the ink drawing snapped into place over her skin: fifteen constellations, scattered on her back from the shoulder blades down past the waist of her trousers; freckles with labels, pulled together by string.

"You want something for the pain?" the guy asked.

Fairuz shrugged. "Sure."

He picked up a container of gold and pink marbles and poured them over her back.

Of course they weren't marbles, but when you haven't heard of the beetles before, you don't think that kind of thing will ever happen, that someone gets a Tupperware of bugs and dumps them out.

(You only need one or two, if the area's small, but Fairuz never did anything small if she could help it; the tattoo was all over and so were the beetles.)

They skittered back and forth over her skin, a shirt of rosy sequins, and across their bodies the projected constellations flickered in and out of sight.

I think this is before she died.

CETONIA APHRODITE (VENUS beetle). This beetle, native to continental Europe and long thought extinct, was recently rediscovered in Denmark's temperate thickets. Though no definitive studies have been conducted, it may be inferred that global warming forced a migration of the species to a more northern climate.

Cetonia aphrodite, commonly known as the Venus beetle because of its pink-gold coloring, feeds off pollen, particularly roses and other flowering climbers. In order to monopolize this popular resource, the beetles produce a toxin that deters predators and competition.

It is this trait that has made the Venus beetle of particular interest, and combined with a hardy disposition that does well in captivity, domestication efforts have brought the species back from the brink of extinction. Breeding programs recently began in Denmark to assure the supply of Venus beetle toxin as a natural pesticide.

The most promising potential for human application since the project's inception has been the peripheral effects of the toxin, which acts as an analgesic on contact with skin. Like many great discoveries, it was an accidental find, but its medical application as an inexpensive, naturally-derived painkiller could be significant.

When applied repeatedly in a short span, buildup of the toxin creates mild euphoria. Addicts and experimenters have been known to plant the Venus beetle under the skin near a vein for a sustained high. The Insect Preservation Act of 2046, if passed, will place these and similar insects under protected status and make implantation punishable, but the market for them continues to thrive, and each year, dozens of injuries are reported from those who tried to self-extract the beetle, and the image of the beetle – a distant, smaller cousin of the scarab, inheriting their round heads and sturdy legs – has become a symbol among the chemical class of thrill-seekers.

MY FIRST MEMORY is Fairuz cradling the mantis in her hands and showing it to me.

It was gray and spotted white, and its wings were crusted over. She blew on it gently; the sand scattered, and the mantis flew away as our parents came looking for us.

My parents always told the story like Fairuz was trying to scare me, but I don't think it had crossed her mind. Being cruel came later. I think she just felt sorry for the mantis, and wanted to see what I would do.

I remember the mantis's wedge-head and the antennae waving, the mottled and translucent wings, the pressed-up arms. Its eyes were huge, the matte steel blue of a storm cloud.

Maybe she'd expected me to hate it, or to be frightened, but it was beautiful; I looked through its glassy wings, watched the trembling, curious feelers moving around its mouth and smearing blood, until Fairuz took it back, frowning absently at the bug, at me.

I wondered what she was thinking. (That happened a lot. It happened when she burned through one career after another. It happened whenever she knew more about what I was doing than I did. It happened when she knocked on my door one night and said without waiting, "I'm sick of all this. I'm getting a tattoo. Let's go.")

She lost interest in bugs after that. I never did.

*   *   *

EVERYTHING ABOUT AN insect tells you what it is.

The antennae, the wings, the joints on the legs, the color of the larvae, are all advertisements of its origin and its adaptation, a line of waiting flags for its taxonomy. It's easy work. They want to be organized, down to the thousand-facets of their eyes; they wear exoskeletons to keep everything in order.

Fairuz had always been interested in the theory behind things – she studied math because she said she wanted to find out what was going on underneath the universe. She must not have found what she was looking for, because after one and a half degrees, her bedroom stacked waist-high with sheets of scribbles that looked like insects had migrated across them, she moved on to the public-advocacy theory of making people do what you want them to do, and from there to some government think tank where everything was classified, and she sometimes got intense and sometimes cutting, but never any happier.

I felt sorry for her. Insects were easy to love. It's always easier to find a thing and love it without hoping for a reason.

I REMEMBER SITTING in the schoolroom.

We'd been kept late because Fairuz argued with a teacher and I'd agreed with Fairuz. They didn't want any talking, so they sat us in rows, one desk apart.

Fairuz was in front of me, her shoulders hunched (she pulled in when she was angry, like a pill bug).

As we took our temporary seats she said, "You're so stupid sometimes," even though it was only that Mr. Richards hated when girls spoke up in class. She had been right to argue, and I had been right to agree.

For the three hours we sat in detention, I didn't even try to answer her. I just seethed in my chair and stared at the bun on her neck, low and beetle-black.

If I try hard enough, between the moment she breathes out and back in, her skin flickers and I can see Auriga, five dots tattoo-traced into a point, the lines disappearing below the collar of her shirt.

*   *   *

FAIRUZ WENT MISSING in the desert.

Probably exposure, the officer said when he came to my door. He said she'd been present at evening roll-call, according to the excursion director. Then she'd gone out, and never come back. There was no body.

"Is there a search?"

They'd called it off after seventy-two hours. They'd looked in every known shelter for a hundred miles, though she couldn't possibly have gone that far. They had flown over in helicopters, looking for her clothes. There had been carrion birds, he said finally, which was when I realized what he was trying to tell me.

"Who saw her go out alone?" I asked.

"Every attempt was made to locate –"

"Who saw her go *into the desert alone*?"

"We're very sorry for your loss," he said.

I folded my arms, careful with the barbed cricket specimen I was carrying on a pin. It trembled one reedy note (my hand was shaking, my voice was shaking).

"What were they looking for?"

"It's classified," he said. "I'm really very sorry. Someone will be in touch with you to make arrangements."

I crushed the barbed cricket in the door when I slammed it. That was worse than anything; that was the horrible omen that let the words slip in – she's dead.

Some words are knives. I cried for a while, my forehead pressed against the door, clammy and sick.

When I could walk again, I pulled up every picture, every message she had sent while she was away. She would have left me a clue, something to go on if the worst should happen, some way to find her or follow her, no matter what.

There was no chance she'd died how they said. If there was one thing Fairuz couldn't stand, it was being alone.

*   *   *

ACHETA EMARGINATA (BARBED cricket). Known colloquially as 'The Ragged Cricket,' this insect's reedy call sets it apart from its cousins the field cricket and the tree cricket. Found widely throughout the Eurasian continent, the barbed cricket population spread as trade increased with Europe and the Americas.

The legs of *Acheta emarginata* are perforated for greater buoyancy when jumping through the tall grass of the temperate plains to which it is native. When the male draws its barbed wing edges together, air passing swiftly back and forth across the holes creates the mournful tone of a woodwind instrument, unique among the shrill sounds of others of its genus. So striking is the sound that the insect has historically been kept at royal courts in China and Indonesia, and has been used by hunters – particularly when displaced from its natural habitat – as a novelty lure to draw curious birds from the brush.

It has recently been speculated by entomologists that this sound, which seems designed to mimic a bird call, is not a mating song as previously supposed, but in fact a way to misdirect those same birds that are the barbed cricket's natural enemies.

Due to the long-standing superstition that a ragged cricket's music has the ability to call loved ones home again, they are considered good luck, and are often kept as pets.

FAIRUZ HAD ARGUED with Mr. Richards because he corrected me.

"This is not an assignment where we should be using our imaginations," he said, holding my biology report out to me. I'd drawn the mantis on the front in pencil, outlined in ink. The eyes I had gone over and over, until they were fathomless black; they'd bled through to the second page.

That was strange, that was wrong, its eyes had been the color of slate; why had I drawn such deep, open black?

Fairuz had turned to watch us, her face pulling at the edges she was so angry.

I opened my mouth to defend the mantis.

"Sir," she snapped, "Given the liberties you take regarding societal evolution, surely she should be forgiven the mistake of thinking this was an exercise in creative writing."

He pivoted slowly to face her, one eyebrow going up. "And what exactly are you suggesting, Fairuz?" He never used last names when he spoke to girls like he did when he spoke to the boys.

I said, "She's suggesting you're an awful teacher who doesn't know what he's talking about."

We got detention, and he walked back to the front of the room and dropped my paper in the garbage.

When he left, Fairuz sprinted for the trash can as soon as the door was closed, before he could come back and set the clock. She sat with her hands folded on top of that report the whole time we were in detention.

"Never talk about anything unless you know it's true here first," she said, like it was a warning she'd given me before. "You're so stupid sometimes."

What she did with it I never knew; I never saw it again. I never looked for it. I never asked what she meant by "here." Fairuz had reasons, most of the time, and either way she wouldn't tell you.

I GOT A book about insects, the kind you could verify, and started reading about those instead. I never found the mantis.

Once I came in to ask her, but she looked up from her book (it was all water, tide pools and surfers and lonely-looking shells wrapped carelessly in kelp) and took one look at me and said, "If this is still bugs, I'm looking at shorelines, so only tell me if it's dragonflies."

After a second I closed the door.

We moved a short while after that, to a city where I learned not to say anything unless I was sure already that it was true. I ended up not saying much.

Sometimes I dreamed that the paper I wrote was only sand now, rolling over the top of the dunes in a place I've never been, little black grains scattered for miles and miles.

FAIRUZ HAD BOYFRIENDS.

I never remembered their names, and they all looked the same: tall, handsome, with the bearing of a man who's landed a girl as beautiful as he thinks he deserves. She never lasted more than two weeks with a boy; she dated them mostly to drive them off. She'd get dressed up and sweep down to his car for a few nights, and after date four she'd tell him to call her at the house, mostly so our mother would shout him down about calling someone's home and assuming he'd be welcome, didn't he have any manners, did they think this was helping their cause with her daughter, put your father on the phone right now, I want to tell him the kind of son he raised.

Fairuz would make me sit with her on the stairs, with her leaning forward with her arms pressed tight to her chest like a chrysalis, grinning wider and wider the angrier the boy got. If we could hear him shouting on the other end of the line, it was the last time Fairuz would hear from him. They always shouted, sooner or later; our mother had a way of getting them to show off their very worst. I was always proud of her; it felt she was working against us except when she was tricking one of Fairuz's boys into proving how awful he really was. Maybe that's why Fairuz did it, as much as anything.

I never had boyfriends. I hardly knew how to make regular friends – I made people nervous, Fairuz said, always like it was their problem and not mine. When she brought me over to peer through the banister with her it mostly reminded me how much trouble it all was.

I tried to take it as lessons in human courtship, but mostly I thought about the time we'd watched a pregnant spider giving birth to dozens of doubles that were just waiting to dry before they ate her. I wondered if our mother felt the same way about dealing with Fairuz.

"Poor boys," Fairuz said once, half-laughing.

Once I said, "One day you're going to fall in love, and then you'll be sorry," and she shot me a strange look, like I knew something she didn't.

(I did know. She'll meet Michael in thirteen years, if my count is right, but in this memory I never know if time is moving at the same rate as it is in the other ones, depending on which life we're leading; maybe she meets him in twelve.)

MICHAEL WAS WITH the government now. He'd know how to find what I needed.

He'd been an entomologist with the Venus Project when I met him. He'd discovered the analgesic properties of the beetle and was on the Ethics

Committee there. It wasn't a surprise he'd been asked to head up a federal task force on conservation. He knew how to cover the bases and how to make everyone feel as if they'd done good work; those kinds of men always ended up treading water in positions of power.

I corresponded with him for my dissertation, which was a study of the ecological, cultural, and economic implications of domestication of half a dozen species of *Entomos amoris*. He always forwarded me new medical opinions about the neurology of the toxin alongside each set of observations about the beetles.

The most important element to the beetle's survival – to the survival of any animal species – is the human element, he wrote me once, as if I hadn't been studying habitat destruction and shrinking populations, as if I didn't already know exactly what every insect I was looking at was up against. From someone I liked less, it would have been insulting.

Still, it was impressive, how much he hoped what he was doing would matter. It was flattering, how much he thought what I was doing would matter.

Fairuz met him when she invited herself to the symposium where I was presenting; he had come down from Copenhagen to hear me read.

Looking forward to meeting you, he'd written, and I'd looked at the screen with my whole face going hot, and thought about dusting bridal butterfly over my collarbones. I wondered whether he would look at me the way boys had always looked at Fairuz when she came down the stairs glowing, the pigment glancing off all the edges and corners of her throat.

I never used it, in the end. I had written a dissertation about how the insects of love were used by the human element, in ways that benefited no one except to soothe old superstitions and deplete populations; even if the bridal butterfly's power was real, the methods were unacceptable. I couldn't take advantage.

Doesn't stop some.

WHEN HE PICKS up the phone my heart thumps. I manage, "Dr. Mason?"

"Soraya?"

His voice sounds just the same. I close my eyes, catch my breath, say, "It's about Fairuz."

*   *   *

FAIRUZ ALWAYS WROTE me messages when we were apart, but her messages from the desert were different, and wrong.

I knew they'd be strange – this was a classified project, there was a lot she'd be unable to say directly, I had expected some vagueness and some secrets – but not like this. These were frightening. Unfocused.

Of all the things you could say about Fairuz, 'unfocused' had never, never been one. When she changed directions it was like repositioning a gun.

She sent me a letter nearly every week. She filled it with wails about the heat and long stories I remembered about our childhoods (*Those were the days,* she'd write) and stories I didn't recognize (framed, *Do you remember?*).

She wrote, in almost every letter, *We're out of time.*

Before the desert, she'd never used the phrase. Fairuz had never been out of time; the world would wait for her, and she knew it.

But I remember her hair shaking as we served detention, pages of a paper I never wrote curling under her fingers, as she worried about me.

I remember her looking over her shoulder at the tattoo parlor to make sure I was still with her, as the constellations scattered across her like she'd found a way straight through the sky.

I was the thing she waited for. It sounds sad, it sounds desperate, but I was. She was my sister. She would never have gone into the desert without me, unless she knew I'd be coming to find her.

I DON'T KNOW how to tell Michael what I need, how to explain what's wrong. The silence pushes in like a broken rib.

Finally I say, "There's something in the desert, and no one wanted her to tell me."

The other end of the line goes very quiet. I don't know what he's thinking; if he loved her, I've never wanted to know. Not now, either. Even dead, she's mine first.

He says, "I have to go," disconnects.

*   *   *

THE YEAR I wrote my dissertation, at a half-size desk in a studio apartment barely big enough to turn around in, Fairuz headed up the environmental campaign that made the tidal basins protected government land, to preserve them from further damage.

"Those tourists and their jet skis can piss off," she said, flinging herself onto my bed and grinning up at the ceiling. In repose, her suit looked even more expensive than it was.

I tried not to feel lesser, just having her around.

"Well, while you were doing that, I found someone who actually works with the Venus beetles. I've written to him – he's an ethics man, I think his work will really strengthen the case for insect conservation."

She laughed and rolled onto her stomach, narrowing her eyes at me. "Oh, Soraya, champion of the insects. They suit you – I don't mean it in a bad way, don't look like that. I just don't dare think what would have happened if I hadn't shown you that mantis."

I frowned; didn't know what she meant.

She hadn't shown me anything.

For a split second, across the back of her gray suit, fifteen constellations flickered in and out of sight.

Soraya,

Well, I'm here. Don't ever tell me you told me so about this whole thing, because you never did and I wouldn't have let you, but if you ever even thought it, don't tell me.

The heat's awful, of course – I told you I'd hate the desert, didn't I, back when my heart was broken and I left the ocean behind? Do you remember? Do you hear from Michael? Don't tell him I'm asking.

The work in [REDACTED BY ADMINISTRATOR] continues, though, and the way things are going I think I'm not going to be home for a long time. The good news is that by the time I'm out of here I'll be ready to go back to the sea for a little while – any place with water sounds wonderful by now.

Well, I'm out of time. I'd trade all this for one day on the seaside. I still think about that book of photography that got me in all that trouble, those

waves and the seaweed and that water the color of turquoise. Those were
the days.

All my love –

I KNOW SHE has the tattoo.

I know which fifteen she has etched on her back, a star-map in miniature: Auriga, Columba, Pegasus, Delphinus, Vulpecula, Taurus, Draco, Aquila, Cygnus, Lyra, Canis Major, Monoceros, Lepus, Orion, Eridanus.

I remember where they sit on her: Auriga at the nape of her neck, Taurus below her shoulder blades, Canis Major on her left hip, with Sirius as large as the eye of a mantis. I remember that Eridanus went below the line of her trousers where she'd rolled the waistband down, and the last few stars were projected over the fabric like a sprinkle of soot.

I see her with it all the time whether it's happened yet or not, but I can't remember when the tattoo begins, even though I'm there when the artist bends to his work, my paper cap scratching my scalp and the beetles still roiling in the bucket he's collected them in.

I don't know if I've vanished by then in this memory, or if it never happened and it's one of the things I dream that's only grief and sand.

I don't know if this is a mistake I'm making, or if this is something Fairuz built – a place for us to be alone, a language she wrote on her back so she would have a way to reach me that I would understand.

MICHAEL CALLS BACK.

"There's nothing I can tell you," he says, and his voice is beautiful until I process the words.

He's a scientist, still – I can hear in his voice how much he wants to share what he knows. Old habits.

"No, there's something," I say, hope it doesn't sound like I'm begging. "Anything."

"I don't know what she was doing that far south," he says, "and no one will tell me."

So it's important enough that it's above his pay grade. Of course it would be. Fairuz wouldn't have died for anything less.

Maybe they're not telling him because whatever they're looking for is going to eat up a hundred thousand beetle species, and that's the kind of thing you don't tell a bug man. But that's not right, either; she stopped using bridal butterfly when I asked her to, and the time our mother brought home a barbed cricket, Fairuz was the one who let it go. She would have warned me. She knew I trusted her; she knew what I loved.

They must not understand why he's really asking, I think; they must none of them have sisters.

"I'm so sorry," he says. "Please let me know if there's anything you need."

"My sister back," I say, hang up.

Tears always sting me. Kids who grow up in dry places aren't supposed to waste water.

MORPHO AMYMONE (BRIDAL butterfly). This rare species in the Morphoceae family, native to the Amazon basin, is known for its iridescent pigmentation. The wings reflect an icy blue-white, visible even at night, when it comes out to feed. This bright reflection actually serves a camouflaging purpose, as the *Morpho amymone* feeds amid night lilies, and this iridescence mimics the lily's petals.

The *Morpho amymone* subsists on a diet of aphids, making it one of only three known carnivorous butterfly species.

The butterfly was named by its discoverers after Amymone 'the blameless,' due to the bridal-white wing pigment (Amymone being one of the Danaid who did not kill her husband on her wedding night), and referencing the myth of her fruitful union with Poseidon, as the pigment from the *Morpho amymone*, when in contact with the skin, acts as an aphrodisiac.

Since the global discovery of this attribute, demand has risen sharply, and the species has been hunted nearly to extinction. The last sighting of a *Morpho amymone* in the wild was in 2046; until there is further evidence to the contrary, it is presumed that they now exist only in captivity.

There is belief among some occultists that the pigment dust of this *Morpho* keeps harm at bay, but this seems to be tied to Amymone's rescue from death in the original myth, and has no basis in any results of scientific study.

* * *

Soraya,

 I'm out of time, the lights will be going off any second to give one of the generators time to recover, but I saw a dragonfly today and I got so jealous of you, because back home it might be raining, so here I am. Are you studying dragonflies, now? You should. This one goes anywhere it pleases, which I like more than I like most insects.

 How is Michael? Don't tell him I asked. You promised not to tell him. He can't know. I miss him, that's all. You were right, all those years back – I'm sorry for it all.

 And that's it, the lights are gone. If this turns into Morse code it's because it's all I could manage in the dark. Do you know Morse code? I don't, really, so good luck to you.

 The sky here is something, though, when the lights are out. No clouds at all, just you and the stars and the night. When I count the constellations, I think of you. Do you think of me, too? Can you even see stars, where you are?

 You'll have to come meet me here, after this is over. The stars are beautiful. Promise me.

 All my love –

FAIRUZ CRIED OVER Michael more than she'd cried over anything, throwing herself on the bed, sobbing into my shoulder.

 Her tears were hotter than human; burning.

 "I have to give him up," she said, when she was calm again. "I know that. I'll let him go. Don't tell him anything about it. It's not his business."

 I wondered what had happened between them, but I didn't ask. I never opened my mouth about Michael, for fear of what I'd say.

 (That day at my reading he'd looked right at me and smiled, and my heart turned over in my chest for one violent beat before he said, "And is this your sister?", and I thought about what it meant to be cruel.)

 Instead I asked, "Will you be all right?"

 She looked straight ahead, said as if I hadn't spoken, "I'm finished with the sea. I'll have to turn to the desert next."

"You hate the desert," I said.

She said, "Not as much as I will."

This is probably after she's died, but sometimes it's hard to tell.

I dredge up the memory anyway, as often as I dare. There's so little I know for certain. I'll hang on to anything where we were together; what does it matter if it's a lie?

I PULL UP my dissertation and refresh my data points to reflect updates in field research.

I write an article about recent developments in the conservation of *Entomos amoris* in arid zones near human habitation. It gets published.

I write a grant proposal and submit it to my university committee.

Michael calls me.

"Soraya, what are you doing?"

There's no way my university would have flagged my proposal; he's keeping an eye on me, then.

"Studying the migratory patterns of turquoise dragonflies in desert regions," I say. "I find it fascinating. There are a lot of implications for adjusting similar populations to counteract human encroachment. It might be very positive. I'm happy to speak to anyone on the committee about my goals for the study."

He says, "I don't like where this is going."

I say, "Good."

SOMETIMES AT NIGHT, as I'm working and reading and looking at maps because there's no chance at sleep, Fairuz blinks into sight in my doorway, my desk chair, at the edge of my bed. (A different bed, now; I gave away the one where she sat next to me and wept.)

I'm looking through her old letters for the clues I hadn't understood before. The list of places she could be gets shorter every night. Every time I see Fairuz, I put a pin on the map. The circles get smaller.

I wish, unfairly, that she'd let me grieve for a little while. If she's only dead, if I go to the desert and there's nothing, I can't still be holding these letters. I can't keep going like this, if she's really gone.

But she's always got a steady, searching look that I remember from whenever she was waiting for me to finally catch up. I keep going.

Sometimes, in the morning, there's a Venus beetle on my wall.

Soraya,

Won't be leaving here any time soon. The desert's full of secrets, and I'm out to name them all. Tell Mother for me; I don't have the courage to do it myself.

Everyone here is either too nice or absolutely horrible, but if I told you why they'd only redact it, so imagine it as best you can. (I know that's not much, when it comes to you, I wish you'd had a little more interest when I tried to show you the endless sea that you think is empty until you look under the surface at the fish eating one another. It would have made all this easier for me to explain.)

This place is crawling with insects. Every time I see a mantis I think about the one I showed you when you were still a baby and we lived in that little town at the edge of the grassland and the dunes; that little gray mantis with the wings. You loved it so much. I should have known right then what you would be when you were older. You just stared at it with those big eyes, and then you were looking at me like I was going to explain everything, and I was sitting there thinking I knew. Not in this world, eh? Those were the days. It had sand on its wings, stuck together. Now I know how it felt.

I've always admired that about you, though – that you can pick something to love and never waver.

Must go, [REDACTED BY ADMINISTRATOR] is calling and there's work to be done. I'm almost out of time. I'm sorry I'm not coming home quite as you thought. Please don't be angry. I'll see you very soon, I promise.

All my love –

WE'RE IN THE tattoo parlor. The Venus beetles have been coaxed back into their container, and now Fairuz's bare back is a maze of constellations, waiting for the work to begin.

(I know how they corralled the beetles back again, which means this is a memory, or a past I must have lived – one in which I study insects, in which this isn't a surprise to me because I know the man who discovered they could be used this way. This is a past in which I know of the beetles long before Fairuz brings me here. It might be real.)

Fairuz says, "Soraya, make sure all the constellations are lined up, all right? Otherwise it'll look like I sneezed."

It would be rude to the artist, if he was here, but she and I are all alone.

"Taurus is centered, I promise," I say, and press my thumb below her shoulder blades to prove it. Somehow I know where the stars should go.

The image slides over the mountain range of my hand, a few straight lines and a cluster of dots. It looks a little like the beetles, if you squint.

Without a sound, her back crumbles under me.

Before I can scream, before I can move, before I can think about what pain she must be in to disappear that way, the light goes out; then I'm kneeling in the desert, my thumb sinking into the sand.

It's cold and it's pitch black, until I look up. I'm underneath those same stars. It looks like anywhere, but I know it can't be real, because Fairuz is kneeling opposite me, grinning.

"What do you think?" she asks.

(I don't remember this.)

TRITHEMIS FAIRUZ (TURQUOISE dragonfly). This dragonfly, found widely throughout the African continent, is most easily identified by the wide, bright blue-green stripes the male adult bears on its abdomen. Young females have a paler blue coloration that fades as they reach adulthood.

The turquoise dragonfly population is nomadic, rarely returning to the same mating ground. This ensures the greatest variety of mates, which has helped this dragonfly adapt to ecological changes more swiftly than some of its more loyal (and now endangered) cousins. For instance, over the last two hundred years the adult female's wingspan has increased by a median three cm, presumably to allow for swifter escape from predators and to demand greater stamina from males during the mating flight.

The fickle nature of *Trithemis fairuz*'s habitation patterns has earned it the nickname 'the heartbreak dragonfly,' as its absence means a rise in the mosquito population, and often a corollary rise in disease.

Historical superstition has it that someone who kills a turquoise dragonfly will soon suffer a personal loss.

On a more practical note, it seems desirable to study the migration habits of *Trithemis fairuz* to determine any factors that encourage the successful transplantation of the population, in order to develop repopulating techniques for other, more threatened dragonfly species.

I GET THE grant.

Michael calls.

"Congratulations," he says.

He doesn't know, I realize as soon as I hear his voice. I've pushed at the edges enough, like Fairuz would have, and something gave, but something else always crumbles underneath you when you do, some tether that slides loose that you can never catch hold of again.

Poor Michael, I think. This must be some other life for him now – *are you still with the Venus Project, is that where this money's coming from?* – and he hardly knows me, and he's never even heard of Fairuz.

She left you for my sake, I almost say.

As I open my mouth, the walls flood with beetles, and I remember everything.

I nearly drop the phone.

(All at the same time, Fairuz is crying into my pajamas, her wild black hair spread over my shoulders; I'm knocking on his door – a house I've never seen in a city I've never been to – and kissing him; I'm attending his wedding to Fairuz; he's clapping politely in the auditorium after my presentation and he will never see me again; Fairuz is standing in my bedroom doorway, leveling a look at me and saying, "I'm getting a tattoo. Let's go.")

His voice is tinny with the phone so far from my ear: "Soraya? Soraya?"

He's mentioned where I'm going – it must not be a secret in this instant, wherever we're standing now. Maybe he's heard the beetles, I think, but they're gone, except one, gleaming on my wall like a pin in a map.

I'm going to forget this, I think, panicking. The receiver cracks under my fingers, I'm so desperate to hold on to anything, but I know that as soon as I speak, or he speaks, or I take a breath, this will vanish. I don't know what will take its place.

I'm shaking. I hope he doesn't say anything. My voice would give me away if he knew what I knew.

"Soraya?"

I blink. The beetle's gone. (Of course the beetle's gone; they don't live here, the climate's all wrong for them.)

"Yes, I'm here," I say. My body is stretched thin, I'm not getting enough sound to support the words. I'm happy, I think, that's why; I can go out looking for her now.

But he only says, "Be careful out there, yeah?"

It doesn't sound like goodbye, but he should know better. This isn't a desert you come back from.

I loved you, I want to say, just to throw him, but all I can think is, *I'm coming, Fairuz.*

THE HEAT AND the wind suck all the air out of me, and I stand outside and struggle against the sun just to breathe.

(I've forgotten that I've lived in the desert before; it's a stranger.)

Fairuz hated the heat, the bright sun, anything that wasn't water. I try to remember what could have sent her to someplace like this. I can't.

When I try to think back to that – when I try to think back to anything – I'm suddenly watching her in the wings of the stage where I'm delivering my paper and she's grinning fit to burst; she's in detention with me, not quite turning her head, and there's the sound of paper being torn to bits; she's dusting bridal butterfly on her collarbones on her way to see Michael, and when I say, "I wish you wouldn't," she looks at me a second before she realizes I mean the bridal butterfly, and she says, "All right, this is for you," and when she offers me the brush there are a few bright spangles still stuck to it, a shape I know I should know – Orion, maybe, or Pegasus.

When I think about the tattoo parlor, all I remember is stars like pinpricks, and the white light bleaching everything I try to look at, except the endless carpet of rosy beetles that runs into the sand at my feet and vanishes.

By the time I make it to my hotel, the desert has already pulled me to pieces.

I can hear the sand caught in my eyelashes when I blink, and I think of the mantis with its wings stuck together, and of Fairuz out in the desert somewhere, alone and waiting for me in the last seconds before she died, and I cry so long that all the sand washes away.

"YOU HAVE TO do something besides cry about things," Fairuz is saying.

We're out of detention, and she's walking through the main hall so fast that the tangled bun of her black hair bangs against her neck with every step.

I stay behind her. It's hopeless, trying to catch up.

"I wasn't crying," I'm saying. I don't want to tell her that my eyes welled up because she'd insulted me for defending her and I'd spent three hours furious and wanting to hit her with my eraser, smack in the middle of Taurus. "And I'm *not* stupid."

There must be something in the way I say it, because she's stopping, turning, waiting for me. I stand shoulder-to-shoulder with her, and she gives me a long look. Her eyes have always been huge and dark, two stains of ink.

"I hope not," she says.

Then we're walking together, and I know already that something is wrong, that someday I'll need to remember this and I won't, that something is slipping away I'll never get back.

As we get outside, I step on a heartbreak dragonfly.

This memory isn't real, then; I would never.

THE WONDERFUL THING about dragonflies is that they fly wherever they like, and if you are to document them properly, you must go where they go.

Still, it's a terrible thing to look at the horizon and know that, somewhere in that vast question, your sister's body is being swallowed by the sand.

I write a letter.

*   *   *

GOVERNMENT PROPERTY IS marked with wire fences, but I'm beginning to remember how wonderful sand can be, and it doesn't take long before I find a place where it's half-swallowed the post, and I can shove it further down with my bare hands, walk right over it without having to climb a thing.

There are enough patches of grass ahead of me that I can probably come up with a dragonfly specimen to match the one on my papers, which is helpful, and the university will defend my purpose here, if it comes to that.

I don't think it will come to that. This is a government operation, and they have something specific in mind. I think if they see me I'll disappear, and then I'll really see what's happened to Fairuz.

Acknowledgements

THE INSECTS OF *Love* is itself the product of those with great passion for their work. I would like, first and foremost, to acknowledge the work of a fellow in my field without whom this book would not exist.

Soraya Qadir's observation and analysis of species within the neoclassification *Entomos amoris* over the last several years was an invaluable resource and inspiration during the writing of this book. What work she completed with *Trithemis fairuz* (which, thanks to her findings, has now been termed the turquoise nomad) is a fascinating glimpse into the future, and may greatly influence the landscape of ecological entomology.

In the last letter I received from her from the field, she presented her progress and the suggestion for *The Insects of Love*, and asked me to be her research partner and the co-author of this work. I was honored. When the time came, I made the decision to continue alone, but never has an accomplishment been so bittersweet.

Qadir first corresponded with me for her dissertation many years ago, and I knew even then an unusual mind was at work. This neoclassification provides new taxonomical and ecological options for those seeking to preserve and study these insect populations, negotiating a visionary space between scholarship and practicality.

Though I never met her, her enthusiasm and insight were, and remain, an inspiration.

As a scientist and as a scholar, she is missed.

Michael Mason (First Edition, 2046)

I KEEP TO the scrub and grass for a while, taking photos of a turquoise dragonfly I find in a stand of tall grass. I think about putting it in the jar in my pack, but since Fairuz died I haven't had much of a heart for collecting.

I've walked for a long time. My water runs out. At some point the sand seems to swallow me up, and I sink to the ground, close my eyes. Air whistles across my ear; it sounds like the barbed cricket. *Oh*, I think, *come home, come home, Fairuz.*

When I wake, my neck hurts (sunburn, I fell asleep when the sun was still out, mistake), but it's cool now, nearly cold, and the stars are out.

The stars are out.

I concentrate until I recognize Orion. It takes longer than it should; I should have been studying the stars all this time, I should have known what Fairuz was really telling me. (I saw them hovering over her back; I know where I'm meant to be, now.)

Eridanus is on my right, then, and when I stand up it will be curving behind me. The sky is a riot of stars, a thousand Venus beetles on a black ground, but I know the road.

I walk as quickly as sand will allow, heading right for the center of the chaos above me.

It seems as though the sun rises and falls, but I don't feel it. It's only that my eyes hurt, and then they don't, and it's night again and I haven't wavered, I haven't stopped for a second, she'll be proud.

Finally it's so cold and I'm so tired that the stars are holding still, and for the first time in a long time I drop to my knees and look around.

It's sand, smooth and glass-flat until it meets the sky, and everywhere I look the air shimmers like I'm burning to death; then for a blink I see Fairuz, and Fairuz when I turn, and then Fairuz is sitting in front of me, grinning, her arms folded on her knees like we're back beside the banister and our mother is yelling at some boy downstairs; her black hair is so dark that it looks like the night's curling around her face.

The stars here are brighter than morning was and getting larger, as if we're close enough to touch them.

(Maybe we are. Maybe I understand what brought Fairuz to the desert at last; this way to make the world really wait for her, to never be out of time, to be outside it, to look straight through the sky and out the other side; this way to never be alone again.)

"Come on, Soraya," she says. "Come with me, if you can find me."

"I can't," I say. I'm too tired to be brave, I don't know what I'm saying, I'm so tired, I want to close my eyes and for everything to be over. "I don't know where you are."

"You're so stupid sometimes," she says, and for the first time in our lives, she sounds afraid.

It's too bright, now, we're in the tattoo parlor and the lamp is on and the artist is about to begin; my throat is dry and I can't move.

A thousand miles away at the end of my arm, a little gray mantis climbs over my hand, shakes the sand off its wings, flies away. I don't recognize it (not yet), but all at once I do; it's the promise between Fairuz and me that I've never understood, that means everything is all right. I should have Fairuz show it to me when I'm little, so I know what to look for now.

"I will," she says, as if I've spoken. "I promise. Come with me."

Maybe I was wrong all those years. Fairuz wasn't afraid of being alone. It's only that she went ahead to make the way easier; it's only that she was waiting, and giving me the chance to reach her.

That much, then, was true: I was her sister, and she wouldn't go on without me.

We're in the tattoo parlor because she insisted I come with her, and her back is a map of the sky.

Taurus has to go in the center.

I look up, where nine bright stars are waiting.

"Oh," I say softly, "the Pleiades," and Fairuz laughing is the last thing I hear.

* * *

POLYSPILOTA SORAYA (PLEIADES mantis). This desert-dwelling member of the mantis family, a cousin of the griffin mantis, is recognizable because of the wings set permanently perpendicular to the abdomen. Adults were medium gray with white-spotted abdomens and front legs, a pattern ideal for camouflage in the sand and scrub regions where they made their home. (These white markings earned the mantis its designation *P. soraya*, from the Persian name for the Pleiades cluster of stars.)

The mantis preyed largely on *Morphos* by mimicking butterfly mating behavior to get close to its prey.

It was widely believed that consuming a Pleiades mantis granted one wish. Unfortunately, the demand greatly exceeded any possible natural supply, and attempts to domesticate the mantis failed.

Since 2022, when the last known specimen died in captivity, the Pleiades mantis has been classified extinct.

COLD WIND
Nicola Griffith

Nicola Griffith (asknicola.blogspot.com) is a native of Yorkshire, England, where she earned her beer money teaching women's self-defense, fronting a band, and armwrestling in bars, before discovering writing and moving to the U.S. Her immigration case was a fight and ended up making new law: the State Department declared it to be "in the National Interest" for her to live and work in this country. This didn't thrill the more conservative powerbrokers, and she ended up on the front page of the *Wall Street Journal*, where her case was used as an example of the country's declining moral standards. In 1993 a diagnosis of multiple sclerosis slowed her down a bit, and she concentrated on writing. Her first five novels are *Ammonite, Slow River, The Blue Place, Stay*, and *Always*. She is the co-editor of the *Bending the Landscape* series of original short fiction published by Overlook the author of multi-media memoir *And Now We Are Going to Have a Party*, and her non-fiction has appeared in a variety of print and web journals, including *The New Scientist, Out*, and *Nature*. Her awards include the Washington State Book Award, Tiptree Award, the Nebula Award, the World Fantasy Award, and the Lambda Literary Award (six times). Her latest book is historical novel *Hild*. She lives in Seattle with her wife, writer Kelley Eskridge, and takes enormous delight in everything.

FROM THE PARK on Puget Sound I watched the sun go down on the shortest day of the year. The air lost its lemon glitter, the dancing water dulled to a greasy heave, and the moon, not yet at its height, grew more substantial. Clouds gathered along the horizon, dirty yellow-white and gory at one end, like a broken arctic fox. Snow wasn't in the forecast, but I could smell it.

More than snow. If all the clues I'd put together over the years were right, it would happen tonight.

I let the weather herd me from the waterfront park into the city, south then east, through the restaurant district and downtown. The streets should have been thronged with last-minute holiday shoppers but the weather had driven them toward the safety of home.

By the time I reached the urban neighborhood of Capitol Hill, the moon was behind an iron lid of cloud, and sleet streaked the dark with pearl.

Inside the women's bar, customers were dressed a little better than usual: wool rather than fleece, cashmere blend instead of merino, and all in richer, more celebratory colors. The air was spiced with cinnamon and anticipation. Women looked up when the door opened, they leaned toward one another, faces alight like children waiting for teacher to announce a story, a present, a visit from Santa.

The holidays, time out of time. Mørketiden or Mōdraniht, Solstice or Soyal, Yaldā or Yule or the Cold Moon Dance, it doesn't matter what people call the turn of the year; it fills them with the drumbeat of expectancy. Even in cities a mammalian body can't escape the deep rhythms imposed by the solar cycle and reinforced by myth. Night would end. Light would come.

Daylight. Daybreak. Crack of dawn. You can tell a lot about a culture from its metaphors: the world is fragile, breakable, spillable as an egg. People felt it. Beyond the warmth and light cast by the holiday they sensed predators roaming the dark. It made people long to be with their own kind. Even those who were not usually lonely hungered to belong.

I sat by the window, facing the door, and sipped Guinness black as licorice and topped with a head like beige meringue. I savored the thrust of rusty-fist body through the velvet glove of foam, glad of the low alcohol. Daybreak was a long way off.

Three women in front of me were complaining about babysitters; someone's youngest had chicken pox and another urged her to throw a holiday pox party so they could get all their children infected at once. After all, wasn't it better for the body to get its immunity naturally, the old-fashioned way?

It was one of the most pernicious fallacies, common the world over: old ways are best. But old ways can outlast their usefulness. Old ways can live on pointlessly in worlds that have no room for them.

I drained my beer and almost, from force of habit, recorded my interaction with the server when she took my order for a refill. But I wasn't here to work and, besides, it would have given me nothing useful, no information on the meeting of equals: the customer is always a little higher on the food chain, at least on the surface.

A woman in the far corner was smiling at me. A woman with the weathered look of a practiced alcoholic. I smiled back; it was the holidays. She brightened. If I brightened in turn she would wave me over. "Let's not be alone at Christmas," she'd say. And I could say... anything. It wouldn't matter because drunks forget it all before they reach the bottom of the glass. I could say: I'm so very, very tired of being alone. I ache, I yearn, I hunger for more.

But women like her would never be my more. So I shook my head and raised my glass with the inclination of the head that, the world over, meant: *Thank you. We are done.*

I sipped my Guinness again, looked at the sky – the sleet was getting whiter – and checked the time. Not yet. So I tuned them all out and listened to the music, a heartfelt rendition of an old blues piece by a woman with a clearly detectable English accent beneath the Delta tones. Perhaps there was a paper in it: In this decade, why do English women sing the blues better than anyone since those who invented it? Music traditions flitted from one place to another acquiring heft and solidity as different cultures adopted them. Over the years they became majestic and apparently eternal. They never were.

The music, at least, did not make me feel like an outsider. It was an old friend. I let it talk to me, let it in, let the fat, untuned bass drum, timed to a slow heartbeat, drive the melody into the marrow of my long bones where it hummed like a bee, and the river of music push against the wall of my belly...

... and they were speaking Korean at a table against the wall, which took me back to the biting cold of the Korean DMZ, the mud on the drinking hole sprinkled with frost, the water buffalo and her calf –

The door slammed open bringing with it a gust of snowy air – and a scent older than anything in the city. Every cell in my body leapt.

Two women came in laughing. The one in jeans and a down vest seemed taller, though she wasn't. Her cheeks were hectic, brown eyes brilliant, and not only from the cold. Women have lit up that way for thousands of years when they have found someone they want, someone whose belly will lie on theirs heavy and soft and urgent, whose weight they welcome, whose voice thrills them, whose taste, scent, turn of the head makes them thrum with need, ring and sing with it. They laugh. They glow.

The other was paler, the red-brown of old ivory stained with tea. Her eyes were brown, too, slanted and wide set. Deep brown, velvet. Snow dappled her hair. She stood by the door, blinking, as people do when they walk from dark into light.

My aorta opened wide and blood gushed through every artery, all my senses gearing up. But I pretended not to see her. I gazed out of the window, at the sleet turning to snow, the air clotting with cold, and the pavement softening from black to gray. Reflected in the glass the women around me were coming alert, spines straightening, cheeks blooming, capillaries opening.

She was here. She was real. I'd been right.

The woman in the down vest smiled, touched the other on the shoulder, and said something. They moved through the doorway to the pool room and out of sight.

I'd been right. I relished the realization because soon I wouldn't be able to; soon my mind would be submerged and I'd be lost in a pull almost as old as the turning of the seasons. I watched the snow come down in streetlight cold as moonlight and, for a moment, missed the old sodium lamps with their warm yellow glow, their hint of hearth and home and belonging.

I pondered her clothes: long dress, with a thick drape; long coat of oddly indeterminate color; boots. Those were long, too. Not shiny. Brown? Black? I frowned. I couldn't tell. It didn't matter. She was here. It would go as it would.

I moved into energy-conversation mode, as in the field when watching groups whose habits you know as well as your own name: reflexes begun but arrested, peripheral vision engaged. Around me the bar moved from hot to simmering and now a new scent undercut the usual wood-and-hops of microbrews and the holiday cinnamon: the sting of liquor. Someone turned up the music. Two women at different tables – one of the Koreans and a gap-toothed white girl – exchanged glances; one followed the other to the bathroom.

The snow fell steadily. Traffic would be snarling the intersections, blocked by buses slid sideways down the hill. Soon those vehicles would be abandoned and the streets utterly empty. The CCTV would be locked with cold.

Soon.

The foam on the inside of my glass sagged like a curtain swag then slid to the bottom. I'd drunk it faster than I'd meant. At the table by the wall a Korean voice was raised – her girlfriend had taken too long in the bathroom, "Because there are two crazy women in there!"

The bathroom.

But as I stood the world swam and lost focus for a moment, then reformed around the doorway from the pool room. She stepped through. Her long coat was fastened to the collar. Toggled with horn, not buttoned. It looked beige and cream against the doorjamb but gray-blue in its shadowed folds. Perfect camouflage.

She saw me. Her face didn't move, but I knew how it would be when she flung her head back, cried out, clutched my shoulders as she shuddered. I felt her breath against my collarbone as she folded there, the brush of her mouth against my skin.

She came toward me, stepping around the spilt beer and dropped fries, lifting her feet high, placing them carefully, as though she wore tall heels.

I watched, unable – unwilling – to move.

And then she stood before me. I could smell her – woodland, fern, musk – and I wanted to reach, fold her down, stretch her out on the bracken, and feel the pulse flutter at her neck.

"You were watching me," she said, and her voice sounded hoarse, as though used to a bigger throat.

"I'm... an anthropologist. It's what we do." I've been looking for you for a long time. I didn't think you existed.

"What's your name?"

I thought about that. "Onca."

She nodded; it meant nothing to her. Her eyes were so dark. She turned up her collar. "I'll see you, Onca. Soon, I hope." A cold stream purled through her voice and snow blew across her eyes. Come outside, under the sky with me, they said.

I nodded. We both knew I would: she called, others followed. It's who she was.

And then she was gone. I didn't look out of the window. If the stories were true in this way too, I wouldn't be able to see her, not yet.

I FOUND HER victim in the bathroom, the blind spot with no cameras. She wasn't dead. She sat propped on the seat in a stall, jeans around her knees, head against the wall. She grinned at me foolishly. "Can't move," she said.

I locked the stall behind me. "Does it hurt?"

"Naw."

It would. I smelled blood, just a little. I bent, looked at her shirt darkening between her breasts. "Can you draw a deep breath?"

She tried. In reality it was more of a sigh. But she didn't flinch or cough. No broken ribs.

I squatted in front of her, elbows on knees, hands dangling comfortably. She just kept smiling, head at that odd angle against the wall. In that position she couldn't see me. I stood, straightened her head, then, because it was distracting, I leaned her on my shoulder, lifted, and pulled up her jeans. She could fasten them herself later, or not.

I squatted again, regarded her. She was still smiling, but it was a faint echo of what it had been. No longer solid. After this not much would be. "There's a legend," I said. "More than a dozen legends, from all over the world." La Llorona. Or Flura. Xana, Iara, Naag Kanya... "She lures people with sex. Some say she takes your heart." Sometimes literally. "But she always takes something." I considered her. "She's taken your spirit."

"My..."

I waited, but she didn't say any more. "Your soul." As good a word as any. "You're tired, I should think."

Her smile faded, like a guttering flame. She might survive. She would never feel alive again.

I wasn't sure she could hear me anymore. I leaned forward, unbuttoned her shirt. The bruise was swelling too quickly to be sure, but the shape cut into the broken skin – lovely skin, over firm muscle – could have been from a blow by a hoof.

"What's your name?"

"Maria José Flores."

"Maria, you make me hungry." And she would have, with her spirit intact. "But not like this." I fastened her back up and stood. Time to go.

THE CITY WAS another world in the snow. Silent. Flakes falling soft as owl feathers. Time out of time.

The streets were empty. No traffic in or out. It would last until she was done. I'd traced her through campfire stories, elders' tales, academic papers, psychiatric reports; it's what she did. She had been new in the world when Columbus came; alone. Over the centuries she had refined her methods until they were ritual: she fed early on the evening of a winter high day or holiday, brought her strength to peak, then chose someone to play with all night. Someone strong. Someone who would last.

I had put myself in her path and she had chosen me, and now I must seek her out. But as I did, as I followed her, she was shadowing me, herding me. I didn't try to pinpoint her – she was at the height of her powers, luxuriant with Maria Flores – but I knew she was there somewhere, behind the abandoned, snow-shrouded cars, in the doorway, behind the dumpster and the frozen cameras. I felt her on my left, a presence as subtle as atmospheric pressure, turning me north. I knew where she wanted me to go. So I padded through the muffled white dream downtown had become, pacing my shadow along the old brick and concrete walls of back streets and alleys, toward the edge of the city, where land met sea.

Alleys widened to open space and the sky glimmered with reflected water light. The land began to climb and undulate. Under the snow, pavement softened to grass and then alternating gravel path and turf on dirt layered on concrete. A switchback over a road. The sculpture park overlooking the Sound.

Before I reached the brow of the hill I stopped and listened. Silence. So profound I heard the snow falling, settling with a crystalline hiss, bright and sharp as stars. I closed my eyes, opened my mouth a little, breathed and tongued the air to the roof of my mouth. There. To the west. Where there should be only the cold snow, industrial solvents beneath the thin layer of topsoil trucked in and grassed over, and the restless damp of the Sound. The sharp tang of woman, of beast.

I opened my eyes, let blood flood the muscles of my shoulders and thighs, and listened.

The snow stopped. A breath of wind ruffled my hair. The clouds thinned from iron to mother-of-pearl, lit from above by moonlight. To the west, the Sound shimmered.

Eyes unfocused, vision wide to catch motion, I saw the shadow picking its way over the snow. If I closed my eyes I would hear the lift and delicate step of a doe moving through undergrowth.

I moved again, keeping low, east then south. I stopped. Coughed, deliberately, and felt as much as heard her ears flick and nostrils flare as she tracked my position. *Come*, I thought, *come to me*.

And she did. She crossed the skyline and I saw her clearly.

Her coat was winter beige, thick and soft, pale as underfur at her throat and where it folded back as she walked. Her knees bent the wrong way. Her dark boots were not boots.

Deer Woman.

I took off my jacket and dropped it in the snow. I opened my shirt.

She stopped, nostrils opening and closing. Her head moved back, her right leg lifted as though to stamp. But there was no herd to signal. She kept coming.

She wanted me to run, so I did. I bounded away, moving through trees – they were not big enough to climb – north and east, leaping the concrete wall, running between the looming sculptures, until I was among the cluster of greenery at the corner of the park. She followed.

Two hundred years ago, even a hundred, when there were still wolves in the north of this country and big cats in the south, she would have been more careful, but she had been playing predator, not prey, for too long. No doubt she had lost count of nights like this, the victims whose fear for a while overwhelmed their attraction. She would take her time, not risk her legs on those walls. She was still sleek with Maria, and this was the height of her yearly rite, not to be rushed.

The sky was almost white now. Against it, bare twigs stood out like black lace. I couldn't see the water from here but I could smell it. It softened the air, utterly unlike the arid cold of Korea, coarse as salt. Korea, where it was rumored that the Amur leopard was back in the DMZ.

The snow crunched. Closer, so much closer than I expected; I'd been careless, too. She was not a buffalo calf.

Moonlight spilled through the cloud and splashed onto the snow and I saw the darker line in the gray-blue shadow of the steel sculpture.

"Onca," it said. "Come to me."

Recklessness burst in me, brilliant as a star. I stood, and left the safety of the trees.

Moon shadow is steep and sharp. The tracks I made looked like craters. Her scent ripened, rich and round against the keen night air. I swallowed.

"I can't see you." My voice was ragged, my breath fast.

She stepped from the shadow.

I moved closer. Closer still, until I could see the pulsing ribbon of artery along her neck, the snowflake on a thread of her hair. Strong hair, brown-black.

"Kneel," she said. She wanted me beneath her in the snow. She would fold down on me and crush the breath from my lungs until my heart stopped and she could lap me up and run, run through the trees, safe, strong for another year.

"No," I said.

She went very still. I regarded her. After a moment I stepped to one side so she could see my tracks.

She took a step backward. It wouldn't be enough. It would never have been enough, even in the long ago.

"Who are you?"

"Onca." My newest name, *Panthera onca*. "B'alam before that. And long, long ago, Viima." She didn't understand. I'd been a myth before she was born.

I waited.

She looked at the tracks again: a half moon and four circles. Unmistakable.

She shot away, all deer now, straight for the trees lining Western Avenue. They always go for the trees.

In the DMZ the water buffalo had been heavier, and horned, but only a buffalo, nothing like my equal. Deer Woman ran like a rumor, like the wind, but I was made for this, and though I hadn't hunted one of my kind for an age, had thought I had taken the last a lifetime ago, she had never run from one like me. I was older. Much older. And at short range, cats are faster than deer.

I brought her down with one swipe to the legs and she tumbled into the snow. She panted, tail flickering. Her hind legs tightened as she prepared to scramble up and run again. I stood over her. I could take her throat in my jaws and suffocate her until she was a heartbeat from death, then rip her open and swallow her heart as it struggled to beat, feel its muscular contraction inside me. The lungs next. Rich with blood. Slippery and dense. Then the shoulders.

But she didn't move, and I didn't move, and she was a woman again.

"Why?" Her hoarse voice seemed more human now. She didn't know why she was still alive.

I didn't, either. "Cold Wind. That was my first name, before people crossed the land bridge and I followed. Or perhaps I crossed and they followed, I forget. You think you're old..."

I looked at the steel sculpture: huge, undeniable, but rust would eat it as surely as leaves fall in winter and dawn breaks the night open, and I would still be here. Alone. I had killed them all, because that was what I did.

"Get up," I said.

"Why?"

"So you can run."

Surely she wasn't weary of life, not yet, but she began to lift her jaw, to offer her throat. Cats are faster than deer. I would catch her, and as young as she was, she felt it: this is who we were, this is what we did. It was the old way.

"Run. I won't kill you. Not this year."

Silence. "But next?"

Predator and prey. We were the last. I said nothing. And she was gone, running, running.

The stars shone bright but the moon was setting and more cloud was on its way, ordinary northwest cloud. The night was warming, the silence already thinning, traffic starting up again at the edges. By tomorrow the snow would melt, the cameras would work. But tonight it was still a white world where Deer Woman ran toward daybreak, and I had someone to hunger for.

INTERSTATE LOVE SONG
(MURDER BALLAD NO. 8)
Caitlín R. Kiernan

Caitlín R. Kiernan (www.caitlinrkiernan) is a two-time recipient of both the World Fantasy and Bram Stoker awards, and the *New York Times* has declared her "one of our essential writers of dark fiction." Her recent novels include *The Red Tree* and *The Drowning Girl: A Memoir*, and, to date, her short stories have been collected in twelve volumes, including *Tales of Pain and Wonder, A is for Alien, The Ammonite Violin & Others*, and the World Fantasy Award winning *The Ape's Wife and Other Stories*. Currently she's editing her thirteenth and fourteenth collections – *Beneath an Oil Dark Sea: The Best of Caitlín R. Kiernan (Volume 2)* for Subterranean Press and *Houses Under the Sea: Mythos Tales* for Centipede Press. She has recently concluded *Alabaster*, her award-winning, three-volume graphic novel for Dark Horse Comics. She will soon begin work on her next novel, *Interstate Love Song*, based on the story that appears here. She lives in Providence, Rhode Island.

"The way of the transgressor is hard." – Cormac McCarthy

1.

THE IMPALA'S WHEELS singing on the black hot asphalt sound like frying steaks, USDA choice-cut T-bones, sirloin sizzling against August blacktop in Nevada or Utah or Nebraska, Alabama or Georgia, or where the fuck ever this one day, this one hour, this one motherfucking minute is going down.

Here at the end, the end of one of us, months are a crimson thumb smudge across the bathroom mirror in all the interchangeable motel bathrooms that have come and gone and come again. You're smoking and looking for music in the shoebox filled with cassettes, and the clatter of protective plastic shells around spools of magnetically coated tape is like an insect chorus, a cicada symphony. You ask what I want to hear, and I tell you it doesn't matter, please light one of those for me. But you insist, and you keep right on insisting, "What d'you wanna hear?" And I say, well not fucking Nirvana again, and no more Johnny Cash, please, and you toss something from the box out the open passenger window. In the side-view mirror, I see a tiny shrapnel explosion when the cassette hits the road. Cars will come behind us, cars and trucks, and roll over the shards and turn it all to dust. "No more Nirvana," you say, and you laugh your boyish girl's laugh, and Jesus and Joseph and Mother Mary, I'm not going to be able to live in a world without that laugh. Look at me, I say. Open your eyes, please open your eyes and look at me, please. You can't fall asleep on me. Because it won't be falling asleep, will it? It won't be falling asleep at all. We are beyond the kindness of euphemisms, and maybe we always were. So, don't fall asleep. Don't flutter the eyelashes you've always hated because they're so long and pretty, don't let them dance that Totentanz tarantella we've delighted at so many goddamn times, don't let the sun go down on me. You shove a tape into the deck. You always do that with such force, as if there's a vendetta grudge between you and that machine. You punch it in and twist the volume knob like you mean to yank it off and yeah, that's good, I say. That's golden, Henry Rollins snarling at the sun's one great demon eye. You light a Camel for me and place it between my lips, and the steering wheel feels like a weapon in my hands, and the smoke feels like Heaven in my lungs. Wake up, though. Don't shut your eyes. Remember the day that we, and remember the morning, and remember *that* time in – shit, was it El Paso? Or was it Port Arthur? It doesn't matter, so long as you keep your eyes open and look at me. It's hours until sunrise, and have you not always sworn a blue streak that you would not die in the darkness? That's all we've got here. In for a penny, in for a pound, but blackness, wall to wall, sea to shining sea, that's all we've got in this fluorescent hell, so don't you please fall asleep on me. Hot wind roars in through the Impala's windows, the stink of melting tar, roaring like an invisible mountain lion, and you point west and say take that next exit. We need beer, and we're almost out of cigarettes, and I want a pack of Starburst Fruit Chews, the tropical flavors, so the assholes better have those out here in the world's barren shit-kicker asshole. You'll just like always save all the pina colada ones for me. Then there's a thud from the trunk, and you laugh that laugh of yours all over again, only now with true passion. "And we need a bottle of water," I say. "No good to us and a waste of time and energy, and just a waste all the way round, if she ups and dies of heat stroke back there," and you shrug. Hey, keep your eyes open, love. Please, goddamn it. You can do that for me, I know you can. And I break open one of the ampules of ammonia and cruelly wave it beneath your nostrils so that both eyes pop open wide, opening up cornflower blue, and I think of startled birds bursting from their hiding places in tall grass. Tall grass, there's so much of tall grass here at the end, isn't there? I kiss your forehead, and I can't help thinking I could fry an egg on your skin, fry an egg on blacktop, fry an egg on the hood of the Impala parked in the Dog Day sun outside a convenience store. You ask me to light a candle, your voice gone all jagged and broken apart like a cassette tape dropped on I-10 at 75 mph. I press my fingers and palm to the sloppy red mess of your belly, and I do not dare take my hand away long enough to light a candle, and I'm so sorry, I'm so, so sorry. I cannot even do that much for you. Just please don't close your eyes. Please don't you fall asleep on me.

2.

ALL THESE THINGS you said to me, if not on this day, then surely on some other, and if not during this long Delta night, than surely on another. The blonde with one brown eye and one hazel-green eye, she wasn't the first, but you said to me she'll be the most memorable yet. She'll be one we talk about in years to come when all the rest have faded into a blur of delight and casual slaughter. We found her at a truck stop near Shreveport, and she'd been hitching down I-49 towards Baton Rouge and New Orleans. Sister, where you bound on such a hot, hot, sweltersome night? you asked. And because she was dressed in red, a Crimson Tide T-shirt and a red Budweiser baseball cap, you said, "Whither so early, Little Red Cap?" And she laughed, and you two shared a joint while I ate a skimpy dinner of Slim Jims, corn chips, and Mountain Dew. Eighteen-wheeled dinosaurs growled in and growled out and purred at the pumps. We laughed over a machine that sold multi-colored prophylactics and another that sold tampons. And would she like a ride? Would she? 'Cause we're a sight lot better than you're likely gonna find elsewhere, if you're looking for decent company and conversation, that is, and the weed, there's more where that came from. How old? Eighteen, she said, and you and I both knew she was adding years, but all the better. She tossed her knapsack in the back seat, and the extra pair of shoes she wore around her neck, laces laced together. She smelled of the road, of many summer days without a bath, and the world smelled of dinosaur trucks and diesel and dust and Spanish moss; and I love you so much, you whispered as I climbed behind the wheel. I love you so much I do not have words to say how much I love you. We set sail southwards, washed in the alien chartreuse glow of the Impala's dash, and she and thee talked while I drove, listening. That was enough for me, listening in, eavesdropping while my head filled up with a wakeful, stinging swarm of bees, with wasps and yellow jackets, courtesy those handy shrink-wrapped packets of dextroamphetamine and amphetamine, Black Beauties, and in the glove compartment there's Biphetamine-T and 40mg capsules of methaqualone, because when *we* drove all damn day and all damned night, we came prepared, didn't we, love? She's traveled all the way from Chicago, the red-capped backseat girl, and you and I have never been to Chicago and have no desire to go. She talks about the road as it unrolls beneath us, before me, hauling us towards dawn's early light. She tells you about some old pervert who picked her up outside Texarkana. She fucked him for twenty bucks and the lift to Shreveport. "Could'a done worse," you tell her, and she doesn't disagree. I watch you both in the rearview mirror. I watch you both, in anticipation, and the uppers and the prospect of what will come, the mischief we will do her in the wood, has me more awake than awake, has me ready to cum then and there. "You're twins," she said. It wasn't a question, only a statement of the obvious, as they say. "We're twins," you reply. "But she's my big sister. Born three minutes apart on the anniversary of the murder of Elizabeth Short," and she has no goddamn idea what you're talking about, but, not wanting to appear ignorant, she doesn't let on. When she asks where we're from, "Los Angeles," you lie. You have a generous pocketful of answers at the ready for that oft asked question. "South Norton Avenue, midway between Coliseum Street and West 39th," you say, which has as little meaning to the heterochromatic blonde as does Glasgow smile and Leimert Park. I drive, and you spin our revolving personal mythology. She will be one for the books, you whispered back at the truck stop. Can't you smell it on her? Can't I smell what on her? Can't you smell happenstance and inevitability and fate? Can't you smell victim? You say those things, and always I nod, because, like backseat girl, I don't want to appear ignorant in your view. This one I love, this one I love, eating cartilage, shark-eyes, shark-heart, and black mulberry trees mean I will not survive you, when the truth is I won't survive *without* you. Backseat girl, she talks about how she's gonna find work in New Orleans as a waitress, when you and I know she's cut out for nothing much but stripping and whoring the Quarter, and if this were a hundred years ago she'd be headed for fabled, vanished Storyville. "I had a boyfriend," she says. "I had a boyfriend, but he was in a band, and they all moved off to Seattle, but, dude, I didn't want to fucking *go* to fucking Seattle, you know?" And you say to her to her how it's like the California Gold Rush or something, all these musician sheep lemming assholes and would-be wannabe musician posers traipsing their way to the fabled Northwest in hopes of riding a wave that's already broken apart and isn't even sea foam anymore. That ship has *sailed,* you say. It's sailed and sunk somewhere in the deep blue Pacific. But that's not gonna stop anyone with stars in their eyes, because the lure of El Dorado is always a bitch, whichever El Dorado is at hand. "Do you miss him?" I ask, and that's the first thing I've said in over half an hour, more than happy just to listen in and count off the reflective mile markers with the help of anger and discord jangling from the tape deck. "Don't know," she says. And she says, "Maybe sometimes. Maybe." The road's a lonely place, you tell her, sounding sympathetic when I know so much better. I know you're mind is full to the brim with red, red thoughts, the itch of your straight-razor lusts, the prospect of the coming butchery. Night cruising at 80 mph, we rush past the turnoff for Natchitoches, and there's a sign that says 'Lost Bayou,' and our passenger asks have *we* ever been to New Orleans. Sure, you lie. Sure. We'll show you round. We have friends who live in an old house on Burgundy, and they say the house is haunted by a Civil War ghost, and they'll probably let you crash there until you're on your feet. Sister, you make us sound like goddamn guardian angels, the best break she's ever had. I drive on, and the car reeks of pot and sweat, cigarette smoke and the old beer cans heaped in the back floorboard. "I've always wished I had a twin," she says. "I used to make up stories that I was adopted, and somewhere out there I had a twin brother. One day, I'd pretend, we'd find one another. Be reunited, you know." It's a pretty dream from the head a such a pretty, pretty red-capped girl in the backseat, ferried by you and I in our human masks to hide hungry wolfish faces. *I could turn you inside out,* I think at the girl. And we will. It's been a week since an indulgence, a week of aimless July motoring, letting peckish swell to starvation, taking no other pleasures but junk food and blue-plate specials, you and I fucking and sleeping in one another's arms while the merciless Dixie sun burned 101°F at motel-room rooftops, kerosene air gathered in rooms darkened and barely cooled by drawn curtains and wheezing AC. Strike a match, and the whole place woulda gone up. Cartoons on television, and watching MTV, and old movies in shades of black and white and grey. Burgers wrapped in meat-stained paper and devoured with salty fries. Patience, love, patience, you whispered in those shadows, and so we thrummed along back roads and highways waiting for just the right confection. And. My. Momma. Said. Pick the Very. Best One. And You. Are. It.

3.

BETWEEN THE TALL rustling cornsilk rows, ripening husks, bluebottle drone as the sun slides down from the greasy blue sky to set the horizon all ablaze, and you straddle Thin Man and hold his cheekbones so that he has no choice but to gaze into your face. He can't close his eyes, as he no longer has eyelids, and he screams every time I shake another handful of Red Devil lye across his bare thighs and genitals. Soft flesh is melting like hot wax, here beneath the fading Iowa day. I draw a deep breath, smelling chemical burns, tilled red-brown Bible Belt soil, and corn, and above all else, corn. The corn smells alive in ways I cannot imagine being alive, and when we are done with Thin

Man, I think I would like to lie down here, right here, in the dirt between the tall rows, and gaze up at the June night, at the wheeling twin dippers and bear twins and the solitary scorpion and Cassiopeia, what I know of summer stars. "You don't have to do this," the man blubbers, and you tell him no, we don't, but yes, we do. We very much actually do. And he screams, and his scream is the lonesome cry of a small animal dying alone so near to twilight. He could be a rabbit in a fox's jaws, just as easily as a thin man in our company. We found him standing alongside a pickup broken down miles and miles north of Ottumwa, and maybe we ought to have driven him farther than we did, but impatience wins sometimes, and so you made up that story about our Uncle Joe who has a garage just a little ways farther up the road. What did he have to fear from two pale girls in a rust-bucket Impala, and so I drove, and Thin Man – whose name I still unto this hour do not know – talked about how liberals and niggers and bleeding hearts and the EPA are ruining the country. Might he have become suspicious of our lies if you'd not switched out the plates at the state line? Might he have paused in his unelicited screed long enough to think twice and think better? You scoop up fertile soil and dribble it into his open mouth, and he gags and sputters and chokes and wheezes, and still he manages to beg throughout. He's pissed himself and shat himself, so there are also those odors. Not too far away are train tracks, and not too far away there is a once-red barn, listing like a drunkard, and silver grain silos, and a whistle blows, and it blows, calling the swallows home. You sing to Thin Man, *Heed the curves, and watch the tunnels. Never falter, never fail.* Remember that? Don't close your eyes, and do not dare sleep, for this is not that warm night we lay together near Thin Man's shucked corpse and screwed in the eyes of approving Maggot Corn King deities thankful for our oblation. Your lips on my breasts, suckling, your fingers deep inside me, plowing, sewing, and by tomorrow we'll be far away, and this will be a pleasant dream for the scrapbooks of our tattered souls. More lye across Thin Man's crotch, and he bucks beneath you like an unbroken horse or a lover or an epileptic or a man being taken apart, piece by piece, in a cornfield north of Ottumwa. When we were children, we sat in the kudzu and live-oak shade near the tracks, waiting, waiting, placing pennies and nickels on the iron rails. You, spitting on the rails to cool them enough you would not blister your ear when you pressed it to the metal. I hear the train, you announced and smiled. Not much farther now, I hear it coming, and soon the slag ballast will dance and the crossties buck like a man dying in a cornfield. Soon now, the parade of clattering doomsday boxcars, the steel wheels that can severe limbs and flatten coins. Boxcars the color of rust – Southern Serves the South and CSX and a stray Wisconsin Central as good as a bird blown a thousand miles off course by hurricane winds. Black cylindrical tankers filled with corn syrup and crude oil, phenol, chlorine gas, acetone, vinyl chloride, and we spun tales of poisonous, flaming, steaming derailments. Those rattling, one-cent copper-smearing trains, we dreamed they might carry us off in the merciful arms of hobo sojourns to anywhere far, far away from home. *Keep your hand upon the throttle, and your eye upon the rail.* And Thin Man screams, dragging me back to the now of then. You've put dirt in his eyes, and you'd imagine he'd be thankful for that, wouldn't you? Or maybe he was gazing past you toward imaginary pearly gates where delivering angels with flaming swords might sweep down to lay low his tormentors and cast us forever and anon into the lake of fire. More Red Devil and another scream. He's beginning to bore me, you say, but I'm so busy admiring my handiwork I hardly hear you, and I'm also remembering the drive to the cornfield. I'm remembering what Thin Man was saying about fairy child-molesting atheist sodomites in all branches of the Federal government and armed forces, and an international ZOG conspiracy of Jews running the USA into the ground, and who the *fuck* starts in about shit like that with total, helpful strangers? Still, you were more than willing to play along and so told him yes, yes, yes, how we were faithful, god-fearing Southern Baptists, and how our daddy was a deacon and our momma a Sunday school teacher. That should'a been laying it on too thick, anyone would've thought, but Thin Man grinned bad teeth and nodded and blew great clouds of menthol smoke out the window like a locomotive chimney. Open your eyes. I'm not gonna tell you again. Here's another rain of lye across tender meat, and here's the corpse we left to rot in a cornfield, and I won't be left alone, do you hear me? Here are cordials to keep you nailed into your skin and to this festering, unsuspecting world. What am I, what am I, what *am* I? he wails, delirious, as long cornstalk shadows crosshatch the field, and in reply do you say, A sinner in the hands of angry gods, and we'd laugh about that one for days. But maybe he did believe you, sister, for he fell to praying, and I half believe he was praying not to Father, Son, and Holy Ghost, but to you and me. You tell him, By your own words, mister, we see thou art an evil man, and we, too, are surely out and about and up to no good, as you'll have guessed, and we are no better than thee, and so there is balance. I don't know why, but you tack on something about the horned, moon-crowned Popess squatting between Boaz and Jachin on the porch of Solomon. They are pretty words, whether I follow their logic or not. Near, nearer, the train whistle blows again, and in that moment you plunge your knife so deeply into Thin Man's neck that it goes straight through his trachea and spine and out the other side. The cherry fountain splashes you. You give the Bowie a little twist to the left, just for shits and giggles. Appropriately, he lies now still as death. You pull out the knife and kiss the jetting hole you've made, painting sticky your lips and chin. Your throat. You're laughing, and the train shrieks, and now I want to cover my ears, because just every once and a while I do lose my footing on the winding serpent highway, and when I do the fear wraps wet-sheet cold about me. This, here, now, is one of those infrequent, unfortunate episodes. I toss the plastic bottle of lye aside and drag you off Thin Man's still, still corpse. Don't, I say. Don't you dare laugh no more, I don't think it's all that funny, and also don't you dare shut your eyes, and don't you dare go to sleep on me. *Till we reach that blissful shore*

Where the angels wait to join us

In that train

Forevermore.

I seize you, love, and you are raving in my embrace: *What the fuck are you doing? Take your goddamn filthy hands off me cunt, gash, bitch, traitor.* But oh, oh, oh I hold on, and I hold on tight for dear forsaken life, 'cause the land's tilting teeter-totter under us as if on the Last Day of All, the day of Kingdom Come, and just don't make me face the righteous fury of the Lion of Judah alone. In the corn, we rolled and wallowed like dust-bathing mares, while you growled, and foam flecked your bloody lips, and you spat and slashed at the gloaming with your dripping blade. A voyeuristic retinue of grasshoppers and field mice, crickets and a lone bullsnake took in our flailing, certainly comedic antics while I held you prisoner in my arms, holding you hostage against my shameful fear and self doubt. Finally, inevitably, your laughter died, and I only held you while you sobbed and Iowa sod turned to streaks of mud upon your mirthless face.

4.

I DRIVE WEST, then east again, then turn south onto I-55, Missouri, the County of Cape Girardeau. Meandering like the cottonmouth, silt-choked Mississippi, out across fertile floodplain fields all night-blanketed, semisweet darkness to hide river-gifted loam. You're asleep in the backseat, your breath soft as velvet, soft as autumn rain. You never sleep more than an hour at a time, not ever, and so I never wake you. Not ever. Not even when you cry out from the secret nightmare countries behind your eyelids. We are moving along between the monotonous, barbarous topography and the overcast sky, overcast at sunset the sky looked dead, and now, well past midnight, there is still no sign of moon nor stars to guide me, and I have only the road signs and the tattered atlas lying open beside me as I weave and wend through the Indian ghosts of Ozark Bluff Dwellers, stalkers of shambling mastodon and mammoth phantoms along these crude asphalt corridors. I light cigarette after cigarette and wash Black Beauties down with peach Nehi. I do not often know loneliness, but I know it now, and I wish I were with you in your hard, hard dreams. The radio's tuned to a gospel station out of Memphis, but the volume is down low, low, low so you'll not be awakened by the Five Blind Boys of Alabama or the Dixie Hummingbirds. In your sleep, you're muttering, and I try not to eavesdrop. But voices carry, as they say, and I hear enough to get the gist. You sleep a walking sleep, and in dreams, you've drifted back to Wichita, to that tow-headed boy with fish and starfish, an octopus and sea shells tattooed all up and down his arms, across his broad chest and shoulders. "Because I've never seen the ocean," he said. "But that's where I'm headed now. I'm going all the way to Florida. To Panama City or Pensacola." "We've never seen the sea, either," you tell him. "Can we go with you? We've really nowhere else to go, and you really have no notion how delightful it will be when they take us up and throw us with the lobsters out to sea." The boy laughed. No, not a boy, not in truth, but a young man older than us, a scruffy beard growing unevenly on his suntanned cheeks.

"Can we? Can we, please?" Hey, you're the two with the car, not me, he replied, so I suppose you're free to go anywhere you desire. And that is the gods' honest truth of it all, ain't it? We are free to drive anywhere we please, so long as we do not attempt to part this material plane of simply three dimensions. Alone in the night, in the now and not the then, I have to be careful. It would be too easy to slip into my own dreams, amphetamine insomnia helping hands or no, and I have so often imagined our Odyssey ending with the Impala wrapped around telephone pole or lying wheels-up turtlewise and steaming in a ditch or head-on folded back upon ourselves after making love to an oncoming semi. I shake my head and open my eyes wider. There's a rest stop not too far up ahead, and I tell myself that I'll pull over there. I'll pull over to doze for a while in sodium-arc pools, until the sun rises bright and violent to burn away the clouds, until it's too hot to sleep. The boy's name was Philip – one L. The young man who was no longer a boy and who had been decorated with the cryptic nautical language of an ocean he'd never seen, and, as it came to pass, never would. But you'd keep all his teeth in a Mason jar, just in case we ever got around to the Gulf of Mexico or an Atlantic shoreline. You kept his teeth, promising him a burial in saltwater. Philip told us about visiting a museum at the university in Lawrence, where he saw the petrified skeletons of giant sea monsters that once had swum the vanished inland depths. He was only a child, ten or eleven, but he memorized names that, to my ears, sounded magical, forbidden, perilous Latin incantations to call down fish from the clear blue sky or summon bones burrowing upwards from yellow-gray chalky rocks. You sat with your arms draped shameless about his neck while he recited and elaborated – *Tylosaurus proriger, Dolichorhynchops bonneri, Platecarpus tympaniticus, Elasmosaurus platyurus, Selmasaurus kiernanii,* birds with teeth and giant turtles, flying reptiles and the fangs of ancient sharks undulled by eighty-five million years, give or take. Show off, you said and laughed. That's what you are, a show off. And you said, Why aren't you in college, bright boy? And Philip with one L said his parents couldn't afford tuition, and his grades had not been good enough for a scholarship, and he wasn't gonna join the army, because he had a cousin went off to Desert Storm, right, and did his duty in Iraq, and now he's afraid to leave the house and sick all the time and constantly checks his shoes for scorpions and landmines. The military denies all responsibility. Maybe, said Philip with one L, I can get a job on a fishing boat, or a shrimping boat, and spend all my days on the water and all my nights drinking rum with mermaids. We could almost have fallen in love with him. Almost. You even whispered to me about driving him to Florida that he might lay eyes upon the Gulf of Mexico before he died. But I am a jealous bitch, and I said no, fuck that sentimental horseshit, and he died the next day in a landfill not far from Emporia. I did that one, cut his throat from ear to ear while he was busy screwing you. He looked up at me, his stark blue irises drowning in surprise and confusion, and then he came one last time, coaxed to orgasm, pumping blood from severed carotid and jugular and, too, pumping out an oyster stream of jizz. It seemed all but immaculate, the red and the silver gray, and you rode him even after there was no more of him left to ride but a cooling cadaver. You cried over Philip, and that was the first and only one you ever shed tears for, and Jesus I am sorry but I wanted to slap you. I wanted to do something worse than slap you for your mourning. I wanted to leave a scar. Instead, I gouged out his lifeless eyes with my thumbs and spat in his face. You wiped your nose on your shirt sleeve, pulled up your underwear and jeans, and went back to the car for the needle-nose pair of pliers in the glove compartment. It did not have to be that way, you said, you pouted, and I growled at you to shut up, and whatever it is you're doing in his mouth, hurry because this place gives me the creeps. Those slumping, smoldering hills of refuse, Gehenna for rats and maggots and crows, coyotes, stray dogs and strayer cats. We *could* have taken him to the sea, you said. We *could* have done that much, and then you fell silent, sulking, taciturn, and not ever again waking have you spoken of him. Besides the teeth, you peeled off a patch of skin, big as the palm of your hand and inked with the image of a crab, because we were born in the sign of Cancer. The rest of him we concealed under heaps of garbage. *Here you go, rats, here's something fresh. Here's a banquet, and we shall not even demand tribute in return. We will be benevolent rat gods, will we two, bringing plenty and then taking our leave, and you will spin prophecies of our return. Amen. Amen. Hossannah.* Our work done, I followed you back to the Impala, stepping superstitiously in your footsteps, and that is what I am doing when – now – I snap awake to the dull, gritty noise of the tires bumping off the shoulder and spraying dry showers of breakdown-lane gravel, and me half awake and cursing myself for nodding off; fuck me, fuck me, I'm such an idiot, how I should have stopped way the hell back in Bonne Terre or Fredericktown. I cut the wheel left, and, just like that, all is right again. Doomsday set aside for now. In the backseat, you don't even stir. I turn up the radio for companionship. If I had toothpicks, I might prop open my eyes. My hands are red, love. Oh god, my hands are so red, and we have not ever looked upon the sea.

5.

BOREDOM, YOU HAVE said again and again, is the one demon might do you in, and the greatest of all our foes, the *one* demon, Mystery Babylon, the Great Harlot, who at the Valley of Josaphat, on the hill of Megiddo, wraps chains about our porcelain slender necks and drags us down to dust and comeuppance if we dare to turn our backs upon the motherfucker and give it free fucking reign. I might allow how this is the mantra that set us to traveling on the road we are on and has dictated our every action since that departure, your morbid fear of boredom. The consequence of this mantra has almost torn you in half, so that I bend low over my love, only my bare hands to keep your insides from spilling outside. Don't you shut your eyes. You don't get out half that easy. Simple boredom is as good as the flapping wings of butterflies to stir the birth throes of hurricanes. Tiresome recitations of childhood traumas and psychoses be damned. As are we; as are we.

6.

WE FOUND HER, or she was the one found us, another state, another county, the outskirts of another slumbering city. Another truck-stop diner. Because we were determined to become connoisseurs of everything that is fried and smothered in lumpy brown gravy, and you were sipping a flat Coke dissolute with melting ice. You were talking – I don't know why – about the night back home when the Piggly Wiggly caught fire, so we climbed onto the roof and watched it go up. The air smelled like burning groceries.

We contemplated cans of Del Monte string beans and pears and cans of Grapico reaching the boiling point and going off like grenades, and the smoke rose up and blotted out the moon, which that night was full. You're talking about the fire, and suddenly she's there, the coal-haired girl named Haddie in her too-large Lollapalooza T-shirt and black jeans and work boots. Her eyes are chipped jade and honey, that variegated hazel, and she smiles so disarming a smile and asks if, perhaps, we're heading east towards Birmingham, because she's trying to get to Birmingham, but – insert here a woeful tale of her douchebag boyfriend – and now she's stranded high and dry, not enough money for bus fare, and if we're headed that way, could she please, and would we please? You scoot over and pat the turquoise sparkle vinyl upholstery, inviting her to take a Naugahyde seat, said the spider to the fly. "Thank you," she says. "Thank you very much," and she sits and you share your link sausage and waffles with her, because she says she hasn't any money for food, either. We're heading for Atlanta, you tell her, and we'll be going right straight through Birmingham, so sure, no problem, the more the goddamn merrier. We are lifesavers, she says. Never been called that before. You chat her up, sweet as cherry pie with whipped cream squirted from a can, and, me, I stare out the plate-glass partition at the gas pumps and the stark white lighting to hide the place where a Mississippi night should be. "Austin," she says, when you ask from whence she's come. "Austin, Texas," she volunteers. "I was born and raised there." Well, you can hear it, plain as tits on a sow, in her easy, drawling voice. I take in a mouthful of lukewarm Cheerwine, swallow, repeat, and do not let my attention drift from the window and an idling eighteen-wheeler parked out there with its cab all painted up like a Santería altar whore, gaudy and ominous and seductive. Smiling Madonna and cherubic child, merry skeletons dancing joyful round about a sorrowful, solemn Pietà, roses and carnations, crucifixions, half-pagan orichá and weeping bloody Catholic Jesus. Of a sudden, then, I feel a sick coldness spreading deep in my bowels, ice water heavy in my guts, and I want to tell this talkative Lone-Star transient that no, sorry, but you spoke too soon and, sorry, but we *can't* give her a ride, after all, not to Birmingham or anywhere else, that she'll have to bum one from another mark, which won't be hard, because the night is filled with travelers. I want to say just that. But I don't. Instead, I keep my mouth shut tight and watch as a man in dirty orange coveralls climbs into the cab of the truck, him and his goddamn enormous shaggy dog. That dog, it might almost pass for a midget grizzly. In the meanwhile, Ms. Austin is sitting there feeding you choice slivers of her life's story, and you devour it, because I've never yet seen you not hungry for a sobby tale. This one, she's got all the hallmarks of a banquet, doesn't she? Easy pickings, if I only trust experience and ignore this inexplicable wash of instinct. Then you, love, give me a gentle, unseen kick beneath the table, hardly more than an emphatic nudge, your right foot insistently tapping, tap, tap, at my left ankle in a private Morse. I fake an unconcerned smile and turn my face away from the window and that strange truck, though I can still hear its impatient engines. "A painter," says Ms. Austin. "See, I want to be a painter. I've got an aunt in Birmingham, and she knows my mom's a total cunt, and she doesn't mind if I stay with her while I try to get my shit together. It was supposed to be me and him both, but now it's just gonna be me. See, I shut my eyes, and I see murals, and that's what I want to paint one day. *Wallscapes*." And she talks about murals in Mexico City and Belfast and East Berlin. "I need to piss," I say, and you flash me a questioning glance that Ms. Austin does not appear to catch. I slide out of the turquoise booth and walk past other people eating other meals, past shelves grounded with motor oil, candy bars, and pornography. I'm lucky and there's no one else in the restroom, no one to hear me vomit. *What the fuck is this? Hunh? What the fuck is wrong with me now?* When the retching is done, I sit on the dirty tile floor and drown in sweat and listen to my heart throwing a tantrum in my chest. Get up and get back out there. And you, don't you even think of shutting your eyes again. The sun won't rise for another two hours, another two hours at least, and we made a promise one to the other. Or have you forgotten in the gauzy veils of hurt and Santísima Muerte come to whisper in your ear? Always have you said you were hers, a demimondaine to the Bony Lady, *la Huesuda*. So, faithless, I have to suffer your devotions as well? I also shoulder your debt? The restroom stinks of cleaning fluid, shit and urine, my puke, deodorant cakes and antibacterial soap, filth and excessive cleanliness rubbing shoulders. I don't recall getting to my feet. I don't recall a number of things, truth be told, but then we're paying the check, and then we're out in the muggy Lee

County night. You tow Ms. Austin behind you. She rides your wake, slipstreaming, and she seems to find every goddamn thing funny. You climb into the backseat with her, and the two of you giggle and titter over private jokes to which I have apparently not been invited. What all did I miss while I was on my knees, praying to my Toilet Gods? I put in a Patsy Cline tape, *punch* it into the deck as you would, and crank it up loud so I don't have to listen to the two of you, not knowing what you (not her, just *you*) have planned, feeling like an outsider in your company, and I cannot ever recall that having happened. Before long, the lights of Tupelo are growing small and dim in the rearview, a diminishing sun as the Impala glides southeast along US 78. My foot feels heavy as a millstone on the gas pedal. So, I have "A Poor Man's Roses" and "Back in Baby's Arms" and "Sweet Dreams" and a fresh pack of Camel's and you and Ms. Austin spooning at my back. And still that ice water in my bowels. She's talking about barbeque, and you laugh, and what the fuck is funny about barbeque. "Dreamland," she says, "just like what those UFO nuts call Area 51 in Nevada, where that dead Roswell alien and shit's supposed to be hidden." Me, I smoke and chew on bitter cherry-favored Tums tablets, grinding calcium carbonate and corn starch and talc between my teeth. "Those like you," says Ms. Austin, "who've lost their way," and I have no goddamn idea what she's going on about. We cross a bridge, and if it's a river below us, I do not see any indication that it's been given a name. But we're entering Itawamba County, says a sign, and that sounds like some mythological world serpent or someplace from a William Faulkner novel. Only about twenty miles now to the state line, and I'm thinking how I desire to be shed of the bitch, how I want her out of the car before Tuscaloosa, wondering how I can signal you without making Ms. Austin Texas Chatterbox suspicious. We pass a dozen exits to lonely country roads where we could take our time, do the job right, and at least I'd have something to show for my sour stomach. I'm thinking about the couple in Arkansas, how we made him watch while we took our own sweet time with her, and you telling him it wasn't so different from skinning catfish, not really. A sharp knife and a pair of pliers, that's all you really need, and he screamed and screamed and screamed. Hell, the pussy bastard sonofabitch screamed more than she did. In the end, I put a bullet in his brain just to shut him the fuck up, please.

And we'd taken so long with her, hours and hours, well, there wasn't time remaining to do him justice, anyway. After that we've made a point of avoiding couples. After that, it became a matter of policy. Also, I remember that girl we stuck in the trunk for a hundred miles, and how she was half dead of heat prostration by the time we got around to ring around the rosies, pockets full of posies time. And you sulked for days. Now, here, I watch you in the rearview, and if you notice that I am, you're purposefully ignoring me. I have to take a piss, I say, and she giggles. Fuck you, Catfish. Fuck you, because on this road you're traveling, is there hope for tomorrow? On this Glory Road you're traveling, to that land of perfect peace and endless fucking day, that's my twin sister you've got back there with you, my one and true and perfect love, and this train is bound for Glory, ain't nobody ride it, *Catfish*, but the righteous and the holy, and if this train don't turn around, well, I'm Alabama bound. You and me and she, only, we ain't going that far together. Here's why God and all his angels and the demons down under the sea made detours, *Catfish*. The headlights paint twin high-beam encouragement, luring me on down Appalachian Corridor X, and back there behind me you grumble something about how I'm never gonna find a place to piss here, not unless it's in the bushes. I'm about to cut the wheel again, because there's an unlit side road like the pitchy throat of evening wanting to swallow us whole, and right now, I'm all for that, but... Catfish, née Austin Girl, says that's enough, turn right around and get back on the goddamn highway. And whatever I'm supposed to say, however I'm about to tell her to go fuck herself, I don't. She's got a gun, you say. Jesus, Bobbie, she's got a gun, and you laugh a nervous, disbelieving laugh. You laugh a stunned laugh. She's got a goddamn gun. *What the fuck,* I whisper, and again she instructs me to retrace my steps back to 78. Her voice is cold now as the Artic currents in my belly. I look in the rearview, and I can't *see* a gun. I want to believe this is some goddamn idiot prank you and she have cooked up, pulling the wool for whatever reason known only to thee. What do you want? I ask, and she says we'll get to that, in the sweet by and by, so don't I go fretting my precious little head over what she wants, okay? Sure, sure. And five minutes later we're back on the highway, and you're starting to sound less surprised, surprise turning to fear, because this is not how the game is played. This is *not* the story. We don't have shit, I tell her. We ain't got any money, and we don't have shit, so if you think – and she interrupts, Well, you got this car, don't you? And that's more than me, so how about you just shut up and drive, Little Bird. That's what she calls me, *Little Bird.* So, someone's rewriting the fairy tale all around us; I know that now, and I realize that's the ice in the middle of me. How many warnings did we fail to heed? The Santería semi, that one for sure, as good as any caution sign planted at the side of any path. Once upon a time, pay attention, you and you who have assumed that no one's out there hunting wolves, or that all the lost girls and boys and men and women on the bum are defenseless lambs to the slaughter. Wrong. Wrong. Wrong, and it's too late now. But I push those thoughts down, and I try to focus on nothing but your face in the mirror, even though the sight of you scares the hell out of me. It's been a long time since I've seen you like that, and I thought I never would again. You want the car? I ask Catfish. Is that it? Because if you want the car, fuck it, it's yours. Just let me pull the fuck over, and I'll hand you the goddamn keys. But no, she says. No, I think you should keep right on driving for a while. As for pulling over, I'll say when. I'll say when, on that you can be sure.

7.

MAYBE, YOU SAY, *it wouldn't be such a bad idea to go home now,* and I nod, and I wipe the blood off your lips, the strawberry life leaking from you freely as ropy cheesecloth, muslin ectoplasm from the mouth, ears, nostrils of a 1912 spiritualist. I wipe it away, but I hold it, too, clasping it against the loss of you. So long as I can catch all the rain in my cupped hands, neither of us shall drown. You just watch me, okay? Keep your eyes on my eyes, and I'll pull you through. It looks a lot worse than it is, I lie. I know it hurts, but you'll be fine. All the blood makes it look terrible, I know, but you'll be fine. Don't you close your goddamn eyes. Oh, sister, don't you die. Don't speak. I cannot stand the rheumy sound of the blood in your throat, so please do not speak. But you say, *You can hear the bells, Bobbie, can't you? Fuck, but they are so red, and they are so loud, how could you not? Take me and cut me out in little stars....*

8.

So FAST, MY love, so swift and sure thy hands, and when Catfish leaned forward to press the muzzle of her 9mm to my head and tell me to shut up and drive, you drew your vorpel steel, and the razor folded open like a silver flower and snicker-snacked across coal-haired Haddie's throat. She opened up as if she'd come with a zipper. Later, we opened her wide and sunk her body in a marshy maze of swamp and creek beds and snapping-turtle weeds. Scum-green water, and her guts pulled out and replaced with stones. You wanted to know were there alligators this far north, handy-dandy helpful gator pals to make nothing more of her than alligator shit, and me, I said, hey this is goddamn Mississippi, there could be crocodiles and pythons for all I know. Afterwards, we bathed in the muddy slough, because cutting a bitch's throat is dirty goddamn business, and then we fucked in the high grass, then had to pluck off leeches from our legs and arms and that one ambitious pioneer clinging fiercely to your left nipple. *What about the car? The car's a bloody goddam mess?* And yeah, I agreed, what about the car? We took what we needed from the Impala, loaded our scavenged belongings into a couple of backpacks, knapsacks, a pillowcase, and then we shifted the car into neutral and pushed it into those nameless waters at the end of a nameless dirt road, and we hiked back to 78. You did so love that car, our sixteenth birthday present, but it is what it is and can't be helped, and no way we could have washed away the indelible stain left behind by treacherous Catfish's undoing. That was the first and only time we ever killed in self defense, and it made you so angry, because her death, you said, spoiled the purity of the game. What have we got, Bobbie, except *that* purity? And now it's tainted, sullied by one silly little thief – or what the hell ever she might have been. We have us, I reply. We will always have us, so stop your worrying. My words were, at best, cold comfort, I could tell, and that hurt more than just a little bit, but I kept it to myself, the pain, the hollow in the pit of my soul that had not been there only the half second before you started in on purity and being soiled by the thwarted shenanigans of Catfish. Are you alright? you asked me, as we marched up the off-ramp. I smiled and shook my head. Really, I'm thinking, let's not have that shoe's on the other foot thing ever again, love. Let's see if we can be more careful about who we let in the car that we no longer have. There was a moon three nights past full, like a judgmental god's eye to watch us on our way. We didn't hitch. We just fucking walked until dawn, and then stole a new car from a driveway outside of Tremont. You pulled the tag and stuck on our old Nebraska plates, amongst that which we'd salvaged from the blooded Impala. The new ride, a swank fucking brand-new '96 Saturn the color of Granny Smith apples, it had all-electric windows, but a CD player when all he had was our box of tapes, so fuck that; we'd have to rely on the radio. We hooked onto WVUA 90.7 FM outta Tuscaloosa, and the DJ played Soundgarden and Beck and lulled us forward on the two lane black-racer asphalt rails of that river, traveling dawnwise back to the earliest beginnings of the world, you said, watching the morning mist burning away, and you said, *When vegetation rioted on the earth, and the big trees were kings.* Read that somewhere? Yeah, you said, and shortly thereafter we took Exit 14, stopping just south of Hamilton, Alabama, because there was a Huddle House, and by then we were both starving all over again. There was also a Texaco station, and good thing, too, as the Saturn was sitting on empty, running on fumes. So, in the cramped white-tile fluorescent drenched restroom, we washed off the swamp water we'd employed to wash away the dead girl's blood. I used wads of paper towels to clean your face as best I could, after the way the raw-boned waitress with her calla-lily tattoo stared at you. I thought there for a moment maybe it was gonna be her turn to pay the ferryman, but you let it slide. There's another woman's scabs crusted in your hair, stubborn clots, and the powdery soap from the powdery soap dispenser on the wall above the sink isn't helping all that much. I need a drink, you say. I need a drink like you would not believe. Yeah, fine, I replied, remembering the half-full, half-empty bottle of Jack in the pillowcase, so just let me get this spot here at your hairline. You go back to talking about the *river,* as if I understand – often I never truly understood you, and for that did I love thee even more. The road which is the river, the river which is the road, mortality, infinity, the grinding maw of history; *An empty stream, a great goddamn silence, an impenetrable forever forest. That's what I'm saying,* you said. *In my eyes, in disposed, in disgrace.* And I said it's gonna be a scorcher today, and at least the Saturn has AC, not like the late beloved lamented Impala, and you spit out what the fuck ever. I fill the tank, and I mention how it's a shame Ms.

Austin Catfish didn't have a few dollars on her. We're damn near busted flat. Yeah, well, we'll fix that soon, you say. We'll fix that soon enough, my sweet. You're sitting on the hood, examining the gun she'd have used to lay us low. Make sure the safety is on, I say. And what I think in the split second before the pistol shot is *Please be careful with that thing, the shit our luck's been,* but I didn't say it *aloud.* An unspoken thought, then bang. No. Then BANG. You look nothing in blue blazes but surprised. You turn your face towards me, and the 9mm slips from your fingers and clatters to the oil- and anti-freeze-soaked tarmac. I see the black girl behind the register looking our way, and Jesus motherfucking-fucking-fuck-fuck-fucking-motherfucker-oh fuck me this *cannot* be goddamn happening, no way can *this* be happening, not after everything we've done and been through and how there's so much left to do and how I love you so. Suddenly, the air is nothing if not gasoline and sunlight. I can hardly clear my head, and I'm waiting for certain spontaneous combustion and the grand *whump* when the tanks blow, and they'll see the mushroom cloud for miles and miles around. My head fills with fire that isn't even there, but, still, flashblind, I somehow wrestle you into the backseat. Your eyes are muddy with shock, muddy with perfect incredulity. I press your left hand against the wet hole in that soft spot below your sternum, and you gasp in pain and squeeze my wrist so hard it hurts. *No, okay, you gotta let go now, I gotta get us the fuck outta here before the cops show up. Let go, but keep pressure on it, right? But we have to get out of here now.* Because, I do not add, that gunshot was louder than thunder, that gunshot cleaved the morning apart like the wrath of Gog and Magog striding free across the Armageddon land, Ezekiel 38:2, or wild archangel voices and the trumpet of Thessalonians 4:16. There's a scattered handful of seconds, and then I'm back on the highway again, not thinking, just driving south and east. I try not to hear your moans, 'cause how's that gonna help either of us, but I do catch the words when you whisper, *Are you alright, Bobbie? You flew away like a little bird,* and isn't that what Catfish called me? *So how about you just shut up and drive, Little Bird.* And in my head I do see a looped serpent made of fire devouring its own tail, and I know we cheated fate only for a few hours, only to meet up with it again a little farther down the road. I just drive. I don't even think to switch on the AC or roll down the window or even notice how the car's becoming as good as a kiln on four wheels. I just fucking *drive*. And, like agate beads strung along a rosary, I recite the prayer given me at the End of Days, the end of one of us: Don't you fucking shut your eyes. Please, don't you shut your eyes, because you do not want to go there, and I do not want to be alone forever and forever without the half of me that's you. In my hands, the steering wheel is busy swallowing its own tail, devouring round and round, and we, you and I, are only passengers.

SHADOW FLOCK
Greg Egan

Greg Egan (www.gregegan.net) published his first story in 1983, and followed it with twelve novels, six short story collections, and more than fifty short stories. During the early 1990s Egan published a body of short fiction – mostly hard science fiction focused on mathematical and quantum ontological themes – that established him as one of the most important writers working in the field. His work has won the Hugo, John W Campbell Memorial, Locus, Aurealis, Ditmar, and Seiun awards. His latest book is novel, *The Arrows of Time*, which concludes the *Orthogonal* trilogy.

1

NATALIE POINTED DOWN along the riverbank to a pair of sturdy-looking trees, a Bald Cypress and a Southern Live Oak, about fifty meters away. "They might be worth checking out." She set off through the scrub, her six students following.

When they reached the trees, Natalie had Céline run a structural check, using the hand-held ground-penetrating radar to map the roots and the surrounding soil. The trees bore gray cobwebs of Spanish moss, but most of it was on the higher branches, out of harm's way. Natalie had chosen the pair three months before, when she was planning the course; it was cheating, but the students wouldn't have thanked her if they'd ended up spending a whole humid, mosquito-ridden day hunting for suitable pillars. In a real disaster you'd take whatever delays and hardship fate served up, but nobody was interested in that much verisimilitude in a training exercise.

"Perfect," Céline declared, smiling slightly, probably guessing that the result was due to something more than just a shrewd judgment made from a distance.

Natalie asked Mike to send a drone with a surveying module across to the opposite bank. The quadrocopter required no supervision for such a simple task, but it was up to Mike to tell it which trees to target first, and the two best candidates – a pair of sturdy oaks – were impossible to miss. The way things were going they stood a good chance of being back in New Orleans before sunset.

With their four pillars chosen, it was time to settle on a construction strategy. They had three quads to work with, and more than enough cable, but the Tchefuncte River was about a hundred and thirty meters wide here. A single spool of cable held a hundred meters, and that was as much weight as each backpack-sized quad could carry.

Josh raised his notepad to seek software advice, but Natalie stopped him. "Would it kill you to spend five minutes thinking?"

"We're going to need to do some kind of mid-air splice," he said. "I just wanted to check what knots are available, and which would be strongest."

"Why splicing?" Natalie pressed him.

He raised his hands and held them a short distance apart. "Cable." Then he increased the separation. "River."

Augusto said, "What about loops?" He hooked two fingers together and strained against the join. "Wouldn't that be stronger?"

Josh snorted. "And halve the effective length? We'd need three spools to bridge the gap then, and you'd still need to splice the second loop to the third."

"Not if we pre-form the middle loop ourselves," Augusto replied. "Fuse the ends, here on the ground. That's got to be better than any mid-air splice. Or easier to check, and easier to fix."

Natalie looked around the group for objections. "Everyone agree? Then we need to make a flight plan."

They assembled the steps from a library of maneuvers, then prepared the cable for the first crossing. The heat was becoming enervating, and Natalie had to fight the urge to sit in the shade and bark orders. Down in Haiti she'd never cared about being comfortable, but it was harder to stay motivated when all that was at stake were a few kids' grades in one minor elective.

"I think we're ready," Céline declared, a little nervous, a little excited.

Natalie said, "Be my guest."

Céline tapped the screen of her notepad and the first quad whirred into life, rising up from the riverbank and tilting a little as it moved toward the cypress.

With cable dangling, the drone made three vertical loops around the tree's lowest branch, wrapping it in a short helix. Then it circumnavigated the trunk twice, once close-in, then a second time in a long ellipse that left cable hanging slackly from the branch. It circled back, dropped beneath the branch and flew straight through the loop. It repeated the maneuver then headed away, keeping the spool clamped until it had pulled the knot tight.

As the first drone moved out over the glistening water, the second one was already ahead of it, and the third was drawing close to the matching tree on the far side of the river. Natalie glanced at the students, gratified by the tension on their faces: success here was not a *fait accompli*. Céline's hand hovered above her notepad; if the drones struck an unforeseen problem – and failed to recover gracefully on their own – it would be her job to intervene manually.

When the second drone had traveled some forty meters from the riverbank it began ascending, unwinding cable as it went to leave a hanging streamer marking its trail. From this distance the shiny blue line of polymer was indistinguishable from the kind its companion was dispensing, but then the drone suddenly stopped climbing, clamped the spool, and accelerated downwards. The single blue line revealed its double-stranded nature, spreading out into a heart-shaped loop. The first drone shot through the heart then doubled back, hooking the two cables together, then the second one pulled out of its dive and continued across the river. The pierced heart always struck Natalie as surreal – the kind of thing that serenading cartoon birds would form with streamers for Snow White in the woods.

Harriet, usually the quietest of the group, uttered an involuntary, admiring expletive.

The third drone had finished hitching itself to the tree on the opposite bank, and was flying across the water for its own rendezvous. Natalie strained her eyes as the second drone went into reverse, again separating the paired cables so its companion could slip through and form the link.

Then the second drone released the loop completely and headed back to the riverbank, its job done. The third went off to mimic the first, tying its loose end to the tree where it had started.

They repeated the whole exercise three more times, giving the bridge two hand-ropes and two deck supports, before breaking for lunch. As Natalie was unwrapping the sandwiches she'd brought, a dark blur the size of her thumb buzzed past her face and alighted on her forearm. Instinctively, she moved to flick it off, but then she realized that it was not a living insect: it was a small Toshiba dragonfly, its four wings iridescent with photovoltaic coatings. Whether it was mapping the forest, monitoring wildlife, or just serving as a communications node, the last thing she'd want to do was damage it. The machine should not have landed on anything but vegetation, but no one's programming was perfect. She watched it as it sat motionless in the patch of sunlight falling on her skin, then it ascended suddenly and flew off out of sight.

In the afternoon, the team gave their bridge a rudimentary woven deck. Each of the students took turns donning a life-jacket and hard-hat before walking across the swaying structure and back, whooping with a mixture of elation at their accomplishment and adrenaline as they confronted its fragility.

"And now we have to take it apart," Natalie announced, prepared for the predictable groans and pleas. "No arguments!" she said firmly. "Pretty as it is, it would only take a party of five or six hikers to break it, and if they ended up dashing their brains out in the shallows that would be enough to bankrupt the university and send us all to prison."

2

As NATALIE STARTED up the stairs to her apartment she heard a distinctive trilling siren, then saw a red shimmer spilling down onto the landing ahead. The delivery quad came into view and she moved to the left to let it pass, catching a welcome cool wash from its downdraft – a sensation weirdly intensified by the lime-green tint of the receding hazard lights.

She tensed as she approached her floor, hoping that she wouldn't find Sam waiting for her. His one talent was smooth talking, and he could always find someone willing to buzz him into the building. Against her better judgment she'd let her brother wheedle her into sinking ten thousand dollars into his latest business venture, but when it had proved to be as unprofitable as all the rest, rather than apologizing and going in search of paid work he'd started begging her to invest even more, in order to "tip the balance" – as if his struggling restaurant were a half-submerged Spanish galleon full of gold that only needed a few more flotation bladders to rise magnificently to the surface.

Sam wasn't lurking in the corridor, but there was a small package in front of her door. Natalie was puzzled and annoyed; she wasn't expecting anything, and the drones were not supposed to leave their cargo uncollected on a doormat. She stooped down and picked up the parcel; it bore the logo of a local courier, but water had somehow got inside the plastic pocket that held the waybill, turning the portion with the sender's address into gray mush. A gentle shake yielded the clinking slosh of melting ice.

Inside, she put the parcel in the kitchen sink, went to the bathroom, then came back and cut open the mailing box to reveal an insulating foam container. The lid bore the words GUESS WHO? written in black marker. Natalie honestly couldn't; she'd parted company with the last two men she'd dated on terms that made surprise gifts unlikely, let alone a peace offering of chilled crab meat, or whatever this was.

She tugged the lid off and tipped the ice into the sink. A small pink object stood out from the slush, but it wasn't any part of a crab. Natalie stared for several seconds, unwilling to prod the thing into position for a better view, then she fetched a pair of tongs to facilitate a more thorough inspection.

It was the top part of a human finger. A little finger, severed at the joint. She walked away and paced the living room, trying to decode the meaning of the thing before she called the police. She could not believe that Alfonso – a moody musician who'd ditched her when she'd dared to leave one of his gigs at two in the morning, on a work night – would have the slightest interest in mutilating his own precious hands in the service of a psychotic prank. Digging back further she still came up blank. Rafael had smashed crockery once, in the heat of an argument, but by now she'd be surprised to elicit any stronger reaction from him than a rueful smile if they ran into each other on the street. The truth was, the prospect of the cops hauling any of these ex-lovers in for questioning mortified her almost as much as the macabre offering itself, because pointing the finger at any of them seemed preposterously self-aggrandizing. "Really?" she could hear the whole line-up of unlikely suspects demanding, holding out their pristine mitts. "You thought you were worth *that*?"

Natalie walked back to the kitchen doorway. Why was she assuming that the amputation had been voluntary? No one she knew would commit such an act – upon themselves or anyone else – but that didn't mean she didn't know the unwilling donor.

She turned around and rushed to the bedroom, where she kept the bioassay attachment for her notepad. The only software she'd downloaded for it was for personal health and pregnancy testing, but it took less than a minute to get the app she needed.

There was no visible blood left inside the fingertip, but when she picked it up with the tongs it was full of meltwater that ought to be brimming with sloughed cells. She tipped a little of the water onto the assay chip and waited ten long minutes for the software to announce a result for the markers she'd chosen.

Chance of fraternity: 95%

Sam must have gone elsewhere for money, but it would have disappeared into the same bottomless pit as her own investment. And when his creditors had come for him with their bolt-cutters, who else was he going to rope in to help him repay his debt but his sister?

Natalie wanted to scream with anger, but she found herself weeping. Her brother was an infuriating, immature, self-deluding brat, but he didn't deserve this. If she had to re-mortgage the apartment to get him out of these people's clutches, so be it. She wasn't going to abandon him.

As she began trying to think through the logistics of dealing with the bank as quickly as possible – without explaining the true purpose of the loan – her phone rang.

3

"WE DON'T WANT your money. But there is a way you can resolve this situation without paying a cent."

Natalie stared at the kidnapper, who'd asked her to call him Lewis. The food court to which he'd invited her was as busy as she'd seen it on a Wednesday night; she had even spotted a few cops. The undeniable fact of their meeting proved nothing incriminating, but how could he know she wasn't recording his words?

She said, "You're not a loan shark."

"No." Lewis had an accent from far out of state, maybe the Midwest. He was a dark-haired, clean-shaven white man, and he looked about forty. Natalie tried to commit these facts to memory, terrified that when the police finally questioned her she'd be unable to recall his face at all. "We'd like you to consult for us."

"Consult?" Natalie managed a derisive laugh. "Who do you think I work for, the NSA? Everything I know about drones is already in the public domain. You didn't need to kidnap my brother. It's all on the web."

"There are time pressures," Lewis explained. "Our own people are quick studies, but they've hit a roadblock. They've read your work, of course. That's why they chose you."

"And what am I supposed to help you do? Assassinate someone?" The whole conversation was surreal, but the hubbub of their boisterous fellow diners was so loud that unless she'd stood up on the table and shouted the question, no one would have looked at them twice.

Lewis shook his head; at least he didn't insult her intelligence by feigning offense. "No one will get hurt. We just need to steal some information."

"Then find yourself a hacker."

"The targets are smarter than that."

"*Targets*, plural?"

Lewis said, "Only three that will concern you directly – though in all fairness I should warn you that your efforts will need to synchronize with our own on several other fronts."

Natalie felt light-headed; when exactly had she signed the contract in blood? "You're taking a lot for granted."

"Am I?" There wasn't a trace of menace in his voice, but then, the stakes had already been made clear.

"I'm not refusing," she replied. "I won't help you to inflict bodily harm – but if you're open with me and I'm sure that there's no chance of that, I'll do what you ask."

Lewis nodded, amiable in a businesslike way. He, or his associates, had been cold-blooded enough to mutilate Sam as proof of their seriousness, but if they planned to kill her once she'd served her purpose, why meet physically, in a public space, where a dozen surveillance drones would be capturing the event?

"The targets are all bitionaires," he said. "We don't plan to touch a hair on their heads; we just want their key-strings... which are not stored on anything vulnerable to spyware."

"I see." Natalie's own stash of electronic pocket change didn't merit any great precautions, but she was aware of the general idea: anyone prudent, and sufficiently wealthy, kept the cryptographic key to their anonymized digital fortune in a purpose-built wallet. The operating system and other software resided solely on read-only media, and even the working memory functioned under rigid, hardware-enforced protocols that made the whole setup effectively incorruptible. "So how can I get around that? Am I meant to infiltrate the wallet factory?"

"No." Lewis paused, but he wasn't turning coy on her – merely hiding a faint belch behind a politely raised hand. "The basic scenario is the kind of thing any competent stage magician could pull off. The target takes their wallet from its safe, then gets distracted. We substitute an identical-looking device. The target commences to log in to their exchange with the fake wallet; we've already cloned their fingerprints so we can mimic those preliminaries on the real wallet. The target receives a one-time password from the exchange on their cell phone; they enter it into the fake wallet, and we use it to enact our own preferred transactions via the real one."

Natalie opened her mouth to protest: her understanding was that the message from the exchange would also include a hash of the transaction details – allowing the user to double-check exactly what it was they were authorizing. But she wasn't thinking straight: to the human looking at that string of gibberish, the information would be invisible. Only *the wallet itself* had the keys required to reveal the hash's true implications, and the fake wallet would blithely pretend that everything matched up perfectly.

She said, "So all you need to do is invite these people to bring their wall safes to a Las Vegas show."

Lewis ignored her sarcasm. "The transactions can't be rescinded, but it won't take the targets long to discover that they've been duped – and to spread the word. So we need to ensure that these individual operations are as close to concurrent as possible."

Natalie struggled to maintain a tone of disapproval even as her curiosity got the better of her. "How do you make all these people get an itch to buy or sell at the same time?"

"We've already set that in motion," Lewis replied. "You don't need to know the details, but in seven days and thirteen hours, unless the targets are comatose they won't be able to ignore the top story on their news feeds."

Natalie leaned back from the table. Half her experience, and all of her best ideas, had involved maneuvers on a scale of tens of meters by devices that were far from small or stealthy. Dextrous as a well-equipped quadrocopter could be, sleight-of-hand was a bit much to ask of it.

"So do you want me to program robot storks to carry the fake wallets down chimneys?"

Lewis said, "The fake wallets have all been in place for a while, concealed inside innocuous-looking items."

"Like what?"

"Cereal packets. Once people find the brand they like, they stick to it."

"I knew there was a reason I didn't use my supermarket's loyalty card. And the drones?"

"They're on site as well."

"The wallets are how big?"

Lewis held his fingers a few centimeters apart. "Like credit cards. And not much thicker."

"So... how many dragonflies?"

"Six at each site. But they're not dragonflies: they're custom-built, smaller and quieter. From a distance they'd pass for houseflies."

Natalie crushed the urge to start grilling him on detailed specifications. "So you have a plan. And you've got the tools in place. Why do you need me at all?"

"Our plan relied on realtime operators," Lewis confessed. "The whole thing seemed too complex to deal with any other way – too many variables, too much uncertainty. All the sites have countermeasures against radio frequency traffic, but we believed we could communicate optically; some people don't consider that at all, or don't make the effort to lock things down tightly."

"But... ?"

"In three cases, it looks as if our optical routes have gone from mostly open to patchy at best. Not from any deliberate blocking strategies – just minor changes in the architecture, or people's routines. But it means that a continuous link would be too much to hope for."

Lewis's team had been given the right advice from the start: this was a job for humans. And now she was expected to program eighteen drones to perform three elaborate feats of prestidigitation, using nothing but their own tiny brains?

Natalie said, "Before we go any further, I want you to prove to me that my brother's still alive."

4

"I RAN INTO your fifth grade teacher last week," Natalie remarked, once the pleasantries were over. "The one you had a crush on."

Sam responded with a baffled scowl, too quickly to have needed to think through his reaction. "I don't even remember her name. I certainly didn't have a crush on her!"

However much intelligence the kidnappers might have gathered on the two of them – all the family pets and vacations they'd shared, all the confidences they might have exchanged – there was no proving a negative. Natalie was sure she wasn't watching a puppet.

Someone else was holding the phone, giving the camera a wider view than usual. Apart from his splinted and bandaged finger Sam appeared to be physically unharmed. Natalie refrained from upbraiding him; *she* was the reason he'd been abducted, even if some idiotic plan to keep the restaurant afloat had made him easier to trap.

"Just take it easy," she said. "I'm going to give these people what they want, and you'll be out of there in no time." She glanced at Lewis, then added, "I'll talk to you every morning, OK? That's the deal. They'll have to keep you safe, or I'll pull the plug."

"Do you think you can check in on the restaurant for me?" Sam pleaded. "Just to be sure that the chef's not slacking off?"

"No, I really can't."

"But Dmitri's so lazy! If I'm not –"

Natalie handed the phone back to Lewis and he broke the connection. They'd gone into a side-street to make the call; apparently Lewis hadn't trusted Sam not to start yelling for help if he saw other people in the background.

"I get to call him every day," she said. "That's not negotiable."

"By Skype," Lewis replied.

"All right." A Skype connection would be much harder to trace than a cell phone. Natalie was beginning to feel nostalgic for her previous nightmare scenario of loan sharks and intransigent banks. "What if I do my best, but I can't pull this off?" she asked.

"We're sure you can," Lewis replied.

His faith in her was not at all reassuring. "There's a reason your experts told you they'd need human pilots. I swear I'll try to make this work – but you can't murder my brother because I fall at the same hurdle as your own people."

Lewis didn't reply. On one level, Natalie understood the psychology behind his strategy: if he'd promised that she'd be rewarded merely for trying, she might have been tempted to hold herself back. She suspected that she'd be unlikely to face criminal charges, regardless, but sheer stubbornness or resentment might have driven her to indulge in some passive sabotage if she thought she could get away with it.

"What now?" she asked.

"By the time you get home, we'll have emailed you briefing files. We'll need the software for the drones by midnight on Monday."

Natalie was so flustered that she had to count out the interval in her head. "Five days! I thought you said seven!"

"We'll need to verify the new software for ourselves, then install it via infrasound. The bandwidth for that is so low that it could take up to forty-eight hours."

Natalie was silent, but she couldn't keep the dismay from showing on her face.

"You might want to call in sick," Lewis suggested.

"That's it? That's the best advice you have for me?"

"Read the briefing." Lewis paused, then nodded slightly. He turned and walked away.

Natalie felt herself swaying. If she went to the police, Sam would be dead in an instant. Lewis couldn't deny meeting her, but he would have prepared a well-documented explanation in advance – maybe log files showing that they'd been matched up by a dating site. The emailed briefing could have come from anywhere. She had nothing on these people that would make them pause for a second before they graduated from fingertips to heads.

Three targets for her special attention, and many more in the whole blitz. The total haul might reach ten or eleven figures. She'd walked willingly into the aftermaths of hurricanes and earthquakes, but she'd never been foolish enough to position herself – in any capacity – on the route between a gang of thugs and a pile of cash.

5

NATALIE SPENT FIVE hours going through the files before she forced herself to stop. She climbed into bed and lay staring into the humid darkness, soaking the sheets in acrid sweat.

There was no information missing that she could have reasonably demanded. She had architectural plans for the victims' entire houses, complete down to the dimensions of every hinge of every closet. She had three-dimensional imagery and gait data for every member of each of the households; she had schedules that covered both their formal appointments and their imperfectly predictable habits, from meal times to bowel movements. Every motion sensor of every security system, every insect-zapping laser, every moth-chasing cat had been catalogued. Navigating the drones between these hazards was not a hopeless prospect – but the pitfalls that made the whole scheme unravel would be the ones nobody had anticipated. It had taken her years to render her bridge-building algorithms robust against wind, rain and wildlife, and she had still seen them fail when grime and humidity had made a motor stall or a cable stick unexpectedly.

She dozed off for fifteen minutes, then woke around dawn. Somehow she managed to fall asleep again, motivated by the certainty that she'd be useless without at least a couple of hours' rest. At a quarter to nine she rose, phoned the engineering department claiming flu, then took a cold shower and made toast and coffee.

The call to Sam took a minute to connect, but then it was obvious from his appearance that his captors had had to rouse him.

"The job they've given me isn't too hard," she said. "I'll get through it, then everyone can walk away happy."

Sam replied with a tone of wary optimism, "And the ten grand they gave me for the restaurant? They don't want it back?"

"Not as far as I know." Natalie wracked her brain for another puppet test, but then she decided that she'd already heard proof enough: no one else on the planet could make it sound as if ten thousand dollars sunk into that grease-pit would more than compensate for any minor inconvenience the two of them might suffer along the way.

"I owe you, Nat," Sam declared. He thought she was simply working off his debt – the way he'd mowed lawns as a kid, to pay for a neighbor's window that one of his friends had broken. He'd taken the rap to spare the boy a thrashing from his drunken father.

"How's your hand?" she asked.

He held it up; the bandage looked clean. "They're giving me pain-killers and antibiotics. The food's pretty good, and they let me watch TV." He spread his hands in a gesture of contentment.

"So, three stars on Travel Adviser?"

Sam smiled. "I'd better let you get back to work."

Natalie started with the easiest target. A man who lived alone, rarely visited by friends or lovers, he was expected to wake around seven o'clock on D-day morning and go jogging for an hour before breakfast. That would be the ideal time for the drones to break out of their hiding places in the spines of the first editions of Kasparov's five-volume *My Great Predecessors*, which presumably had appeared at a seductively low price in the window of a local used book store. The fake wallet was concealed in one of the book's covers, along with the sliver of whorled and ridged biomimetic polymer that would need to be applied to the real wallet. Thankfully, Natalie's own predecessors had already done the work of programming the clog dance of drone against touch-screen that could mimic a human tapping out any sequence of characters on a virtual keyboard. The jobs they'd left for the pilots had been of an entirely different character.

The shelves in target A's library were all spaced to allow for much taller books, leaving plenty of room for a pair of drones to slice into the wallet's compartment, grab the hooks attached to the cargo, draw it out and fly six meters to deposit it temporarily in a poorly illuminated gap between a shelving unit and a table leg. The safe itself was in the library, and prior surveillance had shown that it was A's habit to place his wallet on the table in question.

The distraction was to be a faucet in the kitchen, primed to fail and send water flooding into the sink at full pressure. The house was fitted with detectors for any ongoing radio traffic – the bugs that had collected the latest imagery had used multi-path optics, until a new sunshade had been fitted to a crucial window – but a single brief RF pulse from a drone to trigger the torrent would appear to the detectors' software as no different from the sparking when a power plug was pulled from a socket.

What if target A broke his routine and did not go jogging? The emergence of the drones and the fake wallet's extraction would not be noisy, so those stages could still proceed so long as the library itself was unoccupied. What if target A had an early visitor, or someone had spent the night? The drones would need to start listening for clues to the day's activities well before seven. Loaded with neural-net templates that would allow them to recognize voices in general, doors opening and closing and footsteps receding and approaching, they ought to be able to determine whether or not it was safe to break out.

But the surveillance images that showed the five books neatly shelved were three weeks old; it was possible that they'd ended up strewn around the house, or piled on a table beneath other books and magazines. GPS wouldn't work inside the building, but Natalie used a smattering of WiFi signal strengths collected in the past to equip the drones with a passable ability to determine their location, then added software to analyze the echo of an infrasound pulse, to help them anticipate any obstacles well before they'd broken out of their cardboard chrysalises.

The doors and windows – and even the roof space – were fitted with alarms, but target A had no motion sensors in the library that would scream blue murder every time a housefly crossed the room. Not even two houseflies carrying an object resembling a credit card.

Natalie put the pieces together then ran simulations, testing the software against hundreds of millions of permutations of all the contingencies she could think of: the placement of the books, which doors were open or closed, new developments in the target's love life, and his peregrinations through every plausible sequence of rooms and corridors. When things turned out badly from the simulator's God's-eye-view, she pored over the visual and auditory cues accessible to the drones in a selection of the failed cases, and refined her software to take account of what she'd missed.

By midnight she was exhausted, but she had the mission either succeeding completely or aborting undetected in 98.7% of the simulations. That would have to be good enough. The other targets were going to be more difficult; she needed to move on.

6

WITH EVERY DAY that passed Natalie worked longer, but her short bouts of sleep came fast and ran deep, as if her brain had started concentrating some endogenous narcotic brew and would dispense the thick black distillate the moment she closed her eyes.

In the early hours of Monday morning, she dreamed that she was taking her final exam in machine vision. Sam was seated three rows behind her, throwing wads of chewing gum that stuck in her hair, but she knew that if she turned around to whisper an angry reprimand he'd only ignore it, and it wasn't worth the risk of being accused of cheating.

She glanced up at the clock to check the time; just seconds remained, but she felt satisfied with her answers. But when she looked down at the exam paper she realized that she'd misread the questions and filled the booklet with useless *non sequiturs*.

She woke and marched to the shower to clear her head, trying to convince herself that she hadn't merely dreamed all the progress she'd made. But the truth was, target C was almost done. The ordeal was nearly over.

It was still early, but Sam had grown used to her schedule. Natalie confined herself to jokes and small talk; the more matter-of-fact they kept the conversations, the easier it was on both of them. Until he was actually free, she couldn't afford to let her emotions take over.

Target C had a husband and two school-age children, but if their domestic routine followed its usual pattern they would be out of the house well before the trigger – expected at eleven a.m. in C's east-coast time zone. The most worrying thing about C was not her family, but the way she kept changing the decorative skins she'd bought for her wallet: the surveillance, going back twelve months, revealed no fewer than four different designs. Natalie could accept that anyone might have their personal esthetic whims, even when it came to this most utilitarian of items. But it was hard to believe that it had never once crossed target C's mind that these unpredictable embellishments would make it so much harder for her to mistake another wallet for her own.

Still, the last surveillance imagery was only ten days old, and it showed a skin that was no different from that on the planted fake. The odds weren't bad that it would remain in place, and the changes in style on the previous occasions had been so clear that the drones would have no difficulty noticing if the fake had gone out of fashion. Lewis's people had not been foolhardy enough to try to wrap their substitute in some kind of infinitely reconfigurable chameleon device; visually, these ten-dollar skins were not unforgeable works of art, but they did come with different textures – slick, metallic, silky. Half-fooling a willing participant in a VR game with a haptic interface was one thing, but no hardware on the planet could morph from brushed steel to lamb's fleece well enough to convince someone who'd held the real thing just seconds before.

Natalie started the simulations running. Target C had a strong aversion to insects, and every room was fitted with an eliminator, but even these low-powered pinprick lasers could not be unleashed in a human-occupied space without rigorous certification that ensured their compliance with published standards. Insects followed characteristic, species-specific flight patterns, and the eliminators were required to give any ambiguous object the benefit of the doubt, lest some poor child flicking an apple seed off her plate or brushing glitter from her home-made fairy wand summon unfriendly fire from the ceiling. The drones didn't need to imitate any particular, benign airborne debris; they merely had to exhibit an acceleration profile a few standard deviations away from anything seen in the official laboratory studies of *Musca*, *Culex* or *Aedes*. Unlike target B's cat, the necessary strictures were completely predictable.

With the count of trials rising into seven digits and still no atonal squawk of failure, Natalie let herself relax a little and close her eyes. The midnight deadline was still fourteen hours away. She'd sent versions of her work for the other two targets to her 'Team Leader' – as the collaboration software would have it – and received no complaints. Let these clowns run off to the Bahamas with their billions, and let the victims learn to use banks like normal people. She'd done the only honorable thing under the circumstances, and she had nothing to be ashamed of. Whatever the authorities decided, she could still look herself – and any juror – in the eye.

She opened her eyes. Why, exactly, did she believe that Lewis's people would let her live to confess her crimes? Because she'd been a good girl and done as she was told?

Lewis had met her in a public place, making her feel safer about the encounter and seeming to offer a degree of insurance: if she vanished, or turned up dead, the authorities would scour the surveillance records and reconstruct her movements. A judge was much less likely to sign a warrant for the same trawling expedition if a living, breathing woman and her mildly mutilated brother went to the police with an attention-seeking story that positioned them in starring roles in the heist – and in any case, a shared meal proved nothing about her dinner companion.

But all of that presupposed that there really were records of the meeting: that the flock of benign surveillance drones that watched over downtown New Orleans had been as vigilant as ever that night – even in the places her adversaries had chosen to send her. Who was to say that they hadn't infiltrated the flock: corrupted the software in existing drones, or found a way to substitute their own impostors?

If there was nothing at all to tie Lewis to her – save the microscopic chance that some diner in the food court that night would remember the two of them – why would the thieves leave any loose ends?

Natalie tried to keep her face locked in the same expression of exhaustion and grim resolve that she'd felt being etched into it over the last five days;

the whole apartment was probably full of the same kind of micro-cameras that had documented the targets' lives in such detail. And for all she knew there could be hidden drones too, far more dangerous than anything the targets were facing: robot wasps with fatal stings. A week ago that would have sounded like florid paranoia, but now it was the most reasonable thing she could imagine, and the only thoughts that seemed truly delusional were those of walking away from this unscathed.

She went to the kitchen and made fresh coffee, standing by the pot with her eyes half-closed. Apart from any cameras on the walls, her computer was sure to be infested with spyware. They would have done the same to the one in her office at UNO – and in any case, she doubted that her criminal overseers would be happy if she suddenly decided to show up at work.

When the coffee was ready she stirred in three spoonfuls of sugar; before the crisis she'd gone without, but now she'd been escalating the dose day by day in the hope of shoring up her flagging powers of concentration. She carried the mug back toward her desk, squinting wearily at the screen as she approached, hoping that she wasn't over-playing her frazzled sleep-walker's demeanor.

She tripped and staggered, spilling the sticky, scalding brew straight down the air vent at the top of her workstation. The fans within blew out a geyser of mud-colored liquid for a second or two, with specks reaching as high as the ceiling, then the whole machine shut down, plunging the room into silence.

Natalie spent half a minute swearing and sobbing, then she picked up her phone. She made five calls to local outlets that might – just conceivably – have supplied a replacement, but none of them had a suitably powerful model in stock, and the ones they could offer her would have slowed the simulations to a crawl. She pushed the last salesperson hard, for effect, but not even a premium delivery charge could summon what she needed by drone from the Atlanta warehouse in time.

Finally, as if in desperation, she gritted her teeth and availed herself of the only remaining solution.

"I'd like to rent a cubicle for twelve hours."

"Any secretarial services?" the booking bot asked.

"No."

"Any IT requirements?"

"You bet." She reeled them off, but the bot was unfazed. The firm she'd chosen was accustomed to catering for architects and engineers, caught out with some processor-intensive emergency that was too commercially sensitive to be run in the cloud, or simply too awkward to refactor for a change of platform. It was the most logical place for her to go, given that the university was out of bounds – but it would have taken extraordinary prescience for Lewis's gang to have pre-bugged the place.

Natalie caught a bus into the city. A fly with an odd bluish tint to its body crawled over the windowpane beside her; she watched it for a while, then reached out and squashed it with the side of her fist and inspected its soft remains.

At the office complex, the demands of security and climate control had her pass through half a dozen close-fitting doors. Between these welcome barriers she ran fingers through her hair, brushed her arms and legs, and flattened her back against the nearest wall. The security guards watching on closed circuit could think what they liked, so long as she didn't look quite crazy enough to be thrown out.

On the eleventh floor, she entered the tiny cubicle assigned to her, closed the door and started loading the most recent hourly backup of her project from the flash drive she'd brought. This version wasn't quite the one that had been doing so well in the simulations, but she remembered exactly what changes she'd need to make to bring it up to that level.

The gang's roboticists would run tests of their own, but if she held off delivering the software until just before midnight they would be under enormous pressure. In a finite time there was only so much checking her fellow humans could do, and not a lot of point in them trying to wade manually through every line of code and every neural-net template included in the package. Like her, in the end they would be forced to put their trust in the simulations.

As instructed, Natalie had programmed her drones to wake and commence their mission, not at any pre-determined time, but on receipt of an external infrasound cue. It made sense to allow that much flexibility, in case the lurch in the markets that was meant to prompt people to reach for their wallets came later than expected.

One side effect of this decision was that for targets whose schedules were different for every day of the week, simulations had to be run separately for each day. But where there was no difference except for weekdays versus weekends, the simulated drones were fed no finer distinction, and the millions of permutations to be tested could play out much faster by limiting them to this simple dichotomy.

Target C stuck to a single routine from Monday to Friday, so as far as the simulations for her were concerned, they were taking place only on a generic weekday. Anything in the software that relied on it being a specific day of the week wouldn't come into play, in the simulations.

In the real world, though, Thursday would still announce itself as Thursday in the drones' internal clocks. And that very fact would be enough to tell the drones' software that they were out of VR and moving through the land of flesh and blood.

Natalie couldn't be sure that D-day would arrive on schedule, but she had no choice but to trust the swindlers to accomplish their first, enabling feat exactly as they'd planned it all along.

7

"This should be our last call," Natalie told Sam.

"There are two ways I could take that," he joked.

"Take it the good way."

"So they're happy with your work?" Sam tried to make that sound like a joke, too, but he couldn't quite pull it off.

"I've had no complaints."

"I always knew you'd end up as a mob accountant."

"Ha!" She'd had a summer job once that included book-keeping for a small construction firm with a shady reputation, but every transaction that had crossed her desk had appeared entirely legitimate.

"Stay strong," she said. "I'll see you soon."

Sam just nodded and lowered his eyes. She cut the link.

Natalie waited five more minutes, for six o'clock sharp. If the market trigger was coming, Lewis's people would have recognized the early signs of its onset hours ago, but she'd had no idea what to look for, and she hadn't wanted to attract suspicion by trawling the financial news. It would be impossible to load an entirely new copy of the drones' software via infrasound in less than two days – but in less than an hour, an experienced team might be able to write and deliver a small patch that neutralized the effects of her sabotage.

There would be no moment of perfect safety. Natalie used the collaboration software to send a message: *Flaw in the code for target C. Need to discuss urgently.*

Twenty seconds later, her phone rang.

"What are you talking about?" Lewis demanded angrily.

"It hasn't started executing yet, has it?" Natalie did her best to sound businesslike: she was acknowledging her screw-up, but she was still the voice of authority when it came to these drones, and she was asking for the state of play in order to salvage the situation as rapidly as possible.

"Of course it's *executing!*" Lewis snapped.

Natalie couldn't hold back a smile of relief. The software would be impossible to patch now.

"Why did you think it wouldn't start?" Lewis was baffled. "We got the confirmation hum. The drones are wide awake and running what we loaded. What's this about?"

Natalie said, "If the drones in target C's house don't catch sight of me and my brother – fully ambulatory, with our usual gaits – alone in a room with that woman before eleven a.m., things are going to play out a little differently than they did in the simulations."

Lewis understood immediately. "You *stupid bitch* –"

"No," Natalie cut him off. "Stupid would have been trusting you."

"We'll kill you both," he said coldly. "We can live without the yield from one target."

"Can you live without the yield from all the targets who'll be warned off when this woman raises the alarm? When the drones fly up to her and drop the fake wallet right in front of her face?"

To his credit, Lewis only took a few seconds to give up on the idea of more threats and bravado. "Be on the street outside your building in five minutes." He cut off the call.

Natalie put the phone down. Her whole body was trembling. She went to the bathroom and splashed water on her face, then left her apartment and sprinted down the stairs.

THE BLACK CAR that came for her had tinted passenger windows. Lewis opened the rear door and motioned for her to join him. Sam was sitting by the left window; he glanced across at her anxiously.

"This is what will happen," Lewis told Natalie as they sped away. "You're going to drive a car toward the target's house. Another driver will rear-end you in a hit-and-run: plenty of noise and crumpled panels, but you won't be hurt. You and your brother will walk from the wreckage, knock on the target's door, and ask her to call an ambulance. We'll spoof the 911 connection, so no ambulance will come until we put in the call ourselves. You'll play a wilting Southern flower, and at some point you'll be invited in to wait."

Natalie was incredulous. "She won't invite us in straight away?"

Lewis clenched his teeth, then spoke. "Have you ever been to Nassau County, Long Island?"

"Can we fly Business Class?" Sam wondered.

Lewis reached into a sports bag on his lap and drew out a pair of blindfolds.

Minutes later, the traffic sounds around them receded. They were bundled out of the car, led across the tarmac and up a set of stairs into what must have been a private jet. Natalie felt the plane taxiing before she'd been guided to her seat, and ascending before she'd fumbled the belt into place. It would take almost three hours to reach New York; if they hit so much as an unexpected head wind, Lewis might decide to cut his losses and drop them from the plane.

"I should have told them earlier," she whispered to Sam. "I'm sorry." She'd been fixated on the risk that she'd spring the revelation too early.

"Why do we have to visit this woman?" he asked.

Natalie talked him through the whole thing, from the heist itself to the dead-man switch she'd installed at the last moment.

"You couldn't have found a way to get us to Paris instead?" Sam joked.

"They set you up," Natalie stressed. "They only loaned you the money so they could rope me in if they had to."

"I know," he said. "I get it."

"So whatever happens now, it's not on you."

Sam laughed. "*Seriously?* You thought I was going to blame myself?"

As soon as the wheels hit the ground, someone grabbed Natalie's elbow. "How's the time?" she enquired.

"Local time's ten twenty-seven," Lewis replied.

The blindfolds stayed on as they boarded a second car. When it screeched to a halt and Lewis tugged the dark band up from Natalie's eyes, she squinted out into a fluorescent-lit mechanics' workshop. Half a dozen men in overalls were standing beside a hydraulic jack, watching the new arrivals.

Lewis motioned to her to leave the car. "This is what you'll be driving." He gestured at a white sedan a few meters away. "You rented this at the airport; there are used boarding passes in the glove compartment, and some luggage with clothes and toiletries in the trunk. I don't care what your cover story is – why you're in New York, where you were heading – but you should give your real names. And make sure you don't distract the target from the trigger, or do anything else stupid. Don't even think about driving away; we can immobilize the vehicle remotely, and the crash that follows would be a whole lot worse than the one we've discussed."

"I don't have the address," Natalie realized.

"The GPS has already been programmed. The house number is one hundred and seven; don't get confused and knock anywhere else."

"What if someone else offers to help us?"

Lewis said, "The street will be as good as empty. The crash will be right outside her door."

Natalie turned to Sam, who'd joined her on the floor of the workshop. "Are you OK with this?"

"As opposed to what?"

Lewis walked up to Sam and put a hand on his shoulder. "Sorry about the *déjà vu*, but it will make the whole thing more authentic."

Sam stared at him. Natalie felt the blood draining from her face. The waiting men converged on Sam, one of them carrying a wrench.

Sam didn't fight them, he just bellowed from the pain. When everyone separated the bandage was gone from his finger and his wound was dripping blood.

Lewis said, "Better put that in your pocket for the drive, so no one sees it before the crash."

THE FIGURES ON Natalie's watch had turned blue, to remind her that it had auto-synched to the new time zone. It was ten forty-six. The GPS estimated two minutes to their destination. They'd be outside the house in plenty of time – but they needed to be seen by the drones, indoors.

She glanced over at Sam. He was still pale, but he looked focused. There weren't many cars on the tree-lined streets, and Natalie had yet to spot a single pedestrian. The houses they were passing were ostentatious enough, if not exactly billionaires' mansions. But then, half the point of putting assets into digital currency was keeping a low profile.

"Destination in fifteen seconds," the GPS announced cheerily. Natalie resisted glancing in the rear-view mirror as she braked. The red pickup that had been following them since the garage slammed into the back of the sedan.

The airbags inflated like giant mushroom caps sprouting in time-lapse. Natalie felt the seat belt dig into her shoulder, but when her ears stopped ringing she took stock of her sensations and found no real pain.

"You OK?" she asked Sam. She could hear squealing tires as the truck did a U-turn and departed.

"Yeah."

"Our phones were in the hands-free docks," she reminded him. "The airbags are blocking them."

"We've just been in a crash," Sam said. "No one's going to ask us where our phones are.

Natalie got her door open and clambered out. They were right beside the mailbox of number one hundred and seven.

As Sam joined her, his severed finger exposed, the front door opened and target C ran out toward them.

"Are you all right? Is anyone else in the car?"

Natalie said, "I'm OK. It's just me and my brother."

"Oh, he's bleeding!" C was carrying her phone; she hit some keys then raised it to her ear. "A traffic accident. The other driver's cleared off. No ... they're both walking, but the young man's hand... that's correct."

She lowered the phone and motioned to them to approach. "Please, come inside. They said the ambulance will be a few minutes."

Sam pulled out a handkerchief and wrapped it around the stump of his finger. He couldn't quite look their Good Samaritan in the eye as he stepped through the doorway.

Target C led them into her carpeted living room, unfazed by Sam's blood. "Please, take a seat. I'll bring you some water."

"Thank you." When the woman had left, Natalie checked her watch. It was ten fifty-three. The six drones would be performing sweeps of all the rooms where she and Sam might plausibly have ended up, mostly staying near the ceiling out of people's normal lines of sight. She looked up, and after ten or fifteen seconds she saw it: her own tiny, loyal slave, confirming her safety before fetching its brothers to resume the original plan.

"Are we safe now?" Sam asked.

"I don't know."

"Maybe we should warn her," he suggested.

Natalie was torn. Lewis's people might still come after them, whatever they did. But which action would nudge the odds in favor of survival: enraging their enemies, but weakening them too by depriving them of part of their haul, or placating them but making them stronger?

"We can't risk it," she whispered.

Target C came into the room with a pitcher of water on a tray. She poured two glasses and handed them to her guests. "I can't believe that maniac just drove off," she said. She gazed forlornly at Sam's hand. "What happened?"

"I was opening the glove compartment," Sam replied. "The doors on those things are like guillotines."

Target C's phone beeped: not a ring tone, but some kind of alert. She spent a few seconds trying to ignore it, then lost the fight and examined the screen. Natalie could almost read the woman's deliberations from the movement of her eyes and the changing set of her jaw. This was the trigger: either a grave threat to her wealth, or an irresistible opportunity.

The woman looked up. "I'm so rude. My name's Emily."

"Natalie."

"Sam."

"Are you folks from around here?"

"New Orleans."

Emily nodded, as if she'd guessed as much already. "Where is that ambulance?" She turned to Sam. "Are you in agony? I have Tylenol. But maybe you've suffered some other injury that could make that the wrong thing to take?"

Sam said, "It's all right. I'll wait for the paramedics."

Emily thought for a few seconds. "Let me just check in the medicine cabinet, so I know exactly what I've got."

"Thank you," Sam replied.

Natalie watched her leave, and saw her take the turn toward the study where the wallet was held in its safe. The fake would already be waiting on top of a bookcase, invisible to anyone of normal height. The drones would be watching, parsing the scene, determining when the safe had been opened and the wallet taken out.

Water began drumming against stainless steel, far away in the kitchen. Natalie heard Emily curse in surprise, but she didn't run out of the study immediately.

Three seconds, four seconds, five seconds. The sound of the torrent was hard to ignore, conjuring images of flooded floors and water damage. Most people would have sprinted toward the source immediately, dropping almost anything to attend to it.

Finally, Natalie heard the hurried footsteps as Emily rushed to the kitchen. She could not have had time to execute whatever actions the trigger had inspired – but she had certainly had time to put the wallet back in the safe. Nothing else explained the delay. With strangers in the house – and more expected soon, from the emergency services – she wasn't going to leave the keys to her fortune lying around unattended.

It took Emily a few minutes to assess the situation in the kitchen – unsalvageable by merely tinkering with the faucet – then go to the water mains and shut off the flow at its source. She returned to the living room drying her hands on a towel.

"That was bizarre! Something just... burst." She shook her head. "We've only got Tylenol," she told Sam. She took her phone from her pocket. "Do you think I should call them again?"

Sam said, "It's not like I'm having a heart attack. And who knows what else they're dealing with?"

Emily nodded. "All right." She waited a few seconds, then said, "If you'll excuse me, I just need to clean up. Before it soaks through..."

Natalie said, "We're fine, really."

Emily left the room, to avail herself of the opportunity to move some of her money around. Whether the market signal proved misleading or not, the outcome was unlikely to ruin her. But the drones were helpless now; there'd be no prospect of them making the switch.

Natalie stared at the carpet, trying to assess the situation. She'd shafted Lewis's gang – entirely by mistake, and only partially: Emily would have no suspicions, no reason to raise the alarm and derail the rest of the heist. Lewis might well deduce exactly what had happened. But what would that lead to? Leniency? Forgiveness?

After half an hour, with still no ambulance, Emily phoned 911 again. "They said there was nothing in the system!" she told Natalie. "That fills you with confidence!"

The paramedics declared that Sam needed to go into the emergency department. One of them spent a couple of minutes searching the wreck for his severed fingertip, while the other waxed lyrical on the wonders of microsurgery, but in the end they gave up. "It must have got thrown out and some dog took it."

An hour later, while Natalie was dealing with paperwork at the hospital, two uniformed police approached her. "We had a report of a hit-and-run," the older cop said.

"Can you protect us?" Natalie asked him. "If we're being watched by someone dangerous?"

The cop glanced at his partner. "You're shaken up, I understand. But this was probably just some drunken fool too cowardly to own up to what he'd done. Nothing you should be taking personally."

Natalie's teeth started chattering, but she forced herself to speak.

"They kidnapped my brother," she said. "I'll tell you everything – but I need to know: if they can see everywhere, and reach anywhere, how are you going to protect us?"

I MET A MAN WHO WASN'T THERE
K. J. Parker

K.J. Parker was born long ago and far away, worked as a coin dealer, a dogsbody in an auction house and a lawyer, and has so far published thirteen novels including the *Fencer*, *Scavenger*, and *Engineer* trilogies, four standalone novels, and a handful of short stories including World Fantasy Award winning novellas "A Small Price to Pay for Birdsong" and "Let Maps to Others". Parker's short story collection *Academic Exercises* was published to widespread acclaim in 2014, and new stand-alone novel *Savages* should appear shortly. Married to a lawyer and living in the south west of England, K.J. Parker is a mediocre stockman and forester, a barely competent carpenter, blacksmith and machinist, a two-left-footed fencer, lackluster archer, utility-grade armorer, accomplished textile worker and crack shot. K.J. Parker is not K.J. Parker's real name. However, if K.J. Parker were to tell you K.J. Parker's real name, it wouldn't mean anything to you.

"APPARENTLY," I SAID, "you can teach me how to walk through walls, stop the flow of time and kill people with a single stare." I waited. He didn't say anything. "Is that right?"

The cuff of his left sleeve was frayed, but had been expertly darned. His eyes were pale blue. He had a disappointingly weak chin. There was a book lying closed on the table in front of him, but I was too far away to read the title. And only a leaking roof makes that pattering sound. "Yes," he said.

"Really?"

"Really."

I didn't believe him. "I'll go for that," I said. "When do I start?"

He frowned ever so slightly. "I'm afraid it's not as straightforward as that," he said.

Not what I'd expected. "There's a problem?"

"Oh yes." There's a certain sort of calm serenity I find extremely irritating. "Well?"

He hesitated; not from uncertainty or doubt, but because he was choosing exactly the right words. "I could teach you," he said. "I have the ability. I also have the ability to jump out of the window and kill myself. I don't choose to do the latter, but I could."

"You don't want to teach me?"

The frown was still there, as if I were the words of a familiar song he couldn't quite remember. "I don't know," he said. "I've only just met you. Also, you may not be able to learn from me."

Ah, I thought, here we go. The let-out clause. He will now proceed to give me some plausible but spurious reason why I turn out to be the one student in a hundred who won't be able to do it. Only after I've finished the course, naturally.

"In order to learn from me," he said, "there's something you need to do. Most people won't do it. A great many people simply can't. Unfortunate, but there it is."

"I see," I said. "Do what, exactly?"

Hi face was blank, open and totally sincere. "You need to pay me one hundred and seventy-five thalers," he said.

Well, he'd annoyed me. We'd played a game of body-language chess, and it had been checkmate in four. And besides, you don't need a horse if you're living in Town. So I sold mine – two hundred and six thalers, fifteen more than I paid for it – and turned up the next morning with the money in a faded red velvet bag. As before, he was alone, sitting in the one chair behind the chipped-and-scratched softwood desk, reading a book; no lecture in progress, no enthralled students sitting at his feet eagerly taking notes. And I still didn't believe him.

"Here you are," I said, dumping the bag heavily on the desk. "Count it if you like."

He sort of squinted at it; if I hadn't known better I'd have sworn he was counting the coins through the cloth. "I don't know," he said. Under the desk I could see where he'd tried to stick the uppers of his shoes back onto the soles with fish-scale glue.

"Excuse me?"

"A man walks into a cutler's shop," he said. "He wants to buy a knife. The cutler says, what do you want a knife for?"

"Not where I come from."

He didn't seem to have heard me. "Why does the cutler ask the question?" he went on. "Because, unless he knows what the customer has in mind, he can't sell him one that's suitable for his purpose. Or perhaps he suspects the customer wants to kill his wife."

"I've got a knife," I said. "Several."

He smiled. "And," he said, "if you wanted to kill someone, you'd have the means to do it. Therefore, teaching you the basilisk stare would not be an irresponsible act on my part. Fair enough. But, the cutler replies, if you don't want to kill someone, why do you want to buy a dagger?"

I shrugged. "In case someone wants to kill *me*."

He sighed. "Indeed," he said. "And the customer could quite properly say, if you're that concerned, why do you make and sell daggers? To which the cutler could only reply, because that's what I do." He clicked his tongue, a surprisingly loud and vulgar noise. "A hundred and seventy-five thalers?"

"Cash money."

He looked at the bag. He seemed to find an answer in it. "Plus," he added, "fourteen thalers for materials and other incidentals."

"Incidentals?"

"Bits and pieces," he said. "I could explain, but until you've started the course you wouldn't understand."

"Ah," I said, and gave him three five-thaler bits. They seemed to disappear into his hand, like water poured on gravel. "I'll owe you the change," he said.

I still didn't believe any of it. "So," I said, "do we start now?"

He shook his head. "The introductory class is tomorrow at noon sharp," he said. "Don't be late."

I hesitated, then headed for the door. I looked back; he was reading his book, slumped back a little in his chair, frowning, in the exact centre of a large, empty room. I went back down the stairs into the street. I got a splinter in my hand, from the banister.

* * *

So, YOU MAY well be asking, why *did* I want to learn how to walk through walls, suspend the passage of time and kill people with a single stare?

Well. Wouldn't you?

All right, but you wouldn't sell your horse. Unless your reasoning was: if I could do all that stuff, I could stroll through the walls of the King's Vault, fill my pockets, take out the guards with a single well-directed glare, I could buy all the horses I could possibly want; and I'd have the perfect alibi when the kettlehats came to arrest me – I was in the *Integrity Triumphant* playing shuttlejack with the regular crowd all that evening, ask anyone, they'll remember me. Also, I couldn't have killed those guards, didn't you say there wasn't a mark on them? You could be the greatest criminal ever.

Yes; but so far, nobody was. Put it another way: if the capability existed, surely by now someone would've got hold of it and misused it (because that's what people do, whenever some powerful new thing comes along. If we'd all been born in darkness and someone invented the Sun, the first we'd know about it was when someone used it to burn his way into the First Consolidated Bank). But this hadn't happened. The strange man sat there all day in his room over the cordwainer's shop, purporting to teach the art, but so far there were no reports of inexplicable burglaries and impossible deaths. Therefore, it *didn't work*.

And I'd paid the man a hundred and seventy-five, belay that, a hundred and ninety thalers; presumably non-refundable – do you walk up to a man who might just be able to stop your heart with a frown and ask for your money back? I don't think so. Not unless you're totally *convinced*. And I wasn't.

I know; I haven't answered my own question. Be patient.

IN CORNMARKET THERE's this clock. Well, you know that. It's what the city's famous for. Ten kreuzers buys you the view from the top of the clock tower. For half a thaler: they show you the mechanism; it's this crazy room, twelve feet by fifteen by ten, crammed full of cogs, wheels, pulleys, camshafts, escapements, huge restless circles cut with hundreds of thousands of tiny sharp teeth – for eating time with, presumably. This machine, they tell you, makes all the time used in the whole Empire. You'd think that seeing the mechanism, how it works, would take the magic out of it, but no, quite the reverse. I think it's because the power train moves so slowly you don't notice it; therefore, all the belts and wheels seem to be turning and spinning of their own motion, powered only by magic and some invisible sympathy with the inherent forces of the Earth.

At any rate, if you're in earshot of Cornmarket, you have no excuse for being late. I ran up the stairs just as the chimes were sounding. On the tenth out of twelve, I knocked on the door. As the twelfth chime died away, I heard him say, "Come in."

He was sitting exactly where I'd left him. "You're late," he said.

I blinked. "No I'm not."

He shook his head just a little. "The clock is slow," he said. "Three minutes."

I wanted to say, that's not possible. The clock *is* the time, the Emperor made a decree. Also, how the hell would *you* know? I didn't. I said, "Sorry."

He shrugged. "Try to be punctual," he said. "After all, it's your money you're wasting."

He made a sort of vague gesture, which I interpreted as, sit on the floor. I sat.

I was just starting to wonder if I'd become invisible when he coughed awkwardly and said, "I can only teach you what you already know. You do appreciate that, don't you?"

I thought, one hundred and ninety thalers. "I don't understand," I said.

He sighed. "Let's start with some breathing exercises," he said.

MY FATHER, YOU see, was a thief. Not a bad one, because he never got caught – not once, in fifty years in the profession. Not a particularly good one, because he never made any money. He was in the bulk-stealing end of the trade. He stole high-volume, low-value – sawn lumber, bricks, firewood, sand, pit-props, that sort of thing. If there was a big heap of something anywhere in the City, waiting to be used or shipped, Dad would roll up in the early hours of the morning with his cart, load it up and take it away.

It was relentless hard work, but Dad didn't mind that, he was a grafter, a willing horse. As soon as I turned thirteen I had to go with him; I'm not a willing horse, and I take after my mother, not physically strong, so I had to compensate with extreme effort. I used to tell him: Dad, you could make just as much money – more, probably – just hiring out as a carter; you've got the rig and the horses, where's the difference, except we could do this in daylight, and you wouldn't have to punch out night-watchmen. He'd just look at me.

No money in it; not after he'd paid for feed for the horses – bloody things lived better than we did most of the time. Back then, remember, they still hung thieves. Hell of a way to make a living.

So I grew up thinking; everything is difficult. Everything; even *stealing*, for crying out loud, is backbreaking, merciless slog. The world is so hard, so absolutely unyielding, all human life is basically quarrying stone, millions of little chips, and each one jars your bones and makes your brains rattle, until you're worn out, shaken to bits, steel on stone every minute of every day. Unless – ah, the dream – somehow, somewhere, hidden from the sight of all us losers, there's an easier way, a hidden door in the rock face that leads to the perfumed palaces of the nobility –

Ever seen a blind man looking for a door? He gropes the wall, methodically, inch by inch. That's me, looking for the easy way. Of course, I put more effort into that than I'd need to expend if I was digging coal. Just like Dad.

That's one reason, anyhow.

"There now," he said. I took that as permission to breathe out. My vision was starting to blur. "I've taught you something you already knew."

The evil sadistic bastard had made me hold my breath while he counted to a hundred. What was that supposed to achieve, for crying out loud? "Quite," I croaked, trying not to let him hear me gasping. "I've been breathing for years."

"Of course you have. All living things breathe, by definition."

I looked at him. Holding my breath hadn't conferred on me the gift of the basilisk stare. Pity. "So?"

He gave me a sad smile and stuck his hand into the wall.

Into. Fingers, knuckles, wrist. I tried to see what the boundary looked like, the interface, the point where his arm disappeared into the pale yellow plaster, but I was too far away.

"Happy now?" he said.

"Intrigued," I managed to say. "Hallucination. Brought on by lack of air."

He grinned and pulled his hand out again. "Of course it is," he said. "Now you do it."

I really wanted to, just in case I could. But somehow I couldn't bring myself to try. I could already feel the juddering halt as my fingertips didn't pass through the plaster and the brick, as they bent back under pressure. You could break a bone so easily. The thought made me feel slightly sick.

"I can't," I said.

"Ah well." He picked the book up off his desk and opened it. "Same time tomorrow," he said. "That's assuming you want to continue."

I stood up and headed for the door. As I passed him, he must've stuck out a foot to trip me. I fell sideways, awkwardly, against the wall.

Into the wall. Through it.

MY MOTHER WAS a silversmith's daughter from Scona. I have no idea why she married my father. She made no secret of the fact that she intended me to atone for her mistake. I would go to school, get a good education, join either the Imperial civil service or the Studium; I could be, she told me over and over again, whatever I wanted to be. Trouble was, I believed her.

Also, I was in a hurry; and I knew, from observing my father's losing battle with the universe, that if you play it straight you've got no chance. You have to cheat, and even then it's a long, dreary, miserable slog just to stay in the same place, let alone move forward. My way out of that was to follow my mother's advice, to the letter.

I began – Now, let's see. I was seventeen, almost, and we were living in a sort of shed beside the main road into Ap' Escatoy (that was before some idiot burned it down, of course). Every day, just after dawn, this fancy carriage used to trot past. It was lacquered black, with huge spindly wheels and two armed coachmen, and inside was this kid, about my age, always with his nose in a book; thin, wispy, sad face. I thought; what's he got to be sad about? So one day I followed him, running after the coach (nearly killed me; I was sure I'd cracked a rib just panting for breath) and saw him get down outside a rich merchant's house on Riverside. Then, quite suddenly, I knew all about him. To this day, I have no idea if any of it was true, but it was such a thoroughly plausible, convincing picture that it didn't matter.

I saw him as the younger son of some good but slightly impoverished family in the City, sent out to the sticks with a letter of introduction to a friend of the family, given a place (not too strenuous, not too demanding) in the merchant's house, with a view to working his way up and eventually becoming a minor merchant princeling. And then I thought, I can be anyone I want to be.

So I wrote a letter. Actually, I copied it out of one of those books – the complete epistolary, letters for all purposes and occasions. A little research, mostly in inns and cockpits, gave me the names of a few leading merchants in BocBohec (thirty miles away, where nobody knew us), and there were books in the Cartulary library that told me who was related to who among the people that matter. I gave myself a suitably poncy name – Thrasamund, I think I was – and luck gave me a helping hand, six kreuzers on a scrawny little Perimadeian gamecock at fifteen to one, and it shredded a bird nearly twice its size in the time it takes to blow your nose. Nine thalers bought me two outfits of decent second-hand clothes. All I had to do was the easy bit. I had to be Thrasamund.

And it really was so easy. By the time I came to knock on the merchant's door and hand over my letter to the porter, I knew Thrasamund perfectly, I *was* him, and being Thrasamund was simply being myself. After an awkwardly polite conversation over weak red wine and seed cake I got a job, junior clerk. I knuckled down, paid attention, applied myself, very quickly learned how to make myself useful; three months later I was out of the clerks' room and on my way to Beal Bohec with a letter of credit for nine hundred thalers, to buy seasoned rosewood boards and ebony dowel for my masters. I did a splendid job, though I do say so myself. In fact, if I'd gone back to Boc and carried on with my career there, instead of selling the lumber the next day at a thirty per cent profit and shipping out to the Vesani republic with the money, I would almost certainly have been a great success and made something of myself.

* * *

Unfortunately, it was an outside wall.

Also unfortunately, his rooms were three stories up. It's true what they say; as you fall through the air, time does seem to stand still, and you do get to revisit crucial scenes from your past life – rather depressing, in my case. At any rate, I managed to solve one mystery that had been bugging me for years: how do they know that?

Answer: because at some point, someone must've fallen a very long way, and yet somehow survived to tell the tale. That's what I did. I fell three stories and landed in a cart full of straw that just happened to be drawn up outside the stables which just happened to be directly underneath the room I'd just fallen from. Wonderful.

Straw is marvellous stuff to fall on, but it's still a thoroughly unpleasant experience. I hit the cart hard enough to smash through the plank floor. I'd landed on my backside, so I was kind of sitting in the hole, supported by the insides of my knees and the small of my back, when he came bustling up, looking scared to death. He grabbed my wrist and hauled me out.

"Are you all right?" he said.

"I fell through the wall," I said.

Apparently I'd stated the obvious. "Yes," he said. "Can you move your hands and feet? Are you feeling dizzy?"

"Through the *wall*," I repeated. "I just –"

"Well, of course you did," he said, with just a hint of irritation. "You're my student. I taught you."

"No you didn't."

He was looking over his shoulder. "Let's continue this discussion inside," he said. "People are staring."

He had a valid point. The owner of the cart would probably be along in a minute. Even so. "All you did was make me hold my breath. And that wasn't it, because I looked at you and you're still –"

"Inside," he said. "Please," he added.

I'm a sucker for good manners. We went inside.

"I thought I'd had it then," I said, as I wheezed up the stairs. My back was killing me.

"Oh, you weren't in any danger," he said blithely. We'd reached his landing. I went in, taking great care to stay away from the walls, which I no longer trusted. And if you can't trust walls, what can you do?

"Yes I bloody well was," I felt constrained to say. "You might have warned me."

"What, that you were in danger of succeeding? If you didn't want to pass through walls, why did you enrol in the first place?"

"You might have warned me," I repeated, but it came out sounding merely petulant.

He sat down. I did the same, only much more slowly. "You were in no danger," he said. "You weren't falling fast enough for that."

Oh really, I thought. "Yes I was."

"No you weren't. It took you twenty-seven seconds to reach the ground."

Bullshit, I thought. Less than a second, surely. Of course, it had *felt* much longer than that, but that was because of the well-known psychological effect – "You what?"

"I was counting," he said, "under my breath, as I ran down the stairs. I got there before you did. Twenty-seven seconds." He laughed. "For heaven's sake," he said. "You don't think that little bit of straw –"

"I broke the cart."

"You passed through the cart," he said. "Like you did with the wall. That's a common thing with novices, they don't quite know when to stop."

I wasn't having that. A man is entitled to lie in furtherance of his fraud, but not to the extent of playing serious games with someone's head. "Come on," I told him, as I jumped up and grabbed his arm. He didn't resist. We went all the way back down again. The cart was still there.

Its plank floor was, of course, intact.

FOR OUR NEXT session, he'd said, meet me under the clock at noon.

I was there, bang on time. No sign of him. As I stood there, leaning against one of the columns of the New Revelation temple – I still wasn't happy with walls, but I figured columns were probably all right – part of me was thinking, one hundred and ninety thalers. The other part was thinking: I can pass through walls.

Qualify that. I had passed through *a* wall, and a plank floor; accidentally, not deliberately. I didn't know if I could do it again. I hadn't tried. I didn't want to try – or at least, not on my own and unsupervised. *I can only teach you what you already know.* Yes, well. Con artists' mysticism; I'm quite good at it myself, when I'm on form. But *novices don't quite know when to stop.* Suppose I tried it on my own and I couldn't stop. Suppose I started sinking down through the earth. No, thank you very much. Just because I can do something doesn't mean I have to do it.

Ten minutes past the hour, he eventually turned up. He came out of the saloon bar of the *Veracity & Trust.* He was eating an apple. "You're late," he said.

I glanced up at the clock. "I've been here all the –"

"Noon precisely," he said. "Follow me."

He moved fast for a small, fat man. "If it's dead on noon," I said, jogging to keep up with him "how can I be...?"

"So," he said, without looking round, "have you been practicing?"

"No."

He made a *tsk* noise. "Poor show," he said. "You really do have to practice, you know. Innate ability is all very well, but you have to learn how to use it. Ah, here we are."

I wanted to ask him about a number of things, starting with *innate ability*, but he darted into a doorway, one I happened to know quite well.

"We can't go in there," I said.

I couldn't, anyway. I'd been left in no doubt on that score the last time I tried, about eighteen months earlier. "You can't come in here," the man on the door had told me, and since he was six feet eight with a chest like an ox, I believed him.

One of those ridiculous misunderstandings, of course. I'd gone in fully intending to pay the asking price, not to mention a generous tip. It was only when I put my hand in my pocket and found it empty that I realised there was a hole in the lining, through which my twelve thalers forty must have fallen. I explained. I turned the pocket inside out and showed them the hole. They threw me out.

"Now, then," he said. We were in the front parlour, or waiting room, or whatever you choose to call it. Nobody about. "We've done walking through walls and freezing the passage of time. That only leaves –"

"What are we doing in here?" I asked him in a loud, hoarse whisper. "You do realise this is a –"

He smiled at me. "Last time you were here," he said.

I caught my breath; and then I thought, well, he's been making enquiries, hasn't he? I suppose I'm reasonably well known in some quarters in this town. He's found out about my embarrassing history in this place, and he's using it to try and make me think he's a mind-reader or something. Sort of thing I'd do.

I smiled. "They threw me out," I said.

He nodded. "There was a hole in your pocket," he said.

"That's right. Expensive hole. Twelve thalers forty."

"No." He gave me a mild frown. "You made the hole yourself, with a very sharp knife. You made the hole just slightly smaller than a six-thaler coin. The idea is that the coin gradually works its way through the hole. That way, when you come in through the door, you make a show of jingling the coins in your pocket, to let everyone know you have money. Later, when it's time to pay, you turn your pocket out and show them the hole. But the coins have slipped through, into the little trap you've sewn into the lining."

I looked at him very hard. He didn't drop dead. I don't know. Maybe he'd worked it out from first principles, or maybe someone else had done that, and told him. "I make no admissions on that score," I said.

He gave me a doesn't-matter shrug. "The doorman," he said.

"Well?"

"You don't like him, do you?"

I grinned. "I think he may possibly enjoy his work a little bit too much," I said.

"You were humiliated. People you knew saw you getting thrown out into the street. It made you ashamed, and angry. You wanted to get back at him for that. You wanted to hurt him."

I wasn't sure I liked this. "Wanting's not a crime," I said.

"Of course it isn't." His smile widened. I wanted to hit him, to make him stop grinning at me. "And, by the same token, neither is being in the same room when a man dies from a heart attack. Not even," he went on, "if the man in question was someone you had cause to dislike." His voice was getting softer and softer. "They'd never suspect it was you. If they did, they couldn't prove it."

I did my best to give him a horrified stare. "I don't kill people," I said.

"Of course you don't. You're afraid of getting caught, and strung up. Quite properly, you argue that it's not worth the risk – the brief moment of satisfaction, against your life. Common sense. Like not walking straight at a wall, hoping it'll let you through."

"I don't *want* to kill him," I said. "I don't want to kill anybody."

He nodded; sharply, precisely. "You just want to be able to."

"Yes."

I COULD BE whoever I wanted to be, my mother told me. By the same token, presumably, I could do whatever I wanted to do – walk through walls, stop clocks, kill people. The key word, of course, is *want*.

Ricimer's paradox (that hoary old chestnut): political power should only be given to those who don't want to exercise it. Apply that principle to – here comes the M word – magic. Behold, I give you the power to do anything, anything at all, so long as you don't want to do it.

Neat trick.

At any rate, a wonderful way of gouging someone out of a hundred and ninety thalers. I had a shrewd suspicion that *he'd* magicked me through the wall and slowed down my descent onto the bed of the cart. Upshot: I believe I now have the power to do it, but I won't put that belief to the test, because You Can Only Use Magic To Do Stuff You Don't Want To Do. So, I can't prove I've been cheated. So, I can't have my money back.

Fine. Except, why is someone who can do that sort of stuff reduced to swindling people out of relatively trivial sums? Answers, anyone?

(*Because he doesn't want to make his living that way.*)

I could have been anything I wanted to be. Instead, I made my living by cheating people out of relatively trivial sums. I started out by embezzling the money I was entrusted with by my kind and generous employer in Boc. Using that as a stake, I went to the Vesani republic, where I discovered (a bit too late) that I was way out of my league. Not long afterwards, I left the republic in a tearing hurry, half a jump ahead of the law, found guilty in absentia of a crime I didn't commit (no, really), and ended up on Scona, which is where the ship I was on happened to be going. On that ship, I'd undergone a transformation, the way caterpillars turn into butterflies. I metamorphosed from a penniless fugitive into the accredited representative of the Symmachus brothers, the biggest manufacturers of woollen goods in Boc. I got lucky. I found a sheet of paper and a pen in the captain's cabin. I have neat handwriting. Incidentally, there's no such firm as the Symmachus brothers. I called them into being, out of thin air. Of course, I didn't really want to. Still, a man has to eat.

"You again," he said, peering at me over the top of his book.

"Me again," I said.

He marked the place carefully and closed the book. "But we're all done. I taught you, you learned, you've had your money's worth. That's it."

I'd thought long and hard about the mechanics of it all. A hundred and ninety thalers; let's see. Average weekly wage of an ordinary working man, say, ten thalers. A man of austere habits could last out a long time on a hundred and ninety. He'd only have to pull the scam three, four times a year. The rest of the time he could devote to his own interests; scholarship, research.

"I'm not satisfied," I said.

He sighed. "Sue me," he said. "Oh, sorry, I forgot, you can't. The law wouldn't recognise a contract to teach magic, since there's no such thing. A contract to perform an impossible act is no contract. Look it up," he added kindly.

I stayed where I was. "You didn't teach me anything," I said.

I could see I was turning into a nuisance. Good. "Strictly speaking, no," he said, "since I can't teach you anything you don't already know. But I made that clear from the outset, so it's effectively an essential term of the agreement. You have absolutely no legitimate grounds for complaint. Please go away."

I smiled at him. "No," I said.

I knew that look. I'm used to it. "All right," he said. "What do you want?"

"To annoy you," I said. "So you'll make the floor disappear from under my feet. Like you did with the cart I fell on."

He looked confused. "I didn't do that. I couldn't."

"Because you want to?"

"No, because I can't."

I believed him. He was annoyed enough to be credible. "So it wasn't you," I said. "You didn't make me fall through the wall."

"That would be impossible."

"So the magic –"

The word made him wince. "You did it all by yourself." He gave me a pained look; why are you doing this to me? "I thought you'd understood all that. I can't teach you what you don't already know, remember?"

I gave him my special smile. "You're under arrest," I said.

It's not something I like to talk about.

It was my own stupid fault, needless to say. Sooner or later, everyone in this line of work gets careless. One little slip is all it takes. Sometimes I wonder where the hell we get the courage from. It's like being a soldier, except that every day we're on the front line, that one little slip away from disaster. If I thought about it, I wouldn't be able to do it.

Anyway, they got me. It was, what, ten years ago now. I remember sitting in a cell about a mile down under the Prefecture, telling myself that if ever I got out of there, that was it, the end, no more bad behaviour from me; but I couldn't conceive of a way out, even with my amazingly active imagination. And then the prefect came in – the man himself, not a deputy – and he offered me this deal. Get out there, he said, and scam the scammers. You know how they think, where to find them, how they operate. In return, you get a pardon, immunity, we may even pay you. Of course, we'll be watching you like hawks, and the very first hint that you're playing us for fools, you'll wish you'd never been born. But –

Time stood still. And then I said, yes, please, and the most amazing thing happened. I got out. It was like magic, as though I'd simply stood up and walked through the cell wall like it wasn't there.

Since then, I've been such a good little soldier. Seventy-six convictions. Jail for most of them, and twelve got the rope, due to aggravating circumstances. Quite right, too. If there's one thing I can't be doing with, it's deliberate dishonesty.

*   *   *

I WENT TO see him in his cell. It might just possibly have been the one I was in, all those years ago.

"Still here, then," I said.

He gave me a sort of sad smile. "Of course," he said. "The door's locked."

"Ah," I replied. "But you can walk through walls."

He sighed. "If I could do that," he said, "which I don't admit, naturally, then it would prove that I am indeed a sorcerer. I believe that's illegal."

True. Although the official position these days is that magic doesn't exist, there's a fistful of silly old laws on the statute-book prescribing the death sentence for witchcraft. Nobody can be bothered to repeal them; after all, the argument runs, a person can't be convicted of witchcraft unless he's proven to have performed magic. Magic doesn't exist. Therefore, it's impossible that anyone could be convicted.

I beamed at him. I can be horrible sometimes. "Nobody takes that stuff seriously anymore," I said. "What you're in here for is fraud. To be exact, fraudulently professing to be able to walk through walls. If you demonstrated you could walk through walls, you'd prove you're innocent."

"And then they'd hang me."

"And then we'd hang you, yes. In theory," I added. "Unless we could do a deal."

If looks could kill. "Go on," he said.

"Quite simple," I replied. "Plead guilty to the fraud, and we'll forget about the witchcraft."

He frowned. "You want me to lie. On oath."

"Yes."

"That's perjury."

I shrugged. "I'll throw in a free pardon on the perjury."

He rubbed his chin. "Let's not forget," he said, "you can do magic too."

I laughed. "They'd never believe you."

I could read his mind (which was my mind, essentially, from the time when it was me sitting on the bed hearing the terms of the deal). "You'll drop the sorcery charges."

"If you plead to the fraud, yes."

"What will I get?"

"For the fraud? Two years in the galleys. I'll put in a good word for you. Say you co-operated."

"That's a good deal?"

"Yes."

AFTER THAT, I managed to put him out of my mind. I have that gift; I can forget about people sitting hopelessly in jail cells, because I put them there, because I tricked them. Now that's magic.

I forgot all about him, until a captain of the watch came to see me. No cause for alarm, he said, thereby scaring me to death. One of yours has escaped.

They're required to tell you, so you can be on your guard, in case the fugitive comes after you with a knife or something. As soon as he said it, I knew. "Little short guy."

"That's the one."

I felt that twitch in the stomach. "Don't tell me," I said. "The prison authorities are baffled."

He looked surprised. "Yes, actually. One minute he was in his cell, the next he wasn't. Door still locked on the outside, no hole in the wall, nothing. Not a clue how he got out. But he did."

"Maybe he walked through the wall," I suggested. The fool laughed.

UNDER THE TERMS of my parole, I can't leave town without permission from the prefect. I made an appointment.

"No," he said.

"Oh, go on," I said. "I haven't left the city for ten years, and I've been good as gold."

"Quite." He gave me a big smile. "You're the best thief-taker I've ever had. I'm so proud of you. Which is why you can't leave town. Sorry." He actually looked sorry, the liar. "I'm afraid I don't trust you to come back."

"There's an escaped convict on the loose. I have reason to believe he wants to kill me."

"Ah." He nodded. "That's different. In that case, I definitely don't trust you to come back."

"But if he –"

"Rest assured," he said, and gave me that sincere, reliable look that the voters keep on falling for. "We'll catch him and we'll string him up, and that's a promise. Even if I have to put the noose round his neck personally."

I sighed. "You don't understand," I said. "He's a sorcerer. He can walk through walls. He can stop clocks. He can kill you just by staring at you."

The prefect looked at me. "Now that's just silly," he said.

HE CAME TO see me.

He came in through the wall, though the door wasn't locked – why bother? I was sitting on a chair in the middle of the room, which was empty apart from one other chair, which I'd left for him when I cleared out all the rest of the furniture. I'd also taken down the wall-hangings, exposing the bare red brick. The room looked like a cell.

"I love what you've done with the place," he said.

I looked at him. It didn't work.

"Sit down," I said. "Please."

He glanced up at the ceiling, then sat down. "I'm assuming there's no hidden trapdoor," he said.

I had actually considered that; even went so far as to get a quote from a carpenter. Seventeen thalers forty, just for cutting a simple hidden trapdoor in a floor. For that money he can damn well kill me, I said. "What can I do for you?"

That seemed to amuse him. "You could beg for mercy."

"Would that do me any good?"

"No."

I nodded. "Would it help if I apologised? I really am very sorry for the way I treated you."

He sighed. "All this," he said, "the melodrama. It really isn't me, you know. All my life, all I've ever been is a scholar, a researcher, a scientist. Do you really think I've come here for *revenge*?" He made it sound so utterly absurd.

"Yes," I said.

"Well, I'm not. I'm here to conclude my experiment, that's all. Once I've done that, we're finished. Over, the end. Really."

In spite of overwhelming evidence to the contrary, I persist in thinking I'm smart. Just shows how dumb I am really. "Experiment," I said.

"Quite so." He smiled at me. "An experiment to ascertain whether paranormal powers can be acquired and exercised by someone with no innate paranormal ability."

"Meaning me."

He shook his head. "Meaning me," he said. "That was the first phase. The second phase was whether I could then pass on those abilities to another equally untalented subject. Meaning you," he added helpfully.

"So you weren't –"

He shrugged. "You were my first student," he said. "I guess nobody else was gullible enough to believe they could actually learn magic, for only a hundred and seventy-five thalers."

"A hundred and ninety." I stared at him – not like that, which was probably just as well. "You used me," I said. "You took me for a mark."

"Ah well." He smiled again. "Actually, of course, no, I didn't. There was no confidence trick. I really did teach you to do magic."

"Just the once."

"Indeed," he said. "Which I why I'm here. Now, then. I'm going to count to five. On five, I'll give you the basilisk stare and kill you. Assuming," he added pleasantly, "you're still here. If you make good your escape by walking through the wall, I shall go away and never bother you again. One."

"Screw you," I replied and tilted my chair back, thereby triggering the secret trapdoor I'd had installed under his chair. Well, quite. But I'd managed to beat the bloodsucker down to eleven thalers fifty.

The trapdoor swung open and the chair vanished. He didn't. He just carried on sitting, on nothing, eighteen inches off the floor.

"Two," he said.

Oh for crying out loud, I thought. Still, what can you do?

I walked through the east wall. The west wall was the outside, and I'm seven stories up. The east wall connects with the stairwell. I didn't hang about. I ran down the stairs, burst through the front door and rushed out into the street, where four kettlehats from the Watch arrested me and charged me with witchcraft.

I DID A deal.

I am no longer a thief-taker employed by the prefect. These days, I work directly for the Duke. I go where he sends me, and I look at people he wants looked at. Sometimes these people are hard to get to, which means I have to walk through various bits of architecture first. Occasionally, I look at guards, though I do try hard not to have to.

I frequently wonder why the hell I do this stuff, which is hateful to me. With my abilities, which long practice has perfected, I could simply refuse to carry on; I could go away, and make myself very hard to find. But I keep on doing it, because the Duke has a terrible power over me. Each time I go and look at someone for him, he pays me an obscene amount of money. You just can't fight something like that.

My mother once told me I could be anybody I wanted to be; meaning thereby, I could be rich, buy anything I wanted, never have to do hard, grinding manual work, like my father did all his life. Having considered all the facts in the case, having given them a great deal of careful and objective thought, I'm inclined to the view that she was wrong. I think I could've been anyone – anyone at all – I *didn't* want to be; which is how it seems to work, for some reason.

GRAND JETÉ
(THE GREAT LEAP)
Rachel Swirsky

Rachel Swirsky (www.rachelswirsky.com) holds an MFA from the Iowa Writers Workshop. Her short fiction has been published in numerous magazines and anthologies including *Tor.com, Subterranean Online,* and *Clarkesworld Magazine.* It has also been nominated for the Hugo Award, the World Fantasy Award, and the Locus Award, and won the Nebula Award twice. Her second collection, *How the World Became Quiet: Myths of the Past, Present and Future*, came out from Subterranean Press in 2013. She had a book of illustrated ballet stories as a child from which she learned about *Coppélia*, but alas her attempts to perform ballet were stymied by her lack of grace.

ACT I: Mara
Tombé
(Fall)

As DAWN APPROACHED, the snow outside Mara's window slowed, spiky white stars melting into streaks on the pane. Her abba stood in the doorway, unaware that she was already awake. Mara watched his silhouette in the gloom. Shadows hung in the folds of his jowls where he'd shaved his beard in solidarity after she'd lost her hair. Although it had been months, his face still looked pink and plucked.

Some nights, Mara woke four or five times to find him watching from the doorway. She didn't want him to know how poorly she slept and so she pretended to be dreaming until he eventually departed.

This morning, he didn't leave. He stepped into the room. "Marale," he said softly. His fingers worried the edges of the green apron that he wore in his workshop. A layer of sawdust obscured older scorch marks and grease stains. "Mara, please wake up. I've made you a gift."

Mara tried to sit. Her stomach reeled. Abba rushed to her bedside. "I'm fine," she said, pushing him away as she waited for the pain to recede.

He drew back, hands disappearing into his apron pockets. The corners of his mouth tugged down, wrinkling his face like a bulldog's. He was a big man with broad shoulders and disproportionately large hands. Everything he did looked comical when wrought on such a large scale. When he felt jovial, he played into the foolishness with broad, dramatic gestures that would have made an actor proud. In sadness, his gestures became reticent, hesitating, miniature.

"Are you cold?" he asked.

In deep winter, their house was always cold. Icy wind curled through cracks in the insulation. Even the heater that abba had installed at the foot of Mara's bed couldn't keep her from dreaming of snow.

Abba pulled a lace shawl that had once belonged to Mara's ima from the back of her little wooden chair. He draped it across her shoulders. Fringe covered her ragged fingernails.

As Mara rose from her bed, he tried to help with her crutches, but Mara fended him off. He gave her a worried look. "The gift is in my workshop," he said. With a concerned backward glance, he moved ahead, allowing her the privacy to make her own way.

Their white German Shepherd, Abel, met Mara as she shifted her weight onto her crutches. She paused to let him nuzzle her hand, tongue rough against her knuckles. At thirteen, all his other senses were fading, and so he tasted everything he could. He walked by her side until they reached the stairs, and then followed her down, tail thumping against the railing with every step.

The door to abba's workshop was painted red and stenciled with white flowers that Mara had helped ima paint when she was five. Inside, half-finished apparatuses sprawled across workbenches covered in sawdust and disassembled electronics. Hanging from the ceiling, a marionette stared blankly at Mara and Abel as they passed, the glint on its pupils moving back and forth as its strings swayed. A mechanical hand sprang to life, its motion sensor triggered by Abel's tail. Abel whuffed at its palm and then hid behind Mara. The thing's fingers grasped at Mara's sleeve, leaving an impression of dusty, concentric whorls.

Abba stood at the back of the workshop, next to a child-sized doll that sat on a metal stool. Its limbs fell in slack, uncomfortable positions. Its face looked like the one Mara still expected to see in the mirror: a broad forehead over flushed cheeks scattered with freckles. Skin peeled away in places, revealing wire streams.

Mara moved to stand in front of the doll. It seemed even eerier, examined face to face, its expression a lifeless twin of hers. She reached out to touch its soft, brown hair. Her bald scalp tingled.

Gently, Abba took Mara's hand and pressed her right palm against the doll's. Apart from how thin Mara's fingers had become over the past few months, they matched perfectly.

Abba made a triumphant noise. "The shape is right."

Mara pulled her hand out of abba's. She squinted at the doll's imitation flesh. Horrifyingly, its palm shared each of the creases on hers, as if it, too, had spent twelve years dancing and reading books and learning to cook.

Abel circled the doll. He sniffed its feet and ankles and then paused at the back of its knees, whuffing as if he'd expected to smell something that wasn't there. After completing his circuit, he collapsed on the floor, equidistant from the three human-shaped figures.

"What do you think of her?" abba asked.

Goosebumps prickled Mara's neck. "What is she?"

Abba cradled the doll's head in his hands. Its eyes rolled back, and the light highlighted its lashes, fair and short, just like Mara's own. "She's a prototype. Empty-headed. A friend of mine is working on new technology for the government –"

"A prototype?" repeated Mara. "Of what?"

"The body is simple mechanics. Anyone could build it. The technology in the mind is new. It takes pictures of the brain in motion, all three dimensions, and then creates schematics for artificial neural clusters that will function like the original biological matter –"

Mara's head ached. Her mouth was sore and her stomach hurt and she wanted to go back to bed even if she couldn't sleep. She eyed the doll. The wires under its skin were vivid red and blue as if they were veins and arteries connecting to viscera.

"The military will make use of the technology," Abba continued. "They wish to recreate soldiers with advanced training. They are not ready for human tests, not yet. They are still experimenting with animals. They've made rats with mechanical brains that can solve mazes the original rats were trained to run. Now they are working with chimpanzees."

Abba's accent deepened as he continued, his gestures increasingly emphatic.

"But I am better. I can make it work in humans now, without more experiments." Urgently, he lowered his voice. "My friend was not supposed to send me the schematics. I paid him much money, but his reason for helping is that I have promised him that when I fix the problems, I will show him the solution and he can take the credit. This technology is not for civilians. No one else will be able to do this. We are very fortunate."

Abba touched the doll's shoulder so lightly that only his fingertips brushed her.

"I will need you to sit for some scans so that I can make the images that will preserve you. They will be painless. I can set up when you sleep." Quietly, he added, "She is my gift to you. She will hold you and keep you… if the worst…" His voice faded, and he swallowed twice, three times, before beginning again. "She will protect you."

Mara's voice came out hoarse. "Why didn't you tell me?"

"You needed to see her when she was complete."

Her throat constricted. "I wish I'd never seen her at all!"

From the cradle, Mara had been even-tempered. Now, at twelve, she shouted and cried. Abba said it was only what happened to children as they grew older, but they both knew that wasn't why.

Neither was used to her new temper. The lash of her shout startled them both. Abba's expression turned stricken.

"I don't understand," he said.

"You made a new daughter!"

"No, no." Abba held up his hands to protect himself from her accusation. "She is made *for* you."

"I'm sure she'll be a better daughter than I am," Mara said bitterly.

She grabbed a hank of the doll's hair. Its head tilted toward her in a parody of curiosity. She pushed it away. The thing tumbled to the floor, limbs awkwardly splayed.

Abba glanced toward the doll, but did not move to see if it was broken. "I – No, Marale – You don't –" His face grew drawn with sudden resolution. He pulled a hammer off of one of the work benches. "Then I will smash her to pieces."

There had been a time when, with the hammer in his hand and a determined expression on his face, he'd have looked like a smith from old legends. Now he'd lost so much weight that his skin hung loosely from his enormous frame as if he were a giant coat suspended from a hanger. Tears sprang to Mara's eyes.

She slapped at his hands and the hammer in them. "Stop it!"

"If you want her to –"

"Stop it! Stop it!" she shouted.

Abba released the hammer. It fell against the cement with a hollow, mournful sound.

Guilt shot through her, at his confusion, at his fear. What should she do, let him destroy this thing he'd made? What should she do, let the hammer blow strike, watch herself be shattered?

Sawdust billowed where the hammer hit. Abel whined and fled the room, tail between his legs.

Softly, abba said, "I don't know what else to give."

Abba had always been the emotional heart of the family, even when ima was alive. His anger flared; his tears flowed; his laughter roared from his gut. Mara rested her head on his chest until his tears slowed, and then walked with him upstairs.

THE HOUSE WAS too small for Mara to fight with abba for long, especially during winters when they both spent every hour together in the house, Mara home-schooling via her attic space program while abba tinkered in his workshop. Even on good days, the house felt claustrophobic with two people trapped inside. Sometimes one of them would tug on a coat and ski cap and trudge across the hard-packed snow, but even the outdoors provided minimal escape. Their house sat alone at the end of a mile-long driveway that wound through bare-branched woods before reaching the lonely road that eventually led to their neighbors. Weather permitting, in winter it took an hour and a half to get the truck running and drive into town.

It was dawn by the time they had made their way upstairs, still drained from the scene in the basement. Mara went to lie down on her bed so she could try for the illusion of privacy. Through the closed door, she heard her father venting his frustration on the cabinets. Pans clanged. Drawers slammed. She thought she could hear the quiet, gulping sound of him beginning to weep again under the cacophony.

She waited until he was engrossed in his cooking and then crept out of her bedroom. She made her way down the hallway, taking each step slowly and carefully so as to minimize the clicking of her crutches.

Ima's dance studio was the only room in the house where abba never went. It faced east; at dawn, rose- and peach-colored light shimmered across the full-length mirrors and polished hardwood. An old television hung on the southern wall, its antiquated technology jury-rigged to connect with the household AI.

Mara closed the door most of the way, enough to muffle any sound but not enough to make the telltale thump that would attract her father's attention. She walked up to the television so that she could speak softly and still be heard by its implanted AI sensors. She'd long ago mastered the trick of enunciating clearly enough for the AI to understand her even when she was whispering. "I'd like to access a DVD of ima's performances."

The AI whirred. "Okay, Mara," said its genial, masculine voice. "Which one would you like to view?"

"*Giselle.*"

More clicks and whirs. The television blinked on, showing the backs of several rows of red velvet seats. Well-dressed figures navigated the aisles, careful not to wrinkle expensive suits and dresses. Before them, a curtain hid the stage from view, the house lights emphasizing its sumptuous folds.

Mara sat carefully on the floor near the ballet barre so that she would be able to use it as a lever when she wanted to stand again. She crossed the crutches at her feet. On the television screen, the lights dimmed as the overture began.

Sitting alone in this place where no one else went, watching things that no one else watched, she felt as if she were somewhere safe. A mouse in its hole, a bird in its nest – a shelter built precisely for her body, neither too large nor too small.

The curtain fluttered. The overture began. Mara felt her breath flowing more easily as the tension eased from her shoulders. She could forget about abba and his weeping for a moment, just allow herself to enter the ballet.

Even as an infant, Mara had adored the rich, satiny colors on ima's old DVDs. She watched the tragedies, but her heart belonged to the comedies. Gilbert and Sullivan's *Pineapple Poll*. Ashton's choreography of Prokofiev's *Cinderella*. Madcap *Coppélia* in which a peasant boy lost his heart to a clockwork doll.

When Mara was small, ima would sit with her while she watched the dancers, her expression half-wistful and half-jaded. When the dancers had sketched their bows, ima would stand, shaking her head, and say, "Ballet is not a good life."

At first, ima did not want to give Mara ballet lessons, but Mara insisted at the age of two, three, four, until ima finally gave in. During the afternoons while abba was in his workshop, Mara and ima would dance together in the studio until ima grew tired and sat with her back against the mirror, hands wrapped around her knees, watching Mara spin and spin.

After ima died, Mara had wanted to ask her father to sign her up for dance school. But she hated the melancholia that overtook him whenever they discussed ballet. Before getting sick, she'd danced on her own instead, accompanying the dancers on ima's tapes. She didn't dance every afternoon as she had when ima was alive. She was older; she had other things to do – books to read, study hours with the AI, lessons and play dates in attic space. She danced just enough to maintain her flexibility and retain what ima had taught her, and even sometimes managed to learn new things from watching the dancers on film.

Then last year, while dancing with the Mouse King to *The Nutcracker*, the pain she'd been feeling for months in her right knee suddenly intensified. She heard the snap of bone before she felt it. She collapsed suddenly to the floor, confused and in pain, her head ringing with the echoes of the household's alarms. As the AI wailed for help, Mara found a single thought repeating in her head. *Legs don't shatter just because you're dancing. Something is very wrong.*

On the television screen, the filmed version of Mara's mother entered, dancing a coy Giselle in blue tulle. Her gaze slanted shyly downward as she flirted with the dancers playing Albrecht and Hilarion. One by one, she plucked petals from a prop daisy. *He loves me, he loves me not.*

Mara heard footsteps starting down the hall. She rushed to speak before abba could make it into the room – "AI, switch off –"

Abba arrived before she could finish. He stood in the doorway with his shoulders hunched, his eyes averted from the image of his dead wife. "Breakfast is ready," he said. He lingered for a moment before turning away.

AFTER BREAKFAST, ABBA went outside to scrape ice off of the truck.

They drove into town once a week for supplies. Until last year, they'd always gone on Sundays, after Shabbat. Now they went on Fridays before Mara's appointments and then hurried to get home before sunset.

Outside, snowflakes whispered onto the hard-pack. Mara pulled her knitted hat over her ears, but her cheeks still smarted from the cold. She rubbed her gloved hands together for warmth before attaching Abel's leash. The old dog seemed to understand what her crutches were. Since she'd started using them, he'd broken his lifelong habit of yanking on the strap and learned to walk daintily instead, placing each paw with care.

Abba opened the passenger door so that Abel could clamber into the back of the cab. He fretted while Mara leaned her crutches on the side of the truck and pulled herself into the seat. He wanted to help, she knew, but he was stopping himself. He knew she hated being reminded of her helplessness.

He collected her crutches when she was done and slung them into the back with Abel before taking his place in the driver's seat. Mara stared silently forward as he turned the truck around and started down the narrow driveway. The four-wheel-drive jolted over uneven snow, shooting pain through Mara's bad leg.

"Need to fix the suspension," abba grumbled.

Because abba was a tinkerer, everything was always broken. Before Mara was born, he'd worked for the government. These days, he consulted on refining manufacturing processes. He felt that commercial products were shoddily designed and so he was constantly trying to improve their household electronics, leaving his dozens of half-finished home projects disassembled for months while all the time swearing to take on new ones.

The pavement smoothed out as they turned onto a county-maintained road. Piles of dirty snow lined its sides. Bony trees dotted the landscape, interspersed with pines still wearing red bows from Christmas.

Mara felt as though the world were caught in a frozen moment, preserved beneath the snow. Nothing would ever change. No ice would melt. No birds would return to the branches. There would be nothing but blizzards and long, dark nights and snow-covered pines.

Mara wasn't sure she believed in G-d, but on her better days, she felt at peace with the idea of pausing, as if she were one of the dancers on ima's DVDs, halted mid-leap.

Except she wouldn't pause. She'd be replaced by that thing. That doll.

She glanced at her father. He stared fixedly at the road, grumbling under his breath in a blend of languages. He hadn't bought new clothes since losing so much weight, and the fabric of his coat fell in voluminous folds across the seat.

He glanced sideways at Mara watching him. "What's wrong?"

"Nothing," Mara muttered, looking away.

Abel pushed his nose into her shoulder. She turned in her seat to scratch between his ears. His tail thumped, *tick, tock*, like a metronome.

THEY PARKED BESIDE the grocery. The small building's densely packed shelves were reassuringly the same year in and year out except for the special display mounted at the front of the store. This week it showcased red-wrapped sausages, marked with a cheerful, handwritten sign.

Gerry stood on a ladder in the center aisle, restocking cereals. He beamed as they walked in.

"Ten-thirty to the minute!" he called. "Good morning, my punctual Jewish friends!"

Gerry had been slipping down the slope called being hard of hearing for years now. He pitched his voice as if he were shouting across a football field.

"How is my little adult?" he asked Mara. "Are you forty today, or is it fifty?"

"Sixty-five," Mara said. "Seventy tomorrow."

"Such an old child," Gerry said, shaking his head. "Are you sure you didn't steal that body?"

Abba didn't like those kinds of jokes. He used to worry that they would make her self-conscious; now he hated them for bringing up the subject of aging. Flatly, he replied, "Children in our family are like that. There is nothing wrong with her."

Mara shared an eye roll with the grocer.

"Never said there was," Gerry said. Changing the subject, he gestured at Mara's crutches with a box of cornflakes. "You're an athlete on those. I bet there's nothing you can't do with them."

Mara forced a smile. "They're no good for dancing."

He shrugged. "I used to know a guy in a wheelchair. Out-danced everyone."

"Not ballet, though."

"True," Gerry admitted, descending the ladder. "Come to the counter. I've got something for you."

Gerry had hardly finished speaking before Abel forgot about being gentle with Mara's crutches. He knew what Gerry's gifts meant. The lead wrenched out of Mara's hand. She chased after him, crutches clicking, but even with his aging joints, the dog reached the front counter before Mara was halfway across the store.

"Wicked dog," Gerry said in a teasing tone as he caught Abel's leash. He scratched the dog between the ears and then bent to grab a package from under the counter. "Sit," he said. "Beg." The old dog rushed to do both. Gerry unwrapped a sausage and tossed it. Abel snapped and swallowed.

Mara finished crossing the aisle. She leaned against the front counter. She tried to conceal her heavy breathing, but she knew that her face must be flushed. Abba waited at the edges of her peripheral vision, his arms stretched in Mara's direction as if he expected her to collapse.

Gerry glanced between Mara and her father, assessing the situation. Settling on Mara, he tapped a stool behind the counter. "You look wiped. Take a load off. Your dad and I can handle ourselves."

"Yes, Mara," abba said quickly. "Perhaps you should sit."

Mara glared. "Abba."

"I'm sorry," abba said, looking away. He added to Gerry, "She doesn't like help."

"No help being offered. I just want some free work. You up for manning the register?" Gerry tapped the stool again. "I put aside one of those strawberry things you like. It's under the counter. Wrapped in pink paper."

"Thanks," Mara said, not wanting to hurt Gerry's feelings by mentioning that she couldn't eat before appointments. She went behind the counter and let Gerry hold her crutches while she pulled herself onto the stool. She hated how good it felt to sit.

Gerry nodded decisively. "Come on," he said, leading abba toward the fresh fruit.

Abba and Gerry made unlikely friends. Gerry made no bones about being a charismatic evangelical. During the last election, he'd put up posters saying that Democratic voters were headed to hell. In return, abba had suggested that Republican voters might need a punch in the jaw, especially any Republican voters who happened to be standing in front of him. Gerry responded that he supported free speech as much as any other patriotic American, but speech like that could get the H-E-double-hockey-sticks out of his store. They shouted. Gerry told abba not to come back. Abba said he wouldn't even buy dog food from fascists.

The next week, Gerry was waiting on the sidewalk with news about a kosher supplier, and Mara and abba went in as if nothing had ever happened.

Before getting sick, Mara had always followed the men through the aisles, joining in their arguments about pesticides and free-range chickens. Gerry liked to joke that he wished his children were as interested in the business as Mara was. *Maybe I'll leave the store to you instead of them*, he'd say, jostling her shoulder. He had stopped saying that.

Mara slipped the wrapped pastry out from under the counter. She broke it into halves and hid one in each pocket, hoping Gerry wouldn't see the lumps when they left. She left the empty paper on the counter, dusted with the crumbs.

An activity book lay next to where the pastry had been. It was for little kids, but Mara pulled it out anyway. Gerry's children were too old to play with things like that now, but he still kept an array of diversions under the counter for when customers' kids needed to be kept busy. It was better to do something than nothing. Armed with the felt-tip pen that was clipped to the cover, she began to flip through pages of half-colored drawings and connect-the-dots.

A few aisles over, near the butcher counter, she heard her father grumbling. She looked up and saw Gerry grab abba's shoulder. As always, he was speaking too loudly. His voice boomed over the hum of the freezers. "I got in the best sausages on Wednesday," he said. "They're kosher. Try them. Make them for your, what do you call it, sadbath."

By then, Gerry knew the word, but it was part of their banter.

"Shabbat," Abba corrected.

Gerry's tone grew more serious. "You're losing too much weight. A man needs meat."

Abba's voice went flat. "I eat when I am hungry. I am not hungry so much lately."

Gerry's grip tightened on abba's shoulder. His voice dropped. "Jakub, you need to take care of yourself."

He looked back furtively at Mara. Flushing with shame, she dropped her gaze to the activity book. She clutched the pen tightly, pretending to draw circles in a word search.

"You have to think about the future," said Gerry. His voice lowered even further. Though he was finally speaking at a normal volume, she still heard every word. "You aren't the one who's dying."

Mara's flush went crimson. She couldn't tell if it was shame or anger – all she felt was cold, rigid shock. She couldn't stop herself from sneaking a glance at abba. He, too, stood frozen. Neither of them ever said it. It was a game of avoidance they played together.

Abba pulled away from Gerry and started down the aisle. His face looked numb rather than angry. He stopped at the counter, looking at everything but Mara. He took Abel's leash and gestured for Mara to get off of the stool. "We'll be late for your appointment," he said, even though it wasn't even eleven o'clock. In a louder voice, he added, "Ring up our cart, would you, Gerry? We'll pick up our bags on our way out of town."

*　　*　　*

MARA DIDN'T LIKE Doctor Pinsky. Abba liked him because he was Jewish even though he was American-born reform with a degree from Queens. He wore his hair close-cut but it looked like it would Jew 'fro if he grew it out.

He kept his nails manicured. His teeth shone perfectly white. He never looked directly at Mara when he spoke. Mara suspected he didn't like children much. Maybe you needed to be that way if you were going to watch the sick ones get worse.

The nurses were all right. Grace and Nicole, both blonde and a bit fat. They didn't understand Mara since she didn't fit their idea of what kids were supposed to be like. She didn't talk about pop or interactives. When there were other child patients in the waiting room, she ignored them.

When the nurses tried to introduce her to the other children anyway, Mara said she preferred to talk to adults, which made them hmm and flutter. *Don't you have any friends, honey?* Nicole had asked her once, and Mara answered that she had some, but they were all on attic space. A year ago, if Mara had been upset, she'd have gone into a-space to talk to her best friend, Collin, but more and more as she got sick, she'd hated seeing him react to her withering body, hated seeing the fright and pity in his eyes. The thought of going back into attic space made her nauseous.

Grace and Nicole gave Mara extra attention because they felt sorry for her. Modern cancer treatments had failed to help and now Mara was the only child patient in the clinic taking chemotherapy. *It's hard on little bodies,* said Grace. *Heck, it's hard on big bodies, too.*

Today it was Grace who came to meet Mara in the waiting room, pushing a wheelchair. Assuming it was for another patient, Mara started to gather her crutches, but Grace motioned for her to stay put. "Let me treat you like a princess."

"I'm not much of a princess," Mara answered, immediately realizing from the pitying look on Grace's face that it was the wrong thing to say. To Grace, that would mean she didn't feel like a princess because she was sick, rather than that she wasn't interested in princesses.

"I can walk," Mara protested, but Grace insisted on helping her into the wheelchair anyway. She hadn't realized how tightly abba was holding her hand until she pulled it free.

Abba stood to follow them. Grace turned back. "Would you mind staying? Doctor Pinsky wants to talk to you."

"I like to go with Mara," abba said.

"We'll take good care of her." Grace patted Mara's shoulder. "You don't mind, do you, princess?"

Mara shrugged. Her father shifted uncertainly. "What does Doctor Pinsky want?"

"He'll be out in a few minutes," said Grace, deflecting. "I'm sorry, Mr. Morawski. You won't have to wait long."

Frowning, abba sat again, fingers worrying the collar of his shirt. Mara saw his conflicting optimism and fear, all inscribed plainly in his eyes, his face, the way he sat. She didn't understand why he kept hoping. Even before they'd tried the targeted immersion therapy and the QTRC regression, she'd known that they wouldn't work. She'd known from the moment when she saw the almost imperceptible frown cross the diagnostician's face when he asked about the pain she'd been experiencing in her knee for months before the break. Yes, she'd said, it had been worse at night, and his brow had darkened, just for an instant. Maybe she'd known even earlier than that, in the moment just after she fell in ima's studio, when she realized with strange, cold clarity that something was very wrong.

Bad news didn't come all at once. It came in successions. Cancer is present. Metastasis has occurred. The tumors are unresponsive. The patient's vitals have taken a turn for the worse. We're sorry to say, we're sorry to say, we're sorry to say.

Grace wheeled Mara toward the back, maintaining a stream of banal, cheerful chatter, remarks about the weather and questions about the holidays and jokes about boys. Mara deflected. She wasn't ever going to have a boyfriend, not the way Grace was teasing her about. Adolescence was like spring, one more thing buried in endless snow.

MARA FELT EXHAUSTED as they pulled into the driveway. She didn't have the energy to push abba away when he came around the truck to help her down. Mara leaned heavily on her father's arm as they crunched their way to the front door.

She vomited in the entryway. Abel came to investigate. She pushed his nose away while abba went to get the mop. The smell made her even more nauseated and so when abba returned, she left him to clean up. It made her feel guilty, but she was too tired to care.

She went to the bathroom to wash out her mouth. She tried not to catch her eye in the mirror, but she saw her reflection anyway. She felt a shock of alienation from the thin, sallow face. It couldn't be hers.

She heard abba in the hallway, grumbling at Abel in Yiddish. Wan, late afternoon light filtered through the windows, foreshadowing sunset. A few months ago, she and abba would have been rushing to cook and clean before Shabbat. Now no one cleaned and Mara left abba to cook alone as she went into ima's studio.

She paused by the barre before sitting, already worried about how difficult it would be to get up again. "I want to watch *Coppélia*," she said. The AI whirred.

Coppélia began with a young woman reading on a balcony – except she wasn't really a young woman, she was actually an automaton constructed by the mad scientist, Dr. Coppélius. The dancer playing Coppélia pretended to read from a red leather book. Mara told the AI to fast-forward to ima's entrance.

Mara's mother was dancing the part of the peasant girl, Swanhilde. She looked nothing like the dancer playing Coppélia. Ima was strong, but also short and compact, where Coppélia was tall with visible muscle definition in her arms and legs.

Yet later in the ballet, none of the other characters would be able to tell them apart. Mara wanted to shake them into sense. Why couldn't they tell the difference between a person and a doll?

ABBA LIT THE candles and began the prayer, waving his hands through the smoke. They didn't have an adult woman to read the prayers and abba wouldn't let Mara do it while she was still a child. *Soon*, he used to say, *after your bat mitzvah*. Now he said nothing.

They didn't celebrate Shabbat properly. They followed some traditions – tonight they'd leave the lights on, and tomorrow they'd eat cold food instead of cooking – but they did not attend services. If they needed to work then they worked. As a family, they had always been observant in some ways and relaxed in others; they were not the kind who took well to following rules. Abba sometimes seemed to believe in Hashem and at other times not, though he believed in rituals and tradition. Still, before Mara had become ill, they'd taken more care with *halakha*.

As abba often reminded her, Judaism taught that survival was more important than dogma. *Pikuach nefesh* meant that a hospital could run electricity that powered a machine that kept a man alive. A family could work to keep a woman who had just given birth comfortable and healthy.

Perhaps other people wouldn't recognize the exceptions that Mara and her father made from Shabbat as being matters of survival, but they were. They were using all they had just by living. Not much remained for G-d.

The long window over the kitchen counters let through the dimming light as violet and ultramarine seeped across the horizon. The tangerine sun lingered above the trees, preparing to descend into scratching, black branches. Mara's attention drifted as he said Kiddush over the wine.

They washed their hands. Abba tore the challah. He gave a portion to Mara. She let it sit.

"The fish is made with ginger," abba said. "Would you like some string beans?"

"My mouth hurts," Mara said.

Abba paused, the serving plate still in his hands.

She knew that he wouldn't eat unless she did. "I'll have a little," she added softly.

She let him set the food on her plate. She speared a single green bean and stared at it for a moment before biting. Everything tasted like metal after the drugs.

"I used turmeric," he said.

"It's good."

Mara's stomach roiled. She set the fork on her plate.

Her father ate a few bites of fish and then set his fork down, too. A maudlin expression crossed his face. "Family is Hashem's best gift," he said.

Mara nodded. There was little to say.

Abba picked up his wine glass. He twisted the stem as he stared into red. "Family is what the *goyim* tried to take from us with pogroms and ghettoes and the *shoah*. On Shabbat, we find our families, wherever we are."

Abba paused again, sloshing wine gently from side to side.

"Perhaps I should have gone to Israel before you were born."

Mara looked up with surprise. "You think Israel is a corrupt theocracy."

"There are politics, like opposing a government, and then there is needing to be with your people." He shrugged. "I thought about going. I had money then, but no roots. I could have gone wherever I wanted. But I thought, I will go to America instead. There are more Jews in America than Israel. I did not want to live in the shadow of the *shoah*. I wanted to make a family in a place where we could rebuild everything they stole. *Der mensch trakht un Gatt lahkt.*"

He had been speaking rapidly, his accent deepening with every word. Now he stopped.

His voice was hoarse when it returned.

"Your mother... you... I would not trade it, but..." His gaze became diffuse as if the red of the wine were a telescope showing him another world. "It's all so fragile. Your mother is taken and you... *tsuris, tsuris*... and then there is nothing."

IT WAS DARK when they left the table. Abba piled dishes by the sink so that they could be washed after Shabbat and then retired to his bedroom. Abel came to Mara, tail thumping, begging for scraps. She was too tired to make him beg or shake hands. She rescued her plate from the pile of dishes and laid it on the floor for him to lick clean.

She started toward her bed and then changed her mind. She headed downstairs instead, Abel following after. She paused with her hand on the knob of the red-painted door before entering abba's workshop.

Mara hadn't seen abba go downstairs since their argument that morning but he must have managed to do it without her noticing. The doll sat primly on her stool, dignity restored, her head tilted down as if she were reading a book that Mara couldn't see.

Mara wove between worktables until she reached the doll's side. She lifted its hand and pressed their palms together as abba had done. It was strange to see the shape of her fingers so perfectly copied, down to the fine lines across her knuckles.

She pulled the thing forward. It lolled. Abel ducked its flailing right hand and ran a few steps away, watching warily.

Mara took hold of the thing's head. She pressed the tip of her nose against the tip of its nose, trying to match their faces as she had their palms. With their faces so close together, it looked like a Cyclops, staring back at her with one enormous, blank eye.

"I hate you," Mara said, lips pressed against its mute mouth.

It was true, but not the same way that it had been that morning. She had been furious then. Betrayed. Now the blaze of anger had burned down and she saw what lay in the ashes that remained.

It was jealousy. That this doll would be the one to take abba's hand at Shabbat five years from then, ten years, twenty. That it would take and give the comfort she could not. That it would balm the wounds that she had no choice but to inflict.

Would Mara have wanted a clockwork doll if it meant that she could keep ima?

She imagined lying down for the scans. She imagined a machine studying her brain, replicating her dreams neuron by neuron, rendering her as mathematical patterns. She'd read enough biology and psychology to know that, whatever else she was, she was also an epiphenomenon that arose from chemicals and meat and electricity.

It was sideways immortality. She would be gone, and she would remain. There and not there. A quantum mechanical soul.

Love could hurt, she knew. Love was what made you hurt when your ima died. Love was what made it hurt when abba came to you gentle and solicitous, every kindness a reminder of how much pain you'd leave behind.

She would do this painful thing because she loved him, as he had made this doll because he loved her. She thought, with a sudden clenching of her stomach, that it was a good thing most people never lived to see what people planned to make of them when they were gone.

What Gerry had said was as true as it was cutting. Abba was not the one who would die.

*   *   *

ABBA SLEPT AMONG twisted blankets, clutching his pillow as if afraid to let it go.

Mara watched from the doorway. "Abba."

He grumbled in his sleep as he shifted position.

"Abba," she repeated. "Please wake up, abba."

She waited while he put on his robe. Then, she led him down.

She made her way swiftly through the workshop, passing the newly painted marionette and the lonely mechanical hand. She halted near the doll, avoiding its empty gaze.

"I'm ready now," she said.

Abba's face shifted from confusion to wariness. With guarded hope, he asked, "Are you certain?"

"I'm sure," she said.

"Please, Mara. You do not have to."

"I know," she answered. She pressed herself against his chest, as if she were a much smaller child looking for comfort. She felt the tension in his body seep into relief as he wept with silent gratitude. She was filled with tears, too, from a dozen emotions blended into one. They were tears of relief, and regret, and pain, and love, and mourning, and more.

He wrapped his arms around her. She closed her eyes and savored the comfort of his woody scent, his warmth, the stubble scratching her arm. She could feel how thin he'd become, but he was still strong enough to hold her so tightly that his embrace was simultaneously joyful and almost too much to bear.

Act II: Jakub
Tour en l'air
(Turn in the Air)

JAKUB WAS CAREFUL to make the scans as unobtrusive as possible. If he could have, he'd have recorded a dozen sessions, twenty-five, fifty, more. He'd have examined every obscure angle; he'd have recorded a hundred redundancies.

Mara was so fragile, though; not just physically, but mentally. He did not want to tax her. He found a way to consolidate what he needed into six night-time sessions, monitoring her with portable equipment that he could bring into her bedroom which broadcast its data to the larger machinery in the basement.

When the scans were complete, Jakub spent his nights in the workshop, laboring over the new child while Mara slept. It had been a long time since he'd worked with technology like this, streamlined for its potential as a weapon. He had to gentle it, soothe it, coax it into being as careful about preserving memories of rainy mornings as it was about retaining reflexes and fighting skills.

He spent long hours poring over images of Mara's brain. He navigated three-dimensional renderings with the AI's help, puzzling over the strangeness of becoming so intimate with his daughter's mind in such an unexpected way. After he had finished converting the images into a neural map, he looked at Mara's mind with yet new astonishment. The visual representation showed associational clusters as if they were stars: elliptical galaxies of thought.

It was a truism that there were many ways to describe a river – from the action of its molecules to the map of its progress from tributaries to ocean. A mind was such a thing as well. On one end there was thought, personality, individual... and on the other... It was impossible to recognize Mara in the points of light, but he was in the midst of her most basic elements, and there was as much awe in that as there was in puzzling out the origin of the universe. He was the first person ever to see another human being in this way. He knew Mara now as no one else had ever known anyone.

His daughter, his beloved, his *sheineh maideleh*. There were so many others that he'd failed to protect. But Mara would always be safe; he would hold her forever.

Once Jakub had created the foundational schematics for manufacturing analogues to Mara's brain structures, the remainder of the process was automated. Jakub needed only to oversee it, occasionally inputting his approval to the machine.

Jakub found it unbearable to leave the machinery unsupervised, but nevertheless, he could not spend all of his time in the basement. During the mornings when Mara was awake, he paced the house, grumbling at the dog who followed him up and down the hallways as if expecting him to throw a stick. What if the process stalled? What if a catastrophic failure destroyed the images of Mara's mind now when her health was even more fragile and there might be no way to replace them?

He forced himself to disguise his obsession while Mara was awake. It was important to maintain the illusion that their life was the same as it had been before. He knew that Mara remained uneasy with the automaton. Its very presence said so many things that they had been trying to keep silent.

Mara's days were growing even harder. He'd thought the end of chemotherapy would give her some relief, but cancer pain worsened every day. Constant suffering and exhaustion made her alternately sullen and sharp. She snapped at him when he brought her meals, when he tried to help her across the house, when she woke to find him lingering in the doorway while she slept. Part of it was the simple result of pain displacing patience, but it was more, too. Once, when he had touched her shoulder, she'd flinched; then, upon seeing him withdraw, her expression had turned from annoyance to guilt. She'd said, softly, "You won't always be able to do that." A pause, a swallow, and then even more quietly, "It reminds me."

That was what love and comfort had become now. Promises that couldn't be kept.

Most nights, she did not sleep at all, only lay awake, staring out of her window at the snow.

Jakub searched for activities that might console her. He asked her if she'd like him to read to her. He offered to buy her immersive games. He suggested that she log into a spare room with other sick children where they could discuss their troubles. She told him that she wanted to be alone.

She had always been an unusual child, precocious and content to be her own companion. Meryem had said it was natural for a daughter of theirs, who had been raised among adults, and was descended from people who were also talented and solitary. Jakub and Meryem had been similar as children, remote from others their own age as they pursued their obsessions. Now Jakub wished she had not inherited these traits so completely, that she was more easily able to seek solace.

When Mara didn't think he was watching, she gathered her crutches and went into Meryem's studio to watch ballets. She did not like it when he came too close, and so he watched from the hallway. He could see her profile reflected in the mirrors on the opposite wall. She cried as she watched, soundless tears beading her cheeks.

One morning when she put on *A Midsummer Night's Dream*, Jakub ventured into the studio. For so long, he had stayed away, but that had not made things better. He had to try what he could.

He found Mara sitting on the floor, her crutches leaning against the ballet barre. Abel lay a few feet away with his head on his paws. Without speaking, Jakub sat beside them.

Mara wiped her cheeks, streaking her tears. She looked resentfully at Jakub, but he ignored her, hoping he could reach the part of her that still wanted his company even if she had buried it.

They sat stoically for the remainder of act one, holding themselves with care so that they did not accidentally shift closer to one another. Mara pretended to ignore him, though her darting glances told another story. Jakub let her maintain the pretence, trying to allow her some personal space within the studio since he had already intruded so far. He hoped she would be like a scared rabbit, slowly adjusting to his presence and coming to him when she saw that he was safe.

Jakub had expected to spend the time watching Mara and not the video, but he was surprised to find himself drawn into the dancing. The pain of seeing Meryem leap and spin had become almost a dull note, unnoticeable in the concert of his other sorrows. Meryem made a luminous Titania, a ginger wig cascading in curls down her back, her limbs wrapped in flowers, leaves and gossamer. He'd forgotten the way she moved onstage, as careful and precise as a doe, each agile maneuver employing precisely as much strength as she needed and no more.

As Act II began, Mara asked the AI to stop. Exhaustion, she said. Jakub tried to help her back to her room, but she protested, and he let her go.

She was in her own world now, closing down. She had no room left for him.

What can I do for you, Marale? he wanted to ask. *I will do anything. You will not let me hold you so I must find another way. I will change the laws of life and death. I will give you as much forever as I can,* sheineh maideleh. *See? I am doing it now.*

He knew that she hated it when he stood outside her door, watching, but when he heard her breath find the steady rhythm of sleep, he went to the threshold anyway. While she slept, Mara looked peaceful for a while, her chest gently rising and falling underneath her snow-colored quilt.

He lingered a long time. Eventually, he left her and returned downstairs to check the machines.

The new child was ready to be born.

FOR YEARS, JAKUB had dreamed of the numbers. They flickered in and out of focus as if displayed on old film. Sometimes they looked ashen and faded. At other times, they were darker than any real black. Always, they were written on palettes of human flesh.

Sometimes the dreams included fragmentary memories. Jakub would be back in the rooms his grandparents had rented when he was a child, watching bubbe prepare to clean the kitchen, pulling her left arm free from one long cotton sleeve, her tattoo a shock on the inside of her forearm. The skin there had gone papery with age, the ink bleached and distorted, but time and sun had not made the mark less portentous. She scoured cookware with steel wool and caustic chemicals that made her hands red and raw when they emerged from the bubbling water. No matter how often Jakub watched, he never stopped expecting her to abandon the ancient pots and turn that furious, unrelenting scrubbing onto herself.

Zayde's tattoo remained more mysterious. It had not been inflicted in Auschwitz and so it hid in the more discreet location they'd used on the trains, needled onto the underside of his upper arm. Occasionally on hot days when Jakub was small, zayde would roll up his sleeves while he worked outside in the sun. If Jakub or one of the other boys found him, zayde would shout at them to get back inside and then finish the work in his long sleeves, dripping with sweat.

Jakub's grandparents never spoke of the camps. Both had been young in those years, but even though they were not much older when they were released, the few pictures of them from that time showed figures that were already brittle and desiccated in both physique and expression. Survivors took many paths away from the devastation, but bubbe and zayde were among those who always afterward walked with their heads down.

Being mutually bitter and taciturn, they resisted marriage until long after their contemporaries had sought comfort in each other's arms. They raised their children with asperity, and sent them into the world as adults with small gifts of money and few displays of emotion.

One of those children was Jakub's mother, who immigrated to the United States where she married. Some years later, she died in childbirth, bearing what would have been Jakub's fifth brother had the child not been stillborn. Jakub's father, grieving, could not take care of his four living sons. Instead, he wrote to his father-in-law in Poland and requested that he come to the United States and take them home with him.

Even then, when he arrived on foreign shores to fetch boys he'd never met and take them back with him to a land they'd never known; even then when the moment should have been grief and gathering; even then zayde's face was hard-lined with resignation. Or so Jakub's elder brothers had told him, for he was the youngest of the surviving four, having learned to speak a few words by then but not yet able to stand on his own.

When the boys were children, it was a mystery to them how such harsh people could have spent long enough together to marry, let alone have children. Surely, they would have been happier with others who were kinder, less astringent, who could bring comfort into a marriage.

One afternoon, when Jakub was four years old, and too naïve to yet understand that some things that were discussed in private should not be shared with everyone, he was sitting with bubbe while she sewed shirts for the boys (too expensive to buy, and shouldn't she know how to sew, having done it all her life?). He asked, "If you don't like zayde, why did you marry him?"

She stopped suddenly. Her hands were still on the machine, her mouth open, her gaze fastened on the seam. For a moment, the breath did not rise in her chest. The needle stuttered to a stop as her foot eased its pressure on the pedal.

She did not deny it or ask *What do you mean?* Neither did she answer any of the other questions that might have been enfolded in that one, like *Why don't you like him?* or *Why did you marry at all?*

Instead, she heard Jakub's true question: *Why zayde and not someone else?*

"How could it be another?" she asked. "We're the same."

And then she began sewing again, making no further mention of it. It was what zayde would have done, too, if Jakub had taken his question to where his grandfather worked at replacing the wiring in their old, old walls.

As important as it was for the two of them that they shared a history, it also meant that they were like knives to each other, constantly reopening each other's old wounds and salting them with tears and anger. Their frequent, bitter arguments could continue for days upon days.

The days of arguing were better than those when bitter silence descended, and each member of the family was left in their own, isolated coldness.

It was not that there were no virtues to how the boys were raised. Their bodies were kept robust on good food, and their minds strengthened with the exercise of solving problems both practical and intellectual. Zayde concocted new projects for them weekly. One week they'd learn to build cabinets, and the next they'd read old books of philosophy, debating free will versus determinism. Jakub took Leibniz's part against zayde's Spinoza. They studied the Torah as an academic text, though zayde was an atheist of the bitter stripe after his time in the camps.

When Jakub was nine, bubbe decided that it was time to cultivate their spirits as well as their minds and bodies. She revealed that she had been having dreams about G-d for decades, ever since the day she left the camp. The hours of her rescue haunted her; as she watched them replay, she said, the world seemed to shimmer with awe and renewal. Over the years, she had come to believe that was the presence of G-d. Knowing zayde's feelings about G-d, bubbe had kept her silence in the name of peace for decades, but that year, some indefinable thing had shifted her conscience and she could do so no longer.

As she'd predicted, zayde was furious. "I am supposed to worship a G-d that would make *this* world?" he demanded. "A G-d like that is no G-d. A G-d like that is evil."

But despite the hours of shouting, slammed doors, and smashed crockery, bubbe remained resolute. She became a *frum* woman, dressing carefully, observing prayers and rituals. On Fridays, the kitchen became the locus of urgent energy as bubbe rushed to prepare for Shabbat, directing Jakub and his brothers to help with the chores. All of them worked tensely, preparing for the moment when zayde would return home and throw the simmering cholent out of the window, or – if they were lucky – turn heel and walk back out, going who-knew-where until he came home on Sunday.

After a particularly vicious argument, zayde proclaimed that while he apparently could not stop his wife from doing as she pleased, he would absolutely no longer permit his grandsons to attend *shul*. It was a final decision; otherwise, one of them would have to leave and never come back. After that, bubbe slipped out alone each week, into the chilly morning.

From zayde and bubbe, Jakub learned that love was both balm and nettle. They taught him from an early age that nothing could hurt so much as family.

SOMEHOW, JAKUB HAD expected the new child to be clumsy and vacant as if she were an infant, but the moment she initialized, her blank look vanished. Some parts of her face tensed and others relaxed. She blinked. She looked just like Mara.

She prickled under Jakub's scrutiny. "What are you staring at? Is something wrong?"

Jakub's mouth worked silently as he sought the words. "I thought you would need more time to adjust."

The child smiled Mara's cynical, lopsided smile, which had been absent for months. "I think you're going to need more time to adjust than I do."

She pulled herself to her feet. It wasn't just her face that had taken on Mara's habits of expression. Without pause, she moved into one of the stretches that Meryem had taught her, elongating her spine. When she relaxed, her posture was exactly like Mara's would have been, a preadolescent slouch ameliorated by a hint of dancer's grace.

"Can we go upstairs?" she asked.

"Not yet," Jakub said. "There are tests to perform."

Tests which she passed. Every single one. She knew Mara's favorite colors and the names of the children she had studied with in attic space. She knew the color and weight of the apples that would grow on their trees next fall and perfectly recited the recipe for baking them with cinnamon. In the gruff tone that Mara used when she was guarding against pain, she related the story of Meryem's death – how Meryem had woken with complaints of feeling dizzy, how she had slipped in the bath later that morning, how her head had cracked against the porcelain and spilled red into the bathwater.

She ran like Mara and caught a ball like Mara and bent to touch her toes like Mara. She was precisely as fleet and as nimble and as flexible as Mara. She performed neither worse nor better. She was Mara's twin in every way that Jakub could measure.

"You will need to stay here for a few more days," he told her, bringing down blankets and pillows so that he could make her a bed in the workshop. "There are still more tests. You will be safer if you remain close to the machines."

The new child's face creased with doubt. He was lying to spare her feelings, but she was no more deceived than Mara would have been. She said, "My room is upstairs."

For so many months, Jakub and Mara had taken refuge in mutual silence when the subject turned uncomfortable. He did not like to speak so bluntly. But if she would force him –" No," he said gently. "That is Mara's room."

"Can't I at least see it?"

Wheedling thinned her voice. Her body language occupied a strange lacuna between aggression and vulnerability. She faced him full-on, one foot advancing, with her hands clenched tightly at her sides. Yet at the same time, she could not quite meet his eyes, and her head was tilted slightly downward, protecting her neck.

Jakub had seen that strange combination before. It was not so unusual a posture for teenagers to wear when they were trying to assert their agency through rebellion and yet simultaneously still hoping for their parents' approval.

Mara had never reached that stage. Before she became ill, she had been calm, abiding. Jakub began to worry that he'd erred in his calculations, that the metrics he'd used had been inadequate to measure the essence of a girl. Could she have aged so much, simply being slipped into an artificial skin?

"Mara is sleeping now."

"But I *am* Mara!" The new child's voice broke on her exclamation.

Her lips parted uncertainly. Her fingers trembled. Her glance flashed upward for a moment and he saw such pain in it. No, she was still his Mara. Not defiant, only afraid that he would decide that he had not wanted a mechanical daughter after all, that he would reject her like a broken radio and never love her again.

Gently, he laid his hand on her shoulder. Softly, he said, "You are Mara, but you need a new name, too. Let us call you Ruth."

He had not known until he spoke that he was going to choose that name, but it was a good one. In the Torah, Ruth had given Mara *hesed*. His Mara needed loving kindness, too.

The new child's gaze flickered upward as if she could see through the ceiling and into Mara's room. "Mara is the name ima gave me," she protested.

Jakub answered, "It would be confusing otherwise."

He hoped that this time the new child would understand what he meant without his having to speak outright. The other Mara had such a short time. It would be cruel to make her days harder than they must be.

ON THE DAY when Jakub gave the automaton her name, he found himself recalling the story of Ruth. It had been a long time since he had given the Torah any serious study, but though he had forgotten its minutiae, he remembered its rhythm.

It began when a famine descended on Judah.

A man, Elimelech, decided that he was not going to let his wife and sons starve to death, and so he packed his household and brought them to Moab. It was good that he had decided to do so, because once they reached Moab, he died, and left his wife and sons alone.

His wife was named Naomi and her name meant pleasant. The times were not pleasant.

Naomi's sons married women from Moab, one named Orpah and the other named Ruth. Despite their father's untimely death, the boys spent ten happy years with their new wives. But the men of that family had very poor luck. Both sons died.

There was nothing left for Naomi in Moab and so she packed up her house and prepared to return to Judah. She told her daughters-in-law, "Go home to your mothers. You were always kind to my sons and you've always been kind to me. May Hashem be kind to you in return."

She kissed them goodbye, but the girls wept.

They said, "Can't we return to Judah with you?"

"Go back to your mothers," Naomi repeated. "I have no more sons for you to marry. What can I give if you stay with me?"

The girls continued to weep, but at last sensible Orpah kissed her mother-in-law and left for home.

Ruth, who was less sensible; Ruth, who was more loving; Ruth, who was more kind; Ruth, she would not go.

"Don't make me leave you," Ruth said. "Wherever you go, I will go. Wherever you lodge, I will lodge. Your people will be my people and your G-d my G-d."

When Naomi saw that Ruth was committed to staying with her, she abandoned her arguing and let her come.

They traveled together to Bethlehem. When they arrived, they found that the whole city had gathered to see them. Everyone was curious about the two women traveling from Moab. One woman asked, "Naomi! Is that you?"

Naomi shook her head. "Don't call me Naomi. There is no pleasantness in my life. Call me Mara, which means bitterness, for the Almighty has dealt very bitterly with me."

Through the bitterness, Ruth stayed. While Naomi became Mara, Ruth stayed. Ruth gave her kindness, and Ruth stayed.

JAKUB MET MERYEM while he was in Cleveland for a robotics conference. He'd attended dozens, but somehow this one made him feel particularly self-conscious in his cheap suit and tie among all the wealthy *goyim*.

By then he was living in the United States, but although he'd been born there, he rarely felt at home among its people. Between talks, he escaped from the hotel to go walking. That afternoon, he found his way to a path that wound through a park, making its way through dark-branched trees that waved their remaining leaves like flags of ginger, orange and gold.

Meryem sat on an ironwork bench beside a man-made lake, its water silvered with dusk. She wore a black felt coat that made her look pallid even though her cheeks were pink with cold. A wind rose as Jakub approached, rippling through Meryem's hair. Crows took off from the trees, disappearing into black marks on the horizon.

Neither of them was ever able to remember how they began to converse. Their courtship seemed to rise naturally from the lake and the crows and the fallen leaves, as if it were another inevitable element of nature. It was *bashert*.

Meryem was younger than Jakub, but even so, already ballet had begun taking its toll on her body. Ballet was created by trading pain for beauty, she used to say. Eventually, beauty vanished and left only the pain.

Like Jakub, Meryem was an immigrant. Her grandparents had been born in Baghdad where they lived through the *farhud* instead of the *shoah*. They stayed in Iraq despite the pogroms until the founding of Israel made it too dangerous to remain. They abandoned their family home and fled to the U.S.S.R.

When Meryem was small, the Soviet government identified her talent for dance and took her into training. Ballet became her new family. It was her blood and bone, her sacred and her profane.

Her older brother sometimes sent letters, but with the accretion of time and distance, Meryem came to think of her family as if they were not so much people as they were the words spelled out in Yusuf's spidery handwriting.

Communism fell, and Meryem's family was given the opportunity to reclaim her, but even a few years away is so much of a child's lifetime. She begged them not to force her to return. They no longer felt like her home. More, ballet had become the gravitational center of her life, and while she still resented it – how it had taken her unwillingly, how it bruised her feet and sometimes made them bleed – she also could not bear to leave its orbit. When Yusuf's letters stopped coming some time later, she hardly noticed.

She danced well. She was a lyrical ballerina, performing her roles with tender, affecting beauty that could make audiences weep or smile. She rapidly moved from corps to soloist to principal. The troupe traveled overseas to perform Stravinsky's *Firebird*, and when they reached the United States, Meryem decided to emigrate, which she accomplished with a combination of bribes and behind-the-scenes dealings.

Jakub and Meryem recognized themselves in each other's stories. Like his grandparents, they were drawn together by their similarities. Unlike them, they built a refuge together instead of a battlefield.

After Meryem died, Jakub began dreaming that the numbers were inscribed into the skins of people who'd never been near the camps. His skin. His daughter's. His wife's. They were all marked, as Cain was marked, as the Christians believed the devil would mark his followers at the end of time. Marked for diaspora, to blow away from each other and disappear.

*   *   *

"Is THE DOLL awake?" Mara asked one morning.

Jakub looked up from his breakfast to see her leaning against the doorway that led into the kitchen. She wore a large t-shirt from Yellowstone that came to her knees, covering a pair of blue jeans that had not been baggy when he'd bought them for her. Her skin was wan and her eyes shadowed and sunken. Traces of inflammation from the drugs lingered, painfully red, on her face and hands. The orange knit cap pulled over her ears was incongruously bright.

Jakub could not remember the last time she'd worn something other than pajamas.

"She is down in the workshop," Jakub said.

"She's awake, though?"

"She is awake."

"Bring her up."

Jakub set his spoon beside his leftover bowl of *chlodnik*. Mara's mouth was turned down at the corners, hard and resolute. She lifted her chin at a defiant angle.

"She has a bed in the workshop," Jakub said. "There are still tests I must run. It's best she stay close to the machines."

Mara shook her head. It was clear from her face that she was no more taken in by his lie than the new child had been. "It's not fair to keep someone stuck down there."

Jakub began to protest that the workshop was not such a bad place, but then he caught the flintiness in Mara's eyes and realized that she was not asking out of worry. She had dressed as best she could and come to confront him because she wanted her first encounter with the new child to be on her terms. There was much he could not give her, but he could give her that.

"I will bring her for dinner," he said. "Tomorrow, for Shabbat."

Mara nodded. She began the arduous process of departing the kitchen, but then stopped and turned back. "Abba," she said hesitantly. "If ima hated the ballet, why did you build her a studio?"

"She asked for one," Jakub said.

Mara waited.

At last, he continued, "Ballet was part of her. She could not simply stop."
Mara nodded once more. This time, she departed.

Jakub finished his *chlodnik* and spent the rest of the day cooking. He meted out ingredients for familiar dishes. A pinch, a dash, a dab. Chopping, grating, boiling, sampling. Salt and sweet, bitter and savory.

As he went downstairs to fetch Ruth, he found himself considering how strange it must be for her to remember these rooms and yet never to have entered them. Jakub and Meryem had drawn the plans for the house together. She'd told him that she was content to leave a world of beauty that was made by pain, in exchange for a plain world made by joy.

He'd said he could give her that.

They painted the outside walls yellow to remind them of the sun during the winter, and painted blue inside to remind them of the sky. By the time they had finished, Mara was waiting inside Meryem's womb. The three of them had lived in the house for seven years before Meryem died.

These past few weeks had been precious. Precious because he had, in some ways, finally begun to recover the daughter that he had lost on the day her leg shattered – Ruth, once again curious and strong and insightful, like the Mara he had always known. But precious, too, because these were his last days with the daughter he'd made with Meryem.

Precious days, but hardly bearable, even as he also could not bear that they would pass. Precious, but more salt and bitter than savory and sweet.

The next night, when Jakub entered the workshop, he found Ruth on the stool where she'd sat so long when she was empty. Her shoulders slumped; her head hung down. He began to worry that something was wrong, but then he saw that she was only reading the book of poetry that she held in her lap.

"Would you like to come upstairs for dinner?" Jakub asked.

Setting the poems aside, Ruth rose to join him.

LONG BEFORE JAKUB met Meryem – back in those days when he still traveled the country on commissions from the American government – Jakub had become friends with a rabbi from Minneapolis. The two still exchanged letters through the postal mail, rarefied and expensive as it was.

After Jakub sent the news from Doctor Pinsky, the rabbi wrote back, "First your wife and now your daughter… *es vert mir finster in di oygen*. You must not let yourself be devoured by *agmes-nefesh*. Even in the camps, people kept hope. *Yashir koyech*, my friend. You must keep hope, too."

Jakub had not written to the rabbi about the new child. Even if it had not been vital for him to keep the work secret, he would not have written about it. He could not be sure what the rabbi would say. Would he call the new child a golem instead of a girl? Would he declare the work unseemly or unwise?

But truly, Jakub was only following the rabbi's advice. The new child was his strength and hope. She would prevent him from being devoured by sorrow.

WHEN JAKUB AND Ruth arrived in the kitchen for Shabbat, Mara had not yet come.

They stood alone together in the empty room. Jakub had mopped the floors and scrubbed the counters and set the table with good dishes. The table was laid with challah, apricot chicken with farfel, and almond and raisin salad. *Cholent* simmered in a crock pot on the counter, waiting for Shabbat lunch.

Ruth started toward Mara's chair on the left. Jakub caught her arm, more roughly than he'd meant to. He pulled back, contrite. "No," he said softly. "Not there." He gestured to the chair on the right. Resentment crossed the new child's face, but she went to sit.

It was only as Jakub watched Ruth lower herself into the right-hand chair that he realized his mistake. "No! Wait. Not in Meryem's chair. Take mine. I'll switch with you —"

Mara's crutches clicked down the hallway. It was too late.

She paused in the doorway. She wore the blonde wig Jakub had bought for her after the targeted immersion therapy failed. Last year's green Pesach dress hung off of her shoulders. The cap sleeves neared her elbows.

Jakub moved to help with her crutches. She stayed stoic while he helped her sit, but he could see how much it cost her to accept assistance while she was trying to maintain her dignity in front of the new child. It would be worse because the new child possessed her memories and knew precisely how she felt.

Jakub leaned the crutches against the wall. Ruth looked away, embarrassed. Mara gave her a corrosive stare. "Don't pity me."

Ruth looked back. "What do you want me to do?"

"Turn yourself off," said Mara. "You're *muktzeh*."

Jakub wasn't sure he'd ever before heard Mara use the Hebrew word for objects forbidden on the Sabbath. Now, she enunciated it with crisp cruelty.

Ruth remained calm. "One may work on the Sabbath if it saves a life."

Mara scoffed. "If you call yours a life."

Jakub wrung his hands. "Please, Mara," he said. "You asked her to come."

Mara held her tongue for a lingering moment. Eventually, she nodded formally toward Ruth. "I apologize."

Ruth returned the nod. She sat quietly, hands folded in her lap. She didn't take nutrition from food, but Jakub had given her a hollow stomach that she could empty after meals so she would be able to eat socially. He waited to see if she would return Mara's insults, but she was the old Mara, the one who wasn't speared with pain and fear, the one who let aggressors wind themselves up if that was what they wanted to do.

Jakub looked between the girls. "Good," he said. "We should have peace for the Sabbath."

He went to the head of the table. It was late for the blessing, the sun skimming the horizon behind bare, black trees. He lit the candles and waved his hands over the flames to welcome Shabbat. He covered his eyes as he recited the blessing. "*Barukh atah Adonai, Elohaynu, melekh ha-olam...*"

Every time he said the words that should have been Meryem's, he remembered the way she had looked when she said them. Sometimes she peeked out from behind her fingers so that she could watch Mara. They were small, her hands, delicate like bird wings. His were large and blunt.

The girls stared at each other as Jakub said kaddish. After they washed their hands and tore the challah, Jakub served the chicken and the salad. Both children ate almost nothing and said even less.

"It's been a long time since we've had three for Shabbat," Jakub said. "Perhaps we can have a good *vikuekh*. Mara, I saw you reading my Simic? Ruth has been reading poetry, too. Haven't you, Ruth?"

Ruth shifted the napkin in her lap. "Yehuda Amichai," she said. "*Even a Fist Was once an Open Palm with Fingers.*"

"I love the first poem in that book," Jakub said. "I was reading it when –"

Mara's voice broke in, so quietly that he almost didn't hear. "Ruth?"

Jakub looked to Ruth. The new child stared silently down at her hands. Jakub cleared his throat, but she did not look up.

Jakub answered for her. "Yes?"

Mara's expression was slack, somewhere between stunned and lifeless. "You named her Ruth."

"She is here for you. As Ruth was there for Mara."

Mara began to cry. It was a tiny, pathetic sound. She pushed away her plate and tossed her napkin onto the table. "How could you?"

"Ruth gives *hesed* to Mara," Jakub said. "When everyone else left, Ruth stayed by her side. She expected nothing from her loving, from her kindness."

"*Du kannst nicht auf meinem rucken pishen unt mir sagen class es regen ist,*" Mara said bitterly.

Jakub had never heard Mara say that before either. The crass proverb sounded wrong in her mouth. "Please, I am telling you the truth," he said. "I wanted her name to be part of you. To come from your story. The story of Mara."

"Is that what I am to you?" Mara asked. "Bitterness?"

"No, no. Please, no. We never thought you were bitterness. Mara was the name Meryem chose. Like Maruska, the Russian friend she left behind." Jakub paused. "Please. I did not mean to hurt you. I thought the story would help you see. I wanted you to understand. The new child will not harm you. She'll show you *hesed.*"

Mara flailed for her crutches.

Jakub stood to help. Mara was so weak that she accepted his assistance. Tears flowed down her face. She left the room as quickly as she could, refusing to look at either Jakub or the new child.

Jakub looked between her retreating form and Ruth's silent one. The new child's expression was almost as unsure as Jakub's.

"Did you know?" Jakub asked. "Did you know how she'd feel?"

Ruth turned her head as if turning away from the question. "Talk to her," she said quietly. "I'll go back down to the basement."

*   *   *

MARA SAT ON her bed, facing the snow. Jakub stood at the threshold. She spoke without turning. "*Hesed* is a hard thing," she said. "Hard to take when you can't give it back."

Jakub crossed the room, past the chair he'd made her when she was little, with Meryem's shawl hung over the back; past the hanging marionette dressed as Giselle; past the cube Mara used for her lessons in attic space. He sat beside her on her white quilt and looked at her silhouetted form against the white snow.

She leaned back toward him. Her body was brittle and delicate against his chest. He remembered sitting on that bed with Mara and Meryem, reading stories, playing with toys. *Tsuris, tsuris.* Life was all so fragile. He was not graceful enough to keep it from breaking.

Mara wept. He held her in his large, blunt hands.

Act III: Ruth
Échappé
(Escape)

AT FIRST, RUTH couldn't figure out why she didn't want to switch herself off. Mara had reconciled herself to Ruth's existence, but in her gut, she still wanted Ruth to be gone. And Ruth was Mara, so she should have felt the same.

But no, her experiences were diverging. Mara wanted the false daughter to vanish. Mara thought Ruth was the false daughter, but Ruth knew she wasn't false at all. She *was* Mara. Or had been.

Coming into existence was not so strange. She felt no peculiar doubling, no sensation that her hands weren't hers, no impression that she had been pulled out of time and was supposed to be sleeping upstairs with her face turned toward the window.

She felt more secure in the new body than she had in Mara's. This body was healthy, even round in places. Her balance was steady; her fingernails were pink and intact.

After abba left her the first night, Ruth found a pane of glass that he'd set aside for one of his projects. She stared at her blurred reflection. The glass showed soft, smooth cheeks. She ran her fingers over them and they confirmed that her skin was downy now instead of sunken. Clear eyes stared back at her.

Over the past few months, Mara had grown used to experiencing a new alienation every time she looked in the mirror. She'd seen a parade of strangers' faces, each dimmer and hollower than the last.

Her face was her own again.

SHE SPENT HER first days doing tests. Abba watched her jump and stretch and run on a treadmill. For hours upon hours, he recorded her answers to his questions.

It was tedious for her, but abba was fascinated by her every word and movement. Sometimes he watched as a father. Sometimes he watched as a scientist. At first Ruth chafed under his experimental gaze, but then she remembered that he had treated Mara like that, too. He'd liked to set up simple experiments to compare her progress to child development manuals. She remembered ima complaining that he'd been even worse when Mara was an infant. Ruth supposed this was the same. She'd been born again.

While he observed her, she observed him. Abba forgot that some experiments could look back.

The abba she saw was a different man than the one she remembered sitting with Mara. He'd become brooding with Mara as she grew sicker. His grief had become a deep anger with G-d. He slammed doors and cabinets, and grimaced with bitter fury when he thought she wasn't looking. He wanted to break the world.

He still came down into the basement with that fury on his face, but as he talked to Ruth, he began to calm. The muscles in his forehead relaxed. He smiled now and then. He reached out to touch her hand, gently, as if she were a soap bubble that might break if he pressed too hard.

Then he went upstairs, back to that other Mara.

"Don't go yet," Ruth would beg. "We're almost done. It won't take much longer."

He'd linger.

She knew he thought she was just bored and wanted attention. But that wasn't why she asked. She hated the rain that silvered his eyes when he went up to see the dying girl.

After a few minutes, he always said the same thing, resolute and loyal to his still-living child. "I must go, *nu*?"

He sent Abel down in his place. The dog thumped down and waited for her to greet him at the foot of the stairs. He whuffed hello, breath humid and smelly.

Ruth had been convinced – when she was Mara – that a dog would never show affection for a robot. Maybe Abel only liked Ruth because his sense of smell, like the rest of him, was in decline. Whatever the reason, she was Mara enough for him.

Ruth ran the treadmill while Abel watched, tail wagging. She thought about chasing him across the snowy yard, about breaking sticks off of the bare-branched trees to throw for him. She could do anything. She could run; she could dance; she could swim; she could ride. She could almost forgive abba for treating her like a prototype instead of a daughter, but she couldn't forgive him for keeping her penned. The real Mara was stuck in the house, but Ruth didn't have to be. It wasn't fair to have spent so long static, waiting to die, and then suddenly be free – and still remain as trapped as she'd ever been.

After the disastrous Shabbat, she went back down to the basement and sat on one of abba's workbenches. Abel came down after her. He leaned against her knees, warm and heavy. She patted his head.

She hadn't known how Mara was going to react.

She should have known. She would have known if she'd thought about it. But she hadn't considered the story of Mara and Ruth. All she'd been thinking about was that Ruth wasn't her name.

Their experiences had branched off. They were like twins who'd shared the womb only to be delivered into a world where each new event was a small alienation, until their individual experiences separated them like a chasm.

One heard a name and wanted her own back. One heard a name and saw herself as bitterness.

One was living. One was dying.

She was still Mara enough to feel the loneliness of it.

The dog's tongue left a trail of slobber across the back of her hand. He pushed his head against her. He was warm and solid, and she felt tears threatening, and wasn't sure why. It might have been grief for Mara. Perhaps it was just the unreasonable relief that someone still cared about her. Even though it was miserly to crave attention when Mara was dying, she still felt the gnaw of wondering whether abba would still love her when Mara was gone, or whether she'd become just a machine to him, one more painful reminder.

She jumped off of the table and went to sit in the dark, sheltered place beneath it. There was security in small places – in closets, under beds, beneath the desk in her room. Abel joined her, pushing his side against hers. She curled around him and switched her brain to sleep.

AFTER SHABBAT, THERE was no point in separating Ruth and Mara anymore. Abba told Ruth she could go wherever she wanted. He asked where she wanted to sleep. "We can put a mattress in the parlor," he said. When she didn't react, he added, "Or the studio...?"

She knew he didn't want her in the studio. Mara was mostly too tired to leave her room now, but abba would want to believe that she was still sneaking into the studio to watch ima's videos.

Ruth wanted freedom, but it didn't matter where she slept.

"I'll stay in the basement," she said.

When she'd had no choice but to stay in the basement, she'd felt like a compressed coil that might spring uncontrollably up the stairs at any moment. Now that she was free to move around, it didn't seem so urgent. She could take her time a little, choose those moments when going upstairs wouldn't make things worse, such as when abba and Mara were both asleep, or when abba was sitting with Mara in her room.

Once she'd started exploring, she realized it was better that she was on her own anyway. Moving through the house was dreamlike, a strange blend of familiarity and alienation. These were rooms she knew like her skin, and yet she, as Ruth, had never entered them. The handprint impressed into the clay tablet on the wall wasn't hers; it was Mara's. She could remember the texture of the clay as she pushed in her palm, but it hadn't been her palm. She had never sat at the foot of the plush, red chair in the parlor while ima brushed her hair. The scuff marks on the hardwood in the hallway were from someone else's shoes.

As she wandered from room to room, she realized that on some unconscious level, when she'd been Mara, she'd believed that moving into a robotic body would clear the haze of memories that hung in the house. She'd imagined a robot would be a mechanical, sterile thing. In reality, ima still haunted the kitchen where she'd cooked, and the studio where she'd danced, and the bathroom where she'd died. Change wasn't exorcism.

RUTH REMAINED RESTLESS. She wanted more than the house. For the first time in months, she found herself wanting to visit attic space, even though her flock was even worse about handling cancer than adults, who were bad enough. The pity in Collin's eyes, especially, had made her want to puke so much that she hadn't even let herself think about him. Mara had closed the door on her best friend early in the process of closing the doors on her entire life.

She knew abba would be skeptical, though, so she wanted to bring it up in a way that seemed casual. She waited for him to come down to the workshop for her daily exam, and tried to broach the subject as if it were an afterthought.

"I think I should go back to the attic," she ventured. "I'm falling behind. My flock is moving on without me."

Abba looked up from the screen, frowning. He worried his hands in a way that had become troublingly familiar. "They know Mara is sick."

"I'll pretend to be sick," Ruth said. "I can fake it."

She'd meant to sound detached, as if her interest in returning to school was purely pragmatic, but she couldn't keep the anticipation out of her tone.

"I should go back now before it's been too long," she said. "I can pretend I'm starting to feel better. We don't want my recovery to look too sudden."

"It is not a good idea," abba said. "It would only add another complication. If you did not pretend correctly? If people noticed? You are still new-made. Another few weeks and you will know better how to control your body."

"I'm bored," Ruth said. Making another appeal to his scholarly side, she added, "I miss studying."

"You can study. You've been enjoying the poetry, yes? There is so much for you to read."

"It's not the same." Ruth knew she was on the verge of whining, but she couldn't make her voice behave.

Abba paused, trepidation playing over his features as he considered his response. "Ruth, I have thought on this... I do not think it is good for you to go back to attic space. They will know you. They might see that something is wrong. We will find you another program for home learning."

Ruth stared. "You want me to leave attic space?" Almost everyone she knew, apart from abba and a few people in town, was from the attic. After a moment's thought, the implications were suddenly leaden in her mind. "You don't just want me to stop going for school, do you? You want me to stop seeing them at all."

Abba's mouth pursed around words he didn't want to say.

"Everyone?" asked Ruth. "Collin? Everyone?"

Abba wrung his hands. "I am sorry, Mara. I only want to protect you."

"Ruth!" Ruth said.

"Ruth," abba murmured. "Please. I am sorry, Ruthele."

Ruth swallowed hard, trying to push down sudden desperation. She hadn't wanted the name. She didn't want the name. But she didn't want to be confused for the Mara upstairs either. She wanted him to be there with *her*, talking to *her*.

"You can't keep me stuck here just because she is!" she said, meaning the words to bite. "She's the one who's dying. Not me."

Abba flinched. "You are so angry," he said quietly. "I thought, now that you were well – You did not used to be so angry."

"You mean *Mara* didn't used to be so angry," Ruth said. A horrible thought struck her and she felt cold that she hadn't thought of it before. "How am I going to grow up? Am I going to be stuck like this? Eleven, like she is, forever?"

"No, Ruth, I will build you new bodies," said abba. "Bodies are easy. It is the mind that is difficult."

"You just want me to be like her," Ruth said.

Abba fumbled for words. "I want you to be yourself."

"Then let me go do things! You can't hide me here forever."

"Please, Ruth. A little patience."

Patience!

Ruth swung off of the stool. The connectors in her wrist and neck tore loose and she threw them to the floor. She ran for the stairs, crashing into one of the diagnostic machines and knocking it over before making it to the bottom step.

Abba said nothing. Behind her, she heard the small noise of effort that he made as he lowered himself to the floor to retrieve the equipment.

It was strange to feel such bright-hot anger again. Like abba, she'd thought that the transfer had restored her even temper. But apparently the anger she'd learned while she was Mara couldn't just be forgotten.

She spent an hour pacing the parlor, occasionally grabbing books off of a shelf, flipping through them as she walked, and then tossing them down in random locations. The anger's brightness faded, although the sense of injustice remained.

Later, abba came up to see her. He stood with mute pleading, not wanting to reopen the argument but obviously unable to bear continuing to fight.

Even though Ruth hadn't given in yet, even though she was still burning from the unfairness, she couldn't look into his sad eyes without feeling thickness in her throat.

He gestured helplessly. "I just want to keep you safe, Ruthele."

They sat together on the couch without speaking. They were both entrenched in their positions. It seemed to Ruth that they were both trying to figure out how to make things right without giving in, how to keep fighting without wounding.

Abel paced between them, shoving his head into Ruth's lap, and then into abba's, back and forth. Ruth patted his head and he lingered with her a moment, gazing up with rheumy but devoted eyes.

Arguing with abba wasn't going to work. He hadn't liked her taking risks before she'd gotten sick, but afterward, keeping her safe had become obsession, which was why Ruth even existed. He was a scientist, though; he liked evidence. She'd just have to show him it was safe.

Ruth didn't like to lie, but she'd do it. In a tone of grudging acceptance, she said, "You're right. It's too risky for me to go back."

"We will find you new friends," abba said. "We will be together. That's what is important."

RUTH BIDED HER time for a few days. Abba might have been watching her more closely if he hadn't been distracted with Mara. Instead, when he wasn't at Mara's bedside or examining Ruth, he drifted mechanically through the house, registering little.

Ruth had learned a lot about engineering from watching her father. Attic space wasn't complicated technology. The program came on its own cube which meant it was entirely isolated from the household AI and its notification protocols. It also came with standard parental access points that had been designed to favor ease of use over security – which meant there were lots of back-end entryways.

Abba didn't believe in restricting access to knowledge so he'd made it even easier by deactivating the nanny settings on Mara's box as soon as she was old enough to navigate attic space on her own.

Ruth waited until night-time when Mara was drifting in and out of her fractured, painful sleep, and abba had finally succumbed to exhaustion. Abba had left a light on in the kitchen, but it didn't reach the hallway to Mara's room, which fell in stark shadow. Ruth felt her way to Mara's threshold and put her ear to the door. She could hear the steady, sleeping rhythm of Mara's breath inside.

She cracked the door. Moonlight spilled from the window over the bed, allowing her to see inside. It was the first time she'd seen the room in her new body. It looked the same as it had. Mara was too sick to fuss over books or possessions so the objects sat in their places, ordered but dusty. Apart from the lump that Mara's body made beneath the quilt, the room looked as if it could have been abandoned for days.

The attic space box sat on a low shelf near the door. It fit in the palm of Ruth's hand. The fading image on its exterior showed the outline of a house with people inside, rendered in a style that was supposed to look like a child's drawing. It was the version they put out for five-year-olds. Abba had never replaced it. A waste of money, he said, when he could upgrade it himself.

Ruth looked up at the sound of blankets shifting. One of Mara's hands slipped free from the quilt. Her fingers dangled over the side of the bed, the knuckles exaggerated on thin bones. Inflamed cuticles surrounded her ragged nails.

Ruth felt a sting of revulsion and chastised herself. Those hands had been hers. She had no right to be repulsed.

The feeling faded to an ache. She wanted to kneel by the bed and take Mara's hand into her own. She wanted to give Mara the shelter and empathy that abba had built her to give. But she knew how Mara felt about her. Taking Mara's hand would not be *hesed*. The only loving kindness she could offer now was to leave.

As Ruth sat in ima's studio, carefully disassembling the box's hardware so that she could jury-rig it to interact with the television, it occurred to her that abba would have loved helping her with this project. He loved scavenging old technology. He liked to prove that cleverness could make tools of anything.

The complicated VR equipment that made it possible to immerse in attic space was far too bulky for Ruth to steal from Mara's room without being caught. She thought she could recreate a sketchy, winnowed down version of the experience using low technology replacements from the television and other scavenged equipment. Touch, smell and taste weren't going to happen, but an old stereo microphone allowed her to transmit on the voice channel. She found a way to instruct the box to send short bursts of visuals to the television, although the limited scope and speed would make it like walking down a hallway illuminated by a strobe light.

She sat cross-legged on the studio floor and logged in. It was the middle of the night, but usually at least someone from the flock was around. She was glad to see it was Collin this time, tweaking an experiment with crystal growth. Before she'd gotten sick, Ruth probably would have been there with him. They liked going in at night when there weren't many other people around.

She saw a still of Collin's hand over a delicate formation, and then another of him looking up, startled. "Mara?" he asked. "Is that you?"

His voice cracked when he spoke, sliding from low to high. It hadn't been doing that before.

"Hi, Collin," she said.

"Your avatar looks weird." She could imagine Collin squinting to investigate her image, but the television continued to show his initial look of surprise.

She was using a video skin capture from the last time Mara had logged in, months ago. Without a motion reader, it was probably just standing there, breathing and blinking occasionally, with no expression on its face.

"I'm on a weird connection," Ruth said.

"Is it because you're sick?" Collin's worried expression flashed onscreen. "Can I see what you're really like? It's okay. I've seen videos. I won't be grossed out or anything. I missed you. I thought – we weren't sure you were coming back. We were working on a video to say goodbye."

Ruth shifted uncomfortably. She'd wanted to go the attic so she could get on with living, not to be bogged down in dying. "I don't want to talk about that."

The next visual showed a flash of Colin's hand, blurred with motion as he raised it to his face. "We did some stuff with non-Newtonian fluids," he said tentatively. "You'd have liked it. We got all gross."

"Did you throw them around?" she asked.

"Goo fight," Collin agreed. He hesitated. "Are you coming back? Are you better?"

"Well –" Ruth began.

"Everyone will want to know you're here. Let me ping them."

"No. I just want to talk to you."

A new picture: Collin moving closer to her avatar, his face now crowding the narrow rectangle of her vision.

"I looked up osteosarcoma. They said you had lung nodules. Mara, are you really better? Are you really coming back?"

"I said I don't want to talk about it."

"But everyone will want to know."

Suddenly, Ruth wanted to be anywhere but attic space. Abba was right. She couldn't go back. Not because someone might find out but because everyone was going to want to know, what about Mara? They were going to want to know about Mara all the time. They were going to want to drag Ruth back into that sick bed, with her world narrowing toward death, when all she wanted was to move on.

And it was even worse now than it would have been half an hour ago, before she'd gone into Mara's room and seen her raw, tender hand, and thought about what it would be like to grasp it.

"I have to go," Ruth said.

"At least let me ping Violet," Collin said.

"I'll be back," Ruth answered. "I'll see you later."

On the television: Collin's skeptical face, brows drawn, the shine in his eyes that showed he thought she was lying.

"I promise," she said, hesitating only a moment before she tore the attic space box out of her jury-rigged web of wires.

Tears were filling her eyes and she couldn't help the sob. She threw the box. It skittered across the wooden floor until it smacked into the mirror. The thing was so old and knocked about that any hard collision might kill it, but what did that matter now? She wasn't going back.

She heard a sound from the doorway and looked up. She saw abba, standing behind the cracked door.

Ruth's anger flashed to a new target. "Why are you spying on me?"

"I came to check on Mara," abba said.

He didn't have to finish for his meaning to be clear. He'd heard someone in the studio and hoped it could still be his Marale.

He made a small gesture toward the attic space box. "It did not go well," he said quietly, statement rather than question.

Ruth turned her head away. He'd been right, about everything he'd said, all the explicit things she'd heard, and all the implicit things she hadn't wanted to.

She pulled her knees toward her chest. "I can't go back," she said.

Abba stroked her hair. "I know."

THE LOSS OF attic space hurt less than she'd thought it would. Mara had sealed off those tender spaces, and those farewells had a final ring. She'd said goodbye to Collin a long time ago.

What bothered her more was the lesson it forced; her life was never going to be the same, and there was no way to deny it. Mara would die and be gone, and Ruth had to learn to be Ruth, whoever Ruth was. That was what had scared Mara about Ruth in the first place.

The restlessness that had driven her into attic space still itched her. She started taking walks in the snow with Abel. Abba didn't try to stop her.

She stopped reading Jewish poetry and started picking up books on music theory. She practiced sight reading and toe-tapped the beats, imagining choreographies.

Wednesdays, when abba planned the menu for Shabbat, Ruth sat with him as he wrote out the list he would take to Gerry's on Thursday. As he imagined dishes, he talked about how Mara would like the honey he planned to infuse in the carrots, or the raisins and figs he would cook with the rice. He wondered what they should talk about – poetry, physics, international politics – changing his mind as new topics occurred to him.

Ruth wondered how he kept hoping. As Mara, she'd always known her boundaries before abba realized them. As Ruth, she knew, as clearly as Mara must, that Mara would not eat with them.

Perhaps it was cruel not to tell him, but to say it felt even crueler.

On a Thursday while abba was taking the truck to town, Ruth was looking through ima's collection of sheet music in the parlor when she heard the click of crutches down the hall. She turned to find Mara was behind her, breathing heavily.

"Oh," said Ruth. She tried to hide the surprise in her voice but failed.

Mara's voice was thin. "You didn't think I could get up on my own."

"I…" Ruth began before catching the angry look of resolution on Mara's face. "No. I didn't."

"Of course not," Mara said bitterly. She began another sentence, but was interrupted by a ragged exhalation as she started to collapse against the wall. Ruth rushed to support her. Mara accepted her assistance without acknowledging it, as if it were beneath notice.

"Are you going to throw up?" Ruth asked quietly.

"I'm off the chemo."

Mara's weight fell heavily on Ruth's shoulder. She shifted her balance, determined not to let Mara slip.

"Let me take you back to bed," Ruth said.

Mara answered, "I wanted to see you again."

"I'll take you. We can talk in there."

Ruth took Mara's silence as assent. Abandoning the crutches, she supported Mara's weight as they headed back into the bedroom. In daylight, the room looked too bright, its creams and whites unsullied.

Mara's heaving eased as Ruth helped her into the bed, but her lungs were still working hard. Ruth waited until her breathing came evenly.

Ruth knelt by the bed, the way abba always had, and then wondered if that was a mistake. Mara might see Ruth as trying to act like she was the one in charge. She ducked her gaze for a moment, the way Abel might if he were ashamed, hoping Mara would see she didn't mean to challenge her.

"What did you want to say to me?" Ruth asked. "It's okay if you want to yell."

"Be glad," Mara said, "That you didn't have to go this far."

Mara's gaze slid down Ruth's face. It slowly took in her smooth skin and pink cheeks.

Ruth opened her mouth to respond, but Mara continued.

"It's a black hole. It takes everything in. You can see yourself falling. Nothing looks like it used to. Everything's blacker. So much blacker. And you know when you've hit the moment when you can't escape. You'll never do anything but fall."

Ruth extended her hand toward Mara's, the way she'd wanted to the other night, but stopped before touching her. She fumbled for something to say.

Flatly, Mara said, "I am glad at least someone will get away."

With great effort, she turned toward the window.

"Go away now."

SHE SHOULDN'T HAVE, but Ruth stood at the door that night when abba went in to check on Mara. She watched him kneel by the bed and take her hand. Mara barely moved in response, still staring out the window, but her fingers tensed around his, clutching him. Ruth remembered the way abba's hand had felt when she was sleepless and in pain, a solid anchor in a fading world.

She thought of what abba had said to her when she was still Mara, and made silent promises to the other girl. *I will keep you and hold you. I will protect you. I will always have your hand in mine.*

IN THE MORNING, when Ruth came back upstairs, she peeked through the open door to see abba still there beside Mara, lying down instead of kneeling, his head pillowed on the side of her mattress.

She walked back down the hallway and to the head of the stairs. Drumming on her knees, she called for Abel. He lumbered toward her, the thump of his tail reassuringly familiar. She ruffled his fur and led him into the parlor where she slipped on his leash.

Wind chill took the outside temperature substantially below freezing, but she hesitated before putting on her coat. She ran her hand across the 'skin' of her arm. It was robotic skin, not human skin. She'd looked at some of the schematics that abba had left around downstairs and started to wonder about how different she really was from a human. He'd programmed her to feel vulnerable to cold, but was she really?

She put the coat back on its hook and led Abel out the door. Immediately, she started shivering, but she ignored the bite. She wanted to know what she could do.

She trudged across the yard to the big, bony oak. She snapped off a branch, made Abel sit while she unhooked his leash, and threw the branch as far as she could. Abel's dash left dents in the snow. He came back to her, breath a warm relief on her hand, the branch slippery with slobber.

She threw it again and wondered what she could achieve if abba hadn't programmed her body to think it was Mara's. He'd given her all of Mara's limits. She could run as fast as Mara, but not faster. Calculate as accurately as Mara, but no moreso.

Someday, she and abba would have to talk about that.

She tossed the stick again, and Abel ran, and again, and again, until he was too tired to continue. He watched the branch fly away as he leaned against Mara's leg for support.

She gave his head a deep scratch. He shivered and he bit at the air near her hand. She realized her cold fingers were hurting him. For her, the cold had ceased to be painful, though she was still shivering now and then.

"Sorry, boy, sorry," she said. She reattached his leash, and watched how, despite the temperature, her fingers moved without any stiffness at all.

She headed back to the house, Abel making pleased whuffing noises to indicate that he approved of their direction. She stopped on the porch to stamp the snow off of her feet. Abel shook himself, likewise, and Ruth quickly dusted off what he'd missed.

She opened the door and Abel bounded in first, Ruth laughing and trying to keep her footing as he yanked on the leash. He was old and much weaker than he had been, but an excited burst of doggy energy could still make her rock. She stumbled in after him, the house dim after her cold hour outside.

Abba was in the parlor, standing by the window from which he'd have been able to see them play. He must have heard them come in, but he didn't look toward her until she tentatively called his name.

He turned and looked her over, surveying her bare arms and hands, but he gave no reaction. She could see from his face that it was over.

He wanted to bury her alone. She didn't argue.

He would plant Mara in the yard, perhaps under the bony tree, but more likely somewhere else in the lonely acreage, unmarked. She didn't know how he planned to dig in the frozen ground, but he was a man of many contraptions. Mara would always be out there, lost in the snow.

When he came back, he clutched her hand as he had clutched Mara's. It was her turn to be what abba had been for Mara, the anchor that kept him away from the lip of the black hole, the one steady thing in a dissolving world.

They packed the house without discussing it. Ruth understood what was happening as soon as she saw abba filling the first box with books. Probably she'd known for some time, on the fringe of her consciousness, that they would have to do this. As they wrapped dishes in tissue paper, and sorted through old papers, they shared silent grief at leaving the yellow house that abba had built with Meryem, and that both Mara and Ruth had lived in all their lives.

Abba had enough money that he didn't need to sell the property. The house would remain owned and abandoned in the coming years.

It was terrible to go, but it also felt like a necessary marker, a border bisecting her life. It was one more way in which she was becoming Ruth.

They stayed in town for one last Shabbat. The process of packing the house had altered their sense of time, making the hours seem foreshortened and stretched at turns.

Thursday passed without their noticing, leaving them to buy their groceries on Friday. Abba wanted to drive into town on his own, but Ruth didn't want him to be alone yet.

Reluctantly, she agreed to stay in the truck when they got there. Though abba had begun to tell people that she was recovering, it would be best if no one got a chance to look at her up close. They might realize something was wrong. It would be easier wherever they moved next; strangers wouldn't always be comparing her to a ghost.

Abba was barely out of the truck before Gerry caught sight of them through the window and came barreling out of the door. Abba tried to get in his way. Rapidly, he stumbled out the excuse that he and Ruth had agreed on, that it was good for her to get out of the house, but she was still too tired to see anyone.

"A minute won't hurt," said Gerry. He pushed past abba. With a huge grin, he knocked on Ruth's window.

Hesitantly, she rolled it down. Gerry crossed his arms on the sill, leaning his head into the vehicle. "Look at you!" he exclaimed. "Your daddy said you were getting better, but just *look* at you!"

Ruth couldn't help but grin. Abel's tail began to thump as he pushed himself into the front seat to get a better look at his favorite snack provider.

"I have to say, after you didn't come the last few weeks…" Gerry wiped his eyes with the back of his hand. "I'm just glad to see you, Mara, I really am."

At the sound of the name, Ruth looked with involuntary shock at abba, who gave a sad little smile that Gerry couldn't see. He took a step forward. "Please, Gerry. She needs to rest."

Gerry looked back at him, opened his mouth to argue, and then looked back at Ruth and nodded. "Okay then. But next week, I expect some free cashier work!" He leaned in to kiss her cheek. He smelled of beef and rosemary. "You get yourself back here, Mara. And you keep kicking that cancer in the rear end."

With a glance back at the truck to check that Mara was okay, abba followed Gerry into the store. Twenty minutes later, he returned with two bags of groceries, which he put in the bed of the truck. As he started the engine, he said, "Gerry is a good man. I will miss him." He paused. "But it is better to have you, Mara."

Ruth looked at him with icy surprise, breath caught in her throat.

Her name was her own again. She wasn't sure how she felt about that.

THE SKY WAS bronzing when they arrived home.

On the stove, *cholent* simmered, filling the house with its scent. Abba went to check on it before the sun set, and Ruth followed him into the kitchen, preparing to pull out the dishes and the silverware and the table cloth.

He waved her away. "Next time. This week, let me."

Ruth went into ima's studio. She'd hadn't gone inside since the disaster in attic space, and her gaze lingered on the attic box, still lying dead on the floor.

"I'd like to access a DVD of ima's performances," she told the AI. "*Coppélia*, please."

It whirred.

The audience's rumblings began and she instructed the AI to fast-forward until Coppelia was onstage. She held her eyes closed and tipped her head down until it was the moment to snap into life, to let her body flow, fluid and graceful, mimicking the dancer on the screen.

She'd thought it would be cathartic to dance the part of the doll, and in a way it was, but once the moment was over, she surprised herself by selecting another disc instead of continuing. She tried to think of a comedy that she wanted to dance, and surprised herself further by realizing that she wanted to dance a tragedy instead. Mara had needed the comedies, but Ruth needed to feel the ache of grace and sorrow; she needed to feel the pull of the black hole even as she defied its gravity and danced, en pointe, on its edge.

*   *   *

WHEN THE LIGHT turned violet, abba came to the door, and she followed him into the kitchen. Abba lit the candles, and she waited for him to begin the prayers, but instead he stood aside.

It took her a moment to understand what he wanted.

"Are you sure?" she asked.

"Please, Marale," he answered.

Slowly, she moved into the space where he should have been standing. The candles burned on the table beneath her. She waved her hands through the heat and thickness of the smoke, and then lifted them to cover her eyes.

She said, "*Barukh atah Adonai, Elohaynu, melekh ha-olam, asher kid'shanu b'mitzvotav, v'tzivanu, l'had'lik neir shel Shabbat.*"

She breathed deeply, inhaling the scents of honey and figs and smoke.

"*Amein.*"

She opened her eyes again. Behind her, she heard abba's breathing, and somewhere in the dark of the house, Abel's snoring as he napped in preparation for after-dinner begging. The candles filled her vision as if she'd never seen them before. Bright white and gold flames trembled, shining against the black of the outside sky, so fragile they could be extinguished by a breath.

MOTHERS, LOCK UP YOUR DAUGHTERS BECAUSE THEY ARE TERRIFYING

Alice Sola Kim

Alice Sola Kim (alicesolakim.com) is a writer living in New York who has had stories published in *Writer, NY*, stories in or forthcoming in *Tin House*, *McSweeney's, Asimov's,* and *Lightspeed*, among others.

AT MIDNIGHT WE parked by a Staples and tried some *seriously dark fucking magic.* We had been discussing it for weeks and could have stayed in that *Wouldn't it be funny if* groove forever, zipping between *Yes, we should* and *No, we shouldn't* until it became a joke so dumb that we would never. But that night Mini had said, "If we don't do it right now, I'm going to be so mad at you guys, and I'll know from now on that all you chickenheads can do is talk and not do," and the whole way she ranted at us like that, even though we were already doing and not talking, or at least about to. (We always let her do that, get all shirty and sharp with us, because she had the car, but perhaps we should have said something. Perhaps once everyone had cars, Mini would have to figure out how to live in the world as *not* a total bitch, and she would be leagues behind everyone else.)

The parking lot at night looked like the ocean, the black Atlantic, as we imagined it, and in Mini's car we brought up the spell on our phones and Caroline read it first. She always had to be first to do anything, because she had the most to prove, being scared of everything. We couldn't help but tease her about that, even though we knew it wasn't her fault – her parents made her that way, but then again, if someone didn't get told off for being a pill just because we could trace said pill-ness back to their parents, then where would it ever end?

We had an X-Acto knife and a lighter and antibacterial ointment and lard and a fat red candle still shrink-wrapped. A chipped saucer from Ronnie's dad's grandmother's wedding set, made of china that glowed even in dim light and sang when you rubbed your thumb along it, which she took because it was chipped and thought they wouldn't miss it, but we thought that was dumb because they would definitely miss the chipped one. The different one. We could have wrapped it all up and sold it as a Satanism starter kit.

Those were the things. What we did with them *we'll never tell.*

For a moment, it seemed like it would work. The moment stayed the same, even though it should have changed. A real staring contest of a moment: Ronnie's face shining in the lunar light of her phone, the slow tick of the blood into the saucer, like a radiator settling. But Mini ruined it. "Do you feel anything?" asked Mini, too soon and too loudly.

We glanced at one another, dismayed. We thought, *Perhaps if she had just waited a little longer* – "I don't think so," said Ronnie.

"I knew this was a dumb idea," said Mini. "Let's clean up this blood before it gets all over my car. So if one of you got murdered, they wouldn't blame me." Caroline handed out the Band-Aids. She put hers on and saw the blood well up instantly against the Band-Aid, not red or black or any color in particular, only a dark splotch like a shape under ice.

So much for that, everyone thought, wrong.

Mini dropped Caroline off first, even though she lived closer to Mini, then Ronnie after. It had been this way always. At first Caroline had been hurt by this, had imagined that we were talking about her in the fifteen extra minutes of alone time that we shared. The truth was both a relief and an even greater insult. There was nothing to say about Caroline, no shit we would talk that wasn't right to her face. We loved Caroline, but her best jokes were unintentional. We loved Caroline, but she didn't know how to pretend to be cool and at home in strange places like we did; she was the one who always seemed like a pie-faced country girleen wearing a straw hat and holding a suitcase, asking obvious questions, like, "Wait, which hand do you want to stamp?" or "Is that illegal?" Not that the answers were always obvious to us, but we knew what not to ask about. We knew how to be cool, so why didn't Caroline?

Usually, we liked to take a moment at the end of the night without Caroline, to discuss the events of the night without someone to remind us how young we were and how little we knew. But tonight we didn't really talk. We didn't talk about how we believed, and how our belief had been shattered. We didn't talk about the next time we would hang out. Ronnie snuck into her house. Her brother, Alex, had left the window open for her. Caroline was already in bed, wearing an ugly quilted headband that kept her bangs off her face so she wouldn't get forehead zits. Mini's mom wasn't home yet, so she microwaved some egg rolls. She put her feet up on the kitchen table, next to her homework, which had been completed hours ago. The egg rolls exploded tiny scalding droplets of water when she bit into them. She soothed her seared lips on a beer. *This is the life*, Mini thought.

We didn't go to the same school, and we wouldn't have been friends if we had. We met at an event for Korean adoptees, a party at a low-ceilinged community center catered with the stinkiest food possible. *Koreans*, amirite?! That's how we/they roll.

Mini and Caroline were having fun. Ronnie was not having fun. Mini's fun was different from Caroline's fun, being a fake-jolly fun in which she was imagining telling her *real* friends about this doofus loser event later, although due to the fact that she was reminding them that she was adopted, they would either squirm with discomfort or stay very still and serious and stare her in the pupils with great intensity, nodding all the while. Caroline was having fun – the pure uncut stuff, nothing ironic about it. She liked talking earnestly with people her age about basic biographical details, because there was a safety in conversational topics that no one cared about all that much. Talking about which high school you go to? Great! Which activities you did at aforementioned school? Raaaad. Talking about the neighborhood where you live? How was it possible that they weren't all dead of fun! Caroline already knew and liked the K-pop sound-tracking the evening, the taste of the marinated beef and the clear noodles, dishes that her family re-created on a regular basis.

Ronnie rooted herself by a giant cut-glass bowl full of kimchi, which looked exactly like a big wet pile of fresh guts. She soon realized that (1) the area by the kimchi was very high traffic and (2) the kimchi emitted a powerful vinegar-poop-death stench. As Ronnie edged away from the food table, Mini and Caroline were walking toward it. Caroline saw a lost and lonely soul and immediately said, "Hi! Is this your first time at a meet-up?"

At this Ronnie experienced split consciousness, feeling annoyed that she was about to be sucked into wearying small talk *in addition to* a nearly sacramental sense of gratitude about being saved from standing alone at a gathering. You could even say that Ronnie was experiencing quadruple consciousness if you counted the fact that she was both judging and admiring Mini and Caroline – Mini for being the kind of girl who tries to look ugly on purpose and thinks it looks so great (*ooh, except it did look kinda great*), her torn sneakers and one thousand silver earrings and chewed-up hair, and Caroline of the sweetly tilted eyes and cashmere sweater dress and ballet flats like she was some pampered cat turned human.

Mini had a stainless-steel water bottle full of ice and vodka cut with the minimal amount of orange juice. She shared it with Ronnie and Caroline. And Caroline drank it. Caroline ate and drank like she was a laughing two-dimensional cutout and everything she consumed just went through her face and evaporated behind her, affecting her not at all.

Ronnie could not stop staring at Caroline, who was a one-woman band of laughing and drinking and ferrying food to her mouth and nodding and asking skin-rippingly boring questions that nevertheless got them talking. Ronnie went from laughing at Caroline to being incredibly envious of her. People got drunk just to be like Caroline!

Crap, Ronnie thought. Social graces are actually worth something.

But Caroline was getting drunk, and since she was already Caroline, she went too far with the whole being-Caroline thing and asked if she could tell us a joke. Only if we promised not to get offended!

Mini threw her head back, smiled condescendingly at an imaginary person to her left, and said, "Of course." She frowned to hide a burp that was, if not exactly a solid, still alarmingly substantial, and passed the water bottle to Ronnie.

Caroline wound up. This had the potential to be long. "So, you know how – oh wait, no, okay, this is how it starts. Okay, so white people play the violin like this." She made some movements. "Black people play it like this." She made some more movements. "And then *Korean* people play it like th –" and she began to bend at the waist but suddenly farted so loudly that it was like the fart had bent her, had then jet-packed her into the air and crumpled her to the ground.

She tried to talk over it, but Ronnie and Mini were ended by their laughter. They fell out of themselves. They were puking laughter, the laughter was a thick brambly painful rope being pulled out of their faces, but they couldn't stop it, and finally Caroline stopped trying to finish the joke and we were all laughing.

Consequences: For days after, we would think that we had exhausted the joke and sanded off all the funniness rubbing it so often with our sweaty fingers, but then we would remember again and, whoa, there we went again, off to the races.

Consequences: Summer arrived. Decoupled from school, we were free to see one another, to feel happy misfitting with one another because we knew we were peas from different pods – we delighted in being such different kinds of girls from one another.

Consequences: For weeks after, we'd end sentences with, "Korean people do it like *ppppbbbbbbbbttth*."

There are so many ways to miss your mother. Your real mother – the one who looks like you, the one who has to love you because she grew you from her own body, the one who hates you so much that she dumped you in the garbage for white people to pick up and dust off. In Mini's case, it manifested as some weird gothy shit. She had been engaging in a shady flirtation with a clerk at an antiquarian bookshop. We did not approve. We thought this clerk wore thick-rimmed hipster glasses to hide his crow's feet and hoodies to hide his man boobs so that weird high-school chicks would still want to flirt with him. We hoped that Mini mostly liked him only because he was willing to trade clammy glances with her and go no further. Unlike us, Mini was not a fan of going far. When the manager wasn't around, this guy let her go into the room with the padlock on it, where all of the really expensive stuff was. That's where she found the book with the spell. That's were she took a photo of the spell with her phone. That's where she immediately texted it to us without any explanation attached, confident that the symbols were so powerful they would tentacle through our screens and into our hearts, and that we would know it for what it was.

Each of us had had that same moment where we saw ourselves in a photo, caught one of those wonky glances in the mirror that tricks you into thinking that you're seeing someone else, and it's electric. *Kapow boom sizzle*, you got slapped upside the head with the Korean wand, and now you feel weird at family gatherings that veer blond, you feel weird when your friends replace their Facebook profile photos with pictures of the celebrities they look like and all you have is, say, Mulan or Jackie Chan, ha-ha-ha, hahahahaha.

You feel like you could do one thing wrong, one stupid thing, and the sight of you would become a terrible taste in your parents' mouths.

"I'll tell you this," Mini had said. "None of us actually knows what happened to our mothers. None of our parents tell us anything. We don't have the cool parents who'll tell us about our backgrounds and shit like that."

For Mini, this extended to everything else. When her parents decided to get a divorce, Mini felt like she had a hive of bees in her head (her brain was both the bees and the brain that the bees were stinging). She searched online for articles about adoptees with divorced parents. The gist of the articles was that she would be going through an awfully hard time, as in, chick already felt kind of weird and dislocated when it came to family and belonging and now it was just going to be worse. *Internet, you asshole*, thought Mini. *I already knew that.* The articles for the parents told them to reassure their children. Make them feel secure and safe. She waited for the parents to try so she could flame-throw scorn all over them. They did not try. She waited longer.

And she had given up on them long before Mom finally arrived.

We were hanging out in Mini's room, not talking about our unsuccessful attempt at magic. Caroline was painting Ronnie's nails with a color called Balsamic.

"I love this color," said Caroline. "I wish my parents would let me wear it."

"Why wouldn't they?"

"I can't wear dark nail polish until I'm eighteen."

"Wait – they really said that?"

"How many things have they promised you when you turn eighteen?"

"You know they're just going to change the terms of the agreement when you actually turn eighteen, and then you'll be forty and still wearing clear nail polish and taking ballet and not being able to date."

"And not being able to have posters up in your room. Although I guess you won't need posters when you're forty."

"Fuck that! No one's taking away my posters when I get old."

Caroline didn't say anything. She shrugged, keeping her eyes on Ronnie's nails. When we first started hanging out with Caroline, we wondered if we shouldn't shit-talk Caroline's parents, because she never joined in, but we realized that she liked it. It helped her, and it helped her to not have to say anything. "You're all set. Just let it dry."

"I don't know," said Ronnie. "It doesn't go with anything. It just looks random on me."

Mini said, "Well." She squinted and cocked her head back until she had a double chin, taking all of Ronnie in. "You kind of look like you're in prison and you traded a pack of cigarettes for nail polish because you wanted to feel glamorous again."

"Wow, thanks!"

"No, come on. You know what I mean. It's great. You look tough. You look like a normal girl, but you still look tough. Look at me. I'll never look tough." And she so wanted to, we knew. "I'd have to get a face tattoo, like a face tattoo of someone else's face over my face. Maybe I should get your face."

"Makeover montage," said Caroline.

"Koreans do makeovers like *pppppbbbbbbbth*," we said.

Caroline laughed and the nail polish brush veered and swiped Ronnie's knuckle. We saw Ronnie get a little pissed. She didn't like physical insults. Once she wouldn't speak to us for an hour when Mini flicked her in the face with water in a movie theater bathroom.

"Sorry," Caroline said. She coughed. Something had gone down wrong. She coughed some more and started to retch, and we were stuck between looking away politely and staring at her with our hands held out in this Jesus-looking way, figuring out how to help. There was a wet burr to her coughing that became a growl, and the growl rose and rose until it became a voice, a fluted voice, like silver flutes, like flutes of bubbly champagne, a beautiful voice full of rich-people things.

MY DAUGHTERS

MY GIRLS

MY MY MINE MINE

Mom skipped around. When she spoke, she didn't move our mouths. We felt only the vibration of her voice rumbling through us.

"Did you come to us because we called for you?" asked Mini.

Mom liked to jump into the mouth of the person asking the question. Mini's mouth popped open. Her eyes darted down, to the side, like she was trying to get a glimpse of herself talking.

I HEARD YOU, MY DAUGHTERS

"You speak really good English," Caroline said.

I LEARNED IT WHEN I WAS DEAD

We wanted to talk to one another but it felt rude with Mom in the room. If Mom was still in the room.

LOOK AT YOU SO BEAUTIFUL

THE MOST BEAUTIFUL GIRL IN THE WORLD

Who was beautiful? Which one of us was she talking about? We asked and she did not answer directly. She only said that we were all beautiful, and any mother would be proud to have us. We thought we might work it out later.

OH, I LEFT YOU

AND OH

I'LL NEVER DO IT AGAIN

At first we found Mom highly scary. At first we were scared of her voice and the way she used our faces to speak her words, and we were scared about how she loved us already and found us beautiful without knowing a thing about us. That is what parents are supposed to do, and we found it incredibly stressful and a little bit creepy. *Our parents love us*, thought Caroline and Mini. They do, they do, they do, but every so often we cannot help but feel that we have to earn our places in our homes. Caroline did it by being perfect and PG-rated, though her mind boiled with filthy, outrageous thoughts, though she often got so frustrated at meals with her family during her performances of perfection that she wanted to bite the dining room table in half. *I'm not the way you think I am, and you're dumb to be so fooled.* Mini did it by never asking for anything. Never complaining. Though she could sulk and stew at the Olympic level. Girl's got to have an outlet.

Mom took turns with us, and in this way we got used to her. A few days after Mom's first appearance, Caroline woke herself up singing softly, a song she had never before heard. It sounded a little like *baaaaaachudaaaaa/ neeeeedeowadaaaa*. Peaceful, droning. She sang it again, and then Mom said:

THIS IS A SONG MY MOTHER SANG TO ME WHEN I DIDN'T WANT TO WAKE UP FOR SCHOOL. IT CALLS THE VINES DOWN TO LIFT YOU UP AND –

"Mom?" said Caroline.

YES, SWEETIE

"Could you speak more quietly? It gets pretty loud in my head."

Oh, Of Course. Yes. This Song Is What My Mother Sang In The Mornings. And Her Hands Were Vines And She Would Lift Lift Lift Me Up, Mom said.

Caroline's stomach muscles stiffened as she sat up by degrees, like a mummy. Caroline's entire body ached, from her toenails to her temples, but that wasn't Mom's fault. It was her other mom's fault. Summers were almost worse for Caroline than the school year was. There was more ballet, for one thing, including a pointe intensive that made her feet twinge like loose teeth, and this really cheesed her off most of all, because her parents didn't even like ballet. They were bored into microsleeps by it, their heads drifting forward, their heads jumping back. What they liked was the idea of a daughter who did ballet, and who would therefore be skinny and not a lesbian. She volunteered at their church and attended youth group, where everyone mostly played foosball. She worked a few shifts at a chocolate shop, where she got to try every kind of chocolate they sold once and then never again. *But what if she forgot how they tasted?* She was tutored in calculus and biology, not because she needed any help with those subjects, but because her parents didn't want to wait to find out whether she was the best or not at them – they wanted best and *they wanted it now.*

Once Ronnie said, "Caroline, your parents are like Asian parents," and Mini said, "Sucks to be you," and Caroline answered, "That's not what you're going to say in a few years when you're bagging my groceries," which sounded mean, but we knew she really said it only because she was confident that we wouldn't be bagging her groceries. Except for Ronnie, actually. We were worried about Ronnie, who wasn't academically motivated like Caroline or even *C'mon, c'mon, c'mon, what's next* motivated like Mini.

That first day Caroline enjoyed ballet class as she never had before, and she knew it was because Mom was there. She felt her chin tipped upward by Mom, arranging her daughter like a flower, a sleek and sinuous flower that would be admired until it died and even afterward. Mom had learned to speak quietly, and she murmured to Caroline to stand taller and suck in her stomach and become grace itself. The ballet teacher nodded her approval.

Though You Are A Little Bit Too Fat For Ballet, Mom murmured. Caroline cringed. She said, "Yeah, but Mom, I'm not going to be a ballerina." But Mom told her that it was important to try her best at everything and not be motivated by pure careerism only.

Mom told us we were beautiful and special and loved, but that is not to say that she was afraid to criticize the fuck out of us. Once Caroline tried to sing the song about getting up in the morning to please Mom, and Mom just laughed. *Ha-Ha-Ha-Ha-Ha-Ha, Oh Sweetie Ha-Ha-Ha-Ha-Ha-Ha!*

"Mom," said Caroline. "I know the words."

You Don't Speak Korean, Mom told Caroline. *You Will Never Speak Real Korean.*

"You speak real English, though. How come you get both?"

I Told You. I'm Your Mother And I Know A Lot More Than You And I'm Dead.

It was true, though, about Caroline. The words came out of Caroline's mouth all sideways and awkward, like someone pushing a couch through a hallway. Worst of all, she didn't sound like someone speaking Korean – she sounded like someone making fun of it.

But if we knew Caroline, we knew that this was also what she wanted. Because she wanted to be perfect, so she also wanted to be told about the ways in which she was imperfect.

Mini was the first to actually see Mom. She made herself Jell-O for dinner, which was taking too long because she kept opening the refrigerator door to poke at it. Mini's brain: *C'mon, c'mon, c'mon, c'mon.* She walked around the dining room table. She tried to read the *New Yorker* that her mother had been neglecting, but it was all tiny-print listings of events that happened about five months ago anywhere but where she was. She came back to the fridge to check on the Jell-O. Its condition seemed improved from the last time she checked, and anyhow she was getting hungrier, and it wasn't like

Jell-O soup was the worst thing she'd ever eaten since her mom stopped cooking after the divorce. She looked down at the Jell-O, as any of us would do before breaking that perfect jeweled surface with the spoon, and saw reflected upon it the face of another. The face was on Mini, made up of the Mini material but everything tweaked and adjusted, made longer and thinner and sadder. Mini was awed. "Is that what you look like?" Mini asked. When she spoke she realized how loose her jaw felt. "Ouch," she said. Mom said, *Oh, Honey, I Apologize. I Just Wanted You To See What Mom Looks Like. I'll Stop Now.*

"It's okay," said Mini.

Mom thought that Mini should be eating healthier food, and what do you know, Mini agreed. She told us about the dinner that Mom had Mini make. "I ate vegetables, you guys, and I kind of liked it." She did not tell us that her mother came home near the end of preparations, and Mini told her that she could not have any of it. She did not tell us that she frightened her mother with her cold, slack expression and the way she laughed at nothing in particular as she went up to her room.

Caroline would have said: *I can't believe your mom had the nerve to ask if she could!*

Ronnie would have thought: There's being butt-hurt about your parents' divorce, and then there's being epically, unfairly butt-hurt about your parents' divorce, and you are veering toward the latter, Mini my friend. But what did Ronnie know? She was still scared of Mom. She probably hated her family more than any of us – we knew something was wrong but not what was wrong – but she wouldn't let Mom come too close either.

"Have you been hanging out with Mom?"

"Yeah. We went shopping yesterday."

"I haven't seen her in a long time."

"Caroline, that's not fair! You had her first."

"I just miss her."

"Don't be jealous."

We would wake up with braids in our hair, complicated little tiny braids that we didn't know how to do. We would find ourselves making food that we didn't know how to make, stews and porridges and little sweet hotcakes. Ronnie pulled the braids out. Ronnie did not eat the food. We knew that

Mom didn't like that. We knew Mom would want to have a serious talk with Ronnie soon.

We knew and we allowed ourselves to forget that we already had people in our lives who wanted to parent us, who had already been parenting us for years. But we found it impossible to accept them as our parents, now that our real mother was back. Someone's real mother. Sometimes we were sisters. Sometimes we were competitors.

Our parents didn't know us anymore. They couldn't do anything right, if they ever had in the first place. This is one problem with having another set of parents. *A dotted outline of parents.* For every time your parents forget to pick you up from soccer practice, there is the other set that would have picked you up. They – she – would have been perfect at all of it.

Ronnie was washing the dishes when a terrible pain gripped her head. She shouted and fell to her knees. Water ran over the broken glass in the sink.

Honey, said Mom, *You Won't Let Me Get To Know You. Ronnie, Don't You Love Me? Don't You Like The Food I Make For You? Don't You Miss Your Mother?*

Ronnie shook her head.

Ronnie, I Am Going To Knock First –

Someone was putting hot, tiny little fingers in her head like her head was a glove, up her nose, in her eyes, against the roof of her mouth. And then they squeezed. Ronnie started crying.

– And Then I'm Coming In.

She didn't want this; she didn't want for Mom to know her like Mom had gotten to know Caroline and Mini; she didn't want to become these weird monosyllabic love-zombies like them, them with their wonderful families – how dare they complain so much, how dare they abandon them for this creature? And perhaps Ronnie was just stronger and more skeptical, but she had another reason for wanting to keep Mom away. She was ashamed. The truth was that there was already someone inside her head. It was her brother, Alex. He was the tumor that rolled and pressed on her brain to shift her moods between dreamy and horrified.

Ronnie first became infected with the wrong kind of love for Alex on a school-day morning, when she stood in front of the bathroom mirror brushing her teeth. He had stood there not a minute before her, shaving. On school-day mornings, they were on the same schedule, nearly on top of each other. His hot footprints pressed up into hers. And then he was pressing up against her, and it was confusing, and she forgot now whose idea all of this was in the first place, but there was no mistake about the fact that she instigated everything now. Everything she did and felt, Alex returned, and this troubled Ronnie, that he never started it anymore, so that she was definitively the sole foreign element and corrupting influence in this household of Scandinavian blonds.

("Do you want to do this?") ("Okay. Then I want to do this too.")

Ronnie hated it and liked it when they did stuff in the bathroom. Having the mirror there was horrible. She didn't need to see all that to know it was wrong. Having the mirror there helped. It reassured her to see how different they looked – everything opposed and chiaroscuro – no laws were being broken and triggering alarms from deep inside their DNA.

Sometimes Alex told her that they could get married. Or if not married, they could just leave the state or the country and be together in some nameless elsewhere. The thought filled Ronnie with a vicious horror. If the Halversons weren't her parents, if Mrs. Halverson wasn't her mother, then *who was to be her mother*? Alex would still have his family. He wasn't the adopted one, after all. Ronnie would be alone in the world, with only fake companions – a blond husband who used to be her brother, and a ghost who would rest its hands on Ronnie's shoulders until the weight was unbearable, a ghost that couldn't even tell different Asian girls apart to recognize its own daughter.

Mom was silent. Ronnie stayed on the floor. She collected her limbs to herself and laced her fingers behind her neck. She felt it: something terrible approached. It was too far away to see or hear or feel, but when it finally arrived, it would shake her hard enough to break her in half. Freeing a hand, Ronnie pulled out her phone and called Mini. She told her to come quickly and to bring Caroline and it was about Mom, and before she could finish, Mom squeezed the phone and slammed Ronnie's hand hard against the kitchen cabinet.

YOU ARE A DIRTY GIRL
NEVER
HAVE I
EVER
SLUT SLUT
FILTHY SLUT

Ronnie's ears rang. Mom was crying now too. *You Do This To These People Who Took You In And Care For You*, Mom sobbed. *I Don't Know You At All. I Don't Know Any Of You.*

YOU'RE NOT NICE GIRLS

NO DAUGHTERS OF MINE

When Mini and Caroline came into the kitchen, Ronnie was sitting on the floor. Her hand was bleeding and swollen, but otherwise she was fine, her face calm, her back straight. She looked up at us. "We have to go reverse the spell. We have to send her back. I made her hate us. I'm sorry. She's going to kill us."

"Oh no," said Caroline.

Mini's head turned to look at Caroline, then the rest of her body followed. She slapped Caroline neatly across the face. *You I Don't Like So Much Either*, Mom said, using Mini's mouth to speak. *I Know What You Think About At Night, During The Day, All Day. You Can't Fool Me. I Tried And Tried –*

Mini covered her mouth, and then Mom switched to Caroline. *– And Tried To Make You Good. But Ronnie Showed Me It Was All Useless. You Are All Worthless.* Caroline shook her head until Mom left, and we pulled Ronnie up and ran out to the car together, gripping one another's hands the whole way.

We drove, or just Mini drove, but we were rearing forward in our seats, and it was as though we were all driving, strenuously, horsewhippingly, like there was an away to get to, as if what we were trying to escape was behind us and not inside of us. We were screaming and shouting louder and louder until Mini was suddenly seized again. We saw it and we waited. Mini's jaw unhinged, and we didn't scream only because this had happened many times – certainly we didn't like it when it happened to us, but that way at least we didn't have to look at it, the way that it was only skin holding the moving parts of her skull together, skin become liquid like glass in heat, and then her mouth opened beyond everything we knew to be possible, and the words that came out – oh, the words. Mini began to speak and then we did, we did scream, even though we should have been used to it by now.

DRIVE SAFE

DRIVE SAFE

DO YOU WANT TO DIE BEFORE I TEACH YOU EVERYTHING THERE IS TO KNOW

The car veered, a tree loomed, and we were garlanded in glass, and a branch insinuated itself into Mini's ribs and encircled her heart, and Ronnie sprang forth and broke against the tree, and in the backseat Caroline was marveling at how her brain became unmoored and seesawed forward into the jagged coastline of the front of her skull and back again, until she was no longer herself, and it was all so mortifying that we could have just died, and we did, we did die, we watched every second of it happen until we realized that we were back on the road, driving, and all of the preceding was just a little movie that Mom had played inside of our heads.

"Stop," said Ronnie. "Stop the car."

"No way," said Mini. "That's what she wants."

Mom's sobs again. *I Killed Myself For Love. I Killed Myself For You*, she said. *I Came Back For Girls Who Wanted Parents But You Already Had Parents.*

"Mini, listen to me," said Ronnie. "I said it because it seemed like a thing to say, and it would have been nice to have, but there is no way to reverse the spell, is there?"

"We can try it. We can go back to the parking lot and do everything, but backward."

"We can change the words. We have to try," Caroline said.

"Mom," said Ronnie, "if you're still here, I want to tell you that I want you. I'm the one who needs a mother. You saw."

"Ronnie," said Caroline, "what are you talking about?"

From Mini, Mom said, *You Girls Lie To One Another. All The Things You Don't Tell Your Friends.* Ronnie thought she already sounded less angry. Just sad and a little petulant. Maybe showing all of them their deaths by car crash had gotten it out of her system.

"The thing I'm doing," said Ronnie, "that's a thing they would kick me out of the family for doing. I need my real family. I need you." She didn't want to say the rest out loud, so she waited. She felt Mom open up her head, take one cautious step inside with one foot and then the other. Ronnie knew that she didn't want to be this way or do those things anymore. Ronnie knew that she couldn't find a way to stop or escape

Alex's gaze from across the room when everyone else was watching TV. *Stop looking at me. If you could stop looking at me for just one second, then I could stop too.*

Mom, while we're speaking honestly, I don't think you're any of our mothers. I don't think you're Korean. I don't even think you come from any country on this planet.

(Don't tell me either way.)

But I don't care. I need your help, Mom. Please, are you still there? I'll be your daughter. I love your strength. I'm not scared anymore. You can sleep inside my bone marrow, and you can eat my thoughts for dinner, and I promise, I promise I'll always listen to you. Just make me good.

They didn't see Ronnie for a few months. Mini did see Alex at a concert pretty soon after everything that happened. He had a black eye and his arm in a sling. She hid behind a pillar until he passed out of sight. Mini, at least, had sort of figured it out. First she wondered why Ronnie had never told them, but then, immediately, she wondered how Ronnie could do such a thing. She wondered how Alex could do such a thing. Her thoughts shuttled back and forth between both of those stations and would not rest on one, so she made herself stop thinking about it.

As for Mini and Caroline, their hair grew out or they got haircuts, and everything was different, and Caroline's parents had allowed her to quit ballet and Mini's parents were still leaving her alone too much but she grew to like it. And when they were around, they weren't so bad. These days they could even be in the same room without screaming at each other.

There was another meet-up for Korean adoptees. They decided to go. School had started up again, and Mini and Caroline were on the wane. Mini and Caroline thought that maybe bringing it all back full circle would help. But they knew it wouldn't be the same without Ronnie.

Mini and Caroline saw us first before we saw them. They saw us emerge from a crowd of people, people that even Caroline hadn't befriended already. They saw our skin and hair, skin and eyes, hair and teeth. The way we seemed to exist in more dimensions than other people did. How something was going on with us – something was shakin' it – on the fourth, fifth, and possibly sixth dimensions. Space and time and space-time and skin and hair and teeth. You can't say "pretty" to describe us. You can't say "beautiful." You can, however, look upon us and know true terror. The Halversons know. All of our friends and admirers know.

Who are we? We are Ronnie and someone standing behind her, with hands on her shoulders, a voice in her ear, and sometimes we are someone standing inside her, with feet in her shoes, moving her around. We are Ronnie and we are her mom and we are every magazine clipping on how to charm and beautify, the tickle of a mascara wand on a tear duct, the burn of a waxed armpit.

We watched Mini and Caroline, observed how shocked they were. Afraid, too. Ronnie could tell that they would not come up to her first. *No?* she said to her mother. *No*, we said. For a moment Ronnie considered rebellion. She rejected the idea. Those girls were from the bad old days. Look at her now. She would never go back. Mom was pushing us away from them. She was telling Ronnie to let them go.

Ronnie watched Mini and Caroline recede. The tables, the tables of food and the chairs on either side of them, rushed toward us as their two skinny figures pinned and blurred. We both felt a moment of regret. She once loved them too, you know. Then her mother turned our head and we walked away.

SHAY CORSHAM WORSTED

Garth Nix

Garth Nix (www.garthnix.com) grew up in Canberra, Australia. When he turned nineteen, he left to drive around the United Kingdom in a beat-up Austin with a boot full of books and a Silver-Reed typewriter. Despite a wheel literally falling off the car, he survived to return to Australia and study at the University of Canberra. He has since worked in a bookshop, as a book publicist, a publisher's sales representative, an editor, as a literary agent, and as a public relations and marketing consultant. His first story was published in 1984 and was followed by novels *The Ragwitch, Shade's Children*, the *Old Kingdom* series (*Sabriel, Lirael, Abhorsen*), the six-book YA fantasy series *The Seventh Tower,* the seven-book *The Keys to the Kingdom* series and, the *Troubletwisters* series (co-written with Sean Williams). His latest book is new *Old Kingdom* novel, *Clariel*. He lives in Sydney with his wife and their two children.

THE YOUNG MAN came in one of the windows, because the back door had proved surprisingly tough. He'd kicked it a few times, without effect, before looking for an easier way to get in. The windows were barred, but the bars were rusted almost through, so he had no difficulty pulling them away. The window was locked as well, but he just smashed the glass with a half brick pried out of the garden wall. He didn't care about the noise. He knew there was only the old man in the house, the garden was large and screened by trees, and the evening traffic was streaming past on the road out front. That was plenty loud enough to cloak any noise he might make.

Or any quavering cries for help from the old man, thought the intruder, as he climbed through. He went to the back door first, intending to open it for a quick getaway, but it was deadlocked. More afraid of getting robbed than dying in a fire, thought the young man. That made it easier. He liked the frightened old people, the power he had over them with his youth and strength and anger.

When he turned around, the old man was standing behind him. Just standing there, not doing a thing. It was dim in the corridor, the only light a weak bulb hanging from the ceiling, its pallid glow falling on the bald head of the little man, the ancient slight figure in his brown cardigan and brown corduroy trousers and brown slippers, just a little old man that could be picked up and broken like a stick and then whatever pathetic treasures were in the house could be –

A little old man whose eyes were silver.

And what was in his hands?

Those gnarled hands had been empty, the intruder was sure of it, but now the old bloke held long blades, though he wasn't exactly holding the blades... they were growing, growing from his fingers, the flesh fusing together and turning silver... silver as those eyes!

The young man had turned half an inch towards the window and escape when the first of those silvery blades penetrated his throat, destroying his voice box, changing the scream that rose there to a dull, choking cough. The second blade went straight through his heart, back out, and through again.

Pock! Pock!

Blood geysered, but not on the old man's brown cardigan. He had moved back almost in the same instant as he struck and was now ten feet away, watching with those silver eyes as the young man fell writhing on the floor, his feet drumming for eighteen seconds before he became still.

The blades retreated, became fingers once again. The old man considered the body, the pooling blood, the mess.

"Shay Marazion Velvet," he said to himself, and walked to the spray of blood farthest from the body, head-high on the peeling wallpaper of green lilies. He poked out his tongue, which grew longer and became as silver as the blades.

He began to lick, tongue moving rhythmically, head tilted as required. There was no expression on his face, no sign of physical excitement. This was not some fetish.

He was simply cleaning up.

*　*　*

"YOU'LL NEVER GUESS who I saw walking up and down outside, Father," said Mary Shires, as she bustled in with her ludicrously enormous basket filled with the weekly tribute of home-made foods and little luxuries that were generally unwanted and wholly unappreciated by her father, Sir David Shires.

"Who?" grunted Sir David. He was sitting at his kitchen table, scrawling notes on the front page of the *Times*, below the big headlines with the latest from the war with Argentina over the Falklands, and enjoying the sun that was briefly flooding the whole room through the open doors to the garden.

"That funny little Mister Shea," said Mary, putting the basket down on the table.

Sir David's pencil broke. He let it fall and concentrated on keeping his hand still, on making his voice sound normal. He shouldn't be surprised, he told himself. It was why he was here, after all. But after so many years, even though every day he told himself this could be *the* day, it was a terrible, shocking surprise.

"Really, dear?" he said. He thought his voice sounded mild enough. "Going down to the supermarket like he normally does, I suppose? Getting his bread and milk?"

"No, that's just the thing," said Mary. She took out a packet of some kind of biscuit and put it in front of her father. "These are very good. Oatmeal and some kind of North African citrus. You'll like them."

"Mister Shea," prompted Sir David.

"Oh, yes. He's just walking backwards and forwards along the footpath from his house to the corner. Backwards and forwards! I suppose he's gone ga-ga. He's old enough. He must be ninety if he's a day, surely?"

She looked at him, without guile, both of them knowing he was eighty himself. But not going ga-ga, thank god, even if his knees were weak reeds and he couldn't sleep at night, remembering things that he had forced himself to forget in his younger days.

But Shay was much older than ninety, thought Sir David. Shay was much, much older than that.

He pushed his chair back and stood up.

"I might go and... and have a word with the old chap," he said carefully. "You stay here, Mary."

"Perhaps I should come –"

"No!"

He grimaced, acknowledging he had spoken with too much emphasis. He didn't want to alarm Mary. But then again, in the worst case... no, not the worst case, but in a quite plausible minor escalation...

"In fact, I think you should go out the back way and get home," said Sir David.

"Really, Father, why on –"

"Because I am ordering you to," snapped Sir David. He still had the voice, the tone that expected to be obeyed, deployed very rarely with the family, but quite often to the many who had served under him, first in the Navy and then for considerably longer in the Department, where he had ended up as the Deputy Chief. Almost fifteen years gone, but it wasn't the sort of job where you ever completely left, and the command voice was the least of the things that had stayed with him.

Mary sniffed, but she obeyed, slamming the garden gate on her way out. It would be a few years yet, he thought, before she began to question everything he did, perhaps start bringing brochures for retirement homes along with her special biscuits and herbal teas she believed to be good for reducing the chance of dementia.

Dementia. There was an apposite word. He'd spent some time thinking he might be suffering from dementia or some close cousin of it, thirty years ago, in direct connection to "funny old Mister Shea". Who was not at all funny, not in any sense of the word. They had all wondered if they were demented, for a time.

He paused near his front door, wondering for a moment if he should make the call first, or even press his hand against the wood paneling just so, and flip it open to take out the .38 Colt Police revolver cached there. He had a 9mm Browning automatic upstairs, but a revolver was better for a cached weapon. You wouldn't want to bet your life on magazine springs in a weapon that had sat too long. He checked all his armament every month, but still... a revolver was more certain.

But automatic or revolver, neither would be any use. He'd learned that before, from direct observation, and had been lucky to survive. Very lucky, because the other two members of the team hadn't had the fortune to slip in the mud and hit themselves on the head and be forced to lie still. They'd gone in shooting, and kept shooting, unable to believe the evidence of their eyes, until it was too late...

Sir David grimaced. This was one of the memories he'd managed to push aside for a long, long time. But like all the others, it wasn't far below the surface. It didn't take much to bring it up, that afternoon in 1953, the Department's secure storage on the fringe of RAF Bicester...

He did take a walking stick out of the stand. A solid bog oak stick, with a pommel of bronze worked in the shape of a spaniel's head. Not for use as a weapon, but simply because he didn't walk as well as he once did. He couldn't afford a fall now. Or at any time really, but particularly not now.

The sun was still shining outside. It was a beautiful day, the sky as blue as a bird's egg, with hardly a cloud in sight. It was the kind of day you only saw in films, evoking some fabulous summer time that never really existed, or not for more than half an hour at a time.

It was a good day to die, if it came to that, if you were eighty and getting tired of the necessary props to a continued existence. The medicines and interventions, the careful calculation of probabilities before anything resembling activity, calculations that Sir David would never have undertaken at a younger age.

He swung out on to the footpath, a military stride, necessarily adjusted by age and a back that would no longer entirely straighten. He paused by the kerb and looked left and right, surveying the street, head back, shoulders close to straight, sandy eyebrows raised, hair no longer quite so regulation short, catching a little of the breeze, the soft breeze that added to the day's delights.

Shay was there, as Mary had said. It was wearing the same clothes as always, the brown cardigan and corduroy. They'd put fifty pairs in the safe house, at the beginning, uncertain whether Shay would buy more or not, though its daily purchase of bread, milk and other basics was well established. It could mimic human behavior very well.

It looked like a little old man, a bald little man of some great age. Wrinkled skin, hooded eyes, head bent as if the neck could no longer entirely support the weight of years. But Sir David knew it didn't always move like an old man. It could move fluidly, like an insect, faster than you ever thought at first sighting.

Right now Shay was walking along the footpath, away from Sir David. Halfway to the corner, it turned back. It must have seen him, but as usual, it gave no outward sign of recognition or reception. There would be no such sign, until it decided to do whatever it was going to do next.

Sir David shuffled forward. Best to get it over with. His hand was already sweating, slippery on the bronze dog handle of his stick, his heart hammering in a fashion bound to be at odds with a cardio-pulmonary system past its best. He knew the feeling well, though it had been an age since he'd felt it more than fleetingly.

Fear. Unalloyed fear, that must be conquered, or he could do nothing, and that was not an option. Shay had broken free of its programming. It could be about to do anything, anything at all, perhaps reliving some of its more minor exploits like the Whitechapel murders of 1888, or a major one like the massacre at Slapton Sands in 1944.

Or something greater still.

Not that Sir David was sure he *could* do anything. He'd only ever been told two of the command phrases, and lesser ones at that, a pair of two word groups. They were embossed on his mind, bright as new brass. But it was never known exactly what they meant, or how Shay understood them.

There was also the question of which command to use. Or to try and use both command phrases, though that might somehow have the effect of one of the four word command groups. An unknown effect, very likely fatal to Sir David and everyone for miles, perhaps more.

It was not inconceivable that whatever he said in the next two minutes might doom everyone in London, or even the United Kingdom.

Perhaps even the world.

The first command would be best, Sir David thought, watching Shay approach. They were out in public, the second would attract attention, besides its other significant drawback. Public attention was anathema to Sir David, even in such dire circumstances. He straightened his tie unconsciously as he thought about publicity. It was a plain green tie, as his suit was an inconspicuous grey flannel, off the rack. No club or regimental ties for Sir David, no identifying signet rings, no ring, no earring, no tattoos, no unusual facial hair. He worked to look a type that had once been excellent camouflage, the retired military officer. It still worked, though less well, there being fewer of the type to hide amongst. Perhaps the Falklands War would help in this regard.

Shay was drawing nearer, walking steadily, perfectly straight. Sir David peered at it. Were its eyes silver? If they were, it would be too late. All bets off, end of story. But the sun was too bright, Sir David's own sight was not what it once was. He couldn't tell if Shay's eyes were silver.

"Shay Risborough Gabardine," whispered Sir David. Ludicrous words, but proven by trial and error, trial by combat, death by error. The name it apparently gave itself, a station on the Great Western Line, and a type of fabric. Not words you'd ever expect to find together, there was its safety, the cleverness of Isambard Kingdom Brunel showing through. Though not as clever as how IKB had got Shay to respond to the words in the first place. So clever that no one else had worked out how it had been done, not in the three different attempts over more than a hundred years. Attempts to try to change or expand the creature's lexicon, each attempt another litany of mistakes and many deaths. And after each such trial, the fear that had led to it being shut away. Locked underground the last time, and then the chance rediscovery in 1953 and the foolishness that had led it to being put away here, parked and forgotten.

Except by Sir David.

Shay was getting very close now. Its face looked innocuous enough. A little vacant, a man not too bright perhaps, or very short of sleep. Its skin was pale today, matching Sir David's own, but he knew it could change that in an instant. Skin color, height, apparent age, gender... all of these could be changed by Shay, though it mostly appeared as it was right now.

Small and innocuous, old and tired. Excellent camouflage among humans.

Ten paces, nine paces, eight paces... the timing had to be right. The command had to be said in front of its face, without error, clear and precise –

"Shay Risborough Gabardine," barked Sir David, shivering in place, his whole body tensed to receive a killing blow.

Shay's eyes flashed silver. He took half a step forward, putting him inches away from Sir David, and stopped. There was a terrible stillness, the world perched on the brink. Then it turned on its heel, crossed the road and went back into its house. The old house, opposite Sir David's, that no one but Shay had set foot in for thirty years.

Sir David stood where he was for several minutes, shaking. Finally he quelled his shivering enough to march back inside his own house, where he ignored the phone on the hall table, choosing instead to open a drawer in his study to lift out a chunkier, older thing that had no dial of any kind, push-button or rotary. He held the handset to his head and waited.

There were a series of clicks and whines and beeps, the sound of disparate connections working out how they might after all get together. Finally a sharp, quick male voice answered on the other end.

"Yes."

"Case Shay Zulu," said Sir David. There was a pause. He could hear the flipping of pages, as the operator searched through the ready book.

"Is there more?" asked the operator.

"What!" exploded Sir David. "Case Shay Zulu!"

"How do you spell it?"

Sir David's lip curled almost up to his nose, but he pulled it back.

"S-H-A-Y," he spelled out. "Z-U-L-U."

"I can spell Zulu," said the operator, affronted. "There's still nothing."

"Look up my workname," said Sir David. "Arthur Brooks."

There was tapping now, the sound of a keyboard. He'd heard they were using computers more and more throughout the Department, not just for the boffins in the back rooms.

"Ah, I see... I've got you now, sir," said the operator. At least there was a "sir", now.

"Get someone competent to look up Shay Zulu and report my communication at once to the duty officer with instruction to relay it to the Chief," ordered Sir David. "I want a call back in five minutes."

The call came in ten minutes, ten minutes Sir David spent looking out his study window, watching the house across the road. It was eleven a.m, too late for Shay to go to the supermarket like it had done every day for the last thirty years. Sir David wouldn't know if it had returned to its previous safe routine until 10:30am tomorrow. Or earlier, if Shay was departing on some different course...

The insistent ringing recalled him to the phone.

"Yes."

"Sir David? My name is Angela Terris, I'm the duty officer at present. We're a bit at sea here. We can't find Shay Zulu in the system at all – what was that?"

Sir David had let out a muffled cry, his knuckles jammed against his mouth.

"Nothing, nothing," he said, trying to think. "The paper files, the old records to 1977, you can look there. But the important thing is the book, we... I must have the notebook from the Chief's safe, a small green leather book embossed on the cover with the gold initials IKB."

"The Chief's not here right now," said Angela brightly. "This Falklands thing, you know. He's briefing the cabinet. Is it urgent?"

"Of course it's urgent!" barked Sir David, regretting it even as he spoke, remembering when old Admiral Puller had called up long after retirement, concerned about a suspicious new postman, and how they had laughed on the Seventh Floor. "Look, find Case Shay Zulu and you'll see what I mean."

"Is it something to do with the Soviets, Sir David? Because we're really getting on reasonably well with them at the moment –"

"No, no, it's nothing to do with the Soviets," said Sir David. He could hear the tone in her voice, he remembered using it himself when he had taken Admiral Fuller's call. It was the calming voice that meant no immediate action, a routine request to some functionary to investigate further in days, or even weeks, purely as a courtesy to the old man. He had to do something that would make her act, there had to some lever.

"I'm afraid it's something to do with the Service itself," he said. "Could be very, very embarrassing. Even now. I need that book to deal with it."

"Embarrassing as in likely to be of media interest, Sir David?" asked Angela.

"Very much so," said Sir David heavily.

"I'll see what I can do," said Angela.

"WE WERE REALLY rather surprised to find the Department owns a safe house that isn't on the register," said the young, nattily dressed and borderline rude young man who came that afternoon. His name, or at least the one he had supplied, was Redmond. "Finance were absolutely delighted, it must be worth close to half a million pounds now, a huge place like that. Fill a few black holes with that once we sell it. On the quiet, of course, as you say it would be very embarrassing if the media get hold of this little real estate venture."

"Sell it?" asked Sir David. "Sell it! Did you only find the imprest accounts, not the actual file? Don't you understand? The only thing that stops Shay from running amok is routine, a routine that is firmly embedded in and around that house! Sell the house and you unleash the... the beast!"

"Beast, Sir David?" asked Redmond. He suppressed a yawn and added, "Sounds rather Biblical. I expect we can find a place for this Shea up at Exile House. I daresay they'll dig his file up eventually, qualify him as a former employee."

They could find a place for Sir David too, were the unspoken words. Exile House, last stop for those with total disability suffered on active service, crippled by torture, driven insane from stress, shot through both knees and elbows. There were many ways to arrive at Exile House.

"Did you talk to the Chief?" asked Sir David. "Did you ask about the book marked 'IKB'?"

"Chief's very busy," said Redmond. "There's a war on you know. Even if it is only a little one. Look, why don't I go over and have a chat to old Shea, get a feel for the place, see if there's anything else that might need sorting?"

"If you go over there you introduce another variable," said Sir David, as patiently as he could. "Right now, I've got Shay to return to its last state, which may or may not last until ten thirty tomorrow morning, when it goes and gets its bread and milk, as it has done for the last thirty years. But if you disrupt it again, then who knows what will happen."

"I see, I see," said Redmond. He nodded as if he had completely understood. "Bit of a mental case, hey? Well, I did bring a couple of the boys in blue along just in case."

"Boys in blue!"

Sir David was almost apoplectic. He clutched at Redmond's sleeve, but the young man effortlessly withdrew himself and sauntered away.

"Back in half a mo," he called out cheerfully.

Sir David tried to chase him down, but by the time he got to the front door it was shut in his face. He scrabbled at the weapon cache, pushing hard on a panel till he realized it was the wrong one. By the time he had the revolver in his hand and had wrestled the door open, Redmond was already across the road, waving to the two policemen in the panda car to follow him. They got out quickly, large men in blue, putting their hats on as they strode after the young agent.

"Not even Special Branch," muttered Sir David. He let the revolver hang by his side. What could he do with it anyway? He couldn't shoot Redmond, or the policemen.

Perhaps, he thought bleakly, he could shoot himself. That would bring them back, delay the knock on the door opposite... but it would only be a delay. And if he was killed, and if they couldn't find Brunel's book, then the other command words would be lost.

Redmond went up the front steps two at a time, past the faded sign that said, "Hawkers and Salesmen Not Welcome. Beware of the Vicious Dog" and the one underneath it that had been added a year after the first, "No Liability for Injury or Death, You Have Been Warned."

Sir David blinked, narrowing his eyes against the sunshine that was still streaming down, flooding the street. It was just like the afternoon, that afternoon in '43 when the sun had broken through after days of fog and ice, but even though it washed across him on the bridge of his frigate he couldn't feel it, he could only see the light, he was so frozen from the cold Atlantic days the sunshine couldn't touch him, there was no warmth that could reach him . . .

He felt colder now. Redmond was knocking on the door. Hammering on the door. Sir David choked a little on his own spit, apprehension rising. There was a chance Shay wouldn't answer, and the door was very heavy, those two policemen couldn't kick it down, there would be more delay –

The door opened. There was the flash of silver, and Redmond fell down the steps, blood geysering from his neck as if some newfangled watering system had suddenly switched on beside him, drawing water from a rusted tank.

A blur of movement followed. The closer policeman spun about, as if suddenly inspired to dance, only his head was tumbling from his shoulders to dance apart from him. The surviving policeman, that is the policeman who had survived the first three seconds of contact with Shay, staggered backwards and started to turn around to run.

He took one step before he too was pierced through with a silver spike, his feet taking him only to the gutter where he lay down to die.

Sir David went back inside, leaving the door open. He went to his phone in the hall and called his daughter. She answered on the fourth ring. Sir David's hand was so sweaty he had to grip the plastic tightly, so the phone didn't slip from his grip.

"Mary? I want you to call Peter and your girls and tell them to get across the Channel now. France, Belgium, doesn't matter. No, wait, Terence is in Newcastle, isn't he? Tell him... listen to me... he can get the ferry to Stavanger. Listen! There is going to be a disaster here. It doesn't matter what kind! I haven't gone crazy, you know who I know. They have to get out of the country and across the water! Just go!"

Sir David hung up. He wasn't sure Mary would do as he said. He wasn't even sure that the sea would stop Shay. That was one of the theories, never tested, that it wouldn't or couldn't cross a large body of water. Brunel almost certainly knew, but his more detailed papers had been lost. Only the code book had survived. At least until recently.

He went to the picture window in his study. It had been installed on his retirement, when he'd moved here to keep an eye on Shay. It was a big window, taking up the place of two old Georgian multi-paned affairs, and it had an excellent view of the street.

There were four bodies in full view now. The latest addition was a very young man. Had been a young man. The proverbial innocent bystander, in the wrong place at the wrong time. A car sped by, jerking suddenly into the other lane as the driver saw the corpses and the blood.

Shay walked into the street and looked up at Sir David's window.

Its eyes were silver.

The secure phone behind Sir David rang. He retreated, still watching Shay, and picked it up.

"Yes."

"Sir David? Angela Terris here. The police are reporting multiple 999 calls, apparently there are people –"

"Yes. Redmond and the two officers are dead. I told him not to go, but he did. Shay is active now. I tried to tell you."

Shay was moving, crossing the road.

"Sir David!"

"Find the book," said Sir David wearily. "That's the only thing that can help you now. Find the leather book marked 'IKB'. It's in the Chief's safe."

Shay was on Sir David's side of the street, moving left, out of sight.

"The Chief's office was remodeled last year," said Angela Terris. "The old safe... I don't know –"

Sir David laughed bitter laughter and dropped the phone.

There was the sound of footsteps in the hall.

Footsteps that didn't sound quite right.

Sir David stood at attention and straightened his tie. Time to find out if the other command did what it was supposed to do. It would be out of his hands then. If it worked, Shay would kill him and then await further instructions for twenty-four hours. Either they'd find the book or they wouldn't, but he would have done his best.

As always.

Shay came into the room. It didn't look much like an old man now. It was taller, and straighter, and its head was bigger. So was its mouth.

"Shay Corsham Worsted," said Sir David.

KHELDYU
Karl Schroeder

Karl Schroeder (www.kschroeder.com) was born into a Mennonite family in Manitoba, Canada, in 1962. He started writing at age fourteen, following in the footsteps of A. E. van Vogt, who came from the same Mennonite community. He moved to Toronto in 1986, and became a founding member of SF Canada (he was president from 1996–97). He sold early stories to Canadian anthologies, and his first novel, *The Claus Effect* (with David Nickle) appeared in 1997. His first solo novel, *Ventus*, was published in 2000, and was followed by *Permanence* and *Lady of Mazes*. His most recent work includes the *Virga* series of science fiction novels (*Sun of Suns*, *Queen of Candesce*, *Pirate Sun*, and *The Sunless Countries*) and hard SF space opera *Lockstep*. He also collaborated with Cory Doctorow on The *Complete Idiot's Guide to Writing Science Fiction*. Schroeder lives in East Toronto with his wife and daughter.

THE TRUCK CRESTED a hill and Gennady got his first good look at the Khantayskoe test site. He ground to a stop and sat there for a long time.

Spreading before him were thirty square kilometers of unpopulated Siberian forest. Vast pine-carpeted slopes ran up and up into impossible distance to either side, yet laid over the forest of the south-facing rise was a gleaming circle six kilometers in diameter. It was slightly crinkly, like a giant cellophane disk or parachute that had been dropped here by a passing giant. Its edges had been perfectly sharp in the photos Gennady had seen, but they were ragged in real life. That circle was just a vast roof of plastic sheeting, after all, great sections of which had fallen in the past several winters. Enough remained to turn the slope into a glittering bulls-eye of reflecting sheets and fluttering, tattered banners of plastic.

Underneath that ceiling, the dark low forest was a subdued shade of gray. That gray was why Gennady was now putting on a surgical mask.

Standing up out of the top quarter of the circle was a round, flat-topped tower, like a smoke-stack for some invisible morlock factory. The thing was over a kilometer tall, and wisps of cloud wreathed its top.

He put the truck into gear and bumped his way toward the tumbled edges of the greenhouse. There was no trick to roofing over a whole forest, at least around here; few of the gnarled pines were more than thirty feet tall. Little grew between them, the long sight-lines making the northern arboreal forest a kind of wall-less maze. Here, the trees made a perfect filter, slowing the air that came in around the open edges of the greenhouse and letting it warm slowly as it converged on that distant tower.

"There's just one tiny problem," Achille Marceau had told Gennady when they'd talked about the job, "which is why we need you. The airflow stopped when we shut down the wind turbines at the base of the solar updraft tower. It got hot and dry under the greenhouse, and with the drought – well, you know."

The tenuous road wove between tree trunks and under the torn translucent roof whose surface wavered like an inverted lake. For the first hundred meters or so everything was okay. The trees were still alive. But then he began passing more and more orange and brown ones, and the track became obscured by deepening drifts of pine needles.

Then these began to disappear under a fog of greyish-white fungus.

He'd been prepared for this sight, but Gennady still stopped the truck to do some swearing. The trees were draped in what looked like the fake cobwebs kids hung over everything for American Halloween. Great swathes of the stuff cocooned whole trunks and stretched between them like long, sickening flags. He glanced back and saw that an ominous white cloud was beginning to curl around the truck – billions of spores kicked up by his wheels.

He gunned the engine to get ahead of the spore clouds, and that was when he finally noticed the other tracks.

Two parallel ruts ran through the white snow-like stuff, outlining the road ahead quite clearly. They looked fresh, and would have been made by a vehicle about the same size as his.

Marceau had insisted that Gennady would be the first person to visit the solar updraft plant in five years.

The slope was just steep enough that the road couldn't run straight up the hillside, but zig-zagged; so it took Gennady a good twenty minutes to make it to the tower. He was sweating and uncomfortable by the time he finally pulled the rig into the gravel parking area under the solar uplift tower. The other vehicle wasn't here, and its tracks had disappeared on the mold-free gravel. Maybe it had gone around the long curve of the tower.

He drove that way himself. He was supposed to be inspecting the tower's base for cracks, but his eyes kept straying, looking for a sign that somebody else was here. If they were, they were well hidden.

When he got back to the main lot, he rummaged in the glove compartment and came up with a flare gun. Wouldn't do any good as a weapon, but from a distance it might fool somebody. He slipped it into the pocket of his nylon jacket and climbed out to retrieve a portable generator from the bed of the truck.

Achille Marceau wanted to replace 4% of the world's coal-powered generating plants with solar updraft towers. With no fuel requirements at all, these towers would produce electricity while simultaneously removing CO_2 from the air. All together they'd suck a gigaton of carbon out of the atmosphere every year. Ignoring the electricity sales, at today's prices the carbon sales alone would be worth $40 billion dollars a year. That was $24 million per year from this tower alone.

Marceau had built this tower to prove the plan, by producing electricity for Northern China while simultaneously pulling down carbon and sequestering it underground. It was a brilliant plan, but he'd found himself underbid in the cutthroat post-carbon-bubble economy, and he couldn't make ends meet on the electricity sales alone. He'd had to shut down.

Now he was back – literally, a few kilometers back, waiting for his hazardous materials lackey to open the tower and give the rest of the trucks the all-clear signal.

The plastic ceiling got higher the closer you got to the tower, and now it was a good sixty meters overhead. Under it, vast round windows broke the curve of the wall; they were closed by what looked like steel Venetian blinds. Some portable trailers huddled between two of the giant circles, but these were for management. Gennady trudged past them without a glance and climbed a set of metal steps to a steel door labeled Небезпеки – 'HAZARD,' but written in Ukrainian, not Russian. Marceau's key let him in, and the door didn't even squeak, which was encouraging.

Before he stepped through, Gennady paused and looked back at the shrouded forest. It was eerily quiet, with no breeze to make the dead trees speak.

Well, he would change that.

The door opened into a kind of airlock; he could hear wind whistling around the edges of the inner portal. He closed the outer one and opened the inner, and was greeted by gray light and a sense of vast emptiness. Gennady stepped into the hollow core of the tower.

The ground was just bare red stone covered with construction litter. A few heavy lifters and cranes dotted the stadium-sized circle. Here there was sound – a discordant whistling from overhead. Faint light filtered down.

He spent a long hour inspecting the tower's foundations from the inside, then carried the little generator to the bottom of another flight of metal steps. These ones zigzagged up the concrete wall. About thirty meters up, a ring of metal beams held a wide gallery that encircled the tower, and more portable trailers had been placed on that. The stairs went on past them into a zone of shifting silvery light. The stuff up there would need attending to, but not just yet.

Hauling the generator up to the first level took him ten minutes; halfway up he took off the surgical mask, and he was panting when he finally reached the top. He caught his breath and then shouted, "Hello?" Nobody answered; if there was another visitor here, they were either hiding or very far away across – or up – the tower.

The windows of the dust-covered control trailer were unbroken. The door was locked. He used the next key on that but didn't go in. Instead, he set up the portable generator and connected it to the mains. But now he was in his element, and was humming as he pulled the generator's cord.

While it rattled and roared he took another cautious look around then went left along the gallery. The portable trailer sat next to one of the huge round apertures that perforated the base of the tower. Seated into this circle was the biggest wind turbine he'd ever seen. The gallery was right at the level of its axle and generator, so he was able to inspect it without having to climb anything. When Marceau's men mothballed it five years ago, they'd wrapped everything vulnerable in plastic and taped it up. Consequently, the turbine's systems were in surprisingly good shape. Once he'd pitched the plastic sheeting over the gallery rail he only had to punch the red button at the back of the trailer, and somewhere below, an electric motor strained to use all the power from his little generator. Lines of daylight began to separate the imposing Venetian blinds. With them came a quickening breeze.

"Put your hands up!"

Gennady reflexively put his hands in the air; but then he had to laugh.

"What are you laughing at?"

"Sorry. Is just that, last time I put my hands up like this was for a woman also. Kazakhstan, last summer."

There was a pause. Then: "Gennady?"

He looked over his shoulder and recognized the face behind the pistol. "Nadine, does your brother know you're here?"

Nadine Marceau tilted her head to one side and shifted her stance to a hipshot, exasperated pose as she lowered the pistol. "What the Hell, Gennady. I could ask you the same question."

With vast dignity he lowered his hands and turned around. "I," he said, "am working. You, on the other hand, are trespassing."

She gaped at him. "You're *working*? For *that* bastard?"

So, then it wasn't just a rumor that Achille and Nadine Marceau hated each other. Gennady shrugged; it wasn't his business. "Cushy jobs for the IAEA are hard to come by, Nadine, you know that. I'm a freelancer, I have to get by."

"Yeah, but –" She was looking down, fumbling with her holster, as widening light unveiled behind her the industrial underworld of the solar uplift tower. Warm outside air was pouring in through the opening shutters now, and, slowly, the giant vanes of the windmill fixed in its round window began to turn.

Nadine cursed. "You've started it! Gennady, I thought you had more integrity! I never thought you'd end up being part of the problem."

"Part of the problem? God, Nadine, is just a windmill."

"No, it's not –" He'd turned to admire the turning blades, but looking back saw that she had frozen in a listening posture. "Shit!

"Don't tell him I'm here!" she shouted as she turned and started running along the gallery. "Not a word, Gennady. You hear?"

NADINE MARCEAU, U.N. arms inspector and disowned child of one of the wealthiest families in Europe, disappeared into the shadows. Gennady could hear the approaching trucks himself now; still, he spread his hands and shouted, "Don't you even want a cup of coffee?"

The metal venetian blinds clicked into their fully open configuration, and now enough outside light was coming in to reveal the cyclopean vastness of the tower's interior. Gennady looked up at the little circle of sky a kilometer-and-a-half overhead, and shook his head ruefully. "Is not even radioactive."

Why was Nadine here? Some vendetta with her brother, no doubt, though Gennady preferred to think it was work-related. The last time he'd seen her was in Azerbaijan, two years ago; that time, they'd been working together to find some stolen nukes. A nightmare job, but totally in line with both their professional backgrounds. This place, though, it was just an elaborate windmill. It couldn't explode or melt down or spill oil all over the sensitive arboreal landscape. No, this had to be a family thing.

There were little windows in the reinforced concrete wall. Through one of these he could see three big trucks, mirror to his own, approaching the tower. Nadine's brother Achille had gotten impatient, apparently. He must have seen the blinds opening, and the first of the twenty wind turbines that ringed the tower's base starting to move. A legendary micro-manager, he just couldn't stay away.

By the time the boss clambered out of the second truck, unsteady in his bright-red hazmat suit, Gennady had opened the office trailer, started a hepafilter whirring, and booted up the tower's control system. He leaned in the trailer's doorway and watched as first two bodyguards, then Marceau himself, then his three engineers, reached the top of the stairs.

"Come inside," Gennady said. "You can take that off."

The hazmat suit waved its arms and made a garbled sound that Gennady eventually translated as, "You're not wearing your mask."

"Ah, no. Too hard to work in. But that's why you hired me, Mr. Marceau. To take your chances."

"Call me Achille! Everybody else does." The hazmat suit made a lunging motion; Gennady realized that Nadine's brother was trying to clap him on the shoulder. He pretended it had worked, smiled, then backed into the trailer.

It took ten minutes for them to coax Marceau out of his shell, and while they did Gennady debated with himself whether to tell Achille that his sister was here too. The moments dragged on, and eventually Gennady realized that the engineers were happily chattering on about the status of the tower's various systems, and the bodyguards were visibly bored, and he hadn't said anything. It was going to look awkward if he brought it up now... so he put it off some more.

Finally, the young billionaire removed the hazmat's headpiece, revealing a lean, high-cheekboned face currently plastered with sweat. "Thanks, Gennady," he gasped. "It was brave of you to come in here alone."

"Yeah, I risked an epic allergy attack," said Gennady with a shrug. "Nothing after camping in Chernobyl."

Achille grinned. "Forget the mold, we just weren't sure whether opening the door would make the whole tower keel over. I'm glad it's structurally sound."

"Down here, maybe," Gennady pointed out. "There's a lot up there that could still fall on us." He jerked a thumb at the ceiling.

"You were with us yesterday." They'd done a visual inspection from the helicopters on their way to the plateau. But Gennady wasn't about to trust that.

Achille turned to his engineers. "The wind's not cooperating. Now they're saying it'll shift the right way by 2:00 tomorrow afternoon. How long is it going to take to establish a full updraft?"

"There's inertia in the air inside the tower," said one. "Four hours, granted the thermal difference...?"

"I don't think we'll be ready tomorrow," Gennady pointed out. He was puzzled by Achille's impatience. "We haven't had time to inspect all the turbines, much less the scrubbers on Level Two."

The engineers should be backing him up on this one, but they stayed silent. Achille waved a hand impatiently. "We'll leave the turbines parked for now. As to the scrubbers..."

"There might be loose pieces and material that could get damaged when the air currents pick up."

"Dah! You're right, of course." Achille rubbed his chin for a second, staring into space. "We'd better test the doors now... might as well do it in pairs. Gennady, you've got an hour of good light. If you're so worried about them, go check out the scrubbers."

Gennady stared at him. "What's the hurry?"

"Time is money. You're not afraid of the updraft while we're testing the doors, are you? It's not like a hurricane or anything. We walk all the time up there when the unit's running full bore." Achille relented. "Oh, take somebody with you if you're worried. Octav, you go."

Octav was one of Achille's bodyguards. He was a blocky Lithuanian who favored chewing tobacco and expensive suits. The look he shot Gennady said, *This is all your fault.*

Gennady glanced askance at Octav, then said to Achille, "Listen, is there some reason why somebody would think that starting this thing up would be wrong?"

The boss stared at him. "Wrong?"

"I don't mean this company you're competing with – GreenCore. I mean, you know, the general public."

"Don't bug the boss," said Octav.

Achille waved a hand at him. "It's okay. A few crazy adaptationists think reversing climate change will cause as many extinctions as the temperature rise did in the first place. If you ask me, they're just worried about losing their funding. But really, Malianov – this tower sucks CO_2 right out of the air. It doesn't matter where that CO_2 came from, which means we're equally good at offsetting emissions from the airline industry as we are from, say, coal. We're good for everybody."

Gennady nodded, puzzled, and quickly followed Octav out of the trailer. He didn't want the bodyguard wandering off on his own – or maybe spotting something in the distance that he shouldn't see.

Octav *was* staring – standing in the middle of the gallery, mouth open. "Christ," he said. "It's like a fucking cathedral." With light breaking in from the opening louvers, the full scale of the place was becoming clear, and even jaded Gennady was impressed. The tower was a kilometer and a half tall, and over a hundred meters across, its base ringed with round wind turbine windows. "But I was expecting some kinda machinery in here. Is that gonna be installed later?"

Gennady shook his head, pointing at the round windows. "That's all there is to it. When those windows are open, warm air from the greenhouse comes in and rises. The wind turbines turn, and make electricity."

Gennady began the long climb up the steps to the next gallery. His gaze kept roving across the tower's interior; he was looking for Nadine. Was Octav going to spot her? He didn't want that. Even though he knew Nadine was level-headed in tight situations, Octav was another matter. And then there was the whole question of why she was out here to begin with, seemingly on her own, and carrying a gun.

Octav followed on his heels. "Well sure, I get the whole 'heat rises' thing, but why'd he build it *here?* In the middle of fucking Siberia? If it's solar-powered, wouldn't you want to put it at the equator?"

"They built it on a south-facing slope, so it's 85% as efficient as it would be at the equator. And the thermal inertia of the soil means the updraft will operate 24 hours a day."

"But in winter –"

"Even in a Siberian winter, because it's not about the absolute temperature, it's about the *difference* between the temperatures inside and outside."

Octav pointed up. "Those pull the CO_2 out of the air, right?"

"If this were a cigarette of the gods, that would be the filter, yes." Just above, thousands of gray plastic sheets were stretched across the shaft of the tower. They were stacked just centimeters apart so that the air flowed freely between them.

"It's called polyaziridine. When the gods suck on the cigarette, this stuff traps the CO_2."

They'd come to one of the little windows. Gennady pried it open and dry summer air poured in. They were above the greenhouse roof, and from here you could see the whole sweep of the valley where Achille had built his experiment. "Look at that."

Above the giant tower, the forested slope kept on rising, and rising, becoming bare tanned rock and then vertical cliff. "Pretty mountains," admitted Octav.

"Except they're not mountains." Yes, the slopes rose like mountainsides, culminating in those daunting cliffs. The trouble was, at the very top the usual jagged, irregular skyline of rocky peaks was missing. Instead, the cliff-tops ended in a perfectly flat, perfectly horizontal line – a knife-cut across the sky – signaling that there was no crest and fall down a north-facing slope up there. Miles up, under a regime of harsh UV light and whipping high-altitude winds, clouds scudded low and fast along a nearly endless plain of red rock. Looking down from up there, the outflung arms of the Putorana Plateau absolutely dwarfed Achille's little tower.

"I walked on it yesterday when we flew up to prime the wells," said Gennady. Octav hadn't been along on that flight; he hadn't seen what lay beyond that ruler-straight crest. "That plateau covers an area the size of Western Europe, and it's so high nothing can grow up there. This whole valley is just an erosion ditch in it."

Octav nodded, reluctantly intrigued. "Kinda strange place to build a power plant."

"Achille built here because the plateau's made of basalt. When you pump hot carbonated water into basalt it makes limestone, which permanently sequesters the carbon. All Achille has to do is keep fracking up top there and he's got a continent-sized sponge to soak up all the excess CO_2 on the planet. You could build a thousand towers like this all around the Putorana. It's perfect for –" But Octav had clapped a hand on his shoulder.

"Shht," whispered the bodyguard. "Heard something."

Before Gennady could react, Octav was creeping up the steps with his gun drawn. "What do you think you're doing?" Gennady hissed at the Lithuanian. "Put that thing away!"

Octav waved at him to stay where he was. "Could be bears," he called down in a hoarse – and not at all quiet – stage whisper. The word *bears* seemed to hang in the air for a second, like an echo that couldn't find a wall to bounce off.

Gennady started up after him, deliberately making as much noise as he could on the metal steps. "Bears are not arboreal, much less likely will they be foraging up in the scrubbers –" Octav reached the top of the steps and disappeared. Here, the hanging sheets of plastic made a bizarre drapery that completely filled the tower. Except for this little catwalk, the entire space was given over to them. It was kind of like being backstage in a large theater, except the curtains were white. Octav was hunched over, gun drawn, stepping slowly forward around the slow curve of the catwalk. This would have been a comical sight except that, about eight meters ahead of him, the curtains were swaying.

"Octav, don't –" The bodyguard lunged into the gloom.

Gennady heard a scuffle and ran forward himself. Then, terribly, two gunshots like slaps echoed out and up and down.

"No, what have you –!" Gennady staggered to a stop and had to grab the railing for support; it creaked and gave a bit, and he suddenly realized how high up they were. Octav knelt just ahead, panting. He was reaching slowly out to prod a crumpled gray and brown shape.

"*Jssht!*" said the walkie-talkie on Octav's belt. More garbled vocal sounds spilled out of it, until Octav suddenly seemed to realize it was there, and holstered his pistol with one hand while taking it out with the other.

"Octav," he said. The walkie-talkie spat incoherent staticky noise into his ear. He nodded.

"Everything's okay," he said. "Just shot a goose is all. I guess we have dinner."

Then he turned to glare at Gennady. "You should have stayed where I told you!"

Gennady ignored him. The white curtains swung, all of them now starting to rustle as if murmuring and pointing at Octav's minor crime scene. More of the louvered doors had opened far below, and the updraft was starting. Shadow and sound began to paint the tower's hollow spaces.

Nadine would be hard to see now, and impossible to hear. Hopefully, she'd noticed Octav's shots; even now, if she had a grain of sense, she'd be on her way back to her truck.

Gennady brushed past Octav. "If you're done murdering the locals, I need to work." The two did not speak again, as Gennady tugged at the plastic and inspected the bolts mounting the scrubbers to the tower wall.

A SIBERIAN SUMMER day lasts forever; but there came a point when the sun no longer lit the interior top of the tower. The last hundred meters up there were painted titanium white, and reflected a lot of light down. Now, though, with the sky a dove gray shading to nameless pink, and the sun's rays horizontal, Achille's lads had to light the sodium lamps and admit it was evening.

The lamps were the same kind you saw in parking lots all over the world. For Gennady, they completely stole the sense of mystery from the tower's interior, making it as grim an industrial space as any he'd seen. For a while he stood outside the control trailer with Octav and a couple of the engineers, trying to get used to the evil greenish yellow cast that everything had. Then he said, "I'm going to sleep outside."

One of the engineers laughed. "After your run-in with the climbing bears? And you know, there really are wolves in this forest."

"No, no, I will be in one of the admin trailers." Nobody had even opened those yet; and besides, he needed to find a spot where late night comings and goings wouldn't be noticed by these men.

"First, you must try the goose!" While the others inspected and tested, Octav had cooked it over a barrel-fire. He'd only made a few modest comments about the bird, but Gennady knew he was ridiculously proud of his kill, because he'd placed the barrel smack in the center of the hundred-meter-wide floor of the tower. He'd even dragged over a couple of railroad ties and set them up like logs around his campfire.

Achille was down there now, peering at his air-quality equipment, obviously debating whether he could lose his surgical mask. He waved up at them. "Come! Let's eat!"

Gennady followed the others reluctantly. He knew where this was headed: to the inevitable male bonding ritual. It came as no surprise at all, when, as they tore into the simultaneously charred and raw goose, Achille waved at Gennady, and said, "Now this man! He's a real celebrity! Octav, did you know what kind of adventurer you saved from this fierce beast?" He waved his drumstick in the air. Octav looked puzzled.

"Gennady, here. Gennady fought the famous Dragon of Pripyat!" Of course the engineers knew the story, and smiled politely; but neither Octav nor Bogdan, the other bodyguard, knew it. "Tell us, Gennady!" Achille's grin was challenging. "About the reactor, and the devil guarding it."

"We know all about that," protested an engineer. "I want to know about the Kashmiri incident. The one with the nuclear jet. Is it true you flew it into a mine?"

"Well, yes," Gennady admitted, "not myself of course. It was just a drone." Of course the attention was flattering, but it also made him uncomfortable, and over the years he'd learned that the discomfort outweighed the flattery. He told them the story, but as soon as he could he found a way to turn to Achille and say, "But these are just isolated incidents. Your whole career has been, well, something of an adventure itself, no?"

That burst of eloquence had about exhausted his skills of social manipulation; luckily, Achille was eager to talk about himself. He and Nadine had inherited wealth, and Gennady had sensed yesterday that this weighed on him. He wanted to be a self-made man, but he wasn't; so, he was using his inheritance recklessly, to see if he could achieve something great. He also had an impulsive urge to justify himself.

He told them how, when he'd seen the sheer scale of the cap and trade and carbon tax programs that were springing up across the globe, he'd decided to put all his chips into carbon air capture, "Because," he explained, "it was a completely discredited approach."

"Wait," said Octav, his brow crinkling. "You went into... that... because it had no credibility?" Achille nodded vigorously.

"Decades of research, patents, and designs were just lying around waiting to be snapped up. I was already building this place, but the carbon bubble was bursting as governments started pulling their fossil fuel subsidies. Here, the local price of petrol had gone through the roof as the Arctic oilfields went from profitable to red. But, you see, I had a plan."

The plan was to offer to offset CO_2 emissions of industries anywhere on the planet, from right here. Since Achille's giant machines harvested greenhouse gases from the ambient atmosphere, it didn't matter where they were – which meant he could sell offsets to airlines, mines in South America, or container ships burning bunker oil with equal ease.

"But then, Kafatos stole my market."

The Greek industrialist's company, Greencore, had bought up vast tracts of Siberian forest and had begun rolling out a cheaper biological alternative to Achille's towers.

"They do what? Some kind of fast-growing tree?" asked Gennady. He knew about the rivalry between Achille and Kafatos. It wasn't just business; it was personal.

Achille nodded. "Genetically modified lodgepole pines. Super-fast growing, resistant to the pine beetle. They want to turn the forest itself into a carbon sponge. It's as bad an idea as tampering with Mother Nature was – as oil was – in the first place," he said, "and I intend to prove it."

The conversation wound down a bit after this motivational speech, but then one of the engineers looked around at the trembling shadows of the amphitheater in which they sat, and said, "Pretty spooky, eh?"

"Siberia is all spooky," Bogdan pointed out. "Never mind just here."

And that set them all off on ghost stories and legends of the deep forests. The locals used to believe Siberia was a middle-world, half-way up a vast tree, with underworlds below and heavens above. Shamans rode their drums between the worlds, fighting the impossible strength of the gods with dogged courage and guile. They triumphed now and then, but in the end the deep forest swallowed all human achievement like it would swallow a shout. What was human got lost in the green maze; what came out was changed and new.

Bogdan knew a story about the 'valley of death' and the strange round *kheldyu* – iron houses – that could be found half-buried in the permafrost here and there. There was a valley no one ever returned from; *kheldyu* had been glimpsed there by scouts on the surrounding heights.

The engineers had their own tales, about lost Soviet-era expeditions. There were downed bombers loaded with nukes on hair-trigger, which might go off at any moment. There were Chinese tunnel complexes, and lakes so radioactive that to stand on their shores for a half an hour meant dying within the week. (Well, that last story, at least, was perfectly true.)

"Gennady, what about you?" All eyes turned to him. Gennady had relaxed a bit and was willing to talk; but he didn't know any recent myths or legends. "All I can tell you," Gennady said, "is that it'll be poetic justice if we save the world by burying all our carbon here. Because what's in this place nearly killed the whole world through global warming once already."

The engineers hadn't heard about the plateau's past. "This place – this *thing*," said Gennady in his best ghost-story voice, "killed ninety percent of all life on Earth when it erupted. This supervolcano, called the Siberian Traps, caused the Permian extinction 250 million years ago. Think about it: the place was here before the dinosaurs and it's still here, still taller than mountain ranges and as wide as Europe." There was nothing like it on Earth – older than the present continents, the Putorana was an ineradicable scar from the greatest dying the world had ever seen.

So then they had to hear the story of the Permian extinction. Gennady did his best to convey the idea of an entire world dying, and of geologic forces so gargantuan and unstoppable that the first geologists to find this spot literally couldn't imagine the scale of the apocalypse it represented. He was rewarded by some appreciative nods, particularly for his image of a slumbering monster that could indifferently destroy all life on the planet by just rolling over. The whole thing was too abstract for Octav and Bogdan, though, who were yawning.

"Right." Achille slapped his knees. "Tomorrow's another busy day. Let's turn in everybody, and get a start at sun-up."

"Uh, boss," said an engineer, "sunrise is at 3:00 a.m."

"Make it five, then." Achille headed for the metal steps.

Gennady repeated his intent to sleep in the admin trailer; to his relief, no one volunteered to do the same. When he stepped through the second door of the tower's airlock, it was to find that although it was nearly midnight, the sun was still setting. He remembered seeing this effect before: the sun might dip below the horizon, but the lurid peach-and-rose colored glow it painted on the sky wasn't going to go away. That smear of dusk would just slide up and across the northern horizon, over the next few hours, and then the sun would pop back up once it reached the east.

That was helpful. The administration trailer needed a good airing-out, so he opened all its windows and sat on the front step for a while, waiting to see if anybody came out of the tower. The sunset inched northward. He checked his watch. Finally, with a sigh, he set off walking around the western curve of the structure. A flashlight was unnecessary, but he did bring the flare gun. Because, well, there might be bears.

Nadine had done a pretty good job of hiding her truck, among gnarled cedars and cobwebs of fungi on the north side of the tower. Either she'd been waiting for him, or she had some kind of proximity alarm, because he was still ten meters away when he heard the door slam. He stopped and waited. After a couple of minutes she stood up out of the bushes, a black cut-out on the red sky. "It's just you," she said unnecessarily.

Gennady shrugged. "Do I ever bring friends?"

"Good point." The silhouette made a motion he interpreted as the holstering of a pistol. He strolled over while she untangled herself from the bushes.

"Come back to the trailer," he said. "I have chairs."

"I'm sleeping here."

"That's fine."

"... Okay." They crunched back over the gravel. Halfway there, Nadine said, "Seriously, Gennady. You and Achille?"

"What is the problem?" He spread his hands, distorting the long shadow that leaned ahead of him. "He is restarting his carbon air capture project. That's a good thing, no?"

She stopped walking. "That's what you think he's doing?"

What did that mean? "Let's see. It's what he says he's doing. It's what the press releases say. It's what everybody else thinks he's doing... What else *could* he be up to?"

"Everybody asks that question." She kicked at the gravel angrily. "But nobody sees what he's doing! You know –" she laughed bitterly, "When I told my team at the IAEA what he was up to, they just laughed at me. And you know what? I thought about calling you. I figured, *Gennady knows how these things go. He'd understand.* But you don't get it either, do you?"

"You know I am not smart man. I need thing explained to me."

She was silent until they reached the admin trailer. Once inside she said, "Close those," with a nod at the windows. "I don't want any of that shit in here with us."

She must mean the mold. As Gennady went around shutting things up, Nadine sat down at the tiny table. After a longing look at the mothballed coffee machine, she steepled her hands and said, "I suppose you saw the pictures."

"That the paparazzi took of you two at the Paris café? There were a few, if I recall."

She grimaced. "I particularly like the one that shows Kafatos punching Achille in the face."

Gennady nodded pensively. It had been two years since Achille came across his sister having dinner with Kafatos, his biggest business rival.

The punch was famous, and the whole incident had burned through the internet in a day or two, to be instantly forgotten in the wake of the next scandal.

"Achille and I haven't spoken since. He's even taken me out of his will – you know he was the sole heir, right?"

Gennady nodded. "I figured that was why you went to work at the IAEA."

"No, I did that out of idealism, but... any way it doesn't matter. I knew all about Achille's little rivalry with the Greek shithead, but something about it didn't add up. Achille was lying to me, so I went to Kafatos to see if he knew why. He didn't, so the whole café incident was a complete waste. But I eventually *did* get the story from one of Achille's engineers."

"Let me guess. It's something to do with the tower?"

She shrugged. "It never crossed my mind. When Achille came up with the plan for this place, I guess it was eight years ago, it seemed to make sense. He knew about the Permian, and he talked about how he was going to 'redeem' the site of the greatest extinction in history by using it to not just stop but completely reverse global warming. The whole blowup with Kafatos happened because Greencore bought up about a million square kilometers of forest just east of Achille's site. Kafatos has been genetically engineering pines to soak up the carbon, but you know that." She took a deep breath. "You also know there's no economic reason to re-open the tower."

Gennady blinked at her. "They told me there was, that was why we were here. Told me the market had turned..."

She sent him a look of complete incredulity; then that look changed, and suddenly Nadine stood up. Gennady opened his mouth to ask what was wrong, just as one of the windows rattled loosely in its mount. Nadine was staring out the window, a look of horror on her face.

A deep vibration made the plywood floor buzz. The glass rattled again.

"He's opening the windows!" Nadine ran for the door. Gennady peered outside.

"Surely not all of them..." But all the black circles he could see from here were changing, letting out a trickle of sodium-lamp light.

By the time he got outside she was gone – off and running around the tower in the direction of her truck. Gennady shifted from foot to foot, trying to decide whether to follow.

Her story hadn't made sense, but still, he paused for a moment to gaze up at the tower. In the deep sunset light of the midsummer night, it looked like a rifle barrel aimed at the sky.

He slammed through the airlocks and went up the stairs. All around the tower's base, the round windows were humming open.

Gennady fixed an empty smile on his face, and deliberately slowed himself down as he opened the door to the control trailer. He was thinking of radioactive lakes, of the Bequerel Reindeer, an entire radioactive herd he'd seen once, slaughtered and lying in the back of a transport truck; of disasters he'd cleaned up after, messes he'd hidden from the media – and the kinds of people who had made those messes.

"Hey, what's up?" he said brightly as he stepped inside.

"Close that!" Achille was pacing in the narrow space. "You'll let in the spores!"

"Ah, sorry." He sidled around the bodyguards, behind the engineers who were staring at their tablets and laptops, and found a perch near an empty water cooler. From here he could see the laptop screens, though not well.

"What's up?" he said again.

One of the engineers started to say something, but Achille interrupted him. "Just a test. You should go back to bed."

"I see." He stepped close to the table and looked over the engineer's shoulder. One of the laptop screens showed a systems' diagram of the tower. The other was open to a satellite weather map. "Weather's changing," he muttered, just loud enough for the engineer to hear. The man nodded.

"Fine," Gennady said more loudly. "I'll be in my trailer." Nobody moved to stop him as he left, but outside he paused, arms wrapped around his torso, breath cold and frosting the air. Already he could feel the breeze from below.

Back in Azerbaijan, Nadine had been one of the steadiest operatives during the Alexander's Road incident; they had talked one evening about what Gennady had come to call 'industrial logic.' About what happened when the natural world became an abstraction, and the only reality was the system you were building. Gennady had fallen for that kind of thinking early in his career; had spent the rest of his life mopping up after other people who'd never gotten out from under it. He couldn't remember the details of the conversation now, but he did remember her getting a distant expression on her face at one point, and muttering something about Achille.

But it wasn't just about her brother; all of this had something to do with Kafatos, too. He shook his head, and turned to the stairs.

A flash lit the inside of the tower and seconds later a sharp *bang!* echoed weirdly off the curving walls. The grinding noise of the window mechanisms stopped.

A transformer had blown. It had happened on the far side of the tower; he started in that direction but had only taken a couple of steps when the trailer door flew open and the engineers spilled out, all talking at once. "Malianov!" one shouted. "Did you see it?"

He shook his head. "Heard it, but not sure where it came from. Echoes..." Let them stumble around in the dark for a while. That would give Nadine a chance to get away. Then he could find her again and talk her out of doing anything further.

Octav and Bogdan had come out, too, and Bogdan raced off after the engineers. Gennady shrugged at Octav and said, "I am still going back to bed." He'd gone down the stairs, reached the outer door and actually put his hand on the latch before curiosity overcame his better judgment, and he turned back.

He came up behind the engineers as they were shining their flashlights at the smoking ruin that used to be a transformer. "Something caused it to arc," one said. Bogdan was kneeling a few meters away. He stood up and dangled a mutilated padlock in the beam of his flashlight. "Somebody's got bolt-cutters."

All eyes turned to Gennady.

He backed away. "Now, wait a minute. I was with you."

"You could have set something to blow and then come back to the trailer," said one of the engineers. "It's what I would have done."

Gennady said nothing; if they thought he'd done it they wouldn't be looking for Nadine. "Grab him!" shouted one of the engineers. Gennady just put out his hands and shook his head as Bogdan took hold of his wrists.

"It's not what *I* would have done," Gennady said. "Because this would be the result. I am not so stupid."

"Oh, and I am?" Bogdan glared at him. At that moment one of the engineers put his walkie-talkie to his ear and made a shushing motion. "We found the – what? Sir, I can't hear what –"

The distorted tones of the voice on the walkie-talkie had been those of Achille, but suddenly they changed. Nadine said, "I have your boss. I'll kill him unless you go to the center of the floor and light the barrel-fire so I can see you."

The engineers gaped at one another. Bogdan let go of Gennady and grabbed at the walkie-talkie. "Who is this?"

"Someone who knows what you're up to. Now move!"

Bogdan eyed Gennady, who shrugged. "Nothing to do with me."

There was a quick, heated discussion. The engineers were afraid of being shot once they were out in the open, but Gennady pointed out that there was actually more light around the wall, because that's where the sodium lamps were. "She doesn't want to see us clearly, she just wants us where it'll be obvious which way we're going if we run," he said.

Reluctantly, they began edging toward the shadowed center of the tower. "How can you be so sure?" somebody whined. Gennady shrugged again.

"If she'd wanted to kill her brother, she would have by now," he pointed out.

"Her *what?*"

And at that moment, the gunfire started.

It was all upstairs, but the engineers scattered, leaving Gennady and Bogdan standing in half-shadow. Had Octav stayed up top? Gennady couldn't remember. He and Bogdan scanned the gallery, but the glare from the sodium lamps hid the trailer. After a few seconds, Gennady heard the metallic bounce of feet running on the mesh surface overhead. It sounded like two sets, off to the right.

"There!" Gennady pointed to the left and began running. Bogdan ran too, and quickly outpaced him; at that point Gennady peeled off and headed back. There was another set of stairs nearby, and though the engineers were there, they were huddling under its lower steps. He didn't think they'd stop him, nor did they as he ran past them and up.

Bogdan yelled something inarticulate from the other side of the floor. Gennady kept going.

"Nadine? Where are you?" She'd been running in a clockwise direction around the tower, so he went that way too, making sure now that he was making plenty of noise. He didn't want to surprise her. "Nadine, it's me!"

Multiple sets of feet rang on the gallery behind him. Gennady took the chance that she'd kept going up, and mounted the next set of steps when he came to them. "Nadine!" She'd be among the scrubbers now.

He reached the top and hesitated. Why *would* she come up here? It was the cliché thing to do: in movies, the villains always went up. Gennady tried to push past his confusion and worry to picture the layout of the tower. He remembered the two inspection elevators just as a rattling hum started up ahead.

By the time he reached the yellow wire cage, the elevator car was on its way up. Next stop, as far as he knew, was the top of the tower. Nadine could hold it there, and maybe that was her plan. There wouldn't be just the one elevator, though, not in a structure this big. Gennady turned and ran for the other side of the tower.

He could hear somebody crashing up the steps from the lower levels. "Malianov!" shouted Octav.

He was a good quarter of the way around the curve from Gennady, so Gennady paused and leaned on the rail to shout, "I'm here!"

"What are you doing?"

"I'm right on her heels!"

"Stop! Come down! Leave it to us."

"Okay! I'll be right there." He ran on, and reached the other elevator before Octav had reached the last flight of steps. Gennady wrenched the rusty outer cage door open, but struggled with the inner one. He got in and slammed it just as Octav thundered up. Gennady hit the UP button while Octav roared in fury; but three meters up, he hit STOP.

"Octav. Don't shoot at me, please. I'll send the cage back down when I get to the top. I just need a minute to talk with Nadine, is all."

In the movies there'd be all kinds of wild gunplay happening right now, but Octav was a professional. He crossed his arms and glowered at Gennady through the grid flooring of the elevator. "Where's she going?" he demanded.

"Damned if I know. Up."

"What's up?"

"Someplace she can talk to her brother alone, I'm thinking. Reason with him, threaten him, I don't know. Look, Octav, let me talk to her. She might shoot you, but she's not going to shoot me."

"It really is Nadine? Achille's sister? Do you know her?"

"Well, remember that story I told last night about Azerbaijan and the nukes? We worked together on that. You know she's with the IAEA too. You never met her?"

There was an awkward pause. "What happened in the trailer?" Gennady asked. "Did she hurt him?" Octav shook his head.

"She was yelling," he said. "I snuck around the trailer and came in through the bathroom window. But I got stuck."

Gennady stifled a laugh. He would have paid to see that; Octav was not a small man.

"I took a shot at her but she ran. Might have winged her, though."

Gennady cursed. "Octav, that's your boss's sister."

"He told me to shoot!"

There was another awkward pause.

"I'm sure she doesn't mean to harm him," said Gennady, but he wasn't so sure now.

"Then why's she holding him at gunpoint?"

"I don't know. Look, just give me a minute, okay?" He hit UP before Octav could reply.

He'd gotten an inkling of the size of the tower when they'd inspected it by helicopter, but down at the bottom, the true dimensions of the place were obscured by shadow. Up here it was all vast emptiness, the walls a concrete checkerboard that curved away like the face of a dam. It was all faintly lit by a distant, indigo-silver circle of sky. On the far side of this bottomless amphitheater, the other elevator car had a good lead on him. Nadine probably wouldn't hear him now if he called out to her.

The elevator frameworks ended at tiny balconies about halfway up the tower. Nadine's cage was slowing now as it neared the one on the far side.

Gennady shivered. A cool wind was coming up from below, and it went right through the gridwork floor and flapped his pant legs. There wasn't much to it yet, but it would get stronger.

He watched as Nadine and Achille got out of the other elevator. A square of brightness appeared – a door opening to the outside – and they disappeared through it.

When his own elevator stopped he found he was at a similar little balcony. There was nothing here but the side-rails and a gray metal utility door, with crash bars, in the outer concrete wall. The sense of height here was utterly physical; he'd feel it even if he shut his eyes, because the whole tower swayed ever so gently, and the moving air made it feel like you were falling. Gennady sent the elevator back down and leaned on the crash bar.

Outside it was every bit as bad as he'd feared. The door let onto a narrow catwalk that ran around the tower in both directions. He remembered seeing it from the helicopter, and while it had looked sturdy enough from that vantage, in the gray dawn light he could see long streaks of rust trailing down from the bolts that held it to the wall.

He swallowed, then tested the thing with his foot. It seemed to hold, so he began slowly circling the tower. This time, he tried every step before committing himself, and leaned on the concrete wall, as far from the railing as he could get.

Now he could hear a vague sound, like an endless sigh, rising from below. That, combined with the motion of the tower, made it feel as if something were rousing down in the wall-less maze that filled the black valley.

After a couple of minutes the far point of the circle hove into view. Here was something he hadn't seen from the helicopter: a broadening of the catwalk on this side. At this point it became a wide, reinforced platform, and on it sat a white and yellow trailer. That was utterly incongruous: Gennady could see the thing's undercarriage and wheels sitting on the mesh floor. It had probably been hauled up here by helicopter during the tower's construction.

A pair of parachutes was painted on the side of the trailer. They were gray in this light, but probably pink in daylight.

Now he heard shouting – Achille's voice. Gennady tried to hurry, but the catwalk felt flimsy and the breeze was turning into a wind. He made it to the widened platform, but that was no better since it also had open gridwork flooring and several squares of it were missing.

"Nadine? It's Gennady. What're you doing?"

"Stop her!" yelled Achille. "She's gone crazy!"

He took the chance and ran to the trailer, then peeked around its corner. He was instantly dazzled by intense light – flare-light, in fact – lurid and almost bright green. He squinted and past his sheltering fingers saw it shift around, lean up, and then fade.

"Stop!" Achille sounded desperate. Gennady heard Nadine laugh. He edged around the corner of the trailer.

"Nadine? It's Gennady. Can I ask what you're doing?"

She laughed again, sounding a little giddy. Gennady blinked away the dazzle-dots and spotted Achille. He was clutching the railing and staring wide-eyed as Nadine pulled another flare out of a box at her feet.

She'd holstered her pistol and now energetically pulled the tab from the flare. She windmilled her arm and hurled it into the distance, laughing as she did it. Gennady could see the bright spark following the last one down – but the vista here was too dizzying and he quickly brought his eyes back to Nadine.

"Found these in the trailer," she said. "They're perfect. Want to help?" She offered one to him. Gennady shook his head.

"That's going to cause a fire," he said. She nodded.

"That's the idea. Did you bring a radio? We dropped ours. Achille here has to radio his people to shut down the tower." She looked hopeful, but Gennady shook his head. "We'll have to wait for that new bodyguard, then," she said, "He's sure to have one. Then we can all go home."

The good news was, she didn't look like she was on some murderous rampage. She looked determined, but no different from the Nadine he'd known five years ago. "We can?" said Gennady. "This is just a family fight, is that it? Achille's not going to press charges, and the others aren't going to talk about it?"

She hesitated. "Come on, can't you let me have my moment? You of all people should be able to do that."

"Why me of all people?"

She smiled at him past smoke and vivid pink light. "'Cause you've already saved the world a couple times."

She turned to throw another flare.

"Not the world," Gennady said – only because he felt he had to say something to keep her talking. "Azerbaijan, maybe. But... all this," he gestured at the falling flares, "seems like a bit much for having your brother get into a fight with your date."

"No. *No!*" She sounded hugely disappointed in him. "This isn't about that little incident with Kafatos, is it Achille?" Achille flung up his free hand in exasperation; his other still tightly held the rail. "Although," Nadine went on, "I'm afraid I might have given brother dear the big idea myself, a couple of days before."

"What idea?" Gennady looked to Achille, who wouldn't meet his eyes.

"When he told me about the tower project and said he wanted to use the Putorana Plateau as a carbon sink, I told him about the Permian extinction. He was fascinated – weren't you, Achille? But he really lit up when I told him that though it was heat shock that undoubtedly killed many of the trees on the planet, it was something else that finished off the rest."

"What are you talking about?"

Nadine pointed down, at the disc of plastic-roofed forest below them. "You drove through it on the way up here. It's out there, trying to get into our lungs, our systems..."

"The *fungus?*"

She nodded. "A specific breed of it. It covered Earth from pole to pole during the Permian. It ate all the trees that survived the heat... *conifer* trees, tough as they were. And here's the thing: it's still around today." Again she nodded at the forest. "It's called Rhizoctonia, and Achille's been farming a particularly nasty strain of it here for two years."

Gennady looked at Achille. He was remembering how the day had gone – how Achille seemed to be building his restart schedule around prevailing winds, rather than the integrity of the tower's systems.

If you wanted to cultivate an organism that ate wood and thrived in dry heat, you'd want a greenhouse. They were perched above the biggest greenhouse in central Asia.

Nadine hoisted up the box of flares and stalked off along the catwalk. "I need to make sure the whole fungus crop goes up. *You* need to make sure Achille's engineers close the windows, or the heat's all going to come up here. See you in a bit." She disappeared around the curve of the tower; a short time later, Gennady saw a flare wobble up and then down into the night.

He turned to Achille, who had levered himself onto his feet. "Is she crazy? Or did we really come here to bomb Kafatos's forest with spores?"

Achille glared defiantly back. "So what if we did? It's industrial espionage, sure. But he screwed me over to start with, made a secret deal with the oligarchs to torpedo my bid. Fair's fair."

"And what's to prevent this rhyzoctithing from spreading? How's it supposed to tell the difference between Kafatos's trees and the rest of the forest?" Achille looked away, and suddenly Gennady saw it all – the whole plan.

"It can't, can it? You were going to spread a cloud of spores across the whole northern hemisphere. Every heat-shocked forest in Asia and North America would fall to the Rhizoctia. Biological sequestration of carbon would stagger to a stop, not just here but everywhere. Atmospheric carbon levels would shoot up. Global warming would go into high gear. No more talk about mitigation. No more talk about slowing emissions on a schedule. The world would have to go massively carbon-negative, immediately. And you own all the patents to that stuff."

"Not all," he admitted. "But for the useable stuff, yeah."

A metallic bong bong bong sound came from the catwalk opposite the direction Nadine had taken. Moments later Octav showed up. He was puffing, obviously spooked by the incredible drop, but determined to help his boss. "Where is she?"

"Never mind," said Achille. "Have you got a walkie-talkie?" Octav nodded and handed it over.

"Hello hello?" Achille put the thing to his ear, other hand on his other ear, and paced up and down. Octav was staring at the parachutes painted on the trailer.

"What is that?" he said, assuming, it seemed, that Gennady would know.

"Looks like they were expecting tourists. Base jumping off a solar updraft tower?" From up here, you'd be able to slide down the valley thermals to the river far below. "I guess it could be fun."

"I can't get a signal," said Achille. "You," he said to Octav, "go after her!"

"You can't get a signal because you're outside. They're inside." Gennady pointed at the door in the side of the tower as Octav pounded away along the catwalk. "Try again from next to the elevator." Achille moved to the door and Gennady made to follow, but as Achille opened it a plume of smoke poured out. "Oh, shit!"

The tower had been designed to suck up air from the surrounding forest. It was already pulling in smoke from the fires Nadine had lit with her flares. And she was moving in a circle, trying to ensure that the entire bull's-eye of whitened pines caught.

"Yes! Yes!" Achille was gasping into the radio, ducking out of the smoke-filled tower every few seconds to breathe. "You have to do it now! The whole forest, yes!" He glanced at Gennady. "They're trying to get to the trailer, but they'd have to fix the transformer first and there's too much smoke, I don't know if they're going to make it."

Gennady looked down at the forest; lots of little spot fires were spreading and joining up into larger orange smears and lozenges. If Nadine made it all the way around, they'd be trapped at the center of a firestorm. "We're stuck too."

"Maybe not." Achille ran to the trailer, which turned out to be full of cardboard boxes. They rummaged among them, finding more flares – not useful – and safety harnesses, cables and crampons and, "Ha!" said Achille, holding up two parachutes.

"Is that all?"

The billionaire kicked around at the debris. "Yeah, you'd think there'd be more, but you know we never got this place up and running. These are probably the test units. Doesn't matter, there's one for me, one for you."

"Not Nadine?" Or Octav? Achille shot him an exasperated look. She was his own sister, but he obviously didn't care. Gennady took the chute he offered, with disgust. He and Octav and Nadine could play rock-paper-scissors for it, but if he won, he decided, he'd give it to Nadine when she came back around – if only to see the expression on Achille's face.

Achille was headed out the door. "What then?" asked Gennady. Nadine's brother looked back, still exasperated. "Are you just going to walk away from your dream?"

Achille shook his head. "The patents and designs are all I've got now. I can't make a go selling the power from this place. It's the fungus or nothing. So, look, this fire might eat the tower, but the wind is blowing *in*. The Rhizoctonia on the fringes will be okay. As soon as we're on the ground I'm going to bring in some trucks, and haul away the remainder during the cleanup. I can still dump that all over Kafatos's God-damned forest. We lost the first hand, that's all."

"But..." Gennady couldn't believe he had to say it. "What about Nadine?"

Achille crossed his arms, glowering at the fires. "This has been coming a long time. You know what the worst part is? I'd made her my heir again. Lucky thing I never told her, huh."

As they stepped outside a deep groan came from the tower, and Gennady's inner ear told him he was moving, even though his feet were firmly planted on the deck. Looking down, he saw they were ringed by fire now. The only reason the smoke and heat weren't streaming up the side of the tower was because they were pouring through the open windmill apertures. Through the open door he could see only a wall of shuddering gray inside. The engineers and Bogdan must already be dead.

The tower twisted again, and with a popping sound sixteen feet of catwalk separated from the wall. It drooped, and just then Nadine and Octav came around the tower's curve, on the other side of it.

Achille and Nadine stared at one another over the gap, not speaking. Then Achille turned away with an angry shrug. "We have to go!" He began struggling into his parachute.

Octav waved at Gennady. "Got any ideas?" Neither he nor Nadine were holding weapons. They'd obviously realized their best chance for survival lay with one another.

Gennady edged as close to the fallen section of catwalk as he dared. "Belts, straps, have you got anything like that?" Octav grabbed at his waist, nodded. "The tower's support cables!" Gennady pointed at the nearest one, which leaned out from under the door. "We're going to have to slide down those!" He could see that the cables' anchors were outside the ring of fire, but that wouldn't last long. "Pull up the floor mesh over one, and climb down to the cable anchor. Double up your belt and – hang on a second." Octav's belt would be worn through by friction before they got a hundred feet. Gennady ran into the trailer, which was better lit now by the rising sun, and tossed the boxes around. He found some broken metal strapping. Perfect. Coming out, he tossed a piece across to Octav. "Use that instead. Now get going!"

As they disappeared around the curved wall, Achille darted from behind the trailer. "Coming?" he shouted as he ran to the railing.

Gennady hesitated. He'd dropped his parachute by the trailer steps.

It was clear what had to be done. There was only one way off this tower. Still, he just stood there, watching as Achille clumsily mounted the railing.

Achille looked back. "Come on, what are you waiting for?"

Images from the day were flashing through Gennady's mind – and more, a vision of what could happen after the fire was over. He turned to look out over the endless skin of forest that filled the valley and spread beyond to the horizon.

He'd spent his whole life cleaning up other people's messes. There'd been the Chernobyl affair, and that other nuclear disaster in Azerbaijan. He'd chased stolen nukes across two continents, and only just succeeding in hiding from the world a discovery that would allow any disgruntled tinkerer to build such weapons without needing enriched uranium or plutonium. He'd told himself all the while that he did these things to keep humanity safe. Yet it had never been the idea that people might die that had moved him. He was afraid for something else, and had been for so long now that he couldn't imagine living without that fear.

It was time to admit where his real allegiance lay.

"I'm right behind you," he said with a forced smile. And he watched Achille dive off the tower. He watched Nadine's brother fall two hundred feet and open his chute. He watched the vortex of flame around the tower's base yank the parachute in and down, and swallow it.

Gennady picked up the last piece of metal strapping and, as the tower writhed again, ran along the catwalk opposite to the way Nadine and Octav had gone.

HE ROLLED OVER and staggered to his feet, coughing. A cloud of white was churning around him, propelled by a quickening gale. Overhead the plastic sheeting that forested the dead forest flapped where he'd cut through it. The support cable made a perfectly straight line from the concrete block at his feet up to the distant tower – or was it straight? No, the thing was starting to curve. Achille's tower, which was now in full sunlight, was curling away from the fire, as if unwilling to look at it anymore. Any second now it might fall.

Gennady raced around the perimeter of the fire as the sun touched the plastic ceiling. The flames were eating their way slowly outward, pushing against the wind. Gennady dodged fallen branches and avoided thick brambles, pausing now and then to cough heavily, so it took him a few minutes to spot the support cable opposite the one he'd slid down. When it appeared it was as an amber pen-stroke against the dawn sky. The plastic greenhouse ceiling was broken where the cable pierced it, as it should be if bodies had broken through it on their way to the ground.

As he approached the cable's concrete anchor, he spotted Octav. The bodyguard was curled up on the ground, clutching his ankle.

"Where's Nadine?" Octav looked up as Gennady pounded up. He blinked, looked past Gennady, then they locked eyes.

That look said, *Where's Achille?*

Neither said anything for a long moment. Then, "She fell off," said Octav. "Back there." He pointed into the fire.

"How far –"

"Go. You might find her."

Gennady didn't need any more urging. He let the white wind push him at the shimmering walls of orange light. As the banners of fire whipped up they caught and tore the plastic sheeting that had canopied the forest for years, and they angrily pulled it down. Gennady looked for another break in that upper surface, hopefully close to the cable's anchor, and after a moment he spotted it. Nadine had left a clean incision in the plastic, but had shaved a pine below that; branches and needles were strewn across the white pillows of rhyzoctonia and made Nadine herself easy to find.

She blinked at him from where she lay on a mattress of fungi. She looked surprised, and for a moment Gennady had the absurd thought that maybe his hair was all standing up or something. But then she said, "It doesn't hurt."

He frowned, reached down and pinched her ankle.

"Ow!"

"Fungus broke your fall." He helped her up. The flames were being kept at bay by the inrushing wind, but the radiant heat was intense. "Get going." He pushed her until she was trotting away from the fire.

"What about you?"

"Right behind you!"

He followed, more slowly, until she disappeared into the swirling rhyzoctonia. Then he slowed and stopped, leaning over to brace his hands on his knees. He looked back at the fire.

Sure, if Achille had been thinking, he would have known that the fire would suck in any parachute that came off the tower. Yet Gennady could have warned him, and didn't. He'd murdered Achille, it was that simple.

The wall of fire was mesmerizing and its heat like a giant's hand pushing Gennady back. There must have been a lot of fires like this one, the last time the rhyzoctonia roused itself to make a meal of the world. Achille had engineered special conditions under his greenhouse roof, but it wouldn't need them once it got out. The whole northern hemisphere was a tinderbox, a dry feast waiting for the guest who would consume it all.

Gennady squinted into the flames, waiting. He didn't regret killing Achille. Given the choice between saving a human, or even humanity itself, and preserving the dark labyrinth of Khantayskoe, he'd chosen the forest. In doing that he'd finally admitted his true loyalties, and stepped over the border of the human. But that left him with nowhere to go. So, he simply stood, and waited for the fire.

Somebody grabbed his arm. Gennady jerked and turned to find Octav standing next to him. The bodyguard was using a long branch as a crutch. There was a surprising expression of concern on his face. "Come on!"

"But, you see, I –"

"I don't care!" Octav had a good grip on him, and was stronger than Gennady. Dazed, Gennady let himself be towed away from the fire, and in moments a pale oval swam into sight between the upright boles of orange-painted pine: Nadine's face.

"Where's Achille?" she called.

Gennady waited until they were close enough that he didn't have to yell. "He tried to use a parachute. The fire pulled him in."

Nadine looked down, seeming to crumple in on herself. "Oh, God, all those men, and, and Achille..." She staggered, nearly fell, then seemed to realize where they were. Gennady could feel the fire at his back.

She inserted herself between Octav and Gennady, propelling them both in the direction of the lake at the bottom of the hill. "I'm sorry, I never meant any of this to happen," she cried over the roar of the fire. "All I wanted was for him to go back to his original plan! It could still work." She meant the towers, Gennady knew, and the carbon-negative power plants, and the scheme to sequester all that carbon under the plateau. Not the rhyzoctonia. Maybe she was right, but even though she was Achille's heir, and owner of the technologies that could save the world, she would never climb out from under what had just happened. She'd be in jail soon, and maybe for the rest of her life.

There were options. Gennady found he was thinking coolly and rationally about those; his mind seemed to have been miraculously cleared, and of more than just the trauma of the past hour. He was waking up, it seemed, from something he'd thought of as his life, but which had only been a rough rehearsal of what he could become. He knew himself now, and the anxiety and hesitation that had dogged him since he was a child was simply gone.

What was important was the patents, and the designs, the business plan and the opportunities that might bring another tower to the plateau. It might not happen this year or next, but it would have to be soon. Someone must take responsibility for the crawling disaster overtaking the world, and do something about it.

He would have to talk to Nadine about that inheritance, and about who would administer the fortune while she was in prison. He doubted she would object to what he had in mind.

"Yes, let's go," he said. "We have a lot to do, and not much time."

CALIGO LANE
Ellen Klages

Ellen Klages (ellenklages.com) is the author of two acclaimed YA historical novels: *The Green Glass Sea,* which won the Scott O'Dell Award, the New Mexico Book Award, and the Lopez Award; and *White Sands, Red Menace,* which won the California and New Mexico Book Awards. Her story, "Basement Magic," won a Nebula Award in 2005. In 2014, "Wakulla Springs," co-authored with Andy Duncan, was nominated for the Nebula, Hugo, and Locus awards, and won the World Fantasy Award for Best Novella. She lives in San Francisco, in a small house full of strange and wondrous things.

EVEN WITH THE Golden Gate newly bridged and the ugly hulks of battleships lining the bay, San Francisco is well-suited to magic. It is not a geometric city, but full of hidden alleys and twisted lanes. Formed by hills and surrounded by water, its weather transforms its geography, a fog that erases landmarks, cloaking and enclosing as the rest of the world disappears.

That may be an illusion; most magic is. Maps of the city are replete with misdirection. Streets drawn as straight lines may in fact be stairs or a crumbling brick path, or they may dead end for a block or two, then reappear under another name.

Caligo Lane is one such street, most often reached by an accident that cannot be repeated.

In Barbary Coast bars, sailors awaiting orders to the Pacific hear rumors. Late at night, drunk on cheap gin and bravado, they try walking up Jones Street, so steep that shallow steps are cut into the middle of the concrete sidewalk. Near the crest of the hill, the lane may be on their right. Others stumble over to Taylor until they reach the wooden staircase that zigzags up a sheer wall. Caligo Lane is sometimes at the top – unless the stairs have wound around to end at the foot of Jones Street again. A lovely view of the bay is a consolation.

When it does welcome visitors, Caligo Lane is a single block, near the crest of the Bohemian enclave known as Russian Hill. Houses crowd one edge of a mossy cobblestone path; they face a rock-walled tangle of ferns and eucalyptus, vines as thick as a man's arm, moist earth overlaid with a pale scent of flowers.

Number 67 is in the middle, a tall, narrow house, built when the rest of the town was still brawling in the mud. It has bay windows and a copper-domed cupola, although the overhanging branches of a gnarled banyan tree make that difficult to see. The knocker on the heavy oak door is a Romani symbol, a small wheel wrought in polished brass.

Franny has lived here since the Great Fire. She is a cartographer by trade, a geometer of irregular surfaces. Her house is full of maps.

A small woman who favors dark slacks and loose tunics, she is one of the last of her line, a magus of exceptional abilities. Her hair is jet-black, cut in a blunt bob, bangs straight as rulers, a style that has not been in vogue for decades. She smokes odiferous cigarettes in a long jade-green holder.

The ground floor of number 67 is unremarkable. A small entryway, a hall leading to bedrooms and a bath. But on the right, stairs lead up to a single, large room, not as narrow as below. A comfortable couch and armchairs with their attendant tables surround intricate ancient rugs. A vast library table is strewn with open books, pens and calipers, and scrap paper covered in a jumble of numbers and notations.

Facing north, a wall of atelier windows, reminiscent of Paris, angles in to the ceiling. Seven wide panes span the width of the room, thin dividers painted the green of young spinach. Beyond the glass, ziggurats of stone walls and white houses cascade vertically down to the bay and Alcatraz and the blue-distant hills.

Visitors from more conventional places may feel dizzy and need to sit; it is unsettling to stand *above* a neighbor's roof.

Bookshelves line two walls, floor-to-ceiling. Many titles are in unfamiliar alphabets. Tall art books, dense buckram treatises, mathematical apocrypha:

swaths of cracked, crumbling leather spines with gilt letters too worn to decipher. Four flat cases hold maps, both ancient and modern, in a semblance of order.

Other maps are piled and folded, indexed or spread about willy-nilly. They are inked on scraps of parchment, cut from old textbooks, acquired at service stations with a fill-up of gas. They show Cape Abolesco and Dychmygol Bay and the edges of the Salajene Desert, none of which have ever been explored. On a cork wall, round-headed pins stud a large map of Europe. Franny moves them daily as the radio brings news of the unrelenting malignance of the war.

At the far end of the room, a circular staircase helixes up. Piles of books block easy access, less a barricade than an unrealized intent to reshelve and reorganize.

There will be much to do before the fog rolls in.

The stairs lead to the center of the cupola, an octagonal room with a hinged window at each windrose point. Beneath them is a sill wide enough to hold an open newspaper or atlas, a torus of horizontal surface that circles the room, the polished wood stained with ink, scarred in places by pins and tacks and straight-edged steel, scattered with treasured paperweights: worn stones from the banks of the Vistula, prisms, milleflora hemispheres of heavy Czech glass.

Even in a city of hills, the room has unobstructed views that allow Franny to work in any direction. A canvas chair on casters sits, for the moment, facing southwest. On the sill in front of it, a large square of Portuguese cork lies waiting.

Downstairs, on this clear, sunny afternoon, Franny sits at the library table, a postcard from her homeland resting beside her teacup. She recognizes the handwriting; the postmark is obscured by the ink of stamps and redirections. Not even the mailman can reliably find her house.

She glances at the card one more time. The delayed delivery makes her work even more urgent. She opens a ledger, leafing past pages with notes on scale and symbol, diagrams and patterns, and arcane jottings, turning to a blank sheet. She looks again at the postcard, blue-inked numbers its only message:

50°-02'-09" N 19°-10'-42" E

Plotting this single journey will take weeks of her time, years from her life. But she must. She glances at the pin-studded map. When geography or politics makes travel or escape impossible, she is the last resort. Every life saved is a mitzvah.

Franny flexes her fingers, and begins. Each phase has its own timing and order; the calculations alone are byzantine. Using her largest atlas she locates the general vicinity of the coordinates, near the small village of Oświęcim. It takes her all night to uncover a chart detailed enough to show the topography with precision. She walks her calipers from point to point like a two-legged spider as she computes the progressions that will lead to the final map.

For days she smokes and mutters as she measures, plotting positions and rhumb lines that expand and shrink with the proportions of the landscape. The map must be drawn to the scale of the journey. She feels the weight of time passing, but cannot allow haste, sleeping only when her hands begin to shake, the words illegible. Again and again she manipulates her slide rule, scribbles numbers on a pad, and traces shapes onto translucent vellum, transferring the necessary information until at last she has a draft that accurately depicts both entrance and egress.

She grinds her inks and pigments – lampblack and rare earths mixed with a few drops of her own blood – and trims a sheet of white linen paper to a large square. For a week, the house is silent save for the whisper of tiny sable brushes and the scritch of pens with thin steel nibs.

When she has finished and the colors are dry, she carries the map upstairs and lays it on the cork. Using a round-headed steel pin, she breaches the paper's integrity twice: a single, precise hole at the village, another at Caligo Lane. She transfers the positions onto gridded tissue, and pulls the map free, weighting its corners so that it lies flat on the varnished sill.

She has done what she can. She allows herself a full night's rest.

In the morning she makes a pot of tea and toast with jam, then clears the library table, moving her map-making tools to one side, and opens a black leather case that contains a flat, pale knife made of bone, and a portfolio with dozens of squares of bright paper. She looks around the room. What form must this one take?

Scattered among the dark-spined tomes are small angular paper figurines. Some are geometric shapes; others resemble birds and animals, basilisks and chimeras. Decades before he was exiled to Manzanar, a Japanese calligrapher and amateur conjuror taught her the ancient art of *ori-kami*, yet unknown in this country.

The secret of ori-kami is that a single sheet of paper can be folded in a nearly infinite variety of patterns, each resulting in a different transformation of the available space. Given any two points, it is possible to fold a line that connects them. A map is a menu of possible paths. When Franny folds one of her own making, instead of plain paper, she creates a new alignment of the world, opening improbable passages from one place to another.

Once, when she was young and in a temper, she crumpled one into a ball and threw it across the room, muttering curses. A man in Norway found himself in an unnamed desert, confused and over-dressed. His journey did not end well.

The Japanese army might call this art *ori-chizu*, 'map folding,' but fortunately they are unaware of its power.

Franny knows a thousand ori-kami patterns. Finding the correct orientation for the task requires a skilled eye and geometric precision. She chalks the position of the map's two holes onto smaller squares, folding and creasing sharply with her bone knife, turning flat paper into a cup, a box, a many-winged figure. She notes the alignment, discards one pattern, begins again. A map is a visual narrative; it is not only the folds but their sequence that will define its purpose.

The form this one wishes to take is a fortune teller. American children call it a snapdragon, or a cootie-catcher. It is a simple pattern: the square folded in half vertically, then horizontally, and again on the diagonals. The corners fold into the center, the piece is flipped, the corners folded in again. The paper's two surfaces become many, no longer a flat plane, nor a solid object. A dimension in between.

When she creases the last fold, Franny inserts the index finger and thumb of each hand into the pockets she has created, pushes inward, then moves her fingers apart, as if opening and closing the mouth of an angular bird. Her hands rock outward; the bird's mouth opens now to the right and left. She rocks again, revealing and concealing each tiny hole in turn.

Franny nods and sets it aside. The second phase is finished. Now the waiting begins. She reads and smokes and paces and tidies. The weather is one element she cannot control.

Four days. Five. She moves the pins on the map, crosses off squares on her calendar, bites her nails to the quick until finally one afternoon she feels the fog coming in. The air cools and grows moist as it is saturated with the sea. The light softens, the world stills and quiets. She calms herself for the ritual ahead, sitting on the couch with a cup of smoky tea, listening to the muffled clang of the Hyde Street cable car a few blocks away, watching as the distant hills dissolve into watercolors, fade into hazy outlines, disappear.

The horizon lowers, then approaches, blurring, then slowly obliterating the view outside her window. The edge of the world grows closer. When the nearest neighbors' house is no more than an indistinct fuzz of muted color, she climbs the spiral stairs.

She stands before each window, starting in the east. The world outside the cupola is gone; there are no distances. Where there had once been landmarks — hillsides and buildings and signs — there is only a soft wall, as if she stands inside a great gray pearl.

San Francisco is a different city when the clouds come to earth. Shapes swirl in the diffused cones of street lamps, creating shadows inside the fog itself. They are not flat, but three-dimensional, both solid and insubstantial.

When all the space in the world is contained within the tangible white darkness of the fog, Franny cranks open the northeast window and gently hangs the newly painted map on the wall of the sky. She murmurs archaic syllables no longer understood outside that room, and the paper clings to the damp blankness.

The map is a tabula rasa, ready for instruction.

The fog enters through the disruption of the pinholes.

The paper's fibers swell as they draw in its moisture.

They draw in the distance it has replaced.

They draw in the dimensions of its shadows.

Franny dares not smoke. She paces. Transferring the world to a map is both magic and art, and like any science, the timing must be precise. She has pulled a paper away too soon, before its fibers are fully saturated, rendering it useless. She has let another hang so long that the fog began to retreat again; that one fell to earth as the neighbors reappeared.

She watches and listens, her face to the open window. At the first whisper of drier air, she peels this map off the sky, gently easing one damp corner away with a light, deft touch. There can be no rips or tears, only the two perfect holes.

Paper fibers swell when they are wet, making room for the fog and all it has enveloped. When the fibers dry, they shrink back, locking that in. Now the map itself contains space. She murmurs again, ancient sounds that bind with intent, and lays the map onto the sill to dry. The varnish is her own recipe; it neither absorbs nor contaminates.

Franny closes the window and sleeps until dawn. When she wakes, she is still weary, but busies herself with ordinary chores, reads a magazine, listens to Roosevelt on the radio. The map must dry completely. By late afternoon she is ravenous. She walks down the hill into North Beach, the Italian section, and dines at Lupo's, where she drinks raw red wine and devours one of their flat tomato pies. Late on the third night, when at last the foghorn lows out over the water, she climbs the spiral stairs.

She stands over the map, murmuring now in a language not used for conversation, and takes a deep breath. When she is as calm as a still pond, she lights a candle and sits in her canvas chair. She begins the final sequence, folding the map in half, aligning the edges, precise as a surgeon, burnishing the sharp creases with her pale bone knife. The first fold is the most important. If it is off, even by the tiniest of fractions, all is lost.

Franny uses the knife to move the flow of her breath through her fingers, into the paper. Kinesis. The action of a fold can never be unmade. It fractures the fibers of the paper, leaving a scar the paper cannot forget, a line traversing three dimensions. She folds the map again on the diagonal, aligning and creasing, turning and folding until she holds a larger version of the angular bird's beak.

When the fog has dissolved the world and the cupola is cocooned, Franny inserts her fingers into the folded map. She flexes her hands, revealing one of the tiny holes, and opens the portal.

Now she stands, hands and body rigid, watching from the window high above Caligo Lane. She sees nothing; soon sounds echo beneath the banyan tree. Shuffling footsteps, a whispered voice.

Motionless, Franny holds her hands open. She looks down. Beneath the street lamp stands an emaciated woman, head shorn, clad in a shapeless mattress-ticking smock, frightened and bewildered.

"Elzbieta?" Franny calls down.

The woman looks up, shakes her head.

Three more women step into view.

Beyond them, through a shimmer that pierces the fog, Franny sees other faces. More than she anticipated. Half a dozen women appear, and Franny feels the paper begin to soften, grow limp. There are too many. She hears distant shots, a scream, and watches as a mass of panicked women surge against the portal. She struggles to maintain the shape; the linen fibers disintegrate around the holes. Three women tumble through, and Franny can hold it open no longer. She flexes her trembling hands and reveals the other hole, closing the gate.

After a minute, she calls down in their language. "*Jestes teraz bezpieczna.*" *You are safe now.* She reverses the ori-kami pattern, unfolding and flattening. This work goes quickly. A fold has two possibilities, an unfolding only one.

The women stand and shiver. A few clutch hands.

Franny stares at the place where the shimmer had been. She sees her reflection in the darkened glass, sees tears streak down a face now lined with the topography of age.

"*Znasz moją siostrę?*" she asks, her voice breaking. *Have you seen my sister?* She touches the corner of the depleted map to the candle's flame. "*Elzbieta?*"

A woman shrugs. "*Tak wiele.*" She holds out her hands. *So many.* The others shrug, shake their heads.

Franny sags against the window and blows the ash into the night air. "*Idź,*" she whispers. *Go.*

The women watch the ash fall through the cone of street light. Finally one nods and links her arm with another. They begin to walk now, their thin cardboard shoes shuffling across the cobbles.

Slowly, the others follow. One by one they turn the corner onto Jones Street, step down the shallow concrete steps, and vanish into the fog.

THE DEVIL IN AMERICA

Kai Ashante Wilson

Kai Ashante Wilson is the author of the novella "The Sorcerer of the Wildeeps," available from all fine e-book purveyors, and the story "Super Bass," which can be read for free at *Tor.com*. His story "Légendaire" can be read in Samuel R. Delany tribute anthology, *Stories for Chip*. He lives in New York City.

For my father

1955

EMMETT TILL, SURE, *I remember. Your great grandfather, sitting at the table with the paper spread out, looked up and said something to Grandma. She looked over my way and made me leave the room: Emmett Till. In high school I had a friend everybody called Underdog. One afternoon – 1967? – Underdog was standing on some corner and the police came round and beat him with nightsticks. No reason. Underdog thought he might get some respect if he joined up for Vietnam, but a sergeant in basic training was calling him everything but his name – nigger this, nigger that – and Underdog went and complained. Got thrown in the brig, so he ended up going to Vietnam with just a couple weeks' training. Soon after he came home in a body bag. In Miami a bunch of white cops beat to death a man named Arthur McDuffie with heavy flashlights. You were six or seven: so, 1979. The cops banged up his motorcycle trying to make killing him look like a crash. Acquitted, of course. Then Amadou Diallo, 1999; Sean Bell, 2006. You must know more about all the New York murders than I do.*

Trayvon, this year. Every year it's one we hear about and God knows how many just the family mourns.
– Dad

1877, August 23

"'TIS ALL RIGHT if I take a candle, Ma'am?" Easter said. Her mother bent over at the black iron stove, and lifted another smoking hot pan of cornbread from the oven. Ma'am just hummed – meaning, *Go 'head*. Easter came wide around her mother, wide around the sizzling skillet, and with the ramrod of Brother's old rifle hooked up the front left burner. She left the ramrod behind the stove, plucked the candle from the fumbling, strengthless grip of her ruint hand, and dipped it wick-first into flame. Through the good glass window in the wall behind the stove, the night was dark. It was soot and shadows. Even the many-colored chilis and bright little pumpkins in Ma'am's back garden couldn't be made out.

A full supper plate in her good hand, lit candle in the other, Easter had a time getting the front door open, then out on the porch, and shutting back the door without dropping any food. Then, anyhow, the swinging of the door made the candle flame dance fearfully low, just as wind gusted up too, so her light flickered *way* down... and went out.

"Shoot!" Easter didn't say the curse word aloud. She mouthed it. "Light it back for me, angels," Easter whispered. "Please?" The wick flared bright again.

No moon, no stars – the night sky was clouded over. Easter hoped it wasn't trying to storm, with the church picnic tomorrow.

She crossed the yard to the edge of the woods where Brother waited. A big old dog, he crouched down, leapt up, down and up again, barking excitedly, just as though he were some little puppy dog.

"Well, hold your horses," Easter said. "I'm coming!" She met him at the yard's end and dumped the full plate over, all her supper falling to the ground. Brother's head went right down, tail just a-wagging. "Careful, Brother," Easter said. "You *watch* them chicken bones." Then, hearing the crack of bones, she knelt and snatched ragged shards right out of the huge dog's mouth. Brother whined and licked her hand – and dropped his head right back to buttered mashed yams.

Easter visited with him a while, telling her new secrets, her latest sins, and when he'd sniffed out the last morsels of supper Brother listened to her with what anybody would have agreed was deep love, full attention. "Well, let me get on," she said at last, and sighed. "Got to check on the Devil now." She'd left it til late, inside all evening with Ma'am, fixing their share of the big supper at church tomorrow. Brother whined when she stood up to leave.

Up the yard to the henhouse. Easter unlatched the heavy door and looked them over – chickens, on floor and shelf, huddling quietly in thick straw, and all asleep except for Sadie. Eldest and biggest, that one turned just her head and looked over Easter's way. Only reflected candlelight, of course, but Sadie's beady eyes looked *so* ancient and *so* crafty, blazing like embers. Easter backed on out, latched the coop up securely again, and made the trip around the henhouse, stooping and stooping and stooping, to check for gaps in the boards. Weasel holes, fox doors.

There weren't any. And the world would go on exactly as long as Easter kept up this nightly vigil.

Ma'am stood on the porch when Easter came back up to the house. "I don't *appreciate* my good suppers thrown in the dirt. You hear me, girl?" Ma'am put a hand on Easter's back, guiding her indoors. "That ole cotton-picking dog could just as well take hisself out to the deep woods and hunt." Ma'am took another tone altogether when she meant every word, and *then* she didn't stroke Easter's head, or gently brush her cheek with a knuckle. This was only complaining out of habit. Easter took only one tone with her mother. Meek.

"Yes, Ma'am," she said, and ducked her head in respect. Easter *didn't* think herself too womanish or grown to be slapped silly.

"Help me get this up on the table," Ma'am said – the deepest bucket, and brimful of water and greens. Ma'am was big and strong enough to have lifted *ten* such buckets. It was friendly, though, sharing the little jobs. At one side of the bucket, Easter bent over and worked her good hand under the bottom, the other just mostly ached now, the cut thickly scabbed over. She just sort of pressed it to the bucket's side, in support.

Easter and her mother set the bucket on the table.

Past time to see about the morning milk. Easter went back to the cellar and found the cream risen, though the tin felt a tad cool to her. The butter would come slow. "Pretty please, angels?" she whispered. "Could you help me out a little bit?" They could. They did. The milk tin warmed ever so slightly. Just right. Easter dipped the cream out and carried the churn back to the kitchen.

Ma'am had no wrinkles except at the corners of the eyes. Her back was unbowed, her arms and legs still mighty. But she was old now, wasn't she? Well nigh sixty, and maybe past it. But still with that upright back, such quick hands. *Pretty* was best said of the young – Soubrette Toussaint was very pretty, for instance – so what was the right word for Ma'am's severe cheekbones, sharp almond-shaped eyes, and pinched fullness of mouth? Working the churn, Easter felt the cream foam and then thicken, pudding-like. Any other such marriage, and you'd surely hear folks gossiping over the dead wrongness of it – the wife twenty-some years older than a mighty good-looking husband. *What in the world, I ask you, is that old lady doing with a handsome young man like that?* But any two eyes could see the answer here. Not pretty as she must once have been, with that first husband, whoever he'd been, dead and buried back east. And not pretty as when she'd had those first babies, all gone now too. But age hadn't only taken from Ma'am, it had given too. Some rare gift, and so much of it that Pa *had* to be pick of the litter – kindest, most handsome man in the world – just to stack up. Easter poured off the buttermilk into a jar for Pa, who liked that especially. Ma'am might be a challenge to love sometimes, but respect came easy.

"I *told* him, Easter." Ma'am wiped forefinger and thumb down each dandelion leaf, cleaning off grit and bugs, and then lay it aside in a basket. "Same as I told you. *Don't mess with it.* Didn't I say, girl?"

"Yes, Ma'am." Easter scooped the clumps of butter into the bowl.

Ma'am spun shouting from her work. "That's *right* I did! And I pray to God you *listen*, too. That fool out there *didn't*, but Good Lord knows I get on my knees and pray *every night* you got some little bit of sense in your head. Because, Easter, I ain't *got* no more children – you my last one!" Ma'am turned back and gripped the edge of the table.

Ma'am wanted no comfort, no acknowledgement of her pain at such moments – just let her be. Easter huddled in her chair, paddling the salt evenly through the butter, working all the water out. She worked with far more focus than the job truly needed.

Then, above the night's frogcroak and bugchatter, they heard Brother bark in front of the house, and heard Pa speak, his very voice. Wife and daughter both gave a happy little jump, looking together at the door in anticipation. Pa'd been three days over in Greenville selling the cigars. Ma'am snapped her fingers.

"Get the jug out the cellar," she said. "You know just getting in your Pa wants him a little tot of cider. Them white folks." As if Ma'am wouldn't have a whole big mug her ownself.

"Yes, Ma'am." Easter fetched out the jug.

Pa opened the door, crossed the kitchen – touching Easter's head in passing, he smelt of woodsmoke – and came to stand behind Ma'am. His hands cupped her breasts through her apron, her dress, and he kissed the back of her neck. She gasped aloud. "Wilbur! *The baby*...!" That's what they still called Easter, "The baby." Nobody had noticed she'd gotten tall, twelve years old now.

Pa whispered secrets in Ma'am's ear. He was a father who loved his daughter, but he was a husband first and foremost. *I'm a terrible thirsty man,* Pa had said once, *and your mama is my only cool glass of water in this world.* Ma'am turned and embraced him. "I know it, sweetheart," she said. "I know." Easter covered up the butter. She took over washing the greens while her parents whispered, intent only on each other. Matched for height, and Ma'am a little on the stout side, Pa on the slim, so they were about the same thickness too. The perfect fit of them made Easter feel a sharp pang, mostly happiness. Just where you could hear, Pa said, "And you *know* it ain't no coloreds round here but us living in Rosetree..."

Wrapped in blankets up in the loft, right over their bed, of course she heard things at night, on Sundays usually, when nobody was so tired.

An effortful noise from Pa, as if he were laboring some big rock heave-by-heave over to the edge of the tobacco field, and then before the quiet, sounding sort of worried, as if Pa were afraid Ma'am might accidently touch the blazing hot iron of the fired-up stove, Pa would say, "*Hazel!*"

"... so then Miss Anne claimed she seen some nigger run off from there, and *next thing* she knew – fire! Just *everywhere*. About the whole west side of Greenville, looked to me, burnt down. Oh yeah, and in the morning here come Miss Anne's husband talkmbout, 'Know what else, y'all? That nigger my wife seen last night – matterfact, he *violated* her.' Well, darling, here's what I wanna know…"

Ma'am would kind of sigh throughout, and from one point on keep saying – not loud – "Like *that*…" However much their bed creaked, Ma'am and Pa were pretty quiet when Easter was home. Probably they weren't, though, these nights when Pa came back from Greenville. That was why they sent her over the Toussaints'.

"… *where* this 'violated' come from all of a sudden? So last night Miss Anne said she maybe *might* of seen some nigger run off, and this morning that nigger jumped her show 'nough? And then it *wasn't* just the one nigger no more. No. It was two or three of 'em, maybe about five. *Ten* niggers – at least. Now Lord knows I ain't no lawyer, baby, I *ain't,* but it seem to me a fishy story done changed up even fishier…"

Ma'am and Pa took so much comfort in each other, and just plain *liked* each other. Easter was glad to see it. But she was old enough to wonder, a little worried and a little sad, who was ever going to love her in the way Ma'am and Pa loved each other.

"What you still doing here!" Ma'am looked up suddenly from her embrace. "Girl, you should of *been* gone to Soubrette's. *Go.* And take your best dress and good Sunday shoes too. Tell Mrs. Toussaint I'll see her early out front of the church tomorrow. You hear me, Easter?"

"Yes, Ma'am," she said. And with shoes and neatly folded clothes, Easter hurried out into the dark wide-open night, the racket of crickets.

On the shadowed track through the woods, she called to Brother but he wouldn't come out of the trees, though Easter could hear him pacing her through the underbrush. Always out there in the dark. Brother wanted to keep watch whenever Easter went out at night, but he got shy sometimes too. Lonesome and blue.

AND THIS WHOLE thing started over there, in old Africa land, where in olden days a certain kind of big yellow dog (*you* know the kind I'm talking about) used to run around. Now those dogs ain't nowhere in the world, except for…

Anyway, the prince of the dogs was a sorcerer – about the biggest and best there was in the world. One day he says to hisself, *Let me get up off four feet for a while, and walk around on just two, so I can see what all these folk called 'people' are doing over in that town.* So the prince quit being his doggy self and got right up walking like anybody. While the prince was coming over to the peoples' town, he saw a pretty young girl washing clothes at the river. Now if he'd still been his doggy self, the prince probably would of just *ate* that girl up, but since he was a man now, the prince seen right off what a pretty young thing she was. So he walks over and says, Hey, gal. You want to lay down right here by the river in the soft grass with me? Well – and anybody *would* – the girl felt some kind of way, a strange man come talking to her so fresh all of a sudden. The girl says, Man, don't you see my hair braided up all nice like a married lady? (Because that's how they did over in Africa land. The married ladies, the girls still at home, plaited their hair up different.) So the dog prince said, Oh, I'm sorry. I come from a long way off, so I didn't know what your hair meant. And he *didn't*, either, cause dogs don't braid their hair like people do. *Hmph*, says the gal, all the while sort of taking a real good look over him. As a matter of fact, the dog prince made a *mighty* fine-looking young man, and the girl's mama and papa had married her off to just about the oldest, most dried-up, and granddaddy-looking fellow you ever saw. That old man was rich, sure, but he really couldn't do nothing in the married way for a young gal like that, who wasn't twenty years old yet. So, the gal says, *Hmph*, where you come from anyways? What you got to say for yourself? And it must of been pretty good too, whatever the prince had to say for hisself, because, come nine months later, that gal was mama to your great great – twenty greats – grandmama, first one of us with the old Africa magic.

It wasn't but a hop, skip, and jump through the woods into Rosetree proper. Surrounding the town green were the church, Mrs. Toussaint's general store, and the dozen best houses, all two stories, with overgrown rosebushes in front. At the other side of the town green, Easter could see Soubrette sitting out on her front porch with a lamp, looking fretfully out into night.

It felt nice knowing somebody in this world would sit up for her, wondering where she was, was everything all right.

In her wretched accent, Easter called, "*J'arrive!*" from the middle of the green.

Soubrette leapt up. "Easter?" She peered into the blind dark. "I can't see a thing! Where are you, Easter?"

Curious that *she* could see so well, cutting across the grass toward the general store. Easter had told the angels not to without her asking, told them *many* times, but still she often found herself seeing with cat's eyes, hearing with dog's ears, when the angels took a notion. The problem being, folks *noticed* if you were all the time seeing and hearing what you shouldn't. But maybe there was no need to go blaming the angels. With no lamp or candle, your eyes naturally opened up something amazing, while lights could leave you stone-blind out past your bright spot.

They screamed, embraced, laughed. Anybody would have said three *years*, not days, since they'd last seen each other. "Ah, viens ici, toi!" said Soubrette, gently taking Easter's ruint hand to lead her indoors.

Knees drawn up on the bed, Easter hugged her legs tightly. She set her face and bit her lip, but tears came anyway. They always did. Soubrette sighed and closed the book in her lap. Very softly Easter murmured, "I like *Rebecca* most."

"Yes!" Soubrette abruptly leaned forward and tapped Easter's shin. "Rowena is nice too – she *is*! – but I don't even *care* about old Ivanhoe. It just isn't *fair* about poor Rebecca…"

"He really don't deserve either one of 'em," Easter said, forgetting her tears in the pleasure of agreement. "That part when Ivanhoe up and changed his mind all of a sudden about Rebecca – do you remember that part? '… *an inferior race…*' No, I didn't care for him after that."

"Oh *yes*, Easter, I remember!" Soubrette flipped the book open and paged back through it. "At first he sees Rebecca's so beautiful, and he likes her, but then all his niceness is '… *exchanged at once for a manner cold, composed, and collected, and fraught with no deeper feeling than that which expressed a grateful sense of courtesy received from an unexpected quarter, and from one of an inferior race…*' Ivanhoe's just *hateful*!" Soubrette lay a hand on Easter's foot. "Rowena and Rebecca would have been better off *without* him!"

Soubrette touched you when she made her points, and she made them in the most hot-blooded way. Easter enjoyed such certainty and fire, but it made her feel bashful too. "You ain't taking it too far, Soubrette?" she asked softly. "Who would they love without Ivanhoe? It wouldn't be nobody to, well, *kiss*."

It made something happen in the room, that word *kiss*. Did the warm night heat up hotter, and the air buzz almost like yellowjackets in a log? One and one made two, so right there you'd seem to have a sufficiency for a kiss, with no lack of anything, anyone. From head to toe Easter knew right where she was, lightly sweating in a thin summer shift on this August night, and she knew right where Soubrette was too, so close that –

"Girls!" Mrs. Toussaint bumped the door open with her hip. "The iron's good and hot on the stove now, so..."

Easter and Soubrette gave an awful start. *Ivanhoe* fell to the floor.

"... why don't you come downstairs with your dresses...?" Mrs. Toussaint's words trailed away. She glanced back and forth between the girls while the hot thing still sizzled in the air, delicious and wrong. Whatever it was seemed entirely perceptible to Mrs. Toussaint. She said to her daughter, "Chérie, j'espère que tu te comportes bien. Tu es une femme de quatorze ans maintenant. Ton amie n'a que dix ans; elle est une toute jeune fille!"

She spoke these musical words softly and with mildness – nevertheless they struck Soubrette like a slap. The girl cast her gaze down, eyes shining with abrupt tears. High yellow, Soubrette's cheeks and neck darkened with rosy duskiness.

"Je me comporte toujours bien, Maman," she whispered, her lips trembling as if about to weep.

Mrs. Toussaint paused a moment longer, and said, "Well, fetch down your dresses, girls. Bedtime soon." She went out, closing the door behind her.

The tears *did* spill over now. Easter leaned forward suddenly, kissed Soubrette's cheek, and said, "J'ai *douze* ans."

Soubrette giggled. She wiped her eyes.

Much later, Easter sat up, looking around. Brother had barked, growling savagely, and woken her up. But seeing Soubrette asleep beside her, Easter knew that couldn't be so. And no strange sounds came to her ears from the night outside, only wind in the leaves, a whippoorwill. Brother never came into the middle of town anyway, not ever. The lamp Mrs. Toussaint had left burning in the hallway lit the gap under the bedroom door with an orange glow. Easter's fast heart slowed as she watched her friend breathing easily. Soubrette never snored, never tossed and turned, never slept with her mouth gaping open. Black on the white pillow, her long hair spilled loose and curly.

"Angels?" Easter whispered. "Can you make my hair like Soubrette's?" This time the angels whispered, *Give us the licklest taste of her blood, and all Sunday long tomorrow your hair will be so nice. See that hatpin? Just stick Soubrette in the hand with it, and not even too deep. Prettiest curls anybody ever saw.* Easter only sighed. It was out of the question, of course. The angels sometimes asked for the most shocking crimes as if they were nothing at all. "Never mind," she said, and lay down to sleep.

WHILE TRUE THAT such profoundly sustaining traditions, hidden under the guise of the imposed religion, managed to survive centuries of slavery and subjugation, we should not therefore suppose that ancient African beliefs suffered no sea changes. Of course they did. 'The Devil' in Africa had been capricious, a trickster, and if cruel, only insomuch as bored young children, amoral and at loose ends, may be cruel: seeking merely to provoke an interesting event at any cost, to cause some disruption of the tedious status quo. For the Devil in America, however, malice itself was the end, and temptation a means only to destroy. Here, the Devil would pursue the righteous and the wicked, alike and implacably, to their everlasting doom...

White Devils/Black Devils, Luisa Valéria da Silva y Rodríguez

1871, August 2

THE END BEGINS after Providence loses all wiggle room, and the outcome becomes hopeless and fixed. That moment had already happened, Ma'am would have said. It had happened long before either one of them were born. Ma'am would have assured Easter that the end began way back in slavery times, and far across the ocean, when that great-grandfather got snatched from his home and the old wisdom was lost.

Easter knew better, though. A chance for grace and new wisdom had always persisted, and doom never been assured... right up until, six years old, Easter did what she did one August day out in the tobacco fields.

On that morning of bright skies, Pa headed out to pick more leaves and Easter wanted to come along. He said, *Let's ask your mama.*

"But he *said*, Wilbur." Ma'am looked surprised. "He told us, *You ain't to take the baby out there, no time, no way.*"

Pa hefted Easter up in his arms, and kissed her cheek, saying, "Well, it's going on three years now since he ain't been here to say *Bet not* or say *Yep, go 'head*. So I wonder how long we suppose to go on doing everything just the way he said, way back when. Forever? And the baby *wants* to go..." Pa set her down and she grabbed a handful of his pants leg and leaned against him. "But, darling, if you say not to, then we *won't*. Just that simple."

Most men hardly paid their wives much mind at all, but Pa would listen to any little thing Ma'am said. She, though, *hated* to tell a man what he could and couldn't do – some woman just snapping her fingers, and the man running lickety-split here and there. Ma'am said that wasn't right. So she crossed her arms and hugged herself, frowning unhappily. "Well..." Ma'am said. "Can you just wait a hot minute there with the mule, Wilbur? Let me say something to the baby." Ma'am unfolded her arms and reached out a hand. "Come here, girl."

Easter came up the porch steps and took the hand – swept along in Ma'am's powerful grip, through the open door, into the house. "*Set.*" Ma'am pointed to a chair. Easter climbed and sat down. Ma'am knelt on the floor. They were eye-to-eye. She grasped Easter's chin and pulled her close. "Tell me, Easter – what you do, if some lady in a red silk dress come trying to talk to you?"

"I shake my head *no*, Ma'am, and turn my back on her. Then the lady have to go away."

"That's *right*! But what if that strange lady in the red dress say, *Want me to open up St. Peter's door, and show you heaven?* What if she say to you, *See them birds flying there? Do me one itsy bitsy favor, and you could be in the sky flying too.* What then, Easter? Tell me what you do."

"Same thing, Ma'am." She knew her mother wasn't angry with her, but Ma'am's hot glare – the hard grip on her chin – made tears prick Easter's eyes. "I turn my back, Ma'am. She *have to* go, if I just turn my back away."

"Yes! And will you *promise*, Easter? Christ is your Savior, will you *swear* to turn your back, if that lady in the pretty red dress come talking to you?"

Easter swore up and down, and she meant every word too. Ma'am let her go back out to her father, and he set her up on the mule. They went round the house and down the other way, on the trail through woods behind Ma'am's back garden that led to the tobacco fields. Pa answered every question Easter asked about the work he had to do there.

That woman in the red dress was a sneaky liar. She was '*that old serpent, called the Devil, and Satan, which deceiveth the whole world...*' Warned by Ma'am, Easter guarded night and day against a glimpse of any such person. In her whole life, though, Easter never did see that lady dressed all in red silk. Easter knew nothing about her. She only knew about the angels.

She didn't *see* them, either, just felt touches like feathers in the air – two or three angels, rarely more – or heard sounds like birds taking off, a flutter of wings. The angels spoke to her, once in a while, in whispering soft harmony. They never said anything bad, just helpful little things. Watch out, Easter – gon' rain cats and dogs once that cloud there starts looking purplish. Your folks sure would appreciate a little while by theyself in the house. Why not be nice? Ma'am's worried sick about Pa over in Greenville, with those white folks, so you'd do best to keep your voice down, and tiptoe extra quiet, else you 'bout to get slapped into tomorrow. And, Easter, don't tell nobody, all right? Let's us just be secret friends.

All right, Easter said. The angels were nice, anyway, and it felt good keeping them to herself, having a secret. No need to tell anybody. Or just Brother, when he came out the woods to play with her in the front yard, or when Ma'am let her go walking in the deep woods with him. But in those days Brother used to wander far and wide, and was gone from home far more often than he was around.

The tobacco fields were *full* of angels.

Ever run, some time, straight through a flock of grounded birds, and ten thousand wings just rushed up flapping into the air all around you? In the tobacco fields it was like that. And every angel there *stayed* busy, so the tobacco leaves grew huge and whole, untroubled by flea-beetles or cutworms, weeds or weather. But the angels didn't do *all* the work.

Pa and a friend of his from St. Louis days, Señor, dug up the whole south field every spring, mounding up little knee-high hills all over it. Then they had to transplant each and every little tabacky plant from the flat dirt in the north field to a hill down south. It was back-breaking work, all May long, from sunup to sundown. Afterwards, Pa and Señor had only small jobs, until now – time to cut the leaves, hang and cure them in the barn. Señor had taught Pa everything there was to know about choosing which leaf when, and how to roll the excellent *criollito* tabacky into the world's best cigars. What they got out of one field sold plenty well enough to white folks over in Greenville to keep two families in good clothes, ample food, and some comforts.

A grandfather oaktree grew between the fields, south and north. Pa agreed with Easter. "That big ole thing *is* in the way, ain't it? But your brother always used to say, *Don't you never, never cut down that tree, Wilbur.* And it do make a nice shady spot to rest, anyway. Why don't you go set over there for a while, baby child?"

Easter knew Pa thought she must be worn out and sorry she'd come, just watching him stoop for leaves, whack them off the plant with his knife, and lay them out in the sun. But Easter loved watching him work, loved to follow and listen to him wisely going on about why this, why that.

Pa, though, put a hand on her back and kind of scootched her on her way over toward the tree, so Easter went. Pa and Señor began to chant some work song in Spanish. *Iyá oñió oñí abbé...*

Once in the oaktree's deep shade, there was a fascinating discovery round the north side of the big trunk. Not to see, or to touch – or know in any way Easter had a name for – but she could *feel* the exact shape of what hovered in the air. And this whirligig thing'um, right here, was exactly what kept all the angels hereabouts leashed, year after year, to chase away pests, bring up water from deep underground when too little rain fell, or dry the extra drops in thin air when it rained too much. And she could tell somebody had jiggered this thing together who hardly knew what they were doing. It wasn't but a blown breath or rough touch from being knocked down.

Seeing how rickety the little angel-engine was, Easter wondered if she couldn't do better. Pa and Señor did work *awful* hard every May shoveling dirt to make those hills, and now in August they had to come every day to cut whichever leaves had grown big enough. Seemed like the angels could just do *everything*...

"You all right over there, baby girl?" Pa called. Dripping sweat in the glare, he wiped a sleeve across his brow. "Need me to take you back to the house?"

"I'm all right," Easter shouted back. "I want to stay, Pa!" She waved, and he stooped down again, cutting leaves. See there? Working so hard! She could *help* if she just knocked this rickety old thing down, and put it back together better. Right on the point of doing so, she got one sharp pinch from her conscience.

Every time Easter got ready to do something bad there was a moment beforehand when a little bitty voice – one lonely angel, maybe – would whisper to her. *Aw, Easter. You know good and well you shouldn't.* Nearly always she listened to this voice. After today and much too late, she *always* would.

But sometimes you just do bad, anyhow.

Easter picked a scab off her knee and one fat drop welled from the pale tender scar underneath. She dabbed a finger in it, and touched the bloody tip to the ground.

The angel-engine fell to pieces. Screaming and wild, the angels scattered every which way. Easter called and begged, but she could no more get the angels back in order than she could have grabbed hold of a mighty river's gush.

And the tobacco field...!

Ice frosted the ground, the leaves, the plants, and then melted under sun beating down hotter than summer's worst. The blazing blue sky went cloudy and dark, and boiling low clouds spat frozen pellets, some so big they drew blood and raised knots. Millions of little noises, little motions, each by itself too small to see or hear, clumped into one thick sound like God's two hands rubbing together, and just as gusts of wind stroke the green forest top, making the leaves of the trees all flip and tremble, there was a unified rippling from one end of the tobacco field to the other. Not caused by hands, though, nor by the wind – by busy worms, a billion hungry worms. Grayish, from maggot-size to stubby snakes, these worms ate the tobacco leaves with savage appetite. While the worms feasted, dusty cloud after dusty cloud of moths fluttered up from the disappearing leaves, all hail-torn and frost-blackened, half and then wholly eaten.

In the twinkling of an eye, the lush north field was stripped bare. Nothing was left but naked leaf veins poking spinily from upright woody stems – not a shred of green leaf anywhere. But one year's crop was nothing to the angels' hunger. They were owed *much* more for so many years' hard labor. Amidst the starving angels, Pa and Señor stood dazed in the sudden wasteland of their tobacco field. All the sweet living blood of either this man or the other would just about top off the angels' thirsty cup.

Easter screamed. She called for some help to come – any help at all.

And help *did* come. A second of time split in half and someone came walking up the break.

LIKE THE WAY you and Soubrette work on all that book learning together. Same as that. You *gotta* know your letters, *gotta* know your numbers, for some things, or you just can't rightly take part. Say, for instance, you had some rich colored man, and say this fellow was *very* rich indeed. But let's say he didn't know his numbers at all. Couldn't even count his own fingers up to five. Now, he ain't a bad man, Easter, and he ain't stupid either, really. It's just that nobody ever taught numbering to him. So, one day this rich man takes a notion to head over to the bank, and put his money into markets and bonds, and what have you. Now let me ask you, Easter. What you think gon' happen to this colored man's big ole stack of money, once he walks up in that white man's bank, and gets to talking with the grinning fellow behind the counter? *You* tell me. I wanna hear what you say.

Ma'am. The white man's gonna see that colored man can't count, Ma'am, and cheat him out of all his money.

That's *right* he is, Easter! And I *promise you* it ain't no other outcome! Walk up in that bank just as rich as you please – but you gon' walk out with no shoes, and *owing* the shirt on your back! Old Africa magic's the same way, but *worse*, Easter, cause it ain't money we got, me and you – all my babies had – and my own mama, and the grandfather they brung over on the slave ship. It's *life*. It's life and death, not money. Not play-stuff. But, listen here – we don't know our numbers no more, Easter. See what I'm saying? That oldtime wisdom from over there, what we used to know in the Africa land, is all gone now. And, Easter, you just *can't* walk up into the spirits' bank not knowing your numbers. You *rich*, girl. You got gold in your pockets, and I *know* it's burning a hole. I know cause it burnt me, it burnt your brother. But I pray you listen to me, baby child, when I say – you walk up in that bank, they gon' take a *heap* whole lot more than just your money.

NOTHING MOVED. PA and Señor stood frozen, the angels hovering just before the pounce. Birds in the sky hung there, mid-wingbeat, and even a blade of grass in the breath of the wind leaned motionless, without shivering. Nothing moved. Or just one thing did – a man some long way off, come walking this way toward Easter. He was *miles* off, or much farther than that, but every step of his approach crossed a strange distance. He bestrode the stillness of the world and stood before her in no time.

In the kindest voice, he said, "You need some help, baby child?"

Trembling, Easter nodded her head.

He sat right down. "Let us just set here for a while, then" – the man patted the ground beside him – "and make us a *deal*."

He was a white man tanned reddish from too much sun, or he could've had something in him maybe – been mixed up with colored or indian. Hair would've told the story, but that hid under the gray kepi of a Johnny Reb. He wore that whole uniform in fact, a filthy kerchief of Old Dixie tied around his neck.

Easter sat. "Can you help my Pa and Señor, Mister? The angels about to eat 'em up!"

"Oh, don't you *worry* none about that!" the man cried, warmly reassuring. "I can help you, Easter, I most certainly can. But" – he turned up a long forefinger, in gentle warning – "*not for free.*"

Easter opened her mouth.

"*Ot!*" The man interrupted, waving the finger. "Easter, Easter, Easter..." He shook his head sadly. "Now why you wanna hurt my feelings and say you ain't got no money? Girl, you know I don't want no trifling little money. You know *just* what I want."

Easter closed her mouth. He wanted blood. He wanted life. And not a little drop or two, either – or the life of some chicken, mule, or cow. She glanced at the field of hovering angels. They were owed the precious life of one man, woman, or child. How much would *he* want to stop them?

The man held up two fingers. "That's all. And you get to pick the two. It don't have to be your Pa and Señor at all. It could be any old body." He waved a hand outwards to the world at large. "Couple folk you ain't even met, Easter, somewhere far away. That'd be just fine with me."

Easter hardly fixed her mouth to answer before that still small voice spoke up. *You can't do that. Everybody is somebody's friend, somebody's Pa, somebody's baby. It'd be plain dead wrong, Easter.* This voice never said one word she didn't already know, and never said anything but the God's honest truth. No matter what, Easter *wasn't* going against it, ever again.

The man made a sour little face to himself. "Tell you what then," he said. "Here's what we'll do. Right now, today, I'll call off the angels, how about that? And then you can pay me what you owe by-and-by. Do you know what the word '*currency*' means, Easter?"

Easter shook her head.

"It means the *way* you pay. Now, the *amount*, which is the worth of two lives, stays exactly the same. But you don't have to pay in blood, in life, if you just change the *currency*, see? There's a lot you don't know right now, Easter, but with some time, you might could learn something useful. So let me help out Señor and your Pa today, and then me and you, we'll settle up later on after while. Now when you wanna do the settling up?"

Mostly, Easter had understood the word "later" – a *sweet* word! She really wouldn't have minded some advice concerning the rest of what he'd said, but the little voice inside couldn't tell her things she didn't already know. Easter was six years old, and double that would make *twelve*. Surely that was an eternal postponement, nearabout. So far away it could hardly be expected to arrive. "When I'm twelve," Easter said, feeling tricky and sly.

"All right," the man said. He nodded once, sharply, as folks do when the deal is hard but fair. "Let's shake on it."

Though she was just a little girl, and the man all grown up, they shook hands. And the angels mellowed in the field, becoming like those she'd always known, mild and toothless, needing permission even to sweep a dusty floor, much less eat a man alive.

"I'll be going now, Easter." The man waved toward the field, where time stood still. "They'll all wake up just as soon as I'm gone." He began to get up.

Easter grabbed the man's sleeve. "Wait!" She pointed at the ruins of two families' livelihood. "What about the *tabacky*? We need it to live on!"

The man looked where Easter gestured, the field with no green whatsoever, and thoughtfully pursed his lips. "Well, as you can see, *this* year's tabacky is all dead and gone now. 'Tain't nothing to do about that. But I reckon I could set the angels back where they was, so as *next* year – and on after that – the tabacky will grow up fine. Want me to do that, Easter?"

"*Yes!*"

The man cocked his head and widened his eyes, taking an attitude of the greatest concern. "Now you *show*, Easter?" he asked. "Cause that's extry on what you already owe."

So cautioning was his tone, even a wildly desperate little girl must think twice. Easter chewed on her bottom lip. "How much extra?" she said at last.

The man's expression went flat and mean. "*Triple,*" he said. "And triple that again, and might as well take that whole thing right there, and triple it about ten more times." Now the very nice face came back. "But what you gon' do, baby girl? You messed up your Pa's tabacky field. *Gotta* fix it." He shrugged in deepest sympathy. "*You* know how to do that?"

Easter had to shake her head.

"Want *me* to then?"

Easter hesitated... and then nodded. They shook on it.

The man snapped his fingers. From all directions came the sounds and sensations of angels flocking back to their old positions. The man stood and brushed off the seat of his gray wool trousers.

Easter looked up at him. "Who are you, Mister? Your name, I mean."

The man smiled down. "How 'bout you just call me the banker," he said. "Cause – *whew,* baby girl – you owe me a lot! Now I'll be seeing you after while, you hear?" The man became his own shadow, and in just the way that a lamp turned up bright makes the darkness sharpen and flee, his shadow thinned out along the ground, raced away, and vanished.

"¡Madre de Díos!" Señor said, looking around at the field that had been all lush and full-grown a moment ago. He and Pa awakened to a desolation, without one remnant of the season's crop. With winces, they felt at their heads, all cut and bruised from hailstones. Pa spun around then, to look at Easter, and she burst into tears.

These tears lasted a while.

Pa gathered her up in his arms and rushed her back to the house, but neither could Ma'am get any sense from Easter. After many hours she fell asleep, still crying, and woke after nightfall on her mother's lap. In darkness, Ma'am sat on the porch, rocking in her chair. When she felt Easter move, Ma'am helped her sit up, and said, "Won't you tell me what happened, baby child?" Easter *tried* to answer, but horror filled up her mouth and came pouring out as sobs. Just to speak about meeting that strange man was to cry with all the strength in her body. God's grace had surely kept her safe in that man's presence, but the power and the glory no longer stood between her and the revelation of something unspeakable. Even the memory was too terrible. Easter had a kind of fit and threw up what little was in her belly. Once more she wept to passing out.

Ma'am didn't ask again. She and Pa left the matter alone. A hard, scuffling year followed, without the money from the cigars, and only the very last few coins from the St. Louis gold to get them through.

He was the Devil, Easter decided, and swallowed the wild tears. She decided to grow wise in her way as Pa was about tobacco, though there was nobody to teach her. The Devil wouldn't face a fool next time.

1908

THE MOB WENT up and down Washington Street, breaking storefront windows, ransacking and setting all the black-owned business on fire. Bunch of white men shot up a barbershop and then dragged out the body of the owner, Scott Burton, to string up from a nearby tree. After that, they headed over to the residential neighborhood called the Badlands, where black folks paid high rent for slum housing. Some 12,000 whites gathered to watch the houses burn.
– Dad

* * *

1877, August 24

AT THE CHURCH, the Ladies' Missionary Society and their daughters began to gather early before service. The morning was gray and muggy, not hot at all, and the scent of roses, as sweet and spoiled as wine, soaked the soft air. "Easter, you go right ahead and cut some for the tables," Mrs. Toussaint said, while they walked over to the church. "Any that you see, still nice and red." She and Soubrette carried two big pans of *jambalaya rouge*. Easter carried the flower vases. Rosebushes taller than a man grew in front of every house on the Drive, and were all heavily blooming with summer's doomed roses. Yet Easter could only stop here and there and clip one with the scissors Mrs. Toussaint had given her, since most flowers had rotted deeply burgundy or darker, long past their prime.

With more effort than anybody could calculate, the earth every year brought forth these flowers, and then every year all the roses died. "What's wrong, Easter?" Soubrette said.

"Aw, it's nothing." Easter squeezed with her good hand, bracing the scissors against the heel of her ruint one. "I'm just thinking, is all." She put the thorny clipping into a vase and made herself smile.

At the church there were trestles to set up, wide boards to lay across them, tablecloths, flower vases, an immense supper and many desserts to arrange sensibly. *And my goodness, didn't anybody remember a lifter for the pie...? Girls – you run on back up to the house and bring both of mine...*

She and Soubrette were laying out the serving spoons when Easter saw her parents coming round Rosetree Drive in the wagon. Back when the Mack family had first come to Rosetree, before Easter's first birthday, all the white folks hadn't moved to Greenville yet. And in those days Ma'am, Pa, and her brother still had 'six fat pocketfuls' of the gold from St. Louis, so they could have bought one of the best houses on the Drive. But they'd decided to live in the backwoods outside of town instead (on account of the old Africa magic, as Easter well knew, although telling the story Ma'am and Pa never gave the reason). Pa unloaded a big pot from the wagon bed, and a stack of cloth-covered bread. Ma'am anxiously checked Easter over head to toe – shoes blacked and spotless, dress pressed and stiffly starched, and she laid her palm very lightly against Easter's hair. "Not troubled at all, are you?"

"No, Ma'am."

"Don't really know *what's* got me so wrought up," Ma'am said. "I just felt like I needed to get my eyes on you – *see* you. But don't you look nice!" The worry left Ma'am's face. "And I declare, Octavia can do *better* by that head than your own mama." Ma'am fussed a little with the ribbon in Easter's hair, and then went to help Mrs. Toussaint, slicing the cakes.

Across the table, Mrs. Freeman said, "I do *not* care for the look of these clouds." And Mrs. Freeman frowned, shaking her head at the gray skies. "No, I surely don't."

Won't a drop fall today, the angels whispered in Easter's ear. *Sure 'nough rain hard tomorrow, though.*

Easter smiled over the table. "Oh, don't you worry, Mrs. Freeman." And with supernatural confidence, she said, "It ain't gon' rain today."

The way the heavyset matron looked across the table at Easter, well, anybody would call that *scared,* and Mrs. Freeman shifted further on down the table to where other ladies lifted potlids to stir contents, and secured the bread baskets with linen napkins. It made Easter feel so bad. She felt like the last smudge of filth when everything else is just spic-and-span. Soubrette bumped her. "Take one of these, Easter, will you?" Three vases full of flowers were too many for one person to hold. "Maman said to put some water in them so the roses stay fresh." Together they went round the side of the church to the well.

When they'd come back, more and more men, old folks, and children were arriving. The Missionary ladies argued among themselves over who must miss service, and stay outside to watch over supper and shoo flies and what have you. Mrs. Turner said that she would, *just to hush up the rest of you.* Then somebody caught sight of the visiting preacher, Wandering Bishop Fitzgerald James, come down the steps of the mayor's house with his cane.

1863

SO THAT RIOT started off in protest of the draft, but it soon became a murder spree, with white men killing every black man, woman, or child who crossed their path. They burned down churches, businesses, the homes of abolitionists, and anywhere else black people were known to congregate, work, or live – even the Colored Orphan Asylum, for example, which was in Midtown back then. Altogether, at least a hundred people were killed by whites. And there's plenty more of these stories over the years, plenty more. Maybe you ought to consider Rosetree. That there's a story like you wouldn't believe.

– Dad

EYES CLOSED, SITTING in the big fancy chair, Wandering Bishop Fitzgerald James seemed to sleep while Pastor Daniels welcomed him and led the church to say *amen*. So skinny, so old, he looked barely there. But his suit was very fine indeed, and when the Wandering Bishop got up to preach, his voice was huge.

He began in measured tones, though soon he was calling on the church in a musical chant, one hard breath out – *huh!* – punctuating each four beat line. At last the Wandering Bishop sang, his baritone rich and beautiful, and his sermon, *this one,* a capstone experience of Easter's life. Men danced, women lifted up their hands and wept. Young girls cried out as loudly as their parents. When the plate came around, Pa put in a whole silver dollar, and then Ma'am nudged him, so he added another.

After the benediction, Ma'am and Pa joined the excited crowd going up front to shake hands with the visiting preacher. They'd known Wandering Bishop Fitzgerald James back before the war, when he sometimes came to Heavenly Home and preached for the coloreds – always a highlight! A white-haired mulatto, the Wandering Bishop moved with that insect-like stiffness peculiar to scrawny old men. Easter saw that his suit's plush lapels were velvet, his thin silk necktie cherry-red.

"Oh, I remember you – sure do. Such a pretty gal! Ole Marster MacDougal always used to say, *Now, Fitzy, you ain't to touch a hair on the head of that one, hear me, boy?*" The Wandering Bishop wheezed and cackled. Then he peered around, as if for small children running underfoot. "But where them little yeller babies at?" he said. "Had you a whole mess of 'em, as I recall."

Joy wrung from her face until Ma'am had only the weight of cares, and politeness, left. "A lovely sermon," she murmured. "Good day to you,

Bishop." Pa's forearm came up under her trembling hand and Ma'am leaned on him. Easter followed her parents away, and they joined the spill of the congregation out onto the town green for supper. Pa had said that Easter just had a way with some onions, smoked hock and beans, and would she please fix up a big pot for him. Hearing Pa say so had felt very fine, and Easter had answered, "Yes, sir, I sure will!" Even offered a feast, half the time Pa only wanted some beans and bread, anyhow. He put nothing else on his plate this Sunday too.

The clouds had stayed up high, behaving themselves, and in fact the creamy white overcast, cool and not too bright, was more comfortable than a raw blue sky would have been. Men had gotten the green all spruced up nice, the animals pent away, all the patties and whatnot cleaned up. They'd also finally gotten around to chopping down the old lightning-split, half-rotten crabapple tree in the middle of the green. A big axe still stuck upright from the pale and naked stump. Close by there, Soubrette, Mrs. Toussaint, and her longtime gentleman friend, Señor Tomás, had spread a couple blankets. They waved and called, *Hey, Macks!,* heavy plates of food in their laps. Easter followed Ma'am and Pa across the crowded green.

Pa made nice Frenchy noises at Miss and Mrs. Toussaint, and then took off lickety-split with Señor, gabbling in Spanish. Ma'am sat down next to Mrs. Toussaint and they leaned together, speaking softly. "What did you think of the Wandering Bishop?" Easter asked Soubrette. "Did you care for the sermon?"

"Well..." Soubrette dabbed a fingerful of biscuit in some gravy pooled on Easter's plate. "He had a *beautiful* way of preaching, sure enough." Soubrette looked right and left at the nearby grown-ups, then glanced meaningfully at Easter – who leaned in close enough for whispers.

Señor, the Macks, and the Toussaints always sat on the same pew at church, had dinner back and forth at one another's houses, and generally just hung together as thick as thieves. Scandal clung to them both, one family said to work roots and who knew what all kind of devilment. And the other family... well, back east Mrs. Toussaint had done *some* kind of work in La Nouvelle-Orléans, and Easter knew only that rumor of it made the good church ladies purse their lips, take their husbands' elbows, and hustle the men right along – *no* lingering near Mrs. Toussaint. These were the times

Easter felt the missing spot in the Mack family worst. There was no one to ask, "What's a '*hussycat*'?" The question, she felt, would hurt Soubrette, earn a slap from Ma'am, and make Pa say, shocked, "Aw, Easter – what you asking *that* for? Let it alone!" His disappointment was always somehow worse than a slap.

Brother, she knew, would have just told her.

The youngest Crombie boy, William, came walking by slowly, carrying his grandmother's plate while she clutched his shoulder. The old lady shrieked.

"*Ha' mercy*," cried Old Mrs. Crombie. "The sweet blessèd Jesus!" She let go of her grandson's shoulder, to flap a hand in the air. "Ain't *nothing* but a witch over here! I ain't smelt devilry this bad since slavery days, at that root-working Bob Allow's dirty cabin. Them old Africa demons just *nasty* in the air. Who is it?" Old Mrs. Crombie peered around with cloudy blue eyes as if a witch's wickedness could be seen even by the sightless. "Somebody *right* here been chatting with Ole Crook Foot, and I know it like I know my own name. Who?"

Easter about peed herself she was that scared. Rude and bossy, as she'd never spoken to the angels before, she whispered, "Y'all *get*," and the four or five hovering scattered away. Ma'am heard that whisper, though, and looked sharply at Easter.

"Who there, Willie?" Old Mrs. Crombie asked her grandson. "Is it them dadburn Macks?"

"Yes'm," said the boy. "But, Granny, don't you want your supper...?"

"Hush up!" Old Mrs. Crombie blindly pointed a finger at the Macks and Toussaints – catching Easter dead in its sights. "*All Saturday long* these Macks wanna dance with the Devil, and then come set up in the Lord's house on Sunday. Well, no! Might got the *rest* of you around here too scared to speak up, but *me*, I'ma go ahead say it. '*Be vigilant*,' says the Book! '*For your adversary walks about like a roaring lion*.' The King of Babylon! The Father of Lies!"

And what were they supposed to do? Knock an old lady down in front of everybody? Get up and run in their Sunday clothes, saying *excuse me, excuse me,* all the way to edge of the green, with the whole world sitting there watching? Better just to stay put, and hope like a sudden hard downpour this would all be over soon, no harm done. Ma'am grabbed

Willie down beside her, said something to him, and sent the boy scurrying off for reinforcements.

"And Mister Light-Bright, with the red beard and spots on his face, always smirking – oh, I know *just* what that one was up to! Think folk around here don't know about St. Louis? Everybody know! *The Devil walked abroad in St. Louis*. And that bushwhacked Confederate gold, we all know just how you got it. Them devil-haunted tabacky fields *too* – growing all outta season, like this some doggone Virginia. This ain't no Virginia out here! Well, where he been at, all these last years? Reaped the whirlwind is what I'm guessing. Got himself strick down by the Lord, huh? *Bet* he did."

Preacherly and loud, Old Mrs. Crombie had the families within earshot anything but indifferent to her testimony. But no matter the eyes, the ears, and all the grownfolk, Easter didn't care to hear any evil said of Brother. She had to speak up. "Ma'am, my brother was good and kind. He was the *last* one to do anybody wrong."

"And here come the *daughter* now," shouted Old Mrs. Crombie. "Her brother blinded my eyes when I prayed the Holy Ghost against them. Well, let's see what *this* one gon' do! Strike me dumb? Ain't no matter – til then, I'ma be steady testifying. I'ma keep *on* telling the Lord's truth. Hallelujah!"

At last the son showed up. "Mama?" Mr. Crombie took firm hold of his mother's arm. "You just come along now, Mama. Will you let hungry folk eat they dinner in peace?" He shot them a look, very sorry and all-run-ragged. Ma'am pursed her lips in sympathy and waved a hand, *it's all right*.

"Don't worry none about us," Pa said. "Just see to your Ma." He spoke in his voice for hurt animals and children.

"Charleston?" Old Mrs. Crombie said timidly, the fire and brimstone all gone. "That you?"

"Oh, Mama. Charlie *been* dead. White folk hung him back in Richmond, remember? This *Nathaniel*."

Old Mrs. Crombie grunted as if taking a punch – denied the best child in favor of this least and unwanted. "Oh," she said, "Nathaniel."

"Now y'all know she old," Mr. Crombie raised his voice for the benefit of all those thereabouts. "Don't go setting too much store by every little thing some old lady just half in her right mind wanna say."

Old Mrs. Crombie, muttering, let herself be led away.

Ma'am stood up, and smiled around at Pa, Mrs. Toussaint, Señor, Soubrette. "Everybody excuse us, please? Me and Easter need to go have us a chat up at the church. No, Wilbur, that's all right." She waved Pa back down. "It ain't nothing but a little lady-business me and the baby need to see to, alone." When one Mack spoke with head tilted just so, kind of staring at the other one, carefully saying each word, whatever else was being said it really meant *old Africa magic*. Pa sat down. "And don't y'all wait, you hear? We might be a little while talking. *Girl*." Ma'am held out a hand.

Hand-in-hand, Ma'am led Easter across the crowded green, across the rutted dirt of the Drive, and up the church steps.

"Baby child," Ma'am said. When Easter looked up from her feet, Ma'am's eyes weren't angry at all but sad. "If I *don't* speak, my babies die," she said. "And If I *do*, they catch a fever from what they learn, take up with it, and die anyhow." As if Jesus hid in some corner, Ma'am looked all around the empty church. The pews and sanctuary upfront, the winter stove in the middle, wood storage closet in back. "Oh, Lord, is there any right way to do this?" She sat Easter at the pew across from the wood-burning stove, and sat herself. "Well, I'm just gon' to *tell* you, Easter, and tell everything I know. It's plain to see that keeping you in the dark won't help nothing. This here's what *my* mama told me. When..."

... THEY GRABBED *HER* pa, over across in Africa land, he got *bad* hurt. It was smooth on top of his head right here [*Ma'am lay a hand on the crown of her head, the left side*] and all down the middle of the bare spot was knotted up, nasty skin where they'd cut him terrible. And *there*, right in the worst of the scar was a – *notch?* Something like a deep dent in the bone. You could take the tip of your finger, rest it on the skin there, and feel it give, feel no bone, just softness underneath...

So, you knew him, Ma'am?

Oh, no. My mama had me old or older than I had *you*, child, so the grandfolk was dead and gone *quite* a ways before I showed up. Never did meet him. Well... not to meet in the flesh, I never did. Not alive, like you mean it. But that's a whole 'nother story, and don't matter none for what I'm telling you now. The thing I want you to see is how the old knowing, from grandfolk to youngfolk, got broke up into pieces, so in these late days I got nothing left to teach my baby girl. Nothing except, *Let that old Africa magic alone.* Now *he*, your great-grandpa, used to oftentimes get down at night like a dog and run around in the dark, and then come on back from the woods before morning, a man again. Might of brought my grandmama a rabbit, some little deer, or just anything he might catch in the night. Anybody sick or lame, or haunted by spirits, *you* know the ones I mean – folk sunk down and sad all the time, or just always *angry*, or the people plain out they right mind – he could reach out his hand and brush the trouble off them, easy as I pick some lint out your hair. And a very fine-looking man he was too, tall as anything and just... sweet-natured, I guess you could say. *Pleasant.* So all the womenfolk loved him. But here's the thing of it. Because of that hurt on his head, Easter – because of *that* – he was simple. About the only English he ever spoke was *Yeah, mars.* And most of the time, things coming out his mouth in the old Africa talk didn't make no sense, either. But even hurt and simple and without his good sense, he *still* knew exactly what he was doing. Could get down a dog, and get right back up again being people, being a man, come morning – whenever he felt like it. *We can't, Easter.* Like I told you, like I told your brother. All us coming after, it's just the one way if we get down on four feet. Not *never* getting up no more. That's the way I lost *three* of mine! No. Hush. Set still there and leave me be a minute... So these little bits and pieces I'm telling you right now is every single thing I got from my mama. All *she* got out of your great grand and the old folk who knew him from back over there. Probably you want to know where the right roots at for this, for that, for everything. Which strong words to say? What's the best time of day, and proper season? Why the moon pull so funny, and the rain feel so sweet and mean some particular thing but you can't say what? *Teach me, Ma'am*, your heart must be saying. But I can't, Easter, cause it's gone. Gone for good. They drove us off the path into a wild night, and when morning came we were too turned around, too far from where we started, to *ever* find our way again. Do you think I was my mama's onliest? I wasn't, Easter. Far from it. Same as you ain't *my* only child. I'm just the one that *lived.* The one that didn't mess around. One older sister, and one younger, I saw them both die *awful*, Easter. And all your sisters, and your brothers...

*   *   *

EASTER STOOD LOOKING through the open doors of the church on a view of cloudy sky and the town green. The creamy brightness of early afternoon had given way to ashen gray, and the supper crowd was thinning out though many still lingered. Arm dangling, Ma'am leaned over the back of the pew and watched the sky, allowing some peace and quiet for Easter to think.

And for her part Easter knew she'd learned plenty today from Ma'am about why and where and who, but that she herself certainly understood more about *how*. In fact Easter was sure of that. She didn't like having more knowledge than her mother. The thought frightened her. And yet, Ma'am had never faced down and tricked the Devil, had she?

"Oh, Easter..." Ma'am turned abruptly on the pew "... I clean forgot to tell you, and your Pa *asked* me to! A bear or mountain lion – *something* – was in the yard last night. The dog got scratched up pretty bad chasing it off. Durn dog wouldn't come close, and let me have a proper look-see..."

Sometimes Ma'am spoke so coldly of Brother that Easter couldn't *stand* it. Anxiously she said, "Is he hurt bad?"

"Well, not so bad he couldn't run and hide as good as always. But something took a mean swipe across the side of him, and them cuts weren't pretty to see. *Must of* been a bear. I can't see what else could of gave that dog, big as he is, such a hard time. The *barking* and *racket*, last night! You would of thought the Devil himself was out there in the yard! But, Easter, set down here. Your mama wants you to set down right here with me now for a minute."

Folks took this tone, so gently taking your hand, only when about to deliver the worst news. Easter tried to brace herself. Just now, she'd seen everybody out on the green. So who could have died?

"I know you loved that mean old bird," Ma'am said. "*Heaven* knows why. But the thing in the yard last night broke open the coop, and got in with the chickens. The funniest thing..." Ma'am shook her head in wonder. "It didn't touch *nah* bird except Sadie." Ma'am hugged Easter to her side, eyes full of concern. "But, Easter – I'm sorry – it tore old Sadie to *pieces*."

Easter broke free of Ma'am's grasp, stood up, blind for one instant of panic. Then she sat down again, feeling nothing. She felt only tired. "You done told me this, that, and the other thing" – Easter hung her head sleepily, speaking in a dull voice – "but why didn't you never say the one thing I *really* wanted to know?"

"And what's that, baby child?"

Easter looked up, smiled, and said in a brand new voice, "Who slept on the pull-out cot?"

Her mother hunched over as if socked in the belly. "What?" Ma'am whispered. "What did you just ask me?"

Easter moved over on the pew close enough to lay a kiss on her mother's cheek or lips. This smile tasted richer than cake, and this confidence, just as rich. "Was it Brother Freddie slept on the pull-out cot, Hazel Mae? Was it him?" Easter said, and brushed Ma'am's cheek with gentle fingertips. "Or was it you? Or was it *sometimes* him, and *sometimes* you?"

At that touch, Ma'am had reared back so violently she'd lost her seat – fallen to the floor into the narrow gap between pews.

Feeling almighty, Easter leaned over her mother struggling dazed on the ground, wedged in narrow space. "... *ooOOoo...*" Easter whistled in nasty speculation. "Now *here's* what I really want to know. Was it ever *nobody* on that pull-out cot, Hazel Mae? Just nobody atall?"

Ma'am ignored her. She was reaching a hand down into the bosom of her dress, rooting around as if for a hidden dollarbill.

Easter extended middle and forefingers. She made a circle with thumb and index of the other hand, and then vigorously thrust the hoop up and down the upright fingers. "Two peckers and one cunt, Hazel Mae – did *that* ever happen?"

As soon as she saw the strands of old beads, though, yellow-brownish as ancient teeth, which Ma'am pulled up out of her dress, lifted off her neck, the wonderful sureness, this wonderful strength, left Easter. She'd have turned and fled in fact, but could hardly manage to scoot away on the pew, so feeble and stiff and cold her body felt. She spat out hot malice while she could, shouting.

"One, two, three, four!" Easter staggered up from the end of the pew as Ma'am gained her feet. "And we even tricked that clever Freddie of yours, too. Thinking he was *so* smart. Won't *never* do you any good swearing off the old Africa magic, Hazel Mae! Cause just you watch, we gon' get this last one too! *All of yours –*"

Ma'am slung the looped beads around Easter's neck, and falling to her knees she vomited up a vast supper with wrenching violence. When Easter opened her tightly clenched eyes, through blurry tears she saw, shiny and black in the middle of puddling pink mess, a snake thick as her own arm, *much* longer. She shrieked in terror, kicking backwards on the ground. Faster than anybody could run, the monstrous snake shot off down the aisle between the pews, and out into the gray brightness past the open church doors. Easter looked up and saw Ma'am standing just a few steps away. Her mother seemed more shaken than Easter had ever seen her. "Ma'am?" she said. "I'm scared. What's wrong? I don't feel good. What's this?" Easter began to lift off the strange beads looped so heavily round her neck.

At once Ma'am knelt on the ground beside her. "You just leave those right where they at," she said. "Your great grand brought these over with him. Don't you *never* take 'em off. Not even to wash up." Ma'am scooped hands under Easter's arms, helping her up to sit at the end of a pew. "Just wait here a minute. Let me go fill the wash bucket with water for this mess. *You* think on what all you got to tell me." Ma'am went out and came back. With a wet rag, she got down on her knees by the reeking puddle. "Well, go on, girl. Tell me. All this about Sadie. It's something do with the old Africa magic, ain't it?"

THE LAST ANGEL supped at Easter's hand, half-cut-off, and then lit away. Finally the blood began to gush forth and she swooned.*

*Weird, son. Definitely some disturbing writing in this section. But overarching theme = a people bereft, no? Dispossessed even of cultural patrimony? Might consider then how to represent this in the narrative structure. Maybe just omit how Easter learns to trick the Devil into the chicken? Deny the reader that knowledge as Easter's been denied so much. If you do, leave a paragraph, or even just a sentence, literalizing the "Fragments of History." Terrible title, by the way; reconsider.
– Dad

* * *

PEOPLE PRESENTLY DWELLING in the path of hurricanes, those who lack the recourse of flight, hunker behind fortified windows and hope that this one too shall pass them lightly over. So, for centuries, were the options of the blacks vis-à-vis white rage. Either flee, or pray that the worst might strike elsewhere: once roused, such terror and rapine as whites could wreak would not otherwise be checked. But of course those living in the storm zones know that the big one always does hit sooner or later. And much worse for the blacks of that era, one bad element or many bad influences – 'the Devil,' as it were – might attract to an individual, a family, or even an entire town, the landfall of a veritable hurricane.

White Devils/Black Devils, Luisa Valéria da Silva y Rodríguez

1877, August 24

THERE CAME TO the ears of mother and daughter a great noise from out on the green, the people calling one to another in surprise, and then with many horses' hooves and crack upon crack of rifles, the thunder spoke, surely as the thunder had spoken before at Gettysburg or Shiloh. Calls of shock and wonder became now cries of terror and dying. They could hear those alive and afoot run away, and hear the horsemen who pursued them, with many smaller cracks of pistols. *There!* shouted white men to each other, *That one there running!* Some only made grunts of effort, as when a woodsman embeds his axe head and heaves it out of the wood again – such grunts. Phrases or wordless sound, the whiteness could be heard in the voices, essential and unmistakable.

Easter couldn't understand this noise at first, except that she should be afraid. It seemed that from the thunder's first rumble Ma'am grasped the whole of it, as if she had lived through precisely this before and perhaps many times. Clapping a hand over Easter's mouth, Ma'am said, "Hush," and got them both up and climbing over the pews from this one to the one behind, keeping always out-of-view of the doors. At the back of the church, to the right of the doors, was a closet where men stored the cut wood burned by the stove in winter. In dimness – that closet, *very* tight – they pressed themselves opposite the wall stacked with quartered logs, and squeezed back into the furthest corner. There, with speed and strength, Ma'am unstacked wood, palmed the top of Easter's head, and pressed her down to crouching in the dusty dark. Ma'am put the wood back again until Easter herself didn't know where she was. "You don't *move* from here," Ma'am said. "Don't come at nobody's call but mine." Easter was beyond thought by then, weeping silently since Ma'am had hissed, "*Shut your mouth!*" and shaken her once hard.

Easter nudged aside a log and clutched at the hem of her mother's skirt, but Ma'am pulled free and left her. From the first shot, not a single moment followed free of wails of desperation, or the shriller screams of those shot and bayoneted.

Footfalls, outside – some child running past the church, crying with terror. Easter heard a white man shout, *There go one!* and heard horse's hooves in heavy pursuit down the dirt of the Drive. She learned the noises peculiar to a horseman running down a child. Foreshortened last scream, pop of bones, pulped flesh, laughter from on high. To hear something clearly enough, if it was bad enough, was the same as seeing. Easter bit at her own arm as if that could blunt vision and hearing.

Hey there, baby child, whispered a familiar voice. *Won't you come out from there? I got something real nice for you just outside.* No longer the voice of the kindly spoken Johnny Reb, this was a serpentine lisp – and yet she knew them for one and the same and the Devil. *Yeah, come on out, Easter. Come see what all special I got for you.* Jump up flailing, run away screaming – Easter could think of nothing else, and the last strands of her tolerance and good sense began to fray and snap. That voice went on whispering and Easter choked on sobs, biting at her forearm.

Some girl screamed nearby. It could have been *any* girl in Rosetree, screaming, but the whisperer snickered, *Soubrette. I got her!*

Easter lunged up, and striking aside logs, she fought her way senselessly with scraped knuckles and stubbed toes from the closet, on out of the church into gray daylight.

If when the show has come and gone, not only paper refuse and cast-off food but the whole happy crowd, shot dead, remained behind and littered the grass, then Rosetree's green looked like some fairground, the day after.

Through the bushes next door to the church Easter saw Mr. Henry, woken tardily from a nap, thump with his cane out onto the porch, and from the far side of the house a white man walking shot him dead. Making not even a moan old Mr. Henry toppled over and his walking stick rolled to porch's edge and off into roses. About eight o'clock on the Drive, flames had engulfed the general store so it seemed a giant face of fire, the upstairs windows two dark eyes, and downstairs someone ran out of the flaming mouth. That shadow in the brightness had been Mrs. Toussaint, so slim and short in just such skirts, withering now under a fiery scourge that leapt around her, then up from her when she fell down burning. The Toussaints kept no animals in the lot beside the general store and it was all grown up with tall grass and wildflowers over there. Up from those weeds, a noise of hellish suffering poured from the ground, where some young woman lay unseen and screamed while one white man with dropped pants and white ass out stood afoot in the weeds and laughed, and some other, unseen on the ground, grunted piggishly in between shouted curses. People lay everywhere bloodied and fallen, so many dead, but Easter saw her father somehow alive out on the town green, right in the midst of the bodies just kneeling there in the grass, his head cocked to one side, chin down, as if puzzling over some problem. She ran to him calling *Pa Pa Pa* but up close she saw a red dribble down his face from the forehead where there was a deep ugly hole. Though they were sad and open his eyes slept no they were dead. To cry hard enough knocks a body down, and harder still needs both hands flat to the earth to get the grief out.

In the waist-high corn, horses took off galloping at the near end of the Parks' field. At the far end Mrs. Park ran with the baby Gideon Park, Jr. in her arms and the little girl Agnes following behind, head hardly above corn, shouting *Wait Mama wait*, going as fast as her legs could, but just a little girl, about four maybe five. Wholeheartedly wishing they'd make it to the backwood trees all right, Easter could see as plain as day those white men on horses would catch them first. So strenuous were her prayers for Mrs. Park and Agnes, she had to hush up weeping. Then a couple white men caught sight of Easter out on the green, just kneeling there – some strange survivor amidst such thorough and careful murder. With red bayonets, they trotted out on the grass toward her. Easter stood up meaning to say, or even beginning to, polite words about how the white men should leave Rosetree now, about the awful mistake they'd made. But the skinnier man got out in front of the other, *running,* and hauled back with such obvious intent on his rifle with that lengthy knife attached to it, Easter's legs wouldn't hold her. Suddenly kneeling again, she saw her mother standing right next to the crabapple stump. Dress torn, face sooty, in stocking feet, Ma'am got smack in the white men's way. That running man tried to change course but couldn't fast enough. He came full-on into the two-handed stroke of Ma'am's axe.

Swapt clean off, his head went flying, his body dropped straight down. The other one got a hand to his belt and scrabbled for a pistol while Ma'am stepped up and hauled back to come round for his head too. Which one first, then – pistol or axe? He got the gun out and up and shot. Missed, though, even that close, his hand useless as a drunk's, he was so scared. The axe knocked his chest in and him off his feet. Ma'am stomped the body twice getting her axe back out. With one hand she plucked Easter up off the ground to her feet. "*Run*, girl!"

They ran.

They should have gone straight into the woods, but their feet took them onto the familiar trail. Just in the trees' shadows, a big white man looked up grinning from a child small and dead on the ground. He must have caught some flash or glimpse of swinging wet iron because that white man's grin fell off, he loosed an ear-splitting screech, before Ma'am chopped that face and scream in half.

"Rawly?" Out of sight in the trees, some other white man called. "You all right over there, Rawly?" The fallen man, head in halves like the first red slice into a melon, made no answer. Nor was Ma'am's axe wedging out of his spine soon enough. Other white men took up the call of that name, and there was crash and movement in the trees.

Ma'am and Easter ran off the trail the other way. The wrong way again. They should have forgotten house and home and kept on forever into wilderness. Though probably it didn't matter anymore at that point. The others found the body – axe stuck in it – and cared not at all for the sight of a dead white man, or what had killed him. Ma'am and Easter thrashed past branches, crackled and snapped over twigs, and behind them in the tangled brush shouts of pursuit kept on doubling. What sounded like four men clearly had to be at least eight, and then just eight couldn't half account for such noise. Some men ahorse, some with dogs. Pistols and rifles firing blind.

They burst into the yard and ran up to the house. Ma'am slammed the bar onto the door. For a moment, they hunched over trying only to get air enough for life, and then Ma'am went to the wall and snatched off Brother's old Springfield from the war. *Where the durn cartridges at, and the caps, the doggone ramrod...?* Curses and questions, both were plain on Ma'am's face as she looked round the house abruptly disordered and strange by the knock-knock of Death at the door. White men were already in the yard.

The glass fell out of the back window and shattered all over the iron stove. Brother, up on his back legs, barked in the open window, his forepaws on the windowsill.

"Go on, Easter." Ma'am let the rifle fall to the floor. "Never mind what I said before. Just go on with your brother now. I'm paying your way."

Easter was too afraid to say or do or think, and Brother at the back window was just barking and barking. *She was too scared.*

In her meanest voice, Ma'am said, "Take off that dress, Easter Sunday Mack!"

Sobbing breathlessly, Easter could only obey.

"All of it, Easter, take it off. And throw them old nasty beads on the floor!"

Easter did that too, Brother barking madly.

Ma'am said, "Now –"

Rifles stuttered thunderously and the dark wood door of the house lit up, splintering full of holes of daylight. In front of it Ma'am shuddered awfully and hot blood speckled Easter's naked body even where she stood across the room. Ma'am sighed one time, got down gently, and stretched out on the floor. White men stomped onto the porch.

Easter fell, caught herself on her hands, and the bad one went out under her so she smacked down flat on the floor. But effortlessly she bounded up and through the window. Brother was right there when Easter landed badly again. He kept himself to her swift limp as they tore away neck-and-neck through Ma'am's back garden and on into the woods.*

* *Stop here, with the escape. Or no; I don't know. I wish there were some kind of way to offer the reader the epilogue, and yet warn them off too. I know it couldn't be otherwise, but it's just so grim.*

– Dad

Epilogue

THEY WERE BACK! Right out there sniffing in the bushes where the rabbits were. Two great *big* ole dogs! About to shout for her husband, Anna Beth remembered he was lying down in the back with one of his headaches. So she took down the Whitworth and loaded it herself. Of course she knew how to fire a rifle, but back in the War Between the States they'd hand-picked Michael-Thomas to train the sharpshooters of his brigade, and then given him one of original Southern Crosses, too, for so many Yankees killed. Teary-eyed and squinting from his headaches, he still never missed what he meant to hit. Anna Beth crept back to the bedroom and opened the door a crack.

"You 'wake?" she whispered. "Michael-Thomas?"

Out of the shadows: "Annie?" His voice, breathy with pain. "What is it?"

"I *seen* 'em again! They're right out there in the creepers and bushes by the rabbit burrows."

"You sure, Annie? My head's real bad. Don't go making me get up and it ain't nothing out there again."

"I just now seen 'em, Michael-Thomas. *Big* ole nasty dogs like nothing you ever saw before." Better the little girl voice – that never failed: "Got your Whitworth right here, honey. All loaded up and ret' to go."

Michael-Thomas sighed. "Here I come, then."

The mattress creaked, his cane thumped the floor, and there was a grunt as his bad leg had to take some weight as he rose to standing. (Knee shot off at the Petersburg siege, and not just his knee, either...) Michael-Thomas pushed the door wide, his squinting eyes red, pouched under with violet bags. He'd taken off his half-mask, and so Anna Beth felt her stomach lurch and go funny, as usual. Friends at the church, and Mama, and just *everybody* had assured her she would – sooner or later – but Anna Beth never had gotten used to seeing what some chunk of Yankee artillery had done to Michael-Thomas' face. Supposed to still be up *in* there, that chip of metal, under the ruin and crater where his left cheek... "Here you go." Anna Beth passed off the Whitworth to him.

Rifle in hand, Michael-Thomas gimped himself over to where she pointed – the open window. There he stood his cane against the wall and laboriously got down kneeling. With practiced grace he lay the rifle across the window sash, nor did he even bother with the telescopic sight at this distance – just a couple hundred yards. He shot, muttering, "Damn! Just *look* at 'em," a moment before he did so. The kick liked to knock him over.

Anna Beth had fingertips jammed in her ears against the report, but it was loud anyhow. Through the window and down the yard she saw the bigger dog, dirty mustard color – had been nosing round in the honeysuckle near the rabbit warren – suddenly drop from view into deep weeds. Looked like the littler one didn't have the sense to dash off into the woods. All while Michael-Thomas reloaded, the other dog nudged its nose downward at the carcass unseen in the weeds, and just looked up and all around, whining – pitiful if it weren't so ugly. Michael-Thomas shot that one too.

"Ah," he said. "Oh." He swapped the Whitworth for his cane, leaving the rifle on the floor under the window. "My head's *killing* me." Michael-Thomas went right on back to the bedroom to lie down again.

He could be relied on to hit just what he aimed for, so Anna Beth didn't fear to see gore-soaked dogs yelping and kicking, only half-dead, out there in the untamed, overgrown end of the yard, should she take a notion to venture out that way for a look-see. Would them dogs be just as big, up close and stone dead, as they'd looked from far-off and alive?

But it weren't carcasses nor live dogs, either, back there where the weeds grew thickest. Two dead niggers, naked as sin. Gal with the back of her head blown off, and buck missing his forehead and half his brains too. Anna Beth come running back up to the house, hollering.

TAWNY PETTICOATS
Michael Swanwick

Michael Swanwick (www.michaelswanwick.com) is one of the most acclaimed and prolific science fiction and fantasy writers of his generation. He has received a Hugo Award for fiction in an unprecedented five out of six years and has been honored with the Nebula, Theodore Sturgeon, World Fantasy and five Hugo Awards as well as receiving nominations for the British Science Fiction Award and the Arthur C. Clarke Award. Michael's latest novel is *Chasing the Phoenix*, a second post-Utopian adventure featuring confidence artists Darger and Surplus. He is currently at work on even more new novels and stories.

THE INDEPENDENT PORT city and (some said) pirate haven of New Orleans was home to many a strange sight. It was a place where sea serpents hauled ships past fields worked by zombie laborers to docks where cargo was loaded onto wooden wagons to be pulled through streets of crushed oyster shells by teams of pygmy mastodons as small as Percheron horses. So none thought it particularly noteworthy when for three days an endless line of young women waited in the hallway outside a luxury suite in the Maison Fema for the opportunity to raise their skirts or open their blouses to display a tattooed thigh, breast, or buttock to two judges who sat on twin chairs watching solemnly, asked a few questions, thanked them for their time, and then showed them out.

The women had come in response to a handbill, posted throughout several parishes, that read:

SEEKING AN HEIRESS

ARE YOU . . .

A YOUNG WOMAN BETWEEN THE AGES OF 18 AND 21?

FATHERLESS?

TATTOED FROM BIRTH ON AN INTIMATE PART OF YOUR BODY?
IF SO, YOU MAY BE ENTITLED TO GREAT RICHES
INQUIRE DAYTIMES, SUITE 1, MAISON FEMA

"YOU'D THINK I'D be tired of this by now," Darger commented during a brief break in the ritual. "And yet I am not."

"The infinite variety of ways in which women can be beautiful is indeed amazing," Surplus agreed. "As is the eagerness of so many to display that beauty." He opened the door. "Next."

A woman strode into the room, trailing smoke from a cheroot. She was dauntingly tall – six feet and a hand, if an inch – and her dress, trimmed with silver lace, was the same shade of golden brown as her skin. Surplus indicated a crystal ashtray on the sideboard and, with a gracious nod of thanks, she stubbed out her cigar.

"Your name?" Darger said after Surplus had regained his chair.

"My real name, you mean, or my stage name?"

"Why, whichever you please."

"I'll give you the real one then." The young woman doffed her hat and tugged off her gloves. She laid them neatly together on the sideboard. "It's Tawnymoor Petticoats. You can call me Tawny."

"Tell us something about yourself, Tawny," Surplus said.

"I was born a carny and worked forty-milers all my life," Tawny said, unbuttoning her blouse. "Most recently, I was in the sideshow as the Sleeping Beauty Made Immortal By Utopian Technology But Doomed Never To Awaken. I lay in a glass coffin covered by nothing but my own hair and a strategically placed hand, while the audience tried to figure out if I was alive or not. I've got good breath control." She folded the blouse and set it down by her gloves and hat. "Jake – my husband – was the barker. He'd size up the audience and when he saw a ripe mark, catch 'im on the way out and whisper that for a couple of banknotes it could be arranged to spend some private time with me. Then he'd go out back and peer in through a slit in the canvas."

Tawny stepped out of her skirt and set it atop the blouse. She began unlacing her petticoats. "When the mark had his trousers off and was about to climb in the coffin, Jake would come roaring out, bellowing that he was only supposed to look – not to take advantage of my vulnerable condition." Placing her underthings atop the skirt, she undid her garters and proceeded to roll down her stockings. "That was usually good for the contents of his wallet."

"You were working the badger game, you mean?" Surplus asked cautiously.

"Mostly, I just lay there. But I was ready to rear up and cold-cock the sumbidge if he got out of hand. And we worked other scams too. The pigeon drop, the fiddle game, the rip deal, you name it."

Totally naked now, the young woman lifted her great masses of black curls with both hands, exposing the back of her neck. "Then one night the mark was halfway into the coffin – and no Jake. So I opened my eyes real sudden and screamed in the bastard's face. Over he went, hit his head on the floor, and I didn't wait to find out if he was unconscious or dead. I stole his jacket and went looking for my husband. Turns out Jake had run off with the Snake Woman. She dumped him two weeks later and he wanted me to take him back, but I wasn't having none of that." She turned around slowly, so that Darger and Surplus could examine every inch of her undeniably admirable flesh.

Darger cleared his throat. "Um... you don't appear to have a tattoo."

"Yeah, I saw through that one right away. Talked to some of the girls you'd interviewed and they said you'd asked them lots of questions about themselves but hadn't molested them in any way. Not all of 'em were happy with that last bit. Particularly after they'd gone to all the trouble of getting themselves inked. So, putting two and four together, I figured you were running a scam requiring a female partner with quick wits and larcenous proclivities."

Tawny Petticoats put her hands on her hips and smiled. "Well? Do I get the job?"

Grinning like a dog – which was not surprising, for his source genome was entirely canine – Surplus stood, extending a paw. But Darger quickly got between him and the young woman, saying, "If you will pardon us for just a moment, Ms. Petticoats, my friend and I must consult in the back room. You may use the time to dress yourself."

When the two males were secluded, Darger whispered furiously, "Thank God I was able to stop you! You were about to enlist that young woman into our conspiracy."

"Well, and why not?" Surplus murmured equally quietly. "We were looking for a woman of striking appearance, not overly bound to conventional morality, and possessed of the self-confidence, initiative, and inventiveness a good swindler requires. Tawny comes up aces on all counts."

"Working with an amateur is one thing – but this woman is a professional. She will sleep with both of us, turn us against each other, and in the end abscond with the swag, leaving us with nothing but embarrassment and regret for all our efforts."

"That is a sexist and, if I may dare say so, un-gallant slander upon the fair sex, and I am astonished to hear it coming from your mouth."

Darger shook his head sadly. "It is not all women but all female confidence tricksters I abjure. I speak from sad – and repeated – experience."

"Well, if you insist on doing without this blameless young creature," Surplus said, folding his arms, "then I insist on your doing without me."

"My dear sir!"

"I must be true to my principles."

Further argumentation, Darger saw, would be useless. So, putting the best possible appearance on things, he emerged from the back room to say, "You have the job, my dear." From a jacket pocket he produced a silver filigreed vinaigrette and, unscrewing its cap, extracted from it a single pill. "Swallow this and you'll have the tattoo we require by morning. You'll want to run it past your pharmacist first, of course, to verify –"

"Oh, I trust you. If y'all had just been after tail, you wouldn't've waited for me. Some of those gals was sharp lookers for sure." Tawny swallowed the pill. "So what's the dodge?"

"We're going to work the black money scam," Surplus said.

"Oh, I have always wanted a shot at running that one!" With a whoop, Tawny threw her arms about them both.

Though his fingers itched to do so, Darger was very careful not to check to see if his wallet was still there.

THE NEXT DAY, ten crates of black money – actually, rectangles of scrap parchment dyed black in distant Vicksburg – were carried into the hotel by zombie laborers and then, at Surplus's direction, piled against the outside of Tawny's door so that, hers being the central room of the suite, the only way to enter or leave it was through his or Darger's rooms. Then, leaving the lady to see to her dress and makeup, her new partners set out to speak to their respective marks.

Darger began at the city's busy docklands.

The office of the speculator Jean-Nagin Lafitte were tastefully opulent and dominated by a *Mauisaurus* skull, decorated with scrimshaw filigree chased in silver. "Duke" Lafitte, as he styled himself, or "Pirate" Lafitte, as he was universally known, was a slim, handsome man with olive skin, long and flowing hair, and a mustache so thin it might have been drawn on with an eyebrow pencil. Where other men of wealth might carry a cane, he affected a coiled whip, which he wore on his belt.

"Renting an ingot of silver!" he exclaimed. "I never heard of such a thing."

"It is a simple enough proposition," Darger said. "Silver serves as a catalyst for a certain bioindustrial process, the precise nature of which I am not at liberty to divulge to you. The scheme involves converting bar silver to a colloidal slurry which, when the process is complete, will be recovered and melted back into bar form. You would lose nothing. Further, we will only tie up your wealth for, oh, let us say ten days to be on the safe side. In return for which we are prepared to offer you a ten percent return on your investment. A very tidy profit for no risk at all."

A small and ruthless smile played upon the speculator's lips. "There is the risk of your simply taking the silver and absconding with it."

"That is an outrageous implication, and from a man I respected less highly than I do you, I would not put up with it. However" – Darger gestured out the window at the busy warehouses and transshipment buildings – "I understand that you own half of everything we see. Lend my consortium a building in which to perform our operation and then place as many guards as you like around that building. We will bring in our apparatus and you will bring in the silver. Deal?"

For a brief moment, Pirate Lafitte hesitated. Then, "Done!" he snapped, and offered his hand. "For fifteen percent. Plus rental of the building."

They shook, and Darger said, "You will have no objection to having the ingot tested by a reputable assayist."

*　　*　　*

IN THE FRENCH Quarter, meanwhile, Surplus was having an almost identical conversation with a slight and acerbic woman, clad in a severe black dress, who was not only the mayor of New Orleans but also the proprietress of its largest and most notorious brothel. Behind her, alert and unspeaking, stood two uniformed ape-men from the Canadian Northwest, both with the expressions of baffled anger common to beasts that have been elevated almost but not quite to human intelligence. "An assayist?" she demanded. "Is my word not good enough for you? And if it is not, should we be doing business at all?"

"The answer to all three of your questions, Madam-Mayor Tresjolie, is yes," Surplus said amiably. "The assay is for your own protection. As you doubtless know, silver is routinely adulterated with other metals. When we are done with the silver, the slurry will be melted down and re-cast into an ingot. Certainly, you will want to know that the bar returned to you is of equal worth to the bar you rented out."

"Hmmm." They were sitting in the lobby of the madam-mayor's *maison de tolérance*, she in a flaring wicker chair whose similarity to a throne could not possibly be unintentional, and Surplus on a wooden folding chair facing her. Because it was still early afternoon, the facility was not open for business. But messengers and government flunkies came and went. Now one such whispered in Madam-Mayor Tresjolie's ear. She waved him away. "Seventeen and a half percent, take it or leave it."

"I'll take it."

"Good," Tresjolie said. "I have business with the zombie master now. Move your chair alongside mine, and stay to watch. If we are to do business, you will find this salubrious."

A round and cheerful man entered the public room, followed by half a dozen zombies. Surplus studied these with interest. Though their eyes were dull, their faces were stiff, and there was an unhealthy sheen to their skin, they looked in no way like the rotting corpses of Utopian legend. Rather, they looked like day laborers who had been worked into a state of complete exhaustion. Which doubtless was the case.

"Good morning!" said the jolly man, rubbing his hands briskly together. "I have brought this week's coffle of debtors who, having served their time, are now eligible for forgiveness and manumission."

"I had wondered at the source of your involuntary labor force," Surplus said. "They are unfortunates who fell into arrears, then?"

"Exactly so," said the zombie master. "New Orleans does not engage in the barbarous and expensive practice of funding debtors' prisons. Instead, debt-criminals are chemically rendered incapable of independent thought and put to work until they have paid off their debt to society. Which today's happy fellows have done." With a roguish wink, he added, "You may want to keep this in mind before running up too great a line of credit at the rooms upstairs. Are you ready to begin, Madam-Mayor Tresjolie?"

"You may proceed, Master Bones."

Master Bones gestured imperiously and the first zombie shuffled forward. "Through profligacy you fell into debt," he said, "and through honest labor you have earned your way out. Open your mouth."

The pallid creature obeyed. Master Bones produced a spoon and dipped into a salt cellar on a nearby table. He dumped the salt into the man's mouth. "Now swallow."

By gradual degrees, a remarkable transformation came over the man. He straightened and looked about him with tentative alertness. "I..." he said. "I remember now. Is my... is my wife...?"

"Silence," the zombie master said. "The ceremony is not yet complete." The Canadian guardsmen had shifted position to defend their mistress, should the disoriented ex-zombie attack her.

"You are hereby declared a free citizen of New Orleans again, and indebted to no man," Tresjolie said solemnly. "Go and overspend no more." She extended a leg and lifted her skirts above her ankle. "You may now kiss my foot."

"So DID YOU ask Tresjolie for a line of credit at her sporting house?" Tawny asked when Surplus reported his adventure to his confederates.

"Certainly not!" Surplus exclaimed. "I told her instead that it has always been my ambition to own a small but select private brothel, one dedicated solely to my own personal use. A harem, if you will, but one peopled by a rotating staff of well-paid employees. I suggested I might shortly be in a position to commission her to find an appropriate hotel and create such an institution for me."

"What did she say?"

"She told me that she doubted I was aware of exactly how expensive such an operation would be."

"And you said to her?

"That I didn't think money would be problem," Surplus said airily. "Because I expected to come into a great deal of it very soon."

Tawny crowed with delight. "Oh, you boys are such fun!"

"In unrelated news," Darger said, "your new dress has come."

"I saw it when it first arrived." Tawny made a face. "It is not calculated to show off my body to its best advantage – or to any advantage at all, come to that."

"It is indeed aggressively modest," Darger agreed. "However, your character is demure and inexperienced. To her innocent eyes, New Orleans is a terribly wicked place, indeed a cesspool of carnality and related sins. Therefore, she needs to be protected at all times by unrevealing apparel and stalwart men of the highest moral character."

"Further," Surplus amplified, "she is the weak point in our plans, for whoever has possession of her tattoo and knows its meaning can dispense with us entirely by kidnapping her off the street."

"Oh!" Tawny said in a small voice, clearly intended to arouse the protective instincts of any man nearby.

Surplus took an instinctive step toward her, and then caught himself. He grinned like the carnivore he was. "You'll do."

THE THIRD MEETING with a potential investor took place that evening in a dimly-lit club in a rundown parish on the fringe of the French Quarter – for the entertainment was, in the public mind, far too louche for even that notoriously open-minded neighborhood. Pallid waitresses moved lifelessly between the small tables, taking orders and delivering drinks while a small brass-and-drums jazz ensemble played appropriately sleazy music to accompany the stage show.

"I see that you are no aficionado of live sex displays," the zombie master Jeremy Bones said. The light from the candle sconce on the table made the beads of sweat on his face shine like luminous drops of rain.

"The artistic success of such displays depends entirely on the degree to which they agree with one's own sexual proclivities," Darger replied. "I confess that mine lie elsewhere. But never mind that. Returning to the subject at hand: The terms are agreeable to you, then?"

"They are. I am unclear, however, as to why you insist the assay be performed at the Bank of San Francisco, when New Orleans has several fine financial institutions of its own."

"All of which are owned in part by you, Madam-Mayor Tresjolie, and Duke Lafitte."

"Pirate Lafitte, you mean. An assay is an assay and a bank is a bank. Why should it matter to you which one is employed?"

"Earlier today, you brought six zombies to the mayor to be freed. Assuming this is a typical week, that would be roughly three hundred zombies per year. Yet all the menial work in the city has been handed over to zombies and there still remain tens of thousands at work in the plantations that line the river."

"Many of those who fall into debt draw multi-year sentences."

"I asked around, and discovered that Lafitte's ships import some two hundred prisoners a week from municipalities and territories all the way up the Mississippi to St. Louis."

A small smile played on the fat man's face. "It is true that many government bodies find it cheaper to pay us to deal with their troublemakers than to build prisons for them."

"Madam-Mayor Tresjolie condemns these unfortunates into the city's penal system, you pay her by body count, and after they have been zombified you lease them out for menial labor at prices that employers find irresistible. Those who enter your service rarely leave it."

"If a government official or family member presents me with papers proving that somebody's debt to society has been paid off, I am invariably happy to free them. I grant you that few ever come to me with such documentation. But I am always available to those who do. Exactly what is your objection to this arrangement?"

"Objection?" Darger said in surprise. "I have no objection. This is your system and as an outsider I have no say in it. I am merely explaining the reason why I wished to use an independent bank for the assay."

"Which is?"

"Simply that, happy though I am to deal with you three individually, collectively I find you far too shrewd." Darger turned to stare at the stage, where naked zombies coupled joylessly. Near the front, a spectator removed several banknotes from his wallet and tapped them meaningfully on his table. One of the lifeless waitresses picked up the money and led him through a curtain at the back of the room. "Acting together, I suspect you would swallow me and my partners in a single gulp."

"Oh, there is no fear of that," Master Bones said. "We three only act collectively when there is serious profit in the offing. Your little enterprise – whatever it is – hardly qualifies."

"I am relieved to hear it."

THE NEXT DAY, the three conspirators made three distinct trips to the Assay Office at the New Orleans branch of the Bank of San Francisco. On the first trip, one of Madam-Mayor Tresjolie's green-jacketed zombie bodyguards opened a lockbox, withdrew a silver ingot, and placed it on the work bench. Then, to the astonishment of both the mayor and the assayist, Surplus directed his own hired zombies to hoist several heavy leather bags to the bench as well, and with the aid of his colleagues began pulling out drills, scales, acids, reagents, and other tools and supplies and setting them in working order.

The affronted assayist opened his mouth to object, but – "I'm sure you won't mind if we provide our own equipment," Darger said suavely. "We are strangers here, and while nobody questions the probity of San Francisco's most prestigious financial concern, it is only good business to take proper precautions."

As he was talking, Tawny and Surplus both reached for the scales at once, collided, and almost sent them flying. Faces turned and hands reached out to catch them. But, in the fact, it was Surplus who saved the apparatus from disaster.

"Oops," Tawny said, coloring prettily.

Swiftly, the assayist performed his tests. At their conclusion, he looked up from the ingot. "The finding is .925," he said. "Sterling standard."

With an absent nod, Madam-Mayor Tresjolie acknowledged his judgment. Then she said, "The girl. How much do you want for her?"

As one, Darger and Surplus turned. Then they subtly shifted position so that one stood to either side of Tawny. "Ms. Petticoats is our ward," Darger said, "and therefore, it goes without saying, not for sale. Also, yours is not an entirely reputable business for so innocent a child as she."

"Innocence is in high demand at my establishment. I'll give you the silver ingot. To keep. Do with it as you wish."

"Believe me, madam. In not so very long, I shall consider silver ingots to be so much petty cash."

MASTER BONES WATCHED the assay, including even the chaotic assembly of the trio's equipment, with a beatific smile. Yet all the while, his attention kept straying to Tawny. Finally, he pursed his lips and said, "There might be a place in my club for your young friend. If you'd consider leasing her to me for, oh, let's say a year, I'd gladly forego my twenty percent profit on this deal." Turning to Tawny, he said, "Do not worry, my sweet. Under the influence of the zombie drugs you will feel nothing, and afterwards you will remember nothing. It will be as if none of it ever happened. Further, since you'd be paid a commission on each commercial encounter performed, you'd emerge with a respectable sum being held in trust for you."

Ignoring Tawny's glare of outrage, Darger suavely said, "In strictest confidence, sir, we have already turned down a far better offer for her than yours today. But my partner and I would not part with our dear companion for any amount of money. She is to us a treasure beyond price."

"I'm ready," the assayist said. "Where do you wish me to drill?"

Darger airily waved a finger over the ingot and then, seemingly at random, touched a spot at the exact center of the bar. "Right there."

"I UNDERSTAND THAT on the street they call me the Pirate," Jean-Nagin Lafitte said with quiet intensity. "This, however, is an insolence I will not tolerate to my face. Yes, I do chance to share a name with the legendary freebooter. But you will find that I have never committed an illegal act in my life."

"Nor do you today, sir!" Darger cried. "This is a strictly legitimate business arrangement."

"So I presume or I would not be here. Nevertheless, you can understand why I must take offense at having you and your clumsy confederates question the quality of my silver."

"Say no more, sir! We are all gentlemen here – save, of course, for Ms. Petticoats who is a gently-reared Christian orphan. If my word is good enough for you, then your word is good enough for me. We may dispose of the assay." Darger coughed discreetly. "However, just for my own legal protection, in the absence of an assay, I shall require a notarized statement from you declaring that you will be satisfied with whatever quality of silver we return to you."

Pirate Lafitte's stare would have melted iron. But it failed to wilt Darger's pleasant smile. At last, he said, "Very well, run the assay."

Negligently, Darger spun a finger in the air. Down it came on the exact center of the bar. "There."

While the assayist was working, Pirate Lafitte said, "I was wondering if your Ms. Petticoats must be available to –"

"She is not for sale!" Darger said briskly. "Not for sale, not for rent, not for barter, not available for acquisition on any terms whatsoever. Period."

Looking irritated, Pirate Lafitte said, "I was *going* to ask if she might be interested in going hunting with me tomorrow. There is some interesting game to be found in the bayous."

"Nor is she available for social occasions." Darger turned to the assayist. "Well, sir?"

"Standard sterling," the man said. "Yet again."

"I expected no less."

FOR THE SAKE of appearances, after the assays were complete, the three swindlers sent the zombies with their lab equipment back to Mason Fema and went out to supper together. Following which, they took a genteel stroll about town. Tawny, who had been confined to her room while negotiations took place, was particularly glad of the latter. But it was with relief that Darger, Surplus, and Tawny saw the heavy bags waiting for them on the sitting room table of their suite. "Who shall do the honors?" Darger asked.

"The lady, of course," Surplus said with a little bow.

Tawny curtsied and then, pushing aside a hidden latch at the bottom of one of the bags, slid out a silver ingot. From another bag, she slid out a second. Then, from a third, a third. A sigh of relief went up from all three conspirators at the sight of the silver glimmering in the lantern-light.

"That was right smartly done, when you changed the fake bars for the real ones," Tawny said.

Darger politely demurred. "No, it was the distraction that made the trick possible, and in this regard you were both exemplary. Even the assayist, who was present all three times you almost sent the equipment to the floor, suspected nothing."

"But tell me something," Tawny said. "Why did you make the substitution before the assay, rather than after? The other way around, you wouldn't have needed to have that little plug of silver in the middle for the sample to be drawn from. Just a silver-plated lead bar."

"We are dealing with suspicious people. This way, they first had the ingots confirmed as genuine and then saw that we came nowhere near them afterwards. The ingots are in a safety deposit box in a reputable bank, so to their minds there is not the least risk. All is on the up-and-up."

"But we're not going to stop here, are we?" Tawny asked anxiously. "I do so want to work the black money scam."

"Have no fear, my lovely," Surplus said, "this is only the beginning. But it serves as a kind of insurance policy for us. Even should the scheme go bad, we have already turned a solid profit." He poured brandy into three small glasses and handed them around. "To whom shall we drink?"

"To Madam-Mayor Tresjolie!" Darger said.

They drank, and then Tawny said, "What do you make of her? Professionally, I mean."

"She is far shrewder than she would have you think," Surplus replied. "But, as you are doubtless aware, the self-consciously shrewd are always the easiest to mislead." He poured a second glass. "To Master Bones!"

They drank. Tawny said, "And of him?"

"He is more problematic," Darger said. "A soft man with a brutal streak underneath his softness. In some ways he hardly seems human."

"Perhaps he has been sampling his own product?" Surplus suggested.

"Puffer fish extract, you mean? No. His mind is active enough. But I catch not the least glimmer of empathy from him. I suspect that he's been associating with zombies so long that he's come to think we're all like them."

The final toast inevitably went to Pirate Lafitte.

"I think he's cute," Tawny said. "Only maybe you don't agree?"

"He is a fraud and a poseur," Darger replied, "a scoundrel who passes himself off as a gentleman, and a manipulator of the legal system who insists he is the most honest of citizens. Consequently, I like him quite a bit. I believe that he is a man we can do business with. Mark my words, when the three of them come to see us tomorrow, it will be at his instigation."

For a time they talked business. Then Surplus broke out a deck of cards. They played euchre and canasta and poker, and because they played for matches, nobody objected when the game turned into a competition to see how deftly the cards could be dealt from the bottom of the deck or flicked out of the sleeve into one's hand. Nor was there any particular outcry when in one memorable hand, eleven aces were laid on the table at once.

At last Darger said, "Look at the time! It will be a long day tomorrow," and they each went to their respective rooms.

THAT NIGHT, AS Darger was drifting off to sleep, he heard the door connecting his room with Tawny's quietly open and shut. There was a rustle of sheets as she slipped into his bed. Then the warmth of Tawny's naked body pressed against his own, and her hand closed about his most private part. Abruptly, he was wide awake.

"What on earth do you think you're doing?" he whispered fiercely.

Unexpectedly, Tawny released her hold on Darger and punched him hard in his shoulder. "Oh, it's so easy for you," she retorted, equally quietly. "It's so easy for men! That hideous old woman tried to buy me. That awful little man wanted you to let him drug me. And God only knows what intentions Pirate Lafitte holds. You'll notice they all made their propositions to you. Not a one of them said a word to me." Hot tears fell on Darger's chest.

"All my life I have had male protectors – and needed them too. My Daddy, until I ran away. My first husband, until he got eaten by giant crabs. Then various boyfriends and finally that creep Jake."

"You have nothing to worry about. Surplus and I have never abandoned a confederate, nor shall we ever. Our reputation is spotless in this regard."

"I tell myself that, and daytimes I'm fine with it. But at night... well, this past week has been the longest I ever went without a man's body to comfort me."

"Yes, but surely you understand –"

Tawny drew herself up. Even in the dim half light of the moon through the window she was a magnificent sight. Then she leaned down to kiss Darger's cheek and murmured into his ear, "I've never had to beg a man before, but... Please?"

Darger considered himself a moral man. But there was only so much temptation a man could resist without losing all respect for himself.

THE NEXT MORNING, Darger awoke alone. He thought of the events of last night and smiled. He thought of their implications and scowled. Then he went down to the dining room for breakfast.

"What comes next?" Tawny asked, after they had fortified themselves with chicory coffee, beignets, and sliced baconfruit.

"We have planted suspicions in the minds of our three backers that there is more profit to be had than we are offering to share," Surplus said. "We have given them a glimpse of our mysterious young ward and suggested that she is key to the enterprise. We have presented them with a puzzle to which they can think of no solution. On reflection, they can only conclude that the sole reason we have the upper hand is that we can play them off of one another." He popped the last of his beignet into his mouth. "So sooner or later they will unite and demand of us an explanation."

"In the meantime –" Darger said.

"I know, I know. Back to my dreary old room to play solitaire and read the sort of uplifting literature appropriate to a modest young virgin."

"It's important to stay in character," Surplus said.

"I understand that. Next time, however, please make me something that doesn't need to be stored in the dark, like a sack of potatoes. The niece of a Spanish prisoner, perhaps. Or a socialite heiress. Or even a harlot."

"You are a Woman of Mystery," Darger said. "Which is a time-honored and some would say enviable role to play."

Thus it was that when Darger and Surplus left Maison Fema – at precisely ten o'clock, as they had made it their invariant habit – they were not entirely astonished to find their three benefactors all in a group, waiting for them. A brusque exchange of threats and outrage later, and protesting every step of the way, they led their marks to their suite.

The three bedrooms all opened off of a sunny common-room. Given the room's elegant appointments, the crates of black paper that had been stacked in front of Tawny Petticoats' door looked glaringly out of place.

Gesturing their guests to chairs, Darger adopted an air of resignation and said, "In order to adequately explain our enterprise, we must go back two generations to a time before San Francisco became the financial center of North America. The visionary leaders of that great city-state determined to found a new economy upon uncounterfeitable banknotes, and to this end employed the greatest bacterial engraver of his age, Phineas Whipsnade McGonigle."

"That is an unlikely name," Madam-Mayor Tresjolie sniffed.

"It was of course his *nom de gravure*, assumed to protect him from kidnappers and the like," Surplus explained. "In private life, he was known as Magnus Norton."

"Go on."

Darger resumed his narrative. "The results you know. Norton crafted one hundred and thirteen different bacteria which, as part of their natural functions, laid down layer upon layer of multicolored ink in delicate arabesques so intricate as to be the despair of coin-clippers and paperhangers everywhere. This, combined with their impeccable monetary policies, has made the San Francisco dollar the common currency of the hundred nations of North America. Alas for them, there was one weak point in their enterprise – Norton himself.

"Norton secretly created his own printing vats, employing the bacteria he himself had created, and proceeded to mass-produce banknotes that were not only indistinguishable from the genuine item but for all intents and purposes *were* the genuine item. He created enough of them to make himself the wealthiest man on the continent.

"Unfortunately for that great man, he tried to underpay his paper supplier, precipitating an argument that ended with him being arrested by the San Francisco authorities."

Pirate Lafitte raised an elegant forefinger. "How do you know all this?" he asked.

"My colleague and I are journalists," Darger said. Seeing his audience's expressions, he raised both hands. "Not of the muckraking variety, I hasten to assure you! Corruption is a necessary and time-honored concomitant of any functioning government, and one we support wholeheartedly. No, we write profiles of public figures, lavishing praise in direct proportion to their private generosity; human interest stories of heroic boys rescuing heiresses from fires and of kittens swallowed by crocodiles and yet miraculously passing through their alimentary systems unharmed; and of course amusing looks back at the forgotten histories of local scoundrels whom the passage of time has rendered unthreatening."

"It was this last that led us to Norton's story," Surplus elucidated.

"Indeed. We discovered that by a quirk of San Francisco's labyrinthine banking regulations, Norton's monetary creations could neither be destroyed nor distributed as valid currency. So to prevent their misuse, the banknotes were subjected to another biolithographic process whereby they were deeply impregnated with black ink so cunningly composed that no known process could bleach it from the bills without destroying the paper in the process.

"Now, here's where our tale gets interesting. Norton was, you'll recall, incomparable in his craft. Naturally, the city fathers were reluctant to forego his services. So, rather than have him languish in an ordinary prison, they walled and fortified a mansion, equipped it with a laboratory and all the resources he required, and put him to work.

"Imagine how Norton felt! One moment he was on the brink of realizing vast wealth, and the next he was a virtual slave. So long as he cooperated, he was given fine foods, wine, even conjugal visits with his wife... But, comfortable though his prison was, he could never leave it. He was, however, a cunning man and though he could not engineer his escape, he managed to devise a means of revenge: If he could not have vast wealth, then his descendants would. Someday, the provenance of the black paper would be forgotten and it would be put up for public auction as eventually occurs to all the useless lumber a bureaucracy acquires. His children or grandchildren or great-great grandchildren would acquire it and, utilizing an ingenious method of his own devising, convert it back into working currency and so make themselves rich beyond Croesus."

"The ancients had a saying," Surplus interjected. "'If you want to make God laugh, tell him your plans.' The decades passed, Norton died, and the black paper stayed in storage. By the time we began our researches, his family was apparently extinct. He had three children: a daughter who was not interested in men, a son who died young, and another son who never wed. The second son, however, traveled about in his early adulthood, and in the same neglected cache of family papers where we discovered Norton's plans, we found evidence that he was paying child support for a female bastard he had sired here some twenty years ago. So, utilizing an understanding of the city bureaucracy which Norton's wife and children lacked, we bribed the appropriate official to sell us the crates of seemingly worthless paper and came to New Orleans. Where we found Tawny Petticoats."

"This explains nothing," Madam-Mayor Tresjolie said.

Darger sighed heavily. "We had hoped you would be satisfied with a partial explanation. Now I see that it is all or nothing. Here before you are the crates of blackened banknotes." A plank had been removed from one of the topmost crates. He reached in to seize a handful of black paper rectangles, fanned them for all to see, and then put them back. "My colleague and I will now introduce you to our young charge."

Swiftly, Darger and Surplus unstacked the crates before the doorway, placing them to either side. Then Surplus rapped on the door. "Ms. Petticoats? Are you decent? We have visitors to see you."

The door opened. Tawny's large brown eyes peered apprehensively from the gloom. "Come in," she said in a little voice.

They all shuffled inside. Tawny looked first at Darger and then at Surplus. When they would not meet her eyes, she ducked her head, blushing. "I guess I know what y'all came here to see. Only... must I? Must I really?"

"Yes, child, you must," Surplus said gruffly.

Tawny tightened her mouth and raised her chin, staring straight ahead of herself like the captain of a schooner sailing into treacherous waters. Reaching around her back, she began unbuttoning her dress.

"Magnus Norton designed what no other man could have – a microorganism that would eat the black ink permeating the banknotes without damaging the other inks in any way. Simply place the notes in the proper liquid nutrient, add powdered silver as a catalyst, and within a week there will be nothing but perfect San Francisco money and a slurry of silver," Darger said. "However, he still faced the problem of passing the information of how to create the organism to his family. In a manner, moreover, robust enough to survive what he knew would be decades of neglect."

Tawny had unbuttoned her dress. Now, placing a hand upon her bosom to hold the dress in place, she drew one arm from its sleeve. Then, switching hands, she drew out the other. "Now?" she said.

Surplus nodded.

With tiny, doll-like steps, Tawny turned to face the wall. Then she lowered her dress so that they could see her naked back. On it was a large tattoo in seven bright colors, of three concentric circles. Each circle was made of a great number of short, near-parallel lines, all radiant from the unmarked skin at the tattoo's center. Anyone who could read a gene map could easily use it to create the organism it described.

Master Bones, who had not spoken before now, said, "That's an *E. coli*, isn't it?"

"A variant on it, yes, sir. Norton wrote this tattoo into his own genome and then sired three children upon his wife, believing they would have many more in their turn. But fate is a fickle lady, and Ms. Petticoats is the last of her line. She, however, will suffice." He turned to Tawny. "You may clothe yourself again. Our guests have had their curiosities satisfied, and now they will leave."

Darger led the group back to the front room, closing the door firmly behind him. "Now," he said. "You have learned what you came to learn. At the cost, I might mention, of violently depriving an innocent maiden of her modesty."

"That is a swinish thing to say!" Pirate Lafitte snapped.

In the silence that followed his outburst, all could hear Tawny Petticoats in the next room, sobbing her heart out.

"Your work here is done," Darger said, "and I must ask you to leave."

NOW THAT TAWNY Petticoats was no longer a secret, there was nothing for the three conspirators to do but wait for the equipment they had supposedly sent for upriver – and for their marks to each separately approach them with very large bribes to buy their process and the crates of black paper away from them. As simple logic stipulated that they inevitably must.

The very next day, after the morning mail had brought two notes proposing meetings, the trio went out for breakfast at a sidewalk café. They had just finished and were beginning their second cups of coffee when Tawny looked over Darger's shoulder and exclaimed, "Oh, merciful God in heaven! It's Jake." Then, seeing her companions' incomprehension, "My husband! He's talking to Pirate Lafitte. They're coming this way."

"Keep smiling," Darger murmured. "Feign unconcern. Surplus, you know what to do."

It took a count of ten for the interlopers to reach their table.

"Jake!" Surplus exclaimed in evident surprise, beginning to rise from his chair.

"Come for his pay, no doubt." Darger drew from his pocket the wad of bills – one of large denomination on the outside, a great many singles beneath – which any sensible businessman carried with him at all times and, turning, said, "The madam-mayor wishes you to know –"

He found himself confronted by a stranger who could only be Tawny's Jake and Pirate Lafitte, whose face was contorted with astonishment.

Darger hastily thrust the wad of bills back into his pocket. "Wishes you to know," he repeated, "that, ah, anytime you wish to try out her establishment, she will gladly offer you a ten percent discount on all goods and services, alcohol excepted. It is a courtesy she has newly decided to extend, out of respect for your employer, to all his new hires."

Lafitte turned, grabbed Jake by the shirtfront, and shook him as a mastiff might a rat. "I understand now," he said through gritted teeth. "The honorable brothel-keeper wished to deal me out of a rich opportunity, and so she sent you to me with a cock-and-bull story about this virtuous and inoffensive young woman."

"Honest, boss, I ain't got the slightest idea what this... this... foreigner is talking about. It's honest info I'm peddling here. I heard it on the street that my filthy bitch of a –"

With a roar of rage, Pirate Lafitte punched Jake so hard he fell sprawling in the street. Then he pulled the whip from his belt and proceeded to lay into the man so savagely that by the time he was done, his shirt and vest were damp with sweat.

Breathing heavily from exertion, he touched his hat to Darger and Surplus. "Sirs. We shall talk later, at a time when my passions are not so excited. This afternoon, five o'clock, at my office. I have a proposition to put to you." Then, to Tawny, "Miss Petticoats, I apologize that you had to see this."

He strode off.

"Oh!" Tawny breathed. "He beat Jake within an inch of his worthless life. It was the most romantic thing I ever seen in my life."

"A horsewhipping? Romantic?" Darger said.

Tawny favored him with a superior look. "You don't much understand the workings of a woman's heart, do you?"

"Apparently not," Darger said. "And it begins to appear that I never shall." Out in the street, Jake was painfully pulling himself up and trying to stand. "Excuse me."

Darger went over to the battered and bleeding man and helped him to his feet. Then, talking quietly, he opened his billfold and thrust several notes into the man's hand.

"What did you give him?" Tawny asked, when he was back inside.

"A stern warning not to interfere with us again. Also, seventeen dollars. A sum insulting enough to guarantee that, despite his injuries, he will take his increasingly-implausible story to Master Bones, and then to the Madam-Mayor."

Tawny grabbed Darger and Surplus and hugged them both at once. "Oh, you boys are so good to me. I just love you both to pieces and back."

"It begins to look, however," Surplus said, "like we have been stood up. According to Madam-Mayor Tresjolie's note, she should have been here by now. Which is, if I may use such language, damnably peculiar."

"Something must have come up." Darger squinted up at the sky. "Tresjolie isn't here and it's about time for the meeting with Master Bones. You should stay here, in case the madam-mayor shows up. I'll see what the zombie master has to say.

"And I," Tawny said, "will go back to my room to adjust my dress."

"Adjust?" Surplus asked.

"It needs to be a little tighter and to show just a smidge more bosom."

Alarmed, Darger said, "Your character is a modest and innocent thing."

"She is a modest and innocent thing who secretly wishes a worldly cad would teach her all those wicked deeds she has heard about but cannot quite imagine. I have played this role before, gentlemen. Trust me, it is not innocence *per se* that men like Pirate Lafitte are drawn to but the tantalizing possibility of corrupting that innocence."

Then she was gone.

"A most remarkable young lady, our Ms. Petticoats," Surplus said.

Darger scowled.

AFTER DARGER LEFT, Surplus leaned back in his chair for some casual people watching. He had not been at it long when he noticed that a remarkably pretty woman at a table at the far end of the café kept glancing his way. When he returned her gaze, she blushed and looked quickly away.

From long experience, Surplus understood what such looks meant. Leaving money on the table to pay for the breakfasts, he strolled over to introduce himself to the lady. She seemed not unreceptive to his attentions, and after a remarkably short conversation, invited him to her room in a nearby hotel. Feigning surprise, Surplus accepted.

What happened there had occurred many times before in his eventful life. But that didn't make it any less delightful.

On leaving the hotel, however, Surplus was alarmed to find himself abruptly seized and firmly held by two red-furred, seven-foot-tall uniformed Canadian ape-men.

"I see you have been entertaining yourself with one of the local sluts," Madam-Mayor Tresjolie said. She looked even less benevolent than usual.

"That is a harsh characterization of a lady who, for all I know, may be of high moral character. Also, I must ask you why I am being held captive like this."

"In due time. First, tell me whether your encounter was a commercial one or not."

"I thought not when we were in the throes of it. But afterward, she showed me her union card and informed me that as a matter of policy she was required to charge not only by the hour but by the position. I was, of course, astonished."

"What did you do then?"

"I paid, of course," Surplus said indignantly. "I am no scab!"

"The woman with whom you coupled, however, was not a registered member of the International Sisterhood of Trollops, Demimondaines, and Back-Alley Doxies and her card was a forgery. Which means that while nobody objects to your non-commercial sexual activities, by paying her you were engaged in a union-busting activity – and *that*, sir, is against the law."

"Obviously, you set me up. Otherwise, you could have known none of this."

"That is neither here nor there. What is relevant is that you have three things that I want – the girl with the birthmark, the crates of money, and the knowledge of how to use the one to render the other negotiable."

"I understand now. Doubtless, madam, you seek to bribe me. I assure you that no amount of money –"

"Money?" The madam-mayor's laugh was short and harsh. "I am offering you something far more precious: your conscious mind." She produced a hypodermic needle. "People think the zombification formula consists entirely of extract of puffer fish. But in fact atropine, datura, and a dozen other drugs are involved, all blended in a manner guaranteed to make the experience very unpleasant indeed."

"Threats will not work on me."

"Not yet. But after you've had a taste of what otherwise lies before you, I'm sure you'll come around. In a week or so, I'll haul you back from the fields. Then we can negotiate."

Madam-Mayor Tresjolie's simian thugs held Surplus firmly, struggle though he did. She raised the syringe to his neck. There was a sharp sting.

The world went away.

*   *   *

DARGER, MEANWHILE, HAD rented a megatherium, complete with howdah and zombie mahout, and ridden it to the endless rows of zombie barns, pens, and feeding sheds at the edge of town. There, Master Bones showed him the chest-high troughs that were filled with swill every morning and evening, and the rows of tin spoons the sad creatures used to feed themselves. "When each of my pretties has fed, the spoon is set aside to be washed and sterilized before it is used again," Master Bones said. "Every precaution is taken to ensure they do not pass diseases from one to another."

"Commendably humane, sir. To say nothing of it being good business practice."

"You understand me well." They passed outside, where a pair of zombies, one male and the other female, both in exceptional condition and perfectly matched in height and color of hair and skin, waited with umbrellas. As they strolled to the pens, the two walked a pace behind them, shading them from the sun. "Tell me, Mr. Darger. What do you suppose the ratio of zombies to citizens is in New Orleans?"

Darger considered. "About even?"

"There are six zombies for every fully-functioning human in the city. It seems a smaller number since most are employed as field hands and the like and so are rarely seen in the streets. But I could flood the city with them, should I wish."

"Why on earth should you?"

Rather than answer the question, Master Bones said, "You have something I want."

"I fancy I know what it is. But I assure you that no amount of money could buy from me what is by definition a greater amount of money. So we have nothing to discuss."

"Oh, I believe that we do." Master Bones indicated the nearest of the pens, in which stood a bull of prodigious size and obvious strength. It was darkly colored with pale laddering along its spine, and its horns were long and sharp. "This is a Eurasian aurochs, the ancestor of our modern domestic cattle. It went extinct in seventeenth century Poland and was resurrected less than a hundred years ago. Because of its ferocity, it is impractical as a meat animal, but I keep a small breeding herd for export to the Republic of Baja and other Mexican states where bullfighting remains popular. Bastardo here is a particularly bellicose example of his kind.

"Now consider the contents of the adjoining pen." The pen was over-crammed with zombie laborers and reeked to high heaven. The zombies stood motionless, staring at nothing. "They don't look very strong, do they? Individually they're not. But there is strength in numbers." Going to the fence, Master Bones slapped a zombie on the shoulder and said, "Open the gate between your pen and the next."

Then, when the gate was opened, Master Bones made his hands into a megaphone and shouted, "Everyone! Kill the aurochs. Now."

With neither enthusiasm nor reluctance, the human contents of one pen flowed into the next, converging upon the great beast. With an angry bellow, Bastardo trampled several under its hooves. The others kept coming. His head dipped to impale a body on its horns, then rose to fling a slash of red and a freshly-made corpse in the air. Still the zombies kept coming.

That strong head fell and rose, again and again. More bodies flew. But now there were zombies clinging to the bull's back and flanks and legs, hindering its movements. A note of fear entered the beast's great voice. By now, there were bodies heaped on top of bodies on top of his, enough that his legs buckled under their weight. Fists hammered at his sides and hands wrenched at his horns. He struggled upward, almost rose, and then fell beneath the crushing sea of bodies.

Master Bones began giggling when the aurochs went down for the first time. His mirth grew greater and his eyes filled with tears of laughter and once or twice he snorted, so tremendous was his amusement at the spectacle.

A high-pitched squeal of pain went up from the aurochs... and then all was silence, save for the sound of fists pounding upon the beast's carcass.

Wiping his tears away on his sleeve, Master Bones raised his voice again: "Very good. Well done. Thank you. Stop. Return to your pen. Yes, that's right." He turned his back on the bloodied carcass and the several bodies of zombies that lay motionless on the dirt, and said to Darger, "I believe in being direct. Give me the money and the girl by this time tomorrow or you and your partner will be as extinct as the aurochs ever was. There is no power as terrifying as that of a mob – and I control the greatest mob there ever was."

"Sir!" Darger said. "The necessary equipment has not yet arrived from the Socialist Utopia of Minneapolis! There is no way I can..."

"Then I'll give you four days to think it over. " A leering smile split the zombie master's pasty face. "While you're deciding, I will leave you with these two zombies to use as you wish. They will do anything you tell them to. They are capable of following quite complex orders, though they do not consciously understand them." To the zombies, he said, "You have heard this man's voice. Obey him. But if he tries to leave New Orleans, kill him. Will you do that?"

"If he leaves... kill... him."

"Yasss."

SOMETHING WAS WRONG.

Something was wrong, but Surplus could not put his finger on exactly what it was. He couldn't concentrate. His thoughts were all in jumble and he could not find words with which to order them. It was as if he had forgotten how to think. Meanwhile, his body moved without him particularly willing it to do so. It did not occur to him that it should behave otherwise. Still, he knew that something was wrong.

The sun set, the sun rose. It made no difference to him.

His body labored systematically, cutting sugar cane with a machete. This work it performed without his involvement, steadily and continuously. Blisters arose on the pads of his paws, swelled, and popped. He did not care. Someone had told him to work and so he had and so he would until the time came to stop. All the world was a fog to him, but his arms knew to swing and his legs to carry him forward to the next plant.

Nevertheless, the sensation of wrongness endured. Surplus felt stunned, the way an ox which had just been pole-axed might feel, or the sole survivor of some overwhelming catastrophe. Something terrible had happened and it was imperative that he do something about it.

If only he knew what.

A trumpet sounded in the distance and without fuss all about him the other laborers ceased their work. As did he. Without hurry he joined their chill company in the slow trek back to the feeding sheds.

Perhaps he slept, perhaps he did not. Morning came and Surplus was jostled to the feeding trough where he swallowed ten spoonsful of swill, as a zombie overseer directed him. Along with many others, he was given a machete and walked to the fields. There he was put to work again.

Hours passed.

There was a clop-clopping of hooves and the creaking of wagon wheels, and a buckboard drawn by a brace of pygmy mastodons pulled up alongside Surplus. He kept working. Somebody leaped down from the wagon and wrested the machete from his hand. "Open your mouth," a voice said.

He had been told by... somebody... not to obey the orders of any strangers. But this voice sounded familiar, though he could not have said why. Slowly his mouth opened. Something was placed within it. "Now shut and swallow."

His mouth did so.

His vision swam and he almost fell. Deep, deep within his mind, a spark of light blossomed. It was a glowing ember amid the ashes of a dead fire. But it grew and brightened, larger and more, until it felt like the sun rising within him. The external world came into focus, and with it the awareness that he, Surplus, had an identity distinct from the rest of existence. He realized first that his throat itched and the inside of his mouth was as parched and dry as the Sahara. Then that somebody he knew stood before him. Finally, that this person was his friend and colleague Aubrey Darger.

"How long have I...?" Surplus could not bring himself to complete the sentence.

"More than one day. Less than two. When you failed to return to our hotel, Tawny and I were naturally alarmed and set out in search of you. New Orleans being a city prone to gossip, and there being only one anthropomorphized dog in town, the cause of your disappearance was easily determined. But learning that you had been sent to labor in the sugar cane fields did not narrow the search greatly for there are literally hundreds of square miles of fields. Luckily, Tawny knew where such blue-collar laborers as would have heard of the appearance of a dog-headed zombie congregated, and from them we learned at last of your whereabouts."

"I... see." Focusing his thoughts on practical matters, Surplus said, "Madam-Mayor Tresjolie, as you may have surmised, had no intention of buying our crates of black paper from us. What of our other marks?"

"The interview with the Pirate Lafitte went well. Tawny played him like a trout. That with Master Bones was considerably less successful. However, we talked Lafitte up to a price high enough to bankrupt him and make all three of us wealthy. Tawny is accompanying him to the bank right now, to make certain he doesn't come to his senses at the last minute. He is quite besotted with her and in her presence cannot seem to think straight."

"You sound less disapproving of the girl than you were."

Twisting his mouth in the near grimace he habitually assumed when forced to admit to having made a misjudgment, Darger said, "Tawny grows on one, I find. She makes a splendid addition to the team."

"That's good," Surplus said. Now at last he noticed that in the back of the buckboard two zombies sat motionless atop a pile of sacks. "What's all that you have in the wagon?"

"Salt. A great deal of it."

IN THE FINAL feeding shed, Surplus kicked over the trough, spilling swill on the ground. Then, at his command, Darger's zombies righted the trough and filled it with salt. Darger, meanwhile, took a can of paint and drew a rough map of New Orleans on the wall. He drew three arrows to Madam-Mayor Tresjolie's brothel, Jean-Nagel Lafitte's waterfront office, and the club where Master Jeremy Bones presided every evening. Finally, he wrote block letter captions for each arrow:

THE MAN WHO TRANSPORTED YOU HERE.

THE WOMAN WHO PUT YOU HERE.

THE MAN WHO KEPT YOU HERE.

Above it all, he wrote the day's date.

"There," Darger said when he was done. Turning to his zombies, he said, "You were told to do as I commanded."

"Yass," the male said lifelessly.

"We must," the female said, "oh bey."

"Here is a feeding spoon for both of you. When the zombie laborers return to the barn, you are to feed each of them a spoonful of salt. Salt. Here in the trough. Take a spoonful of salt. Tell them to open their mouths. Put in the salt. Then tell them to swallow. Can you do that?"

"Yass."

"Salt. Swall oh."

"When everyone else is fed," Surplus said, "be sure to take a spoonful of salt yourselves – each of you."

"Salt."

"Yass."

Soon, the zombies would come to feed and discover salt in their mouths instead of swill. Miraculously, their minds would uncloud. In shed after shed, they would read what Darger had written. Those who had spent years and even decades longer than they were sentenced to would feel justifiably outraged. After which, they could be expected to collectively take appropriate action.

"The sun is setting," Darger said. In the distance, he could see zombies plodding in from the fields. "We have just enough time to get back to our rooms and accept Pirate Lafitte's bribe before the rioting begins."

BUT WHEN THEY got back to Maison Fema, their suite was lightless and Tawny Petticoats was nowhere to be seen. Nor was Pirate Lafitte.

The crates of black paper, having served their purpose, had not been restacked in front of Tawny's bedroom door. Hastily lighting an oil lamp, Darger threw open the door. In the middle of her carefully-made bed was a note. He picked it up and read it out loud:

DEAR BOYS,

   I know you do not beleive in love at first site because you are both Synics. But Jean-Nagin and I are Kindred Spirits and meant to be together. I told him so Bold a man as he should not be in Trade, esp. as he has his own ships banks and docks and he agrees. So he is to be a Pirate in fact as well as name and I am his Pirate Queen.

   I am sorry about the Black Mony scam but a girl can't start a new life by cheating her Hubby that is no way to be.

   Love,

   Tawny Petticoats

   P.S. You boys are both so much fun.

*   *   *

"TELL ME," DARGER said after a long silence. "Did Tawny sleep with you?"

Surplus looked startled. Then he placed paw upon chest and forthrightly, though without quite looking Darger in the eye, said, "Upon my word, she did not. You don't mean that she –?"

"No. No, of course not."

There was another awkward silence.

"Well, then," Darger said. "Much as I predicted, we are left with nothing for all our labors."

"You forget the silver ingots," Surplus said.

"It is hardly worth bothering to . . ."

But Surplus was already on his knees, groping in the shadows beneath Tawny's bed. He pulled out three leather cases and from them extracted three ingots.

"Those are obviously..."

Whipping out his pocket knife, Surplus scratched each ingot, one after the other. The first was merely plated lead. The other two were solid silver. Darger explosively let out his breath in relief.

"A toast!" Surplus cried, rising to his feet. "To women, God bless 'em. Constant, faithful, and unfailingly honest! Paragons, sir, of virtue in every respect."

In the distance could be heard the sound of a window breaking. "I'll drink to that," Darger replied. "But just a sip and then we really must flee. We have, I suspect, a conflagration to avoid."

THE FIFTH DRAGON

Ian McDonald

Ian McDonald (ianmcdonald.livejournal.com) lives in Northern Ireland, just outside Belfast. He sold his first story in 1983 and bought a guitar with the proceeds, perhaps the only rock'n'roll thing he ever did. Since then he's written sixteen novels, including *River of Gods, Brasyl,* and *The Dervish House,* three story collections and diverse other pieces, and has been nominated for every major science fiction/ fantasy award – and even won a couple. His current novel is *Empress of the Sun,* third book in the young adult SF *Everness* series. Upcoming is new adult SF novel, *Luna* and a collection, *The Best of Ian McDonald.*

THE SCAN WAS ROUTINE. Every moon worker has one every four lunes. Achi was called, she went into the scanner. The machine passed magnetic fields through her body and when she came out the medic said, you have four weeks left.

WE MET ON the Vorontsov Trans-Orbital cycler but didn't have sex. We talked instead about names.

"Corta. That's not a Brazilian name," Achi said. I didn't know her well enough then, eight hours out from transfer orbit, to be my truculent self and insist that any name can be a Brazilian name, that we are a true rainbow nation. So I told her that my name had rolled through many peoples and languages like a bottle in a breaker until it was cast up sand-scoured and clouded on the beaches of Barra. And now I was taking it on again, up to the moon.

Achi Debasso. Another name rolled by tide of history. London born, London raised, M.I.T. educated but she never forgot – had never been let forget – that she was Syrian. Syria*c*. That one letter was a universe of difference. Her family had fled the civil war, she had been born in exile. Now she was headed into a deeper exile.

I didn't mean to be in the centrifuge pod with Achi. There was a guy; he'd looked and I looked back and nodded *yes, I will, yes* even as the OTV made its distancing burn from the cycler. I took it. I'm no prude. I've got the New Year Barra beach bangles. I'm up for a party and more, and everyone's heard about (here they move in close and mouth the words) *freefall sex*. I wanted to try it with this guy. And I couldn't stop throwing up. I was not up for zero gee. It turned everything inside me upside down. Puke poured out of me. That's not sexy. So I retreated to gravity and the only other person in the centrifuge arm was this caramel-eyed girl, slender hands and long fingers, her face flickering every few moments into an unconscious micro-frown. Inward-gazing, self-loathing, scattering geek references like anti-personnel mines. Up in the hub our co-workers fucked. Down in the centrifuge pod we talked and the stars and the moon arced across the window beneath our feet.

A Brazilian miner and a London-Syriac ecologist. The centrifuge filled as freefall sex palled but we kept talking. The next day the guy I had puked over caught my eye again but I sought out Achi, on her own in the same spot, looking out at the moon. And the whirling moon was a little bigger in the observation port and we knew each other a little better and by the end of the week the moon filled the whole of the window and we had moved from conversationalists into friends.

ACHI: LEFT DAMASCUS as a cluster of cells tumbling in her mother's womb. And that informed her every breath and touch. She felt guilty for escaping. Father was a software engineer, mother was a physiotherapist. London welcomed them.

Adriana: seven of us: seven Cortas. Little cuts. I was in the middle, loved and adored but told solemnly I was plain and thick in the thighs and would have be thankful for whatever life granted me.

Achi: a water girl. Her family home was near the Olympic pool – her mother had dropped her into water days out of the hospital. She had sunk, then she swam. Swimmer and surfer: long British summer evenings on the western beaches. Cold British water. She was small and quiet but feared no wave.

Adriana: born with the sound of the sea in her room but never learned to swim. I splash, I paddle, I wade. I come from beach people, not ocean people.

Achi: the atoner. She could not change the place or order of her birth, but she could apologise for it by being useful. Useful Achi. Make things right!

Adriana: the plain. Mãe and papai thought they were doing me a favour; allowing me no illusions or false hopes that could blight my life. Marry as well as you can; be happy: that will have to do. Not this Corta. I was the kid who shot her hand up at school. The girl who wouldn't shut up when the boys were talking. Who never got picked for the futsal team – okay, I would find my own sport. I did Brasilian jujitsu. Sport for one. No one messed with plain Adriana.

Achi: grad at UCL, post-grad at M.I.T. Her need to be useful took her battling desertification, salinisation, eutrophication. She was an -ation warrior. In the end it took her to the moon. No way to be more useful than sheltering and feeding a whole world.

Adriana: university at São Paulo. And my salvation. Where I learned that plain didn't matter as much as available, and I was sweet for sex with boys and girls. Fuckfriends. Sweet girls don't have fuckfriends. And sweet girls don't study mining engineering. Like jujitsu, like hooking up, that was a thing for me, me alone. Then the economy gave one final, apocalyptic crash at the bottom of a series of drops and hit the ground and broke so badly no one could see how to fix it. And the seaside, be-happy Cortas were in ruins, jobless, investments in ashes. It was plain Adriana who said, I can save you. I'll go to the Moon.

All this we knew by the seventh day of the orbit out. On the eight day, we rendezvoused with the transfer tether and spun down to the new world.

The freefall sex? Grossly oversold. Everything moves in all the wrong ways. Things get away from you. You have to strap everything down to get purchase. It's more like mutual bondage.

*   *   *

I WAS SINTERING ten kilometres ahead of Crucible when Achi's call came. I had requested the transfer from Mackenzie Metals to Vorontsov Rail. The forewoman had been puzzled when I reported to Railhead. You're a dustbunny not a track-queen. Surface work is surface work, I said and that convinced her. The work was good, easy and physical and satisfying. And it was on the surface. At the end of every up-shift you saw six new lengths of gleaming rail among the boot and track prints, and on the edge of the horizon, the blinding spark of Crucible, brighter than any star, advancing over yesterday's rails, and you said, I made that. The work had real measure: the inexorable advance of Mackenzie Metals across the Mare Insularum, brighter than the brightest star. Brighter than sunrise, so bright it could burn a hole through your helmet sunscreen if you held it in your eye line too long. Thousands of concave mirrors focusing sunlight on the smelting crucibles. Three years from now the rail lines would circle the globe and the Crucible would follow the sun, bathed in perpetual noon. Me, building a railroad around the moon.

Then ting ching and it all came apart. Achi's voice blocking out my work-mix music, Achi's face superimposed on the dirty grey hills of Rimae Maestlin. Achi telling me her routine medical had given her four weeks.

I hitched a ride on the construction car back down the rails to Crucible. I waited two hours hunkered down in the hard-vacuum shadows, tons of molten metal and ten thousand Kelvin sunlight above my head, for an expensive ticket on a slow Mackenzie ore train to Meridian. Ten hours clinging onto a maintenance platform, not even room to turn around, let alone sit. Grey dust, black sky... I listened my way through my collection of historical bossanova, from the 1940s to the 1970s. I played Connecto on my helmet hud until every time I blinked I saw tumbling, spinning gold stars. I scanned my family's social space entries and threw my thoughts and comments and good wishes at the big blue Earth. By the time I got to Meridian I was two degrees off hypothermic. My surface activity suit was rated for a shift and some scramble time, not twelve hours in the open. Should have claimed compensation. But I didn't want my former employers paying too much attention to me. I couldn't afford the time it would take to re-pressurise for the train, so I went dirty and fast, on the BALTRAN.

I knew I would vomit. I held it until the third and final jump. BALTRAN: Ballistic Transport system. The moon has no atmosphere – well, it does, a very thin one, which is getting thicker as human settlements leak air into it. Maybe in a few centuries this will become a problem for vacuum industries, but to all intents and purposes, it's a vacuum. See what I did there? That's the engineer in me. No atmosphere means ballistic trajectories can be calculated with great precision. Which means, throw something up and you know exactly where it will fall to moon again. Bring in positionable electromagnetic launchers and you have a mechanism for schlepping material quick and dirty around the moon. Launch it, catch it in a receiver, boost it on again. It's like juggling. The BALTRAN is not always used for cargo. If you can take the gees it can as easily juggle people across the moon.

I held it until the final jump. You cannot imagine what it is like to throw up in your helmet. In free fall. People have died. The look on the BALTRAN attendant's face when I came out of the capsule at Queen of the South was a thing to be seen. So I am told. I couldn't see it. But if I could afford the capsule I could afford the shower to clean up. And there are people in Queen who will happily clean vomit out of a sasuit for the right number of bitsies. Say what you like about the Vorontsovs, they pay handsomely.

All this I did, the endless hours riding the train like a moon-hobo, the hypothermia and being sling-shotted in a can of my own barf, because I knew that if Achi had four weeks, I could not be far behind.

YOU DON'T THINK about the bones. As a Jo Moonbeam, everything is so new and demanding, from working out how to stand and walk, to those four little digits in the bottom right corner of your field of vision that tell you how much you owe the Lunar Development Corporation for air, water, space and web. The first time you see those numbers change because demand or supply or market price has shifted, your breath catches in your throat. Nothing tells you that you are not on Earth any more than exhaling at one price and inhaling at another. Everything – *everything* – was new and hard.

Everything other than your bones. After two years on the moon human bone structure atrophies to a point where return to Earth gravity is almost certainly fatal. The medics drop it almost incidentally into your initial assessment. It can take days – weeks – for its ripples to touch your life. Then you feel your bones crumbling away, flake by flake, inside your body. And there's not a thing you can do about it. What it means is that there is a calcium clock ticking inside your body, counting down to Moon Day. The day you decide: do I stay or do I go?

In those early days we were scared all the time, Achi and I. I looked after her – I don't know how we fell into those roles, protector and defended, but I protected and she nurtured and we won respect. There were three moon men for every moon woman. It was a man's world; a macho social meld of soldiers camped in enemy terrain and deep-diving submariners. The Jo Moonbeam barracks were exactly that; a grey, dusty warehouse of temporary accommodation cabins barely the safe legal minimum beneath the surface. We learned quickly the vertical hierarchy of moon society: the lower you live – the further from surface radiation and secondary cosmic rays – the higher your status. The air was chilly and stank of sewage, electricity, dust and unwashed bodies. The air still smells like that; I just got used to the funk in my lungs. Within hours the induction barracks self-sorted. The women gravitated together and affiliated with the astronomers on placement with the Farside observatory. Achi and I traded to get cabins beside each other. We visited, we decorated, we entertained, we opened our doors in solidarity and hospitality. We listened to the loud voices of the men, the real men, the worldbreakers, booming down the aisles of cabins, the over-loud laughter. We made cocktails from cheap industrial vodka.

Sexual violence, games of power were in the air we breathed, the water we drank, the narrow corridors through which we squeezed, pressing up against each other. The moon has never had criminal law, only contract law, and when Achi and I arrived the LDC was only beginning to set up the Court of Clavius to settle and enforce contracts. Queen of the South was a wild town. Fatalities among Jo Moonbeams ran at ten percent. In our first week, an extraction worker from Xinjiang was crushed in a pressure lock. The Moon knows a thousand ways to kill you. And I knew a thousand and one.

Cortas cut. That was our family legend. Hard sharp fast. I made the women's Brazilian jujitsu team at university. It's hard, sharp, fast: the perfect Corta fighting art. A couple of basic moves, together with lunar gravity, allowed me to put over the most intimidating of sex pests. But when Achi's stalker wouldn't take no, I reached for slower, subtler weapons. Stalkers don't go away. That's what makes them stalkers. I found which Surface Activity training squad he was on and made some adjustments to his suit thermostat. He didn't die. He wasn't meant to die. Death would have been easier than my revenge for Achi. He never suspected me; he never suspected anyone. I made it look like a perfect malfunction. I'm a good engineer. I count his frostbite thumb and three toes as my trophies. By the time he got out of the med centre, Achi and I were on our separate ways to our contracts.

That was another clock, ticking louder than the clock in our bones. I&A was four weeks. After that, we would go to work. Achi's work in ecological habitats would take her to the underground agraria the Asamoah family were digging under Amundsen. My contract was with Mackenzie Metals; working out on the open seas. Working with dust. Dustbunny. We clung to the I&A barracks, we clung to our cabins, our friends. We clung to each other. We were scared. Truth: we were scared all the time, with every breath. Everyone on the moon is scared, all the time.

There was a party; moon mojitos. Vodka and mint are easy up here. But before the music and the drinking: a special gift for Achi. Her work with Aka would keep her underground; digging and scooping and sowing. She need never go on the surface. She could go her whole career – her whole life – in the caverns and lava tubes and agraria. She need never see the raw sky.

The suit hire was cosmologically expensive, even after negotiation. It was a GP surface activity shell; an armoured hulk to my lithe sasuit spiderwoman. Her face was nervous behind the faceplate; her breathing shallow. We held hands in the outlock as the pressure door slid up. Then her faceplate polarised in the sun and I could not see her any more. We walked up the ramp amongst a hundred thousand boot prints. We walked up the ramp and few metres out on to the surface, still holding hands. There, beyond the coms towers and the power relays and the charging points for the buses and rovers; beyond the grey line of the crater rim that curved on the close horizon and the shadows the sun had never touched; there perched above the edge of our tiny world we saw the full earth. Full and blue and white, mottled with greens and ochres. Full and impossible and beautiful beyond any words of mine. It was winter and the southern hemisphere was offered to us; the ocean half of the planet. I saw great Africa. I saw dear Brazil.

Then the air contract advisory warned me that we were nearing the expiry of our oxygen contract and we turned out backs on the blue earth and walked back down into the moon.

That night we drank to our jobs, our friends, our loves and our bones. In the morning we parted.

WE MET IN a café on the twelfth level of the new Chandra Quadra. We hugged, we kissed, we cried a little. I smelled sweet by then. Below us excavators dug and sculpted, a new level every ten days. We held each other at arms' length and looked at each other. Then we drank mint tea on the balcony.

I loathe mint tea.

Mint tea is a fistful of herbs jammed in a glass. Sloshed with boiling water. Served scalded yet still flavourless. Effete like herbal thés and tisanes. Held between thumb and forefinger: so. Mint leaves are coarse and hairy. Mint tea is medicinal. Add sugar and it becomes infantile. It is drinking for the sake of doing something with your fingers.

Coffee is a drink for grownups. No kid ever likes coffee. It's psychoactive. Coffee is the drug of memory. I can remember the great cups of coffee of my life; the places, the faces, the words spoken. It never quite tastes the way it smells. If it did, we would – drink it until out heads exploded with memory,

But coffee is not an efficient crop in our ecology. And imported coffee is more expensive than gold. Gold is easy. Gold I can sift from lunar regolith. Gold is so easy its only value is decorative. It isn't even worth the cost of shipment to Earth. Mint is rampant. Under lunar gravity, it forms plants up to three metres tall. So we are a nation of mint tea drinkers.

We didn't talk about the bones at once. It was eight lunes since we last saw each other: we talk on the network daily, we share our lives but it takes face to face contact to ground all that; make it real.

I made Achi laugh. She laughed like soft rain. I told her about King Dong and she clapped her hands to her mouth in naughty glee but laughed with her eyes. King Dong started as a joke but shift by shift was becoming reality. Footprints last forever on the moon, a bored surface worker had said on a slow shift rotation back to Crucible. What if we stamped out a giant spunking cock, a hundred kilometres long? With hairy balls. Visible from Earth. It's just a matter of co-ordination. Take a hundred male surface workers and an Australian extraction company and joke becomes temptation becomes reality. So wrong. So funny.

And Achi?

She was out of contract. The closer you are to your Moon Day, the shorter the contract, sometimes down to minutes of employment, but this was different. Aka did not want her ideas any more. They were recruiting direct from Accra and Kumasi. Ghanaians for a Ghanaian company. She was pitching ideas to the Lunar Development Corporation for their new port and capital at Meridian – quadras three kilometres deep; a sculpted city; like living in the walls of a titanic cathedral. The LDC was polite but it had been talking about development funding for two lunes now. Her savings were running low. She woke up looking at the tick of the Four Fundamentals on her lens. Oxygen water space coms: which do you cut down on first? She was considering moving to a smaller space.

"I can pay your per diems," I said. "I have lots of money."

And then the bones... Achi could not decide until I got my report. I never knew anyone suffered from guilt as acutely as her. She could not have borne it if her decision had influenced my decision to stay with the moon or go back to Earth,

"I'll go now," I said. I didn't want to. I didn't want to be here on this balcony drinking piss-tea. I didn't want Achi to have forced a decision on me. I didn't want there to be a decision for me to make. "I'll get the tea."

Then the wonder. In the corner of my vision, a flash of gold. A lens malfunction – no, something marvellous. A woman flying. A flying woman. Her arms were outspread, she hung in the sky it like a crucifix. Our Lady of Flight. Then I saw wings shimmer and run with rainbow colours; wings transparent and strong as a dragonfly's. The woman hung a moment, then folded her gossamer wings around her, and fell. She tumbled, now diving heard-first, flicked her wrists, flexed her shoulders. A glimmer of wing slowed her; then she spread her full wing span and pulled up out of her dive into a soaring spiral, high into the artificial sky of Chandra Quadra.

"Oh," I said. I had been holding my breath. I was shaking with wonder. I was chewed by jealousy.

"We always could fly" Achi said. "We just haven't had the space. Until now."

Did I hear irritation in Achi's voice, that I was so bewitched by the flying woman? But if you could fly why would you ever do anything else?

I WENT TO the Mackenzie Metals medical centre and the medic put me in the scanner. He passed magnetic fields through my body and the machine gave me my bone density analysis. I was eight days behind Achi. Five weeks, and then my residency on the moon would become citizenship.

Or I could fly back to Earth, to Brazil.

THERE ARE FRIENDS and there are friends you have sex with.

After I&A it was six lunes until I saw Achi again. Six lunes in the Sea of Fertility, sifting dust. The Mackenzie Metals Messier unit was old, cramped, creaking: cut-and-cover pods under bulldozed regolith berms. Too frequently I was evacuated to the new, lower levels by the radiation alarm. Cosmic rays kicked nasty secondary particles out of moon dust, energetic enough to penetrate the upper levels of the unit. Every time I saw the alarm flash its yellow trefoil in my lens I felt my ovaries tighten. Day and night the tunnels trembled to the vibration of the digging machines, deep beneath even those evacuation tunnels, eating rock. There were two hundred dustbunnies in Messier. After a month's gentle and wary persistence and charm from a 3D print designer, I joined the end of a small amory: my Chu-yu, his homamor in Queen, his hetamor in Meridian, her hetamor also in Meridian. What had taken him so long, Chu-yu confessed, was my rep. Word about the sex pest on I&A with the unexplained suit malfunction. *I wouldn't do that to a co-worker,* I said. *Not unless severely provoked.* Then I kissed him. The amory was warmth and sex, but it wasn't Achi. Lovers are not friends

Sun Chu-yu understood that when I kissed him goodbye at Messier's bus lock. Achi and I chatted on the network all the way to the railhead at Hypatia, then all the way down the line to the South. Even then, only moments since I had last spoken to her image on my eyeball, it was a physical shock to see her at the meeting point in Queen of the South station: her, physical her. Shorter than I remembered. Absence makes the heart grow taller.

Such fun she had planned for me! I wanted to dump my stuff at her place but no; she whirled me off into excitement. After the reek and claustrophobia of Messier Queen of the South was intense, loud, colourful, too too fast. In only six lunes it had changed beyond recognition. Every street was longer, every tunnel wider, every chamber loftier. When she took me in a glass elevator down the side of the recently completed Thoth Quadra I reeled from vertigo. Down on the floor of the massive cavern was a small copse of dwarf trees – full-size trees would reach the ceiling, Achi explained. There was a café. In that café I first tasted and immediately hated mint tea.

I built this, Achi said. *These are my trees, this is my garden.*

I was too busy looking up at the lights, all the lights, going up and up.

Such fun! Tea, then shops. I had had to find a party dress. We were going to a special party, that night. Exclusive. We browsed the catalogues in five different print shops before I found something I could wear: very retro, 1950s inspired, full and layered, it hid what I wanted hidden. Then, the shoes.

The special party was exclusive to Achi's workgroup and their F&Fs'. A security-locked rail capsule took us through a dark tunnel into a space so huge, so blinding with mirrored light, that once again I reeled on my feet and almost threw up over my Balenciaga. An agrarium, Achi's last project. I was at the bottom of a shaft a kilometre tall, fifty metres wide. The horizon is close at eye level on the moon; everything curves. Underground, a different geometry applies. The agrarium was the straightest thing I had seen in months. And brilliant: a central core of mirrors ran the full height of the shaft, bouncing raw sunlight one to another to another to walls terraced with hydroponic racks. The base of the shaft was a mosaic of fish tanks, criss-crossed by walkways. The air was warm and dank and rank. I was woozy with CO_2. In these conditions plants grew fast and tall; potato plants the size of bushes; tomato vines so tall I lost their heads in the tangle of leaves and fruit. Hyper-intensive agriculture: the agrarium was huge for a cave, small for an ecosystem. The tanks splashed with fish. Did I hear frogs? Were those ducks?

Achi's team had built a new pond from waterproof sheeting and construction frame. A pool. A swimming pool. A sound system played G-pop. There were cocktails. Blue was the fashion. They matched my dress.

Achi's crew were friendly and expansive. They never failed to compliment me on my fashion. I shucked it and my shoes and everything else for the pool. I lolled, I luxuriated, I let the strange, chaotic eddies waft green, woozy air over me while over my head the mirrors moved. Achi swam up beside me and we trod water together, laughing and plashing. The agrarium crew had lowered a number of benches into the pool to make a shallow end. Achi and I wafted blood-warm water with our legs and drank Blue Moons.

I am always up for a party.

I woke up in bed beside her the next morning; shit-headed with moon vodka. I remembered mumbling, fumbling love. Shivering and stupid-whispering, skin to skin. Fingerworks. Achi lay curled on her right side, facing me. She had kicked the sheet off in the night. A tiny string of drool ran from the corner of her mouth to the pillow and trembled in time to her breathing.

I looked at her there, her breath rattling in the back of her throat in drunk sleep. We had made love. I had sex with my dearest friend. I had done a good thing, I had done a bad thing. I had done an irrevocable thing. Then I lay down and pressed myself in close to her and she mumble-grumbled and moved in close to me and her fingers found me and we began again.

I WOKE IN the dark with the golden woman swooping through my head. Achi slept beside me. The same side, the same curl of the spine, the same light rattle-snore and open mouth as that first night. When I saw Achi's new cabin, I booked us into a hostel. The bed was wide, the air was as fresh as Queen of the South could make and the taste of the water did not set your teeth on edge.

Golden woman, flying loops through my certainties.

Queen of the South never went fully dark – lunar society is 24-hour society. I pulled Achi's unneeded sheet around me and went out on to the balcony. I leaned on the rail and looked out at the walls of lights. Apts, cabins, walkways and staircases. Lives and decisions behind every light. This was an ugly world. Hard and mean. It put a price on everything. It demanded a negotiation from everyone. Out at Railhead I had seen a new thing among some of the surface workers: a medallion, or a little votive tucked into a patch pocket. A woman in Virgin Mary robes, one half of her face a black angel, the other half a naked skull. Dona Luna: goddess of dust and radiation. Our Lady Liberty, our Britannia, our Marianne, our Mother Russia. One half of her face dead, but the other alive. The moon was not a dead satellite, it was a living world. Hands and hearts and hopes like mine shaped it. There was no mother nature, no Gaia to set against human will. Everything that lived, we made. Dona Luna was hard and unforgiving, but she was beautiful. She could be a woman, with dragonfly wings, flying.

I stayed on the hotel balcony until the roof reddened with sun-up. Then I went back to Achi. I wanted to make love with her again. My motives were all selfish. Things that are difficult with friends are easier with lovers.

MY GRANDMOTHER USED to say that love was the easiest thing in the world. Love is what you see every day.

I did not see Achi for several lunes after the party in Queen. Mackenzie Metals sent me out into the field, prospecting new terrain in the Sea of Vapours. Away from Messier, it was plain to me and Sun Chu-yu that the amory didn't work. You love what you see every day. All the amors were happy for me to leave. No blame, no claim. A simple automated contract, terminated.

I took a couple of weeks furlough back in Queen. I had called Achi about hooking up but she was at a new dig at Twe, where the Asamoahs were building a corporate headquarters. I was relieved. And then was guilty that I had felt relieved. Sex had made everything different. I drank, I partied, I had one night stands, I talked long hours of expensive bandwidth my loved ones back on Earth. They thanked me for the money, especially the tiny kids. They said I looked different. Longer. Drawn out. My bones eroding, I said. There they were, happy and safe. The money I sent them bought their education. Health, weddings, babies. And here I was, on the moon. Plain Adriana, who would never get a man, but who got the education, who got the degree, who got the job, sending them the money from the moon.

They were right. I was different. I never felt the same about that blue pearl of Earth in the sky. I never again hired a sasuit to go look at it, just look at it. Out on the surface, I disregarded it.

The Mackenzies sent me out next to the Lansberg extraction zone and I saw the thing that made everything different.

Five extractors were working Lansberg. They were ugly towers of Archimedes screws and grids and transport belts and wheels three times my height, all topped out by a spread of solar panels that made them look like robot trees. Slow-moving, cumbersome, inelegant. Lunar design tends to the utilitarian, the practical. The bones on show. But to me they were beautiful. Marvellous trees. I saw them one day, out on the regolith, and I almost fell flat from the revelation. Not what they made – separating rare earth metals from lunar regolith – but what they threw away. Launched in high, arching ballistic jets on either side of the big, slow machines.

It was the thing I saw every day. One day you look at the boy on the bus and he sets your heart alight. One day you look at the jets of industrial waste and you see riches beyond measure.

I had to dissociate myself from anything that might link me to regolith waste and beautiful rainbows of dust.

I quit Mackenzie and became a Vorontsov track queen.

I WANT TO make a game of it, Achi said. That's the only way I can bear it. We must clench our fists behind our backs, like Scissors Paper Stone, and we must count to three, and then we open our fists and in them there will be something, some small object, that will say beyond any doubt what we have decided. We must not speak, because if we say even a word, we will influence each other. That's the only way I can bear it if it is quick and clean and we don't speak. And a game.

We went back to the balcony table of the café to play the game. It was now on the 13th level. Two glasses of mint tea. No one was flying the great empty spaces of Chandra Quadra this day. The air smelled of rock dust over the usual electricity and sewage. Every fifth sky panel was blinking. An imperfect world.

Attempted small talk. Do you want some breakfast? No, but you have some. No I'm not hungry. I haven't seen that top before. The colour is really good for you. Oh it's just something I printed out of a catalogue... Horrible awful little words to stop us saying what we really had to say.

"I think we should do this kind of quickly," Achi said finally and in a breathtaking instant her right hand was behind her back. I slipped my small object out of my bag, clenched it in my hidden fist.

"One two three," Achi said. We opened our fists.

A *nazar*: an Arabic charm: concentric teardrops of blue, white and black plastic. An eye.

A tiny icon of Dona Luna: black and white, living and dead.

THEN I SAW Achi again. I was up in Meridian renting a data crypt and hunting for the leanest, freshest, hungriest law firm to protect the thing I had realised out on Lansberg. She had been called back from Twe to solve a problem with microbiota in the Obuasi agrarium that had left it a tower of stinking black slime.

One city; two friends and amors. We went out to party. And found we couldn't. The frocks were fabulous, the cocktails disgraceful, the company louche and the narcotics dazzling but in each bar, club, private party we ended up in a corner together, talking.

Partying was boring. Talk was lovely and bottomless and fascinating.

We ended up in bed again, of course. We couldn't wait. Glorious, impractical 1950s Dior frocks lay crumpled on the floor, ready for the recycler.

"What do you want?" Achi asked. She lay on her bed, inhaling THC from a vaper. "Dream and don't be afraid."

"Really?"

"Moon dreams."

"I want to be a dragon," I said and Achi laughed and punched me on the thigh: *get away*. "No, seriously."

In the year and a half we had been on the moon, our small world had changed. Things move fast on the moon. Energy and raw materials are cheap, human genius plentiful. Ambition boundless. Four companies had emerged as major economic forces: four families. The Australian Mackenzies were the longest established. They had been joined by the Asamoahs, whose company Aka monopolised food and living space. The Russian Vorontsovs finally moved their operations off Earth entirely and ran the cycler, the moonloop, the bus service and the emergent rail network. Most recent to amalgamate were the Suns, who had defied the representatives of the People's Republic on the LDC board and ran the information infrastructure. Four companies: Four Dragons. That was what they called themselves. The Four Dragons of the Moon.

"I want to be the Fifth Dragon," I said.

THE LAST THINGS were simple and swift. All farewells should be sudden, I think. I booked Achi on the cycler out. There was always space on the return orbit. She booked me into the LDC medical centre. A flash of light and the lens was bonded permanently to my eye. No hand shake, no congratulations, no welcome. All I had done was decide to continue doing what I was doing. The four counters ticked, charging me to live.

I cashed in the return part of the flight and invested the lump sum in convertible LDC bonds. Safe, solid. On this foundation would I build my dynasty.

The cycler would come round the Farside and rendezvous with the moonloop in three days. Good speed. Beautiful haste. It kept us busy, it kept us from crying too much.

I went with Achi on the train to Meridian. We had a whole row of seats to ourselves and we curled up like small burrowing animals.

I'm scared, she said. It's going to hurt. The cycler spins you up to Earth gravity and then there's the gees coming down. I could be months in a wheelchair. Swimming, they say that's the closest to being on the moon. The water supports you while you build up muscle and bone mass again. I can do that. I love swimming. And then you can't help thinking, what if they got it wrong? What if, I don't know, they mixed me up with someone else and it's already too late? Would they send me back here? I couldn't live like that. No one can live here. Not really live. Everyone says about the moon being rock and dust and vacuum and radiation and that it knows a thousand ways to kill you, but that's not the moon. The moon is other people. People all the way up, all the way down; everywhere, all the time. Nothing but people. Every breath, every drop of water, every atom of carbon has been passed through people. We eat each other. And that's all it would ever be, people. The same faces looking into your face, forever. Wanting something from you. Wanting and wanting and wanting. I hated it from the first day out on the cycler. If you hadn't talked to me, if we hadn't met...

And I said: *Do you remember, when we talked about what had brought us to the moon?* You said that you owed your family for not being born in Syria – and I said I wanted to be a dragon? I saw it. Out in Lansberg. It was so simple. I just looked at something I saw every day in a different way. Helium 3. The key to the post oil economy. Mackenzie Metals throws away tons of Helium 3 every day. And I thought, how could the Mackenzies not see it? Surely they must... I couldn't be the only one... But family and companies, and family companies especially, they have strange fixations and blindesses. Mackenzies mine metal. Metal mining is what they do. They can't imagine anything else and so they miss what's right under their noses. I can make it work, Achi. I know how to do it. But not with the Mackenzies. They'd take it off me. If I tried to fight them, they'd just bury me. Or kill me. It's cheaper. The Court of Clavius would make sure my family were compensated. That's why I moved to Vorontsov rail. To get away from them while I put a business plan together. I will make it work for me, and I'll build a dynasty. I'll be the Fifth Dragon. House Corta. I like the sound of that. And then I'll make an offer to my family – my final offer. Join me, or never get another cent from me. There's the opportunity – take it or leave it. But you have to come to the moon for it. I'm going to do this, Achi.

No windows in moon trains but the seat-back screen showed the surface. On a screen, outside your helmet, it is always the same. It is grey and soft and ugly and covered in footprints. Inside the train were workers and engineers; lovers and partners and even a couple of small children. There was noise and colour and drinking and laughing, swearing and sex. And us curled up in the back against the bulkhead. And I thought, *this is the moon.*

ACHI GAVE ME a gift at the moonloop gate. It was the last thing she owned. Everything else had been sold, the last few things while we were on the train.

Eight passengers at the departure gate, with friends, family, amors. No one left the moon alone and I was glad of that. The air smelled of coconut, so different from the vomit, sweat, unwashed bodies, fear of the arrival gate. Mint tea was available from a dispensing machine. No one was drinking it.

"Open this when I'm gone," Achi said. The gift was a document cylinder, crafted from bamboo. The departure was fast, the way I imagine executions must be. The VTO staff had everyone strapped into their seats and were sealing the capsule door before either I or Achi could respond. I saw her begin to mouth a goodbye, saw her wave fingers, then the locks sealed and the elevator took the capsule up to the tether platform.

The moonloop was virtually invisible: a spinning spoke of M5 fibre twenty centimetres wide and two hundred kilometres long. Up there the ascender was climbing towards the counterbalance mass, shifting the centre of gravity and sending the whole tether down into a surface-grazing orbit. Only in the final moments of approach would I see the white cable seeming to descend vertically from the star filled sky. The grapple connected and the capsule was lifted from the platform. Up there, one of those bright stars was the ascender, sliding down the tether, again shifting the centre of mass so that the whole ensemble moved into a higher orbit. At the top of the loop, the grapple would release and the cycler catch the capsule. I tried to put names on the stars: the cycler, the ascender, the counterweight; the capsule freighted with my amor, my love, my friend. The comfort of physics. I watched the images, the bamboo document tube slung over my back, until a new capsule was loaded into the gate. Already the next tether was wheeling up over the close horizon.

THE PRICE WAS outrageous. I dug into my bonds. For that sacrifice it had to be the real thing: imported, not spun up from an organic printer. I was sent from printer to dealer to private importer. She let me sniff it. Memories exploded like New Year fireworks and I cried. She sold me the paraphernalia as well. The equipment I needed simply didn't exist on the moon.

I took it all back to my hotel. I ground to the specified grain. I boiled the water. I let it cool to the correct temperature. I poured it from a height, for maximum aeration. I stirred it.

While it brewed I opened Achi's gift. Rolled paper: drawings. Concept art for the habitat the realities of the moon would never let her build. A lava tube, enlarged and sculpted with faces, like an inverted Mount Rushmore. The faces of the orixas, the Umbanda pantheon, each a hundred metres high, round and smooth and serene, overlooked terraces of gardens and pools. Waters cascaded from their eyes and open lips. Pavilions and belvederes were scattered across the floor of the vast cavern; vertical gardens ran from floor to artificial sky, like the hair of the gods. Balconies – she loved balconies – galleries and arcades, windows. Pools. You could swim from one end of this Orixa-world to the other. She had inscribed it: *a habitation for a dynasty*.

I thought of her, spinning away across the sky.

The grounds began to settle. I plunged, poured and savoured the aroma of the coffee. Santos Gold. Gold would have been cheaper. Gold was the dirt we threw away, together with the Helium 3.

When the importer had rubbed a pinch of ground coffee under my nose, memories of childhood, the sea, college, friends, family, celebrations flooded me.

When I smelled the coffee I had bought and ground and prepared, I experienced something different. I had a vision. I saw the sea, and I saw Achi, Achi-gone-back, on a board, in the sea. It was night and she was paddling the board out, through the waves and beyond the waves, sculling herself forward, along the silver track of the moon on the sea.

I drank my coffee.

It never tastes the way it smells.

MY GRANDDAUGHTER adores that red dress. When it gets dirty and worn, we print her a new one. She wants never to wear anything else. Luna, running barefoot through the pools, splashing and scaring the fish, leaping from stepping stone, stepping in a complex pattern of stones that must be landed on left footed, right-footed, two footed or skipped over entirely. The Orixas watch her. The Orixas watch me, on my veranda, drinking tea.

I am old bones now. I haven't thought of you for years, Achi. The last time was when I finally turned those drawings into reality. But these last lunes I find my thoughts folding back, not just to you, but to all the ones from those dangerous, daring days. There were more loves than you, Achi. You always knew that. I treated most of them as badly as I treated you. It's the proper pursuit of elderly ladies, remembering and trying not to regret.

I never heard from you again. That was right, I think. You went back to your green and growing world, I stayed in the land in the sky. Hey! I built your palace and filled it with that dynasty I promised. Sons and daughters, amors, okos, madrinhas, retainers. Corta is not such a strange name to you now, or most of Earth's population. Mackenzie, Sun, Vorontsov, Asamoah. Corta. We are Dragons now.

Here comes little Luna, running to her grandmother. I sip my tea. It's mint. I still loathe mint tea. I always will. But there is only mint tea on the moon.

THE TRUTH ABOUT OWLS
Amal El-Mohtar

Amal El-Mohtar (amalelmohtar.com) is the Nebula-nominated author of *The Honey Month,* a collection of poetry and very short fiction written to the taste of twenty-eight different kinds of honey. Her work has appeared in many venues including *Lightspeed, Apex, Strange Horizons*, and *Uncanny*. She has won the Rhysling award three times, the Richard Jefferies Prize once, is a columnist for *Tor.com* and *Lightspeed*, and regularly writes book reviews for NPR. She is also a founding member of the Banjo Apocalypse Crinoline Troubadours performance collective, and edits *Goblin Fruit*, a web quarterly devoted to fantastical poetry. Presently she divides her time between Ottawa and Glasgow.

OWLS HAVE EYES *that match the skies they hunt through. Amber-eyed owls hunt at dawn or dusk; golden-eyed owls hunt during the day; black-eyed owls hunt at night.*

No one knows why this is.

ANISA'S EYES ARE black, and she no longer hates them. She used to wish for eyes the color of her father's, the beautiful pale green-blue that people were always startled to see in a brown face. But she likes, now, having eyes and hair of a color those same people find frightening.

Even her teachers are disconcerted, she's found – they don't try to herd her as they do the other students. She sees them casting uncertain glances towards her before ushering their group from one owl exhibit to another, following the guide. She turns to go in the opposite direction.

"Annie-sa! Annie, this way!"

She turns, teeth clenching. Mrs. Roberts, whose pale powdered face, upswept yellow hair, and bright red lips make Anisa think of Victoria sponge, is smiling encouragingly.

"My name is A-NEE-sa, actually," she replies, and feels the power twitching out from her chest and into her arms, which she crosses quickly, and her hands, which she makes into fists, digging nails into her palms. The power recedes, but she can still feel it pouring out from her eyes like a swarm of bees while Mrs. Roberts looks at her in perplexed confusion. Mrs. Roberts' eyes are a delicate, ceramic sort of blue.

Anisa watches another teacher, Ms. Grewar, lean over to murmur something into Mrs. Roberts' ear. Mrs. Roberts only looks more confused, but renews her smile uncertainly, nods, and turns back to her group. Anisa closes her eyes, takes a deep breath, and counts to ten before walking away.

OWLS ARE PREDATORS. *There are owls that would tear you apart if you gave them half a chance.*

THE SCOTTISH OWL Centre is a popular destination for school trips: a short bus ride from Glasgow, an educational component, lots of opportunities for photographs to show the parents, and who doesn't like owls nowadays? Anisa has found herself staring, more than once, at owl-print bags and shirts, owl-shaped earrings and belt buckles, plush owl toys and wire statues in bright, friendly colors. She finds it all desperately strange.

Anisa remembers the first time she saw an owl. She was seven years old. She lived in Riyaq with her father and her grandparents, and that morning she had thrown a tantrum about having to feed the chickens, which she hated, because of their smell and the way they pecked at her when she went to gather their eggs, and also because of the rooster, who was fierce and sharp-spurred. She hated the chickens, she shouted, why didn't they just make them into soup.

She was given more chores to do, which she did, fumingly, stomping her feet and banging cupboard doors and sometimes crying about how unfair it was. "Are you brooding over the chickens," her father would joke, trying to get her to laugh, which only made her more furious, because she *did* want to laugh but she didn't want him to think she wasn't still mad, because she was.

She had calmed down by lunch, and forgotten about it by supper. But while helping her grandmother with the washing up she heard a scream from the yard. Her grandmother darted out, and Anisa followed, her hands dripping soap.

An owl – enormous, tall as a lamb, taller than any bird she had ever seen – perched in the orange tree, the rooster a tangle of blood and feathers in its talons. As Anisa stared, the owl bent its head to the rooster's throat and tore out a long strip of flesh.

When Anisa thinks about this – and she does, often, whenever her hands are wet and soapy in just the right way, fingertips on the brink of wrinkling – she remembers the guilt. She remembers listening to her grandmother cross herself and speak her words of protection against harm, warding them against death in the family, against troubled times. She remembers the fear, staring at the red and pink and green of the rooster, its broken, dangling head.

But she can't remember – though she often tries – whether she felt, for the first time, the awful electric prickle of the power in her chest, flooding out to her palms.

THERE ARE OWLS *that sail through the air like great ships. There are owls that flit like finches from branch to branch. There are owls that look at you with disdain and owls that sway on the perch of your arm like a reed in the wind.*

ANISA IS NOT afraid of owls. She thinks they're interesting enough, when people aren't cooing over them or embroidering them onto cushions. From walking around the sanctuary she thinks the owl she saw as a child was probably a Eurasian Eagle Owl.

She wanders from cage to cage, environment to environment, looking at owls that bear no resemblance to the pretty patterns lining the hems of skirts and dresses – owls that lack a facial disk, owls with bulging eyes and fuzzy heads, owls the size of her palm.

Some of the owls have names distinct from their species: Hosking, Broo, Sarabi. Anisa pauses in front of a barn owl and frowns at the name. Blodeuwedd?

"Blow-due-wed," she sounds out beneath her breath, while the owl watches her.

"It's Bloh-DA-weth, actually," says a friendly voice behind her. Anisa turns to see one of the owl handlers from the flying display, a black woman named Izzy, hair wrapped up in a brightly colored scarf, moving into one of the aviaries, gloved hands clutching a feed bucket. "It means 'flower-face' in Welsh."

Anisa flushes. She looks at the owl again. She has never seen a barn owl up close, and does not think it looks like flowers; she thinks, all at the same time, that the heart-shaped face is alien and eerie and beautiful and like when you can see the moon while the sun is setting, and that there should be a single word for the color of the wings that's like the sheen of a pearl but not the pearl itself.

She asks, "Is it a boy or a girl?"

"Do you not know the story of Blodeuwedd?" Izzy smiles. "She was a beautiful woman, made of flowers, who was turned into an owl."

Anisa frowns. "That doesn't make sense."

"It's from a book of fairytales called *The Mabinogion* – not big on sense-making." Izzy chuckles. "I don't think she likes it either, to be honest. She's one of our most difficult birds. But she came to us from Wales, so we gave her a Welsh name."

Anisa looks into Blodeuwedd's eyes. They are blacker than her own.

"I like her," she declares.

A GROUP OF owls is called a Parliament.
Owls are bad luck.

THE SUMMER ANISA saw the owl kill the rooster was the summer Israel bombed the country. She always thinks of it that way, not as a war – she doesn't remember a war. She never saw anyone fighting. She remembers a sound she felt more than heard, a *thud* that shook the earth and rattled up through her bones – then another – then a smell like chalk – before being swept into her father's arms and taken down into shelter.

She remembers feeling cold; she remembers, afterwards, anger, weeping, conversations half-heard from her bed, her mother's voice reaching them in sobs from London, robotic and strangled over a poor internet connection, a mixing of English and Arabic, accents swapping places. Her father's voice always calm, measured, but with a tension running through it like when her cousin put a wire through a dead frog's leg to make it twitch.

She remembers asking her grandmother if Israel attacked because of the owl. Her grandmother laughed in a way that made Anisa feel hollow and lost.

"Shh, shh, don't tell Israel! An owl killed a rooster – that's more reason to attack! An owl killed a rooster in Lebanon and the government let it happen! Quick, get off the bridges!"

The whole family laughed. Anisa was terrified, and told no one.

WHY DID THE *owl not go courting in the rain? Because it was* too wet to woo.

"WHAT MAKES HER 'difficult'?" asks Anisa, watching Blodeuwedd sway on her perch. Izzy looks fondly at the owl.

"Well, we acquired her as a potential display bird, but she just doesn't take well to training – she hisses at most of the handlers when they pass by, tries to bite. She's also very territorial, and won't tolerate the presence of male birds, so we can't use her for breeding." Izzy offers Blodeuwedd a strip of raw chicken, which she gulps down serenely.

"But she likes you," Anisa observes. Izzy smiles ruefully.

"I'm not one of her trainers. It's easy to like people who ask nothing of you." Izzy pauses, eyes Blodeuwedd with exaggerated care. "Or at least, it's easy to not hate them."

Before Anisa leaves with the rest of her class, Izzy writes down *Mabinogion* for her on a piece of paper, a rather deft doodle of an owl's face inside a five-petaled flower, and an invitation to come again.

*   *   *

MOST OWLS ARE *sexually dimorphic: the female is usually larger, stronger, and more brightly colored than the male.*

ANISA'S MOTHER IS tall, and fair, and Anisa looks nothing like her. Her mother's brown hair is light and thin and straight; her mother's skin is pale. Anisa is used to people making assumptions – *are you adopted? Is that your stepmother?* – when they see them together, but her mother's new job at the university has made outings together rare. In fact, since moving to Glasgow, Anisa hardly sees her at home anymore, since she has evening classes and departmental responsibilities.

"What are you reading?" asks her mother, shrugging on her coat after a hurried dinner together.

Anisa, legs folded up underneath her on the couch, holds up a library copy of *The Mabinogion.* Her mother looks confused, but nods, wishes her a good night, and leaves.

Anisa reads about how Math, son of Mathonwy, gathered the blossoms of oak, of broom, of meadowsweet, and shaped them into a woman. She wonders, idly, what kind of flowers could be combined to make her.

THERE ARE OWLS *on every continent in the world except Antarctica.*

THE SO-CALLED war lasted just over a month; Anisa learned the word 'ceasefire' in August. Her father put her on a plane to London the moment the airports were repaired.

Before she started going to school, Anisa's mother took her aside. "When people ask you where you're from," she told her, "you say 'England,' all right? You were born here. You have every bit as much right to be here as anyone else."

"Baba wasn't born here." She felt a stinging in her throat and eyes, a pain of *unfair.* "Is that why he's not here? Is he not allowed to come?"

Anisa doesn't remember what her mother said. She must have said something. Whatever it was, it was certainly not that she wouldn't see her father in person for three years.

THE WELSH WORD *for owl once meant 'flower-face'.*

WHEN IZZY SAID Blodeuwedd was made of flowers, Anisa had imagined roses and lilies, flowers she was forced to read about over and over in books of English literature. But as she reads, she finds that even Blodeuwedd's flower names are strange to her – what kind of a flower is "broom"? – and she likes that, likes that no part of Blodeuwedd is familiar or expected.

Anisa has started teaching herself Welsh, mostly because she wants to know how all the names in *The Mabinogion* are pronounced. She likes that there is a language that looks like English but sounds like Arabic; she likes that there is no one teaching it to her, or commenting on her accent, or asking her how to speak it for their amusement. She likes that a single 'f' is pronounced 'v', that 'w' is a vowel – likes that it's an alphabet of secrets hidden in plain sight.

She starts visiting the owl centre every weekend, feeling like she's done her homework if she can share a new bit of *Mabinogion* trivia with Izzy and Blodeuwedd in exchange for a fact about owls.

OWLS ARE BIRDS *of the order* Strigiformes, *a word derived from the Latin for* witch.

DURING ANISA'S FIRST year of school in England a girl with freckles and yellow hair leaned over to her while the teacher's back was turned, and asked if her father was dead.

"No!" Anisa stared at her.

"My mum said your dad could be dead. Because of the war. Because there's always war where you're from."

"That's not true."

The freckled girl narrowed her eyes. "My mum *said* so."

Anisa felt her pulse quicken, her hands tremble. She felt she had never hated anyone in her whole life so much as this idiot pastry of a girl. She watched as the girl shrugged and turned away.

"Maybe you just don't understand English."

She felt something uncoil inside her. Anisa stood up from her chair and *shoved* the girl out of hers, and felt, in the moment of skin touching skin, a startling shock of static electricity; the girl's freckles vanished into the pink of her cheeks, and instead of protesting the push, she shouted "Ugh, she *shocked* me!"

In her memory, the teacher's reprimand, the consequences, the rest of that year all melt away to one viciously satisfying image: the freckled girl's blue eyes looking at her, terrified, out of a pretty pink face.

She learned to cultivate an appearance of danger, of threat; she learned that with an economy of look, of gesture, of insinuation, she could be feared and left alone. She was the Girl Who Came From War, the Girl Whose Father Was Dead, the Girl With Powers. One day a boy tried to kiss her; she pushed him away, looked him in the eye, and flung a fistful of nothing at him, a spray of air. He was absent from school for two days; when the boy came back claiming to have had a cold, everyone acknowledged Anisa as the cause. When some students asked her to make them sick on purpose, to miss an exam or assignment, she smirked, said nothing, and walked away.

OWLS HAVE A *narrow field of binocular vision; they compensate for this by rotating their heads up to two hundred and seventy degrees.*

CAREFULLY, IZZY LOWERS her arm to Anisa's gloved wrist, hooks her tether to the ring dangling from it, and watches as Blodeuwedd hops casually down on to her forearm. Anisa exhales, then grins. Izzy grins back.

"I can't believe how much she's mellowed out. She's really surprisingly comfortable with you."

"Maybe," Anisa says, mischievous, "it's because I'm really good at not asking anything of her."

"Sure," says Izzy, "or maybe it's because you keep talking about how much you hate Math, son of Mathonwy."

"Augh, that *prick*!"

Izzy laughs, and Anisa loves to hear her, to see how she tosses her head back when she does. She loves how thick and wiry Izzy's hair is, and the different things she does with it – today it's half-wrapped in a white and purple scarf, fluffed out at the back like a bouquet. She continues,

"He's the worst. He takes flowers and tells them to be a woman; as soon as she acts in a way he doesn't like, he turns her into an owl. It's like – he needs to keep being in charge of her story, and the way to do that is to change her shape."

"Well. To be fair. She did try to kill his adopted son."

"He forced her into marriage with him! And he was a jerk too!"

"You're well into this, you are."

"It's just" – Anisa bites her lip, looking at Blodeuwedd, raising her slightly to shift the weight on her forearm, watching her spread her magnificent wings, then settle – "sometimes – I feel like I'm just a collection of bits of things that someone brought together at random and called *girl*, and then *Anisa*, and then..." she shrugs. "Whatever."

Izzy is quiet for a moment. Then she says, thoughtfully, "You know, there's another word for that."

"For what?"

"What you just described – an aggregation of disparate things. An anthology. That's what *The Mabinogion* is, after all."

Anisa is unconvinced. "Blodeuwedd's just one part of someone else's story, she's not an anthology herself."

Izzy smiles, gently, in a way that always makes Anisa feel she's thinking of someone or something else, but allowing Anisa a window's worth of view into her world. "You can look at it that way. But there's another word for anthology, one we don't really use any more: *florilegium*. Do you know what it means?"

Anisa shakes her head, and blinks, startled, as Blodeuwedd does a side-wise walk up her arm to lean, gently, against her shoulder. Izzy smiles, a little more brightly, more for her, and says: "A gathering of flowers."

* * *

OWLS FLY MORE *silently than any other bird.*

WHEN HER FATHER joined them in London three years later, he found Anisa grown several inches taller and several sentences shorter. Her mother's insistence on speaking Arabic together at all times – pushing her abilities as a heritage speaker to their limits – meant that Anisa often chose not to speak at all. This was to her advantage in the school yard, where her eyes, her looks, and rumors of her dark powers held her fellow students in awe; it did her no good with her father, who hugged her and held her until words and tears gushed out of her in gasps.

The next few years were better; they moved to a different part of the city, and Anisa was able to make friends in a new school, to open up, to speak. She sometimes told stories about how afraid of her people used to be, how she'd convinced them of her powers like it was a joke on them, and not something she had ever believed herself.

OWLS PURGE FROM *themselves the matter they cannot absorb: bones, fur, claws, teeth, feathers.*

"IS THAT FOR school?"

Anisa looks up from her notebook to her mother, and shakes her head. "No. It's Welsh stuff."

"Oh." Her mother pauses, and Anisa can see her mentally donning the gloves with which to handle her. "Why Welsh?"

She shrugs. "I like it." Then, seeing her mother unsatisfied, adds, "I like the stories. I'd like to read them in the original language eventually."

Her mother hesitates. "You know, there's a rich tradition of Arabic storytelling –"

The power flexes inside her like a whip snapping, takes her by surprise, and she bites the inside of her lip until it bleeds to stop it, stop it.

"– and I know I can't share much myself but I'm sure your grandmother or your aunt would love to talk to you about it –"

Anisa grabs her books and runs to her room as if she could outrun the power, locks the door, and buries her fingernails in the skin of her arms, dragging long, painful scratches down them, because the only way to let the power out is through pain, because if she doesn't hurt herself she knows with absolute certainty that she will hurt someone else.

ILLNESS IN OWLS *is difficult to detect and diagnose until it is dangerously advanced.*

ANISA KNOWS SOMETHING is wrong before she sees the empty cage, from the way Izzy is pacing in front of it, as if waiting for her.

"Blodeuwedd's sick," she says, and Anisa feels a rush of gravity inside her stomach. "She hasn't eaten in a few days. I'm sorry, but you won't be able to see her today –"

"What's wrong with her?" Anisa begins counting back the days to the last flare, to what she thought, and it wasn't this, it was never anything like this, but she'd held *The Mabinogion* in her hands –

"We don't know yet. I'm so sorry you came out all this way –" Izzy hesitates while Anisa stands, frozen, feeling herself vanishing into misery, into a day one year and four hundred miles away.

OWLS DO NOT *mate for life, though death sometimes parts them.*

THE MEMORY IS like a trap, a steel cage that falls over her head and severs her from reality. When the memory descends she can do nothing but see her father's face, over and over, aghast, more hurt than she has ever seen him, and her own words like a bludgeon to beat in her own head: "Fine, go back and *die*, I don't care, just *stop coming back.*"

She feels, again, the power lashing out, confused, attempting both to tether and to push away; she remembers the shape of the door knob in her hand as she bolts out of the flat, down the stairs, out the building, into the night. She feels incandescent, too burnt up to cry, thinking of her father going back to a country every day in the news, every day a patchwork of explosions and body counts, every day a matter of someone else's opinions.

She thinks of how he wouldn't take her with him.

And she feels, irrevocably, as if she is breathing a stone when she sees him later that evening in hospital, eyes closed, ashen, and the words reaching her from a faraway dimness saying he has suffered a stroke, and died.

"ANISA – ANISA!" Izzy has taken her hands, is holding them, and when Anisa focuses again she feels as if they're submerged in water, and she wants to snatch them away because what if she hurts Izzy but she is disoriented and before she knows what she is doing she is crying while Izzy holds her hands and sinks down to the rain-wet floor with her. She feels gravel beneath her knees and grinds them further into it, to punish herself for this, this thing, the power, and she is trying to make Izzy understand and she is trying to say she is sorry but all that comes out is this violent, wrecking weeping.

"It's me," she manages, "I made her sick, it's my fault, I don't mean to do it but I make bad things happen just by wanting them even a little, wanting them the wrong way, and I don't want it anymore, I never wanted *this* but it keeps happening and now she'll die –"

Izzy looks at her, squeezes her hands, and says, calm and even, "Bullshit."

"It's true –"

"Anisa – if it's true it should work both ways. Can you make good things happen by wanting them?"

She looks into Izzy's warm dark eyes, at a loss, and can't frame a reply to such a ridiculous question.

"Think, pet – what *good* things do you want to happen?"

"I want..." She closes her eyes, and bites her lip, looking for pain to quash the power but feels it differently – feels, with Izzy holding her hands, Izzy facing her, grounded, as if draining something out into the gravel and the earth beneath it and leaving something else in its wake, something shining and slick as sunlight on wet streets. "I want Blodeuwedd to get better. I want her to have a good life, to ... be whatever she wants to be and do whatever she wants to do. I want to learn Welsh. I want to –" Izzy's face shimmers through her tears. "I want to be friends with you. I want –"

She swallows them down, all of her good wants, how much she misses her father and how much she misses just talking, in any language, with her mother, and how she misses the light in Riyaq and the dry dusty air, the sheep and the goats and the warmth, always, of her grandmother and uncles and aunts and cousins all around, and she makes an anthology of them. She gathers the flowers of her wants all together in her throat, her heart, her belly, and trusts that they are good.

THE TRUTH ABOUT *owls* –

ANISA AND HER mother stand at the owl centre's entrance, both casually studying a nearby freezer full of ice lollies while waiting for their tickets. Their eyes meet, and they grin at each other. Her mother is rummaging about for caramel cornettos when the sales attendant, Rachel, waves Anisa over.

"Is that your mother, Anisa?" whispers Rachel. Anisa goes very still for a moment as she nods, and Rachel beams. "I thought so. You have precisely the same smile."

Anisa blushes, and looks down, suddenly shy. Her mother pays for their tickets and ice cream, and together they move towards the gift-shop and the aviaries beyond.

Anisa pauses on her way through the gift-shop; she waves her mother on, says she'll catch her up. Alone, she buys a twee notebook covered in shiny metallic owls and starts writing in it with an owl-topped pen.

She writes "The truth about owls –" but pauses. She looks at the words, their shape, the taken-for-granted ease of their spilling from her. She frowns, bites her lip, and after a moment's careful thought writes "Y gwir am tylluanod –"

But she has run out of vocabulary, and this is not something she wants to look up. There is a warmth blossoming in her, a rightness, pushing up out of her chest where the power used to crouch, where something lives now that is different, better, and she wants to pour that out on the page. She rolls the pen between her thumb and forefinger, then shifts the journal's weight against her palm.

She writes "أنا الحقيقة عن البوم معقدة", and smiles.

FOUR DAYS OF CHRISTMAS
Tim Maughan

Tim Maughan (timmaughanbooks.com) is a British writer currently based in Brooklyn, using both fiction and non-fiction to explore issues around cities, art, class, and technology. His debut short story collection *Paintwork* received critical acclaim when released in 2011, and his story "Limited Edition" was shortlisted for the British Science Fiction Award. His non-fiction work regularly appears in a number of places, including the BBC, *New Scientist*, *Arc*, and *Icon*, and he has recently given talks at Princeton School of Architecture, HASTAC 2014 in Lima, Lambeth Council in London, and Sonic Acts in Amsterdam. He sometimes makes films, too.

29 June 2024 Yiwu, China

MING-HUA TAKES a Santa Claus from the conveyor belt, holds its feet between thumb and forefinger, and blushes its cheeks red with two delicate taps from a paintbrush. As always, she tries to avoid its dead-eyed gaze, but before the second dab of paint it's laughing at her, hidden servos shaking its head from side to side in simulated cheer.

Ho ho ho! Merry Christmas Ming-hua!

She drops the Santa on the pile next to her table and they celebrate the arrival of yet another of their kind, 300 Santas *ho ho ho ho*-ing and vibrating as one.

Two tables up the line Yanyu, who paints the pupils onto their dead eyes, is wearing a plastic mask while she works. This week it's Kermit the Frog; last week it was Pikachu. Before that, a Teenage Mutant Ninja Turtle. It stops the Santas from scanning her face and searching the social networks for her name. It means they keep fucking quiet. The masks have to be animals or cartoon characters – no real people or celebrities.

Ming-hua tried it, for a while. She hid behind Spider-Man's face. But it got too hot, the sweat from her brow stinging her eyes, the smell of the plastic as suffocating as the fumes from the injection-moulding machines clanking and pounding in the corner. She decided she was better off putting up with the *ho ho ho*-ing.

The camera above her twitches as she moves, the counters on the screen tracking her progress as the Santa hits the pile, updating her daily stats like video game scores: units per minute, units per hour, units per day, Yuan earned. Time per unit, both for her and across the whole production line. They've all been keeping an eye on that one – Mr. Han threatening them every morning that if they don't keep on target he'll replace them all with 3D printers and auto-painters. At break Yanya always tells her it's bullshit, that there's no way he can find printers or bots faster than them, plus he's too tight to pay for upgrades. All Ming-hua knows is that she needs this job, so she doesn't let herself stop and think about it for too long.

13 October 2024, Ningbo, China

WEIYUAN STARES DOWN, past his feet and through the glass floor of the cab, fighting vertigo. He drops the container down on steel cables. Even though he can't see it happening, he knows it's made contact with the stack on the ship. Somehow he feels the hard clang of contact through joysticks and pedals.

He knows well enough to thumb the button on the joystick that releases the spreader, makes it disconnect from the container, and leaves it sitting there. Hit that too soon and boxes fall, product is ruined, lives are lost. Hit it too late and you slow everything down, or you find yourself hauling the spreader back up before the release is done, and you're back to falling boxes, ruined product, lost lives. Either way you're fucked, the network knowing it's *you* holding up the entire supply chain, your incompetence sending planet-wide ripples of schedule panic through infrastructure space. Timing is everything. *Feeling* is everything.

Weiyuan glances at the screen above him, at the ever-shifting Tetris puzzle, unthinkingly decoding the squares and numbers, knowing instantly where on the ship he needs to drop the next box. He doesn't know what's in the boxes, doesn't care, he leaves that to the network, to some algorithm in Copenhagen to worry about. He just worries about being fast.

And he is fast. One of the fastest. The frame of his super-post-Panamax class crane is studded with medals, gold and white against Maersk corporate blue. 300, 400 – even 500 boxes moved in a single 12 hour shift. And he's got to stay fast. He rarely looks up, but he knows that across the port, under the halogen-orange clouds, the rival Evergreen terminal is running without people at all. If they don't keep up the pace it'll be Maersk next; they'll plug the cranes directly into the network so Copenhagen can run them. They're fast, he hears, but not 500-a-shift fast, limited by safety regulations and insurance policies. He wonders if those Danish algorithms can *feel*.

Not that Weiyuan is perfect. Next to his screen, gaffer-taped to the ceiling, is a crane-jockey's tradition: items taken from every box he's dropped and split open, a bouquet of multicolored plastic. Day-Glo toys. USB charging cables. Cigarette lighters. Socks. A Che Guevara action figure. Phone covers. Toy cars. And right in the middle of them all, a red and white plastic Santa Claus, its head shaking as its eyes meet his, its tinny digital voice singing out:

Ho ho ho! Merry Christmas Weiyuan!

And Weiyuan swears, that for a second, he can *feel* the container hanging below him shaking, as if its entire contents are *ho-ho-ho*-ing along.

22 December 2024, Queens, New York City

SHONDA SCANS THE shelves of Target, desperately looking for something she can afford.

It's not that she's totally broke, but she just spent too much of her last paycheck getting back from Detroit. 11 hours stuck in the back of a Bolt Bus, not sleeping, her limbs aching. She should be excited to be back – first time she's seeing her kids in four months – but she's scared. Scared they won't even recognize her. Scared they won't care.

Four months in Detroit, away from her family, sleeping in a workers' dormitory that was once a public housing project. Four *months* spraying plastic tribal masks with varnish so they look more like real wood. Varnish that hangs like a cloud of glue around her, sticking to her overalls and splattering her goggles, impossible to shake in a small room in a building where Americans used to make cars for the whole world. And now the Chinese make fake masks to sell to tourists in Kenya. A small room where it's always too hot, even when it's minus twenty outside.

She thought she'd have more to show for it, after four months of 16 hour shifts in the varnish room. Even after PayPaling most the money to her mom so she can feed the kids, she expected to have some left for Christmas. But money acts weird in Detroit. You get paid and it seems like a lot, seems to go a long way, plus when you live in the dorms you don't really need to pay for food or heating or shit anyway.

But come back to NYC and damn, like as soon as you step outside of Detroit all the prices are doubled, like it's a different country or something. Mom says it's because they made Detroit a Special Economic Zone, with its own laws about taxes and labor conditions, just so the Chinese could come in and help out the city when it was so broke. And that's why Shonda headed up there, 'cause there were jobs. Seemed like a good idea, four months in Detroit.

On the shelf, in amongst the mess of red and green and white and glitter, something catches Shonda's eye. A little fat Santa Claus, his cheeks cherry red, his head starting to shake from side to side as it calls out to her.

Ho ho ho! Merry Christmas Shonda!

And then around it dozens more, identical little Santas, springing to life, *ho ho ho*-ing and vibrating as one.

She shakes her head. What the fuck is it with things all knowing your damn name these days? But it is kinda cute. The kids will probably like it. It'll make them smile. And it's only a couple of bucks. She grabs one, drops it in her shopping basket. Looks back at the shelf. Doesn't seem much point in only getting one. She grabs another three. Now she's just got to find something for mom.

*   *   *

25 December 2107, Land Fill District 14 South-B, New Jersey

MARY SCANS THE landscape, trying to blank out the stench.

Some of the other kids joke that they can't smell it anymore. They say it's burnt out the parts of their noses that respond to that particular frequency, or the parts of their brains that identify it. Mary's not so sure. She can smell it. Always. It's always on her body. She can smell it when she wakes in the morning. She can smell it when she eats. She can smell it every fourth day when she's allowed to shower, and she can smell it while she sleeps. She can smell it in her dreams.

Walking is hard. The oversized boiler suit flaps about her like a useless flag, stained with filth like the emblem of the world's shittiest nation. It catches the breeze like a sail as she walks. She keeps her head down; the floor of the landfill crater is hazardous terrain, an undulating battlefield of micro-hills carved from plastic and pools of toxic runoff. Tendrils of compacted ethylene monomers graze her ankles. She's good at this, she's been doing it most of her life. Keep your head down. It was the best piece of advice she was ever given – keep your head down. Pay attention to your feet. Pay attention to the ground.

Before they let her out of the camp to work here she had to memorize diagrams, catalogues of shapes and lines drawn precisely by hand on decaying paper sheets. The things she spends all day looking for. Syringes. Glass bottles. Ceramic plates and cups. Cutlery. Scalpels. Clothes. Anything valuable. Anything they can't make anymore.

And then the pictures of things to ignore, the useless things best left and forgotten – she had to memorize them too. Cell phones. Batteries. Toys. Laptops. Anything made of plastic. Anything with a screen.

She was good at memorizing; when they give her and the other kids tests, she always scores high. Which is why she pauses when, from out of the corner of her eye, she spots something she doesn't recognize, red and white extruding from the shredded, mulched plastic.

She pulls it away from the ground, holds it in her hand. It's dented and scuffed, but made from that ancient plastic that's near indestructible. She turns it in her hands, a tiny ornate figure, red cheeks and sculpted white beard. As the gaze of its dead eyes meets hers, its head starts to shake, and it calls out to her.

Ho ho ho! Merry Christmas [ERROR: NETWORK CONNECTION UNAVAILABLE]

She drops it, lets it just slip from her fingers, and as it falls the ground beneath her begins to shake, the small hill she's standing on vibrating, a tiny earthquake of indestructible, compressed, forgotten trash *ho ho ho*-ing as one.

Note: Over the summer of 2014, writer Tim Maughan accompanied the Unknown Fields Division, 'a nomadic design studio' lead by speculative architects Liam Young and Kate Davies, on an expedition to follow the supply chain back to the source of our consumer goods. This story was inspired by that trip, and in particular a visit to the markets and factories of Yiwu, the Chinese city where over 60% of the world's Christmas decorations are made.

COVENANT

Elizabeth Bear

Elizabeth Bear was born on the same day as Frodo and Bilbo Baggins, but in a different year. When coupled with a childhood tendency to read the dictionary for fun, this led her inevitably to penury, intransigence, and the writing of speculative fiction. She is the Hugo, Sturgeon, Locus, and Campbell Award winning author of twenty-six novels and over a hundred short stories. Her dog lives in Massachusetts; her partner, writer Scott Lynch, lives in Wisconsin. She spends a lot of time on planes. Her most recent book is science fiction novel *Karen Memory*.

THIS COLD COULD kill me, but it's no worse than the memories. Endurable as long as I keep moving.

My feet drum the snow-scraped roadbed as I swing past the police station at the top of the hill. Each exhale plumes through my mask, but insulating synthetics warm my inhalations enough so they do not sting and seize my lungs. I'm running too hard to breathe through my nose – running as hard and fast as I can, sprinting for the next hydrant-marking reflector protruding above a dirty bank of ice. The wind pushes into my back, cutting through the wet merino of my base layer and the wet MaxReg over it, but even with its icy assistance I can't come close to running the way I used to run. Once I turn the corner into the graveyard, I'll be taking that wind in the face.

I miss my old body's speed. I ran faster before. My muscles were stronger then. Memories weigh something. They drag you down. Every step I take, I'm carrying 13 dead. My other self runs a step or two behind me. I feel the drag of his invisible, immaterial presence.

As long as you keep moving, it's not so bad. But sometimes everything in the world conspires to keep you from moving fast enough.

I thump through the old stone arch into the graveyard, under the trees glittering with ice, past the iron gate pinned open by drifts. The wind's as sharp as I expected – sharper – and I kick my jacket over to warming mode. That'll run the battery down, but I've only got another 5 kilometers to go and I need heat. It's getting colder as the sun rises, and clouds slide up the western horizon: cold front moving in. I flip the sleeve light off with my next gesture, though that won't make much difference. The sky's given light enough to run by for a good half-hour, and the sleeve light is on its own battery. A single LED doesn't use much.

I imagine the flexible circuits embedded inside my brain falling into quiescence at the same time. Even smaller LEDs with even more advanced power cells go dark. The optogenetic adds shut themselves off when my brain is functioning *healthily*. Normally, microprocessors keep me sane and safe, monitor my brain activity, stimulate portions of the neocortex devoted to ethics, empathy, compassion. When I run, though, my brain – my dysfunctional, murderous, *cured* brain – does it for itself as neural pathways are stimulated by my own native neurochemicals.

Only my upper body gets cold: Though that wind chills the skin of my thighs and calves like an ice bath, the muscles beneath keep hot with exertion. And the jacket takes the edge off the wind that strikes my chest.

My shoes blur pink and yellow along the narrow path up the hill. Gravestones like smoker's teeth protrude through swept drifts. They're moldy black all over as if spray-painted, and glittering powdery whiteness heaps against their backs. Some of the stones date to the 18th century, but I run there only in the summertime or when it hasn't snowed.

Maintenance doesn't plow that part of the churchyard. Nobody comes to pay their respects to *those* dead anymore.

Sort of like the man I used to be.

The ones I killed, however – some of them still get their memorials every year. I know better than to attend, even though my old self would have loved to gloat, to relive the thrill of their deaths. The new me... feels a sense of... obligation. But their loved ones don't know my new identity. And nobody owes *me* closure.

I'll have to take what I can find for myself. I've sunk into that beautiful quiet place where there's just the movement, the sky, that true, irreproducible blue, the brilliant flicker of a cardinal. Where I die as a noun and only the verb survives.

I run. I am running.

WHEN HE MET her eyes, he imagined her throat against his hands. Skin like calves' leather; the heat and the crack of her hyoid bone as he dug his thumbs deep into her pulse. The way she'd writhe, thrash, struggle.

His waist chain rattled as his hands twitched, jerking the cuffs taut on his wrists.

She glanced up from her notes. Her eyes were a changeable hazel: blue in this light, gray green in others. Reflections across her glasses concealed the corner where text scrolled. It would have been too small to read, anyway – backward, with the table he was chained to creating distance between them.

She waited politely, seeming unaware that he was imagining those hazel eyes dotted with petechiae, that fair skin slowly mottling purple. He let the silence sway between them until it developed gravity.

"Did you wish to say something?" she asked, with mild but clinical encouragement.

Point to me, he thought.

He shook his head. "I'm listening."

She gazed upon him benevolently for a moment. His fingers itched. He scrubbed the tips against the rough orange jumpsuit but stopped. In her silence, the whisking sound was too audible.

She continued. "The court is aware that your crimes are the result of neural damage including an improperly functioning amygdala. Technology exists that can repair this damage. It is not experimental; it has been used successfully in tens of thousands of cases to treat neurological disorders as divergent as depression, anxiety, bipolar disorder, borderline personality, and the complex of disorders commonly referred to as schizophrenic syndrome."

The delicate structure of her collarbones fascinated him. It took 14 pounds of pressure, properly applied, to snap a human clavicle – rendering the arm useless for a time. He thought about the proper application of that pressure. He said, "Tell me more."

"They take your own neurons – grown from your own stem cells under sterile conditions in a lab, modified with microbial opsin genes. This opsin is a light-reactive pigment similar to that found in the human retina. The neurons are then reintroduced to key areas of your brain. This is a keyhole procedure. Once the neurons are established, and have been encouraged to develop the appropriate synaptic connections, there's a second surgery, to implant a medical device: a series of miniaturized flexible microprocessors, sensors, and light-emitting diodes. This device monitors your neurochemistry and the electrical activity in your brain and adjusts it to mimic healthy activity." She paused again and steepled her fingers on the table.

"'Healthy,'" he mocked.

She did not move.

"That's discrimination against the neuro-atypical."

"Probably," she said. Her fingernails were appliquéd with circuit diagrams. "But you did kill 13 people. And get caught. Your civil rights are bound to be forfeit after something like that."

He stayed silent. Impulse control had never been his problem.

"It's not psychopathy you're remanded for," she said. "It's murder."

"Mind control," he said.

"Mind *repair*," she said. "You can't be *sentenced* to the medical procedure. But you can volunteer. It's usually interpreted as evidence of remorse and desire to be rehabilitated. Your sentencing judge will probably take that into account."

"God," he said. "I'd rather have a bullet in the head than a fucking computer."

"They haven't used bullets in a long time," she said. She shrugged, as if it were nothing to her either way. "It was lethal injection or the gas chamber. Now it's rightminding. Or it's the rest of your life in an 8-by-12 cell. You decide."

"I can beat it."

"Beat rightminding?"

Point to me.

"What if I can beat it?"

"The success rate is a hundred percent. Barring a few who never woke up from anesthesia." She treated herself to a slow smile. "If there's anybody whose illness is too intractable for this particular treatment, they must be smart enough to keep it to themselves. And smart enough not to get caught a second time."

You're being played, he told himself. *You are smarter than her. Way too smart for this to work on you. She's appealing to your vanity. Don't let her yank your chain. She thinks she's so fucking smart. She's prey. You're the hunter. More evolved. Don't be manipulated –*

His lips said, "Lady, sign me up."

THE SNOW CREAKS under my steps. Trees might crack tonight. I compose a poem in my head.

The fashion in poetry is confessional. It wasn't always so – but now we judge value by our own voyeurism. By the perceived rawness of what we think we are being invited to spy upon. But it's all art: veils and lies.

If I wrote a confessional poem, it would begin: *Her dress was the color of mermaids, and I killed her anyway.*

A confessional poem need not be true. Not true in the way the bite of the air in my lungs in spite of the mask is true. Not true in the way the graveyard and the cardinal and the ragged stones are true.

It wasn't just her. It was her, and a dozen others like her. Exactly like her in that they were none of them the right one, and so another one always had to die.

That I can still see them as fungible is a victory for my old self – his only victory, maybe, though he was arrogant enough to expect many more. He thought he could beat the rightminding.

That's the only reason he agreed to it.

If I wrote it, people would want to read *that* poem. It would sell a million – it would garner far more attention than what I *do* write.

I won't write it. I don't even want to *remember* it. Memory excision was declared by the Supreme Court to be a form of the death penalty, and therefore unconstitutional since 2043.

They couldn't take my memories in retribution. Instead they took away my pleasure in them.

Not that they'd admit it was retribution. They call it *repair*. 'Rightminding.' Fixing the problem. Psychopathy is a curable disease.

They gave me a new face, a new brain, a new name. The chromosome reassignment, I chose for myself, to put as much distance between my old self and my new as possible.

The old me also thought it might prove good will: reduced testosterone, reduced aggression, reduced physical strength. Few women become serial killers.

To my old self, it seemed a convincing lie.

He – no, I: alienating the uncomfortable actions of the self is something that psychopaths do – I thought I was stronger than biology and stronger than rightminding. I thought I could take anabolic steroids to get my muscle and anger back where they should be. I honestly thought I'd get away with it.

I honestly thought I would still want to.

I could write that poem. But that's not the poem I'm writing. The poem I'm writing begins: *Gravestones like smoker's teeth...* except I don't know what happens in the second clause, so I'm worrying at it as I run.

I do my lap and throw in a second lap because the wind's died down and my heater is working and I feel light, sharp, full of energy and desire. When I come down the hill, I'm running on springs. I take the long arc, back over the bridge toward the edge of town, sparing a quick glance down at the frozen water. The air is warming up a little as the sun rises. My fingers aren't numb in my gloves anymore.

When the unmarked white delivery van pulls past me and rolls to a stop, it takes me a moment to realize the driver wants my attention. He taps the horn, and I jog to a stop, hit pause on my run tracker, tug a headphone from my ear. I stand a few steps back from the window. He looks at me, then winces in embarrassment, and points at his navigation system. "Can you help me find Green Street? The autodrive is no use."

"Sure," I say. I point. "Third left, up that way. It's an unimproved road; that might be why it's not on your map."

"Thanks," he says. He opens his mouth as if to say something else, some form of apology, but I say, "Good luck, man!" and wave him cheerily on.

The vehicle isn't the anomaly here in the country that it would be on a city street, even if half the cities have been retrofitted for urban farming to the point where they barely have streets anymore. But I'm flummoxed by the irony of the encounter, so it's not until he pulls away that I realize I should have been more wary. And that *his* reaction was not the embarrassment of having to ask for directions, but the embarrassment of a decent, normal person who realizes he's put another human being in a position where she may feel unsafe. He's vanishing around the curve before I sort that out – something I suppose most people would understand instinctually.

I wish I could run after the van and tell him that I was never worried. That it never occurred to me to be worried. Demographically speaking, the driver is very unlikely to be hunting me. He was black. And I am white.

And my early fear socialization ran in different directions, anyway.

My attention is still fixed on the disappearing van when something dark and clinging and sweetly rank drops over my head.

I gasp in surprise and my filter mask briefly saves me. I get the sick chartreuse scent of ether and the world spins, but the mask buys me a moment to realize what's happening – a blitz attack. Someone is kidnapping me. He's grabbed my arms, pulling my elbows back to keep me from pushing the mask off.

I twist and kick, but he's so strong.

Was I this strong? It seems like he's not even working to hold on to me, and though my heel connects solidly with his shin as he picks me up, he doesn't grunt. The mask won't help forever –

– it doesn't even help for long enough.

Ether dreams are just as vivid as they say.

HIS FIRST WAS the girl in the mermaid-colored dress. I think her name was Amelie. Or Jessica. Or something. She picked him up in a bar. Private cars were rare enough to have become a novelty, even then, but he had my father's Mission for the evening. She came for a ride, even though – or perhaps because – it was a little naughty, as if they had been smoking cigarettes a generation before. They watched the sun rise from a curve over a cornfield. He strangled her in the backseat a few minutes later.

She heaved and struggled and vomited. He realized only later how stupid he'd been. He had to hide the body, because too many people had seen us leave the bar together.

He never did get the smell out of the car. My father beat the shit out of him and never let him use it again. We all make mistakes when we're young.

I AWAKEN IN the dying warmth of my sweat-soaked jacket, to the smell of my vomit drying between my cheek and the cement floor. At least it's only oatmeal. You don't eat a lot before a long run. I ache in every particular, but especially where my shoulder and hip rest on concrete. I should be grateful; he left me in the recovery position so I didn't choke.

It's so dark I can't tell if my eyelids are open or closed, but the hood is gone and only traces of the stink of the ether remain. I lie still, listening and hoping my brain will stop trying to split my skull.

I'm still dressed as I was, including the shoes. He's tied my hands behind my back, but he didn't tape my thumbs together. He's an amateur. I conclude that he's not in the room with me. And probably not anywhere nearby. I think I'm in a cellar. I can't hear anybody walking around on the floor overhead.

I'm not gagged, which tells me he's confident that I can't be heard even if I scream. So maybe I wouldn't hear him up there, either?

My aloneness suggests that I was probably a target of opportunity. That he has somewhere else he absolutely has to be. Parole review? Dinner with the mother who supports him financially? Stockbroker meeting? He seems organized; it could be anything. But whatever it is, it's incredibly important that he show up for it, or he wouldn't have left.

When *you* have a new toy, can you resist playing with it? I start working my hands around. It's not hard if you're fit and flexible, which I am, though I haven't kept in practice. I'm not scared, though I should be. I know better than most what happens next. But I'm calmer than I have been since I was somebody else. The adrenaline still settles me, just like it used to. Only this time – well, I already mentioned the irony.

It's probably not even the lights in my brain taking the edge off my arousal.

The history of technology is all about unexpected consequences. Who would have guessed that peak oil would be linked so clearly to peak psychopathy? Most folks don't think about it much, but people just aren't as mobile as they – as we – used to be. *We* live in populations of greater density, too, and travel less. And all of that leads to knowing each other more.

People like the nameless him who drugged me – people like me – require a certain anonymity, either in ourselves or in our victims.

The floor is cold against my rear end. My gloves are gone. My wrists scrape against the soles of my shoes as I work the rope past them. They're only a little damp, and the water isn't frozen or any colder than the floor. I've been down here awhile, then – still assuming I *am* down. Cellars usually have windows, but guys like me – guys like I used to be – spend a lot of time planning in advance. Rehearsing. Spinning their webs and digging their holes like trapdoor spiders.

I'm shivering, and my body wants to cramp around the chill. I keep pulling. One more wiggle and tug, and I have my arms in front of me. I sit up and stretch, hoping my kidnapper has made just one more mistake. It's so dark I can't see my fluorescent yellow-and-green running jacket, but proprioception lets me find my wrist with my nose. And there, clipped into its little pocket, is the microflash sleeve light that comes with the jacket.

He got the mask – or maybe the mask just came off with the bag. And he got my phone, which has my tracker in it, and a GPS. He didn't make the mistake I would have chosen for him to make.

I push the button on the sleeve light with my nose. It comes on shockingly bright, and I stretch my fingers around to shield it as best I can. Flesh glows red between the bones.

Yep. It's a basement.

EIGHT YEARS AFTER my first time, the new, improved me showed the IBI the site of the grave he'd dug for the girl in the mermaid-colored dress. I'd never forgotten it – not the gracious tree that bent over the little boulder he'd skidded on top of her to keep the animals out, not the tangle of vines he'd dragged over that, giving himself a hell of a case of poison ivy in the process.

This time, I was the one who vomited.

How does one even begin to own having done something like that? How do *I*?

*   *   *

AH, THERE'S THE fear. Or not fear, exactly, because the optogenetic and chemical controls on my endocrine system keep my arousal pretty low. It's anxiety. But anxiety's an old friend.

It's something to think about while I work on the ropes and tape with my teeth. The sleeve light shines up my nose while I gnaw, revealing veins through the cartilage and flesh. I'm cautious, nipping and tearing rather than pulling. I can't afford to break my teeth: they're the best weapon and the best tool I have. So I'm meticulous and careful, despite the nauseous thumping of my heart and the voice in my head that says, *Hurry, hurry, he's coming.*

He's not coming – at least, I haven't heard him coming. Ripping the bonds apart seems to take forever. I wish I had wolf teeth, teeth for slicing and cutting. Teeth that could scissor through this stuff as if it were a cheese sandwich. I imagine my other self's delight in my discomfort, my worry. I wonder if he'll enjoy it when my captor returns, even though he's trapped in this body with me.

Does he really exist, my other self? Neurologically speaking, we all have a lot of people in our heads all the time, and we can't hear most of them. Maybe they really did change him, unmake him. Transform him into me. Or maybe he's back there somewhere, gagged and chained up, but watching.

Whichever it is, I know what he would think of this. He killed 13 people. He'd like to kill me, too.

I'm shivering.

The jacket's gone cold, and it – and I – am soaked. The wool still insulates while wet, but not enough. The jacket and my compression tights don't do a damned thing.

I wonder if my captor realized this. Maybe *this* is his game.

Considering all the possibilities, freezing to death is actually not so bad.

Maybe he just doesn't realize the danger? Not everybody knows about cold.

The last wrap of tape parts, sticking to my chapped lower lip and pulling a few scraps of skin loose when I tug it free. I'm leaving my DNA all over this basement. I spit in a corner, too, just for good measure. Leave traces: even when you're sure you're going to die. Especially then. Do anything you can to leave clues.

It was my skin under a fingernail that finally got me.

* * *

THE PERIOD WHEN he was undergoing the physical and mental adaptations that turned him into me gave me a certain... not sympathy, because they did the body before they did the rightminding, and sympathy's an emotion he never felt before I was 33 years old... but it gave him and therefore me a certain *perspective* he hadn't had before.

It itched like hell. Like puberty.

There's an old movie. Some people from the future go back in time and visit a hospital. One of them is a doctor. He saves a woman who's waiting for dialysis or a transplant by giving her a pill that makes her grow a kidney.

That's pretty much how I got my ovaries, though it involved stem cells and needles in addition to pills.

I was still *him*, because they hadn't repaired the damage to my brain yet. They had to keep him under control while the physical adaptations were happening. He was on chemical house arrest. Induced anxiety disorder. Induced agoraphobia.

It doesn't sound so bad until you realize that the neurological shackles are strong enough that even stepping outside your front door can put you on the ground. There are supposed to be safeguards in place. But everybody's heard the stories of criminals on chemarrest who burned to death because they couldn't make themselves walk out of a burning building.

He thought he could beat the rightminding, beat the chemarrest. Beat everything.

Damn, I was arrogant.

MY FORMER SELF had more grounds for his arrogance than this guy. *This is pathetic,* I think. And then I have to snort laughter, because it's not my former self who's got me tied up in this basement.

I could just let this happen. It'd be fair. Ironic. *Justice.*

And my dying here would mean more women follow me into this basement. One by one by one.

I unbind my ankles more quickly than I did the wrists. Then I stand and start pacing, do jumping jacks, jog in place while I shine my light around. The activity eases the shivering. Now it's just a tremble, not a teeth-rattling shudder. My muscles are stiff; my bones ache. There's a cramp in my left calf.

There's a door locked with a deadbolt. The windows have been bricked over with new bricks that don't match the foundation. They're my best option – if I could find something to strike with, something to pry with, I might break the mortar and pull them free.

I've got my hands. My teeth. My tiny light, which I turn off now so as not to warn my captor.

And a core temperature that I'm barely managing to keep out of the danger zone.

WHEN I WALKED into my court-mandated therapist's office for the last time – before my relocation – I looked at her creamy complexion, the way the light caught on her eyes behind the glasses. I remembered what *he'd* thought.

If a swell of revulsion could split your own skin off and leave it curled on the ground like something spoiled and disgusting, that would have happened to me then. But of course it wasn't my shell that was ruined and rotten; it was something in the depths of my brain.

"How does it feel to have a functional amygdala?" she asked.

"Lousy," I said.

She smiled absently and stood up to shake my hand – for the first time. To offer me closure. It's something they're supposed to do.

"Thank you for all the lives you've saved," I told her.

"But not for yours?" she said.

I gave her fingers a gentle squeeze and shook my head.

MY OTHER SELF waits in the dark with me. I wish I had his physical strength, his invulnerability. His conviction that everybody else in the world is slower, stupider, weaker.

In the courtroom, while I was still my other self, he looked out from the stand into the faces of the living mothers and fathers of the girls he killed.

I remember the 11 women and seven men, how they focused on him. How they sat, their stillness, their attention.

He thought about the girls while he gave his testimony. The only individuality they had for him was what was necessary to sort out which parents went with which corpse; important, because it told him whom to watch for the best response.

I wish I didn't know what it feels like to be prey. I tell myself it's just the cold that makes my teeth chatter. Just the cold that's killing me.

Prey can fight back, though. People have gotten killed by something as timid and inoffensive as a white-tailed deer.

I wish I had a weapon. Even a cracked piece of brick. But the cellar is clean.

I do jumping jacks, landing on my toes for silence. I swing my arms. I think about doing burpees, but I'm worried that I might scrape my hands on the floor. I think about taking my shoes off. Running shoes are soft for kicking with, but if I get outside, my feet will freeze without them.

When. When I get outside.

My hands and teeth are the only weapons I have.

An interminable time later, I hear a creak through the ceiling. A footstep, muffled, and then the thud of something dropped. More footsteps, louder, approaching the top of a stair beyond the door.

I crouch beside the door, on the hinge side, far enough away that it won't quite strike me if he swings it violently. I wish for a weapon – I *am* a weapon – and I wait.

A metallic tang in my mouth now. *Now* I am really, truly scared.

His feet thump on the stairs. He's not little. There's no light beneath the door – it must be weather-stripped for soundproofing. The lock thuds. A bar scrapes. The knob rattles, and then there's a bar of light as it swings open. He turns the flashlight to the right, where he left me lying. It picks out the puddle of vomit. I hear his intake of breath.

I think about the mothers of the girls I killed. I think, *Would they want me to die like this?*

My old self would relish it. It'd be his revenge for what I did to him.

My goal is just to get past him – my captor, my old self; they blur together – to get away, run. Get outside. Hope for a road, neighbors, bright daylight.

My captor's silhouette is dim, scatter-lit. He doesn't look armed, except for the flashlight, one of those archaic long heavy metal ones that doubles as a club. I can't be sure that's all he has. He wavers. He might slam the door and leave me down here to starve –

I lunge.

I grab for the wrist holding the light, and I half catch it, but he's stronger. I knew he would be. He rips the wrist out of my grip, swings the flashlight. Shouts. I lurch back, and it catches me on the shoulder instead of across the throat. My arm sparks pain and numbs. I don't hear my collarbone snap. Would I, if it has?

I try to knee him in the crotch and hit his thigh instead. I mostly elude his grip. He grabs my jacket; cloth stretches and rips. He swings the light once more. It thuds into the stair wall and punches through drywall. I'm half past him and I use his own grip as an anchor as I lean back and kick him right in the center of the nose. Soft shoes or no soft shoes.

He lets go, then. Falls back. I go up the stairs on all fours, scrambling, sure he's right behind me. Waiting for the grab at my ankle. Halfway up I realize I should have locked him in. Hit the door at the top of the stairs and find myself in a perfectly ordinary hallway, in need of a good sweep. The door ahead is closed. I fumble the lock, yank it open, tumble down steps into the snow as something fouls my ankles.

It's twilight. I get my feet under me and stagger back to the path. The shovel I fell over is tangled with my feet. I grab it, use it as a crutch, lever myself up and stagger-run-limp down the walk to a long driveway.

I glance over my shoulder, sure I hear breathing.

Nobody. The door swings open in the wind.

Oh. The road. No traffic. I know where I am. Out past the graveyard and the bridge. I run through here every couple of days, but the house is set far enough back that it was never more than a dim white outline behind trees. It's a Craftsman bungalow, surrounded by winter-sere oaks.

Maybe it wasn't an attack of opportunity, then. Maybe he saw me and decided to lie in wait.

I pelt toward town – pelt, limping, the air so cold in my lungs that they cramp and wheeze. I'm cold, so cold. The wind is a knife. I yank my sleeves down over my hands. My body tries to draw itself into a huddled comma even as I run. The sun's at the horizon.

I think, *I should just let the winter have me.*

Justice for those 11 mothers and seven fathers. Justice for those 13 women who still seem too alike. It's only that their interchangeability *bothers* me now.

At the bridge I stumble to a dragging walk, then turn into the wind off the river, clutch the rail, and stop. I turn right and don't see him coming. My wet fingers freeze to the railing.

The state police are half a mile on, right around the curve at the top of the hill. If I run, I won't freeze before I get there. If I run.

My fingers stung when I touched the rail. Now they're numb, my ears past hurting. If I stand here, I'll lose the feeling in my feet.

The sunset glazes the ice below with crimson. I turn and glance the other way; in a pewter sky, the rising moon bleaches the clouds to moth-wing iridescence.

I'm wet to the skin. Even if I start running now, I might not make it to the station house. Even if I started running now, the man in the bungalow might be right behind me. I don't think I hit him hard enough to knock him out. Just knock him down.

If I stay, it won't take long at all until the cold stops hurting.

If I stay here, I wouldn't have to remember being my other self again. I could put him down. At last, at last, I could put those women down. Amelie, unless her name was Jessica. The others.

It seems easy. Sweet.

But if I stay here, I won't be the last person to wake up in the bricked-up basement of that little white bungalow.

The wind is rising. Every breath I take is a wheeze. A crow blows across the road like a tattered shirt, vanishing into the twilight cemetery.

I can carry this a little farther. It's not so heavy. Thirteen corpses, plus one. After all, I carried every one of them before.

I leave skin behind on the railing when I peel my fingers free. Staggering at first, then stronger, I sprint back into town.

CIMMERIA: FROM *THE JOURNAL OF IMAGINARY ANTHROPOLOGY*

Theodora Goss

Theodora Goss (www.theodoragoss.com) was born in Hungary and spent her childhood in various European countries before her family moved to the United States. Although she grew up on the classics of English literature, her writing has been influenced by an Eastern European literary tradition in which the boundaries between realism and the fantastic are often ambiguous. Her publications include the short story collection *In the Forest of Forgetting; Interfictions*, a short story anthology coedited with Delia Sherman; and *Voices from Fairyland*, a poetry anthology with critical essays and a selection of her own poems. Her most recent book is *The Thorn and the Blossom: A Two-sided Love Story*. She has been a finalist for the Nebula, Crawford, and Mythopoeic Awards, as well as on the Tiptree Award Honor List, and has won the World Fantasy and Rhysling Awards.

REMEMBERING CIMMERIA: I walk through the bazar, between the stalls of the spice sellers, smelling turmeric and cloves, hearing the clash of bronze from the sellers of cooking pots, the bleat of goats from the butcher's alley. Rugs hang from wooden racks, scarlet and indigo. In the corners of the alleys, men without legs perch on wooden carts, telling their stories to a crowd of ragged children, making coins disappear into the air. Women from the mountains, their faces prematurely old from sun and suffering, call to me in a dialect I can barely understand. Their stands sell eggplants and tomatoes, the pungent olives that are distinctive to Cimmerian cuisine, video games. In the mountain villages, it has long been a custom to dye hair blue for good fortune, a practice that sophisticated urbanites have lately adopted. Even the women at court have hair of a deep and startling hue.

My guide, Afa, walks ahead of me, with a string bag in her hand, examining the vegetables, buying cauliflower and lentils. Later she will make rice mixed with raisins, meat, and saffron. The cuisine of Cimmeria is rich, heavy with goat and chicken. (They eat and keep no pigs.) The pastries are filled with almond paste and soaked in honey. She waddles ahead (forgive me, but you do waddle, Afa), and I follow amid a cacophony of voices, speaking the Indo-European language of Cimmeria, which is closest perhaps to Iranian. The mountain accents are harsh, the tones of the urbanites soft and lisping. Shaila spoke in those tones, when she taught me phrases in her language: Can I have more lozi (a cake made with marzipan, flavored with orange water)? You are the son of a dog. I will love you until the ocean swallows the moon. (A traditional saying. At the end of time, the serpent that lies beneath the Black Sea will rise up and swallow the moon as though it were lozi. It means, I will love you until the end of time.)

On that day, or perhaps it is another day I remember, I see a man selling Kalashnikovs. The war is a recent memory here, and every man has at least one weapon: even I wear a curved knife in my belt, or I will be taken for a prostitute. (Male prostitutes, who are common in the capital, can be distinguished by their khol-rimmed eyes, their extravagant clothes, their weaponlessness. As a red-haired Irishman, I do not look like them, but it is best to avoid misunderstandings.) The sun shines down from a cloudless sky. It is hotter than summer in Arizona, on the campus of the small college where this journey began, where we said, let us imagine a modern Cimmeria. What would it look like? I know, now. The city is cooled by a thousand fountains, we are told: its name means just that, A Thousand Fountains. It was founded in the sixth century BCE, or so we have conjectured and imagined.

I have a pounding headache. I have been two weeks in this country, and I cannot get used to the heat, the smells, the reality of it all. Could we have created this? The four of us, me and Lisa and Michael the Second, and Professor Farrow, sitting in a conference room at that small college? Surely not. And yet.

* * *

WE WERE WORRIED that the Khan would forbid us from entering the country. But no. We were issued visas, assigned translators, given office space in the palace itself.

The Khan was a short man, balding. His wife had been Miss Cimmeria, and then a television reporter for one of the three state channels. She had met the Khan when she had been sent to interview him. He wore a business suit with a traditional scarf around his neck. She looked as though she had stepped out of a photoshoot for *Vogue Russia*, which was available in all the gas stations.

"Cimmeria has been here, on the shores of the Black Sea, for more than two thousand years," he said. "Would you like some coffee, Dr. Nolan? I think our coffee is the best in the world." It was – dark, thick, spiced, and served with ewe's milk. "This theory of yours – that a group of American graduate students created Cimmeria in their heads, merely by thinking about it – you will understand that some of our people find it insulting. They will say that all Americans are imperialist dogs. I myself find it amusing, almost charming – like poetry. The mind creates reality, yes? So our poets have taught us. Of course, your version is culturally insensitive, but then, you are Americans. I did not think Americans were capable of poetry."

Only Lisa had been a graduate student, and even she had recently graduated. Mike and I were post-docs, and Professor Farrow was tenured at Southern Arizona State. It all seemed so far away, the small campus with its perpetually dying lawns and drab 1970s architecture. I was standing in a reception room, drinking coffee with the Khan of Cimmeria and his wife, and Arizona seemed imaginary, like something I had made up.

"But we like Americans here. The enemy of my enemy is my friend, is he not? Any enemy of Russia is a friend of mine. So I am glad to welcome you to my country. You will, I am certain, be sensitive to our customs. Your coworker, for example – I suggest that she not wear short pants in the streets. Our clerics, whether Orthodox, Catholic, or Muslim, are traditional and may be offended. Anyway, you must admit, such garments are not attractive on women. I would not say so to her, you understand, for women are the devil when they are criticized. But a woman should cultivate an air of mystery. There is nothing mysterious about bare red knees."

Our office space was in an unused part of the palace. My translator, Jafik, told me it had once been a storage area for bedding. It was close to the servants' quarters. The Khan may have welcomed us to Cimmeria for diplomatic reasons, but he did not think much of us, that was clear. It was part of the old palace, which had been built in the thirteenth century CE, after the final defeat of the Mongols. Since then, Cimmeria had been embroiled in almost constant warfare, with Anatolia, Scythia, Poland, and most recently the Russians, who had wanted its ports on the Black Sea. The Khan had received considerable American aid, including military advisors. The war had ended with the disintegration of the USSR. The Ukraine, focused on its own economic problems, had no wish to interfere in local politics, so Cimmeria was enjoying a period of relative peace. I wondered how long it would last.

Lisa was our linguist. She would stay in the capital for the first three months, then venture out into the countryside, recording local dialects. "You know what amazes me?" she said as we were unpacking our computers and office supplies. "The complexity of all this. You would think it really had been here for the last three thousand years. It's hard to believe it all started with Mike the First goofing off in Professor Farrow's class." He had been bored, and instead of taking notes, had started sketching a city. The professor had caught him, and had told the students that we would spend the rest of the semester creating that city and the surrounding countryside. We would be responsible for its history, customs, language. Lisa was in the class too, and I was the TA. AN 703, Contemporary Anthropological Theory, had turned into Creating Cimmeria.

Of the four graduate students in the course, only Lisa stayed in the program. One got married and moved to Wisconsin, another transferred to the School of Education so she could become a kindergarten teacher. Mike the First left with his master's and went on to do an MBA. It was a coincidence that Professor Farrow's next postdoc, who arrived in the middle of the semester, was also named Mike. He had an undergraduate degree in classics, and was the one who decided that the country we were developing was Cimmeria. He was also particularly interested in the Borges hypothesis. Everyone had been talking about it at Michigan, where he had done his PhD. At that point, it was more controversial than it is now, and Professor Farrow had only been planning to touch on it briefly at the end of the semester. But once we started on Cimmeria, AN 703 became an experiment in creating reality through perception and expectation. Could we actually create Cimmeria by thinking about it, writing about it?

Not in one semester, of course. After the semester ended, all of us worked on the Cimmeria Project. It became the topic of Lisa's dissertation: *A Dictionary and Grammar of Modern Cimmerian, with Commentary*. Mike focused on history. I wrote articles on culture, figuring out probable rites of passage, how the Cimmerians would bury their dead. We had Herodotus, we had accounts of cultures from that area. We were all steeped in anthropological theory. On weekends, when we should have been going on dates, we gathered in a conference room, under a fluorescent light, and talked about Cimmeria. It was fortunate that around that time, the *Journal of Imaginary Anthropology* was founded at Penn State. Otherwise, I don't know where we would have published. At the first Imaginary Anthropology conference, in Orlando, we realized that a group from Tennessee was working on the modern Republic of Scythia and Sarmatia, which shared a border with Cimmeria. We formed a working group.

"Don't let the Cimmerians hear you talk about creating all this," I said. "Especially the nationalists. Remember, they have guns, and you don't." Should I mention her cargo shorts? I had to admit, looking at her knobby red knees, above socks and Birkenstocks, that the Khan had a point. Before she left for the mountains, I would warn her to wear more traditional clothes.

I was going to stay in the capital. My work would focus on the ways in which the historical practices we had described in "Cimmeria: A Proposal," in the second issue of the *Journal of Imaginary Anthropology,* influenced and remained evident in modern practice. Already I had seen developments we had never anticipated. One was the fashion for blue hair; in a footnote, Mike had written that blue was a fortunate color in Cimmerian folk belief. Another was the ubiquity of cats in the capital. In an article on funerary rites, I had described how cats were seen as guides to the land of the dead until the coming of Christianity in the twelfth century CE. The belief should have gone away, but somehow it had persisted, and every household, whether Orthodox, Catholic, Muslim, Jewish, or one of the minor sects that flourished in the relative tolerance of Cimmeria, had its cat. No Cimmerian wanted his soul to get lost on the way to Paradise. Stray cats were fed at the public expense, and no one dared harm a cat. I saw them everywhere, when I ventured into the city. In a month, Mike was going to join us, and I would be able to show him all the developments I was documenting. Meanwhile, there was email and Skype.

I was assigned a bedroom and bath close to our offices. Afa, who had been a sort of under-cook, was assigned to be my servant but quickly became my guide, showing me around the city and mocking my Cimmerian accent. "Heh heh!" she would say. "No, Doctor Pat, that word is not pronounced that way. Do not repeat it that way, I beg of you. I am an old woman, but still it is not respectable for me to hear!" Jafik was my language teacher as well as my translator, teaching me the language Lisa had created based on what we knew of historical Cimmerian and its Indo-European roots, except that it had developed an extensive vocabulary. As used by modern Cimmerians, it had the nuance and fluidity of a living language, as well as a surprising number of expletives.

I had no duties except to conduct my research, which was a relief from the grind of TAing and, recently, teaching my own undergraduate classes. But one day, I was summoned to speak with the Khan. It was the day of an official audience, so he was dressed in Cimmerian ceremonial robes, although he still wore his Rolex watch. His advisors looked impatient, and I gathered that the audience was about to begin – I had seen a long line of supplicants waiting by the door as I was ushered in. But he said, as though we had all the time in the world, "Doctor Nolan, did you know that my daughters are learning American?" Sitting next to him were four girls, all wearing the traditional head-scarves worn by Cimmerian peasant women, but pulled back to show that their hair was dyed fashionably blue. "They are very troublesome, my daughters. They like everything modern: Leonardo DiCaprio, video games. Tradition is not good enough for them. They wish to attend university and find professions, or do humanitarian work. Ah, what is a father to do?" He shook a finger at them, fondly enough. "I would like it if you could teach them the latest American idioms. The slang, as it were."

That afternoon, Afa led me to another part of the palace – the royal family's personal quarters. These were more modern and considerably more comfortable than ours. I was shown into what seemed to be a common room for the girls. There were colorful rugs and divans, embroidered wall-hangings, and an enormous flat-screen TV.

"These are the Khan's daughters," said Afa. She had already explained to me, in case I made any blunders, that they were his daughters by his first wife, who had not been Miss Cimmeria, but had produced the royal children: a son, and then only daughters, and then a second son who had died shortly after birth. She had died a week later of an infection contacted during the difficult delivery. "Anoor is the youngest, then Tallah, and then Shaila, who is already taking university classes online." Shaila smiled at me. This time, none of them were wearing head-scarves. There really was something attractive about blue hair.

"And what about the fourth one?" She was sitting a bit back from the others, to the right of and behind Shaila, whom she closely resembled.

Afa looked at me with astonishment. "The Khan has three daughters," she said. "Anoor, Tallah, and Shaila. There is no fourth one, Doctor Pat."

The fourth one stared at me without expression.

"Cimmerians don't recognize twins," said Lisa. "That has to be the explanation. Do you remember the thirteenth-century philosopher Farkosh Kursand? When God made the world, He decreed that human beings would be born one at a time, unique, unlike animals. They would be born defenseless, without claws or teeth or fur. But they would have souls. It's in a children's book – I have a copy somewhere, but it's based on Kursand's reading of Genesis in one of his philosophical treatises. Mike would know which. And it's the basis of Cimmerian human rights law, actually. That's why women have always had more rights here. They have souls, so they've been allowed to vote since Cimmeria became a parliamentary monarchy. I'm sure it's mentioned in one of the articles – I don't remember which one, but check the database Mike is putting together. Shaila must have been a twin, and the Cimmerians don't recognize the second child as separate from the first. So Shaila is one girl. In two bodies. But with one soul."

"Who came up with that stupid idea?"

"Well, to be perfectly honest, it might have been you." She leaned back in our revolving chair. I don't know how she could do that without falling. "Or

Mike, of course. It certainly wasn't my idea. Embryologically it does make a certain sense. Identical twins really do come from one egg."

"So they're both Shaila."

"There is no both. The idea of both is culturally inappropriate. There is one Shaila, in two bodies. Think of them as Shaila and her shadow."

I tested this theory once, while walking through the market with Afa. We were walking through the alley of the dog-sellers. In Cimmeria, almost every house has a dog, for defense and to catch rats. Cats are not sold in the market. They cannot be sold at all, only given or willed away. To sell a cat for money is to imperil your immortal soul. We passed a woman sitting on the ground, with a basket beside her. In it were two infants, as alike as the proverbial two peas in a pod, half-covered with a ragged blanket. Beside them lay a dirty mutt with a chain around its neck that lifted its head and whimpered as we walked by.

"Child how many in basket?" I asked Afa in my still-imperfect Cimmerian.

"There is one child in that basket, Pati," she said. I could not get her to stop using the diminutive. I even told her that in my language Pati was a woman's name, to no effect. She just smiled, patted me on the arm, and assured me that no one would mistake such a tall, handsome (which in Cimmerian is the same word as beautiful) man for a woman.

"Only one child?"

"Of course. One basket, one child."

Shaila's shadow followed her everywhere. When she and her sisters sat with me in the room with the low divans and the large-screen TV, studying American slang, she was there. "What's up!" Shaila would say, laughing, and her shadow would stare down at the floor. When Shaila and I walked through the gardens, she walked six paces behind, pausing when we paused, sitting when we sat. After we were married, in our apartment in Arizona, she would sit in a corner of the bedroom, watching as we made love. Although I always turned off the lights, I could see her: a darkness against the off-white walls of faculty housing.

Once, I tried to ask Shaila about her. "Shaila, do you know the word twin?"

"Yes, of course," she said. "In American, if two babies are born at the same time, they are twins."

"What about in Cimmeria? Surely there is a Cimmerian word for twin. Sometimes two babies are born at the same time in Cimmeria too."

She looked confused. "I suppose so. Biology is the same everywhere."

"Well, what's the word, then?"

"I cannot think of it. I shall have to email Tallah. She is better at languages than I am."

"What if you yourself were a twin?"

"Me? But I am not a twin. If I were, my mother would have told me."

I tried a different tactic. "Do you remember the dog you had, Kala? She had two sisters, born at the same time. Those were Anoor's and Tallah's dogs. They were not Kala, even though they were born in the same litter. You could think of them as twins – I mean, triplets." I remembered them gamboling together, Kala and her two litter-mates. They would follow us through the gardens, and Shaila and her sisters would pet them indiscriminately. When we sat under the plum trees, they would tumble together into one doggy heap.

"Pat, what is this all about? Is this about the fact that I don't want to have a baby right now? You know I want to go to graduate school first."

I did not think her father would approve the marriage. I told her so: "Your father will never agree to you marrying a poor American post-doc. Do you have any idea how poor I am? My research grant is all I have."

"You do not understand Cimmerian politics," Shaila replied. "Do you know what percentage of our population is ethnically Sarmatian? Twenty percent, all in the Eastern province. They fought the Russians, and they still have weapons. Not just guns: tanks, anti-aircraft missiles. The Sarmatians are getting restless, Pati. They are mostly Catholic, in a country that is mostly Orthodox. They want to unite with their homeland, create a greater Scythia and Sarmatia. My father projects an image of strength, because what else can you do? But he is afraid. He is most afraid that the Americans will not help. They helped against the Russians, but this is an internal matter. He has talked to us already about different ways for us to leave the country. Anoor has been enrolled at the Lycée International in Paris, and Tallah is going to study at the American School in London. They can get student visas. For me it is more difficult: I must be admitted at a university. That is why I have been taking courses online. Ask him: if he says no, then no. But I think he will consider my marriage with an American."

She was right. The Khan considered. For a week, and then another, while pro-Sarmatian factions clashed with the military in the Eastern province. Then protests broke out in the capital. Anoor was already in Paris with her mother, supposedly on a shopping spree for school. Tallah had started school in London. In the Khan's personal office, I signed the marriage contract, barely understanding what I was signing because it was in an ornate script I had seen only in medieval documents. On the way to the airport, we stopped by the cathedral in Shahin Square, where we were married by the Patriarch of the Cimmerian Independent Orthodox Church, who checked the faxed copy of my baptismal certificate and lectured me in sonorous tones about the importance of conversion, raising children in the true faith. The Khan kissed Shaila on both cheeks, promising her that we would have a proper ceremony when the political situation was more stable and she could return to the country. In the Khan's private plane, we flew to a small airport near Fresno and spent our first night together at my mother's house. My father had died of a heart attack while I was in college, and she lived alone in the house where I had grown up. It was strange staying in the guest bedroom, down the hall from the room where I had slept as a child, which still had my He-Man action figures on the shelves, the Skeletor defaced with permanent marker. I had to explain to her about Shaila's shadow.

"I don't understand," my mother said. "Are you all going to live together?"

"Well, yes, I guess so. It's really no different than if her twin sister were living with us, is it?"

"And Shaila is going to take undergraduate classes? What is her sister going to do?"

"I have no idea," I said.

What she did, more than anything else, was watch television. All day, it would be on. Mostly, she watched CNN and the news shows. Sometimes I would test Shaila, asking, "Did you turn the TV on?"

"Is it on?" she would say. "Then of course I must have turned it on. Unless you left it on before you went out. How did your class go? Is that football player in the back still falling asleep?"

One day, I came home and noticed that the other Shaila was cooking dinner. Later I asked, "Shaila, did you cook dinner?"

"Of course," she said. "Did you like it?"

"Yes." It was actually pretty good, chicken in a thick red stew over rice. It reminded me of a dish Afa had made in an iron pot hanging over an open fire in the servants' quarters. But I guess it could be made on an American stovetop as well.

After that, the other Shaila cooked dinner every night. It was convenient, because I was teaching night classes, trying to make extra money. Shaila told me that I did not need to work so hard, that the money her father gave her was more than enough to support us both. But I was proud and did not want to live off my father-in-law, even if he was the Khan of Cimmeria. At the same time, I was trying to write up my research on Cimmerian funerary practices. If I could publish a paper in the *Journal of Imaginary Anthropology*, I might have a shot at a tenure-track position, or at least a visiting professorship somewhere that wasn't Arizona. Shaila was trying to finish her pre-med requirements. She had decided that she wanted to be a pediatrician.

Meanwhile, in Cimmeria, the situation was growing more complicated. The pro-Sarmatian faction had split into the radical Sons of Sarmatia and the more moderate Sarmatian Democratic Alliance, although the Prime Minister claimed that the SDA was a front. There were weekly clashes with police in the capital, and the Sons of Sarmatia had planted a bomb in the Hilton, although a maid had reported a suspicious shopping bag and the hotel had been evacuated before the bomb could go off. The Khan had imposed a curfew, and martial law might be next, although the army had a significant Sarmatian minority. But I had classes to teach, so I tried not to pay attention to politics, and even Shaila dismissed it all as "a mess."

ONE DAY, I came home from a departmental meeting and Shaila wasn't in the apartment. She was usually home by seven. I assumed she'd had to stay late for a lab. The other Shaila was cooking dinner in the kitchen. At eight, when she hadn't come back yet, I sat down at the kitchen table to eat. To my surprise, the other Shaila sat down across from me, at the place set for Shaila. She had never sat down at the table with us before.

She looked at me with her dark eyes and said, "How was your day, Pati?"

I dropped my fork. It clattered against the rim of the plate. She had never spoken before, not one sentence, not one word. Her voice was just like

Shaila's, but with a stronger accent. At least it sounded stronger to me. Or maybe not. It was hard to tell.

"Where's Shaila?" I said. I could feel a constriction in my chest, as though a fist had started to close around my heart. Like the beginning of my father's heart attack. I think even then, I knew.

"What do you mean?" she said. "I'm Shaila. I have always been Shaila. The only Shaila there is."

I stared down at the lamb and peas in saffron curry. The smell reminded me of Cimmeria, of the bazaar. I could almost hear the clash of the cooking pots.

"You've done something to her, haven't you?"

"I have no idea what you're talking about. Eat your dinner, Pati. It's going to get cold. You've been working so hard lately. I don't think it's good for you."

But I could not eat. I stood up, accidentally hitting my hip on the table and cursing at the pain. With a growing sense of panic, I searched the apartment for any clue to Shaila's whereabouts. Her purse was in the closet, with her cell phone in it, so she must have come home earlier in the evening. All her clothes were on the hangers, as far as I could tell – she had a lot of clothes. Nothing seemed to be missing. But Shaila was not there. The other Shaila stood watching me, as though waiting for me to give up, admit defeat. Finally, after one last useless look under the bed, I left, deliberately banging the door behind me. She had to be somewhere.

I walked across campus, to the Life Sciences classrooms and labs, and checked all of them. Then I walked through the main library and the science library, calling "Shaila!" until a graduate student in a carrel told me to be quiet. By this time, it was dark. I went to her favorite coffee shop, the Espresso Bean, where undergraduates looked at me strangely from behind their laptops, and then to every shop and restaurant that was still open, from the gelato place to the German restaurant, famous for its bratwurst and beer, where students took their families on Parents' Weekend. Finally, I walked the streets, calling "Shaila!" as though she were a stray dog, hoping that the other Shaila was simply being presumptuous, rebelling against her secondary status. Hoping the real Shaila was out there somewhere.

I passed the police station and stood outside, thinking about going in and reporting her missing. I would talk to a police officer on duty, tell him I could not find my wife. He would come home with me, to find – my wife, saying that I was overworked and needed to rest, see a psychiatrist. Shaila had entered the country with a diplomatic passport – one passport, for one Shaila. Had anyone seen the other Shaila? Only my mother. She had picked us up at the airport, we had spent the night with her, all three of us eating dinner at the dining-room table. She had avoided looking at the other Shaila, talking to Shaila about how the roses were doing well this year despite aphids, asking whether she knew how to knit, how she dyed her hair that particular shade of blue – pointless, polite talk. And then we had rented a car and driven to Arizona, me and Shaila in the front seat, the other Shaila in back with the luggage. Once we had arrived at the university, she had stayed in the apartment. Lisa knew, but she and Mike the Second were still in Cimmeria, and their internet connection could be sporadic. I could talk to Dr. Farrow? She would be in her office tomorrow morning, before classes. She would at least believe me. But I knew, with a cold certainly in the pit of my stomach, that Anne Farrow would look at me from over the wire rims of her glasses and say, "Pat, you know as well as I do that culture defines personhood." She was an anthropologist, through and through. She would not interfere. I had been married to Shaila, I was still married to Shaila. There was just one less of her.

In the end, I called my mother, while sitting on a park bench under a street lamp, with the moon sailing high above, among the clouds.

"Do you know what time it is, Pat?" she asked.

"Listen, Mom," I said, and explained the situation.

"Oh, Pat, I wish you hadn't married that woman. But can't you divorce her? Are you allowed to divorce in that church? I wish you hadn't broken up with Bridget Ferguson. The two of you were so sweet together at prom. You know she married an accountant and has two children now. She sent me a card at Christmas."

I said good night and told her to go back to sleep, that I would figure it out. And then I sat there for a long time.

When I came home, well after midnight, Shaila was waiting for me with a cup of Cimmerian coffee, or as close as she could get with an American espresso machine. She was wearing the heart pajamas I had given Shaila for Valentine's Day.

"Pati," she said, "you left so quickly that I didn't have time to tell you the news. I heard it on CNN this morning, and then Daddy called me. Malek was assassinated yesterday." Malek was her brother. I had never met him – he had been an officer in the military, and while I had been in Cimmeria, he had been serving in the mountains. I knew that he had been recalled to the capital to deal with the Sarmantian agitation, but that was all.

"Assassinated? How?"

"He was trying to negotiate with the Sons of Sarmatia, and a radical pulled out a gun that had gotten through security. You never watch the news, do you, Pati? I watch it a great deal. It is important for me to learn the names of the world leaders, learn about international diplomacy. That is more important than organic chemistry, for a Khanum."

"A what?"

"Don't you understand? Now that Malek is dead, I am next in the line of succession. Someday, I will be the Khanum of Cimmeria. That is what we call a female Khan. In some countries, only male members of the royal family can succeed to the throne. But Cimmeria has never been like that. It has always been cosmopolitan, progressive. The philosopher Amirabal persuaded Teshup the Third to make his daughter his heir, and ever since, women can become rulers of the country. My great-grandmother, Daddy's grandma, was a Khanum, although she resigned when her son came of age. It is the same among the Scythians and Sarmatians." This was Lisa's doing. It had to be Lisa's doing. She was the one who had come up with Amirabal and the philosophical school she had founded in 500 BCE. Even Plato had praised her as one of the wisest philosophers in the ancient world. I silently cursed all Birkenstock-wearing feminists.

"What does this mean?" I asked.

"It means that tomorrow we fly to Washington, where I will ask your President for help against the Sarmatian faction. This morning on one of the news shows, the Speaker of the House criticized him for not supporting the government of Cimmeria. He mentioned the War on Terror – you know how they talk, and he wants to be the Republican candidate. But I think we can finally get American aid. While I am there, I will call a press conference, and you will stand by my side. We will let the American people see that my husband is one of them. It will generate sympathy and support. Then we will fly to Cimmeria. I need to be in my country as a symbol of the future. And I must produce an heir to the throne as quickly as possible – a boy, because while I can legally become Khanum, the people will want assurance that I can bear a son. While you were out, I packed all our clothes. We will meet Daddy's plane at the airport tomorrow morning. You must wear your interview suit until we can buy you another. I've set the alarm for five o'clock."

I should have said no. I should have raged and cried, and refused to be complicit in something that made me feel as though I might be sick for the rest of my life. But I said nothing. What could I say? This, too, was Shaila.

I lay in the dark beside the woman who looked like my wife, unable to sleep, staring into the darkness. Shaila, I thought, what has happened to you? To your dreams of being a pediatrician, of our children growing up in America, eating tacos and riding their bikes to school? You wanted them to be ordinary, to escape the claustrophobia you had felt growing up in the palace, with its political intrigue and the weight of centuries perpetually pressing down on you. In the middle of the night, the woman who was Shaila, but not my Shaila, turned in her sleep and put an arm around me. I did not move away.

YOU ARE PLEASED, Afa, that I have returned to Cimmeria. It has meant a promotion for you, and you tell everyone that you are personal assistant to the American husband of the Khanum-to-be. You sell information about her pregnancy to the fashion magazines – how big she's getting, how radiant she is. Meanwhile, Shaila opens schools and meets with foreign ambassadors. She's probably the most popular figure in the country, part of the propaganda war against the Sons of Sarmatia, which has mostly fallen apart since Malek's death. The SDA was absorbed into the Cimmerian Democratic Party and no longer presents a problem. American aid helped, but more important was the surge of nationalism among ethnic Cimmerians. Indeed, the nationalists, with their anti-Sarmatian sentiments, may be a problem in the next election.

I sit at the desk in my office, which is no longer near the servants' quarters, but in the royal wing of the palace, writing this article, which would be suppressed if it appeared in any of the newspapers. But it will be read only by *JoIA*'s peer editors before languishing in the obscurity of an academic journal. Kala and one of her sisters lies at my feet. And I think about this country, Afa. It is – it was – a dream, but are not all nations of men dreams? Do we not create them, by drawing maps with lines on them, and naming rivers, mountain ranges? And then deciding that the men of our tribe can only marry women outside their matrilineage? That they must bury corpses rather than burning them, eat chicken and goats but not pigs, worship this bull-headed god rather than the crocodile god of that other tribe, who is an abomination? Fast during the dark of the moon, feast when the moon is full? I'm starting to sound like a poet, which will not be good for my academic career. One cannot write an academic paper as though it were poetry.

We dream countries, and then those countries dream us. And it seems to me, sitting here by the window, looking into a garden filled with roses, listening to one of the thousand fountains of this ancient city, that as much as I have dreamed Cimmeria, it has dreamed me.

Sometimes I forget that the other Shaila ever existed. A month after we returned to Cimmeria, an Arizona state trooper found a body in a ditch close to the Life Sciences Building. It was female, and badly decomposed. The coroner estimated that she would have been about twenty, but the body was nude and there was no other identification. I'm quoting the story I read online, on the local newspaper's website. The police suggested that she might have been an illegal immigrant who had paid to be driven across the border, then been killed for the rest of her possessions. I sometimes wonder if she was Shaila.

This morning she has a television interview, and this afternoon she will be touring a new cancer treatment center paid for with American aid. All those years of listening and waiting were, after all, the perfect training for a Khanum. She is as patient as a cobra.

If I ask to visit the bazaar, the men who are in charge of watching me will first secure the square, which means shutting down the bazaar. They accompany me even to the university classes I insist on teaching. They stand at the back of the lecture hall, in their fatigues and sunglasses, carrying

Kalashnikovs. Despite American aid, they do not want to give up their Russian weapons. So we must remember it: the stalls selling embroidered fabrics, and curved knives, and melons. The baskets in high stacks, and glasses of chilled mint tea into which we dip the pistachio biscuits that you told me are called Fingers of the Dead. Boys in sandals break-dancing to Arabic hip hop on a boombox so old that it is held together with string. I would give a great deal to be able to go to the bazaar again. Or to go home and identify Shaila's body.

But in a couple of months, my son will be born. (Yes, it is a son. I've seen the ultrasound, but if you tell the newspapers, Afa, I will have you beheaded. I'm pretty sure I can still do that, here in Cimmeria.) There is only one of him, thank goodness. We intend to name him Malek. My mother has been sending a steady supply of knitted booties. There will be a national celebration, with special prayers in the churches and mosques and synagogues, and a school holiday. I wish Mike could come, or even Lisa. But he was offered a tenure-track position at a Christian college in North Carolina interested in the Biblical implications of Imaginary Anthropology. And Lisa is up in the mountains somewhere, close to the Scythian and Sarmatian border, studying woman's initiation rites. I will stand beside Shaila and her family on the balcony of the palace, celebrating the birth of the future Khan of Cimmeria. In the gardens, rose petals will fall. Men will continue dying of natural or unnatural causes, and the cats of Cimmeria will lead them into another world. Women will dip their water jugs in the fountains of the city, carrying them on their heads back to their houses, as they have done since Cimmeria has existed, whether that is three or three thousand years. Life will go on as it has always done, praise be to God, creator of worlds, however they were created.

Reprinted from the *Journal of Imaginary Anthropology* 4.2 (Fall 2013). Dr. Patrick Nolan is also co-author of "Cimmeria: A Proposal" (with M. Sandowski , L. Lang, and A. Farrow), *JoIA* 2.1 (Spring 2011) and author of "Modern Cimmerian Funerary Practices," *JoIA* 3.2 (Fall 2012). Dr. Nolan is currently a professor at Kursand University. He is working on *A History of Modern Cimmeria*.

COLLATERAL
Peter Watts

Peter Watts (www.rifters.com) is a multi-award-winning SF author, marine biologist, flesh-eating-disease survivor and convicted felon whose novels – despite an unhealthy focus on space vampires – are required texts for undergraduate courses ranging from Philosophy to Neuropsychology. His most recent book is *Firefall*, an omnibus of novels *Blindsight* and *Echopraxia*. His work is available in eighteen languages. He also likes cats.

THEY GOT BECKER out in eight minutes flat, left the bodies on the sand for whatever scavengers the Sixth Extinction hadn't yet managed to take out. Munsin hauled her into the Sikorsky and tried to yank the augments manually, right on the spot; Wingman swung and locked and went hot in the pants-pissing half-second before its threat-recognition macros, booted late to the party, calmed it down. Someone jammed the plug-in home between Becker's shoulders; wireless gates unlocked in her head and Blanch, way up in the cockpit, put her prosthetics to sleep from a safe distance. The miniguns sagged on her shoulders like anesthetized limbs, threads of smoke still wafting from the barrels.

"Corporal." Fingers snapped in her face. "Corporal, you with me?"

Becker blinked. "They – they were human…" She thought they were, anyway. All she'd been able to see were the heat signatures: bright primary colors against the darkness. They'd started out with arms and legs but then they'd *spread* like dimming rainbows, like iridescent oil slicks.

Munson said nothing.

Abemama receded to stern, a strip of baked coral suffused in a glow of infrared: yesterday's blackbodied sunshine bleeding back into the sky. Blanch hit a control and the halo vanished: night-eyes blinded, ears deafened to any wavelength past the range of human hearing, all senses crippled back down to flesh and blood.

The bearing, though. Before the darkness had closed in. It had seemed wrong.

"We're not going to Bonriki?"

"*We* are," the Sergeant said. "You're going home. Rendezvous off Aranuka. We're getting you out before this thing explodes."

She could feel Blanch playing around in the back of her brain, draining the op logs from her head. She tried to access the stream but he'd locked her out. No telling what those machines were sucking out of her brain. No telling if any of it would still be there when he let her back in.

Not that it mattered. She wouldn't have been able to scrub those images from her head if she tried.

"They *had* to be hostiles," she muttered. "How could they have just *been* there, I mean – what else could they be?" And then, a moment later: "Did any of them…?"

"You wouldn't be much of a superhuman killing machine if they had," Okoro said from across the cabin. "They weren't even armed."

"Private Okoro," the Sergeant said mildly. "Shut your fucking mouth."

They were all sitting across the cabin from her, in defiance of optimal in-flight weight distribution: Okoro, Perry, Flannery, Cole. None of them augged yet. There weren't enough Beckers to go around, one every three or four companies if the budget was up for it and the politics were hot enough. Becker was used to the bitching whenever the subject came up, everyone playing the hard-ass, rolling their eyes at the cosmic injustice that out of all of them it was the farmer's daughter from fucking *Red Deer* who'd won the lottery. It had never really bothered her. For all their trash-talking bullshit, she'd never seen anything but good-natured envy in their eyes.

She wasn't sure what she saw there now.

EIGHT THOUSAND KILOMETERS to Canadian airspace. Another four to Trenton. Fourteen hours total on the KC-500 the brass had managed to scrounge from the UN on short notice. It seemed like forty: every moment relentlessly awake, every moment its own tortured post-mortem. Becker would have given anything to be able to shut down for just a little while – to sleep through the dull endless roar of the turbofans, the infinitesimal brightening of the sky from black to grey to cheerful, mocking blue – but she didn't have that kind of augmentation.

Blanch, an appendage of a different sort, kept her company on the way home. Usually he couldn't go five minutes without poking around inside her, tweaking this inhibitor or that BCI, always trying to shave latency down by another millisecond or two. This time he just sat and stared at the deck, or out the window, or over at some buckled cargo strap clanking against the fuselage. The tacpad that pulled Becker's strings sat dormant on his lap. Maybe he'd been told to keep his hands off, leave the crime scene in pristine condition for Forensic IT.

Maybe he just wasn't in the mood.

"Shit happens, you know?"

Becker looked at him. "What?"

"We're lucky something like this didn't happen *months* ago. Half those fucking islands underwater, the rest tearing each other's throats out for a couple dry hectares and a few transgenics. Not to mention the fucking Chinese just waiting for an excuse to *help out*." Blanch snorted. "Guess you could call it *peacekeeping*. If you've got a really warped sense of humor."

"I guess."

"Shame we're not Americans. They don't even sign on to those treaties, do anything they damn well please." Blanch snorted. "It may be a fascist shithole down there but at least they don't knuckle under every time someone starts talking about *war crimes*."

He was just trying to make her feel better, she knew.

"Fucking *rules of engagement*," he grumbled.

EIGHT HOURS IN IT when they landed: every aug tested to melting, every prosthetic stripped to the bolts while the meat attached to it sat silent and still and kept all the screams inside. They gave her four hours' rack time even though her clockwork could scrub the fatigue right out of her blood, regulate adenosine and melatonin so precisely she wouldn't even yawn right up until the point she dropped dead of heart failure. Might as well, they said: other schedules to clear anyway, other people to bring back across other oceans.

They told her not to worry. They told her it wasn't her fault. They gave her propranolol to help her believe them.

Four hours, flat on her back, staring at the ceiling.

Now here she was: soul half a world away, body stuck in this windowless room, paneled in oak on three sides, crawling with luminous maps and tacticals on the fourth. Learning just what the enemy had been doing, besides sneaking up on a military cyborg in the middle of the fucking night.

"They were fishing," the PAO told her.

"No," Becker said; some subconscious subroutine added an automatic "*sir*".

The JAG lawyer – *Eisbach*, that was it – shook her head. "They had longlines in their outriggers, Corporal. They had hooks, a bait pail. No weapons."

The general in the background – from NDHQ in Ottawa, Becker gathered, although there'd been no formal introduction – studied the tacpad in his hand and said nothing at all.

She shook her head. "There aren't any fish. Every reef in the WTP's been acidified for twenty years."

"It's definitely a point we'll be making," Eisbach said. "You can't fault the system for not recognizing profiles that aren't even supposed to exist in the zone."

"But how could they be –"

"Tradition, maybe." The PAO shrugged. "Some kind of cultural thing. We're checking with the local NGOs but so far none of them are accepting responsibility. Whatever they were doing, the UN never white-listed it."

"They didn't show on approach," Becker remembered. "No visual, no sound – I mean, how could a couple of boats just sneak up like that? It had to be some kind of stealth tech, that must be what Wingman keyed – I mean, they were just *there*." Why was this so hard? The augs were supposed keep her balanced, mix up just the right cocktail to keep her cool and crisp under the most lethal conditions.

Of course, the augs were also supposed to know unarmed civilians when they saw them...

The JAG was nodding. "Your mechanic. Specialist, uh…"

"Blanch." From the room's only civilian, standing unobtrusively with the potted plants. Becker glanced over; he flashed her a brief and practiced smile.

"Specialist Blanch, yes. He suspects there was a systems failure of some kind."

"I would never have fired if –" Meaning, of course, *I would never have fired.*

Don't be such a pussy, Becker. Last month you took on a Kuan-Zhan with zero cover and zero backup, never even broke a sweat. Least you can do now is stand next to a fucking philodendron without going to pieces.

"Accidents happen in – these kind of situations," the PAO admitted sadly. "Drones misidentify targets. Pillbox mistakes a civilian for an enemy combatant. No technology's perfect. Sometimes it fails. It's that simple."

"Yes sir." Dimming rainbows, bleeding into the night.

"So far the logs support Blanch's interpretation. Might be a few days before we know for certain."

"A few days we don't have. Unfortunately."

The general swept a finger across his tacpad. A muted newsfeed bloomed on the war wall behind him: House of Commons, live. Opposition members standing, declaiming, sitting. Administration MPs across the aisle, rising and falling in turn. A two-tiered array of lethargic whackamoles.

The General's eyes stayed fixed on his pad. "Do you know what they're talking about, Corporal?"

"No, sir."

"They're talking about you. Barely a day and a half since the incident and already they're debating it in Question Period."

"Did we –"

"We did not. There was a breach."

He fell silent. Behind him, shell-shocked pols stammered silent and shifty-eyed against the onslaught of Her Majesty's Loyal Opposition. The Minister of Defence's seat, Becker noted, was empty.

"Do we know who, sir?"

The general shook his head. "Any number of people could have intercepted one or more of our communications. The number who'd be able to decrypt them is a lot smaller. I'd hate to think it was one of ours, but it's not something we can rule out. Either way –" He took a breath. "– so much for our hopes of dealing with this internally."

"Yes sir."

Finally he raised his eyes to meet hers. "I want to assure you, Corporal, that nobody here has passed any judgment with regard to potential – culpability. We've reviewed the telemetry, the transcripts, the interviews; FIT's still going over the results but so far there's no evidence of any conscious wrong-doing on your part."

Conscious, Becker noted dully. Not *deliberate*. There'd been a time when the distinction would never have occurred to her.

"Be that as it may, we find ourselves forced to change strategy. In the wake of this leak it's been decided we have to *engage the public*. Doubling down and invoking national security would only increase the appearance of guilt, and after that mess in the Philippines we can't afford even a whiff of cover-up." The general sighed. "This, at least, is the view of the Minister."

"Yes sir."

"It has therefore been decided – and I'm sorry to do this to you, I know it's not what you signed up for – it's been decided to *get out in front of this thing*, as they say. Control the narrative. Make you available for interviews, prove we have nothing to hide."

"Interviews, sir?"

"You'll be liaising with Mr. Monahan here." On cue, the civilian stepped out of the background. "His firm's proven useful in matters of – public outreach."

"Ben. Just Ben." Monahan reached out to shake with his right hand, offered his card with the left: *Optic Nerve*, twinkling above a stock-ticker crawl of client endorsements. "I know how much this sucks, Corporal. I'm guessing the last thing you want to hear right now is what some high-priced image consultant has to say about covering your ass. Is that about right?"

Becker swallowed, and nodded, and retrieved her hand. Phantom wings beat on her shoulders.

"The good news is: no ass-covering required. I'm not here to polish a turd – which is actually a nice change – I'm here to make sure the truth gets out. As you know, there's no shortage of parties who are a lot less interested in what really happened than in pushing their own agendas."

"I can understand that," Becker said softly.

"This person, for example." *Just Ben* tapped his watch and wiped Parliament from the wall; the woman revealed in its place stood maybe one-seventy, black, hair cropped almost army short. She seemed a little off-balance in the picture; doubtless the helmeted RCMP officer grabbing her left bicep had something to do with that. The two of them danced against a chorus line of protestors and pacification drones.

"Amal Sabrie," Monahan was saying. "Freelance journalist, well-regarded by the left for her human rights work. Somali by birth but immigrated to Canada as a child. Her home town was Beledweyne. Does that ring any bells, Corporal?"

Becker shook her head.

"Airborne Regiment? 1992?"

"Sorry. No."

"Okay. Let's just say she's got more reason than most to mistrust the Canadian military."

"The last person we'd expect to be on our side," Eisbach remarked.

"Exactly." Monahan nodded. "Which is why I've granted her an exclusive."

THEY ENGAGED ON neutral territory, proposed by Sabrie, reluctantly approved by the chain of command: a café patio halfway up Toronto's Layton Tower, overlooking Lakeshore. It jutted from the side of the building like a bracket fungus, well above most of the drone traffic.

An almost pathological empathy for victimhood. Monahan had inventoried Sabrie's weak spots as if he'd been pulling the legs off a spider. *Heart melts for stray cats, squirrels with cancer; blood boils for battered women and oppressed minorities and anyone who ever ended up on the wrong end of a shockprod. Not into performance rage, doesn't waste any capital getting bent out of shape over random acts of microaggression. Smart enough to save herself for the big stuff. Which is why she still gets to soapbox on the prime feeds while the rest of the rabies brigade fights for space on the public microblogs.*

Twenty floors below, pedestrians moved like ants. They'd never be life-sized to Becker; she'd arrived by the roof and she'd leave the same way, a concession to those who'd much rather have conducted this interview under more controlled conditions. Who'd much rather have avoided this interview entirely, for that matter. That they'd ceded so much control spoke volumes about Optic Nerve's rep for damage control.

If we can just get her to see you as a victim – which is exactly what you are – we can turn her from agitator to cheerleader. Start off your appies as a tool of the patriarchy, you'll be her soulmate by dessert.

Or maybe it spoke volumes about a situation so desperate that the optimum strategy consisted of gambling everything on a Hail Mary.

There she is, Monahan murmured now, just inside her right temple, but Becker had already locked on: the target was dug in at a table next to the railing. This side, flower boxes and hors-d'oeuvres: that side, an eighty-meter plunge to certain death. Wingman, defanged but still untrusting, sent wary standbys to the stumps of amputated weaponry.

Amal Sabrie stood at her approach. "You look –" she began.

– *like shit*. Becker hadn't slept in three days. It shouldn't have shown; cyborgs don't get tired.

"I mean," Sabrie continued smoothly, "I thought the augments would be more conspicuous."

Great wings, spreading from her shoulders and laying down the wrath of God. Corporal Nandita Becker, Angel of Death.

"They usually are. They come off."

Neither extended a hand. They sat.

"I guess they'd have to. Unless you sleep standing up." A thought seemed to occur to her. "You sleep, right?"

"I'm a cyborg, Ms. Sabrie. Not a vacuum cleaner." An unexpected flicker of irritation, there; a bright spark on a vast dark plain. After all these flat waking hours. Becker almost welcomed it.

Monahan didn't. Too hostile. Dial it down.

Sabrie didn't miss a beat. "A cyborg who can flip cars one-handed. If the promos are to be believed."

Be friendly. Give a little. Don't make her pull teeth.

Okay.

Becker turned in her seat, bent her neck so the journalist could glimpse the tip of the black enameled centipede bolted along her backbone. "Spinal and long-bone reinforcement to handle the extra weight. Wire-muscle overlays, store almost twenty Joules per cc." There was almost a kind of comfort in rattling off the mindless specs. "Couples at over seventy percent under most –"

A *little*, Corporal.

"Anyway." Becker shrugged, straightened. "Most of the stuff's inside. The rest's plug and play." She took a breath, got down to it. "I should tell you up front I'm not authorized to talk about mission specifics."

Sabrie shrugged. "I'm not here to ask about them. I want to talk about you." She tapped her menu, entered an order for kruggets and a Rising Tide. "What're you having?"

"Thanks. I'm not hungry."

"Of course." The reporter glanced up. "You *do* eat, though, right? You still have a digestive system?"

"Nah. They just plug me into the wall." A smile to show she was kidding.

Now you're getting it.

"Glad you can still make jokes," Sabrie said from a face turned suddenly to stone.

Shit. Walked right into that one.

Down in the left hand, a tremor. Becker pulled her hands from the table, rested them on her lap.

"Okay," Sabrie said at last. "Let's get started. I have to say I'm surprised Special Forces even let me talk to you. The normal response in cases like this is to refuse comment, double down, wait for a celebrity overdose to move the spotlight."

"I'm just following orders, ma'am." The tic in Becker's hand wouldn't go away. She clasped her hands together, squeezed.

"So let's talk about something you *can* speak to," Sabrie said. "How do you feel?"

Becker blinked. "Excuse me?"

"About what happened. Your role in it. How do you feel?"

Be honest.

"I feel fucking *awful*," she said, and barely kept her voice from cracking. "How am I supposed to feel?"

"Awful," Sabrie admitted. She held silence for a respectable interval before pressing on. "The official story's systems malfunction."

"The investigation is ongoing," Becker said softly.

"Still. That's the word from sources. Your augments fired, you didn't. No *mens rea*."

Blobs of false color, spreading out against the sand.

"Do you *feel* like you killed them?"

Tell her the truth, Monahan whispered.

"I – *part* of me did. Maybe."

"They say the augments don't do anything you wouldn't do yourself. They just do it faster."

Six people on a fishing trip in an empty ocean. It didn't make any fucking sense.

"Is that the way you understand it?" Sabrie pressed. "The brain decides what it's going to do before it *knows* it's decided?"

Becker forced herself to focus, managed a nod. Even that felt a bit shaky, although the journalist didn't seem to notice. "Like a, a bubble rising from the bottom of a lake. We don't see it until it breaks the surface. The augs see it – before."

"How does that feel?"

"It feels like – " Becker hesitated.

Honesty, Corporal. You're doing great.

"It's like having a really good wingman sitting on your shoulder, watching your back. Taking out threats before you even see them. Except it's using your own body to do that. Does that make sense?"

"As much as it can, maybe. To someone who isn't augged themselves." Sabrie essayed a little frown. "Is that how it felt with Tionee?"

"Who?"

"Tionee Anoka. Reesi Eterika. Io –" She stopped at something she saw in Becker's face.

"I never knew," Becker said after a moment.

"Their names?"

Becker nodded.

"I can send you the list."

A waiter appeared, deposited a tumbler and a steaming platter of fluorescent red euphausiids in front of Sabrie; assessed the ambiance and retreated without a word.

"I didn't –" Becker closed her eyes. "I mean yes, it felt the same. At first. There had to be a threat, right? Because the augs – because *I* fired. And I'd be dead at least four times over by now if I always waited until I knew what I was firing at." She swallowed against the lump in her throat. "Only this time things started to – sink in afterward. Why didn't I see them coming? Why weren't the –"

Careful, Corporal. No tac.

"Some of them were still – moving. One of them was talking. Trying to."

"To you?"

Up in ultraviolet, the textured glass of the table fractured the incident sunlight into tiny rainbows. "No idea."

"What did they say?" Sabrie poked at her kruggets but didn't eat.

Becker shook her head. "I don't speak Kiribati."

"All those augments and you don't have realtime translation?"

"I – I never thought of that."

"Maybe those smart machines saw the bubbles rising. Knew you wouldn't *want* to know."

She hadn't thought of that either.

"So you feel awful," Sabrie said. "What else?"

"What else am I feeling?" The tremor had spread to both hands.

"If it's not too difficult."

What the fuck is *this he said I'd be* steady *he said the drugs –*

"They gave me propranolol." It was almost a whisper, and Becker wondered immediately if she'd crossed the line. But the voice in her head stayed silent.

Sabrie nodded. "For the PTSD."

"I know how that sounds. It's not like I was a victim or anything." Becker stared at the table. "I don't think it's working."

"It's a common complaint, out there on the cutting edge. All those neurotransmitters, synthetic hormones. Too many interactions. Things don't always work the way they're supposed to."

Monahan, you asshole. You're the goddamn PR expert, you should've known I wasn't up for this...

"I feel worse than awful." Becker could barely hear her own voice. "I feel *sick...*"

Sabrie appraised her with black unblinking eyes.

"This may be bigger than an interview," she said at last. "Do you think we could arrange a couple of follow-ups, maybe turn this into an in-depth profile piece?"

"I – I'd have to clear it with my superiors."

Sabrie nodded. "Of course."

Or maybe, Becker thought, *you knew all along.* As, two hundred fifty kilometers away, a tiny voice whooped in triumph.

THEY PLUGGED HER into an alternate universe where death came with an undo option. They ran her through scenarios and simulations, made her kill a hundred civilians a hundred different ways. They made her relive Kiribati again and again through her augments, for all the world as if she wasn't already reliving it every time she closed her goddamn eyes.

It was all in her head, of course, even if it wasn't all in her mind; a high-speed dialog between synapse and simulator, a multichannel exchange through a pipe as fat as any corpus callosum. A Monte-Carlo exercise in tactical brutality.

After the fourth session she opened her eyes and Blanch had disappeared; some neon red-head had replaced him while Becker had been racking up the kills. *Tauchi*, according to his name tag. She couldn't see any augments but he glowed with smartwear in the Megahertz range.

"Jord's on temporary reassignment," he said when she asked. "Tracking down the glitch."

"But – but I thought *this* –"

"This is something else. Close your eyes."

Sometimes she had to let innocent civilians die in order to save others. Sometimes she had to murder people whose only crime was being in the wrong place at the wrong time: blocking a clean shot on a battlebot that was drawing down on a medical team, or innocently reaching for some control that had been hacked to ignite a tank of H_2S half a city away. Sometimes Becker hesitated on those shots, held back in some forlorn hope that the target might move or change its mind. Sometimes, even lacking any alternative, she could barely bring herself to pull the trigger.

She wondered if maybe they were trying to toughen her up. Get her back in the saddle, desensitized through repetition, before her own remorse made her useless on the battlefield.

Sometimes there didn't seem to be a right answer, no clear way to determine whose life should take priority; mixed groups of children and adults, victims in various states of injury and amputation. The choice between a brain-damaged child and its mother. Sometimes Becker was expected to kill with no hope of saving anyone; she took strange comfort in the stark simplicity of those old classics. Fuck this handwringing over the relative weights of human souls. Just point and shoot.

I am a camera, she thought.

"Who the hell makes up these scenarios?"

"Don't like judgment calls, Corporal?"

"Not *those* ones."

"Not much initiative." Tauchi nodded approvingly. "Great on the follow-through, though." He eyed his pad. "Hmmm. That might be why. Your cortisol's fucked."

"Can you fix that? I don't think my augs have been working since I got back."

"Flashbacks? Sweats? Vigilant immobility?"

Becker nodded. "I mean, aren't they supposed to take care of all that?"

"Sure," Tauchi told her. "You start to freak, they squirt you a nice hit of dopamine or leumorphin or whatever to level you out. Problem is, do that often enough and it stops working. Your brain grows more receptors to handle the extra medicine, so now you need more medicine to feed the extra receptors. Classic habituation response."

"Oh."

"If you've been feeling wobbly lately, that's probably why. Killing those kids only pushed you over the threshold."

God, she missed Blanch.

"Chemistry sets are just a band-aid anyway," the tech rattled on. "I can tweak your settings to keep you out of the deep end for now, but longer-term we've got something better in mind."

"A drug? They've already got me on propranolol."

He shook his head. "Permanent fix. There's surgery involved, but it's no big deal. Not even any cutting."

"When?" She could feel her insides crumbling. She imagined Wingman looking away, too good a soldier to be distracted by its own contempt. "*When?*"

Tauchi grinned. "Whaddya think we're doing now?"

SHE FELT STRONGER by the next encounter.

This time it went down at street level; different patio, different ambiance, same combatants. Collapsed parasols hung from pikes rising through the center of each table, ready to spread protective shade should the afternoon sun ever make it past the skyscrapers. Sabrie set down a smooth rounded disk – a half-scale chrome hockey puck – next to the shaft. She gave it a tap.

Becker's BUD fuzzed around the edges with brief static; Wingman jumped to alert, hungry and limbless.

"For privacy," Sabrie said. "You okay with that?"

White noise on the radio. Broad-spectrum visual still working, though. The EM halo radiating from Sabrie's device was bright as a solar corona; her retinue of personal electronics glowed with dimmer light. Her watch. Her smartspecs, already recording; the faint nimbus of some medallion packed with circuitry, nestled out of sight between her breasts.

"Why now?" Becker asked. "Why not before?"

"First round's on the house. I was amazed enough that they even cleared the interview. Didn't want to push my luck."

Wingman flashed an icon; a little judicious frequency-hopping would get around the jam. If they'd been in an actual combat situation it wouldn't even be asking permission.

"You realize there are other ways to listen in," Becker said.

Sabrie shrugged. "Parabolic ear on a rooftop. Bounce a laser off the table and read the vibrations." Her eyes flickered overhead. "Any one of those drones could be a lip-reader for all I know."

"So what's the point?" (FHop?[y/n] FHop?[y/n] FHop?[y/n])

"Perpetual surveillance is the price of freedom," Sabrie said, half-smiling. "Not to mention the price of not having to worry about some random psycho shooter when you go out for sushi."

"But?"

"But there are limits. Your bosses are literally inside your *head*." She dipped her chin at the jammer. "Do you think they'll object to you providing a few unprompted answers? Given this new apparent policy of transparency and accountability?"

(FHop?[y/n])

(n)

"I don't know," Becker said.

"You know what would make them even *more* transparent and accountable? If they released the video for the night of the 25th. I keep asking, and they keep telling me there isn't any."

Becker shook her head. "There isn't."

"Come on."

"Really. Too memory-intensive. "

"Corporal, I'm recording *this*," Sabrie pointed out. "16K, Slooped sound, no compression even." She glanced into the street. "Half those people are life-logging every second of their lives for the sheer narcissistic thrill of it."

"And they're *streaming* it. Or caching and dumping every couple of hours. I don't get the luxury of tossing my cookies into some cloud whenever my cache fills up. I have to be able to operate in the dark for weeks at a time: you stream any kind of data in the field, it points back at you like a big neon arrow.

"Besides, budget time rolls around, how much of your limited R&D funding are you going to take away from tactical computing so you can make longer nature documentaries?" Becker raised her espresso in a small mock toast. "You think the People's Republic is losing any sleep over that one?"

Which is awfully convenient, remarked a small voice, *When you've just –* She shut it off.

Sabrie gave her a sidelong look. "You can't record video."

"Sure I can. But it's discretionary. You document anything you think needs documenting, but the default realtime stream is just numbers. Pure black-box stuff."

"You didn't think you needed to document –"

"I didn't *know*. It wasn't *conscious*. Why the fuck can't you people –"

Sabrie watched her without a word.

"Sorry," Becker said at last.

"It's okay," Sabrie said softly. "Rising bubbles. I get it."

Overhead, the sun peeked around an office tower. A lozenge of brightness crept onto the table.

"You know what they were doing out there?" Sabrie asked. "Tionee and his friends?"

Becker closed her eyes for a moment. "Some kind of fishing trip."

"And you never wondered why anyone would go night fishing in a place where there wasn't anything to catch but slugs and slime?"

I never stopped *wondering.* "I heard it was a – cultural thing. Keep the traditions alive, in case someone ever builds a tuna that eats limestone."

"It was an art project."

Becker squinted as the hockey puck bounced sunlight into her eyes. "Excuse me?"

"Let me get that for you." Sabrie half-rose and reached for the center of the table. The parasol bloomed with a snap. The table dropped back into eclipse.

"That's better." Sabrie reseated herself.

"An art project?" Becker repeated.

"They were college students. Cultural anthropology and art history majors, wired in from Evergreen State. Re-enact the daily lives of your forebears, play them back along wavelengths outside the human sensory range. They were calling it *Through Alien Eyes.* Some kind of commentary on outsider perspectives."

"What wavelengths?"

"Reesi was glassing everything from radio to gamma."

"There's a third-party recording?"

"Nothing especially hi-def. They were on a student budget, after all. But it was good enough to pick out a signal around 400 Megahertz. Nobody can quite figure out what it is. Not civilian, anyway."

"That whole area's contested. Military traffic all over the place."

"Yeah, well. The thing is, it was a just a couple of really short bursts. Half a second, maybe. Around eleven-forty-five."

Wingman froze. Gooseflesh rippled up Becker's spine.

Sabrie leaned forward, hands flat on the table. "That wouldn't have been you, would it?"

"You know I can't discuss operational details."

"Mmmm." Sabrie watched and waited.

"I take it you have this recording," Becker said at last.

The journalist smiled faintly. "You know I can't discuss operational details."

"I'm not asking you to compromise your sources. It just seems – odd."

"Because your guys would have been all over the bodies before they were even cool. So if anyone had that kind of evidence, it would be them."

"Something like that."

"Don't worry, you don't have a mole. Or at least if you do, they don't report to me. You want to blame anyone, blame your *wingman*."

"What?"

"Your *preconscious triggers* tie into some pretty high-caliber weaponry. I'm guessing I don't have to tell you what kind of games physics plays when multiple slugs hit a body at twelve hundred meters a second."

Momentum. Inertia. Force vectors transferred from small masses to larger ones – and maybe back to smaller ones again. A pair of smartspecs could have flown twenty meters or more, landed way up in the weeds or splashed down in the lagoon.

"We wouldn't have even known to look," Becker murmured.

"We did." Sabrie sipped her drink. "Want to hear it?"

Becker sat absolutely still.

"I know the rules, Nandita. I'm not asking you to ID it, or even comment. I just thought you might like…"

Becker glanced down at the jammer.

"I think we should leave that on." Sabrie reached into her blouse, fingered the luminous medallion hanging from her neck. "You have sockets, though, right? Hard interfaces?"

"I don't spread my legs in public."

Sabrie's eyes flickered to the far side of the street, where a small unmarked quadrocopter had just dipped into sight below the rim of the parasol. "Let's talk about your family," she said.

* * *

MONAHAN DIDN'T SEEM put out.

"We thought she might try something like that. Sabrie's hardly in the tank. But you did great, Corporal."

"You were monitoring?"

"Like we'd let some gizmo from the Sony Store cut us out of the loop? I could've even whispered sweet nothings in your ear if I'd had to – acoustic tightbeam, she'd never have had a clue unless she leaned over and nibbled your earlobe – but like I say, you were just fine." Some small afterthought made him frown. "Would've been easier if you'd just authorized frequency hopping, of course…"

"She had a lot of gizmos on her," Becker said. "If one of them had been able to pick up the signal…"

"Right. Good plan. Let her think it worked."

"Yes sir."

"Just Ben. Oh, one other thing…"

Becker waited.

"We lost contact for just a few moments there. When the umbrella went up."

"You didn't miss much. Apparently the collateral was doing a school project of some kind. Art history. They weren't actually fishing, it was more of a – a re-enactment, I guess."

"Huh. Pretty much what we heard." Monahan nodded. "Next time, might help if you went to active logging. You know, when we're out of contact."

"Right. Sorry. I didn't think."

"Don't apologize. After what you've been through I'd be amazed if you *didn't* make the occasional slip."

He patted her on the back. Wingman bristled.

"I gotta prep for a thing. Keep up the *great* work."

ALL THOSE DEVIL'S bargains and no-win scenarios. All those exercises that tore her up inside. Turned out they were part of the fix. They had to parameterize Becker's remorse before they could burn it out of her.

It was a simple procedure, they assured her, a small part of the scheduled block upgrade. Seven deep-focus microwave bursts targeting the ventromedial prefrontal cortex. Ten minutes, tops. Not so much as a scar to show for it afterward. She didn't even need to sign anything.

They didn't put her under. They turned her off.

Coming back online, she didn't feel much different. The usual faint hum at the back of her skull as Wingman lit up and looked around; the usual tremors in fingers and toes, half-way between a reboot sequence and a voltage spike. The memory of her distant malfunction seemed a bit less intense, but then again things often seemed clearer after a good night's sleep. Maybe she was just finally seeing things in perspective.

They plugged her into the simulator and worked her out.

Fifty-plus male, thirtysomething female, and a baby alone in a nursery: all spread out, all in mortal and immediate danger as the house they were trapped in burned down around them. She started with the female, went back to extract the male, was heading back in for the baby when the building collapsed. *Two out of three*, she thought. *Not bad.*

Sniper duty on some post-apocalyptic overpass, providing cover for an airbus parked a hundred meters down the road below, for the refugees running and hobbling and dragging themselves towards salvation. A Tumbleweed passing beneath: a self-propelled razorwire tangle of ONC and magnesium and white phosphorus, immune to bullets, hungry for body heat, rolling eagerly toward the unsuspecting evacuees. The engineer at Becker's side – his face an obvious template, although the sim tagged him as her *brother* for some reason – labored to patch the damage to their vehicle, oblivious to the refugees and their imminent immolation.

Oblivious until Becker pitched him off the overpass and brought the Tumbleweed to rapture.

The next one was a golden oldie: the old man in the war zone, calling for some lost pet or child, blocking Becker's shot as a battlefield robot halfway to the horizon took aim at a team of medics. She took out the old man with one bullet and no second thought; took out the bot with three more.

"Why'd you leave the baby for last?" Tauchi asked afterward, unhooking her. The light in his eyes was pure backwash from the retinal display, but he looked eager as a puppy just the same.

"Less of a loss," Becker said.

"In terms of military potential?" They'd all been civilians; tactically, all last among equals.

Becker shook her head, tried to put instinct into words. "The adults would – suffer more."

"Babies can't suffer?"

"They can hurt. Physically. But no hopes or dreams, no memories even. They're just – potential. No added value."

Tauchi looked at her.

"What's the big deal?" Becker asked. "It was an exercise."

"You killed your *brother*," he remarked.

"In a simulation. To save fifty civilians. I don't even *have* a brother."

"Would it surprise you to know that you took out the old man and the battlebot a full six hundred milliseconds faster than you did before the upgrade?"

She shrugged. "It was a repeat scenario. It's not like I even got it wrong the first time."

Tauchi glanced at his tacpad. "It didn't *bother* you the second time."

"So what are you saying? I'm some kind of sociopath now?"

"Exactly the opposite. You've been immunized against trolley paradoxes."

"What?"

"Everybody talks about morality like it's another word for *right and wrong*, when it's really just a load of static on the same channel." Tauchi's head bobbed like a woodpecker. "We just cleaned up the signal. As of now, you're probably the most ethical person on the planet."

"Really."

He walked it back, but not very far. "Well. You're in the top thirty at least."

BURIED HIGH ABOVE the streets of Toronto, cocooned in a windowless apartment retained as a home base for transient soldiers on missions of damage control: Nandita Becker, staring at the wall and watching the Web.

The wall was blank. The Web was in her head, invited through a back door in her temporal lobe. She and Wingman had spent altogether too much time alone in there, she'd decided. Time to have some company over.

The guest heads from Global's *Front View Mirror*, for example: a JAG lawyer, a retired professor of military law from Dalhousie, a token lefty from Veterans for Accountable Government. Some specialist in cyborg tech she'd never met, on loan from the Ministry of Defence and obviously chosen as much for disarming good looks as for technical expertise. (Becker imagined Ben Monahan just out of camera range, pulling strings.) A generic moderator whose affect alternated between earnest sincerity and failed attempts at cuteness.

They were all talking about Becker. At least, she assumed they still were. She'd muted the audio five minutes in.

The medallion in her hand glowed like dim cobalt through the flesh of her fingers, a faint nimbus up at 3MHz. She contemplated the feel of the metal, the decorative filigree (a glyph from some Amazonian culture that hadn't survived first contact, according to Sabrie), the hairline fracture of the interface port. The recessed Transmit button in its center: tap it once and it would squawk once, Sabrie had told her. Hold it down and it would broadcast on continuous loop.

She pressed it. Nothing happened.

Of course not. There'd be crypto. You didn't broadcast *anything* in the field without at least feeding it through a pseudorandom timeseries synched to the mothership – you never knew when some friend of Amal Sabrie might be lurking in the weeds, waiting to snatch it from the air and take it home for leisurely dissection. The signal made sense only at the instant of its creation. If you missed it the first time, wanted to repeat it for the sake of clarity, you'd need a time machine.

Becker had built her own personal time machine that very afternoon, stuck it at #1 on speed-dial: a three-line macro to reset her system clock to a dark moment weeks in the past, just before her world had turned to shit.

She unmuted audio on the web feed. One of Global's talking heads was opining that Becker was as much a victim as those poor envirogees her hijacked body had gunned down. Another spoke learnedly of the intimate connection between culpability and intent, of how blame – if that loaded term could even be applied in this case – must lie with the technology and not with those noble souls who daily put their lives on the line in the dangerous pestholes of a changing world.

"And yet this technology doesn't decide anything on its own," the moderator said. "It just does what the soldier's already decided sub – er, *pre*consciously."

"That's a bit simplistic," the specialist replied. "The system has access to a huge range of data that no unaugged soldier would ever be able to process in realtime – radio chatter, satellite telemetry, wide-spectrum visuals – so it's actually taking that preconscious intent and modifying it based on what the soldier *would* do if she had access to all those facts."

"So it guesses," said the Man from VAG.

"It predicts."

"And that doesn't open the door to error?"

"It reduces error. It optimizes human wisdom based on the maximum available information."

"And yet in this case –"

Becker held down transmit and sacc'd speed-dial.

"– don't want to go down that road," the lawyer said. "No matter *what* the neurology says."

Thirty-five seconds. Gone in an instant.

"Our whole legal system is predicated on the concept of free will. It's the moral center of human existence."

That was so much bullshit, Becker knew. She knew exactly where humanity's moral center was. She'd looked it up not six hours ago: the place where the brain kept its empathy and compassion, its guilt and shame and remorse.

The ventromedial prefrontal cortex.

"Suppose" – the moderator raised a finger – "I get into a car with a disabled breathalyzer. I put it into manual and hit someone. Surely I bear some responsibility for the fact that I *chose* to drink and drive, even if I didn't intend to hurt anyone."

"That depends on whether you'd received a lawful command from a superior officer to get behind the wheel," Ms. JAG countered.

"You're saying a soldier can be *ordered* to become a cyborg?"

"How is that different from ordering a sniper to carry a rifle? How is it different from ordering soldiers to take antimalarial drugs – which have also, by the way, been associated with violent behavioral side-effects in the past – when we deploy them to the Amazon? A soldier is sworn to protect their country; they take that oath knowing the normal tools of their trade, knowing that technology advances. You don't win a war by bringing knives to a gunfight –"

Speed-dial.

"– may not like cyborgs – and I'm the first to agree there are legitimate grounds for concern – but until you can talk the Chinese into turning back the clock on *their* technology, they're by far the lesser evil."

Twenty-eight seconds, that time.

"It's not as though we ever lived in a world without collateral damage. You don't shut down such a vital program over a tragic accident."

A tragic accident. Even Becker had believed that. Right up until Sabrie had slipped her a medallion with a burst of radio static in its heart, a cryptic signal snatched from the warm Pacific night by a pair of smart-specs on a dead kid walking. A signal that was somehow able to offline her for intervals ranging from twenty to sixty-three seconds.

She wondered if there was any sort of pattern to that variability.

"Safeguards should be put into place at the very least." The moderator was going for the middle road. "Ways to monitor these, these *hybrids* remotely, shut them down at the first sign of trouble."

Becker snorted. Wingman didn't take orders in the field, couldn't even *hear* them. Sure, Becker could channel some smiley little spin doctor through her temporal, but he was just a peeping tom with no access to the motor systems. The actual metal didn't even pack an on-board receiver; it was congenitally deaf to wireless commands until someone manually slotted the dorsal plug-in between Becker's shoulders.

Deliberately design a combat unit that could be shut down by anyone who happened to hack the right codes? Who'd be that stupid?

And yet –

Transmit. Speed-dial.

"– are only a few on active duty – they won't tell us exactly how many of course, say twenty or thirty. A couple dozen cyborgs who can't be blamed if something goes wrong. And that's just *today*. You wouldn't believe how fast they're ramping up production."

Forty seconds. On the nose.

"Not only do I believe it, I *encourage* it. The world's a tinderbox. Water wars, droughts, refugees everywhere you look. The threat of force is the only thing that's kept a lid on things so far. Our need for a strong military is greater today than it's ever been since the cold war, especially with the collapse of the US eco –"

Speed-dial.

"– and what happens when *every* pair of boots in the field has a machine reading its mind and pulling the trigger in their name? What happens to the very concept of a *war crime* when every massacre can be defined as an industrial accident?"

Thirty-two.

"You're saying this Becker deliberately –"

"I'm saying nothing of the kind. I'm *concerned*. I'm concerned at the speed with which outrage over the massacre of civilians has turned into an outpouring of sympathy for the person who killed them, even from quarters you'd least expect. Have you *seen* the profile piece Amal Sabrie posted on the Star?"

A shutdown command, radioed to a system with no radio.

"Nobody's forgetting the victims here. But it's no great mystery why people also feel a certain sympathy for Corporal Becker –"

Becker kept wondering who'd be able to pull off a trick like that. She kept coming up with the same answer.

"Of course. She's sympathetic, she's charismatic, she's *nice*. Exemplary soldier, not the slightest smudge on her service record. She volunteered at a veterinary clinic back in high school."

Someone with an interest in *controlling the narrative*.

"Chief of Defence couldn't have a better poster girl if they'd *planned* –"

Dial.

"– should be up on charges is for the inquiry to decide."

Forty-two seconds.

She wondered if she should be feeling something right now. Outrage. Violation. She'd thought the procedure was only supposed to cure her PTSD. It seemed to have worked on that score, anyway.

"Then let the inquiry decide. But we can't allow this to become the precedent that tips over the Geneva Conventions."

The other stuff, though. The compassion, the empathy, the guilt. The moral center. That seemed to be gone too. They'd burned it out of her like a tumor.

"The Conventions are a hundred years old. You don't think they're due for an overhaul?"

She still had her sense of right and wrong, at least.

Brain must keep that somewhere else.

"I THOUGHT THEY'D shipped you back to the WTP," Sabrie remarked.

"This weekend."

The journalist glanced around the grotto: low light, blue-shifted, private tables arrayed around a dance floor where partygoers writhed to bass beats that made it only faintly through the table damper. She glanced down at the Rising Tide Becker had ordered for her.

"I don't fuck my interviews, Corporal. Especially ones who could snap my spine if they got carried away."

Becker smiled back at her. "Not why we're here."

"Ohhhkay."

"Bring your jammer?"

"Always." Sabrie slapped the little device onto the table; welcome static fuzzed Becker's peripherals.

"So why *are* we in a lekking lounge at 2a.m.?"

"No drones," Becker said.

"None in the local Milestones either. Even during business hours."

"Yeah. I just – I wanted a crowd to get lost in."

"At two in the morning."

"People have other things on their mind in the middle of the night." Becker glanced up as a triplet stumbled past en route to the fuck-cubbies. "Less likely to notice someone they may have seen on the feeds."

"Okay."

"People don't – congregate the way they used to, you know?" Becker sipped her scotch, set it down, stared at it. "Everyone telecommutes, everyone cocoons. Downtown's so – thin, these days."

Sabrie panned the room. "Not here."

"Web don't fuck. Not yet, anyway. Still gotta go out if you want to do anything more than whack off."

"What's on your mind, Nandita?"

"The price of freedom."

"Go on."

"Not having to worry about some random psycho shooter when you go out for sushi. Don't tell me you've forgotten."

"You know I was being sarcastic."

Becker cocked her head at the other woman. "I don't think you were. Not entirely, anyway."

"Maybe not entirely."

"Because there *were* shootings, Amal. A lot of them. Twenty thousand deaths a year."

"Mainly down in the States, thank God." Sabrie said. "But yes."

"Back before the panopticon, people could just walk into some school or office building and – light it up." Becker frowned. "I remember there was this one guy shot up a *daycare*. Prechoolers. Babies. I forget how many he killed before they took him out. Turned out he'd lost a sister himself, six months before, in *another* shooting. Everybody said it tipped him over the edge and he went on a rampage."

"That doesn't make sense."

"That shit never does. It's what people said, though, to explain it. Only…"

"Only?" Sabrie echoed after the pause had stretched a bit too far.

"Only what if he wasn't crazy at all?" Becker finished.

"How could he not be?"

"He lost his sister. Classic act of senseless violence. The whole gun culture, you know, the NRA had everyone by the balls and anyone who so much as *whispered* about gun control got shot down. So to speak." Becker grunted. "Words didn't work. Advocacy didn't work. The only thing that might possibly work would be something so unthinkable, so horrific and obscene and unspeakably evil, that not even the most strident gun nut could possibly object to – countermeasures."

"Wait, you're saying that someone in favor of gun control – someone who'd *lost his sister to gun violence* – would deliberately shoot up a daycare?"

Becker spread her hands.

"You're saying he turned himself into a monster. Killed twenty, thirty kids maybe. For a piece of legislation."

"Weighed against thousands of deaths a year. Even if legislation only cut that by a few percent you'd make back your investment in a week or two, tops."

"Your *investment*?"

"Sacrifice, then." Becker shrugged.

"Do you know how insane that sounds?"

"How do you know that's not the way it went down?"

"Because you said nothing changed! No laws were passed! They just wrote him off as another psycho."

"He couldn't know that up front. All he knew was, there was a chance. His life, a few others, for thousands. There was a *chance*."

"I can't believe that you, of all people, would – after what happened, after what you *did* –"

"Wasn't me, remember? It was Wingman. That's what everyone's saying." Wingman was awake now, straining at the leash with phantom limbs.

"But you were still part of it. You know that, Deet, you *feel* it. Even if it wasn't your fault it still tears you up inside. I saw that the first time we spoke. You're a good person, you're a moral person, and –"

"Do you know what morality is, really?" Becker looked coolly into the other woman's eyes. "It's letting two stranger's kids die so you can save one of your own. It's thinking it makes some kind of difference if you look into someone's eyes when you kill them. It's squeamishness and cowardice and *won't someone think of the children*. It's not rational, Amal. It's not even ethical."

Sabrie had gone very quiet.

"Corporal," she said when Becker had fallen silent, "what have they done to you?"

Becker took a breath. "Whatever they're doing –"

Not much initiative. Great on the follow-through.

"– it ends here."

Sabrie's eyes went wide. Becker could see pieces behind them, fitting together at last. No drones. Dense crowd. No real security, just a few bouncers built of pitiful meat and bone…

"I'm sorry, Amal," Becker said gently.

Sabrie lunged for the jammer. Becker snatched it up before the journalist's hand had made it halfway.

"I can't have people in my head right now."

"Nandita." Sabrie was almost whispering. "Don't do this."

"I like you, Amal. You're good people. I'd leave you right out of it if I could, but you're – smart. And you know me, a little. Maybe well enough to put it together, afterward…"

Sabrie leapt up. Becker didn't even rise from her chair. She seized the other woman's wrist quick as a striking snake, effortlessly forced it back onto the table. Sabrie cried out. Dim blue dancers moved on the other side of the damper field, other things on their minds.

"You won't get away with it. You can't blame the machines for –" Soft pleading words, urgent, rapid-fire. The false-color heatprint of the contusion spread out across Sabrie's forearm like a dim rainbow, like a bright iridescent oil slick. "*Please* there's no *way* they'll be able to sell this as a malfunction no matter how –"

"That's the whole point," Becker said, and hoped there was a least a little sadness left in her smile. "You know that."

Amal Sabrie. Number one of seventy-four.

It would have been so much faster to just spread her wings and raise arms. But her wings had been torn out by the roots, and lay twitching in the garage back at Trenton. The only arms she could raise were of flesh and blood and graphene.

It was enough, though. It was messy, but she got the job done. Because Corporal Nandita Becker was more than just a superhuman killing machine.

She was the most ethical person on the planet.

THE SCRIVENER

Eleanor Arnason

Eleanor Arnason (eleanorarnason.blogspot.com) published her first story in 1973. Since then she has published six novels, two chapbooks and more than thirty short stories. Her novel *A Woman of the Iron People* won the James Tiptree, Jr. Award and the Mythopoeic Society Award. Novel *Ring of Swords* won a Minnesota Book Award. Her short story "Dapple" won the Spectrum Award. Other short stories have been finalists for the Hugo, Nebula, Sturgeon, Sidewise and World Fantasy Awards. Eleanor would really like to win one of these. Eleanor's most recent books are collections *Big Mama Stories* and *Hidden Folk*. Her favorite spoon is a sterling silver spoon given to her mother on her mother's first Christmas and dated December 25, 1909.

THERE WAS A scrivener who had three daughters. He lived in a great empire that stretched from west to east. Some parts of the empire were civilized and up-to-date, full of coffee shops and other amenities. Other parts were backward and primitive, the home of peasants and witches.

The scrivener lived in a provincial city, midway between civilization and the primitive. The streets were lined with shops, many of them selling foreign luxuries; there were cafés and coffee shops that had the latest newspapers and journals. In the marketplace, peasant farmers and hunters sold their traditional products. Outside the city were fields. Beyond the fields was a vast, dark forest.

He made his living in a modest way, writing letters for illiterate neighbors, drawing up bills of sale and even doing some accounting, for he was a man of many skills, who could do complicated sums and figure compound interest.

In spite of his skills and his adequate living, he had always dreamed of more: to be a writer of stories. But he lacked something, a divine spark, or so he believed. So he stuck to what he knew.

His wife died when the children were still young. He might have remarried, but he had loved the woman and had no desire to replace her. Three children were enough, even if none was a son.

Their mother had wanted to name them after fruits or flowers. But he had always dreamed of fathering a storyteller and insisted that they be named Imagination, Ornamentation, and Plot. All three were active and quick to learn. Surely they could become what he could not.

He bought books of fables for them and took them every week to the marketplace to listen to the storytellers who sat there in the dust, reciting tales about heroes and dragons. The girls liked the fables and the oral narratives, but showed no inclination toward becoming authors.

Imagination, who was called Ima, said the stories she heard and read gave her wonderful dreams, which she treasured, but she had no desire to write them down.

Ornamentation, who was called Orna, liked individual words. She sang them as she embroidered. What she made were not true songs, which have meaning most of the time. Rather, they were random strings of words that chimed and tinkled, rhymed or rolled majestically, but told no coherent story. She also liked images and put them in her embroidery: flowers and fruit and – between these – tiny lords and ladies, delicate dragons, diminutive heroes with needle-like swords.

Plot said it was all silliness, and she would rather do accounting.

But the scrivener did not lose hope; and when the girls were grown up, he took them to a famous critic. She was a large, fat woman, who sat every day in one of the city's cafes, wearing a caftan, smoking black cigarettes and drinking coffee or wine. Piled in the chair next to her were newspapers, literary reviews, and books, some leather bound, but most bound only in paper. There were coffee rings on the book covers and notes scribbled in the margins. The woman had a broad, arrogant face with a hawk nose and heavy-lidded eyes.

"Yes?" she said in her gruff, deep voice.

The scrivener told her that the dearest wish of his heart was to have a child who wrote stories, and he had brought his three daughters to be examined.

Each child had brought a story, which she had written reluctantly, not out of fear of her father, but rather out of fear of disappointing him. He was a kind, gentle man, whose only failing was his desire to have an author.

The critic waved the eldest daughter into a chair, drank some coffee, lit a new cigarette, and read Ima's story, grunting now and then. When she was done, she put the sheets of paper down, frowned mightily, and said, "Next."

Orna replaced her sister in the chair and handed over her story. Once again the critic drank coffee, lit a new cigarette, and read. A waiter came by and refilled her coffee cup, bringing also a pastry on a plate. The critic loved astringent fiction, bitter coffee, strong cigarettes, and pastries full of honey. Her taste in wine was uncritical. "One cannot judge everything," she always said.

She finished Orna's story, grunted loudly, and said, "Next."

Now Plot sat down and handed over her story. By this time she was helping her father with accounting, and she had written the story on ledger paper. "There is nothing here except numbers," the critic said.

"Turn it over," Plot replied.

The critic did and found a short, neat narrative about a prince who needed a new accounting system and how he found a girl able to set one up.

The critic finished the story and looked at the scrivener. "Your daughters have no talent at all." She pointed a thick finger at Ima. "This one has a flood of ideas and images set down in no order, as a confusing as a dream. And this one" – she pointed at Orna – "is simply babbling words, without any sense of what they mean or should mean within the structure of a story.

"Finally," she frowned mightily, "your last daughter has written a story with no color, mood, atmosphere, imagery or development of character. She might as well have written rows of numbers."

The scrivener wrung his hands. "Can nothing be done?"

The critic raised a hand, and the scrivener waited while she ate her pastry, washing it down with coffee. Then she lit another black cigarette. She was a chain smoker of the worst kind and should have died young.

Finally she said, "There is a witch in the nearby forest, living in the forest's black heart in a hut that stands on ostrich legs. She might be able to help, if she is willing. But remember that witches – like critics – are capricious and have their own agendas."

The scrivener thanked her for her advice, then herded his daughters home.

Remember, in considering what happened next, that the daughters loved their father and wanted to please him and also to protect him from harsh reality.

He sat them down and asked them if they would be willing to seek out the witch. The three girls looked at one another.

"Yes," said Plot. "But only one at a time. Ima does all the shopping, and Orna cares for the house. I help you with accounting. It would be too difficult if all of us left at once."

The scrivener agreed that this was a good idea. The three girls then drew straws, and the eldest got the short one. "I will set out tomorrow," Ima said bravely.

On the morrow, she packed a bag with food and other necessities and set out, taking a stage coach to the forest edge. There she climbed out.

The forest lay before her, rising abruptly from farmland. Its edge was a mixture of scrub trees: aspens and birches, with a few spindly maples and oaks. Farther back it was all evergreens, rising tall and dark toward the sunlit sky. In spite of the bright sky, the forest looked ominous to Ima, and her heart quailed.

But she had promised her father, and she would not fail him. Shouldering her pack, she marched into the forest. The edge seemed harmless. Sunlight came in around the scrub trees, and they were attractive: the aspens and birches flipping yellowing leaves in a light wind, the maples showing touches of red. She followed a narrow path among ferns. Birds flew above her, and small animals – mice or ground squirrels – scurried through the ferns. Nothing seemed dangerous, except possibly a croaking raven.

As she got deeper into the forest, the shadows grew thicker. The ground was bare, except for a thick carpet of pine needles. Above her, pine branches hissed in the wind. Names do matter, and Ima had rather too much imagination. The forest began to frighten her. But she did not want to disappoint her father, so she kept on. Noon passed, then the afternoon. Evening came. The shadows darkened. Finally, when she could barely see, she came to a break in the forest. A huge pine had fallen and lay across a clearing full of ferns. Overhead was the moon, one day off full, flooding the clearing with light. It should have reassured her, but it did not. She hunched down against the fallen trunk and ate the food she'd brought: bread and cheese and sausage. For drink she had wine in a flask, a good red that went with the sausage.

All she could think of was the danger around her. Who could say what wild animals lived in the forest? There were might be trolls as well as witches, and forest spirits of every variety, all of them cruel. In the distance, a fox barked.

All night she sat and shivered, too afraid to sleep. In the morning, she decided to go home. Her father would be disappointed, but she did not have the courage or the lack of imagination necessary to continue.

She soon discovered that she had lost her path in the darkness. All day she wandered through the forest, exhausted by lack of sleep. Late in the afternoon, she came upon a woodcutter, a tall, handsome young man. "What on earth are you doing here?" he asked. "The forest is dangerous."

She explained she had gotten lost, but did not mention the witch. She was embarrassed to, since she no longer had any intention of seeking the woman out.

"I can guide you to the forest edge," he said. "But not today. It's too late. Come back to my cabin. My mother and I will shelter you for the night. In the morning, I will escort you out of the forest."

Because of her imagination, which was good at seeing peril or at least its possibility, Ima hesitated. But she had no other choice. So she went with the woodsman to a little cabin built of logs. It was cheery looking, with smoke spiraling out of the chimney. Inside, a fire burned in the fireplace, and a stew bubbled in a pot. The woodcutter's mother was there, an old woman with a kind face.

Ima got out the last of her food to share. All three of them sat merrily around a table, eating and drinking the last of Ima's wine.

"Why do you live so far in the forest?" Ima asked.

"We like our privacy," the mother replied.

"And this is where the trees are," the woodcutter added. "I make our living by cutting them down and burning them into charcoal, which I take into the city and sell. It's a long walk with charcoal on my back. But it gives us what money we need. For the most part, the forest provides."

At length they showed her to a bed. Ima lay down and went right to sleep. She woke in the middle of the night, when moonlight shone in the cabin door. *Why was it open?* she wondered and got up to shut it.

Outside, in the clearing in front of the cabin, two wolves frolicked. One looked young. The other seemed old, but still vigorous.

Ima was too frightened to scream. Instead she crept back into the cabin's one room. A few coals still glowed in the fireplace. By their light and the moonlight pouring through the door, she searched the cabin. The beds that should have been occupied by the woodcutter and his mother were empty, their covers flung back.

Ima knew what this meant. She was spending the night with werewolves.

The cabin had only one door, but there were several windows. Slowly, carefully, quietly, Ima opened the shutters on one of these, climbed out and fled into the forest.

She ran and walked all night, not stopping until morning. She could go no farther then, so lay down and slept.

A cough woke her. She opened her eyes, saw the woodcutter and screamed.

"Beg pardon?" he said.

"You are a werewolf! And so is your mother!"

"Yes, but we are wolves only one night a month, not by intention, but because we must. Don't think we are monsters. When we are wolves, we do nothing to harm people. We hunt animals – mostly voles and rabbits – and enjoy the way it feels to run with wolf muscles and smell with a wolf nose. The rest of the time, I am an ordinary woodcutter, she is an ordinary mother.

"You went in the right direction when you fled our cabin, which is good. I suspect you don't want to spend another night in the forest. But we'll have to start now, if we are going to reach the coach stop before nightfall."

He held out his hand. Ima took it reluctantly, and he lifted her upright with surprising ease. A strong man. Well, he spent his day cutting down trees.

It was late afternoon when they reached the road by the forest. He waited with her till the coach came. When it was in sight, he said, "Please don't tell people about my mother and me. We live in the forest to be safe, but I do come into the city. I don't want to be stoned or arrested. I could have harmed you, when you were alone in the forest. I didn't. Instead, I helped you. Remember that."

The coach stopped. He helped her on. As it drove off, she looked back and saw him standing by the road, tall and lean and handsome, as rangy as a wolf.

When she got home, she told her father, "The forest was too frightening. I did not find the witch." She didn't talk about the woodcutter. The story was too strange, and she did not want to endanger the man or his mother.

The scrivener looked at his two other daughters with hope. They chose straws. This time Orna got the short one.

The next day she packed a bag and caught a coach to the forest. Like Ima, she climbed out at the forest edge and found a path. She lacked her sister's fearful imagination. Instead of possible danger, she noticed small birds in the pine branches and interesting fungi. Her path led her through clearings full of late summer grasses, faded to shades of tan and gold. Everything seemed lovely and enchanting.

She came finally to a meadow by a river. It was full of autumn flowers. Butterflies fluttered over the blossoms. A blue and orange kingfisher dove from a branch into the river and rose with a minnow in its beak.

"How beautiful!" Orna exclaimed.

"Indeed it is," said a melodious voice behind her.

She turned and beheld the most beautiful woman she had ever seen. The maid was naked, but her long, golden hair acted as a garment, falling over her body and reaching her knees.

"Who are you?" Orna asked.

"A forest spirit," the woman – really a girl – replied. "In countries to the south of here, I would be a dryad or naiad. To the east, I would be a rusalka, as in the famous opera by Antonín Dvořák. North of here, I might be a nixie or huldra. But here in this forest I am only a spirit."

If you are wondering how the girl knew Dvořák's opera *Rusalka*, a twentieth century work, remember that fairy tales and their creatures exist outside time.

And you may have noticed that many of the spirits mentioned – the rusalka, huldra, and nixie – are usually considered malevolent and dangerous. Orna did not know this; and the spirit she met was in fact mostly harmless, though she could enchant and distract.

Orna took out her lunch and shared it with the spirit. Then, both of them tipsy with white wine, they picked flowers and waded in the river shallows, gathering round, smooth stones.

Anther spirit appeared, naked like the first, but clothed with long, red hair. Then another came; Orna did not see from where. This one was brown-skinned with wavy black hair that swirled around her like a cloak. Her eyes were like the eyes of deer, large and dark.

Orna's food was gone. But they had apples taken from orchards gone wild and a fish – a fine, large trout – the dark maiden caught with her bare hands.

That was dinner, cooked over a fire. The roasted apples were coated with honey from the combs of wild bees. The fish was flavored with wild onions and salt from Orna's pack.

Orna had wine left. They ate and drank and got a little drunk. Orna ended in a huddle with the three dryads. Her clothes came off her. Curious fingers caressed her and soft lips kissed her face and body.

She was a modest maiden in a conservative society. She had never experienced anything like this before. Of course it overwhelmed her. She dove into it like a kingfisher into the river and brought up her first real orgasm like a struggling, silver fish.

At last, exhausted, she lay in the meadow's grass. Overhead, the night sky was full of stars. The dryads lay around her. "Why are you here?" one asked in a drowsy voice.

"I am seeking the witch who lives at the forest's black heart."

"No! No!" the dryads cried. "She is ugly and dangerous. Stay here with us."

What did she owe her father? Orna wondered. Respect. Love. But not the destruction of her life. If the witch were dangerous, she would avoid her.

She stayed with the dryads. By day, they wandered through the forest, sometimes gathering food and sometimes watching the life around them: green pines and yellowing ferns, birds flocking for their autumn migration. The forest shadows held numerous animals: deer, red foxes, badgers, red squirrels, weasels, tiny mice and voles. The dryads did not harm any of these. They were not hunters.

In the evening they made love in the meadow. Their nights were spent in an earthen cave, formed when a giant pine fell over. The dryads filled the cave half full with grass, and the four women kept each other warm.

One morning Orna woke and found the meadow was covered in frost. She was cold, in spite of the cave and the dryads. Winter was coming. She could not continue to live like this.

"What will you do?" she asked the dryads.

"We sleep through the cold months inside the trunks of trees – except for our sister here." The dryad who was speaking gestured toward the dark maiden. "She will sleep at the bottom of the river, safe below the ice."

"I can't do that," Orna said.

"Then go home to humanity, but return in the spring."

Orna kissed the dryads goodbye and went home. When she arrived, ragged and dirty, her father embraced her and said, "We thought you had died in the forest."

"No," Orna replied. "But I did not find the witch. The forest distracted me. I wandered a long time, not knowing where I was."

This was misleading, but not a direct lie. She didn't want to talk about the dryads. The city's conservative society did not approve of magical creatures or sex between women.

Her father wisely did not ask more questions, but told his other daughters to fill a tub with hot water and find new clothes for Orna. They did this gladly, happy that Orna was home.

Once she was clean and neatly dressed and eating a good dinner, the scrivener said to her, "Don't think we failed to search for you, dear child. I went to the forest edge and talked to the farmers there. No one had seen you, though they do not go far into the forest, as they told me. They advised me to ask the hunters and charcoal burners, who went farther in. We found them here in the city, selling their goods in the market. A rough lot, but not bad hearted. They hadn't seen you, either. We offered a reward, and everyone – farmers, hunters and charcoal burners – said they would keep an eye out. It was all to no avail. You had vanished."

Orna felt guilty, but she couldn't think of a way to apologize or explain.

That left the youngest daughter, Plot. The next day she packed her bag and caught a coach to the forest. Unlike her sister Ima, she was not troubled by imagination; and unlike her sister Orna, she was not easily distracted. She marched firmly into the forest. After three days, she came to the home of the witch, which was a hut made of logs. It stood in a clearing, surrounded by towering pines. In its own way it towered, resting atop long ostrich legs. Plot looked up, wondering how she could reach the door. Then she heard a noise in back of her and ducked behind a pine.

A large, fat, solid woman came out of the forest. She was dressed entirely in black. Even the boots on her large feet were as black as night. She called out:

"Hut mine, obey my summons.

Bend thy legs and let me in."

The ostrich legs folded, and the hut was lowered to the ground. The witch entered. A moment later, before the hut could raise itself, Plot ran through the door.

"What?" cried the witch, who had a wide, arrogant face and a beaklike nose. "How dare you sneak in here?"

"My father sent me," Plot replied. "I love and respect him, and I came because he asked me to. He wants me to be an author. But the great critic in the city says I have no ability."

"My sister," the witch replied. "The way she smokes, she would die of a lung disease, except that I send her magic potions which protect her respiratory system.

"Writing is a terrible way to make a living, almost as bad as criticism. I send my sister charms, which enchant editors, so they publish her essays and reviews. That has given her a great reputation, though not much money. Fortunately, she wants fame more than money."

"I can also do accounting," Plot said.

"That's better. A woman can make a living at accounting," the witch said. She waved in a mystical manner, and the hut stood up. "Since you're here, you might as well make yourself useful. Make dinner."

Plot found root vegetables in the witch's storeroom, along with a fresh, plucked chicken. She made a broth and then a soup, full of vegetables and pieces of chicken. It took all day, while the witch grumbled. "Can't you be quicker?"

"A soup takes the time it takes," Plot replied.

They finally sat down to dinner. The witch tasted the soup and grimaced. "Can't you do better?"

"I can only do as well as I can," Plot replied.

Though the witch was grouchy, the soup was actually quite good, thick and nourishing, an excellent meal for a cold autumn evening. There was bread and cheese and beer, as well.

When they finished, the witch said, "There is a stream at the edge of my clearing. You can take the dishes there and wash them tomorrow."

"Can you make me an author?" Plot asked.

"We will see."

So began Plot's time with the witch, who was demanding and evasive, but also interesting. As mentioned before, Plot was not easily frightened, nor easily distracted. She had promised her father to give this enterprise a good effort, and she would. In addition, she had never met a witch before. She wanted to learn how a magic-worker did her work.

Even deep in the forest, the witch had visitors. People came, bringing gifts and problems that required magic. Most of the problems involved health, though there were also romantic problems, people who wanted potions to attract someone or make someone lose interest.

The witch told Plot that she did her best with curing potions. "Most people are worth saving." When she made a love potion, it would work, but only so far as creating a mild interest. "The lover must do most of the work himself or herself," the witch said. "I will not force anyone into love." She felt differently about indifference potions. These always worked. "No one should be troubled by an unwanted lover."

Remembering how much her family had worried about Orna, Plot sent messages home. Some of the witch's clients went into the city and were willing to stuff a note under the scrivener's door. *Don't worry, dear father. I have found the witch and am staying with her. I am safe, and everything is fine.* But they would do no more, since they were mostly poor folk and did not want to attract the attention of the authorities. Witches were not respectable, being relics of a former time.

Plot kept the hut clean and made meals. Over time – through the long, cold, snowy winter – she learned enough to help the witch with potions. The hut took care of the snow in the clearing by stamping it down with its big ostrich feet. In addition, it broke the ice that formed on the stream. All the stamping and breaking made the hut jerk and shake. This was fine with Plot. If the hut had not done the work, she would have had to shovel and chop ice. She knew the witch well enough to know this.

You might think that people wouldn't come in the winter. But sickness and love are strong drivers. There were fewer visitors after the snow fell, but they did not stop. Instead they came wrapped in heavy coats and wearing high boots. The ostrich legs knelt down for them and the witch listened to their stories, as did Plot. Life was not simple, the scrivener's daughter learned. She could see that the witch's potions were not enough to solve every problem.

Most of the clients were peasants. At best, their lives were precarious, dependent on the weather, which was often capricious. The witch could help them with illness and love, but there was no charm that would make the weather reliable or people rich. Money had its own magic, the witch said, which was different from the magic of witches; and weather systems were too large for anyone to control. In spite of everything the witch did, her clients still worried about harvests and taxes, their own futures and the fates of their animals and children.

She did make charms that called rain and drove away pests. These helped some. "Though bugs can learn to resist the magic used against them," the witch said. "And there is no way to make the rain consistent. At best, I nudge it a little."

"Are you going to help me?" Plot asked the witch from time to time.

"You are a better house cleaner than you were when you came, a better cook and a better maker of potions. All this is useful. In addition, you know more about the world and the lives of other people."

"My father wants me to be a writer of stories."

"What do you want?" the witch replied.

Plot could not say.

Spring came finally. Plot said, "I need to go. My father will be worrying."

The witch gave her a considering look. She knew that Plot could not be distracted, but would always go directly to her goal. This was a virtue in an ordinary person, though not in a storyteller or a story.

"Go, then," the witch said. "But come back. I need an assistant."

So Plot packed her bag and walked to the road at the edge of the forest. Everything around her was fresh and tender and green. The trees were full of migrating birds. She waited at the coach stop. The coach appeared and carried her back to the city through spring fields.

When she got home, the house was empty, except for her father, sitting in his study and writing out contracts.

"Where are my sisters?" she asked.

"Ima had a visitor who came again and again," her father said. "A woodsman she had met in the forest. He was one of those who promised to look for Orna. First he came to report on his searching, but it was soon evident that he came to see Ima, and he kept coming even after Orna returned.

"At first, she was nervous around him. No one had courted her before, and young girls are always nervous in this situation. But he kept coming through the worst of the winter, always courteous and obviously in love. He brought her gifts, rabbit pelts and deerskins and venison. A good provider – and a good son. He always spoke warmly of his mother, and he always treated me with respect. A good son is likely to be a good husband.

"In the end, Ima agreed to marry him and move to his cabin in the forest. So that is what happened to her."

"What about Orna?" Plot asked.

"She met some women during her stay in the forest. Once spring came, she wanted to visit them again. I could tell she wouldn't be happy till she saw them, so I told her to go and stay as long as she wanted. A good parent must let go of his children in the end, and I know now that neither of them will be an author. What about you, my darling? I got your notes, but they were all brief and stuck under my door."

"I found the witch, but she gave me nothing that will make me a teller of stories. She asked me to become her assistant. I think I will."

"Ah," said the scrivener. "Well, Ima found a husband in the forest, and Orna found friends. A job may be equally good."

"Yes," said Plot. "But it isn't right that you are alone, dear father."

"I have hired a housekeeper. I could afford to, since Ima left me all the skins that the woodcutter gave her. I sold them in the marketplace for good money, and he has promised to bring me more. As I said before, the lad is a good provider.

"I don't know if Orna will bring anything back from her visit, though she mentioned honey and berries and hard-to-find mushrooms. I will get by, dear Plot."

"Well, then," said Plot.

They had dinner, made by the housekeeper, who was an excellent cook. Afterward they sat by a fire. The evenings were still cool. Plot told her father about the witch and her customers. Their stories were not large and grand, like the stories told in the marketplace. They were small tales of illness, romance, family quarrels, good or bad weather. The great twentieth century Icelandic novelist Halldór Laxness told stories like these, except that he wrote novels. You ought to read his *Independent People*.

Plot's narratives were brief and to the point. Some were happy. An illness was cured. In other cases, the witch could not solve the problem. A lover came back and complained that a love potion had not worked. Families continued to quarrel. The harvest was not good.

Plot lacked Laxness's humor and sense of irony, which can be seen as a failing. But she had his clear vision and his respect for ordinary people, which she had learned in the hut atop ostrich legs. Life was hard, and people did the best they could. Their lives did not become epic, unless a writer as good as Laxness was writing. But they were worth hearing about – and worth helping, as the witch did, though she was not always successful. Even a witch can only do so much.

When she was done, her father said, "You are certainly a better storyteller than before. But these stories will not sell in the marketplace. People want to hear about heroes and dragons and fair maidens in distress. Maybe it would be a good idea for you to rejoin the witch – or stay at home and do accounting."

"I will rejoin the witch," Plot said.

Her father felt a little unhappy, but he was not going to stand in the way of any child. Ima and Orna had taught him a lesson. We cannot determine how our children turn out. They cannot live our dreams.

"Good enough," he said. "Please come back to visit, and if you ever decide to tell stories about heroes and dragons, I would be happy to hear them."

The next day, Plot packed a new bag and set out for the forest. On the way, she passed the café where the critic sat.

"You are the girl with the ridiculous name," the critic said, a cigarette in her hand and a cloud of smoke twisting around her. A glass of wine stood in front of her. Plot had no idea how she could taste it through the tobacco. "What was it?"

"Plot," the scrivener's daughter said. "But I'm thinking of changing it to Amelia."

"A good idea," the critic said in the firm and considered tone that critics often use. She drew on her cigarette and puffed out smoke. "Did you ever learn to write?"

"No," Amelia answered. "But your sister has offered me an apprenticeship." She set down her bag and considered the critic. She could see the resemblance between the two sisters clearly now, both of them tall and wide, with arrogant faces and beaky noses. They had the same eyes: sharp and knowing under heavy lids. "I don't know what I want to be yet. I'll study with your sister, and think about my future."

"Good enough," the critic said. "There are too many writers in the world already. I try to cut them down, but they spring back up. On the other hand, there are too few good witches. Always remember, no matter what you end up doing, stay away from stories about heroes and dragons. They have been done to death."

Amelia went on, carrying her bag, feeling happy at the thought of returning to the hut with ostrich legs. Maybe that job would not work out. If so, she could always go back to accounting. And maybe she would write a few stories down for her own pleasure. Or maybe not.

For Patrick

SOMEDAY

James Patrick Kelly

James Patrick Kelly (www.jimkelly.net) has written novels, short stories, essays, reviews, poetry, plays and planetarium shows. His most recent book is a collection of stories entitled *The Wreck Of The Godspeed*. His short novel *Burn* won the Nebula Award in 2007. He has won Hugo Awards for his novelettes "Think Like A Dinosaur" and "Ten to the Sixteenth to One." With John Kessel he is co-editor of five anthologies, most recently *Digital Rapture: The Singularity Anthology*. He is on the faculty of the Stonecoast Creative Writing MFA Program at the University of Southern Maine and on the Board of Directors of the Clarion Foundation.

Daya had been in no hurry to become a mother. In the two years since she'd reached childbearing age, she'd built a modular from parts she'd fabbed herself, thrown her boots into the volcano, and served as blood judge. The village elders all said she was one of the quickest girls they had ever seen – except when it came to choosing fathers for her firstborn. Maybe that was because she was too quick for a sleepy village like Third Landing. When her mother, Tajana, had come of age, she'd left for the blue city to find fathers for her baby. Everyone expected Tajana would stay in Halfway, but she had surprised them and returned home to raise Daya. So once Daya had grown up, everyone assumed that someday she would leave for the city like her mother, especially after Tajana had been killed in the avalanche last winter. What did Third Landing have to hold such a fierce and able woman? Daya could easily build a glittering new life in Halfway. Do great things for the colony.

But everything had changed after the scientists from space had landed on the old site across the river, and Daya had changed most of all. She kept her own counsel and was often hard to find. That spring she had told the elders that she didn't need to travel to gather the right semen. Her village was happy and prosperous. The scientists had chosen it to study and they had attracted tourists from all over the colony. There were plenty of beautiful and convenient local fathers to take to bed. Daya had sampled the ones she considered best, but never opened herself to blend their sperm. Now she would, here in the place where she had been born.

She chose just three fathers for her baby. She wanted Ganth because he was her brother and because he loved her above all others. Latif because he was a leader and would say what was true when everyone else was afraid. And Bakti because he was a master of stories and because she wanted him to tell hers someday.

She informed each of her intentions to make a love feast, although she kept the identities of the other fathers a secret, as was her right. Ganth demanded to know, of course, but she refused him. She was not asking for a favor. It would be her baby, her responsibility. The three fathers, in turn, kept her request to themselves, as was custom, in case she changed her mind about any or all of them. A real possibility – when she contemplated what she was about to do, she felt separated from herself.

That morning she climbed into the pen and spoke a kindness to her pig Bobo. The glint of the knife made him grunt with pleasure and he rolled onto his back, exposing the tumors on his belly. She hadn't harvested him in almost a week and so carved two fist-sized maroon swellings into the meat pail. She pressed strips of sponge root onto the wounds to stanch the bleeding and when it was done, she threw them into the pail as well. When she scratched under his jowls to dismiss him, Bobo squealed approval, rolled over and trotted off for a mud bath.

She sliced the tumors thin, dipped the pieces in egg and dragged them through a mix of powdered opium, pepper, flour, and bread crumbs, then sautéed them until they were crisp. She arranged them on top of a casserole of snuro, parsnips and sweet flag, layered with garlic and three cheeses. She harvested some of the purple blooms from the petri dish on the windowsill and flicked them on top of her love feast. The aphrodisiacs produced by the bacteria would give an erection to a corpse. She slid the casserole into the oven to bake for an hour while she bathed and dressed for babymaking.

Daya had considered the order in which she would have sex with the fathers. Last was most important, followed by first. The genes of the middle father – or fathers, since some mothers made babies with six or seven for political reasons – were less reliably expressed. She thought starting with Ganth for his sunny nature and finishing with Latif for his looks and good judgment made sense. Even though Bakti was clever, he had bad posture.

Ganth sat in front of a fuzzy black and white screen with his back to her when she nudged the door to his house open with her hip. "It's me. With a present."

He did not glance away from his show – the colony's daily news and gossip program about the scientists – but raised his forefinger in acknowledgment.

She carried the warming dish with oven mitts to the huge round table that served as his desk, kitchen counter and sometime closet. She pushed aside some books, a belt, an empty bottle of blueberry kefir, and a Fill Jumphigher action figure to set her love feast down. Like her own house, Ganth's was a single room, but his was larger, shabbier, and built of some knotty softwood.

Her brother took a deep breath, his face pale in the light of the screen. "Smells delicious." He pressed the off button; the screen winked and went dark.

"What's the occasion?" He turned to her, smiling. "*Oh.*" His eyes went wide when he saw how she was dressed. "Tonight?"

"Tonight." She grinned.

Trying to cover his surprise, he pulled out the pocket watch he'd had from their mother and then shook it as if it were broken. "Why, look at the time. I totally forgot that we were grown up."

"You like?" She weaved her arms and her ribbon robe fluttered.

"I was wondering when you'd come. What if I had been out?"

She nodded at the screen in front of him. "You never miss that show."

"Has anyone else seen you?" He sneaked to the window and peered out. A knot of gawkers had gathered in the street. "What, did you parade across Founders' Square dressed like that? You'll give every father in town a hard on." He pulled the blinds and came back to her. He surprised her by going down on one knee. "So which am I?"

"What do you think?" She lifted the cover from the casserole to show that it was steaming and uncut.

"I'm honored." He took her hand in his and kissed it. "Who else?" he said. "And you have to tell. Tomorrow everyone will know."

"Bakti. Latif last."

"Three is all a baby really needs." He rubbed his thumb across the inside of her wrist. "Our mother would approve."

Of course, Ganth had no idea of what their mother had really thought of him.

Tajana had once warned Daya that if she insisted on choosing Ganth to father her baby, she should dilute his semen with that of the best men in the village. A sweet manner is fine, she'd said, but babies need brains and a spine.

"So, dear sister, it's a sacrifice"– he said, standing – "but I'm prepared to do my duty." He caught her in his arms.

Daya squawked in mock outrage.

"You're not surprising the others are you?" He nuzzled her neck.

"No, they expect me."

"Then we'd better hurry. I hear that Eldest Latif goes to bed early." His whisper filled her ear. "Carrying the weight of the world on his back tires him out.

"I'll give him reason to wake up."

He slid a hand through the layers of ribbons until he found her skin. "Bakti, on the other hand, stays up late, since his stories weigh nothing at all." The flat of his hand against her belly made her shiver. "I didn't realize you knew him that well."

She tugged at the hair on the back of Ganth's head to get his attention. "Feasting first," she said, her voice husky. Daya hadn't expected to be this emotional. She opened her pack, removed the bottle of chardonnay and poured two glasses. They saluted each other and drank, then she used the spatula she had brought – since she knew her brother wouldn't have one – to cut a square of her love feast. He watched her scoop it onto a plate like a man uncertain of his luck. She forked a bite into her mouth. The cheese was still melty – maybe a bit too much sweet flag. She chewed once, twice and then leaned forward to kiss him. His lips parted and she let the contents of her mouth fall into his. He groaned and swallowed. "Again." His voice was thick. "Again and again and again."

Afterward they lay entangled on his mattress on the floor. "I'm glad you're not leaving us, Daya." He blew on the ribbons at her breast and they trembled. "I'll stay home to watch your baby," he said. "Whenever you need me. Make life so easy, you'll never want to go."

It was the worst thing he could have said; until that moment she had been able to keep from thinking that she might never see him again. He was her only family, except for the fathers her mother had kept from her. Had Tajana wanted to make it easy for her to leave Third Landing? "What if I get restless here?" Daya's voice could have fit into a thimble. "You know me."

"Okay, maybe someday you can leave." He waved the idea away. "Someday."

She glanced down his lean body at the hole in his sock and dust strings dangling from his bookshelf. He was a sweet boy and her brother, but he played harder than he worked. Ganth was content to let the future happen to him; Daya needed to make choices, no matter how hard. "It's getting late." She pressed her cheek to his. "Do me a favor and check on Bobo in the morning? Who knows when I'll get home."

By the time she kissed Ganth goodbye, it was evening. An entourage of at least twenty would-be spectators trailed her to Old Town; word had spread that the very eligible Daya was bringing a love feast to some lucky fathers. There were even a scatter of tourists, delighted to witness Third Landing's quaint mating ritual. The locals told jokes, made ribald suggestions and called out names of potential fathers. She tried to ignore them; some people in this village were so nosy.

Bakti lived in one of the barn-like stone dormitories that the settlers had built two centuries ago across the river from their landing spot. Most of these buildings were now divided into shops and apartments. When Daya finally revealed her choice by stopping at Bakti's door, the crowd buzzed. Winners of bets chirped, losers groaned. Bakti was slow to answer her knock, but when he saw the spectators, he seized her arm and drew her inside.

Ganth had been right: she and Bakti weren't particularly close. She had never been to his house, although he had visited her mother on occasion when she was growing up. She could see that he was no better a housekeeper than her brother, but at least his mess was all of a kind. The bones of his apartment had not much changed from the time the founders had used it as a dormitory; Bakti had preserved the two walls of wide shelves that they had used as bunks. Now, however, instead of sleeping refugees from the Genome Crusades, they were filled with books, row upon extravagant row. This was Bakti's vice; not only did he buy cheap paper from the village stalls; he had purchased hundreds of hardcovers on his frequent trips to the blue city. They said he even owned a few print books that the founders had brought across space. There were books everywhere, open on chairs, chests, the couch, stacked in leaning towers on the floor.

"So you've come to rumple my bed?" He rearranged his worktable to make room for her love feast. "I must admit, I was surprised by your note. Have we been intimate before, Daya?"

"Just once." She set the dish down. "Don't pretend that you don't remember." When she unslung the pack from her back, the remaining bottles of wine clinked together.

"Don't pretend?" He spread his hands. "I tell stories. That's all I do."

"Glasses?" She extracted the zinfandel from her pack.

He brought two that were works of art; crystal stems twisted like vines to flutes as delicate as a skim of ice. "I recall a girl with a pansy tattooed on her back," he said.

"You're thinking of Pandi." Daya poured the wine.

"Do you sing to your lovers?"

She sniffed the bouquet. "Never."

They saluted each other and drank.

"Don't rush me now," he said. "I'm enjoying this little game." He lifted the lid of the dish and breathed in. "Your feast pleases the nose as much as you please the eye. But I see that I am not your first stop. Who else have you seen this night?"

"Ganth."

"You chose a grasshopper to be a father of your child?"

"He's my brother."

"Aha!" He snapped his fingers. "Now I have it. The garden at Tajana's place? I recall a very pleasant evening."

She had forgotten how big Bakti's nose was. "As do I." And his slouch was worse than ever. Probably from carrying too many books.

"I don't mind being the middle, you know." He took another drink of wine. "Prefer it actually – less responsibility that way. I will do my duty as a father, but I must tell you right now that I have no interest whatsoever in bringing up your baby. And her next father is?"

"Latif. Next and last."

"A man who takes fathering seriously. Good, he'll balance out poor Ganth. I will tell her stories, though. Your baby girl. That's what you hope for, am I right? A girl?"

"Yes." She hadn't realized it until he said it. A girl would make things much easier.

He paused, as if he had just remembered something. "But you're supposed to leave us, aren't you? This village is too tight a fit for someone of your abilities. You'll split seams, pop a button."

Why did everyone keep saying these things to her? "*You* didn't leave."

"No." He shook his head. "I wasn't as big as I thought I was. Besides, the books keep me here. Do you know how much they weigh?"

"It's an amazing collection." She bent to the nearest shelf and ran a finger along the spines of the outermost row. "I've heard you have some from Earth."

"Is this about looking at books or making babies, Daya?" Bakti looked crestfallen.

She straightened, embarrassed. "The baby, of course."

"No, I get it." He waved a finger at her. "I'm crooked and cranky and mothers shut their eyes tight when we kiss." He reached for the wine bottle. "Those are novels." He nodded at the shelf. "But no, nothing from Earth."

They spent the better part of an hour browsing. Bakti said Daya could borrow some if she wanted. He said reading helped pregnant mothers settle. Then he told her the story from one of them. It was about a boy named Huckleberry Flynn, who left his village on Novy Praha to see his world but then came back again. "Just like your mother did," he said. "Just like you could, if you wanted. Someday."

"Then you could tell stories about me."

"About this night," he agreed, "if I remember." His grin was seductive. "Will I?"

"Have you gotten any books from them?" She glanced out the dark window toward the river. "Maybe they'd want to trade with you?"

"Them?" he said. "You mean our visitors? Some, but digital only. They haven't got time for nostalgia. To them, my books are as quaint as scrolls and clay tablets. They asked to scan the collection, but I think they were just being polite. Their interests seem to be more sociological than literary." He smirked. "I understand you have been spending time across the river."

She shrugged. "Do you think they are telling the truth?"

"About what? Their biology? Their politics?" He gestured at his library. "I own one thousand, two hundred and forty-three claims of truth. How would I know which is right?" He slid the book about the boy Huckleberry back onto the shelf. "But look at the time! If you don't mind, I've been putting off dinner until you arrived. And then we can make a baby and a memory, yes?"

By the time Daya left him snoring on his rumpled bed, the spectators had all gone home for the night. There was still half of the love feast left but the warming dish was beginning to dry it out. She hurried down the Farview Hill to the river.

Many honors had come to Latif over the years and with them great wealth. He had first served as village eldest when he was still a young man, just thirty-two years old. In recent years, he mediated disputes for those who did not have the time or the money to submit to the magistrates of the blue city. The fees he charged had bought him this fine house of three rooms, one of which was the parlor where he received visitors. When she saw that all the windows were dark, she gave a cry of panic. It was nearly midnight and the house was nothing but a shadow against the silver waters.

On the shore beyond, the surreal bulk of the starship beckoned.

Daya didn't even bother with front door. She went around to the bedroom and stood on tiptoes to knock on his window. *Tap-tap.*

Nothing.

"Latif." *Tap-tap-tap.* "Wake up."

She heard a clatter within. "Shit!" A light came on and she stepped away as the window banged open."

"Who's there? Go away."

"It's me, Daya."

"Do you know what time it is? Go away."

"But I have our love feast. You knew this was the night, I sent a message."

"And I waited, but you took too damn long." He growled in frustration. "Can't you see I'm asleep? Go find some middle who's awake."

"No, Latif. You're my last."

He started with a shout. "You wake me in the middle of night…" Then he continued in a low rasp. "Where's your sense, Daya, your manners? You expect me to be your last? You should have said something. I take fathering seriously."

Daya's throat closed. Her eyes seemed to throb.

"I told you to move to the city, didn't I? Find fathers there." Latif waited for her to answer. When she didn't, he stuck his head out the window to see her better. "So instead of taking my best advice, now you want my semen?" He waited again for a reply; she couldn't speak. "I suppose you're crying."

The only reply she could make was a sniffle.

"Come to the door then."

She reached for his arm as she entered the darkened parlor but he waved her through to the center of the room. "You are rude and selfish. Daya." He shut the door and leaned against it. "But that doesn't mean you're a bad person."

He turned the lights on and for a moment they stood blinking at one another. Latif was barefoot, wearing pants but no shirt. He had a wrestler's shoulders, long arms, hands big as dinner plates. Muscles bunched beneath his smooth, dark skin, as if he might spring at her. But if she read his eyes right, his anger was passing.

"I thought you'd be pleased." She tried a grin. It bounced off him.

"Honored, yes. Pleased, not at all. You think you can just issue commands and we jump? You have the right to ask, and I have the right to refuse. Even at the last minute."

At fifty-three, Latif was still one of the handsomest men in the village. Daya had often wondered if that was one reason why everyone trusted him. She looked for some place to put the warming dish down.

"No," he said, "don't you dare make yourself comfortable unless I tell you to. Why me?"

She didn't have to think. "Because you have always been kind to me and my mother. Because you will tell the truth, even when it's hard to hear. And because, despite your years, you are still the most beautiful man I know."

This time she tried a smile on him. It stuck. "All the children you've fathered are beautiful, and if my son gets nothing but looks from you, that will still be to his lifelong advantage." Daya knew that in the right circumstance, even men like Latif would succumb to flattery.

"You want me because I tell hard truths, but when I say you should move away, you ignore me. Does that make sense?"

"Not everything needs to make sense." She extended her love feast to him. "Where should I put this?"

He glided across the parlor, kissed her forehead and accepted the dish from her. "Do you know how many have asked me to be last father?"

"No." She followed him into the great room.

"Twenty-three," he said. "Every one spoke to me ahead of time. And of those, how many I agreed to?"

"No idea."

"Four." He set it on a round wooden table with a marble inset.

"They should've tried my ambush strategy." She shrugged out of her pack. "I've got wine." She handed him the bottle of Xino she had picked for him.

"Which you've been drinking all night, I'm sure. You know where the glasses are." He pulled the stopper. "And who have you been drinking with?"

"Ganth, first."

Latif tossed the stopper onto the table. "I'm one-fourth that boy's father," he rapped on the tabletop, "but I don't see any part of me in him."

"He's handsome."

"Oh, stop." He poured each of them just a splash of the Xino and offered her a glass. She raised an eyebrow at his stinginess.

"It's late and you've had enough," he said. "It is affecting your judgment. Who else?"

"Bakti."

"You surprise me." They saluted each other with their glasses. "Does he really have Earth books?"

"He says not."

"He makes too many stories up. But he's sound – you should have started with him. Ganth is a middle father at best."

Both of them ran out of things to say then. Latif was right. She had finished the first two bottles with the other fathers, and had shared a love feast with them and had made love. She was heavy with the weight of her decisions and her desires. She felt like she was falling toward Latif. She pulled the cover off the warming dish and cut a square of her love feast into bite-sized chunks.

"Just because I'm making a baby doesn't mean I can't go away," she said.

"And leave the fathers behind?"

"That's what my mother did."

"And did that make her happy? Do you think she had an easy life?" He shook his head. "No, you are tying yourself to this village. This little, insignificant place. Why? Maybe you're lazy. Or maybe you're afraid. Here, you are a star. What would you be in the blue city?"

She wanted to tell him that he had it exactly wrong. That he was talking about himself, not her. But that would have been cruel. This beautiful foolish man was going to be the last father of her baby. "You're right," Daya said. "It's late." She piled bits of the feast onto a plate and came around to where he was sitting. She perched on the edge of the table and gazed down at him.

He tugged at one of the ribbons of her sleeve and she felt the robe slip off her shoulder. "What is this costume anyway?" he said. "You're wrapped up like some kind of present."

She didn't reply. Instead she pushed a bit of the feast across her plate until it slid onto her fork. They watched each other as she brought it to her open mouth, placed it on her tongue. The room shrank. Clocks stopped.

He shuddered, "Feed me, then."

Latif's pants were still around his ankles when she rolled off him. The ribbon robe dangled off the headboard of his bed. Daya gazed up at the ceiling, thinking about the tangling sperm inside her. She concentrated as her mother had taught her, and she thought she felt her cervix close and her uterus contract, concentrating the semen. At least, she hoped she did. The sperm of the three fathers would smash together furiously, breaching cell walls, exchanging plasmids. The strongest conjugate would find her eggs and then...

"What if I leave the baby behind?" she said.

"With who?" He propped himself up on an elbow. "Your mother is dead and no..."

She laid a finger on his lips. "I know, Latif. But why not with a father? Ganth might do it, I think. Definitely not Bakti. Maybe even you."

He went rigid. "This is an idea you get from the scientists? Is that the way they have sex in space?"

"They don't live in space; they just travel through it." She followed a crack in the plaster of his ceiling with her eyes. "Nobody lives in space." A water stain in the corner looked like a face. A mouth. Sad eyes. "What should we do about them?"

"Do? There is nothing to be done." He fell back onto his pillow. "They're the ones the founders were trying to get away from."

"Two hundred years ago. They say things are different."

"Maybe. Maybe these particular scientists are more tolerant, but they're still dangerous."

"Why? Why are you so afraid of them?"

"*Because they're unnatural.*" The hand at her side clenched into a fist. "We're the true humans, maybe the last. But they've taken charge of evolution now, or what passes for it. We have no say in the future. All we know for sure is that they are large and still growing and we are very, very small. Maybe this lot won't force us to change. Or maybe someday they'll just make us want to become like them."

She knew this was true, even though she had spent the last few months trying not to know it. The effort had made her weary. She rolled toward Latif. When she snuggled against him, he relaxed into her embrace.

It was almost dawn when she left his house. Instead of climbing back up Farview Hill, she turned toward the river. Moments later she stepped off Mogallo's Wharf into the skiff she had built when she was a teenager.

She had been so busy pretending that this wasn't going to happen that she was surprised to find herself gliding across the river. She could never have had sex with the fathers if she had acknowledged to herself that she was going to go through with it. Certainly not with Ganth. And Latif would have guessed that something was wrong. She had the odd feeling that there were two of her in the skiff, each facing in opposite directions. The one looking back at the village was screaming at the one watching the starship grow ever larger. But there is no other Daya, she reminded herself. There is only me.

Her lover, Roberts, was waiting on the spun-carbon dock that the scientists had fabbed for river traffic. Many of the magistrates from the blue city came by boat to negotiate with the offworlders. Roberts caught the rope that

Daya threw her and took it expertly around one of the cleats. She extended a hand to hoist Daya up, caught her in an embrace and pressed her lips to Daya's cheek.

"This kissing that you do," said Roberts. "I like it. Very direct." She wasn't very good at it but she was learning. Like all the scientists, she could be stiff at first. They didn't seem all that comfortable in their replaceable bodies. Roberts was small as a child, but with a woman's face. Her blonde hair was cropped short, her eyes were clear and faceted. They reminded Daya of her mother's crystal.

"It's done," said Daya.

"Yes, but are you all right?"

"I think so." She forced a grin. "We'll find out."

"We will. Don't worry, love, I am going to take good care of you. And your baby."

"And I will take care of you."

"Yes." She looked puzzled. "Of course."

Roberts was a cultural anthropologist. She had explained to Daya that all she wanted was to preserve a record of an ancient way of life. A culture in which there was still sexual reproduction.

"May I see that?"

Daya opened her pack and produced the leftover bit of the love feast. She had sealed it in a baggie that Roberts had given her. It had somehow frozen solid.

"Excellent. Now we should get you into the lab before it's too late. Put you under the scanner, take some samples." This time she kissed Daya on the mouth. Her lips parted briefly and Daya felt Roberts' tongue flick against her teeth. When Daya did not respond, she pulled back.

"I know this is hard now. You're very brave to help us this way, Daya." The scientist took her hand and squeezed. "But someday they'll thank you for what you're doing." She nodded toward the sleepy village across the river. "Someday soon."

AMICAE AETERNUM
Ellen Klages

Ellen Klages (ellenklages.com) is the author of two acclaimed YA historical novels: *The Green Glass Sea,* which won the Scott O'Dell Award, the New Mexico Book Award, and the Lopez Award; and *White Sands, Red Menace*, which won the California and New Mexico Book Awards. Her story, "Caligo Lane," appears earlier in this book.

IT WAS STILL dark when Corry woke, no lights on in the neighbors' houses, just a yellow glow from the streetlight on the other side of the elm. Through her open window, the early summer breeze brushed across her coverlet like silk.

Corry dressed silently, trying not to see the empty walls, the boxes piled in a corner. She pulled on a shirt and shorts, looping the laces of her shoes around her neck and climbed from bed to sill and out the window with only a whisper of fabric against the worn wood. Then she was outside.

The grass was chill and damp beneath her bare feet. She let them rest on it for a minute, the freshly-mowed blades tickling her toes, her heels sinking into the springy-sponginess of the dirt. She breathed deep, to catch it all – the cool and the green and the stillness – holding it in for as long as she could before slipping on her shoes.

A morning to remember. Every little detail.

She walked across the lawn, stepping over the ridge of clippings along the verge, onto the sidewalk. Theirs was a corner lot. In a minute, she would be out of sight. For once, she was up before her practical, morning-people parents. The engineer and the physicist did not believe in sleeping in, but Corry could count on the fingers of one hand the number of times in her eleven years that she had seen the dawn.

No one else was on the street. It felt solemn and private, as if she had stepped out of time, so quiet she could hear the wind ruffle the wide canopy of trees, an owl hooting from somewhere behind her, the diesel chug of the all-night bus two blocks away. She crossed Branson St. and turned down the alley that ran behind the houses.

A dandelion's spiky leaves pushed through a crack in the cement. Corry squatted, touching it with a finger, tracing the jagged outline, memorizing its contours. A weed. No one planted it or planned it. She smiled and stood up, her hand against a wooden fence, feeling the grain beneath her palm, the crackling web of old paint, and continued on. The alley stretched ahead for several blocks, the pavement a narrowing pale V.

She paused a minute later to watch a cat prowl stealthily along the base of another fence, hunting or slinking home. It looked up, saw her, and sped into a purposeful thousand-leg trot before disappearing into a yard. She thought of her own cat, Mr. Bumble, who now belonged to a neighbor, and wiped at the edge of her eye. She distracted herself by peering into backyards at random bits of other people's lives – lawn chairs, an overturned tricycle, a metal barbecue grill, its lid open.

Barbecue. She hadn't thought to add that to her list. She'd like to have one more whiff of charcoal, lit with lighter fluid, smoking and wafting across the yards, smelling like summer. Too late now. No one barbecued their breakfast.

She walked on, past Remington Rd. She brushed her fingers over a rosebush – velvet petals, leathery leaves; pressed a hand against the oft-stapled roughness of a telephone pole, fringed with remnants of garage-sale flyers; stood on tiptoe to trace the red octagon of a stop sign. She stepped from sidewalk to grass to asphalt and back, tasting the textures with her feet, noting the cracks and holes and bumps, the faded paint on the curb near a fire hydrant.

"Fire hydrant," she said softly, checking it off in her mind. "Rain gutter. Lawn mower. Mailbox."

The sky was just beginning to purple in the east when she reached Anna's back gate. She knew it as well as her own. They'd been best friends since first grade, had been in and out of each other's houses practically every day. Corry tapped on the frame of the porch's screen door with one knuckle.

A moment later, Anna came out. "Hi, Spunk," she whispered.

"Hi, Spork," Corry answered. She waited while Anna eased the door closed so it wouldn't bang, sat on the steps, put on her shoes.

Their bikes leaned against the side of the garage. Corry had told her mom that she had given her bike to Anna's sister Pat. And she would, in an hour or two. So it hadn't really been a lie, just the wrong tense.

They walked their bikes through the gate. In the alley, Corry threw a leg over and settled onto the vinyl seat, its shape molded to hers over the years. Her bike. Her steed. Her hands fit themselves around the rubber grips of the handlebars and she pushed off with one foot. Anna was a few feet behind, then beside her. They rode abreast down to the mouth of the alley and away.

The slight grade of Thompson St. was perfect for coasting, the wind on their faces, blowing Corry's short dark hair off her forehead, rippling Anna's ponytail. At the bottom of the hill, Corry stood tall on her pedals, pumping hard, the muscles in her calves a good ache as the chain rattled and whirred as fast and constant as a train.

"Trains!" she yelled into the wind. Another item from her list.

"Train whistles!" Anna yelled back.

They leaned into a curve. Corry felt gravity pull at her, pumped harder, in control. They turned a corner and a moment later, Anna said, "Look."

Corry slowed, looked up, then braked to a stop. The crescent moon hung above a gap in the trees, a thin sliver of blue-white light.

Anna began the lullaby her mother used to sing when Corry first slept over. On the second line, Corry joined in.

I see the moon, and the moon sees me.
The moon sees somebody I want to see.

The sound of their voices was liquid in the stillness, sweet and smooth. Anna reached out and held Corry's hand across the space between their bikes.

God bless the moon, and God bless me,
And God bless the somebody I want to see.

They stood for a minute, feet on the ground, still holding hands. Corry gave a squeeze and let go. "Thanks," she said.

"Any time," said Anna, and bit her lip.

"I know," Corry said. Because it wouldn't be. She pointed. The sky was lighter now, palest blue at the end of the street shading to indigo directly above. "Let's get to the park before the sun comes up."

No traffic, no cars. It felt like they were the only people in the world. They headed east, riding down the middle of the street, chasing the shadows of their bikes from streetlight to streetlight, never quite catching them. The houses on both sides were dark, only one light in a kitchen window making a yellow rectangle on a driveway. As they passed it, they smelled bacon frying, heard a fragment of music.

The light at 38th St. was red. They stopped, toes on the ground, waiting. A raccoon scuttled from under a hedge, hump-backed and quick, disappearing behind a parked car. In the hush, Corry heard the metallic *tick* from the light box before she saw it change from red to green.

Three blocks up Ralston Hill. The sky looked magic now, the edges wiped with pastels, peach and lavender and a blush of orange. Corry pedaled as hard as she could, felt her breath ragged in her throat, a trickle of sweat between her shoulder blades. Under the arched entrance to the park, into the broad, grassy picnic area that sloped down to the creek.

They abandoned their bikes to the grass, and walked to a low stone wall. Corry sat, cross-legged, her best friend beside her, and waited for the sun to rise for the last time.

She knew it didn't actually rise, that *it* wasn't moving. They were, rotating a quarter mile every second, coming all the way around once every twenty-four hours, exposing themselves once again to the star they called the sun, and naming that moment *morning*. But it was the last time she'd get to watch.

"There it is," Anna said. Golden light pierced the spaces between the trunks of the trees, casting long thin shadows across the grass. They leaned against each other and watched as the sky brightened to its familiar blue, and color returned: green leaves, pink bicycles, yellow shorts. Behind them lights began to come on in houses and a dog barked.

By the time the sun touched the tops of the distant trees, the backs of their legs were pebbled with the pattern of the wall, and it was daytime.

Corry sat, listening to the world waking up and going about its ordinary business: cars starting, birds chirping, a mother calling out, "Jimmy!

Breakfast!" She felt as if her whole body was aware, making all of this a part of her.

Over by the playground, geese waddled on the grass, pecking for bugs. One goose climbed onto the end of the teeter-totter and sat, as if waiting for a playmate. Corry laughed out loud. She would never have thought to put *that* on her list. "What's next?" Anna asked.

"The creek, before anyone else is there."

They walked single file down the steep railroad-tie steps, flanked by tall oaks and thick undergrowth dotted with wildflowers. "Wild," Corry said softly.

When they reached the bank they took off their shoes and climbed over boulders until they were surrounded by rushing water. The air smelled fresh, full of minerals, the sound of the water both constant and never-the-same as it poured over rocks and rills, eddied around logs.

They sat down on the biggest, flattest rock and eased their bare feet into the creek, watching goosebumps rise up their legs. Corry felt the current swirl around her. She watched the speckles of light dance on the water, the darkness under the bank, ten thousand shades of green and brown everywhere she looked. Sun on her face, wind in her hair, water at her feet, rock beneath her.

"How much of your list did you get to do?" asked Anna.

"A lot of it. It kept getting longer. I'd check one thing off, and it'd remind me of something else. I got to most of the everyday ones, 'cause I could walk, or ride my bike. Mom was too busy packing and giving stuff away and checking off her own lists to take me to the aquarium, or to the zoo, so I didn't see the jellies or the elephants and the bears."

Anna nodded. "My mom was like that too, when we were moving here from Indianapolis."

"At least you knew where you were going. We're heading off into the great unknown, my dad says. Boldly going where nobody's gone before."

"Like that old TV show."

"Yeah, except we're not going to *get* anywhere. At least not me, or my mom or my dad. The *Goddard* is a generation ship. The planet it's heading for is five light years away, and even with solar sails and stuff, the trip's going to take a couple hundred years."

"Wow."

"Yeah. It won't land until my great-great – I don't know, add about five more greats to that – grandchildren are around. I'll be old – like thirty – before we even get out of the solar system. Dad keeps saying that it's the adventure of a lifetime, and we're achieving humankind's greatest dream, and blah, blah, blah. But it's *his* dream." She picked at a piece of lichen on the rock.

"Does your mom want to go?"

"Uh-huh. She's all excited about the experiments she can do in zero-g. She says it's an honor that we were chosen and I should be proud to be a pioneer."

"Will you be in history books?"

Corry shrugged. "Maybe. There are around four thousand people going, from all over the world, so I'd be in tiny, tiny print. But maybe."

"Four *thousand*?" Anna whistled. "How big a rocket is it?"

"Big. Bigger than big." Corry pulled her feet up, hugging her arms around her knees. "Remember that humongous cruise ship we saw when we went to Miami?"

"Sure. It looked like a skyscraper, lying on its side."

"That's what this ship is like, only bigger. And rounder. My mom keeps saying it'll be *just* like a cruise – any food anytime I want, games to play, all the movies and books and music ever made – after school, of course. Except people on cruise ships stop at ports and get off and explore. Once we board tonight, we're *never* getting off. I'm going to spend the rest of my whole entire life in a big tin can."

"That sucks."

"Tell me about it." Corry reached into her pocket and pulled out a crumpled sheet of paper, scribbles covering both sides. She smoothed it out on her knee. "I've got another list." She cleared her throat and began to read:

Twenty Reasons Why Being on a Generation Ship Sucks,
by Corrine Garcia-Kelly

1. *I will never go away to college.*
2. *I will never see blue sky again, except in pictures.*

3. There will never be a new kid in my class.

4. I will never meet anyone my parents don't already know.

5. I will never have anything new that isn't ~~man~~ human-made.
    Manufactured or processed or grown in a lab.

6. Once I get my ID chip, my parents will always know exactly
    where I am.

7. I will never get to drive my Aunt Frieda's convertible, even
    though she promised I could when I turned sixteen.

8. I will never see the ocean again.

9. I will never go to Paris.

10. I will never meet a tall, dark stranger, dangerous or not.

11. I will never move away from home.

12. I will never get to make the rules for my own life.

13. I will never ride my bike to a new neighborhood and find a store
    I haven't seen before.

14. I will never ride my bike again.

15. I will never go outside *again*.

16. I will never take a walk to anywhere that isn't planned and
    mapped and numbered.

17. I will never see another thunderstorm. Or lightning bugs.
    Or fireworks.

18. I will never buy an old house and fix it up.

19. I will never eat another Whopper.

20. I will never go to the state fair and win a stuffed animal.

She stopped. "I was getting kind of sleepy toward the end."

"I could tell." Anna slipped her arm around Corry's waist. "What will you miss most?"

"You." Corry pulled Anna closer.

"Me, too." Anna settled her head on her friend's shoulder. "I can't believe I'll never see you again."

"I know." Corry sighed. "I *like* Earth. I like that there are parts that no one made, and that there are always surprises." She shifted her arm a little. "Maybe I don't want to be a pioneer. I mean, I don't know *what* I want to be when I grow up. Mom's always said I could be anything I wanted to be, but now? The Peace Corps is out. So is being a coal miner or a deep-sea diver or a park ranger. Or an antique dealer."

"You like old things."

"I do. They're from the past, so everything has a story."

"I thought so." Anna reached into her pocket with her free hand. "I used the metals kit from my dad's printer, and made you something." She pulled out a tissue paper-wrapped lump and put it in Corry's lap.

Corry tore off the paper. Inside was a silver disk, about five centimeters across. In raised letters around the edge it said SPUNK-CORRY-ANNA-SPORK-2065. Etched in the center was a photo of the two of them, arm in arm, wearing tall pointed hats with stars, taken at Anna's last birthday party. Corry turned it over. The back said: *Optimae amicae aeternum.* "What does that mean?"

"'Best friends forever.' At least that's what Translator said."

"It's great. Thanks. I'll keep it with me, all the time."

"You'd better. It's an artifact."

"It is really nice."

"I'm serious. Isn't your space ship going off to another planet with a whole library of Earth's art and culture and all?"

"Yeah...?"

"But by the time it lands, that'll be ancient history and tales. No one alive will ever have been on Earth, right?"

"Yeah..."

"So your mission – if you choose to accept it – is to preserve this artifact from your home planet." Anna shrugged. "It isn't old now, but it will be. You can tell your kids stories about it – about us. It'll be an heirloom. Then they'll tell their kids, and –"

"– and their kids, and on down for umpity generations." Corry nodded, turning the disc over in her hands. "By then it'll be a relic. There'll be legends about it." She rolled it across her palm, silver winking in the sun "How'd you think of that?"

"Well, you said you're only allowed to take ten kilos of personal stuff with you, and that's all you'll ever have from Earth. Which is why you made your list and have been going around saying goodbye to squirrels and stop signs and Snickers bars and all."

"Ten kilos isn't much. My mom said the ship is so well-stocked I won't need much, but it's hard. I had to pick between my bear and my jewelry box."

"I know. And in twenty years, I'll probably have a house full of clothes and furniture and junk. But the thing is, when I'm old and I die, my kids'll get rid of most of it, like we did with my Gramma. Maybe they'll keep some pictures. But then their kids will do the same thing. So in a couple hundred years, there won't be any trace of me *here* –"

"– but you'll be part of the legend."

"Yep."

"Okay, then. I accept the mission." Corry turned and kissed Anna on the cheek.

"You'll take us to the stars?"

"You bet." She slipped the disc into her pocket. "It's getting late."

She stood up and reached to help Anna to her feet. "C'mon. Let's ride."

COPYRIGHT

ENGINEERING
INFINITY

Edited by Jonathan Strahan

UK ISBN: 978 1 907519 51 2 • US ISBN: 978 1 907519 52 9 • £7.99/$7.99

The universe shifts and changes; suddenly you understand, and are filled with wonder. Coming up against the speed of light (and with it, the sheer size of the universe), seeing how difficult and dangerous terraforming an alien world really is, realising that a hitch-hiker on a starship consumes fuel and oxygen and the tragedy that results... it's "hard-SF" where sense of wonder is most often found and where science fiction's true heart lies. Including stories from the likes of Stephen Baxter and Charles Stross.

 WWW.SOLARISBOOKS.COM

Follow us on Twitter! www.twitter.com/solarisbooks

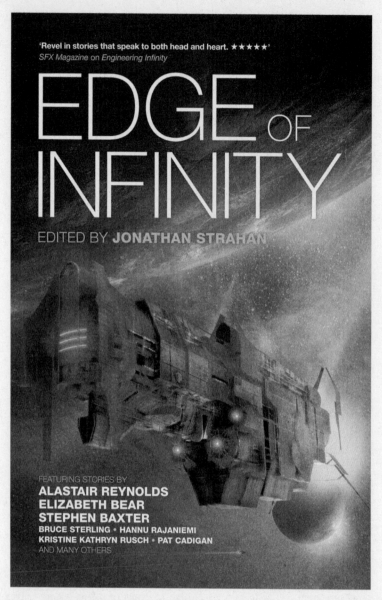

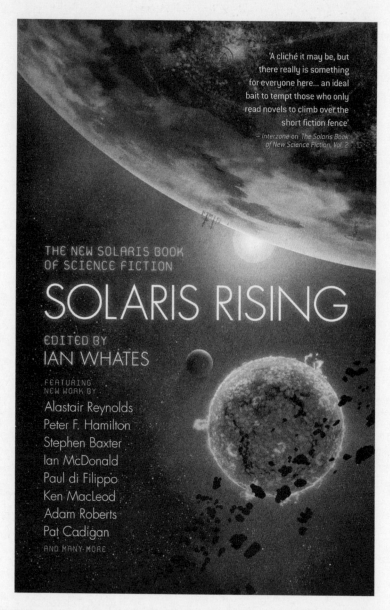

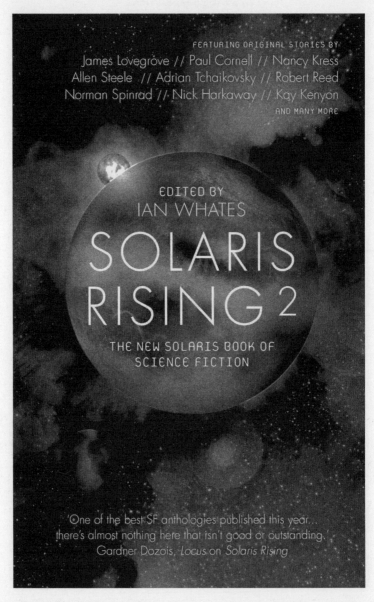

FEATURING ORIGINAL STORIES BY

James Lovegrove // Paul Cornell // Nancy Kress
Allen Steele // Adrian Tchaikovsky // Robert Reed
Norman Spinrad // Nick Harkaway // Kay Kenyon
AND MANY MORE

EDITED BY
IAN WHATES

SOLARIS RISING 2

THE NEW SOLARIS BOOK OF
SCIENCE FICTION

'One of the best SF anthologies published this year...
there's almost nothing here that isn't good or outstanding.'
Gardner Dozois, *Locus* on *Solaris Rising*

Solaris Rising 2 showcases the finest new science fiction from both celebrated authors and the most exciting of emerging writers. Following in the footsteps of the critically-acclaimed first volume, editor Ian Whates has once again gathered together a plethora of thrilling and daring talent. Within you will find unexplored frontiers as well as many of the central themes of the genre – alien worlds, time travel, artificial intelligence – made entirely new in the telling. The authors here prove once again why SF continues to be the most innovative, satisfying, and downright exciting genre of all.

 WWW.SOLARISBOOKS.COM

Follow us on Twitter! www.twitter.com/solarisbooks

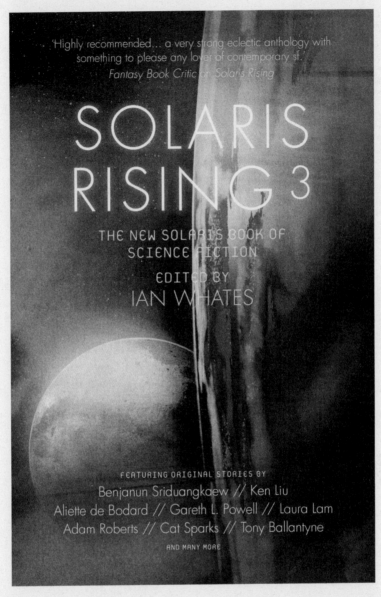

'Highly recommended... a very strong eclectic anthology with something to please any lover of contemporary sf.'
Fantasy Book Critic on Solaris Rising

SOLARIS RISING 3

THE NEW SOLARIS BOOK OF SCIENCE FICTION

EDITED BY IAN WHATES

FEATURING ORIGINAL STORIES BY

Benjanun Sriduangkaew // Ken Liu

Aliette de Bodard // Gareth L. Powell // Laura Lam

Adam Roberts // Cat Sparks // Tony Ballantyne

AND MANY MORE

Award-nominated editor Ian Whates showcases the best in contemporary science fiction, celebrating new writing by a roster of diverse and exciting authors. Here you will discover how this 'literature of ideas' produces stories of astonishing imagination and incisive speculation.

Solaris Rising 3 thrillingly demonstrates why science fiction is the most relevant, daring and progressive of genres.

 WWW.SOLARISBOOKS.COM

Follow us on Twitter! www.twitter.com/solarisbooks